CRIMSON
IN THE WATER

TSAI YULING'S DRAMATIC EARLY LIFE
IN SUBTROPICAL SOUTH-EAST CHINA
BETWEEN 1934 AND 1945

NIGEL BEAUMONT

authorHOUSE®

AuthorHouse™ UK Ltd.
500 Avebury Boulevard
Central Milton Keynes, MK9 2BE
www.authorhouse.co.uk
Phone: 08001974150

First published by AuthorHouse   3/22/2011

ISBN: 978-1-4567-7503-2 (sc)

For my very good sons Antonius and Ollie
(their speaking Chinese a constant wonder to their father)

PREFACE

Meaning of words and names sometimes appearing:
Doli - wide-rimmed conical hat useful against the sun and rains
K'ang - peasant bed
Li - distance measurement of about one third of a mile
Name chop - artist's red-paste signature imprinted by pressing a carved wood-
　　　piece
Sampan - near flat-bottom boat normally used inland on rivers
Chang-o - mythological moon goddess
Chinese New Year also called the Spring Festival - the lunar New Year festival
　　　period end January-February
Manchu - the ruling Qing dynasty 1644-1911, the final dynasty
Manchukuo - Japanese name for their puppet state of occupied Manchuria
　　　1932-45
Zhongguo - 'the Middle Kingdom' (i.e., China) as the Chinese called their country.

Fictional Chinese and Japanese characters in the novel:
Except for the cameo appearance of Chiang Kai-shek, all characters actually
appearing are entirely fictional (in particular Colonel later General Huang,
General Toyamo and Air Colonel Hijiya) and are in no way based on historical
persons.

Fictional and actual place names:
The story takes place in Fujian province, China, during parts of the 1930s
and 40s. Apart from the name of the province, all scenes are set in entirely
fictional places except for Amoy (now Xiamen) i.e. Tuxieng, Mingon and Wuyi
Court are fictional, as is Manchuria's Valley of Heroes of the Twentieth Year.
However, references often occur to real places in China such as Fuzhou and
Nanjing. Chinese readers in particular should note that this novel is a journey
into the imagination; it does not seek historical or landscape accuracy, although
historical events are followed reasonably closely date-wise.

Spelling of characters' names:
The name of a Chinese person starts with the family name, often followed by two hyphenated personal names. But in line with some western writers, the author has combined the second and third names for easier reading. So the 'hero' of the book, whose name would normally be written Tsai Yu-ling, becomes Tsai Yuling. However, the historical figures Chiang Kai-shek and Sun Yat-sen have been left with their well-known hyphenated names.

Chinese history: A few historical dates and events may be of interest:

1911/12	Fall of Qing (Manchu) final dynasty, 1st Year of Chinese Republic
1911-27	Era of rule of warlords over parts of China
1926	Nationalists (Kuomintang/KMT/the Whites) begin to unify China under Sun Yat-sen, then Chiang Kai-shek (the Generalissimo)
1927-37	Rise of the Chinese Communist Party/CCP/the Reds 1st Chinese Civil War: Nationalist -v- Communist
1931	Japan colonizes Manchuria, sets up puppet Manchukuo government
1934–1935	October-to-October 'The Long March' (Communist retreat from Nationalist encirclement in Jiangsi province to Communist capital Yan'an in mountains, Mao Tse-tung becoming their leader)
1937	Japanese invasion of China's main coastal areas including Peking, Shanghai, Canton, and Nationalist capital Nanjing, Chiang Kai-shek's Nationalists making new capital further west at Chongqing
1944	Japanese offensive 'Operation Ichigo' taking more of central and southern China
1945 May	German surrender, end of World War II in Europe
1945 Aug/Sep	Japanese surrender, end of World War II in Far East
1946-49	2nd Chinese Civil War, ending with Communist victory and Nationalist flight to the island of Formosa/Taiwan

List of main characters for easier reference of Chinese names:
Alinga - family pet name for Yuling
Ashenga - daughter of Mr Wu, furniture maker, Mingon
Ayi - younger brother of Yuling
CCP - the Chinese Communist Party, the Reds
Chang - resistance fighter
Dajuan - personal maid to Madame Huang

Chiang Kai-shek (the Generalissimo), Nationalist leader of the KMT, the Whites

Fainan- wife of Jinjin

Fang Lamgang - see Lam below

Hijiya - Japanese Air Colonel

Ho Chitian - priest of the Temple of the Five Concubines, Tuxieng

Huang Mingchang - Nationalist Colonel, later General

Huang Huihua - see Huihua

Huang Shanghan - see Shanghan

Huihua (or Hua) - daughter of Colonel later General and Madame Huang

Janping - Luo Janping, daughter of tea plantation owner at Dongang

Jinjin - uncle of Yuling, brother-in-law of Wenlie

KMT/Kuomintang - the Nationalists' party, the Whites

Koo Guanglu - Art Professor at Suodin

Lam - Fang Lamgang 'the Imbecile'

Lee - private secretary to Colonel later General Huang

Ma - Nationalist military officer

Madame Huang - wife of Colonel/General Huang, mother of Huihua and
Shanghan

Meibei - peasant farmer's wife

Nanako - Japanese young woman

Sanchi - Doctor Chen's daughter

Shanghan - son of Colonel/General and Madame Huang, younger brother of
Huihua

Su - Chief Doctor, see Ya Ya below

Sun Yat-sen - founder of modern China, died 1926, his testamentary Three
Principles: the unification of China, popular government by and for the
people, social and economic reforms

Tan Zhiyong - tea merchant

Tsai Peiheng - grandfather of Yuling and Ayi

Tsai Wenlie - see Wenlie below

Tsai Yuling - (or Alinga) see Yuling below

Wang - servant to the Huangs

Wenlie - mother of Yuling and Ayi

Whites - see KMT

Wu - furniture maker in Mingon

Xuiey - cook to the Huangs

Ya Ya - familiar name for Professor Su, Chief Doctor of Tuxieng Hospital

Yiying - personal maid to Huihua

Yuling - Tsai Yuling, elder son of Tsai Peijinn and Tsai Wenlie, family pet
name Alinga

Zen Yahan - monk, East Gate Monastery, Mingon

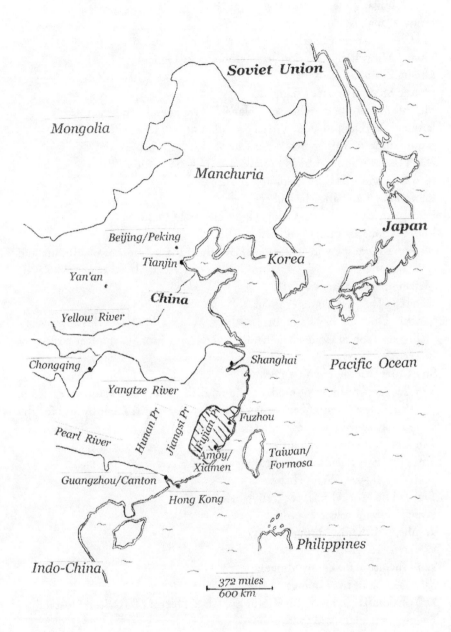

Soviet Union

Mongolia

Manchuria

Beijing/Peking

Tianjin

Yan'an

China

Yellow River

Chongqing

Yangtze River

Hunan Pr

Jiangsi Pr

Pearl River

Fujian Pr

Fuzhou

Amoy/
Xiamen

Guangzhou/Canton

Hong Kong

Indo-China

Korea

Japan

Pacific Ocean

Shanghai

Taiwan/
Formosa

Philippines

372 miles
600 km

1

September 1934, the 23rd Year of the Republic,
Fujian Province, Zhongguo (Chinese name for China).

Lam was not mad or half mad but a simpleton; his brain was slow and often uncomprehending, and he had never been able to speak. He could hear, and he could understand some of the things said to him; he knew kindness and its opposite, that he needed to eat and to rest, and that in the hills were his *friends*.

He was a small lightly built man in early middle age, with black hair that usually was wild. But he was not wild, he was gentle. His full name was Fang Lamgang, but everyone in Tuxieng called him the Imbecile, or Imbecile to his face, although to three people only (the three who loved him) and to the peasant farmer of one of them he was simply Lam.

Tuxieng was a large inland town standing on one side of a wide river, the uplands rising impressively beyond rice farms and orchards on the other, dark green hills that were subtropical, uninhabited and dangerous.

Although his usual state was one of melancholic resignation, that state rarely showed on a face often smiling to the world whether people were nice to him or nasty. But this particular day he was feeling happy and expectant. He had left his dilapidated shack at the side of the blue-tiled Temple of the Five Concubines, after being given a breakfast by the only priest there, the tiny old man who looked after him for all the years he could remember. His foot had healed and he was making his way to the hills. The previous day, he had visited one of the markets, and some of the vegetable traders had given him throwaways; the old sack he now carried was heavy, but that did not worry him, it made his whole being thrill to think who would soon be munching his provisions.

He never walked to the hills if it was raining or cold. The priest always told him when he should not make the journey, and he had seen his sack and said nothing.

Lam did not know that the priest prayed for him every single day, especially for his safety in the uplands, and prayed for the stout peasant woman called Meibei who lived at the base of the hills proper, the farmer's wife with the large wart on her forehead. The priest knew from Meibei that she always tried to protect Lam, and often fed him, and that he ran down to her tiny mud cottage if storms came.

When she and her husband harvested the rice and it was drying on the ground, they would give Lam the job he liked best, to hit away the hens using a long stick with feathers at the end, as the chicks were fast and tried to pinch the grains.

Of all the townsfolk and peasants, Meibei was the kindest to him. Sometimes she took him into her arms, and when this happened it always sent him into happy slow chattering, which he could never stop until well after the embrace. Hers were the only eyes he felt completely safe to look into, though he was also comfortable with the old woman who sometimes brought him food to his shack by the temple. Most people shied away from him, left him alone which was what he wanted. But some could be unpleasant, laughing at him, calling him names he did not understand, pushing him or throwing things at him, which always made him frightened so that he chattered in a different way and fast.

The journey from the temple to the little farm was long, taking him through part of the town, over the main bridge crossing the big river, then for several li along a road through gently rising countryside, before crossing another bridge, small and sagging, made of bamboo and rope, that served the last peasant dwellings under the hills. As he walked there, he loved the anticipation of being with his four-legged friends, especially when he could see Meibei's terrace paddies in the distance and the trees higher up that he would be going through.

But now, he had nearly reached Meibei's first rice paddy, and yet he couldn't see at all far, not the rising terraces or the trees, they were hidden by mist. When he walked upwards along the track after clambering across the shaking bridge - the track that passed the path leading the short distance to the mud cottage - he could just see the farmer waving to him, and could make out the old water buffalo sitting beside the flat stone near the cottage ('Lam's stone' Meibei called it, where he usually squatted); but the small dwelling itself was blanked out.

Sometimes hunters went into the hills; but no one else ventured there, certainly not townsfolk, and woodsmen never touched the area. Apart from big cats in the higher forests, the hunters were very wary of the wild horses, they were unpredictable and aggressive, small, fast and many. In former days, they only got through them by using warning shots or picking off the leaders. The horses had learnt the danger of the guns, and usually kept away when man occasionally appeared.

It never ceased to astonish strong-minded Meibei and her quiet husband that Lam spent whole days and even some nights near the horses. One hunter told them that he had seen upwards of a hundred of the beasts in an open patch on the hillside, with the little man in the middle of them.

As Lam moved up the track, he wondered if some of the horses would find him in the mist. He knew they roamed a large area that lay below the forests, forests he never went near for the unknown dangers he sensed.

Once passed the highest terrace, carefully he crossed the stepping stones of the little stream that fed the terraces; he always chattered at this point, didn't want to slip and fall into the water, which sometimes happened when running down from storms. Then he walked on by the farmer's red warning post, and continued up through the first trees until soon he reached a more open but still-rising landscape of bush and hillside rocks …and animal tracks.

He placed his sack under a large rock that projected from the sloping ground like a thick roof, the rock that for years had been his shelter from rains and sudden storms. He had learnt the hard way that the horses, though small, could not get at his sack if he put it back far enough.

He hated the storms, never understanding when they were coming, and was often caught out. If it was just rain, he would crouch under his rock and wait for hours for it to stop; and if it did not, he would eventually get down to the cottage drenched. But if lightning and thunder came, he would chatter fast in fear, and when he dared, he would run back to Meibei and then not leave her side.

Tufts of grass were thick under the roof of stone, giving him a comfortable home in the hills. And on a good day, he could stand on top of the rock and look down to see the highest terrace through the trees. He felt safe there, and although he was scared of the occasional snake he came across, they never seemed to be around the rock.

*

Lam now sits on top of his overhang with legs dangling over the edge, watching whorls of mist breaking up. He feels surprised that none of his friends have appeared.

Some neighing, faint but distinct, comes to his ears from well above him. He listens, can distinguish different horse noises and movements - their neighs, whinnies, snorts and stamps - and knows that the sound he is hearing means

3

that some are disturbed. The neighing stops for a short while, then begins again.

He scrambles down and starts walking in the direction of the noise. The intermittent neighing grows louder, and the mist clears to one side of him offering up bushes of red berries.

Just as he feels he shouldn't go any further, he crests a rise and sees five horses in a clear patch about thirty paces ahead on flatter ground, one a favourite, and they have encircled something on their track.

He moves two steps closer. Some of the horses are snorting, their nostrils quivering. All suddenly turn and look towards him. As one begins stamping the ground, he becomes frightened, thinks they have disturbed a vipers' nest among a very low heap of rocks that he can see on the ground. Usually he feels safe with his friends, but he knows better than to be near them if they are agitated, or worse fighting.

He is about to go back to his rock when two come galloping up to him, stopping near, ears moving backwards and forwards. He sees them look to their companions, and soon the other three are rushing towards him, and in no time the favourite has nosed him hard in his chest and he loses his balance, crying out as he falls.

He sits on the ground bewildered, because the horse has never done that before. His wrist is painful, and he sees it has streaks of dirt, and that bobbles of dark red blood are appearing.

He scrambles up about to turn and run, now certain that the small rocks and vipers could chase him. But he is concerned for the favourite horse that nosed him, as it has galloped back to the danger, its head is lowered, and it is moving a front leg in the air but without touching the rocks.

He hunches and watches, and knows that his chattering has become loud and fast, and that his hands are shaking including the one that stings. And he wants the horse to get away from the track, though he can tell that the pawing is not of the hostile kind.

The favourite turns to face him. Rays of the sun burst through the mist; they catch its straggling hair, light brown tinted with stripes of grey.

It whinnies.

The rocks move.

Lam's body jerks upright, his eyes become big, and for a moment he is mesmerized, he thinks hundreds of snakes are about to spring at the horse and curl round the head and bite it to death.

And now he expects the rocks to rise up too, they'll roll and crash into him and make him fall again. So he starts running back, and his chattering has become high-pitched cries of fear.

But he hasn't gone more than a few strides when he hears two powerful whinnies from the favourite, followed by some from the others, and they make him stop.

He looks back. Snakes haven't sprung up, and the favourite is still close to the low rocks, and they are not rolling. Lam sees more sun streaking through the mist, and as he reads the horse's behaviour, rays light up parts of the track, and he realizes that what is on the ground might not be moving rocks or writhing vipers or some other animal or animals dangerous to him and the horses: the favourite, who loves to be stroked on both sides of the neck at the same time, who gives him comforting nudges and sits near him keeping the others away, might be wanting to show him something.

He creeps half sideways through the other four horses, and as he approaches, he senses the favourite has grown calm. More courage comes, and a few further steps and he sees that someone is lying on the ground - a head is raised.

The snorting and neighing so close, the shaking of the hard dusty ground under him, these make the person lying on his side picture wild horses and expect his end to come …from tramples or kicks or bites.

And when there is neither blow nor bite, when horse noises stop and there seems to be silence, he tries to see around him; but his eyes will not focus, he can only make out the blur of an animal's head right above him.

A snort of warm air onto his face jolts his vision, and he looks up at nostrils and at an eye bulging through hair.

But very soon, through sheer weakness and resignation, his eyes close, and he goes into a state of semi-being where his mind forgets what he has just seen.

Sometime later - how long he does not know - a strange sound starts to register with him. It grows into a loud murmuring that is close to him, it is bringing him back to the horse with the bulging eye; there is something else nearby, and when he manages to focus a second time, he sees that a man is looking down at him - another human being - and knows that he is not alone in his world.

He holds the focus, wants to say something but finds he can't, and the man isn't speaking to him though there is a kind of smile on the face, there is only this murmuring, and the body is moving from side to side. And the next moment the man is trying to pick him up, pain is shooting through the bad arm making him cry out as he sees better the animal so close; and for an instant, despite the pain, he is strangely comforted by the view of its whole head, and feels that the eyes, the brain of the horse, are looking right into him.

His head now rests against a bony chest, and the man has begun walking, more utterances pouring from the mouth. Other horses come into view, and as he passes them there bursts into his mind an old horse with its nose in a

5

bucket; it is drinking water, and its eyes are dark brown; but where he has seen such a horse does not come to him, his only concern being the pain and that he might be dropped.

Not long after, he is put roughly on the ground, and is too weak to look up to see the man standing near him; but he hears the loud panting.

Soon he is being carried again, and the thought that the man must be taking him to other human beings, to safety from the tigers, lifts his spirits.

The third time they stop and he is put down, he sees that they are among trees on a downward slope. The man has now left him, and he thinks he is being abandoned. But as he watches him disappear, he spots a rice terrace well below; it is in sunlight that shows through wisps of mist lingering among the trees; and although it is the first time since leaving the cavern floor that he has thought of paddy fields, he knows that food is being grown, and it makes him want to walk there. He tries to move so he can stand, but all strength has gone; he can only lie where he has been left, and soon he drifts into the unconscious again.

That's strange, the peasant farmer thinks to himself as he looks up from his lowest paddy. His hands are full of unwanted grasses and plucked weeds, and he can see Lam coming down the track after passing through the birch trees that shimmer in the new sun; Lam has already crossed the little stream and has passed the top terrace.

He turns to his wife; she is in another row a few paces behind, her back bent in the high rice that two weeks earlier had been drained of its water.

'Eh! Why's he coming down so soon? Looks like he's half running!'

Meibei comes upright under her wide-brimmed doli, and grimaces; her eyes are not good, but she can make out Lam moving faster than his usual slowness, almost like when he runs to her from the storms. She is puzzled: on good-weather days he normally stays up there near the beasts.

'What's he doing!' her husband exclaims as they see Lam leave the track and start along one of their mud embankments between two terraces; they have never seen Lam on the embankments before; they always thought he was afraid of falling over the edge into a lower paddy, especially if there was water.

Lam is some way from them when he scrambles down the embankment and into their field. A large flock of rice birds rises from the paddy, swoops over him, and almost at once disappears into the higher terrace.

'Off, Lam! Get off!' the farmer shouts, much against his mild nature.

But their little friend keeps wading through the rice towards them, and he is wildly gesticulating, something else they have never seen him do; they can hear his calls of alarm, and his usual smiling expression looks to have taken a frightened turn.

Meibei has joined her husband by the time Lam reaches them, and she is shocked to see him in such a nervous state; he is so out of breath that he just stands in front of her gasping, his upper body moving dramatically.

'What's wrong with you, Lam?' she says loudly. 'Been stung, or seen a horse fight?'

Lam steps forward and begins tugging her upper sleeve, and she sees that the other hand is grazed, has blood, and thinks he has come for her help. She is about to take his hand away when, to her surprise, her husband pushes him and he falls over into the rice. 'What you doing!' the farmer calls out, half raising the hand holding the grasses and weeds, though he has no intention to use it.

'Leave him be, he's hurt himself,' Meibei says, pointing to the hand, before leaning down and helping Lam up. 'Why's my Lam coming through our paddy like this?'

She watches him turn towards the birches, and his arms wave again. He looks back at her, and she reads fear ...and is he begging her to go with him to see something?

'Could be horses careering down like four years ago,' the farmer says. 'Have to warn them off, I'll fetch the gun.'

'You'd better,' she replies looking towards Lam. 'Come on, come with Meibei.' She signals to the simpleton, and nods to her cottage that she knows he loves.

But Lam surprises her, he is taking backward steps through the rice, his chattering towards her as strong and fast as ever. Then he turns. Normally she can tell what he is thinking or wanting, yet it doesn't seem to be about the grazed hand. Maybe her husband is right: if many horses come running through the terraces, they could lose much of the crop, it would be a disaster, they could face starvation.

'That's right Lam, leave us and walk on the embankment,' the farmer calls now more kindly. He shakes his head and starts for the cottage.

Meibei remains puzzled watching her little friend, he seems to be heading to whatever has alarmed him, towards the track that leads into the trees; or perhaps he'll be turning down to the sagging bamboo bridge and return to town, to Tuxieng.

She resumes her position in the paddy, and soon is weeding again.

A few minutes later she looks up to see that her husband has placed his gun on the nearby embankment, and is coming back to her; he hasn't used it recently; they don't have much ammunition left and it is too expensive for them to buy. The mist has gone, and she knows that the sun is now working on the crop soon be harvested; parts are already becoming a gentle yellow-brown; and thankfully the snails that were destructive of some of the earlier crop that year have not been much in evidence.

There is no sign of Lam. She now thinks that one of the horses must have died to make him so agitated. Only once has she been with him up the track past their top terrace and over the stream; and when she came to the red warning post that her husband banged into the ground just a short way before the first birches, she had refused to follow Lam any higher, knowing he wanted to show her his friends; but she was terrified of them.

The person on the ground among the trees has been drifting in and out of consciousness, feeling his body becoming ever colder, knowing he is entering that state of life-threatening coldness he experienced on the cavern floor before the fever came. But the rice terrace that he'd seen keeps returning to his mind, and when he hears again the man's strange utterances, he finds some strength to look up, and sees him properly for the first time.

He is picked up with difficulty, with pain as before, and the walking resumes. This time he is held in a way that enables him to see better; they are coming out of the trees, there is water tumbling nearby, they are on a path descending towards the rice terrace, there are other terraces below, and now he knows beyond doubt that the man is trying to help him.

Meibei, standing well behind her husband, straightens and screws her eyes. She sees the figure she knows to be Lam walking down from the birches, though this time he seems to be moving very slowly. 'Lam's coming again,' she calls, 'is he holding something?'

Her husband looks up, blood draining from his head so he cannot make out what the simpleton might have. He smiles to himself that Lam could have caught a peacock for all he cares, so long as he doesn't trample through the terraces again.

'He'd better take his treasure to town,' he calls back. 'If he comes through the fields, I'll...' He stops in shock, seeing somebody in Lam's arms near the red warning post, and the next moment he yells: 'Lam's carrying someone!' and begins jumping through the rice towards the embankment and letting grasses fall from his hand.

Meibei is startled - he can't be, Lam's too small to carry a hunter if one is injured, and hunters are always in two's or three's, and they let her know when they are going up into the dangerous hills, and no one has passed in months. But she thinks she can make out the legs of an injured or dead foal, and starts for the mud steps.

Lam sees the farmer and is now hardly moving, his burden too heavy to hold much longer. When he hears his name, he stops and puts the person on the ground.

Reaching the simpleton completely out of breath, the farmer can hardly believe his eyes: a hunter is lying on the track in badly ripped clothes, alive but shockingly injured, the head and body are covered in wounds, one foot has a sandal and the other is bare, and the fellow seems to be trying to look up at him.

He kneels, and as he takes in the dull eyes and a face and neck full of cuts, he receives a further shock: he is looking at a youth whose age it is impossible to guess at from his state, sixteen, fourteen...

He shouts and waves to his wife who is still some way down the track, and turns back to the youth. 'Who are you? What you doing in the hills? How you get these injuries?'

The mouth opens but no words come, the youth merely staring up at him.

All sorts of things go through the farmer's mind: he might die on them, because part of the head and one of the hands look terrible, then what would they do? And how did he get up the track? He must have been taken by a hunter who hadn't told them. Surely Lam couldn't have taken him.

Meibei reaches her husband and lets out a cry. With difficulty she also kneels, her chest heaving as she tries to draw in longer breaths, and for a while she is unable to speak.

Lam has moved a few paces off the track and has stopped chattering; he is standing quietly, his head turned towards the mud cottage - his refuge - and the smile to the world has fully returned.

'It's a young lad and he can't talk or he don't answer,' the farmer says looking at her in fear.

'What's...what's your name dear?' she finally gets out.

She thinks he gives her the strangest look. 'Don't ...you don't know your name!' She turns to her husband. 'Where's your village?' he asks. 'Or Tuxieng,' she adds. 'You come from town?'

They don't get an answer. Meibei unties a wide hessian sash from around her middle, folds it, and puts it carefully under the head, noticing that part of the hair has been scorched. 'Your father do this to you? Tell me.' She looks into the eyes. They stare back at her, and she thinks death could be approaching.

The farmer takes off his doli and wipes his brow on his sleeve. They agree that they have to get the lad to the cottage, do what they can for him if he lives, and get him into Tuxieng, find the Doctor Chen they've heard about in North District; or they might get him to the apothecary's shop they've seen; but they have never been near the hospital at the other end of the town.

Meibei's husband works his arms under the body, and as he picks the lad up there is a pitiful cry. Meibei helps put the better arm round her husband's neck, thinking the head and the other raw-looking hand are so bad that she doesn't know what to do to help.

They walk down the track. 'What you doing in the hills?' the farmer asks again. 'Hunters take you and you got lost? How long you been up there?'

There is no reply.

They reach their tiny cottage without stopping, go inside, and put him on their k'ang, their hard-mud bed. As her husband goes out to create a makeshift stretcher, Meibei, hot and sweating, looks down at a boy she now thinks might be about fourteen. 'You sure you don't know your family? Your father, give me his name.'

The boy remains silent, the eyes telling her that he may not have taken in what she said.

She goes through a curtain, soon coming back with a bowl of lukewarm rice milk, to find him trying to turn onto his right side, the head trembling and tears falling. She cries out, puts the bowl on the floor spilling some of the milk, and touches part of the cheek where there is no cut. 'You're safe with me,' she says hearing her voice quiver. But the cheek is cold, and it makes her again think of death, except that he is crying.

She finds a cloth and dabs the wetness where she can. 'See this?' She touches the large wart in the middle of her forehead. 'Keep weeping an' you'll grow one, when you get better.' She tries to smile, stops the dabbing, and keeps the back of her forefinger against the cheek, telling him she wants him to drink the milk.

The tears soon stop, and she brings the bowl to his lips. Holding the back of his head as best she can, she praises him after he has taken the first sip, and again with the next. He takes a third, but when he doesn't open his mouth the fourth time, she places the bowl at the end of the k'ang and releases his head onto her pillow, the pillow filled with hair from the old nanny goat they used to have but had no money to replace.

She turns to the tiny shrine in a niche in the corner, to the happy Buddha. She whispers: 'Help me! I'm sure I've lost my younger son to the revolutionary struggle, but don't let this one go.' She looks back and sees that the eyes have closed. 'Don't go an' die on Meibei!' she calls out, 'we're getting you to a doctor.' She doesn't add that they never go near any doctor; there are very few in any case, and peasants like them have no money and cannot afford to offer enough rice or much else in kind.

She stays by the k'ang anxiously listening to the boy's breathing, watching his chest, occasionally giving him a nudge and telling him that she is beside him. But the eyes remain closed.

The woman's presence, and her touch and her voice - its strong dialect - have consoled the boy; most words he understood, some not. But now, despite the milk, he feels himself succumbing; he is drifting away from her, the voice is getting ever fainter …until he hears it no more …and thinks of nothing, not the woman or the cold within him, not the horse's breath or the chattering man who carried him…

10

...and the smiling girl is coming back, she is again beside him in the slippery stream in the warm sunshine, he is laughing down to the colourful ripples as she cuffs him ...and as he turns, her expression changes to serious and he begins to understand what her eyes are telling him: that she helped him at the boulder, he must feel the power of the sun within his body and must listen out for the peasant woman's voice, and when he hears it, hold onto it...

...and the image of the girl starts to disappear, he is beginning to hear once more the woman, as though her voice comes from over a hill, her faint words are growing louder, he is coming back to pain in a hand ...and when his cheek feels the warmth and strokes of the woman's rough fingers and he hears her telling him to open his eyes and not go away from her again and to take more rice milk, he looks up at her anxious and kind face, and his will to stay alive returns...

Meibei's husband comes back with a makeshift stretcher. The simpleton, who has been squatting on 'Lam's stone' close to the old buffalo, stands behind. Meibei has already looked at his grazed hand and told him that it would heal in a day or two.

The farmer places the stretcher on part of the k'ang, and when he has the boy lying on it, he makes Lam take hold of a pole at the back, and tells him not to let go, not to drop it. Meibei has the other pole beside Lam, and they lift the boy and take him out of their mud cottage and onto the path.

It is impossible to stretcher him over the sagging bridge, and the farmer struggles to carry him. Once across, they continue with the stretcher, the farmer and Meibei often having to tell Lam to keep his end up.

A traveller going the same way reaches them and takes over from Meibei and Lam, much to her relief; her legs have been giving her bad trouble for months; she didn't think she could have held the stretcher all the way to the start of town.

Before she turns back, she says to the boy: 'I'll come and see you, so you get better mind!'

She remains very worried for his life, and watches as the two men continue down the gentle incline towards Tuxieng, Lam following them. When they go out of sight through a worn-out bamboo grove that straddles the road, she makes two supplications to the gods: for the recovery of the seriously injured boy, and for her two revolutionary sons, although she feels in her bones that her younger one is dead. Being at heart a supporter of the Communists does not stop her from praying, sometimes.

*

11

'The wild horses! In the hills!' The doctor in his forties wearing a blue skullcap finds it almost impossible to believe, his left eye starting to twitch as he stands beside his young medical apprentice outside the high gate of his courtyard, looking down at the most extraordinary patient ever brought to him. 'Did you see anybody with him apart from this man?' He looks at the peasant farmer, and nods towards the smiling simpleton who stands a few steps away moving as if swaying. 'And what's his name? Is he the father?'

He is shocked at the state of the boy. He takes in at once that part of the head is scorched, that the left hand is badly burnt on its upper side, and that there appears to be some injury through torn clothing in the area of a shoulder. He cannot think how the boy came by such burns and cuts, except to have been in a fire and in thorny forest. He wonders if the strange little man is the deranged father who took him into the hills - no sane person would dare go there, except a hunter, as the peasant farmer said.

The farmer gives Lam's full name, adding that he has no wife or children, and then looks at the boy. 'Lad don't speak, he can't say where he's from.'

Doctor Chen glances again at the simpleton. 'Do you know where he lives?'

'Five Concubines temple.' The farmer shuffles. 'Wife give the lad rice milk, was that right?'

The doctor doesn't answer. The farmer and traveller place the boy on a bed as instructed, and retire to the door. 'We'll be going,' the farmer says, half looking at the traveller before making a short bow towards the doctor whose back is already turned. The medical apprentice returns the bow. 'I'll take the poles then,' the farmer adds, going towards his makeshift stretcher.

Again the doctor says nothing; he is placing cushions to support his patient's neck and the back of the head, and is looking at the head. 'Fetch my mother,' he barks at the medical apprentice. 'And bring warm water and towels.'

They make the boy drink from a bowl of tepid green tea mixed with a little ginger. Then they remove the single sandal - the other foot being without - and begin to cut away the trousers, parts of which have stuck to some of the wounds. A thin sheet is placed over the lower body. An old lady with white hair has come to stand nearby.

'Can you talk?' the doctor asks as he looks through the shirt at the left shoulder and upper arm. 'Good heavens, what's happened to you here?' He stares at the boy in astonishment. 'You've been badly bitten by a...' But he doesn't want to guess. 'And you're missing a finger. What animal did this?'

There is no answer, only vacancy in the eyes. Doctor Chen cuts away the shirt, and looks closer at severe puncture marks.

He turns back to the boy. 'Can you speak, say anything?' He receives another blank look. He sits down at the edge of the bed. 'Did that strange man leave you in the hills? Do this if yes.' He nods and waits.

No head movement comes. 'You can't tell me where you live? Or your family name?'

'Or you mother's name?' the old lady adds.

A puzzled expression comes over the boy's face. The doctor is about to stop his questions when to his relief the boy whispers 'No.'

'Ah good, you can talk. Tell me how old you are?' Again there is no answer.

'Tell me who is your best friend, or tell me the name of anyone you can think of, anyone.'

The boy stares up at him.

'During the night there is the moon. During the day there is the... do you know?'

The doctor feels the boy is searching him. 'Sun,' he hears.

'Good! Very good! And how many fingers am I showing you?' He hides his thumb.

Slow eyes look at the hand. 'Four' comes back the weak answer.

'Excellent! And what town are we in?'

The doctor waits. Again he receives no reply.

He looks at the hand. 'How did you get these burns? Did you fall into a fire, or did someone push you, do you recall?' The puzzled look returns.

'Tell me the first thing you can remember.' The boy frowns, and there is a long silence. 'Go on,' the old lady says, trying to encourage. The eyes turn to her, and she smiles back.

'...nearly drowned...' he is speaking a little louder '...couldn't see...' The eyes are filling.

The old lady bends nearer, wanting to take hold of the right hand that is not burnt; but she hesitates as it has its cuts, so she holds two of the fingers. 'My son's a good doctor, you'll be alright.'

'Were you in a boat?' the doctor asks, wondering if hunters might have made a boat in the hills, to fish at some high lake.

'...got out...'

'Did the boat sink?'

Again the boy frowns. '...cavern...'

'A cavern! What were you doing in a cavern? Who took you there, your father, or someone else?'

Now the boy has a look of anguish.

'You don't know who took you into a cavern? Or did you go there alone? Try to tell us.'

The boy is staring again at the old lady. The doctor asks: 'Did you have these injuries when you got out of the cavern?'

The boy appears to be thinking, then nods towards the doctor's mother. 'Well done,' she says.

The doctor continues: 'What did you do after getting out? Was anybody with you at that stage?'

The boy looks back at him, and the head shakes a little as if he wants to say No again. Then he speaks: '...forest ...followed streams ...lake...'

The legs jerk under the thin sheet, and there is a look of sheer panic as the boy says something Doctor Chen doesn't catch.

The medical apprentice whispers into the doctor's ear.

'Tigers! You saw tigers!' Doctor Chen straightens and reads terror, putting a hand over the legs to calm the movement. 'They can't have attacked you,' he asks in disbelief. He glances at the punctures in the shoulder and upper arm, badly swollen and red but relatively clean; he would have expected severe rips if from teeth or claws of tiger. He waits for some confirmation or explanation, but none comes.

The doctor talks with his mother, and she goes out of the room. A minute later she returns with a cup of thinned chicken broth, some of which the boy sips.

A girl of fifteen, her hair very short, comes into the room and gapes. 'Ah, Sanchi!' her father calls as he stands up from the bed. He beckons her and the medical apprentice into the corridor.

The doctor closes the door, leaving his mother with the boy. 'Run as quickly as you can to Ya Ya, ask him to come straight over or to send another hospital doctor, and they're to bring the carrier, that's important. Tell him we're treating a boy of about thirteen who has burns to a hand and his head and cuts all over him.' The doctor looks with concern from daughter to medical apprentice and back. 'It seems he's been in forests in the uplands for some days, and he has a serious animal bite. He was brought down from the area of the wild horses. And tell him he encountered tigers, that'll bring him!'

The girl catches her breath. 'Off with you!' he says, firmly patting the side of her arm.

'Is he going to be alright father?' But her father is already leading the medical apprentice through into his surgery, and waves a hand at her to go.

The surgery is cluttered. Chinese medical pictures hang tilted at varying angles from the walls, the floor is hardly to be seen for all the ledgers and papers and half-open drawers and a desk vying for space, and the desk itself is piled high with old equipment and books. In the annex preparation room, bottles and tins and bowls small and large stand among medicine grinders, herbs, roots, and more drawers, some with their labels hanging loose.

'You will never forget what you have just seen,' Doctor Chen says to the medical apprentice. 'For the rest of your life this examination will stay with you. We will have to treat some of his wounds, poor child, so be prepared for him to cry out. And when I tell you to hold him, you do so firmly, don't let me down. I'll leave Professor Su to deal with the burns.' He sighs. 'You realize the boy is in shock, he can't say much of what's happened to him. Hopefully he'll soon start remembering who he is and his home, which part of Tuxieng or what village he comes from.'

It takes over an hour for Professor Su - the Chief Doctor of Tuxieng Hospital and known affectionately by many as Doctor Ya Ya - to arrive with the girl Sanchi. They come in a four-wheeled carrier pulled by two men; part of the carrier is covered by tarpaulin over a bamboo frame.

When Doctor Chen hears his daughter returning with his old friend, he feels great relief and goes to greet him, talking briefly before leading him to the patient.

'Greetings, boy without a name!' the Chief Doctor says in seemingly high spirits, but masking enormous surprise despite his friend having warned him what to expect. He bows to the old lady, and she nods respectfully and stands up from the bed. 'I'm Doctor Ya Ya, and I'm glad to hear you have eaten something. Keep eating, keep drinking!' He looks over his glasses as warmly as he can. 'We're going to help you get better, and I want you to say to yourself that all your injuries will heal, you are already feeling stronger, keep saying that to yourself!'

The Chief Doctor is about to continue, when he receives the faintest of smiles, a look that tells him there is every reason to hope for recovery, every reason but one.

'I'm going to quickly examine you, I won't hurt you, I won't touch you at all hard, don't worry. Then we have our carrier to take you to my hospital, you will like it there, the gardens are the best in all southern China, they are waiting for you!'

Although Professor Su has immediately taken in the state of the head and the burnt hand, he bends over and looks first at the animal puncture wounds in the shoulder and upper arm, the part that most worries him, and retains his smile.

When he moves to the head, he asks without looking at the boy: 'Do you remember being in a fire?' He waits, gets no reply, and looks back kindly at him. 'Have you been in an explosion? What hit you on the top of your head? You have a clean cut and it's not deep, it's already healing, that's good, isn't it. Can you remember anything about it?'

'No,' the boy answers more clearly, and Doctor Chen thinks there is more strength in the voice, their young patient is already starting to perk up.

The Chief Doctor moves to the chest, then to the middle part of the body, in places pressing but not talking. Then he asks: 'Does your tummy hurt?' The boy nods. 'When did you last eat a meal?' The Chief Doctor receives a blank look. 'You don't remember when you last had a meal, some rice in your home, or in the hills maybe?' There is no response. 'And you can't tell us who was with you in the hills?' The boy gives the puzzled look again. 'How many days do you think you spent there?' The eyes close, come open, but the boy shakes his head.

They turn him partly onto his right side and look at the back. Finally the Chief Doctor examines the burnt hand.

The two men leave the room, followed by Sanchi and the medical apprentice. Professor Su says to his friend: 'As you say, amnesia, but blessings be he can talk. Obviously not horse marks. My guess is wildcat, except...' he hesitates, '...the punctures seem bigger. Can't be tiger, I've seen what they can do, anyway he wouldn't have survived.'

'A young one?' Sanchi chips in.

The face of the Chief Doctor gives away his doubt. He continues: 'Perhaps he was lying on the ground, sleeping on his side, and somehow the animal didn't pursue the attack. Very strange.'

The doctor friends agree that the boy must have been taken into the hills, dangerous though that would have been, and that the simpleton called Fang Lamgang who brought him to the peasants was the obvious suspect, since the farmer said the man often went up there. They do not think the boy himself is simple or walked there alone, though if he came from one of the villages, he might have. They agree it is much more likely that the simpleton made a fire, and the fire somehow exploded to cause the burns, though the loss of the little finger on the burnt hand was another puzzling feature - had the animal torn it off? They think the boy must have been abandoned after the fire or explosion, suffered the animal attack, and the simpleton went back for him later and brought him down, possibly not knowing what he had done. They also agree that the burnt hand, nasty though it looked, would heal largely by itself by growing new skin with the help of pig-fat applications at the hospital.

'We'll notify the police and town elders,' Doctor Chen says, 'we can give a description of the boy, some family must be missing him, or can be found if he was abandoned. I've given you an interesting one, Ya Ya.'

'You certainly have, unique.' The Chief Doctor pauses. 'Wandering in the uplands, what he must have been through! And he's lucky the animal didn't rupture a main artery. It's infection developing from that attack that I'm concerned about, as long as there are no internal injuries, and I don't think there are. At least none of the wounds look ulcerated, which surprises me when he's been in subtropical forest.'

16

2

Some three weeks earlier

The first thunderclap shook the wooden house in the early darkness and made the mother jump. She was standing with her father-in-law on a raised platform leading to the main door of their home, watching her son running through a courtyard lit by more flashes of lightning.

But as he ran to them up the steps, her fright was far less than the alarm she next felt when the old man delivered his unexpected invitation to the boy to accompany him into the uplands. She saw her son's look of surprise, his expectation caught in the glow of blue-tasselled lanterns swaying in the threatening air.

'The tigers have gone haven't they grandfather?' the boy gasped as the thunder trailed off.

'You'll need this my son,' the old man said, going past them just inside the house. He removed a sheathed long-blade hunting knife hanging by a cord from the wall, fondled the leather and stepped back onto the platform and handed it over. 'It belonged to your father, one of my presents when he was sixteen. Haven't seen any tigers near the Hut for thirty years, they're further in the hills.' He stroked one side of his long drooping moustache but did not look at the mother, though he guessed what she was thinking. They watched the boy undo the bind and pull the blade half way. 'The first time I took your father he was about your age or a bit older. You can help repair the Hut. And there's the lake, we can fish. You'll see birds and animals you've not seen before. Will you come?'

'Yes,' the boy answered towards his mother, no longer hesitant, as more sheets of lightning split the sky from the direction of the rapids.

The grandfather smiled at his daughter-in-law. 'I'll tell the school, Wenlie. I may not get there again, legs won't be up to it. We'll go the day after tomorrow,

17

rain or not, well before sunrise. We need to catch the sampan from the rapids. Be ready.'

Tsai Wenlie tried to hide her fear and did not speak. Lively though she was by nature, she had rarely crossed her father-in-law since coming into the Tsai family, patriarchal respect and obedience to the older generation being integral parts of their society. But her son sensed her anxiety, and ever after, when recalling the ghastly feeling she had on that night of storms, she would tell people that she was filled with foreboding.

Yuling, eleven years old soon to become twelve, was called 'Alinga' in the Tsai family. He was tall and well-built for his age, his shoulders and arms already showing growing muscle development.

He had one brother, Ayi, two years younger.

Their father had died three years earlier in battle during the Japanese invasion of Manchuria, and shortly afterwards their grandfather had begun calling each of them *my son* and they liked it. They knew that when their grandfather was not working, he disappeared into the lonely hills for weeks at a time, usually with one of the uncles, and that the Hut was completely isolated, had been in the family for nearly half a century, from well before the 1911 fall of the final dynasty. They always thought that his wrinkled face and weathered skin came from those journeys. And they loved the grey drooping moustache that fell long, left and right below the chin.

The next day, while his grandsons were out of the house, the old man spoke to Wenlie. 'We'll stay the night with the Luos, and one night or maybe two coming back. We'll be gone three weeks, and should be home the third day of the ninth moon. But if the weather is bad, don't be concerned, we'll get back when we can.' He chuckled. 'And don't mention the Luos to Alinga, I want to surprise him.'

Luchian, their town standing high above the river behind ancient three-sided walls - the river navigable each way though not directly below because of rapids - was an old market town on a small plateau beneath low hills to the west, hills that contained the burial grounds.

Six months after her husband was killed, Wenlie had left her coastal home in the east and taken the boys inland to Luchian to live with her father-in-law and uncle Jinjin, moving for two reasons: they would grow up in a larger family atmosphere, as Jinjin had three very young girls, and she was frightened that the Japanese colonization of Manchuria might be extended to include more of her motherland including parts of eastern coastal China - what soldiers might do to her and possibly to her two boys she did not like to dwell on.

She was a music and drama teacher at Luchian's boys-only junior school, in her early thirties, of well above average height and carrying herself with an air of friendly self-assurance; and in that respect she was different from most women in her society, obedient yes to her father-in-law, but not always meek or submissive in the presence of other men in the family or outside - it was as though she had taken on some of her husband's authority, to which she liked to add a little acting in her dealings with people.

For many months after the formal end of her period of mourning, Wenlie had felt unable to take part in the festivals, folklore plays and operas she loved. But recently, she had taken to the stage again and was receiving much applause for her acting and singing, though only she knew that she was doing it for her husband - the theatre and her teaching were the best means she had to alleviate the pain in her heart, apart from being with the sons she adored.

Yuling and Ayi loved their grandfather, and knew that at sixty-three he was old but not very old. He had been the first in the family to go to school, and had been so promising that he went on to a new university in Shanghai to become an engineer. The rise of the family from poverty was due to him. He was mellow and reflective, and in their earlier years they remembered him often singing. Nature was special to him, particularly birds, and when he read them books of the wild he became animated, his clipped speech full of colour and playing on their imagination. His collection of stuffed birds in a wooden outhouse, its windows of thick paper, never failed to excite them, not only the large birds of prey but also the smaller more colourful ones; some were mounted, others fixed to upright strips of wood, and all were named. He loved talking to bird vendors, inspecting their cages at the end of bamboo shoulder-poles, checking that the thrushes and mynah birds were kept in good condition; if they were not, his gentle nature took a different turn. And the boys knew that he was clever, had built bridges, roads and dams in the south.

Only once had Yuling felt his grandfather's rare anger. As a three-year-old he had come with his parents and toddler brother westwards up the rivers to visit his grandparents in Luchian for the Ancestors Feast Day celebrations, the occasion when families gathered to honour their dead. He had gone into a room and found the old man dozing in a favourite chair, the head and upper part of the body much tilted, and it seemed to his young eyes that one side of the moustache droops was too long, much longer than the other. Scissors lay on the table. He had seen his mother use them, and he thought that his grandfather would be happy to wake up and find the droops at equal length. He was pleased with himself when after two or three goes he had managed to snip off most of what seemed the longer side, without his grandfather waking.

'Grandfather! What have you done to your moustache?' his mother later asked wide-eyed, 'you look like a clown!' His grandfather began feeling the moustache, and received a terrible shock when his fingers were unable to find one side of the droops. 'My hair's diseased!' he exclaimed in alarm. Then they

19

discovered the open scissors and saw the hair on the floor. Yuling's mother and grandmother tried to protect him, but he received a good smacking. And until he and his parents and brother returned to their home in the east, his grandfather - who cut off a large length of the other droop to make it equal - dozed in his favourite chair with a thin muslin covering his face, and even went to sleep on his k'ang that way.

'Precious Alinga,' Wenlie said embracing Yuling the night before the journey, 'you must be brave like your father, and you *must* stick to grandfather, you understand me? It's a long way, and the uplands are not without dangers.'

    That night he felt great excitement and slept fitfully. He was woken early, his mother pressing on his hand, her face anxious in the light of a candle. As he climbed off his k'ang while his brother Ayi remained asleep nearby, his mother whispered to him: 'I've prepared a shoulder sack for you, it shouldn't be too heavy. When you reach the Hut, kneel at our little shrine, you'll see it overlooks the escarpment, I helped Papa build it. Pray for your safe return my sweet, and for his continuing journey.' She did not mention the bliss she had felt on her only visit to the Hut shortly after her marriage. Alone with her husband, she had experienced a feeling so overwhelming that only the joy in the hours after the birth of each baby came close.

The sky seemed unusually black to Yuling as he followed his grandfather into the lane, noticing the old man was carrying a rifle as well as a sack. Some of the dwellings glowed dimly red from candles that continued to burn, their house shrines giving him a feeling of security, of the permanence of things: it was mid-autumn, the air was pleasant and warm, and well before midday he knew it would be hot.

    At the end of the lane, where it met one of Luchian's two streets, a much larger corner shrine greeted them, full-glowing in the dark. There was nobody about. But as they approached the last few shacks of the town, a dog with half a tail, a friend to Yuling, stood at the edge of the road as if expecting him. This was the bitch that always followed for a while. Yet now, although he called her, the dog would not move. 'That's strange,' he said, 'she *always* comes to me.'

    The old man said nothing, hoped it was not portentous, and told himself to pay daily homage to the hill and forest spirits at the little shrine by the Hut. May my health remain reasonable up there, he said to himself.

    At first the grandfather walked in front, hardly looking to see if his grandson was keeping up. At one stage he pointed to the only bright object in the heavens. 'Venus,' he said quietly, 'it's a planet not a star, the horizon starts changing soon.'

    Yuling had already noticed that it was not as dark as he first thought; he was easily able to see for some distance; they were passing rolling paddy fields of well-growing rice, an occasional chained buffalo sleeping along a track.

'What if there are bandits?' he asked.

'Unlikely.' The old man tapped the side of the rifle. There was a short silence except for the crunch of sandals on impacted earth. 'Peasant dwellings,' he added, pointing towards vague low shapes appearing through the dark. 'If they hear trouble, they'll be out to check and help us. We're not interesting to bandits. You know why farm shacks are so far back? So they can see people coming, have time to defend themselves.'

Well into their walk, his grandfather started to hum, and soon to his surprise he was singing, the songs coming one after the other, sometimes with full words, sometimes just the melody, and they seemed to carry Yuling along. He had loved it when his father and grandfather had sung with the uncles, his mother accompanying them on her zither and often joining in. But he had not heard his grandfather sing since his father's death.

During one of the sadder songs, when the voice faltered Yuling turned. 'Are you crying, grandfather?'

'My son, there are two types of people on this earth. The ones who go happily from one song to another, they like the tunes, the words, they sing along or move their bodies. But do they really feel deep emotion? I don't think so. And there are the others, they are brought up sharp, the music grips them, they live in it and feel their souls touched. Your grandmother and your father were in the first group, your mother and me, we're in the second, music moves us, is great joy.' The old man let out a sigh. 'And sometimes, whether it's joyful or sad, we can't stop the odd tear.'

The road started descending towards the river. By the time they arrived at the rapids and could see ahead of them the outline of the lonely temple, the eastern horizon was brightening, although Yuling thought the sun was taking forever to appear. Many years earlier, on the last stretch of their journey inland to visit his grandparents, his father had brought them to this place. They were strapped to their parents' backs, and he remembered Ayi being frightened by the fiery dragons at the roof-ends of the temple.

As the old road took them along the side of the rapids, the noise of a mighty gong rent the air; it was being hit several times, the vibrating sounds blocking out the babbles of the river.

'Sunrise soon,' the old man said, putting a hand across his chest to hold his sack from slipping. 'This temple has never been attacked by bandits, over centuries, their code of honour. Sometimes townsfolk use it as end-stops for processions.'

They passed ancient stone tablets and went through doors in a wall and into a courtyard, confronted by statues of two armed gods larger than men, standing on either side of the main path. Great banyan trees with snaking roots and long-hanging hair semi-circled the path that led to the steps of the inner sanctuary.

Yuling could see the golden Buddha at the back; it was well candle-lit, with flowers in vases decorating the floors and tables below the statue. And he could hear a monk quietly intoning.

His grandfather placed a coin into a wooden box and took up a wad of votive money and several incense sticks. 'Offer these in honour to our ancestors, and to help them and us on our separate journeys,' the old man said, dividing the coloured notes between them and moving to one of the open burners. They put the notes into the fire, two or three at a time.

Walking to a bronze incense urn, greyish-black and heavily embossed, they lit the sticks and bowed up and down in prayer towards the Buddha, holding the sticks in front of them in closed hands.

...Ayi and me, Yuling said in his mind, we remember the voyage along the river, or rather I do, I think he only remembers the dragons on the roof. Grandfather is taking me to the uplands, so please protect us. And Papa, you told me you saw some tigers near the Hut a long time ago when you were young. Keep them away. I miss you, I love you, mother still loves you... He stopped, had noticed how much brighter the sky had become, and began to imagine what the Hut would be like.

The hand on his arm jerked him from his thoughts. He followed his grandfather up into the sanctuary, and they knelt on cushioned prayer mats, and said more prayers.

A few minutes later they were walking away from the temple. But the sun did not arrive for several more minutes, until they were approaching the river landing where the rapids ended, when Yuling felt the power of the great fireball as it rose over the low hills.

A sampan with a shabby semi-circular roof moved gently in the water, roped at each end to heavy stones. Four people had already gathered waiting to board. Other rickety boats were moored to the banks on either side of the river.

Nearby, a man with an old horse had set up a stall; the animal was unhitched from its cart. As his grandfather bargained for newly-cooked rice and some dates, Yuling looked carefully at the horse. He had seen much better ones in his first home in the east, but domestic horses were rare inland. He watched it drinking from a bucket, its hair covering the eyes, and when it looked up he studied those eyes, such small features in a great head, he thought, but large close up. He noticed the eyeballs had different browns in their darkness, and was fascinated by the length of the eyelashes, and by the long bulging veins down the head. There seemed to be sadness and a mystery in those eyes, and he told himself that he would soon draw a horse's head side-on.

Half way into the morning's journey down-river, the landscape began to change; where before there had been flat or rolling paddy fields, now narrow terraces of rice curved along the contours of ground rising more sharply, and they were passing the odd fruit orchard and sugar plantation.

'Beginning of the uplands, dark green, dense and primitive,' his grandfather said in his clipped way of talking, pointing from the open back of the sampan just as a reserve oarsman took over handling the long oar. 'Have a surprise for you, remember the Luos? We're staying tonight, old friends, they've a tea plantation. Your father liked them, admired their wine jars. Have a look at them, beautifully painted with jasmine and wild rose.' The old man smiled across the river. 'And he liked their daughter Janping. Good thing he didn't marry her! They don't know you're coming, that's my surprise for them.'

'Were those the people I met at Papa's service?' His grandfather nodded. Yuling remembered that before the procession moved off to the trumpets and the drums, he was introduced to an elderly tea planter and his daughter Luo Janping, a pretty woman though strange and emotional; she looked rather like his mother but smaller. Near the end of the service and after the whole family had bowed in unison three times towards the plaque, deeply, reverentially - the plaque that carried his father's name, though the body lay in an unknown soldier's grave far away in southern Manchuria - he had watched as the Luchian friends and citizens then made their three bows together as a group, and he had been startled when Janping kept crying out at each bow, which she seemed to make deeper and longer than anyone else.

They disembarked at Dongang shortly before midday, and walked in the shadows of a winding lane, its high walls draped with bougainvillea and geranium that hung between old lanterns.

Stopping at a thick door in the walls, the old man knocked hard and called out. Soon they could hear exclamations, people scampering towards them on the other side. Yuling watched a broad smile come over his grandfather's face, and when the door was opened they were greeted by loud shouts from three grinning adults: the elderly plantation owner and pretty Janping who Yuling recognised, and an elderly woman.

Janping was immediately looking at him. His grandfather barely had time to say that he'd brought his eldest grandchild, before Yuling found himself being hugged. At first she wouldn't release him, but when she did after prompting from the older woman, he managed to bow quickly to her parents, and they laughed and semi-bowed back with hands clasped and raised. There was such a chattering greeting going on that he thought he had never seen his grandfather so happy for a long time.

Over lunch in the courtyard under a bamboo roof covering below the raised house, he learnt that his grandfather and Janping's father had been college friends in Shanghai, and that the Luo tea plantation was on the other side of the Zass River, the connecting river that they would be crossing in the morning to start the trek proper into the hills.

Later that hot afternoon, the old woman handed him a drawing pad and a cigar box full of chalks. 'Your grandfather says you are a very good drawer, better than he is and that's saying something. They are coloured chalks, we haven't used them for years, so I'd like to see what you can do, as I like art.'

A few suggestions were made, and he decided to draw the well in a corner of the courtyard. Its pail leaned at an angle on the side of the rim, and a big gum tree and flowering hibiscus were a good backdrop.

As he was half through his drawing, Janping came down the wooden steps from the house, a large parrot on her shoulder. Yuling was at once fascinated with the bird of many colours, especially its blue, green and yellow feathers, and by its very long tail.

He stood up and soon began stroking its crown, and Janping gasped but did not pull back. At first only its eyes moved. But Yuling was watching, and when the upward lunge came, quickly he took his hand away as the squawking started.

'He's vicious,' old Luo called through the din while Janping was trying to soothe the bird. 'Take care, don't go near Genghis!'

He continued looking at the parrot. It calmed down and inclined its head towards him, appeared to be eyeing him. Before Janping could move away, he was touching its chest under the gouge beak, and it was letting him. 'Look at this,' Janping exclaimed, 'he never lets anyone near, except me of course!' He took a sideways look at his grandfather and caught the pleasure on his weather-beaten face.

At the evening meal he listened to the men talking about China's problems, especially what was happening just over the provincial border. 'It's appalling the Nationalist government let the Reds take over Jiangsi against the rights of the landowners,' old Luo exclaimed. 'They're even in pockets here in Fujian. We should never have let the Reds gather their armies. They start controlling the peasants, and it would have been the towns next if the government hadn't stopped them. They cause chaos. The country would break up if they got their way.'

'They're encircled,' his grandfather replied, 'trapped, the Nationalists will wipe them out. But social reforms are needed or the countryside will explode. The level of poverty is intolerable, we're the fortunate ones.'

'If the peasantry need reforms, not at my expense, and not at the expense of other people's property and livelihoods.'

Yuling's mind had begun to drift. The men were now talking about the Japanese '...loathe the devils,' he heard old Luo say, 'their militarism and emperor-worship, they are imperialist dogs...' But he was thinking about the colours of the parrot. And there had been some mention of a foreigner in the past in his family, a woman.

He was too tired to listen further.

That night he slept fully; the pleasure in the intimacy of his grandfather's friends warmed his heart; he felt at home with these people who had known his father, close in spirit to them, close to his father again.

Over breakfast, he heard that the weather remained good but could change, though rains were not expected. He listened as his grandfather told the friends when they would return. 'We'll come back down even if it's raining, unless it's bad in which case just wait for us.'

Old Luo replied: 'If you get down too late for the last ferry, stay in the cottage, we'll leave the door unlocked and come over the next morning.'

Accompanied by Janping, they walked through the twisting streets of Dongang until they came to the Zass River, where Yuling saw the old ferry in the water. He took hold of ropes on either side of step planks, and followed the other two down to a floating platform. They had come for the first crossing an hour after daybreak.

His grandfather pointed to three birds sitting on the ferry's railing. 'Cormorants, wonderful fish-catchers, I've seen one trying to swallow a water snake.'

The river was low with some of its mud banks exposed. Wooden houses stood on the town side, some on stilts near the bank. On the far side the vegetation was lush among palm trees of every shape and angle; and behind the trees, row upon row of tea bushes climbed the hillsides towards higher darker subtropical forest.

Once over the river, they walked up through the extensive plantation, with Janping escorting them to the last of the bushes. There she said to Yuling: 'You're to consider me your aunt, and if anything happens to me, you must have Genghis.' She turned to her father's old friend. 'Look after the boy, Peiheng.'

Yuling felt apprehensive as he followed his grandfather up the path and into the forest. His three weeks of adventure had begun. 'You're not taking the rifle,' he said.

'Too heavy. I've borrowed a revolver, it'll do, and there are guns at the Hut.'

The narrow path wound its way through undergrowth of bush and creeper. Above them the canopy of trees blocked out direct sun, but they could see their way well enough, particularly when shafts of bright light penetrated.

25

At first his grandfather had difficulty; he was breathing hard and wanting frequent rests, and Yuling wondered if they would have to turn back. But after a while they settled into a rhythm and the rests were less needed.

'The noise of the birds is amazing!' he exclaimed, looking upwards from under his doli.

'It grows less as the day gets hotter.'

'Will we meet hunters?'

'Possibly, if they're up there. But they mightn't be around when we pass. We'll come to three of their huts, they're well spaced out, ours is the fourth and last, further on. We couldn't get through these forests if the hunters didn't keep this track open.' The old man stopped and took a small cloth tucked into his belt and mopped his face and neck.

When eventually they came to a clearing, they took a further rest beside a stream, drinking and enjoying cold water on their faces. Sitting on a low flat rock, the old man rolled up his trousers and began rubbing a liquid on his calves. 'I must have sat on this rock a hundred times,' he said, handing Yuling the bottle. 'Rub this in, my son.'

'What is it?'

'Tiger ointment, legs benefit.'

Yuling began to massage the back of his right leg, and asked: 'When will we get to the Hut?'

'Normally takes six hours from the top of the plantation including rests, but we'll take seven or more. We're well into the first stretch, all uphill, sometimes steep as you see. Then we descend into two valleys and go up again, they're not bad, plenty of water to drink. By early afternoon we'll be where the hills level off, and we can rest at a hut if we need to. Then there are the lakes, we head for second tallest peak, that's a good direction pointer. If you're too tired, I promised your mother we'd stay the night at the third hut. The final stretch is through a short forest and up a small ravine, you'll like the great boulders.'

'What are the animals? Janping told me to watch out.'

'No need to be concerned, they stay away. Lizards. And keep an eye out for resting snakes on the path in warm spots.' The old man smiled, knowing Yuling liked reptiles.

'And no tigers?'

The smile went. 'I told you, there *were* tigers, many. My father shot some, but he preferred not to, used to say they were magnificent cats but cowards at heart, frightened of human noise unless trapped or hungry. I killed two myself in my twenties. The hunters finished them off years ago where we're going. When my father built the Hut we lost a coolie, he just disappeared one evening, we never heard a thing. We kept rattle-tins, tigers hate that. I'll teach you to use the revolver, but you're not old enough yet for a bigger gun.'

'Panthers?'

'Maybe a few, they're shy, won't see them. Hunters get one occasionally.'

The ointment seemed to help Yuling, but the strap of his sack rubbing against the shoulder had become a trial, and he moved it to the other.

They reached a hunters' hut at the top of the first valley, but there was no sign of men. They were able to throw water over their heads from a nearby pool, and cooled their feet. The sun beat down on them by the water, and they were glad of their dolis.

As they crossed one of the streams of the second valley and were walking upwards again, they found that for a short stretch new vegetation had overgrown the path to knee height.

'Hunters haven't been this far for a while,' his grandfather said, 'we'll be undisturbed, that's how I like it.' The old man began hacking with a curved farm knife that had been strapped to his sack. 'We're not far from the plateau lakes, we can see further then, the going's easier.'

Yuling also helped to cut away the growth, using his father's hunting knife, and soon they were through.

When they finally came out of the forest, they stopped at a second hut and had a snack under the drooping branches of an old larch. Yuling could see two lakes, the first stretching some distance, another smaller one behind it; the landscape was rocky and dotted with little trees.

His grandfather pointed to two blue peaks in the distance. 'We aim for the right hand one, go round the right of the lakes.'

It took them over two hours to get past the second smaller lake, and as they approached the last of the hunters' huts, the old man said: 'I'm finished for a while, got to rest here.'

Each was suffering from pains in legs and shoulders, and Yuling knew that his grandfather was carrying rice and other provisions, as well as the revolver and the farm knife. In the last stretch, he'd often seen him pursing his lips. At least a welcome cooling change had come in the weather, with clouds filling the sky from the east. 'The sun's gone,' he said as his grandfather pushed open a creaking door.

Some time later he was woken. 'We've rested too long, you were fast asleep,' the old man said with a serious look, before reverting to his gentle smile that sometimes made Yuling remember his own father. 'Darkness can come quickly if the clouds get thicker. Can you keep going, or shall we stay here, walk the last part in the morning? Could be raining then, makes clambering up the ravine more difficult. If we keep on, we can have supper in the Hut, maybe outside with a fire. Then you can sleep long.'

They went on, and soon were walking again in lighter forest, still following a rough track. They had only trudged a little way when Yuling began to feel faint and flopped to the ground. 'I'm sorry…' he gasped.

The old man sat beside him. 'Put your head between your legs, I'll rub some ointment on you.'

A couple of minutes later he was given water and two betel nuts to chew. 'You've done well, better than your father when he first came as a boy. We can go back to the last hut, do the rest tomorrow if you prefer. We're not far now.'

Yuling's legs hurt, but the faintness had soon gone. He was about to say he wanted to return to the last hut when his grandfather added: 'Lie like this!' He watched him stretch out, the revolver resting between them in its holster. 'Look up through the trees, take deep breaths, you'll feel better, an old army trick. We'll have a conversation looking at the sky, you start.'

Yuling lay with his knees up, at first wondering what to say. Then he asked: 'How did mother walk all this way?'

There was a chuckle. 'Ah, my son, when in love you can do anything, move the moon or the earth. Your mother is plucky, always was, she showed that the first time your father brought her to us. And she's wise, invokes the help of the gods. You may think I'm hard on her sometimes, but she knows my admiration, and she's good-looking and talented. I love her acting, her mimics, wonderful!' There was a pause. 'Your father chose well.'

'Did he think of marrying Janping?'

'He did!' There was another laugh. 'He asked me about her as a wife. I said yes she was attractive, but scatterbrained. They were close, but then he met your mother and it was love at once, though she needed some persuading I believe.'

'Why?'

'Maybe she didn't want to be married to an engineer like me, away on projects. Maybe she thought his face too long!'

Yuling stretched his legs out and looked across, catching the smile to the trees. He said nothing, turned back and listened to the buzzing of insects.

Not long after he asked: 'You said to the Luos that we have a foreigner in the family, who was that?'

No answer came; his grandfather had just groaned and was trying to stand. 'Come! We've got to keep going.'

They came to yet another stream and walked beside it against the flow. 'This feeds the lakes we passed. Further up it divides and goes down a second ravine into a different area.'

Yuling hardly listened; he was now desperate to reach the Hut and finally rest. When they entered the base of the narrow ravine, he was shocked to see how steep it was. But his grandfather told him that the Hut was not far over the top, and this spurred him on.

28

Huge grey-streaked marble rocks overhung the narrow stream that tumbled towards them in a succession of waterfalls to their left.

'The Buddha boulder' his grandfather called out with a nod, 'named by my father.' On the far side of a pool into which one of the waterfalls cascaded, Yuling saw a huge upright boulder sitting majestically under the rock face, bulging in the middle like the Enlightened One.

The light grew ever weaker as they made their way slowly up through the ravine. Sometimes they had to use both hands in the narrow twisting path between the rocks, his grandfather struggling and again needing frequent stops.

When they reached the top and the stream became more level, the old man said: 'Mustn't stop, we'll be there in fifteen minutes. Bang these with your father's knife from now on, as loud as you can. Nothing to worry about.'

Yuling was surprised, immediately frightened to be handed two tins loosely tied that came from his grandfather's sack. For the first time on the long trek up, his grandfather had the revolver out of its holster and pointing.

As they approached the last of the boulders on their left, one that the water curled round, Yuling was striking the tins, thinking of big cats, aching limbs and the safety of a building he was about to see. And when they tramped past the boulder, he was too anxious and too tired to notice that it divided the stream, that part of the water went into another direction.

A few minutes later they were crossing the shallow stream, and when he stepped from the water, it took him a few seconds in the murky light to realize that some way ahead was the outline of a small building with curling ends.

'Definitely my last visit, couldn't do this again,' he heard the old man say as they trudged the final stretch.

They reached the Hut and threw down their sacks and he watched his grandfather take a stone and bang out a wedge in a wooden brace. He followed him inside, waited while a candle was lit, and asked where he could lie. He had forgotten they were to have something to eat.

Before the grandfather had time to light a small kerosene lamp, the grandson was lying on a k'ang deep in the unconscious.

3

...the great bird flew up through the invisible currents of air...rising high above the escarpment to keep sight of her human admirer and a young one...wanting no bangs as her calls to her mate circling the forest below pierced the vast silence...

'**H**ear something my son?' the old man called, his way of greeting the boy he loved, and who he greatly admired for his youthful artistic talent.

Yuling walked stiff and slow through the open door of the Hut, into the brightness of a sun well in the sky, and saw his grandfather adding sticks to a small fire. Further on, he could see a path going through rocky terrain, with a few trees on either side before it disappeared into a wood.

He stopped and listened. 'The fire?'

'Go higher!'

He turned; there was a light breeze and some rustling.

'Trees?'

'Higher!'

In his grandfather's smile he read the love; and there was contentment in the eyes. He looked up, wondering what was meant; the clouds on the last part of the trek had gone.

Shrill mewing came to his ears, cries rising and falling and echoing through the limitless sky, and he saw a bird of prey gliding high above them. He was about to answer when another magnificent bird came swooping up over the Hut from the escarpment side.

'Black kites,' his grandfather said, 'but they're dark brown not black. Their ancestors were here when my father first came. They're greeting us. Look at those wings with their finger-like feathers, and notice the fantail. What power, what grace!'

They craned their necks and watched in silence for several seconds. Then the old man looked down. 'Take this, fetch some water, you're perfectly safe.'

Some fear came to Yuling as he was handed a bucket and pointed to the stream. He noticed a long-barrel shotgun a few paces away, its muzzle propped against a sapling.

'Just don't go out of sight Alinga, don't wander.' The use of his pet name in the family rather than the usual 'my son' only added to the fear - he wasn't going to wander.

'Shouldn't I have the tins?' he asked. His grandfather shook his head.

As he walked over an area of short grass strewn with half-sunken rocks, the aches in his legs and shoulders told him he had achieved something special the previous day. Half way to the stream he looked back to the sight of the old man watching him, shotgun in hand.

He reached the water, looked around, dipped the bucket and filled it only partly, and took it back as quickly as he could without trying to run.

While his grandfather prepared a meal, he went to the other side of the Hut to see the escarpment. The little wooden building with its weather-worn curling roof-ends stood well back from the edge.

Two narrow round pillars supported a small portico to a closed door, the portico's little roof making him think of ancient boats, their bows rising to the sky.

Painted on the portico's door, from top to bottom, a fierce celestial guardian looked out in full armour, eyes blazing, sword ready to strike at evil spirits that dared to come near. The painting looked old and was behind a heavy glaze. Yuling's mother had mentioned the little shrine but not this painting. He felt a degree of comfort; now he had the warrior's protection as well as his grandfather's.

On either side of the portico, glassless windows with shutters gave panoramic views. Under a shutter, a cedar wood bench stood against the wall. One shutter was open, through which he could see a room with a reddish middle column and two unlit lanterns hanging from the ceiling.

He looked over the escarpment down to forests, parts of which were covered by morning mists. Above the mists the sky was clear, the hills in the far distance gleaming in the light of the sun.

He thought he could see one of the lakes they had passed, and guessed the direction of the Luo tea plantation, though there was no sign of the Zass River or Dongang on the other side. Where his home town Luchian was he had no idea, and he wondered what his brother Ayi and three younger girl cousins would think if they could see where he was.

A whiff of incense came to him from the stream side of the Hut, and he walked the few paces to the shrine his parents had built. It was a small edifice of rocks not much taller than himself, the statue of the Buddha looking out over the forests, its gold paint peeling, the lower part blackened by candle smoke.

He remembered his mother's instruction to kneel, but the stone slab had bird droppings and looked hard. He remained standing, thanking the spirits of the hills for helping him reach the Hut. His grandfather walked over and stayed silently beside him.

A minute later they were squatting on the ground near the fire over bowls of rice and strips of dried fish. The old man said: 'You're the fourth generation to come here. I helped my father build the Hut. It took us two full springs and autumns. Sometimes the rains were so heavy we couldn't leave the tents, so we read and played mah-jong. Twenty coolies made this clearing, we got rid of rocks, trees, bushes, everything, and we cut the planks to size. But we never worked at daybreak or dusk, too dangerous.'

Yuling knew the danger referred to. 'Why did your father come so far into these hills?'

'Loved everything to do with nature, saw the potential when hunting with friends, knew he'd be alone. I could happily go to the next world from here, the birds would take me.'

Yuling caught the look to the sky; the comment frightened him, and he thought of his grandfather becoming ill, or worse...

After they had eaten, he went inside to inspect the Hut, at once coming into a small passage, more an alcove, with two rooms leading off on either side. In the alcove, white bowls of metal sat on a table, one half filled with the water he had brought from the stream. Two long-barrel guns lay horizontally in a rack, a third space empty. Nearby rested the holstered revolver, above work-tools and fishing gear in open boxes on the floor.

In the room to his left he could see the k'angs he and his grandfather had slept on. To his right, through a partly drawn ring-curtain of colourful phoenixes was the room with the red column and the lanterns that he'd seen from outside. And as he went in, strong sunlight came at an angle through the open shutter, brightening the column's crudely painted flower motifs running up its curvature.

Another very large k'ang, made of stone and big enough to sleep three people, he thought, stood on one side of the room - a sitting or sleeping area that on unusually cold days he knew could become a wood-stove underneath. At the shutter end of the k'ang, a framed photograph of his grandmother stood on a shelf; he remembered her only a little as he was five when she died. And beside the frame hung a board with pieces of paper tagged. Rough-hewn benches with loose cushions faced each other against the walls, a shelving of books above one of them, a large and strange technical drawing pinned nearby on the wall. A table on one side of the small portico door held a lamp.

Pushing through another curtain displaying peacocks, he found himself in a very small cooking area, its own door to the outside facing the latrine shack several paces away and the path to the wood.

That first day they rested, except that he was shown how to load, hold firmly, aim and fire the revolver, and how not to shoot from too long a range.

They took turns to aim at a tree, and although he found the handgun heavy with a tendency to rise when fired, he soon learnt to control this.

The following morning they went to a lake on the far side of the wood, Yuling carrying the revolver in the holster strapped to his shoulder.

'I hope we don't see a tiger,' he said as they came out through the trees.

The old man jiggled his favourite old shotgun. 'We won't, not here. Would hate to kill one after all these years.'

Within a few days, Yuling felt he was learning more about life than ever before. Using his father's long-blade hunting knife, he helped clear thorny vine that had spread in places round the base of the Hut. They went into an area where he was shown trees that his grandfather said existed as a species millions of years earlier. He learnt to recognize certain birds. And he fished at the lake, sometimes from the bank between clumps of reed, sometimes a little in the cold water.

On one occasion when they caught more fish than they needed, his grandfather stood by the lake and said in his short way of speaking: 'My son, moments like this make me content, I like it here more than anywhere, can feel the spirits of the air, in the wind, in the trees and mists, they make music and talk in my ear, drive away my sorrows.'

One late afternoon, after helping knock nails into some of the loose planks in the walls of the Hut, and after digging and pulling up nearby unwanted saplings, Yuling was told: 'You're the best drawer in the family. When the sun descends over the hills, go half way to the stream and draw the Hut and hills from there. Don't include me in it. Take the revolver, have it out on a stone, I won't be far. I'll give you some ink, use it first but don't overdo it, leave lines unfinished, then draw sparingly with the pencils. Don't be frightened to use colour.'

He liked the idea and the compliment, and was excited to be handed paper on a board, together with a feather pen in a small glass of ink, and coloured pencils his grandfather had sharpened. He had already noticed that the Hut contained a number of surprising objects that family and friends must have brought up over the years, including a mounted hawk, two drums, a zither, and the engineer's drawing of the Sun Yat-sen Bridge, the drawing he had seen pinned up.

He no longer had any fear walking with his grandfather to the lake or going alone to collect water from the stream. The evening was still, and he felt inspired sitting on a low flat rock. The revolver was beside him out of its holster. He was looking back to the Hut and over the escarpment, and he could see his grandfather reading outside the main door facing the wood.

Streaks of late sun under the horizon came up from the distant hills, colouring the partly cloudy sky in yellows, oranges and reds that reflected in the small building's sweeping roof and its curling ends. His parents' shrine cast a dramatic shadow on the grass.

The ink that he applied with the feather pen, sometimes licking the tip to reduce strength, created a sharp liveliness to his drawing, especially at the curling ends and at the top of the escarpment, and as he worked the pencils he knew instinctively that he was doing well.

Just before finishing, he was so absorbed in his idea to include the black kites that he took little notice when his grandfather came to stand behind. Carefully he placed the wings of a bird of prey high over his escarpment in the top left of the picture. He was wondering where to place the second bird when he heard the cough, and turned.

'Just one bird, I think. May I?' The old man bent down and took the board with its drawing. Without a word but beckoning, his grandfather walked back towards the Hut, Yuling following in silence. When his grandfather went in, Yuling stayed at the door thinking his picture might not have pleased. But after a very short while he was being called, and he found him beaming and pointing to the shelf. 'See, I've pinned it up, goes well near your grandmother. Very good, my son, I love it, so does she.'

'Tell me about father,' Yuling asked during their second week as they squatted in the dark by a low fire near the little shrine. His mother had told him things, but he had never liked to ask his grandfather, knowing the grief. Now he felt he could. 'What happened to him, grandfather?'

The old man looked towards the fire. 'You know he wasn't a soldier, but the armies in Manchuria needed technically-minded men. He'd done some military training, could build defences, barriers and get up wooden and metal river-crossings. They were fleeing an onslaught by Nipponese infantry, there was artillery and bombing. His unit was caught at night, some General's stupidity, he ordered them to retreat through the wrong valley and they went straight into an ambush...' His grandfather stopped and looked up at the early night sky. Yuling turned to the embers in the fire, thinking he would hear no more. After a short while the old man continued: 'Only a few escaped in the darkness, the rest died in the valley. Fighting went on for several hours. A few escaped, and one soldier reported seeing your father and another man carrying a wounded soldier away, then all three fell.' The old man's voice had begun to shake, and Yuling felt his own tears swelling; in the dying fire he imagined seeing the explosions of warfare. 'The hardest thing for your mother and me, we can't visit the valley. It's not the distance, we'd go, but the Japanese give no details and won't allow visitors. The Manchurians are supposed to be back in charge but they're not.'

Half way into their stay the weather turned nasty, each developing headaches in the afternoon as they saw the approaching dark clouds that already blanked out the furthest hills. His grandfather had warned the previous day that they might be in for a typhoon from the Pacific, one that could last long.

They brought in firewood and three latrine buckets washed in the stream. It became ever darker, and they watched the panoramic view quickly fading. The wind increased, they closed and braced the shutters, and did the same to the door of the small portico. The celestial warrior would not stop the storm and would get very wet, Yuling thought, now understanding the reason for the heavy glaze.

The first splatters of rain falling on the roof were loud, but he never expected what hit them barely half a minute later, not the noise of thunder after lightning, but of rain and wind crashing on them with such force that he was sure the shutters must fly in at any moment and the Hut would be twisted round and blown over the escarpment. He had never felt so frightened of the elements, and remembered his father telling him about the colossal noise inside a waterfall by the Yangtze.

But his grandfather seemed to take it all in his stride, coming over to his bench and shouting in his ear: 'Sit on the k'ang, my son,' pointing to the end near the red column, 'you can read or go to sleep, or try to!'

Yuling detected the giggling but couldn't hear it, and felt reassured knowing that his grandfather had survived many such storms. As he took a book and climbed onto the stone k'ang and its cushions, he watched the old man sit at the other end near his drawing, a quilt over the shoulders. Soon they were reading under the light of the single lamp.

The storm's first battering of the Hut lasted several hours, during parts of which Yuling managed to sleep but only fitfully.

When the first lull came he asked: 'The foreigner in grandmother's family, who was he?'

The old man looked at the photograph. 'Ah, a Frenchman, a trader who seduced your grandmother's grandmother. He took a Fujian girl, she was only fourteen, made her his wife in some false marriage contract, but her family didn't find out until afterwards. They protested and brought a suit against the foreigner. The French Consul ordered him to leave China, probably didn't want him to cause more trouble. The western dogs thought themselves superior, abused their position, still do, it's even worse now. The girl had a baby by the man, another girl. She wasn't allowed to keep it and the child was taken into care by Christian missionaries in Amoy, grew up in an orphanage. She became very good-looking, well educated and sought after. Your grandmother was one of her children. When I was to marry your grandmother, my family paid respectful visits to exchange presents, and my future mother-in-law told me her history. So your grandmother's mother was half French, very tall and elegant. You may get your height from her more than from your mother, and your nose as well.' He smiled at Yuling. 'She was friendly to me, we discussed all the religions. She was Christian, her husband and children Buddhist. She told me she had no problem praying to the Christ in our temples, with her family around her.'

The next morning, during another lull in the stormy weather, Yuling was asked what he was reading, and showed a book on snakes. 'It was on the top shelf,' he said, 'I like the different colours and the patterns on the skins. Look at this one!' He held up the front cover.

The old man laughed and shook his head. 'They've got in here.'

'In the Hut!'

'Ten years ago. Your father and uncle Jinjin were here, we were returning from shooting. Coming towards the lake, we were very surprised to count three snakes in the space of maybe fifty paces. Different types. And they all seemed to be moving ahead of us or to the side, quite fast, in the direction of the water. That worried us, you don't often come across snakes. And less than a minute later we saw another. Then an earthquake started, a deep, sickening, unworldly noise, the ground shook for several seconds, we held each other and prayed for our lives. Those snakes knew what was coming when they left their holes. We got back to the Hut, I opened the door, and a small yellow one, they can be the most dangerous, slithered in, disappeared in this room. We tried to isolate it, blocked the way to the little kitchen and the bedroom. Your father stayed in the alcove with a stick, Jinjin in the kitchen, I came in here but couldn't find it, poked everywhere, beat everything and we stamped. We decided to keep the doors open hoping it would sneak away. The worst thought we had was when going to bed in case it was still around, but there was no sign. I slept badly that night and we kept sticks in our hands.' The old man burst into laughter. Yuling remained concerned. 'First thing in the morning we searched again. Began to relax that day. By the following day we were certain it must have got out, found a hole in the wall.'

Yuling thought the end of the story had come, and felt sorry for the snake, that it had been scared by the stamping and banging.

'That evening your uncle Jinjin was sitting on your cushion,' the old man pointed, 'and thought his backside was having spasms, then shot up screaming the snake was under him. I lifted the cushion and beat it on the head.'

Yuling's eyes widened. 'Did you kill it?'

The old man chuckled. 'Fourth or fifth time.'

Yuling didn't see the funny side; they should have got the snake into a sack and put it out.

The old man caught the thought. 'You may like snakes and lizards, my son, but please not in the Hut!'

They had nearly three days of recurring fierce winds and torrential rains. When finally better weather arrived, they were relieved to be able to go outside again. But from the escarpment they could see only the far-away hills; thick mists that rose from the forests covered all the nearer hills and valleys.

In the middle of the third week, his grandfather told him they would soon have to make the return journey down to the plantation friends. He was given certain cleaning and clearing tasks, one of them to wash the towels in the stream.

He was in two minds - he'd loved their time in the hills, but he wanted to get home to tell all that he'd experienced and seen.

On their last full day before they were due to return to the Luo household, they sat on a narrow promontory into the lake in the glory of the late afternoon sun. Yuling had placed the holstered revolver on the ground beside his grandfather's favourite single-barrel shotgun. Neither had taken their dolis with them; on this last afternoon, his grandfather had said that he preferred not to wear one, that he wanted to savour everything around him ...and above in the sky.

'Sad moment,' the old man said looking at him, 'I don't expect to be able to get here again.' Yuling felt the bond between them, a bond that had strengthened over the days they had spent together. 'But *you* will, you can take me every time you come here, bring your father too, then you'll know we're happy.' His grandfather paused. 'We'll have excellent weather tomorrow, see the wispy clouds?'

Yuling looked up, and then picked a stone and threw it into the water, watching the ripples as his grandfather began to talk about one of the engineering jobs he had done.

'...and in south Guangdong we built a small dam...' a stick was being used at their feet to show how a river had been temporarily moved '...problem was to get through the bedrock to divert the...' The old man stopped in mid-sentence, dropped the stick, grabbed the shotgun and began getting up as quickly as he could.

Yuling was startled by the sudden movement, tigers immediately coming to his mind for the first time in many days, and he grabbed the holster, leapt up and took the revolver out, letting the holster fall and removing the safety catch. At first he couldn't see the big cat that he thought had frightened his grandfather.

'Look, my son!' he heard him whisper, 'what a present for the Luos!' He caught sight of a mountain hare with huge ears, and felt immense relief; the animal was on its hind legs looking at them from about forty paces not far from the water's edge on their side of the small lake. Apart from the banging of the tins and the first hour of the storm, this was the only seriously frightening experience he had had in their time in the uplands.

The hare was now crouching by a low bush, still looking towards them. 'Cartridge too big for the poor thing,' Yuling heard, 'doesn't matter, can't miss unless it runs, they're fast, can swerve.'

He was standing immediately to his grandfather's right. Quickly he put the revolver back on the ground, clamped his hands over his ears, and preferred to look down, telling the animal to run, he definitely did not want it killed.

He waited. No blast came. He looked slightly up at his grandfather while keeping his hands over his ears. He caught him cursing, and wondered if the gun had jammed or there was some problem with the cartridge, hoping there was.

When he thought his grandfather was about to fire, he lowered his head again, glimpsing that the hare hadn't moved and feeling sad, and the next moment an ear-splitting explosion shattered his world as a force hurled him sideways onto hard ground and searing pains shot through his head and a hand as if they had been plunged into a furnace and knives were cutting through him.

He lay stunned, his ears throbbing; he was trying to scream but nothing came out.

The smell of explosive and burning hair came to clear his mind enough for him to realize he was on fire. He managed to stand, staggered down the promontory's short slope, and let himself fall through reeds into the lake. As he went under he blacked out, but the pain brought him fast back to consciousness, his feet felt the bottom and his right hand tried to hold some of the reeds.

Using his legs to push himself out of the water, he collapsed onto the start of the slope, with the right side of his head against the ground; he was hardly able to breathe, only rapid panting being possible as he lay soaked, shivering and in shock.

The volcano in the left hand forced him to look along the ground. Upper parts of the hand between the wrist and the finger-joints near the nails seemed red-raw with patches of black, and the skin was no more. He raised his head to look closer, moved the hand up, and the little finger dangled loose, the further horror making him drop the hand to the ground.

Grandfather... He wriggled himself up the slope crying out, and saw his grandfather lying just a few paces away, the back facing him, the hair at the side of the head strangely dark and matted, the shirt smouldering at the neck. There was no movement.

His shivering grew worse. He tried to raise himself with his good hand, but only succeeded at the third attempt, and as he got to his feet he nearly fell back, his legs felt so weak.

He lurched forward, the smell of cordite entered his nostrils, and when he reached his grandfather and went on one knee, he saw close-up the dreadful state of the hair.

He knew his grandfather was unconscious, that he would have to wake him and dampen the collar. He called to him and gently pushed the back of the shoulder. There was no response. He pushed harder twice more, but still his grandfather did not stir, and small flames were coming round the neck of the shirt. He lent over thinking to smother the fire with his own wet shirt or the lower part of his grandfather's, and looked down at the imploded blackened face of death; bone and the hollow of an eye-socket were exposed and the nose was gone.

No scream came; he was filled with such terror that he jumped up as best he could and turned away, choking and stumbling the short distance to the beginning of the promontory.

The top of his head made him stop; one side felt white hot, and he believed he might still be on fire. He raised his good hand, and as he was feeling shrivelled wet hair on the left side, he touched something small and jagged that fell out. He looked at the object on the ground, and thought it was a sizeable splinter from his skull - he was going to die. He had not seen the shotgun in pieces on the other side of his grandfather. In his shock, it did not occur to him that the gun had exploded and that a sliver of wood had struck him; nor could he know that the cut in his skull was not deep, that his fall into the lake had loosened the sliver.

The only tiny comfort coming to him was the warmth he began to feel from the evening sun; his shivering was lessening.

He thought of the Hut, had to reach it, it had the medicine tin, but would he make it there alive... Then he thought he'd have to pull his grandfather, but soon realized that would be impossible.

Tigers! He looked around, now sure they were in the area, near him. Where was the revolver! He was confused, the holster and gun must have fallen off him when he fell into the lake, he was defenceless ...or had he left it in the Hut...

The stick came to his mind, the one his grandfather had used to outline the river in the ground, and near it he remembered putting the revolver. He *had* to have it, had to go back to his grandfather's body. But he dared not look, and the thought made him shake more as the sickening smell of explosive remained in the air.

Quickly he turned, and saw the body and the handgun close to one of the legs. For a few seconds he hesitated. Then he lurched forward looking only to the ground, and when he reached the revolver he caught sight of the barrel of his grandfather's shotgun; it was broken from the rest of the gun.

He picked up the revolver and staggered off the promontory. He went back along the side of the lake in the direction of the wood path, the revolver growing ever heavier in his hand so that most of the time he had to let his right arm hang.

He tried to get relief for the burnt hand by moving it in the air, but it made no difference to the agony and he kept crying out. He even thought of throwing lake water over it, but could not bring himself to do it.

Weakness forced him to stop several times along the lake and through the wood; but he dared not kneel or sit on the ground, for fear of animal attack. When eventually he came round the final bend in the wood path and saw the Hut, he had his first genuine feeling of relief - he would reach the safety of its wooden walls, and he might not after all be going to die ...or not immediately.

He tugged at the door with the revolver, went inside, and dropped it on the table by the water jugs in the little alcove.

Only able to use the good hand, he pulled a wooden bar across the door.

He went straight to the tin box and found several pieces of cloth, some tape, rusty scissors, and a small iodine bottle, corked and similar to the one his mother used.

Pulling out the cork, he smelt inside, his nostrils filling with water, and he knew he could not use it, would lose consciousness or could die from shock if he applied the liquid to the burnt hand.

Why he did what came next, or from where he got the strength of mind, he didn't think about. The dangling little finger seemed no longer part of him. He took hold of it, pulled, and it came easily away and he let it fall. He looked at his terrible hand, surprised no blood gushed out.

He thought about covering the burn with one of the cloths he had washed in the stream. But he couldn't do it; like the iodine, he couldn't let anything touch it.

His plight and terrifying loneliness hit him again. He closed one of the shutters they had left open on the side of the Hut looking out over the escarpment.

The door to the small portico was closed, but the inner bar not applied, so he pushed it in place. Somehow that door worried him less than the other two that faced the wood path and the lake where his grandfather lay.

The inside of the Hut was now in semi-darkness, though narrow shafts of light came through the side of one of the shutters enough for him to see. From the alcove he managed to pull a table to lean against the main door that he had barred.

The kitchen door to the outside needed securing, and he began pulling one of the benches from the main room. But as he was doing so his good hand lost its grip and he fell, his nose hitting the round column in the middle of the room and his shoulder taking the impact of the floor.

The nose was not cut, but struggling to his feet, blood poured out.

More than anything, he knew he had to buttress the kitchen door. He tried taking deep breaths to stop the bleeding, but it was no use. He pulled the bench through the peacock curtain until it stood firmly against the door. As he staggered back through the main room and the alcove and into his bedroom with the two k'angs, blood continued dropping onto the floors.

He got onto his k'ang and faced the ceiling, pinching the top of his nose. When the bleeding eventually stopped, he stayed there for a while, and for the first time since the shocking event at the lake, he found himself crying, overwhelmed by the pains and by the knowledge that his beloved grandfather was dead, an adult, his protector...

By the time he sat up and kicked off his still-sodden sandals, the tears had stopped and the room was much darker. Through the alcove, he could see that the evening rays no longer penetrated the room with the column, and the horror of spending the dark night there alone made him tremble.

His clothes had partly dried in the stagger back from the lake. The front of the shirt was covered in blood, and he only just managed to get it off without touching the upper part of the burnt hand. He dropped the shirt on the floor. With equal difficulty he put on his other shirt.

But a front headache had started, and soon it became worse than the headache he had had before the storm, forcing him to lie back on the k'ang.

That blackened face kept coming into his mind, so he desperately tried to think of his mother, to conjure her look, her smile; but all that came was her look of anxiety in the candlelight as she woke him that early first morning before they started the trip to the hills. His inner voice cried out for her, the answering silence only adding to his fearful loneliness.

He got the lamp working just before complete darkness came, and carried it into the tiny kitchen area, where he ate some of the rice they had left in a bowl; but he could only manage two small amounts.

Feeling extremely thirsty, he drank straight from the quarter-full water jug. Then he walked back to one of the metal bowls in the alcove and washed away dried blood from his nose and mouth and from near the left ear where some had trickled from the head wound.

When he again lay down he felt no safer despite the lamp on the floor and the revolver by his right hand. He didn't know what scared him more: the Hut in darkness with evil spirits around who would know his grandfather wasn't there to protect him, or the Hut lit by the lamp, attracting tigers and other animals, other terrors of the night. The armed celestial guardian painted on the outside of the little portico's door overlooking the escarpment never came into his shocked mind.

He thought about turning down the wick to reduce the light, but he could not do it because the darkness beyond the phoenix curtain also frightened him.

That night the wind became strong and shook the Hut, adding to his misery. He kept the injured hand resting as much as possible on his chest, worried that if he managed to sleep he could roll onto it.

After time unknown, he succumbed to a pain-filled sleep of sorts, though three times he left his k'ang to carry the lamp, to check that the table and bench were still buttressing the doors facing the wood.

4

Vibrating fear consumed Yuling's mind and body from the moment he finally got off the k'ang. His grandfather kept saying the tigers had been killed off in that part of the uplands, but he didn't believe it.

The lamp on the floor still burned, but he gave it no thought, was not going to spend the day and another fearful night there at the mercy of the evil spirits. Nor did he think of waiting to be rescued, because no one would come for days and he could die - part of his skull had fallen out, the hand looked shocking, and the pain... He had to get down to the plantation as quickly as he could ...if he could ...and maybe hunters were now at the nearest hut, or at one of the others by the path, then he might be saved, they could deal with his wounds...

His legs felt much stronger. The headache had gone. The wind was no more. The second pair of strap-sandals his mother had packed gave him some reassurance once he could get them on using the good hand. He still wore his bloodstained long trousers, but they were now dry from the lake.

And something else told him he could not remain: he looked at the k'ang that his grandfather had slept on the first two nights, and thought of the body lifeless on the promontory.

He was thirsty and drank. After eating more of the rice, he put the rest into a small bag of cashew nuts, the remains of the nuts they had brought with them; the bag went into his sack.

His main protection the revolver was fully loaded. He took up some bullets from the ammunition box; the metal felt cold but reassuring, such a contrast to the fire in the other hand. He let them drop one by one into the sack, then scooped up more and dropped them straight in.

He looked for his father's hunting knife but couldn't find it, though he found the sheath by the gun rack. He couldn't remember when he had last used it - or had his grandfather been using it? He gave up the search just as he saw his doli hanging from the wall - if he'd worn the hat at the lake, he might not have the fiercely stinging head wound, and now it was impossible to wear.

He listened, pushed away the table from the main door facing the wood, pulled back the bar and waited. He quarter opened the door and met sunshine, and as he looked towards the wood, a primeval shudder ran through him - he was willing his grandfather to be walking towards him along the path, but knew...

Carefully he placed the sack round his neck so not to touch the head, and took up the revolver, pushing the door wider with his foot. He could see the stream, the direction they had come from when he first saw the curling roof-ends of the little building in that murky light seemingly so long ago.

He wanted to step out but found it almost impossible because the right leg would not move; he cried inwardly that he had the gun and all he needed was to begin walking.

A slit down the hinge side of the door enabled him to see the nearby latrine shack, that no animal, nothing nasty was waiting for him. He pushed the door fully against a wooden support in the ground, and started out.

A few steps on, and a cry so penetrating from a huge black kite launching itself off the top of the nearby shrine made him turn and run back while it flew away below the rim of the escarpment. As he pulled the door behind him, he caught a glimpse of the hunting knife in the ground by the side of the Hut, remembering he'd been using it to cut creepers. His heart was beating fast and the left hand was throbbing and making him gasp, and his eyes were filling.

'...you must be brave like your father...' He tried to invoke his mother's words but they did not help; he heard the second part of her injunction: that he had to stick to grandfather, and as he stood by the water bowls pointing the gun at the door, the trembling began again.

Minutes passed, breathing became easier, trembling reduced. At last he remembered the celestial warrior. He went to the door facing the escarpment, removed the brace and opened it slowly. The eyes blazed, the sword stood ready in the mighty gloves, he believed the defending spirit had seen him through the night ...help me get down to the plantation, he begged, but the guardian continued staring.

He closed the painted door, didn't want to leave by that escarpment side ...the huge bird. Once more he moved out of the main door and looked in all directions: no bird was on his parents' shrine. He pulled the knife from the ground and put it straight into the sack; the long blade wasn't as big as the warrior's sword, but his father had held the knife, and the thought added to his keenness to start the long trek back down the path to the nearest of the hunters' huts.

Thankful to be again holding the revolver, his mind was possessed with one thought only: to fire if he saw anything. He very nearly pulled the trigger when passing the back of the small shrine, sure that a bird would swoop up from the escarpment with talons outstretched. And as he drew closer to the stream, he expected a tiger to run at him from every bush or rock, the gun waving as if by its own volition.

On reaching the water he took a look back to see that he was not being stalked, saw the Hut for the last time, and started to follow the flow in its decline towards the ravine on that side of the water.

The morning sun beat down. He wanted to throw water over his head but dare not, knowing that if he collapsed he would be at the mercy of the wild.

...the trek up to the Hut ...had they crossed the stream to the side he was on ...he thought so but wasn't sure, they'd crossed so many from one side or the other and he'd been exhausted when banging those tins... the tins! ...why hadn't he thought of them, it wasn't dawn or dusk but noise was supposed to frighten them away... It didn't occur to him that with only the good hand to use, he could not have held the revolver and rattled the tins at the same time.

A few minutes later he came level with the rock that was not far from the top of the ravine, and saw the water dividing round it. He became more confused, because his stream seemed to be going away from the other and had started flowing fast. If he crossed and made his way to the other stream, he could fall in, black out as he had in the lake, only for longer, he could get swept down ...no he'd keep going, cross later, the waters must link up somewhere in the ravine...

He made his way well past the rock, and was soon descending through other rocks on either side of him, and the landscape looked familiar and he was beginning to feel a little less frightened; he'd made a fair start and realized he could keep going, so long as his legs remained reasonably strong and the head got no worse despite the sun.

But very soon he was forced to put the revolver in the sack to free his right hand for balance, making him feel more exposed than ever. As he picked his way not far from the cascading water on his left, he knew he was having far more difficulty than on the way up three weeks earlier, and often he had to stop for fear he might fall.

...wasn't there a path up the ravine, it was narrow and sometimes petered out but grandfather always found it again... yes, he was sure there was one, and there was certainly a path in the last part of the forest, the forest he could see below him ...if he could just get there, it would be frightening with shadows and noises, but the path wasn't long, and the hunters' hut by its lake wasn't much further on.

The forest came ever closer; he was getting to the end of the ravine and soon could have the gun back in his hand ...the Buddha boulder! ...he'd just remembered the giant rock, where was it, why couldn't he see it ...his eyes searched the larger boulders but none of them seemed like the one his grandfather had nodded to.

He turned to the water that was just a few scrambling steps away; it was tumbling less steeply than at the top of the ravine, but still loud and looking dangerous. He wasn't able to spot the path on the other side, but if he could soon cross, he was sure to find it, and then he would definitely see the boulder from that side.

The burnt hand kept making him grimace, but it wasn't the absolute agony he'd had at the lake and afterwards, and he noticed that if he kept it raised to his middle, the pain lessened a little.

The day was growing hotter, and thirst overcame him. He removed the sack from round his head, and looked inside for the gun, feeling huge relief when bringing it out. He placed it on small stones, and scooped up water with the right hand, drinking several times and experiencing a lift of spirits.

He moved more easily towards the ravine's end, this time holding the gun. As he followed the stream into the forest, he thought of his mother and longed to be with her at home, under her protection; she wouldn't know his terrible situation and what was happening to him.

The noises of the forest kept making him start. More than ever he felt vulnerable, and very soon he needed the knife to cut his way through, again forced to return the gun to the sack, and hating doing so.

He looked across the water; it wasn't deep now and was wider than in the ravine and not so fast, and he became very hopeful he would at last find the path. He stepped in, the coldness of the water on his long trousers and the lower part of his legs feeling really good. He reached the other side remembering that on the trek up, the path in the final stretch of forest had been close to the water; his grandfather had pointed out a giant lizard basking on a stone in the stream; the reptile would have fascinated Yuling if he hadn't been so tired and keen to reach the Hut.

But he couldn't see the path! It *must* be here ...maybe just a few further steps through the undergrowth, then I'll see it and it'll be alright, no more hacking.... He hacked at right angles to the stream, very soon coming into sword grass up to his middle and trying to trample it down with his sandals, pushing his way through with the knife, holding the burnt hand close to his middle for fear grasses could touch it.

Several blades came back at him, and one cut his trousers above the right knee though not into his leg, and it forced him to stop. He searched for the path, but saw only more sword grass and hanging thick creepers that barred the way.

He returned to the water's edge, flopped onto a stone, and looked at his leg through the trousers.

A flock of parakeets flew down to the edge of the stream not far below him, and soon they were dipping their beaks in the water. One or two went half in, opened their feathers and started splashing. He knew they hadn't seen him, and they took him back to Janping's parrot: these were smaller than Genghis but just as colourful, and he thought of the crayon drawing of the well that he had made in the Luos' courtyard, and yearned to be back there, to be safe.

He picked the knife up and recrossed, and for the first time since leaving the Hut, he realized that he could be going along a different stream to the one they had followed on the way up. But he knew he wouldn't have the strength to go all the way back through the rocks to the top of the ravine, to the boulder where the water divided; he couldn't start again; the further away he got from the Hut in the rough direction of the plateau lakes, the further away from tigers ...and this stream he was following, it must lead out of the forest to the hunters' hut, it *must*...

He continued picking his way beside the flowing water, very relieved to find no more sword grass; though sometimes insects pestered him, and he wondered if his hand wound was attracting them although none settled.

The stream took many turns. At one stage, glad to be in the shade of trees near the water's edge, he noticed that his head was stinging a lot less. If he could just keep going, if nothing attacked him... at any moment he was ready to drop the knife and reach for the gun, but how quickly could he get it out...

Two other streams on his side joined the one he was following, giving him no choice but to cross them, and after the second he looked despairingly at the water, begging it to lead him to the hut and its small lake nearby.

Just after he had difficulty getting over a fallen tree, his ears caught a strange sound not far ahead, and soon he realized he was coming to the top of a waterfall. When he reached it, he could see part of a pool at the base, and that the water continued its course through the forest.

He moved to the right, trying not to go far from the tumbling water, knowing he had to reach the pool. But some of the rocks he passed were large and forced him to move further away, and again he had to put the gun in the sack and use the knife. At the edge of the stream, he'd been able to look out for animals on the other side of the water and sometimes ahead; but now he found himself in the thick of forest with very little view.

He came to a particularly large rock that he hoped to go round, and froze because there was commotion just ahead in the undergrowth, some animal was near him. He dropped the knife and frantically tried to get into the sack round his head, and as his fingers touched the gun-barrel, a wild cat leapt up to the top of the rock and looked down at him, its eyes menacing under dark stripes leading to the ears, light through the forest's canopy catching its brown face and accentuating white areas.

He could hardly breathe, was sure it was about to spring at him, his hand a flapping wing as he pulled the gun from the sack, and just as he got it out, the animal jumped back and he saw another cat darting away to his right, firing twice into the undergrowth, the noise deafening though he soon took in the sound of screeching birds flying away. The gun was shaking so much that when he pointed it towards the top of the rock expecting the first cat to reappear, he had to lay the barrel on his raised forearm of the bad hand before he could fire, something his grandfather had taught him, and when he pulled the trigger the bullet ricocheted off the rock.

'...they're more frightened than us...' his grandfather had said on the way to the ginkgo trees, '...they're shy...'

...no! that was panthers ...stop shaking he screamed within, go back, they'll kill me I know they will... He fired again into the undergrowth where the first shots had gone ...only two bullets left, then must reload and it'll be impossible with only one hand unless I put the gun on the ground...

He felt the blade of his father's knife resting on his right foot ...go down Alinga... his mother is beseeching ...down I tell you, to the pool... Sweat was pouring from him as he tried to look round, quickly putting the revolver by his foot and picking up the knife and thrusting it into the sack, then taking hold of the gun again and pointing it now at the rock, now into the undergrowth.

The sound of the falls came to his ears ...maybe the shots have frightened them... The hand holding the gun grew calmer, and he started to edge his way past the left side of the rock, the side away from the wild cat he'd seen disappearing into the undergrowth. With each further step and no attack he drew more courage. ...if only I can reach the pool, if they don't come for me I can reload...

He came back to near the plunging water about three-quarters down the side of the falls, hesitating for several seconds before daring to put the revolver in the sack, but it was the only way he could keep his balance as he struggled the last part.

When he reached the bottom he let himself fall onto his back into short grass not far from the base of the falls but in the full glare of the sun. He was panting and spent, had energy only enough to pull out the gun and rest it on pebbles, his finger on the trigger.

The grass was wet. Soon he propped himself up against a rock, feeling gentle spray sweeping over him. A hollowed stone looking like a wok was close, it was covered in dark green moss, and before he realized what he was doing, the hand had left the gun and he was stroking the damp moss, it was, thick, soft and spongy, seemed comforting, and the cooling sprays were not making the burns any worse.

His strength began to return. He walked to a shady part of the pool where the view about him was greater and he could reload away from the spray.

The reloading seemed to take forever, and his relief when done was enormous. Hunger came. He ate some of the rice and the nuts as fast as he could - this was no place to stay, he remained terrified, was sure he was being watched by those menacing eyes.

The zigzag course of what was now a small river beyond the pool soon became easier to follow, the gradient less steep than above the waterfall. He was able to go a considerable distance with the revolver in his hand and without too much undergrowth impeding him, because torrential summer rains had created a narrow flood channel of mud and small rocks on his side of the water, mud that had largely dried since the typhoon storm the previous week.

Sometimes he thought about crossing again, believing the plateau lakes must be somewhere below him to the left. But always the water seemed too deep, and he could not see a flood channel on the far side, let alone the path he yearned to find.

When the dry channel came to an end in the river, he continued to follow the side of the water as best he could, until it led him into an area of marshland in a valley between low hills. He could make out a lake ahead through many rushes, and knew at once that it was not the small lake by the hunters' hut; and there had been no nearby hills at the plateau lakes.

Further desperation set in; there would be no hut to shelter at or men to help him, and more than ever he feared he was being led into another part of the uplands, away from the Luo tea plantation.

He had to be careful not to get into bog, and went a little back into the forest for higher ground, always trying to keep sight of the rushes. When he passed the marsh and saw the lake again, it was the middle of the afternoon and his strength had all but gone.

He lay partly in shadow under trees just above the lake, his eyes level with the tops of the high rushes nearby. He began to watch blue-green dragonflies flying among the slender stems; for a time they seemed to take his mind from his perilous situation, and slowly, without realizing, his eyes were closing...

...the chirping of cicadas woke Yuling to a sun now getting low, and he was more than ever frightened: if he found nowhere to hide before it got dark, he was sure he would be killed in the night. He looked at the rushes: they would be no protection, he could be smelt, and anyway he couldn't lie in wet ground; and with the injured hand he couldn't climb into one of the trees either, or even if he managed to, he would be caught or could fall out.

He began walking, the gun by his side feeling very heavy. He had gone some distance when he was brought up sharp seeing a snake curled up on a low rock a few paces in front, and he knew at once it was a cobra, that by its size it was not a king cobra but could spit and was venomous and if he went any closer it would feel his vibrations even through its rock.

Not wanting to waste a bullet or use one on a snake, he edged his way to the side and was soon past it. The snake remained curled up. He thought again of his mother; she might have called the snake a good spirit, might have blessed it for not attacking him. He looked back ...let me find the hut by the lake ...your great ancestor covered the sun with its hood so that Lord Buddha could meditate in the cool ...protect me, don't let me be bitten by other snakes, and keep scorpions away ...I try to like you ...please don't let wild cats come near me again...

He reached the end of the lake, and picked up what he thought was the same river; it had definitely quickened and was wider than the first streams, and it was so deep that he could not see stones at the bottom - no possibility to cross. Worse, it seemed to be moving to the right, away from where he kept thinking he should be heading.

The sky had turned to a red that seemed redder than the colour in his drawing of the Hut over the escarpment. But it gave him no thrill as it had when he'd made the drawing, only an ever-growing fear. And he had a new problem: every time he took a step, the heel of his left foot sharply stabbed inside the sandal - a blister.

The river brought him round yet another bend and then gave him a shock: the valley he had been walking through came to an abrupt end. Rising slopes of forest in front and to the sides formed a semi-circular barrier, and not far ahead the water disappeared into a big cave.

Evening had come, trees and rocks cast their shadows, he couldn't go on much longer. He moved closer to the cave. The roof on his side of the river seemed as high as a tall building, and it sloped sharply down the other side; the water itself filled the whole entrance, no banks inside, and directly in front of him a landslide of stones and mud obscured part of the right side of the entrance.

He sat down at the foot of a dead tree that had broken in two with the upper part embedded in the ground at an angle. It was the only place he could think to lie, and he resigned himself to curling up there.

As he was pulling out some bullets to put beside the gun, something caught his eye. Well above the water, near where the landslide higher up seemed to connect with the cave, a narrow ledge or shelf disappeared inside. He looked closer, and wondered if he could reach it, and if it might be some protection, wide enough and not sloping.

He returned the gun to the sack and started clambering upwards ...help me help me... he mimed thinking of no person or gods in particular, desperate to reach anywhere that might be safer than the ground and the embedded tree. As he used his tired legs and aching hand to haul himself further up, the blistered heel stabbed at every movement.

When he finally reached just below the projection, he was able to push the sack onto what was a flattish rock shelf about two paces wide. Holding the palm of his burnt hand against his chest, he wriggled himself up and collapsed onto the shelf just inside the cave, too weak even to think whether anything might be lurking along the shelf, or that he should get the gun out.

He lay without moving, his eyes closed, and he heard the water rushing below against the walls of the cave.

A few minutes later, dull redness through the skin of his eyelids told him the sky still had some strength. When he sat up with his back against the shelf wall and looked down at the entrance, he was surprised to see how high he had reached above the river. The water outside the cave and a little way in had taken on a deep mauve colour, and the red in the sky was turning to grey.

Thirst came again. He wished he had drunk before starting the climb; but at least he felt safer for the night to come, so long as he did not fall off the shelf.

In the fast receding light, he looked more closely at where he was. Above him the wall on his side created a ceiling not much higher than himself, and then the cave's wall rose to its highest point before arching down the other side. The river itself curved, flowing into darkness on his side. Low down on the opposite wall, he could make out small areas of vegetation clinging to ridges close to the waterline.

He got to his feet with little headroom to spare, held the sack in his good hand and edged further in. He sat down half facing the entrance, with the sack at the end of his feet. The air was much cooler inside the cave, but at least he was dry; only the sandals remained damp.

Very hungry, he put his hand in the sack, touching first the handle of the knife and taking it out, placing it beside him just as his stomach began to cramp. He lent forward trying to ease the discomfort. He felt again inside the sack, and touched the gun but was looking for the small bag containing what was left of the nuts and rice. He took out the bag, and devoured the remains.

The stomach spasms would not stop. He bent more forward, trying at the same time to release his left foot from the sandal, but the strap of the sandal caught against the burst blister, and his leg jerked and hit hard against the sack, and as he cried out, the sack disappeared over the edge before he could catch it.

Soon he heard the splash - his main protection, the revolver, had gone.

He grabbed the knife and pointed it into the dark to his right. High-pitched noises started coming from somewhere inside the cave, noises that grew loud and soon blocked out the sounds of the quick-flowing water below him. He guessed they were bats but wasn't at all sure.

At the point when he was wondering if to leave the shelf and stay just outside on the landslide, several large bats flew past him out to the late evening air, and he felt some relief; he had watched bats with his family in Luchian, and knew they did not land on humans. But these were much bigger, and several times he waved the long blade high in front of him just in case.

Darkness came quickly, and with it a lessening of the noise of the bats, though he was able to make out that some still flew in and out. Great weariness set in, and he went into sleep lying on his right side clutching the knife, his back against the rock.

When he woke it was night, and he knew at once where he was and that his hand had freed from the knife. He felt for it and sat up. The bat noises had gone, and only the sounds of the river came to his ears. He could see nothing inside the cave, but was able indistinctly to make out the shape of the entrance and the river coming in, as well as the outline of part of the landslide he had hauled himself up. He guessed there was a mist outside.

Very relieved still to be safe, he let himself doze. But the cave had become cold, and sleep did not so easily come this time.

He was thinking of his brother Ayi - their playing with the dog with half a tail - when he heard something above the sounds of the river, some faint but definite noise coming from the direction of the entrance. Immediately his hand tightened on the knife's handle as he peered out trying to see what might be in the mist.

A few seconds later the hairs rose at the back of his neck when he saw movement outside the cave on the far bank. He strained to see better, and the dim outline of a big cat came to him, bigger than a wild cat, he thought. It made him hold his breath …don't come …don't come my side… He got to his feet …go away, go away… He edged further into the cave, frightened he might tumble over the edge of the rock shelf, and caught another look at the vague shape that he was sure had moved nearer the entrance.

The knife's blade hit stone above him, dislodging some fragment that hit his shoulder but did no harm. Rock soon pushed his head down so he could go no further. He felt so weak that he longed to sit again.

The big cat's outline disappeared. He remained fully alert, clutching the knife, looking down towards the entrance and the far bank outside, trying to penetrate the dark mist.

As the minutes went by, gradually his fearful alarm began to ease, and a hope came …if it doesn't know I'm here, if it's gone well away, if I can just see the night through and wake up in the morning, I can try to reach the top of the hill above here, and maybe I'll see the lake at last …and the hut…

...the night is her domain...the scent she has picked up is coming from the other side of the drink-cool water inside or very near the big hole...instinct tells her what danger the man-animal poses...she's smelt man before and got out of its way or come across its scent only when the danger passed...

...now she raises her head and draws in the air...other scents come to her but are of no interest because her senses tell her this one is close and injured and trapped unless it leaves...and even then she'll have it...

...stealthily she moves forward catching sight of the man-animal on one of her lairs... and as she starts upwards in the undergrowth its scent all but disappears...

...but when she comes back down on the far side of the big hole, the smell returns and grows ever stronger until it becomes so powerful that just below the entrance to her resting place she stops and hugs the ground...but not for long...

Yuling's mind has quietened, but his legs are hurting badly from standing. He is about to sit, when he is returned to panic by hissing that is coming from his side of the cave just outside the shelf, from the landslide...

...she jumps up and crouches and sees man-animal's eyes and senses its youth and smells its injuries and hears its terror as sensations course through her and she knows her prey is caught...the kill easy...the after a feast...

...and the next moment he is screaming at the dark form as his heart thumps from head to toe, he can still hear the hissing between his screams as immediately he bends lower, instinct making him turn his left side to the big cat while keeping the firmness of the rock against his lower back for securer stand, he is thrashing his father's knife across his left shoulder but tilting to the right, and when he sees it coming and catches flashes in the eyes, time no longer exists for Yuling as he tilts more, feels the knife being hit, his upper body is pierced, the shelf is giving way, and he is falling for an eternity with the beast clutching him...

...with the animal under him, his back takes the impact of the water and they go deep; and as his body begins to rise, his brain registers that the jaws have released, before part of it shuts down.

5

Air...air... the boy was choking after swallowing as he surfaced, was being swept along in blackness, desperately trying to keep his head above water in an elemental struggle for survival. One of his legs hit something rock-like, and when his body collided with an object and an arm held to it, the head stayed up and more air entered his heaving lungs. The object, like a rough pole, seemed fixed, the water now pushing hard against him as he hung on.

He began to edge along the object, but found he couldn't move one arm from which unaccountable throbbing pain was coming in the shoulder and the hand. At the end of the pole came something more substantial, and as he took hold of a second protrusion, his knees hit stones. Somehow he moved over them, and found he was leaving the water. Choking more, he collapsed onto his front, his mouth and whole body shivering from fearful cold.

The spluttering grew less. When he tried to stir he could hardly move. He managed to turn himself onto the side that wasn't hurting, and got to his knees using an elbow and an arm on pebbles he couldn't see.

He stretched out the arm and touched another protrusion, and the branch of a tree came to his mind. He hauled himself up and felt along it to a trunk that he realized was on its side.

He didn't know where he was, or why he'd been in water, or why he was in complete darkness, or why one arm was severely hurting and immovable. All he knew was that he had nearly drowned in fast flowing water, and that he was in some hellish underworld. He had no concept of personal identity or belonging. He didn't think about animals, or about people.

He touched the trunk again, and his fingers felt grooves. Managing to sit against it, he put the good hand to the shoulder area of his other arm, but very soon withdrew because through ripped clothing came a warm ooze - his mind told him it was his life force. He felt lower down, and when he touched the hand he shrieked.

In his agony he never registered the echoes around him.

Time passed. Breathing grew easier and lengthened; the shivering lessened, and he entered into a semi-aware state where all that mattered was that his body was warming. His entire world was his body, the tree trunk, the pebbles, and the sound of the water so close.

He came out of that state feeling positively hot, despite the soaked clothing and sodden sandals. He stretched out his hand to the water and bathed his face, touching part of his head where there was some bearable stinging; the hair felt strange.

Many times the discomfort of the pebbles made him move from his lying or sitting position. The wound fever grew worse, with no relief when he threw water over himself.

More time passed. Whether he was conscious or not he hardly knew. But as he was turning over a pebble with the right hand, he thought there might be a change in the darkness.

And soon, through the palest of light he understood that some sort of dome was over him. When parts of a huge rock roof came into profile, he knew he was in a cavern, and that a sun must be arriving to lighten his underworld.

He had not stood since leaving the water. Now feeling hotter than ever, he struggled to his feet and kept his balance by leaning against the tree trunk he was beginning to make out; and as he looked higher, he was surprised to see sky through part of what he believed was an opening in the roof of the cavern.

Dark patches on the ceiling came into view. And he could even see areas of the water - an underground river flowing out of darkness into darkness.

Light penetrated further. Rocks on the cavern floor took shape, as did the tree that had stopped him, which was half in, half out of the water. And it was not the only tree. Above him were other trees lying scattered at all angles on a causeway of earth stretching towards the top of the cavern. Although he did not know it, part of a hillside had collapsed inwards.

He stood again, looked at what he would have to climb if he was to try to leave the cavern, and thought that if he could reach the opening, he might find where he was and see somebody, anybody, to help him and to give him some food, because he felt very very hungry and his stomach kept tightening.

Again he was forced to sit. How long he remained by the tree trunk he did not know, though he realized he no longer felt so hot. What caused him to stir was a beam of direct sunlight that made the water sparkle near him, and when he looked up towards the causeway, he could see the sun at the top of the opening, and realized that if he moved just a few paces, he would be in its direct power.

He was now able to look at the bad hand, and was shocked at its state; but a grandfather, a gun explosion, a hut, and a lake were buried deep in some recess of the brain, as was an animal attack. When he tried to look at the shoulder and upper arm, he was unable to see the wounds through a ripped shirt, unaware that a big cat's teeth had punctured.

He picked his way over to the brighter part of the cavern floor, and for a little while he felt the rays of the sun warming his clothes. When the sun disappeared above the opening, he curled up and went into a partial sleep.

The sound of splashing water stirred him, but he could not see what was making it, because much of the river and the cavern floor were again in darkness. The wound fever had almost gone, and when he stood, his legs felt more strength. After drinking from the river, he began to move up, bit by bit, through the causeway debris.

Many times he had to stop, sometimes for long periods; his legs ached, the back of a heel was sore and troublesome, and the useless arm made the climbing very hard. But little by little, over earth and rocks and trees, he went higher.

His final stop was not far from the top, and there he was too exhausted even to stay awake, resting his head on hard earth.

Much later he came back to himself, and managed to climb the last part to the opening: he wasn't fearful, simply had no idea what to expect; he was leaving a cavern that had been a tomb, and was coming to a world of daylight where he hoped he would find people.

Warmth greeted him at the opening, but at once he became alarmed to see that he was in a forest on a hillside with no other view except the sky, no person to call to, no dwelling. Clouds covered the part of the sky that he could see through the trees.

He was at a loss to know what to do, thinking he might be in some unpeopled world all his own. His throat and mouth were nastily dry. He went back into the cavern and sat on a patch of earth by low plants with short leaves, plucking a few leaves and sucking them, then chewing. But this gave no comfort, and when he tried to swallow the leaves, he couldn't. Though he felt ravenous, no food came to his mind.

As the light faded, creatures he knew by sight but couldn't name started flying in and out of the opening. He'd noticed them while climbing, their dark shapes hanging from parts of the cavern roof. But when he had last seen them never came to him. He wasn't afraid - he and they seemed to be living separate lives in the same place.

He realized that night would be arriving; he did not feel particularly frightened, and knew he would have to lie where he was and try to keep warm. His mouth and throat still felt very dry, but it was out of the question to go all the way back down to the flowing water at the cavern floor.

As night descended it grew cooler, and he went back into the cavern and lay down behind a collapsed tree. Soon he was asleep.

Sometime later a shrill cry from outside woke him to immediate fright, though he envisaged no animal. He looked over the tree and saw to one side of the opening small bright lights that seemed to hover in the dark. To his surprise some of them vanished and reappeared in the middle. He thought he had seen them somewhere before, sensed they would do him no harm, and the fright left him. He watched them until the last light suddenly disappeared, and then he curled up again and returned to sleep.

The fireflies moved on.

Thick clouds filled the early morning sky when he went to the opening. The sun that had brought him back to life on the cavern floor was well hidden, and there was a breeze. Although he was cold, he sensed there might soon be a warming of the strange forest that was now his world. He thought only of his parched throat, hunger, and that he had to try to go through this forest to find someone, and quickly.

He was about to start his descent when he caught sight of a bird not far away, circling low over the forest; and although this was the first time birds had come into his mind, he knew them. He watched its flight. Soon he began thinking he had seen a bird like it before. And when it flew in his direction with its head and powerful beak looking down as if searching, there flashed into his mind a similar bird, one he had touched, it was dead and mounted, its colours different browns, its wings outspread as if in flight; he even recalled a feeling of wonder at the smoothness of the feathers.

He held the image, and as the bird in the sky turned away, he saw himself inside a wooden outhouse with windows of thick paper; and other birds of different sizes and colours were pressing on his memory, as bird after bird materialized in his thoughts; he was among a large collection of stuffed birds, and he could see the plaques though not the names.

The memory door closed as thirst brought him back to the present. Several times he stroked dewy grasses, licking the moisture off his fingers and the palm of the right hand. Then he started edging his way down the slope, surprised how difficult it was to get through the undergrowth, and soon taking up a thin broken branch to help him push back tree creepers. At least the sore at the back of the heel hurt less.

The noises of the forest made him picture more birds, but in the blockage of his mind no animal or reptile entered his thoughts. Further and further he descended as he pushed his way through. And just as he was recalling the echoing cries of the bird he had seen, he heard the sound he'd been longing for, and after a few further steps was looking at water and throwing down the branch and walking straight into a little stream, drinking with unimaginable relief, hardly noticing that new cuts round his ankles and the lower parts of his legs were stinging in the water through the trousers.

A few seconds on and his stomach tightened. He bent to ease the discomfort, bird noises in the forest seemed to grow louder, and as he looked down at a partly submerged stone, a word burst through. 'Buzzard!' he exclaimed towards the stone, surprised at the sound of his voice and repeating it in his mind.

The stomach eased. He took up the thin branch feeling better, and began following the stream. It brought him into an area of sweet-smelling trees, cones abundant on branches, dead trees standing or lying among the living.

He flopped by a rotting trunk, and as he touched it, several pieces of severely decayed wood came away showing greyish white larvae half the size of his thumb. He took three or four into his hand and they went into his mouth and he swallowed. Hunger tore at him and he did it again, this time chewing for a moment; the grubs were not unpleasant, and he did it a third time.

A light rain was falling. He stumbled on through the forest and began to call out, longing for human answer. The rain remained gentle, and the water led him to a larger stream. He crossed, but now the stream seemed to go on endlessly without much descending. It still flowed through semi-forest, but he could tell that the landscape was changing; the trees and hanging creepers were no longer so many or the undergrowth so thick or so prickly and hurting.

He came to a lake that gave him his first hope that people might be nearby, though he was still in wild country. Long-beaked birds stood in shallow water, and an extraordinary noise from near them came to his ears, a sound he felt he had heard somewhere before.

Soon he came to a green pool not part of the lake proper, and found it alive with croaking frogs, their name coming to him a few seconds after he saw them. Something told him they were food, he could try to catch and kill one, tear at it. He still had the thin branch, and tried to beat one, then another; but it was no good, his arm did not have enough strength and they jumped easily away.

He pressed on along the side of the lake through sparse trees and rocks. The rain had stopped, but he was now walking straight into gusts of wind.

As he was part way along the lake and passing a rock no higher than himself, he let out a stifled cry into the wind and jumped back. Tigers! The word exploded inside his head before the barrier slammed shut on all else but fear. He knew them, although it was as if he had never thought of animals before.

His legs began shaking as he arched against the rock, so unexpected was this danger. There were two, some way ahead on his side, one near the water's edge; it was facing the lake and shaking its head with something in its mouth, while the other looked on with its back to him.

And then he was running, dropping the branch that was making him slow, he had to get back to where the stream came in, was staggering past trees and more rocks, and the strap of a sandal was coming loose, he was trying to keep his foot in it but the sandal fell off, and he ran on, several times he looked back, his world now perilous, his survival no longer dependant only on finding some human being to help him.

He reached the stream at the start of the lake, but now his eyes had black red spots that were blurring his vision, he couldn't see back properly, didn't know if they were following, and only just managed not to fall into mud as again he tried to look behind him, inwardly shrieking ...must cross...get to those trees...other side of the lake...only chance...growth's thicker...no they'll see me, they'll swim through the water, they'll get me...

He looked up at the sloping hillside and was soon struggling away from the stream and the lake, and getting cut all over including his face as he climbed ever upwards, always gasping for breath, unable to stop himself crying out, sure he was hearing the tigers coming up from below, the image of the one violently shaking its powerful head uppermost in his terrified mind.

Unexpectedly, it became easier to keep going; although it was always uphill, much of the thorny undergrowth had gone, the ground now dark and charred and easier on the foot that was badly missing its sandal. Trees had been severely burnt into stumps, and creepers had all but disappeared; here and there new vegetation had sprouted.

The spots had gone and he began to hope, to think the tigers would have caught him if they'd followed. It didn't occur to him that he'd been downwind of them, that they had not heard or smelt him.

At last he crested the hill. He dropped to the dark earth and wanted to close his eyes, to be taken away to a better place, to no tigers or fear, to no running or pain.

The wind on his face felt fresh and cooling, and the sun was making a short appearance.

When his chest eased, he got to his feet. The view over the fire-destroyed part of the forest took his eyes to a flatter area well below, where something small shone in the middle distance. He imagined some person's roof caught in the fleeting sun, though he also thought it could be another dangerous lake. The day was advancing. The roof seemed his only chance; he had to try to reach it.

It took him a long time to get down to the end of the burnt area in another valley; and by then, after many rests usually at streams, evening had come. Fast moving clouds covered the sky, and the wind was stronger than ever.

He plunged back into swirling forest, eventually coming to a wide stream flowing slower than the ones he had seen since leaving the cavern.

Taking a rest near the edge, with the wind at his back and chewing on a leaf trying again to get some nourishment, he was startled to see a long green snake slither into the water just a few paces above him, the first time he'd thought of snakes. He wasn't frightened, and watched it swimming effortlessly past him in the gentle flow, its head strong out of the water as it glided between small rocks.

Almost forgetting about his own state, he followed as best he could along the side of the stream, and saw the snake come out of the water further down and disappear. The snake had its home, he thought, its place of safety...

The light of the day was going. Not counting the nights in the cavern, he had the strangest feeling he'd been in this same situation before: alone in nature and very frightened as night approached; it was as if this was the only world he knew.

Ahead, further along on the other side of the water, he saw something that gave him hope: a boulder that might be some protection against the elements, though not against tigers. The water was shallow, and as he began to cross, his feet kept slipping on the bed of the stream, especially the foot with the sandal. Several times he nearly fell.

He pulled a stone from the water, held it at shoulder height ready to throw, and reached the other side. Fear of waiting tigers meant he couldn't stop his hand from shaking as he moved round the boulder, the wind clawing at his torn shirt and trousers.

But he was alone.

He gathered more stones, and sat below an overhang that partly faced the water. He felt reasonably protected from some of the wind, but knew that if the tigers or others found him he wouldn't hear them, and he kept trembling as much from that thought as from the growing cold.

He remained vigilant with his hand over the stone, until through great weariness the eyes could stay open no longer and the upper body sagged. Not even the gusts in his face could hold him from sleep, and he went deep.

The courtly girl with a flower in her hair, coming down to him at the boulder, appeared in the night sky from the direction of the moon. She was about his age, but he did not know her. And her silk robe, high at the neck and down to bare feet, radiated a lovely deep red that stunned him. Feeling very lonely and confused, he asked her to help him up. 'Get up yourself, Tsai Yuling!' she laughed. As he tried and was falling back, she bent down and caught him with an arm in a beautiful sleeve, an arm that seemed to be as strong as a man's, and as soon as he stood beside her, the night changed to day though the moon still glowed. 'We'll walk in the water,' she said as she pulled him into the stream, the stream he was now beside at the boulder, to the middle, the girl firm-footed on the slippery bed and not caring that her robe was wet half way to her knees. She was on his left, firmly holding his injured arm in hers, they each saw that it was injured, but there was no pain. They were treading with the flow of the water, talking away, she was often laughing and always looking at him with happy, friendly, trusting eyes. And when she removed her arm and he thought he was sure to fall in the water, he felt the playful slaps on his back and the cuffs on his head, not once but several times, and his fear of falling and his loneliness and his confusion disappeared. And as she held to him again, he too began laughing, marvelling at the ripples that reflected the rich colour of her robe in different tones of red that sparkled in the water. 'Keep walking, don't give up, don't give up, I'll see you to your rescuer,' he heard her say just before waking.

The night wind had almost gone. In his wakeful state, his immediate fright of tigers miraculously left him as he felt strongly comforted by the clearest lingering image of the girl in the silk robe, the only person to come into his mind since scrambling out of the water in the blackness of the cavern. He derived a feeling of certainty that she was real, that she was keeping him from more harm, and leading him, that he would soon meet someone to help him. Still curled up with his fingers touching the stone, he began to imagine her sitting barefoot beside him, magically on each side, protecting him, that if the tigers came she would whisk him into the air and then lead them away.

And when he kept hearing scurrying noises near his head that told him small creatures shared his boulder (though he couldn't envisage what they might be), he wasn't frightened; the memory of the dream told him that mother nature would do him no harm. Soon he was thinking of the long green snake gliding through the water, and it returned him to sleep.

A new day of silver-white mist met the boy's eyes. He was lying full stretch under part of a large spider web; it was drooping and angled from the boulder to a thorny bush by his feet, pearls of dew decorating the whole web. This time he did visualize the spider, but he couldn't see one and no name came to him for the trapper and its trap.

And his next thought was that of the tigers he'd seen, and the next that he couldn't last much longer. The dream never came to him, and the name the girl called him had disappeared beyond reach.

He felt extremely weak as he moved from under the web, and only just managed to stand. Mist covered everything. All he could see was the immediate overhang of the boulder, and the thorn bush and some vegetation at the water's edge; but the stream itself was hidden. Where the sky should have been, a faint glow of yellow in one area permeated the mist.

He bent down with great difficulty, picked up the stone he had held in the night, and started walking slowly into the whiteness, keeping as close as he could to the stream's vegetation.

A few steps on and he turned to look back: the boulder had vanished and he had no view of anything except small rocks just to his right.

He tried to keep going, and soon stumbled into a large bush with red berries. He dropped the stone and snatched at three or four, biting into them, and his mouth erupted and he spat them out.

Staggering on without the stone, he no longer thought where the edge of the stream might be, and did not realize that he had moved away from the water. His legs just took him, nearly fell under him when he stopped, and carried him further when they found any strength.

Nor did he think more of tiger attack, or register the calling of birds, or care that pale tree trunks were slowly coming into view close to him, or notice that the grey leaves of evergreens were changing to luminous transparent green as the sun began to pierce the thinning mist. He did not realize that he had left forest and come into sloping more open country, that he had begun to follow downwards an animal track.

His head hung. He went further, but was soon brought back to reality by the sound of hooves coming fast towards him, and before he had time to look up, he felt a great rush of air, and the panic of seeing the tigers at the lake returned with a vengeance although the image of a horse also came into his mind.

He half turned but was too slow, the animal had vanished into a patch of mist now more yellow than white.

Frantically he looked to his front, saw a piece of wood just ahead to one side of the track, and when he managed to reach it and was trying to pick it up, he heard snorting, and the next moment a horse he again didn't see brushed past him and he fell.

Somehow he hauled himself to his feet without the piece of wood and lurched a few more faltering steps. But a terrible faintness was overcoming him, his legs were giving way, and soon he was crashing once more to the ground.

As the track beneath him heaved, his ears filled with the stamping of hooves like the pounding of festival drums, and he gave himself up.

6

At the Tsai home (grandfather Tsai Peiheng's house in Luchian) an urgent discussion took place after the hand-delivered message came during the midday meal.

> Peiheng and Yuling not arrived two days ago when said or yesterday. Weather Good. Very worried one of them injured or ill. Not sure way to Hut. Send Rescuers. Luos.

Wenlie felt shock, immediately reminded of the foreboding she had in the lightning storm when her father-in-law made his invitation to her elder son. But she tried not to think the worst. There was good reason to hope that if one of them was injured or ill, they could survive until her brother-in-law Jinjin got to them in the next two days, unless the injury or illness was very serious and had occurred many days earlier. She also told herself that they could well have reached the Luos by the time Jinjin reached Dongang. She cursed that she could not go with him, her left foot remaining very sore from tripping on a stage a few days earlier.

'No, Wenlie, you'll hold us up,' her brother-in-law said, 'neighbour Xinxiang will come with me, I'm sure. He's been up there before, and we'll go at once.'

Hastily Wenlie made up a medicine bag while Jinjin went to see the neighbour.

'Best take handguns,' Xinxiang said, 'rifles too heavy.'

The men took the land route to Dongang, as there were no afternoon sampans leaving Luchian travelling downriver. They were not troubled by rain on their fast walk, but the last part of the journey was in the dark and became windy against them and held them up. They arrived at the Luo house well after midnight, deeply troubled to find that the two had still not arrived.

The following morning the ferryman was late again, and they reached the far side of the river shortly before nine on a very misty day. Janping accompanied them, as she wanted to make sure that they started at the right point from the top of the plantation, though Jinjin knew the path perfectly well.

Apart from the pistols, they took only one bag between them, containing Wenlie's medical supply and some provisions. They were glad that the wind had gone, but early in the trek the mists that lingered through the forest added to their concern.

The mists went, and it soon became warm; they had good cover in the forest, but in the open of the plateau lakes the sun blazed down. Their fears grew as they reached each hut and found no sign of the two, though Jinjin kept repeating that the chances had to be good that they would find his father and nephew waiting to be rescued for some reason.

They reached the top of the ravine and came through the final stream in the middle of the afternoon when a breeze was up. They could see the main door of the Hut facing the wood; it was open and flapping, and each man immediately sensed possible disaster but said nothing.

As they ran the last part, Jinjin called out for his father, and when they reached the door and were about to enter, Xinxiang pointed to bloodstains on the floor just inside the Hut. Jinjin let out a cry. 'I can't go in,' he said turning away, his eyes taking in the small shrine nearby.

Soon he heard one of the shutters being opened, and a few seconds later Xinxiang was gasping. 'What have you found?' Jinjin called out in fear looking back to the door.

'They're not here,' his companion shouted, 'but it's terrible, looks like they've been attacked, or...'

Slowly Jinjin entered; he saw more bloodstains, the table was placed oddly near the door, and the small alcove was in a mess. When he came to Yuling's blood-streaked shirt and the sandals on the floor near the k'angs, he too gasped.

'The little cooking area's also bad,' Xinxiang said coming towards him. 'Lots of blood. Were they trying to barricade themselves in? Do bandits ever come this far, maybe they've been taken hostage?'

Jinjin shook his head not knowing what to think. As he was going towards the phoenix curtain he spotted part of a broken pencil on the floor near the white basins. Something made him pick it up, and when he did so he cried out, dropped the object and ran outside starting to retch.

Xinxiang ran after him. For a short while Jinjin was unable to speak. When he recovered, he told the neighbour of the gruesome find: a shrivelled finger; it had to be Alinga's he said, but wasn't sure.

They sat on the ground a few paces from the door, their handguns beside them. They agreed that Yuling must have suffered some terrible injury to his chest or head and taken off his shirt, and it looked as though he alone had tried to barricade himself in, Jinjin saying that his father would never have created such a mess, thinking of the matches and clothing and lamp on the floor. And he had noticed his father's favourite gun was missing.

'Could a lone tiger have come back to this part of the uplands,' Xinxiang suggested, 'attacked them? Maybe Yuling was also attacked but got back.' He grimaced, wanting to add that the animal could have taken the boy later, but said nothing more.

For a while Jinjin did not answer; he was gazing along the path to the wood. He thought the idea of a wandering tiger a possibility. He'd never heard of bandits there; they would not have come so far in, with only one path to use and the rest of the forests practically impenetrable except around the plateau lakes; and if they had, he found it hard to believe they would have hurt an old man and a boy, unless his father had become foolishly angry at the breaking of his solitude, his peace, and shot at them. As to hunters, murder was inconceivable; they were good men, unless one of them had been crazed and alone. The state of the Hut showed no signs that men had been there; if they had, the other guns and the ammunition would have gone.

'Father could have had heart failure,' he said, 'he might still be alive somewhere near us. But if Alinga was left alone...' He stopped, imagining a tiger or some other animal attacking his nephew. The discarded bloodied shirt came to his mind; if it had been a tiger, the boy wouldn't have been able to get back to the Hut. He looked towards the stream frowning.

They went back inside, to the two remaining long-barrel guns, deciding to search the immediate area including the wood, and then to separate if they found nothing, Jinjin to go roughly southward, Xinxiang to the east and to include the lake area. They would search as best they could, and agreed to return to the Hut within two hours. If the search failed, they would look in the other areas. If either found something significant or spotted tiger, he was to fire and they would return to the Hut.

Jinjin had been searching the area of rocks and trees on the far side of the stream and was thinking how hopeless the task was, when he heard a shot. He ran back to the Hut and waited. Many minutes passed, and when Xinxiang did not appear, he started walking along the path that led through the wood to the lake.

He had gone some distance when he saw his neighbour coming slowly round a corner, fifty paces or so from him. He called out, but Xinxiang gave him no answer, was looking down, and Jinjin ran towards him fearing the worst. When he came near, Xinxiang looked up through tears.

'Your father...' Xinxiang was shaking his head, 'I've found him at the lake, his body...' Jinjin let out a cry, put down the gun and covered his face with his hands. 'The shotgun's in pieces, it must have exploded and...' Xinxiang touched his friend's arm, 'you mustn't go, very bad state, I had difficulty identifying him, he's been lying there a long time.' Xinxiang thought of the sickening smell of death that came to him. 'I walked round the lake but there's no sign of Yuling. Maybe he was caught in the gun explosion or was attacked by an animal sometime later, either would explain the blood.'

Several minutes passed before Jinjin stopped his crying. Evening had come. 'We're exhausted,' Xinxiang said, picking up both guns. 'We'd better go back to the Hut, I can tidy a little and we can decide what to do with your father's...' But he couldn't finish the sentence.

'We'll have to look for Alinga,' Jinjin said very quietly to the ground. 'What are we going to tell Wenlie?'

Xinxiang could find no answer. To him it was clear the boy must have suffered a painful and lonely death somewhere near them, and he desperately hoped they would not find the body, not after what he'd just seen.

Back at the Hut, Jinjin remained distraught and could hardly touch the food Janping had packed. He too couldn't bear the thought that they might find Alinga. He asked: 'How are we going to carry my father down?'

Xinxiang shook his head. 'Impossible. Animals or birds...' again not finishing, 'we must bury him by the lake. I'll do it all if you want, but it'll take some time.'

Jinjin nodded. 'Just cover father first, then I'll help.'

Xinxiang suggested that they start at first light, adding they would have to watch out just in case a lone tiger had returned. There was lots of open space at the lake, so they should spot one. If they could complete the grave within two or three hours, they could then look for Yuling, and if they didn't find him, they could go back down in the afternoon and evening to reach the plantation cottage in darkness, or they might stay at the last of the hunters' huts.

They rose early. The weather was overcast, and they came to the lake heavy laden: guns, pickaxe, spade, blankets. Jinjin recoiled when he caught sight of the body, and as they drew near to the promontory, he could not go further but fell to his knees and looked away while his companion covered it.

They began looking for a place to dig. Their first few attempts hit rock. But in a dip not far from the promontory stood a sentinel hemlock tree that Jinjin knew well, and near it they were able to cut into the ground, Xinxiang suggesting the dip might have been part of the lake in former times.

It took them well over two hours to reach a depth sufficient to prevent animal penetration. Jinjin could not face the task of helping to pull his father's body to the tree; his companion made him go well away, and did that shocking task alone.

Before refilling, they prayed in silence, Jinjin asking the gods to give his father a safe journey in the next world and to allow him to return one day to a good new life. They spent another hour completing the grave, putting on top and around it as many rocks and stones as they could find. Then Jinjin handed incense sticks to Xinxiang; they lit them and placed them at each end of the mound.

Exhausted, they rested by the lake, for a time neither speaking. Then Jinjin said: 'There are no birds, where are they? There are always some here. It's so quiet.'

Xinxiang flung the broken pieces of the gun far into the lake, and they walked back to the Hut in silence, each realizing they had not enough time to look for Yuling's body and also get all the way down to the plantation. Much against their earlier hopes, they were forced to spend a second night at the Hut. Although physically and emotionally drained, they knew they had to try to look properly for the boy's body, for his mother's sake.

That afternoon they split up again, this time to explore the two ravines. They agreed it was too dangerous to scramble through the forested base of the escarpment, though they knew there was a possibility that injured Yuling could have fallen over the edge. Jinjin got back first, and finding his friend had not returned, he wrote a note that he was going again round the lake area and further on, and asked Xinxiang to scour the wood.

They found no trace of Yuling. Afterwards they spent an unhappy evening. The next morning they began their return under another cloudy day, Jinjin taking Yuling's drawing of the Hut in sunset; it had his signature near the top right-hand corner, drawn in red in the shape of a rectangular name chop of a Chinese artist.

They reached the tea plantation in the early part of a sunless afternoon, and as they came down through the last bushes and could see the Luo cottage, they heard Janping's shout from a window, and were soon startled to see Wenlie following her out and hobbling a little; despite her sore foot, she must somehow have got herself to a sampan at the Luchian river landing at the end of the rapids.

Wenlie was consumed by dread as soon as she saw that the men were alone and the way they walked. She could not make herself go towards them but stayed near the entrance. Janping said something to her, but she didn't take it in.

When the men reached them, Wenlie watched her brother-in-law try to speak. But he wasn't looking at her, and her mind went into absolute panic. She saw him nudge Xinxiang, and she turned frantically to the neighbour, catching his eye.

Xinxiang found he too could hardly talk, could not look at the mother for long, and lowered his head. 'We found …we found Tsai Peiheng …his body…'

Janping let out a long cry, Wenlie soon pulling at her sleeve to silence her, '...by the lake, the gun was in pieces ...must have exploded...'

Wenlie broke in: 'Alinga?'

Xinxiang felt the fearful gaze. He stammered: 'We couldn't find him, lots of ...lots of...'

'His shirt was on the floor, Wenlie, it was full of blood,' Jinjin managed to say, now looking at his brother's widow through the tears coming to him as Wenlie's hands went to her mouth and Janping let out a second cry.

'There were marks everywhere,' Xinxiang added looking up at Janping, gaining more voice following Jinjin's courage, 'bad mess, he must have been alone, there was a table near the main door and a bench against the kitchen door...' He hesitated, still not looking at the mother. 'The lamp was on the floor, it had burnt itself out. Maybe he was caught in the gun explosion and got back to the Hut.' He didn't dare mention his thought that an animal might have taken him afterwards, or the gruesome find on the floor. 'We searched many areas, he must have left the Hut and got lost. We couldn't look at the base of the escarpment as it's just too difficult to...'

'How long ago?' Wenlie cut in again voice trembling.

The neighbour swallowed and looked sideways to Jinjin. 'Many days, maybe seven or more, Tsai Peiheng's body was in a very bad state.'

Janping was now crying out at nearly every comment.

Jinjin shook his head and said quietly: 'Alinga couldn't have survived up there for long ...not so injured...' his voice was breaking up again, '...if he'd tried to get down ...couldn't have gone far, no sign in the ravines...'

'Just in case,' Xinxiang continued where he thought Jinjin had left off, 'we searched in the other huts too, and around them.'

'We had to bury father...' Jinjin added, but he didn't want to describe it.

A short and terrible silence followed, when even Janping was quiet. Then Wenlie sank to her knees. Janping followed and was soon sobbing. Each man squatted and avoided looking at the women.

No tears came to Wenlie, no cries came from her; she was numb, was staring at the first tea bushes but hardly seeing them. A minute or two passed with the men quietly weeping and Janping crying in fitful bursts. When Jinjin raised his head and saw the look in Wenlie's eyes, he touched Janping on the shoulder, and she finally stopped her outpouring.

Wenlie was looking up towards the forests. She saw the body of her son lying cold and exposed somewhere in the hills or under the escarpment. She thought of the moment he was born, when she had experienced indescribable joy and gratitude. She thought of her younger son, now brother-less.

Her whisper was barely audible. 'I have now lost two of my family, my husband and my Alinga.' She had wanted to say 'my beautiful Alinga' but found she could not, it was too painful to acknowledge she would never see him again. She drew in a deep breath and let it out slowly. 'I will never know where either of them lies, and that is too much for any person to bear, and horribly, horribly cruel for Ayi.'

Still she could not cry. She wished her heartbeat would stop. She wished she could join her beloved son on his journey in the next world.

They took the rickety ferry back across the Zass River to Janping's frightened parents, to the desolation in the plantation owner's house. Old Mrs Luo held Wenlie's hand, and shortly afterwards she collapsed and became inconsolable.

The next day Jinjin and Xinxiang escorted her back to Luchian on one of the sampans. For much of the river journey it lightly rained. When they disembarked at the landing before the Luchian rapids, Wenlie was quietly weeping. As they walked slowly passed the temple near the rapids, she looked at the stone tablets and shook her head. 'I cannot go in, the gods have punished me, why I do not know. Their jealousies have taken their reward.'

Later that day, the family shielded her from many callers, though she gave a slight nod in agreement to see the kindly head teacher of her school.

The following morning she did not appear from her room, and Jinjin's wife Fainan found her in her nightclothes, bent forward in a chair and staring at the floor. The bed had not been slept in. 'Wenlie, I'll help you get dressed, then we'll have something small to eat. If you don't want to see any visitors, we can say you're not to be disturbed.'

Fainan received no answer, saw no flicker of understanding. Since the previous evening, a frightening change had come over the grief-stricken face. Shortly after the death of Wenlie's husband three years earlier, Fainan had gone to comfort and help her in Fuzhou, and had admired how courageous she had been, how well she had coped, seeing her put all her love into the two boys. But now it was as though life itself had left her, and when Fainan tried to help her up, there was no response. She decided to bring her some food.

The family took turns to sit with her, but she seemed only to recognise Ayi, holding him weakly to her breasts, touching his hair though she did not speak. Otherwise, she wept from her chair or looked with vacant eyes.

What Wenlie experienced was an all-powerful black despair much worse than the terrible sickness she felt physically. It was as though she had been lowered through a small hole to the bottom of a deep deep well, the rope had been lifted, and she had heard the casing being shut far above her and clamped; eternal darkness had enveloped her.

7

'The Imbecile took him there all right,' one of the two policemen said to the tiny old priest, Ho Chitian, opposite the altar to the third goddess. They were at the Temple of the Five Concubines, and Lam was not at his shack beside the temple when they came for him. 'The boy's lucky he wasn't killed by the man, or by the horses for that matter. We heard he's got burns and cuts all over him, and the medical apprentice said the Imbecile looked sheepish. He must have had him up there for days. We're on our way to the farmers under the hills, and if we find him, we'll bring him back and...'

'But Lam is a gentle child of nature,' the timid priest bravely interrupted, 'and he couldn't have taken him, he had a septic toe for days, I was treating it. He only went there yesterday, the first time in a couple of weeks.'

'He could have taken the boy before that,' the second policeman said, 'left him with some food, and gone back for him.'

'He can't control anybody. A thirteen-year-old you say?' The old priest shook his head. 'That's really not possible. Speak to the farmers, especially the woman.'

Two hours later, as they were pulling themselves across the sagging bridge after interviewing the peasant farmers, one of the policemen called back: 'She's aggressive, isn't she! They're Reds! I'll check if we've got them on the list. The Imbecile saved his life! Ha! When the lad remembers, we'll have him.'

'Has any family reported a boy missing?' the elder asked the policemen just inside Tuxieng's Kuomintang police building.

'No sir, not recently,' one replied.

'Don't you think that is strange if you're right about the Imbecile? I've seen him around, and he doesn't look as though he could do such a thing.'

'We don't believe the priest,' the policeman said, 'he's hiding something. The boy could be one of the abandons, it's likely the Imbecile found him in the street or on the road outside town and took him to the hills.'

The elder looked thoughtful; he knew Ho Chitian from processions and burials, a shy priest with humans but a fierce adversary of demons and evil spirits. He also knew how powerless the town was to stop young girls being sold as labour or as wives or simply being thrown out by their parents and left to fend for themselves. But boys being kicked out by their families was less common. Usually the cause was the parents' inability to feed all the children, or the father's bankruptcy; there had been a number of such cases in the famine a few years back. He said: 'I'll arrange for posters to be put up in Three Principles Square and at the Pagoda, just in case someone knows of a boy who is no longer with his family. I'll also let the newspaper know.'

'May we have your order to lock him up, sir, when we find him?' the second policeman asked. 'He could be a danger again.'

'You say the hospital expects the boy to start remembering soon. No, use the leg chains, let him stay with the priest, he feeds him.'

Meibei saw the man coming towards her cottage and went along an embankment of a terrace high with rice to meet him. Following the visit of the two unpleasant policemen, she guessed it was something to do with the boy.

When the man introduced himself as the senior reporter for the Tuxieng News, she insisted he ask his questions outside, not inside, her little mud cottage, and beckoned to her husband who was already coming over.

'Kuomintang send you? Tell you straight, don't like your paper, can't read but we hear bad things about you Whites, you won't print the truth, will you!' Her husband reached them and bowed to the man. 'Reds been doing good things in Jiangsi for peasants like us, an' what you do, attack farmers an' kill 'em! You Whites have probably killed my younger son. Hope you get a bloody nose!'

The reporter was taken aback. 'I'm sorry about your son. Please, I'm a newspaper man, not the military.' But he became bold, wasn't going to be lectured to by a peasant woman. 'Yes, we support the government. Communists are a threat, they undermine the countryside and towns wherever they appear, the sooner they give up or join the Whites the better, or there'll be a bloodbath.'

'Pfut!' she shouted into his face. 'Been enough blood already, you've been butchering your own people.'

The reporter felt threatened and stepped back. He looked at the farmer. In an agitated voice he said: 'I've not come to argue. All I need is to get the story, then I'll leave you in peace.'

'Let him speak,' Meibei's husband urged.

She growled: 'So what you want to know then?'

The man asked them to tell him what happened the previous morning, and wrote in a notebook as Meibei spoke, her husband adding a few words here and there.

When the reporter made some comment that told Meibei the police believed 'the Imbecile' was implicated with the boy's injuries, she waded into him. 'Don't you say that! Lam's never been violent, an' what he did was amazing considering who he is. You'd better print he went back to rescue the boy when we didn't understood what he was trying to tell us, you'd better!'

'That's not true,' the man replied, 'he's been violent before. We did an article on him two years back when he ran amok in the market.'

'Lam ran amok!' she cried. 'Should be ashamed of yourself! We heard you wrote a rotten article after you talked to the market man. Nobody likes him anyway, you didn't talk to others, did you, eh? That man accused him of pinching carrots and then soaked him in filthy water. Now you write an article that Lam's a hero, you hear me!'

'I can't do that,' the man protested, 'the police...'

Meibei exploded. 'Off with you!' she shouted, raising an arm. But the man was already moving back, and he nearly tumbled as he clipped the side of Lam's stone. 'If I hears you've written rubbish saying Lam's hurt the boy, I'll have all the farmers hereabouts march on you with so much sludge, you'll be in the middle of it an' you won't be able to get into your precious building, I'm telling you! Now leave us alone!'

The reporter walked down the path as fast as he could without seeming to run. A stone hit the ground to one side and skidded away. 'Lam's the name, understand! Fang Lamgang,' he heard.

*

During the second day of the boy's admission to the hospital, he had a memory recall. Crying out from the morning treatment by young doctor Li who was applying ointment to a leg wound, he saw himself with a younger boy he believed to be his brother: they were near the end of a town, his town he thought, and they were running with a dog that had only part of a tail.

He asked the doctor to stop, and told him. When the doctor asked him the name of his brother and which end of Tuxieng he meant, he tried hard to think but could not answer. Doctor Li praised him and reminded him to keep telling them every time he recalled anything.

That afternoon the fifteen-year-old girl with short hair, Doctor Chen's daughter Sanchi, visited the hospital and found the boy lying on a bed in the men's ward; the long room was crammed with patients, families and helpers. She thought he was already looking more alert. His left arm was now in a sling. 'What am I to call you?' she asked.

She received a blank look. A student in the next bed said: 'We've already called him Yamin, it's my name, he says he likes it.'

She sat him up, and gave him a vegetable and rice soup containing fresh ginger root and amber, suggested by her father's friend Ya Ya, the Chief Doctor; she had prepared it in the hospital's communal kitchens, and she told him that the families of two other patients had agreed to share their meals with him until his family was found.

She talked to him about her father and about the Chief Doctor, friends from their student days in Amoy. 'You know why we call him Doctor Ya Ya and not Professor Su?' The boy shook his head. 'My father says he was always questioning the teachers, and one was a foreigner, a German I think, and he picked it up. At first the teachers didn't like all his questions, but they soon discovered he was very clever. He's going to start a nursing college if he can collect the money, it'll be the first inland in Fujian province.' She saw the boy looking puzzled. 'You know what a nurse is, don't you?' Again he shook his head. 'I'm going to become one, they work with the doctors, do what the helpers and families do here, only we won't cook.'

She stayed with him for a time, making most of the talk, and then went to find her father's friend.

'Sanchi, he's not opening up to us,' the Chief Doctor told her. 'You know what I want you to do dear, more than anything: touch him as much as he'll let you, hold him if you can, but watch the left side. I know this is not our Chinese way, and it's a strange thing to ask when he's not your family, but the power of touch is one of our most important weapons in healing, and I'm sure he's more likely to talk to you than to me. Try to get him to tell you everything he can recall up to the time the farmer found him. He has now told us he thinks he was in the hills for two or three days, but he can't tell us anything about what animal caused the punctures, and the first thing he recalls is nearly drowning. And ask him about the simpleton, get him to think and see if he remembers seeing him before, because it's very possible the man led him into the hills.'

On the third day after the rescue, Meibei set off early for the hospital that she had never seen at the far end of the town. She'd wanted to go the previous day but her hips and legs had given her trouble. She was fearful for the boy, kept thinking of him when he lay so weak and injured on her k'ang. If he hadn't already died, and the doctors were now going to tell her that he was likely to, she had decided to stay with him, and had told her husband so, though he hadn't liked it. And she had prepared something special for the boy to take, a strong herbal medicine she made that she learnt from her grandmother.

She walked with difficulty through the countryside to the edge of Tuxieng, taking more than three hours, the heavy clouds and gloomy atmosphere

73

seeming to affect her legs for the worse. Once into the town, she didn't want to pay even the minimal price of man-pulled rickshaws, because as peasant farmers they were heavily in debt to their pawnbroker landlord. But she could hail tradesmen's carts if there was room for her, and this way she got two good rides.

'He lives,' the older of two hospital receptionists told her, 'but you can't see him and that's flat, he's badly injured and you're not from family.' The woman was seated on a stool below a high table.

Meibei was very relieved the boy had not died, but wasn't going to take No for an answer. 'Course I can see him, I found him didn't I!' She lent as far over the high table as she could. 'You tell me where he is or I'll get angry and tip this over you.' She began shaking the table.

The woman turned on her stool and shouted a name. Meibei saw a very large man with high cheekbones stand up; he was in a nearby annex, and she realized he might come over and try to manhandle her out.

She looked quickly round. A young man she thought might be a doctor was coming along the passage. With the very big man coming up behind her, she walked to him in her waddle-way and collared him. 'I kept boy alive,' she said without bow or introduction, 'we found him, he couldn't talk, we got him to Doctor Chen, I've walked a long way, an' now I'm here I require to see him, it needn't be for long mister doctor, I just want to see how he's doing, see he's getting everything proper.'

She was lucky. Doctor Li took to her peasant directness and strong dialect, and spoke briefly to the older receptionist. He signalled to the Mongolian guard to leave them. 'Come along then. Our patient can talk now, but don't be with him for more than ten minutes.'

As they reached the next floor, she gasped: 'I'm not a tiger! Slow down! Legs bad.' The doctor stopped near an open window, Meibei finding the air refreshing. 'Another flight, I'm afraid,' he said.

She struggled up the last steps, and was breathing so heavily that she only just managed to talk. 'Hear me ...boy can live with us if nobody come for him ...' she tried to take another breath, '.... we're honest peasants, had two boys...' She had no more breath to mention her fear that she had lost a son in the revolutionary struggle.

She found the boy sitting up on a bed in the middle of a room full of people, the crowded scene a new and troubling experience for her. He seemed to her better and worse; his face had life in it, but he had a sling and bandages.

As she pushed through people visiting a young man in the next bed, what warmed her big heart was the boy's smile of recognition. She requisitioned a stool from one of the other visitors, and sat down with huge relief.

'You give us real fright with all your injuries, thought you were hunter at first, getting better?' The boy nodded. 'Still don't know your name?' He told her people were calling him Yamin. She put a small bag on the bed. 'What you doing in them hills, it's dangerous up there! Your family take you then an' you got lost? We never saw you going up our track. You got Lam to thank for saving you, he brought you down to us.'

He didn't answer her questions, though he told her he did not think he had a family.

He asked her about Lam, and she told him he was a simple man who could not talk, that he did nobody any harm, and that he loved being with the nasty horses. She made him smile when she demonstrated how Lam used a bamboo pole and feathers to hit the hens away from the rice grains, his favourite job. Laughter came from the student in the next bed and from his visitors; they were already listening.

'Call me Meibei like everyone does,' she said in her direct way. 'Could be your family threw you out. When you get better, visit me an' we'll talk.' She rubbed one of her thighs. 'They give me real trouble. We'll be harvesting soon, an' after that you can help us if you want.'

He made her laugh loud when telling her he couldn't always understand her. Then he said something that made her want to hug him, like the sons she used to hug, because he didn't have a family who wanted him: he asked if she would be coming back to see him.

She took a small bottle from her bag, pulled the cork and handed it to him. 'Here, you drink this, husband says it's best medicine in all China.'

Without hesitating, he took it to his mouth and drank her potion.

Shortly after Meibei left, one of the women helpers gave the boy a drawing pad with pencils, some of them coloured. That afternoon Sanchi again visited 'Yamin' and saw the first two pages, and when he told her he drew the pictures, she scolded him, feeling sad to discover he was a liar. 'I don't believe you,' she cried, certain they had been done by another patient or by a visitor. The first page showed a well-executed pencil drawing of the entire window behind the bed, branches of a weeping willow shown through it. The second page she found beautiful and moving; it seemed to be a night scene, a girl was fully drawn and appeared to be leaning down towards a boy who was only half drawn and crouching beside a huge rock as if frightened, the rock filling much of the right side background which she thought wonderfully lined; the only colour was the girl's darkish red robe.

'I watched him do them,' the student in the next bed said, 'he doesn't know who she is, it's not his sister, at least he doesn't think so.'

Looking at the girl in the picture, Sanchi said: 'You were copying this one from a book!' She watched him shaking his head, half at her and half towards the student. 'Then you've seen a picture like this before, at your home maybe? She an angel, isn't she, and he's done something wrong?'

He told her it was from a dream. But she still didn't believe him. She said: 'Then draw this table,' she touched the table at the end of his bed, 'and get in the two bottles.' She giggled and looked at the student.

The boy remained sitting up in bed, left arm in the sling, and placed the pad on his other side. He looked at the objects for a few seconds, and then began to draw.

Sanchi was astonished seeing the fluency of his pencil work, and noticed that he did not look up, he seemed to have remembered what he'd quickly studied.

Very soon she began jumping up and down in quick steps of delight. 'Told you so!' the student laughed.

But he did not seem to be distracted by them; he looked up, studied more, and resumed drawing. She watched as he worked the proportions and angles of the tabletop and the bottles, seeing that he did not simply produce cold lines, that each movement of his hand appeared to bring the picture ever more to life. And he seemed able to create shadow as he went along, sometimes using a thicker pencil. She thought to herself how strange that a family could throw out such a boy, and was about to comment that the bottles needed to be bluish when he told her he preferred to leave the drawing without colour. He soon completed it, handing her the pad.

She was so impressed that she called to some other patients and their families to look at the pictures. When she handed the open pad back to him, she asked warmly: 'Can I have the second one Yamin, the angel and the boy, it's so good.' She was sure he would give it her, and knew it would really please her father and grandmother to see it.

But a look of concern had come into the eyes. He closed the pad and seemed to be staring at its blank cover. Then he looked at her, and to her surprise shook his head.

When she left, she went straight to the Chief Doctor's office. Professor Su was interested to hear about Yamin's unusual talent, but he told her that what was exercising his mind, apart from the amnesia and the treatments, was the terrifying nightmares the boy had started. The other patients were being disturbed because he was sometimes screaming. He had decided to move him to a room away from the ward, it was not an ideal room as it was rather large; the night-carers would be told to get to him quickly when he had the bad dreams, in the hope he might remember something useful; if memories were of family or Tuxieng, or names or buildings, the family might be traced.

As soon as he finished, Sanchi offered to sleep in the room in a second bed, an offer that the Chief Doctor thought kind and useful, because he was aware she and the boy were developing a friendship that could only help his patient.

He said: 'He told me he's terrified of tigers coming into the room and taking him away, and of spirits and dragons attacking him. Don't sleep in the room, but we'll put a bed for you outside his door. Get your father's permission, and tell him we'll have a double screen round you to give you privacy.'

That night she slept in the passage, and was twice woken by his cries; but apart from quieting and comforting him, she learnt nothing.

*

It is the afternoon on the fourth day of the unidentified boy's admission. Professor Su is smiling at Sanchi, though she knows her father's friend very well, senses there is concern behind the smile. 'Take him one of your mother's books on animals, especially if it includes big cats,' he says.

When she goes into the boy's room, he has just woken from a nap. He had slept very badly in the night, and so had she (in the passage); she too feels tired.

He seems pleased to see her, and she sits on the bed on his right side.

'Do you like any of the pictures in this book, Yamin? It belonged to my mother, she died when I was born. I love all her books, and can bring some more if you want.'

The boy starts looking at the pictures, and they immediately interest him. 'They're good drawings,' he says, pointing to two monkeys hanging from a branch. He turns the page, sees a wild horse depicted running, and frowns.

'You don't like horses, do you,' she says.

He looks at the older girl who is kind to him, who he clings to after his nightmares, and thinks about the moment when he first realized there was a horse's head very close to him as he lay on the ground; and then a man was looking down at him; and he recalls the horses he'd seen when the man was carrying him - in those tight arms, somehow they hadn't frightened him. He says: 'I'm not sure, do you?'

'No I don't!' Sanchi has hardly ever seen a horse, and thinks about the dangerous ones she has heard about in the hills.

The boy turns other pages and comes to a snake with its body raised to attack; he knows its type, but his mind won't give him the name; he also thinks of the green snake he followed in that wind as it swam between small rocks in the stream. Then he reads the word *Cobra*, instantly having a memory flash of passing a small cobra curled on a stone, one he has seen somewhere recently, he is sure, though it hadn't been about to strike as in the picture. 'That's wrong,' he says in her direction, 'the hood's too big.' Sanchi laughs.

She watches Yamin looking at more pages, until suddenly his eyes widen as if in horror, and he slams the book shut with his good hand.

'Why did you do that?' she asks astonished, taking hold of her mother's book and turning it round to herself on the bed. She begins flipping through the pages, stops at one and looks up. The face that meets her frightens her to death.

'Is this what attacked you?' she asks in disbelief without turning the book back to him. But already the lips are trembling, and quickly she takes gentle hold of his right hand just as the left arm jerks in its sling. And the next moment the legs also jerk and the book falls to the floor.

'You're alright Yamin!' she calls as the hand in hers clenches and nastily catches her fingers, and he is now shaking so hard that she is forced to pull her hand away. She shouts for help and leaps off the bed.

His body is leaning towards her, the head turns as if to look over his left side, and before she can catch the right hand, it is rising across the sling to the left shoulder as if holding something, as if defending against a danger she cannot see.

'Yamin, I'm here!' she cries 'we're in the hospital!' as she tries to buttress him from falling off the bed, a shiver running through her because now she feels the presence of evil in the room.

A plump woman comes running in and goes to the other side of the bed, telling Yamin he is safe with them, he is to feel her hands. The helper takes his right hand firmly in both of hers.

'Shuyuan there are bad spirits in the air,' Sanchi says to the helper.

The shaking grows less, and Sanchi is able to push Yamin back more or less to an upright position, with relief seeing he has come to recognize her again. The helper brings the hand to rest on the bed.

The older woman's presence dispels Sanchi's fear of spirits. The girl picks up the book and soon finds what she wants, though does not show it to Yamin. 'Did a black leopard attack you,' she asks quietly, glancing at the helper, 'a panther?'

He doesn't answer her.

At once she leaves the helper to stay with him, and goes straight to see the Chief Doctor. But he is leaving his office in a hurry, only having time to listen quickly and to tell her that he is grateful for all she is doing. 'You'll make an excellent nurse,' he calls as he walks away, 'your mother would be proud of you. When do you go to Amoy?'

A conversation took place in the Chief Doctor's office later that afternoon. Young Doctor Li, who had led the forthright peasant woman to Yamin and who had been treating the burnt hand, was answering the Chief Doctor's question about handling memory loss caused by shock.

'Teaching and the books show that a patient's mind normally heals itself within hours of the bad event,' the young man was saying with confidence, 'certainly within a day, two at the most, although very occasionally it might be longer as appears to be the case with Yamin. A patient can be prompted but should never be pushed. As he's already starting to recall the attack, the rest is sure to come very soon.'

Professor Su answered: 'Yes I agree, Li. But a doctor must always try to think in an original way. Exceptionally, might it not be in a patient's interest to jolt the mind, use shock to relieve shock? Is the patient, in this case a child, suffering in the brain too much and for too long? What about these terrible nightmares? If they continue and his amnesia stays for many more days, you and I are going to be very worried, because part of the brain could be searching for its anchor and giving out negative messages to the body, and these could prevent his physical improvement or make him worse. In this strangest of cases, if there is a possibility that Yamin carries infection from the attack, infection that can in the next few days or weeks develop into serious illness, might not a brain remaining in shock enable the infection to grow, rather than hinder it through nature's brilliant ways? There's the strongest connection between the brain and the physical well-being of the body, as you know.'

The next morning, after another bad night with Yamin, Sanchi was passing the front desk when one of the receptionists told her that Doctor Ya Ya wanted to speak to her and that he was outside in the gardens.

When Professor Su saw her, he beckoned, but continued his conversation with the gardener after she reached him; they were discussing the route of a procession through the gardens for the forthcoming festival.

He soon finished and put a hand on her shoulder, leading her back towards the front entrance.

'Sometimes I think I'd rather be a gardener than a doctor,' he chuckled. 'Now, what are we going to do about our young friend? He's in the grip of the worst shock I've ever encountered, and he's not telling us much about what he *does* remember.'

'Maybe he got a double shock,' Sanchi replied, 'from the animal and from being burnt.'

The Chief Doctor stopped beside a tall fuchsia cascading pink flowers, took his hand away from the girl's shoulder and touched one of the flowers.

'That's an intelligent thing to say and probably partly true. But I think there must have been some sort of explosion first, and although it could have severely confused him, the appalling burns would have prevented him going into amnesic shock. No, my guess is, it was the animal attack that caused this.' He looked closely at the girl. 'I want you to be with me while I try something on him, it mightn't work mind you, but I must ask you not to interrupt me, please don't say anything except to comfort him.'

*

The boy stands by a table in his room; he is playing dominoes against himself, hoping Sanchi will soon come, when he hears the usual greeting: 'It's Doctor Ya Ya again!' as the Chief Doctor enters, followed by the girl.

He both fears and likes Doctor Ya Ya. But except for the warm sesame oil on his head and temples, he dreads some of the treatments, the applications, always worried the doctor is thinking up something else painful for him.

Nor could he answer his questions. One was whether he remembered being by a fire where there was an explosion, or near fireworks that might have burst around him; another was about handling kerosene lamps, and another about being in a forest fire. All he could say was that he'd walked for a long time through a part of forest that had been burnt, and that he saw no fires and didn't fall into any hot areas.

But he likes the smiling friendliness of the doctor and the tufted eyebrows and the glasses sitting low on the nose, and he knows he can draw him, and might do so quietly.

The Chief Doctor feels apprehensive, but says cheerfully: 'Now Yamin, you and me and Sanchi are going to have a competition here and now, yes a competition to see who can do the best drawing of an animal, we'll draw a panther and get one of the helpers to decide the winner.' Immediate fear comes into the boy's eyes, but he continues: 'If it's Sanchi, I'll treat her and her father to a meal. If it's me, you'll have to clean my office with one hand!' He smiles broadly at his patient. 'And if it's you, I'll let you walk in the gardens with Tari our huge Mongolian, he can tell you all about life in his country, if you can understand him!' He looks to the girl and back. 'Sanchi says you saw a picture in her mother's book and it frightened you. You need never be frightened of panthers again, I can assure you, you won't come across them, and I never have.' He knows those last words will be little comfort, but keeps up his unconcerned manner. 'I'm a good drawer you know, I reckon I'm better than you, watch me!' His smile erupts into laughter, the glasses nearly falling off so that he has to put up a hand to stop them. 'I'm going to do the best picture of a panther I can, I'll try to put it lying on a fallen trunk, what do you think?'

Without waiting for an answer, he places his student-days drawing pad and some pencils on the table at the end of the bed, opens the pad, and begins slowly to turn the pages in front of the boy.

80

'Look at this one, I did it on the Yangtze near Wuhan, d'you like it? The hills look good don't you think, they were blue.' He shows it to Sanchi. 'Right, time to draw! Watch me you two!' He places the pad back on the table, finds a clean page, and begins drawing.

And he starts to hum.

At first Yamin turns away, doesn't want to look. But after a while he realizes Sanchi is closely watching the doctor, and he begins to follow the movements of the hand.

The humming continues. He notices at once that Doctor Ya Ya is left-handed and quite good at drawing, as good as… A woman comes into his mind, someone he believes he knows; and still watching the hand, he tries to catch her more clearly, and sees himself in a room with other boys, and the woman is demonstrating some art and using colours. He looks towards Sanchi, but her gaze remains on the drawing, which he sees is taking early shape. The art teacher's face disappears, then comes again and this time stays, and he knows he is in a school. As he tries to think of the teacher's name, the plump helper enters.

'Oh, I'm disturbing!' she says.

'No, no,' Professor Su calls back without looking, 'come in Shuyuan, you're just the person to help us.' The doctor has not completed the outline of his reclining animal, but he is already adding some early hatching under the head. Straightening, he looks towards the helper who has stayed by the half-open door. 'You're our perfect judge, you speak your mind! We're going to draw a panther, each of us, and I want you to find us some coloured pencils or crayons, especially blacks and greys, but browns and yellows as well, and bring them as soon as possible. When we've finished, you've got to say if mine is the best. Hurry!'

The helper looks surprised. 'Doctor Ya Ya, why do you want colours, a panther's black isn't it?'

'Branch and background. Now off with you!'

Professor Su turns again to his drawing, concentration on his face as he mumbles in his patient's direction that he has to finish the area of the back and then return to the ears, they are worrying him.

'This is good, don't you think Yamin?' Sanchi says a minute later and meaning it.

The boy looks up from watching the doctor; he has already thought that the body outline too short; but he cannot make himself answer, though he likes the position of the animal on a tree branch.

Professor Su takes the pad to his chest. 'Of course it is. Enough! You may look no more my friends, and you cannot see my work until I have added shading and colouring and until you've each done a drawing for me, then we'll ask Shuyuan who's the winner, that's a fair deal, no?'

Without allowing the boy time to say anything, he turns away, carefully tears off his sheet from the pad, hands the girl his pad with two pencils, and points the boy to his own. As he goes to the window he calls back: 'There's no copying out of books allowed! And you can do any panther you like Yamin, standing, sitting, with cubs, up a tree, whatever you want, but don't copy Sanchi, and don't copy me or you'll lose!'

The plump helper returns, reads the boy's alarm, and goes to him. 'Here are the colours, Yamin, you'll do well.' She hands him a thin wooden box, gently touching his good arm and whispering so the Chief Doctor won't hear: 'Show him! A panther's not difficult is it, like a huge tabby cat only darker!'

'No Shuyuan, those colours are for me first!' her boss says. Her hand goes to her mouth to cover her embarrassment, and she hears: 'I'm going to demonstrate to my young friends what truly good drawing is all about, and they are going to see if they can do better, which I doubt.'

'Yamin's very good, Doctor Ya Ya,' she replies, taking the thin box from the boy and going over to the window. 'Did you see the one he did of the student patient in the men's ward?'

'So I hear. No I haven't seen it, but I'm not afraid, I came top in my art class when I was sixteen.' The Chief Doctor gives a big wink to the helper, one he intends his patient to see, then turns his back on them, bends over his sheet and starts to colour. Without looking round he calls out: 'Shuyuan, stay until my friends have started their drawings, then come back and judge after twenty minutes.'

'Twenty minutes!' exclaims Sanchi.

'Well, maybe a little longer,' he mutters head down.

A couple of minutes pass. The humming continues, to which are added the doctor's occasional exclamations, sometimes of exasperation though more often satisfaction.

Sanchi herself is soon expressing open annoyance at her own efforts.

Then there is complete silence.

Professor Su looks down to his beautiful gardens, and wills his patient to come out of the shock. He says a prayer of thanks to the gods that no infection has so far manifested from the bite. And he asks the Lord Buddha to guide him at that important moment, to help him as a doctor to do the right thing.

When he dares to look round, he sees that Shuyuan has left the room, Sanchi is standing at the table engrossed in her drawing, and the gods be further praised, the boy is kneeling, his body upright beside the bed, his left arm resting on the bed in its sling ...and he is drawing. The Chief Doctor fully expected his patient to have found the task too frightening, and had considered what he should do in that event, deciding he would just have to rely on his own instincts at the time. He had already told himself that if Yamin did surprisingly respond to the challenge of the competition, or even made a decent start, he would show himself to be remarkably brave; the doctor and his wife had been talking about how horrific the attack must have been.

He did not know that while the plump helper had been in the room, she had again whispered into Yamin's ear, this time that she would give him a present '…if you beat Doctor Ya Ya.' Sanchi had heard the comment just as she was starting to draw. 'Or give it to me if I win,' she had whispered back.

The young doctor comes in to remind his chief that he is wanted in his office for an appointment with the Provincial Inspector who has just arrived.

Professor Su turns from the window. 'Well tell him to wait, I'm in a competition! No, tell him I'll be there shortly, but I won't! Take him round the gardens, Li. Ask him if he's seen finer ones anywhere in the province. Tell him the patients say they recover just by looking at them, and we respectfully ask him, no, we *expect* him to put that in his report!'

When the junior doctor leaves, Professor Su watches the boy who is still working on his drawing. Sanchi lets out another sigh, and as she does so he notices that the boy's hand has started to shake a little, and he sees him look up frightened to the girl.

'How are you doing?' he asks as he goes over to the bed, immediately surprised to be looking at an unfinished drawing already of remarkable strength. 'My, it's coming along well! Here, have these colours.' He places the thin box on the bed. 'Courage my friend, keep it going!'

The hand continues shaking. The doctor thinks the shape of the animal is extraordinary: it is the sinuous form of a big cat approaching the viewer at an angle, and he tells himself that he would have had great difficulty imagining such movement and producing the dimensions so quickly. But as to the head, only the outline has been attempted, the features not drawn at all.

He kneels down by his patient. 'I'm not going to touch your drawing Yamin, but why don't you complete the head and eyes with me beside you, I can make suggestions. If you like them you can go ahead, and if you don't, just do your own drawing, any panther don't forget.'

The boy is now looking at him with the fear. The doctor holds his smile. 'Advice wanted, Sanchi!'

The girl comes round the bed, at first staring at the drawing in obvious admiration. 'Do the nose first, then complete the ears, and then get in the eyes, do it in that order Yamin, but hurry, Shuyuan will be back soon. Yes, get the nose done first.'

She returns to her table. The Chief Doctor remains kneeling beside the boy, for whom he feels enormous sympathy and now a liking and respect after just a few days - the way the boy speaks, his extraordinary talent, his look of intelligence and the fact he can read, these tell him that Yamin must surely come from a good family, so how such a family could have abandoned him, or how he'd become lost without a local family reclaiming him, he finds mystifying.

He nods for him to continue, and to his relief his patient takes the girl's advice and starts on the nose. He gives him early encouragement and keeps a hand near the side of the pad so the boy can see it, would feel he is in the company of a helpful adult, is safe whatever goes on in his imaginings.

As he watches the head of the beast come alive with the second eye, Professor Su finds himself holding his breath, and knows he has never seen so powerful an animal picture.

'We've got serious competition, my dear!' he jokes, touching the boy in the middle of the back where he knows there are no sores. 'Get in some background Yamin, and maybe you'd prefer not to use colour, the drawing is looking good as it is.' He laughs. 'Ha! I don't want you to do too well, do I!'

A look of annoyance comes over Sanchi's face, and he asks her what's wrong. 'My drawing's not good, the body's too long,' she replies.

Yamin looks quickly at her.

Professor Su stands up saying he knows how off-putting it can be to have someone looking over the shoulder. He encourages the young ones to continue, and walks to the door. When he opens it, the helper is waiting, and he indicates with his hand that she is to enter after five minutes.

He returns to the window, finds another tune to hum, and sees below him that the gardener is speaking with the man he assumes must be the Inspector. Turning round, he watches his patient - an amazing young artist indeed - and notices that his genial advice has been ignored, that a brown-colour pencil is in the hand.

As he goes back to the bed, he catches Sanchi's eye and puts a finger of silence to his lips.

He sits on the bed facing the kneeling boy. 'I think you've about finished, don't you?'

He takes hold of the pad and studies the drawing. This is the next important moment, and the doctor decides to go straight in. 'This is an excellent picture, I congratulate you. It's the beast that attacked you, isn't it? You remembered the animal when Sanchi showed you the book. So if you are able to remember the attack, you can tell Sanchi and me what happened just afterwards. How did you get away? Don't forget you're perfectly safe with us, there are no nasty animals or spirits here in my hospital!'

For a moment the doctor feels his patient is looking through him. Then the boy stares at the wooden floor.

'We fell into water.'

'We? You mean you and the animal, or you had someone who fell in with you, that man who carried you?'

The boy seems puzzled. 'It grabbed my shoulder and the shelf gave way.'

'Where were you?'

'The cavern,' Sanchi says quietly.

'Ah yes, you and the animal fell into water in a cavern.'

The boy nods to the floor.

'If the animal was holding you, it would have dragged you out of the water, or...' The near unimaginable scene, and something in the eyes, make the doctor think of height. 'How high was this shelf, above the water I mean, as high as a tall man?'

The boy looks up distressed towards Sanchi just as the helper enters. The woman seems ready to enquire about the drawings, but the doctor urgently signals her from the bed not to speak, and she stays just inside the door.

'Higher?'

The boy nods, still at Sanchi.

'As high as this ceiling?'

A finger points upwards, and the doctor is astonished. 'Higher! Twice as high as this room?'

The doctor watches the head tilt right back, before it comes down again.

Professor Su thinks for a moment. 'Do you remember going into the water?'

The boy's eyes widen in horror towards the bed .

'What happened in the water,' he encourages, 'tell us.'

There is a silence. Then '...deep, couldn't breathe...'

His patient shudders, so the doctor from his position on the bed places a hand on the boy's right shoulder. 'And the animal? Did it pull you to a bank?'

'It let go of me, the water took me into blackness, I was choking and couldn't keep my head up...' words are now pouring out '...I hit a tree and got out, it was so cold, and the pain...' the shuddering continues '...and then the sun came and I could see the cavern and I climbed up...'

'Well spoken! And you got out of the cavern, and you didn't see the panther again but you saw a tiger?'

The eyes grow big again, and Professor Su knows he must soon end his questions, doesn't want to put him to further anguish, can ask more later.

'Two,' the boy says to him through tears, making the plump helper at the door catch her breath, 'I ran away and they didn't come after me...'

Sanchi has gone to comfort him and is now kneeling with him.

'You've done splendidly Yamin to tell us all this,' the Chief Doctor says getting off the bed, 'I'm proud of you. You've remembered the terrifying attack and falling into the water. And you've told us a bit about what happened afterwards. Can you remember getting into the cavern before the animal came along, anything at all?'

The boy is now clinging to Sanchi. He shakes his head against her shoulder. She comes partly free, turns his head to her and asks: 'You still don't know your real name or where you live?' The fifteen-year-old (who hopes to be a nurse) looks up at her father's friend, guessing he won't have minded her question. But Yamin gives her no answer, and rubs away his wetness with the good hand.

'Doesn't matter, you're getting better,' the doctor says, 'I told you you would! Sometime later, not now, I'd like to hear more about what else you saw, you were in nature and I like nature. Or talk with Sanchi, her mother loved all living creatures, even insects! Now, don't think any more about it, the time has come to let our judge decide.'

He turns to the plump helper. 'What do you think of these, Shuyuan?' He places the three drawings on the bed while Sanchi helps Yamin to his feet. 'We're not telling you who did which! Say first what you think.'

The helper studies them. She assumes Doctor Chen's daughter would have produced something good, so isn't sure which is hers and which is the boy's; she has already admired his pictures; she has never seen the doctor's work, unaware he can draw well.

'This creeping animal, the eyes, it's frightening,' she says pointing to the one she thinks could be Yamin's. 'And this one with the animal looking towards mountains, the colours are good, yes the best colours, but…' she hesitates, '…is it a panther, looks too nice, and it's a bit long.' She is studying Sanchi's picture but thinks it is the Chief Doctor's.

Professor Su winks at his patient and grins at the girl. The helper looks at the third drawing. 'The panther on a branch up a tree: it's quite realistic, I like the leaves covering part of the head. Is that a sun or a full moon?'

'Thank you Shuyuan!' Professor Su says as Sanchi giggles. 'Now tell us which is the winner.'

The helper pauses and then points to the creeping beast, and Sanchi claps her hands. 'It's too good, I like its darkness, it's not coloured but…'

'I knew it!' the doctor exclaims. 'You've chosen well, it's Yamin's drawing. And if you look carefully, it is in fact quite subtly coloured.' Pointing to his own, he says: 'That's mine, and it's a moon! Panthers go out at night, I think.' The helper looks embarrassed. 'Oh dear,' he adds, 'I've got to meet the Inspector!'

When the Chief Doctor called on Sanchi's father, it was with a purpose. He told his friend that he was now more confident that the boy would not be carrying infection from the bite. Yamin had recalled the attack and other small pre-shock elements of his life, including people although not names. It could well be that falling into the water at the cavern was his saving in three senses: the animal disappeared, the water acted as an immediate cleanser of the punctures, and if, as seemed likely, the burns occurred first, they would also have received a cleansing. He said that the few enquiries so far made to the police and at his hospital (from families claiming they had lost a boy) did not match or were not genuine. After a further week, Yamin should be able to leave the hospital, and he would need a temporary home if his memory still had not come back and no one had claimed him or his family had not been found. He asked his friend to consider taking the boy into his home for up to a month, after which they would know for certain there was no infection; he added that a home atmosphere would surely help him further, and it would be easier for Sanchi, as it was undesirable she should sleep in the passage for long.

Sanchi was not present when the doctor friends talked. But when she came back from late school and her father told her what Ya Ya had said and that he had agreed to have Yamin for a month if needed, she embraced him.

8

After the old Luos had said their tearful farewells to Wenlie, Jinjin and Xinxiang, they felt ghastly, the plantation owner's wife saying the loss of their old friend was hard to take but the loss of the boy was harder. Each kept bursting into tears, old Luo crying out that he'd lost a brother, someone he'd always admired from their turbulent student years, when they marched against their own weak Manchu dynasty government and against the many 'imperialist foreign dogs' having concession territories in China.

Janping had cried her heart out, and now that the three had left, she felt very low and listless, that life was cruel, kept dangling jewels in front of her, then snatching them away as if laughing gods were mocking. Her heart bled for Wenlie, even though not so many years earlier she had hated her, had wished her dead for taking away the man she'd set her heart on.

She thought most about Yuling, and now that he must have died, the haphazardness and cruelty of life hit her once more. Occasionally she imagined a miracle - that he would turn up at the plantation - but she knew that to be a delusion. Of all the hardships in life, she thought the worst must be the loss of a child. And she was sure Genghis was also mourning; the parrot's appetite had diminished, he seemed very subdued.

Since the two men had returned from the Hut three days earlier with their terrible news, her father had not taken the ferry over to his plantation; he felt unable to organize the workers or to conduct business, fearing he would break down. She knew he didn't have much confidence in her, so was surprised when he told her '...to keep things going...' warning her that a potential new tea buyer had to be seen that very morning at Dongang's largest inn, '...he wants to inspect the plantation and the warehouse, show him round, his name is Tan Zhiyong, I can't leave this to a worker.'

With no enthusiasm she walked to the inn and found the buyer waiting. She gave the first bow, he reciprocated gracefully, and she introduced herself.

'My father asks you to forgive him that he cannot meet you himself, but we have just suffered a tragedy. He's lost his best friend and I've lost my beautiful boy, well not mine but I was great friends with his father, he was killed in Manchuria you know.'

The man shuffled, clearly embarrassed. 'I can come another time,' he said, 'say in three or four weeks if your father prefers.' He hesitated. 'Or perhaps he would allow me to take a look on my own? The weather's been so changeable, excellent a week ago, but not the last few days, and yesterday was bad. Perhaps I ought to see the plantation while the rains stay away?'

Janping knew the man had come many li, might have spent a large part of the previous rainy day reaching Dongang. And her first impression was favourable, in fact very. Tan Zhiyong was about her age - thirty or a bit more - and she was much taken by his long fingernails, and by a thin silk neck-scarf he loosely sported; it was in beautiful yellow, her favourite colour, one end draped behind his back.

'No no, you must certainly see it!' she replied. 'I will be glad to show you, really.'

He raised his clasped hands and smiled politely.

The rains had made the Zass River muddy, but the flow was not too fast for the old ferry to operate. As they crossed, the sun kept shining through clouds, giving the lush vegetation on either side of the river a particularly lovely character, as the buyer pointed out to her.

Once over the river, she avoided going close to the cottage where she and Wenlie had met the men, but took him into the lower part of the plantation, glad he wore boots as the ground was slippery. When they reached a part of the tea bushes where women were working, she noticed some of them smiling at each other, and soon understood the reason - the dashing yellow scarf. This made her inwardly laugh, and for the first time since the tragedy, she felt somewhat better - this potential buyer with the yellow scarf was taking her mind off her sadness.

'You've a much larger plantation than I realized,' he said, pointing to where bushes followed the contours and disappeared. 'Does it stretch round the hill?'

'Yes' she replied and nodded. She saw him look up towards the hills. 'My grandfather cleared these hillsides,' she went on, 'there's a fire-break up there, and many years ago my father came running home very worried because of a forest fire, but luckily the winds came from over there.' She pointed westwards. 'We were spared, but other plantations were ruined, it was awful for the families and workers.'

'I remember, I'd just started in teas,' he said.

'See these bushes,' she continued, 'they're on slopes going down like this.' Her arm tilted. 'When we have the ocean storms, they don't affect us so much because the rains go down there to the river.' She nodded again, towards the Zass.

On the return crossing, while Janping had both hands on a wooden railing and was watching a large colony of white egrets perched in a cluster of tall palms, the tea buyer on her left said to her: 'I like what I see, and will report to my boss. Please tell your father that I cannot say if we will be placing an order, but if we do, it's likely to be quite a large one because...'

'Good, good, good!' Janping said unable to hold herself back, and turning to him.

The tea buyer's face went into a half smile. 'We're feeling a lot more confident now the Reds have gone, and good riddance. Do you think your father will be able to meet a big order?'

'Of course he can!' She was now looking straight into the eyes of the handsome man, and one of her hands moved a little along the railing towards the long nails of one of his hands, though he was not holding the railing. The smile at her became broad, and her heart missed a beat.

'First you'll need to know how much we want, roughly!' he said. 'I'd say about two hundred sacks.'

As he spoke, she became aware that he had given her a look telling her he wasn't only thinking of the business in hand. She blushed and quickly looked down to the brown water; and what they were talking about went clear out of her head.

'How many people live in your town?' she asked with false interest and without looking up again. 'It's big isn't it, we went there some years ago, we went on to Canton you know.' Through the side of her eye, she saw that he had also turned to the water, and his right hand was now on the railing quite near her left.

'A hundred thousand maybe, more if you count the outlying areas. It's a good place to live if you can't be in Fuzhou or Amoy. We've excellent tea houses and restaurants. And there are always things happening, sometimes not so good!' He laughed.

Janping laughed too, and thought his hand with its long nails was nearly touching hers, and that if it did, she would try her hardest not to move hers away. She heard him say '...and a few months ago we lost an elder I knew, he took his own life through shame, he felt family loss of face because one of his sons joined the Reds. Then there's a sect of women, the newspaper has just reported that they have not taken food for over a week, about twenty of them, they're not being allowed to build a temple to follow some weird religion from the Gobi.'

The ferry had reached the middle of the river, and a breeze was up. Janping saw the tea buyer turn his head towards the white egrets in the palm trees. She looked quickly up at him, couldn't help herself, her mind now in a whirl. But she wasn't able to gaze for long, was soon staring back to the muddy water and telling herself that she had never met a man like this one, so colourful in dress and manner.

He was continuing to talk (and she was pleased) '...and there's a strange story about a boy who has lost his memory...' She let the voice flow over her, it was so musical, and while he was talking, part of the neck-scarf blew off his shoulder and across her face, its masculine scent was captivating, and she wasn't going to remove the scarf, not immediately, as she didn't think he'd noticed. And she didn't want the breeze to take it away either, she wanted to hold on to her moment of excitement.

She let go of the railing and caught the silk's end and playfully held it to her nose, breathing in, very glad he was talking on unawares.

'Oh, forgive me!' he suddenly exclaimed when he realized what had happened, retrieving the scarf while their eyes met, Janping knowing at once that he was finding her attractive. For a moment, as she looked away but half watched him re-tie his scarf, she allowed a coy smile to remain, which she hoped he would see.

She was about to ask where he had bought the silk, when he looked down to the water, she following still lost in the manly scent and his looks at her. She came back to listening about his town when he mentioned festivals '...the best in Fujian, we have carnivals, theatres, operas, dragon races. I've been in a boat for thirteen years but we never win, though last year we came second.'

She caught his smile to the river, and wanted the ferry to go round and round in circles so they could stay at the wooden railing forever.

'Hey, is this ferry safe?' he exclaimed looking up at her. 'The water seems to be getting higher!'

She felt light-hearted, and against their culture of genuine or affected shyness, she threw caution to the breeze, inclined her head as close as she dared, and pointed to the ferryman, whispering in Tan Zhiyong's ear: 'He's the danger, not the ferry! If he's drunk and we're in mid-stream, we worry!'

They parted company at the corner of the winding main street leading to the inn. When they bowed to each other, Janping gave him a look of sadness, one she hoped he would interpret the way she meant.

As she walked home, she felt again the unfairness of life, that such a dream-of-a-man did not live in Dongang, that she might never see him again. Then she told herself that he must be married, was unavailable; but it didn't make her feel any better.

Approaching her parents' house, the sorrows over the recent tragedy came back to haunt. She told her parents what the tea buyer had said, and that there was a good possibility of a big order. But her father was depressed, didn't thank her, and there was no usual drinking to an expected order.

For the rest of the day Janping thought mainly of Tan Zhiyong. She spoke about him to her parrot in the courtyard, asking if the brushing of the scented scarf across her face wasn't a good augury. Genghis gave a favourable and detailed answer, the squawking going on for a long time.

But by the end of the day she felt low, and when she went to her bed, she was very melancholic, thinking of that terrible moment when she and Wenlie saw the two men coming down the plantation path without the old friend and the lovely boy.

In the early hours she woke with a start, sitting bolt upright in the darkness of her room, wide-awake and hearing the parrot calling her from his hooded cage down the passage. Yet Genghis had never disturbed before at night, never.

As she tried to put the parrot from her mind, she wanted to remember what the tea buyer had said on the return ferry, just after he had mentioned a women's religious sect. But the continuing on-off squawking, the look Tan Zhiyong had given her when he retrieved his scarf, and her image of his strong arms paddling hard with his festival crew as they raced through the water kept interfering.

She lay back on her pillow, closed her eyes, and tried to let her mind go quiet. It took her back to the parrot; thankfully he too had gone silent. He had liked Yuling; that had greatly impressed her. Like the grandfather, the boy must have had something special about him to be accepted by her bird. Now it was all so horribly sad.

At first she could not go back to sleep, and started naming the colours of the bird and then guessing the number of feathers on his wings.

She was about to doze off when the parrot began calling again, and she found herself pushing back the thin quilt and leaving her bed. Once outside the insect net, she lit a lamp, turned it low, and crept along the passage towards her father's study, past Genghis who she shushed without looking under the hood, the parrot immediately stopping his noise.

In the study she took down a box from head height, opened it on the table, and removed several papers. Turning up the wick, she discarded a few of the papers before stopping at one. She untied a ribbon, unfolded a map and began looking at it, her finger tracing rivers and stopping at towns, Mr Tan's in particular.

Soon she felt immensely sad, fell into a chair, closed her eyes and returned to sleep.

Sometime later she woke and took the lamp back to her room. But her mind allowed her little further sleep, and when she got up feeling exhausted, she found that it was still early and her parents had not stirred.

Without daring to consider the consequences of what she was doing, she packed a small shoulder bag with one change of clothes - a robe - and her wash-kit, and made sure she was taking enough of her own money, money she kept in her room. She thought about her distraught father and the plantation, telling herself that he would manage somehow. She scribbled a note.

> *Dear Father, dearest Mother. Don't be concerned, I am not ill but*
> *still feel very very sad and I just have to get away, I will be back*
> *within four days or so, promise, promise, promise.*
> *Your loving daughter, Janping.*
> *Mother, please feed Genghis and make sure the muck is cleared*
> *and water changed. Thanks, thanks, thanks. Watch the beak.*

She removed the hood from the cage. Her parrot began making gentle noises, and she was sure he was agreeing what she was doing.

Forgetting to put back the maps and other papers strewn over the table, she went out of the house, down into the courtyard and through the thick door in the high wall.

The night sky was beginning to turn. She walked along the winding main street, past the Yuan temple that had stood for five hundred years, and took the road that followed the Zass River for part of the way, the road that would eventually cross the confluence of two rivers at the Sun Yat-sen Bridge. She was heading in the direction of the handsome tea buyer's town.

As she walked into the countryside with the first light coming from below the horizon, she caught up with a middle-aged man travelling the same way, and when he told her he was also going to the bridge, she asked if she could accompany him for her own safety. He replied that it would be an honour, but that he could not walk fast.

In the long periods of silence when they did not talk, she sometimes felt hot with embarrassment when thinking that Mr Tan might have stayed at the inn a second night and started his return journey early that very morning, that she could be catching him up, or more likely he was catching her up. Or, when she reached his town, they could bump into each other, and then he would be very surprised, he could think she was following him, though she could explain; but her behaviour might lead to the loss of the hoped-for order.

Many hours later they crossed the famous bridge. She thought again of grandfather Tsai Peiheng, their old friend who had been the main engineer in the building of the bridge ten years earlier, shortly before the great revolutionary leader had died. Peiheng and her father had often spoken about Sun Yat-sen, saying it had been a tragedy for all China when he died before his Three Principles had been achieved, and that since his death, China had been in ever greater turmoil, politically divided, and the Manchurian parts a puppet state under Japanese control.

She parted company with the traveller at the far end of the bridge, and had to wait before taking a boat.

In the evening she reached her destination and went to the Great Mandarin, one of the better hotels that a passenger on the boat had recommended; she had not sought an inn because some might be seedy, or there might be suspicion of a single woman alone there.

The first newspaper the elderly receptionist handed her - she could tell he was an opium smoker by the reddish swollen eyes and the continual muttering - was several weeks old, much to her annoyance. The spur of the moment journey she had made, this drugged receptionist, and now the unreality of what she was seeking made her reluctant to open the second newspaper he gave her, though she could see that it was just a few days old.

She walked slowly up the stairs to her room on the first floor; it overlooked two tea houses standing on either side of a large pawnbroker. She flopped into a cushioned teak chair and opened the Tuxieng News.

It had four pages, and as she skimmed through the first three and turned in dismay to the fourth and was thinking to drop the paper on the floor, her eyes alighted on what she was looking for: the story she believed the tea buyer had mentioned on the ferry.

Unclaimed boy with memory-loss survives dangerous uplands. Her mind began to race. A Tuxieng boy had been lost in the hills. She was now fairly sure that was what the tea buyer mentioned when his scented scarf blew across her face; the boy had lost his memory - so strange. She read on.

> A boy of about thirteen from Tuxieng or a neighbouring village is being treated in the hospital of respected Professor Su for burns and multiple wounds and cuts and for amnesia sustained after wandering in forest in the hills east of Tuxieng. Professor Su says it is too early to predict a full recovery though he is firmly optimistic. The police and hospital are anxious for the boy's family to come forward or be found. Dumb man Fang Lamgang, well known in the markets by another name, is credited with carrying the boy from the area of the wild horses down to the nearest farm, where the peasant farmer and a traveller took him to respected Doctor Chen in North District. Police hope the boy's memory returns soon so they can investigate if Fang took him to the hills

or if he was dumped there by family. They do not believe he would have gone there alone. Clearly the boy will not come from a family of our esteemed reader class, though surprisingly he can read and write. But readers may know of servants, shopkeepers, tenant farmers, citizens and peasants who have a boy recently missing. Information to the KMT at Han Street. Posters have been placed in the town.

Janping looked down to the busy street. A lad was nodding vigorously to an old man, and then ran off. Turning back to the paper, her doubts grew large as she realized the article was reporting on a Tuxieng boy - it couldn't be Yuling.

She watched carts and rickshaws and pedestrians passing beneath her. She thought about Tan Zhiyong, his nails and the scarf, and imagined he had returned home to a wife who at that very moment was cuddling him in a house not far from her hotel. That thought made her feel very lonely and foolish about her spontaneous useless journey - she could almost hear her father's curses when her parents read the note.

The next morning she dressed in her robe, and much in two minds, she took a rickshaw to the hospital, carrying a lady's pink umbrella lent by the hotel. Heavy rains had fallen overnight, though they seemed to have abated; the streets were very wet, the rickshaw puller apologising that he couldn't go his usual speed for fear of slipping.

She began to relax through the bustle of the traffic; she had liked Tuxieng on her previous visit, and spotted the restaurant she and her father had eaten at. She recalled the riverboats to Amoy and the exciting sea voyage they had taken to Canton.

But when she reached the hospital, she realized she had not prepared herself for the moment at hand. She walked through the drenched and steamy subtropical gardens, soon coming to the entrance doors.

She went inside, passed a shrine bedecked with flowers, and walked along a hallway, lanterns of every colour hanging from the ceiling.

Two women sat behind a high table at the reception end of the hallway, one middle-aged, the other younger; only the tops of their heads showed.

As Janping leaned over the table, the older woman, sour looking, eyed her in an unfriendly manner, and her courage began to fail.

'I have come to ask about a boy here, he's badly injured I've read, he was found in the uplands, lost his memory, unbelievable, it's in this newspaper.' She fumbled in her shoulder bag, and produced the page, holding it for them to see. 'Can I see him?' Her voice had started to shake.

The women remained seated. The older one barked: 'What's your interest?'

Janping gulped. 'I would like to see if this boy is …if he might be the son of a friend of mine. I know it's unlikely, he's been missing in the uplands you see, we thought he was dead but…'

'Well if he was missing up there he's certainly dead, isn't he!' the woman sniggered. 'When was he missing, and anyway where do you come from? So you're not claiming to be the mother then?'

'No, I'm a close friend, I'm from Dongang, he was with his grandfa…'

'Dongang! That's by the Zass River on the other side of the uplands!'

'Yes, I know, I've just come from there,' Janping could hardly speak, her throat had dried, 'there was …there was some accident…'

'Well of course we haven't got a boy from Dongang!' The woman looked at her younger colleague. 'Another enquiry and the stupidest!'

'But all I need do is see your boy, then…' Janping stopped in mid-sentence because the woman had begun calling to a male colleague whose wide back she had just spotted; he was sitting at a table in an annex.

The sour receptionist left her stool and went part way to him, and Janping saw that when the man stood up he was enormous. From his features and rugged face, she took him to come from one of the Mongol regions. The woman talked quietly to him, and soon he looked her way.

Then he began walking towards the reception table. He came round it to her. In a strong accent and deep voice he said looking down frowning: 'Woman, you leave. Boy no yours.' Before she could answer, he had grabbed her right arm and was forcing her to turn.

'Let me go! Let me go!' she protested trying to pull away from him but to no effect.

'Go away,' the officious receptionist said. 'Leave or else.'

Sizing up the man towering over her, Janping's courage began to return despite the grip, and a scheme formed in her head. Surprising herself, she told them in a calmer tone that she would leave, made a move that he allowed, and began to walk back under the multi-coloured lanterns toward the entrance doors, the big man staying with her and relaxing his hold as they went, almost to the point of letting her go by the time they had reached the shrine.

Just before the entrance doors she stopped. She gave a womanly look into his large eyes, and in a quiet and gentle voice she asked him to tell her which floor the boy was on, so that she could inform his family, who she hoped to contact very soon.

'Boy top floor,' he said, 'you no see.'

She thanked him and walked through the doors.

A light rain had begun, and she opened the hotel's umbrella. When she reached the road, she looked back through the gardens and could see the entrance doors through severely drooping bushes. The big man had not followed her out.

She looked at the long three-storey building, and decided which part seemed to have the most windows. With a beating heart she walked to a position underneath them, leaned back, and as rain fell on her face despite the umbrella, she began shouting. 'Help me somebody, help me! I want to speak to someone. Can you come and talk with me!' She stopped to draw breath. 'There's a boy you have, he's on the top floor, he was found in the hills. Hello! Would somebody answer me!'

She moved the umbrella the better to cover her head. Soon several windows and shutters were being partly opened, and people began looking out from each level.

'I'm looking for Tsai Yuling, he's eleven, no he's twelve, no he's ...' she wanted to say he's dead but stopped herself just in time - what madness was this, Yuling had died somewhere near the Hut - '...can anyone help me? You've got a boy, he's lost his memory, can I speak to a doctor? Oh please someone!...' She was now looking at a man in an open window close to her at ground level; he was staring at her with a wok in his hand, as if he was in some kitchen, but he didn't speak and she managed to keep her voice going '...I want to see the boy, I might know him.'

A woman directly over her, from the floor above, shouted angrily for her to stop the noise; and someone else, a man from further away, called out that there was a boy in his ward the other day who couldn't remember who he was or where he came from.

Janping heard him. She was trying to locate the voice from several people now looking out, when she saw the huge man and the sour receptionist running along a path towards her, and the receptionist had begun yelling at her.

The man with the wok smiled and told her she was in trouble, and nearly the next moment the huge man had reached her and seized her arm holding the umbrella.

'Pick her up Tari and throw her out of the grounds!' the receptionist called out as she ran up.

Janping found herself being turned to the horizontal, blood rushing to her head and the umbrella being pulled from her hand and falling to the ground.

She was now being carried along some other path. She tried to cry that she should be put down, but found she couldn't speak. And the woman was running behind them. 'I'll deliver you to the police,' she was shouting, 'you'll rot in prison if you come near us again.'

Two other men also came running out of the building, and Janping, whose head was partly facing them, caught sight of them and managed to yell for help.

'Tari, put the woman down,' one of the men called as she saw him lean to the ground for the umbrella.

When the men reached them, Janping had been restored to her standing position, and in the rain was smoothing down her robe and her hair.

The younger man shouted into her face. 'What are you doing disturbing us like this? We're a hospital!' He raised the umbrella to cover his head, and let his companion get a little under it. 'Why were you shouting? What do you want?'

'Doctor Li, she's crack-brained!' the receptionist said breathlessly, droplets running down her face. 'She's been asking about Yamin, but she's from Dongang!'

'Dongang!' he exclaimed towards Janping.

'He's hurting me!' she said grimacing towards him. 'Tell him to let go, I'm a plantation owner's daughter, not some crazed woman!'

The young doctor signalled, and when she was released, she put up a hand to stroke her arm thinking it would be bruised, and noticed that many more windows were now open with people looking towards them.

She moved under the eave of a shed close by. In a faltering voice she said: 'I want to see the boy you've got, I know he's not likely to be Yuling, that's my friend's boy, he must have died with his grandfather, but his body wasn't found you see...'

'Just a minute. Who is this Yuling? Which part of town is he from?'

'No, no, no, he's not from here, he's from Luchian. His father...'

'From Luchian? How can the boy we've got come from Luchian? He was found in our part of the uplands. Madam, I don't...'

'Peiheng took him to the Hut, it's in the hills, it's a long walk from our plantation, that's at Dongang...'

'Peiheng?'

'Yes, Yuling's grandfather but he died.'

The receptionist sneezed, before also moving under the roof; but it was too low for the Mongolian.

'Where is this hut?' Doctor Li asked.

'I don't know, I looked on the map, it could be in the hills somewhere near here, couldn't it?'

The young doctor turned under the pink umbrella towards his companion, and looked back at her. 'I doubt there's a hut where our patient was found.' He paused. 'The grandfather died, you said. Why did he take this boy into the hills?'

'You see they both loved birds, and my parrot...'

'How old is the boy you're talking about?'

'He's twelve, well he would have been the other day, but he's tall for his age.' Janping wiped some rain from her cheek, then pleaded with her eyes. 'One look, please doctor, then I'll go, promise, promise.'

The young doctor stared at her. 'Stay here, you're under hospital arrest at the moment.'

He walked with his companion a few paces away behind sodden sad-looking oleander bushes.

'Huh!' exclaimed the receptionist, giving Janping a look of contempt.

They soon returned. 'We'll allow you to view the boy, but only from behind glass doors. He will walk towards you, and our guard will hold you. On no account will you call out or say one word, our patient is in shock and there are other patients about. If you disobey, you'll be handed to the police, we will not tolerate any more scenes.'

Janping felt immense relief. 'Oh thank you, thank you, you don't need to worry, no more scenes. May I have my umbrella back, it's the Great Mandarin's you see.'

In the rush to find what the shouting was about, the young doctor hadn't realized that the umbrella belonged to the woman, and returned it with a short apology, reluctantly as the rain was coming down harder.

The hospital staff ran back to the entrance doors as quickly as they could, though Janping walked carefully under the umbrella, the guard staying close by her looking very wet. She was taken up flights of stairs and along a passage. After a right turn, they came to doors between corridors, with window glass in the upper parts.

'Place your hands behind your back please, and remember, not a word.' Doctor Li nodded to the guard, who took hold of one of Janping's arms, this time less firmly.

The doctor's companion went through the doors, and walked for quite some way down the corridor, Janping following him with her eyes, seeing him stop and begin to talk to someone who was out of view.

She now felt she was in a drama entirely of her own making, that she was about to prove to herself what a melodramatic fool she knew she could be, that she was on a wild-goose chase and would be ashamed by her own folly. She thought what she could say before leaving the hospital - no doubt the older receptionist would shower her with abuse.

Her expression had already taken on an embarrassed smile when she saw a boy come out to meet the man.

The man and boy began walking towards her.

Her first reaction was tremendous disappointment, her part smile vanishing; she was indeed a fool, this was not Yuling, though the patient was about the same height; not the smiling, fine-looking, self-assured boy she had seen with his grandfather at the courtyard door before their trek into the hills; not the boy with the enquiring look who had so marvellously stroked Genghis. The young patient coming towards her had an arm in a sling, part of the head looked severely cropped, and the expression seemed vacant.

But as the boy drew closer, goose pimples started running along Janping's arms, and with each further step that he took, her head began to clear, and when the man brought him to a stop about four paces from the glass, her mind registered the truth and she let out a cry and dropped the umbrella.

She didn't realize Doctor Li was observing her. Her arm freed itself from the Mongolian's hold and she began fast clapping in unbelievable joy, calling out 'Yuling! Yuling! Yuling!', her smile becoming so broad that she thought her cheeks would burst. And soon tears started to flow, and as she took a final look before the vision blurred, she tried to fall to her knees but the huge man had re-taken hold of the arm and was keeping her up.

Between her outbursts, she never heard the doctor telling him to let her go, and when she was kneeling on the floor she began sobbing with relief and excitement - her intuition, her brilliant intuition had been right.

Eventually she heard the young doctor asking her to control herself, that he wanted to take her to meet the Chief Doctor. He helped her up.

On the way to the office on the ground floor, Janping began to collect herself, asking the doctor why Yuling's arm was in a sling. The young man replied that their patient Yamin had been attacked by a panther, and that he had nasty burns to a hand. But the animal information did not make a special impression on her mind because it was running fast: how was she going to tell Wenlie, what would her own parents now say about her action, how could she get to see exciting tea merchant Tan Zhiyong to tell him, to search his eyes, so he could give her more wonderful looks, that very day if possible...

Professor Su had been at the back of the building; he hadn't heard the woman shouting at the windows from the front gardens, or the resulting commotion. He was very surprised when his rather wet young colleague came into his office to say that a plantation owner's daughter, a woman in her early thirties perhaps, was outside his office, and that he ought to see her because she claimed to know of a boy lost in the uplands very recently, so had been allowed to view Yamin from behind glass doors; the young doctor added that she seemed very genuine, she had fallen on her knees crying and saying she knew the boy and his family and that they came not from the town but from Luchian.

The Chief Doctor was at once dismissive, wondering how a woman of apparently good standing - if she really was a plantation owner's daughter - could come up with such a claim. And when he heard that a grandfather had taken a boy of eleven or twelve into the hills above Dongang to look at birds, and that the grandfather was found dead but the boy was not found, he became even more sceptical. 'Li, could you as a boy or now as a man walk alone and severely injured through these wild hills from Dongang to Tuxieng!' His young colleague gave him no reply.

But he did not want to offend him. 'Alright, I'll see her quickly, I have a question that will show her dishonesty, unless she's insane of course, and disprove her straight away.'

He went out and greeted the woman, introducing himself and telling her she could call him Doctor Ya Ya if she liked, as many people did. He asked her name and where she lived, and saw that she was well-dressed though looked somewhat dishevelled from the rain. Against his better judgement and despite the excited manner she displayed, he decided out of courtesy to invite her into his office.

He showed her to a chair, and sat behind his desk. His young colleague remained standing.

'Tell me madam, what do you know of the boy you have just seen.'

'It's Yuling, I just can't believe it!' The woman began shaking her head. 'He's alive, oh it's so wonderful, I must send a message to Wenlie, they won't believe it's true. What's happened to his head? I must see him and comfort…'

'Please,' he interrupted, 'one thing at a time. Allow me to point out that a boy from Luchian cannot possibly be found wandering in our hills, can he? And certainly nobody can come here from Dongang through the uplands.' He raised a hand to prevent the woman answering. 'You say a grandfather has died leaving a boy of twelve, and that he has walked here?'

'Yes, Peiheng took Yuling to the Hut, I saw them off from the top of the plantation, we waved to each other. Poor Peiheng! He was such a…'

'This hut. Where is it exactly?'

Professor Su felt the woman gave him a strange look.

'I've no idea, somewhere in the hills, I've never been there but my father has, I went to my father's library in the middle of the night, that was only the night before last, and I looked on a map but couldn't find it but I saw the river and followed it all the way to here, Wenlie won't believe this, and my father's going to…'

'Yes, yes, but how did the grandfather die? Of old age or some illness perhaps?'

'How did he die, how did he die?' came the reply, the Chief Doctor realizing he should never have invited this woman into his office, that she was trying to think up a story; possibly she had lost a child and was hoping she might be given custody of his patient once Yamin got better. He was wondering if she was unstable, when she added: 'Well his gun blew up, didn't it, Jinjin found him dead, he's Yuling's uncle you know.'

Professor Su's eyebrows rose. 'This uncle, he saw the gun?'

'Yes, it was broken in pieces by the lake, Yuling wasn't there, just the body, it must have been horrible, they had to bury…'

'And you told Doctor Li that this boy - you know his family I understand - comes from Luchian?'

'Yes, his father was my …well, we were very very close, he was killed by the Japanese you see, it was terrible, the funeral I mean, everyone was crying, and now I've just met another man, he's a tea merchant…'

'Forgive me again! Tell me, does your boy …what is the family name by the way?'

'Tsai, and the wonderful tea buyer's name, I wouldn't be here if it wasn't for him…'

The Chief Doctor broke in again. 'Excuse me once more for interrupting, madam,' -while the gun explosion was genuinely interesting, the impossibility of walking through those hills and forests was self-evident, and he was going to ask his defining question to end this fruitless interview - 'but does this boy - Yuling you say - have something special about him, a particular talent?'

'Of course he does, doctor! He's amazing with birds, Genghis never lets anyone touch him, never, only me naturally, but Yuling stroked him and Genghis loved it, you should…'

'Genghis?'

'Yes my lovely parrot, he was on my shoulder and he stroked him, you should have seen his reaction, we couldn't believe it, he gets that from Peiheng, he has a collection of stuffed birds you know.'

The Chief Doctor gave his young colleague a certain look, and stood up.

'Well, thank you for coming. Our patient is in shock, and we expect him to remember who he is very shortly, or we certainly hope so.'

The woman got up. 'Take me to him Doctor Yo Yo, I must see him at once to comfort him for Wenlie's…'

'Doctor Ya Ya,' the young doctor corrected.

She was becoming demanding the Chief Doctor thought. 'I'm afraid no one may see our patient apart from two visiting friends he has made. I want to keep it that way, you understand me, so that he is not unnecessarily confused.' Through his smile he tried to hide that he was sure this emotional woman was either making up her story or talking about another boy; she had failed his litmus test.

'But if I see Yuling he might know me, his memory could come back!' the woman protested.

'No madam, for medical reasons he must not be disturbed.' He led her to the door. 'But thank you for coming in.'

As he bowed to her, the woman said: 'I'll be back with Tsai Wenlie very soon,' and she returned the bow.

He made no answer.

Doctor Li escorted the woman away, and felt acute embarrassment, catching the unusual frown at him on Professor Su's face. And when they passed the reception, he watched in further shame as the excitable woman leant over the side of the table. 'I hope you didn't get too wet,' he heard her say, 'I'm so happy to have identified my lovely boy, well he's my friend's boy, he's Tsai Yuling you know, and he must have walked all the way through the hills from the Hut above Dongang.'

*

Much later that day, after evening has come, a messenger arrives at the Tsai house in Luchian, Jinjin accepting the envelope. It is addressed strangely, to himself and his sister-in-law *Tsais Jinjin and Wenlie*. He and his wife Fainan are outside the front of the house under the light of an oil lamp, helping their six-year-old daughter finish a papier-mâché mask for a part in a children's street play, one that Wenlie would normally have directed but couldn't in her continuing terrible state. Jinjin assumes the sender has mixed up Wenlie's name for his wife's, and can't think why anybody would want to send him a written message; he hadn't ordered materials from another town for his small building business.

He begins to read, and the words *Yuling* and *alive* jump out at him, and for a moment he thinks his eyes or the lamplight are playing tricks. Fainan picks up that it might be important and also reads the paper in her husband's hand.

> *Found Yuling alive, Genghis helped, deliriously happy, promise true, just seen him in Tuxieng hospital badly injured but walked towards me, Doctor Ya Ya says is getting better but has lost his memory. Wenlie, bring money and clothes for long stay. Am at the Great Mandarin. Must run to find a wonderful tea man Tan Zhiyong.*
> *Luo Janping.*

Jinjin is about to shout when Fainan pushes her hand in front of his mouth. Then she hugs him with all her might. 'Tuxieng! Tuxieng!' he keeps saying in her arms. 'It's possible! It's really possible!'

Fainan releases herself; she has started crying and has set off their daughter.

Jinjin picks the girl up. 'Alinga's alive, sweetie, he's got through the hills, it's incredible, so injured but somehow...' He does a little jig with her, then stops himself, his nose touching hers. 'Don't say anything to Ayi, we've got to tell Aunt Wenlie first.'

The adults go into the kitchen, followed by the girl. Wenlie is sitting on a low stool at a table; she is cutting apples, a job Fainan has given her. Ayi is in neighbour Xinxiang's house with other boys.

Fainan goes up to her, puts hands on her shoulders and looks down at a forlorn face. 'Wenlie, look at me, listen carefully, you must promise to listen, and you must believe us, we've some truly wonderful news.' She removes her hands and turns to her husband.

Jinjin bends down and shows the message, unable to hide his excitement. 'This is from Janping, Wenlie. Alinga's alive, she's found him in a hospital in Tuxieng. He's alive!'

He waits for her reaction but none comes. 'It says he's injured but getting better.' He reads the words to her, his voice shaking.

Wenlie is feeling her usual numbness, a vast emptiness. She hears her brother-in-law's words, sees the incredulous smile on his face and the paper in his hand ...but she isn't accepting what he has said, isn't reading the message.

She looks up at Fainan, and starts exploring her expression, seeing the wet on her cheeks. Slowly she puts the knife on the table and takes hold of the paper.

This time, Fainan says to herself, she appears to be reading it.

Several seconds later Wenlie lets out such a cry that it makes the girl run from the room. She begins trembling, and as Jinjin repeats that her Alinga is alive, she gives herself into Fainan's arms, still clutching the paper.

9

From the moment the possibility penetrated Wenlie's mind that her son might have survived, she couldn't believe how much her spirits had risen. But although she desperately wanted to accept the message, she wasn't able to put away the thought that over-emotional Janping could have temporarily lost her mind because of the tragedy, or had at best been foolishly horribly mistaken, at worst was deliberately avenging herself that her man had been taken from her.

These terrifying ideas seemed to grow larger as she read the message over and over again, allowing herself to think more freely. Parts rang so false: Genghis the nasty parrot, a hospital doctor with a nonsensical name, and *a wonderful tea man*; and she couldn't imagine her lively son losing his memory. Her concerns made her strangely unwilling to rush over to a place she knew well by name on the other side of the uplands but had never visited.

She mentioned her dark thoughts to her brother-in-law and his wife. 'You know what she's like,' she said searching Fainan's face yet again.

'Of course she's found him, she *saw* him!' Jinjin exclaimed. 'Even Janping couldn't be mistaken about something so important, she can't have gone mad, and she's not evil Wenlie.'

Despite Jinjin and Fainan's assurances, deep down she was fearful. She packed little, only one change of clothes, and boots against the rains. After taking a little money from a small box that belonged to her husband, she went to her jewellery case. Whether from the superstition of thinking it might make the news come true, or from the comforting memory of her childhood family, she took out the brooch her parents had given her at her wedding, the jade and emerald brooch that had been her grandmother's.

On the river journeys that Wenlie and Jinjin took the next morning, the constant rain did nothing to dispel Jinjin's own misgivings. Perhaps his wife was wrong, that Janping really could be mentally disturbed, or in her neurotic excitement she had simply mistaken the boy in the hospital for Alinga. He remembered the bloodied shirt and the dreadful little object on the floor that had not been mentioned to the women. He asked himself how he was going to deal with his sister-in-law if the boy turned out not to be Alinga after all; he would hardly know what to do, would miss Fainan at such a shattering moment.

Wenlie picked up his fear. Looking closely at him she said: 'Jinjin, when we get to the hospital, you go in and see their boy first, then come and tell me quietly, you can just shake your head and we'll leave quickly.'

The request made Jinjin even more fearful.

As the boat approached Tuxieng, the bad weather they had been having for several days finally cleared, and they arrived at the hotel in evening sunshine.

Janping was in the lounge talking away with Tan Zhiyong. She had written him a note, the hotel had delivered it to his company's office, but in her elation she had failed to say where she was staying, and he had gone to a number of inns and hotels before finding her.

On seeing the travellers come through the doors, she at once leapt up and embraced Wenlie, excitedly telling her and Jinjin that they should all go straight away to the hospital. Then she turned and told them that they must meet her new friend, 'the gentleman who helped me find Yuling.'

She found Wenlie's reaction to her embrace and to the introduction most odd. There was hardly a bow to Tan Zhiyong, and no raised clasped hands in respectful greeting, only a strained smile without any words of gratitude. Janping was shocked. So she explained further, saying that Mr Tan had mentioned to her on the ferry about an article in a Tuxieng newspaper, of a boy found wandering in the hills who had lost his memory.

Although she was pleased when Jinjin politely thanked her new friend, she was surprised and hurt that stern-faced Wenlie had lowered her eyes to the floor. She told them about being saved from the Mongolian, and that a panther had attacked Yuling, but that he had 'of course' survived, and said that Doctor Ya Ya might still be at the hospital if they went straight away. 'We'll be there in twenty minutes, Wenlie,' she added with encouragement.

On hearing about the animal, Wenlie found it even less likely that the boy she had been brought to see was her son. She didn't ask about the Mongolian. 'No,' she replied, shaking her head as she looked briefly at the man she had been introduced to. 'I am tired Janping, I'd rather go tomorrow.' She begged to be forgiven, bowed a little deeper, and turned.

*

The next morning, without taking breakfast, they take two rickshaws, Wenlie and Janping in one, Jinjin in another. Janping warns Wenlie to expect Yuling to look lost, telling her that his hair is cut and strange. But Wenlie makes no comment, and hardly speaks on the journey.

At the reception, Janping says over the table to the officious woman: 'I have brought the mother and uncle of Tsai Yuling, we wish to see the boy, so kindly inform Doctor Ya Ya, he told me I could call him that you know, tell him we are here will you.'

The woman stands up and eyes them. She says loudly to Janping: 'Professor Su, the Chief Doctor, is not in yet. You're wasting our time and his, he won't want to see you, you didn't properly identify our patient Yamin.'

Jinjin audibly catches his breath, Wenlie looking at him as he reads her thought.

'What do you mean!' Janping exclaims. 'I *saw* him, it *was* Yuling. The doctor was very pleased, he....'

'Not what I heard, lady.' The receptionist notices the reaction of the visitors and says grumpily: 'Well, seeing as you've come a long way, wait over there.' She points to chairs and sits down on her stool.

Janping continues remonstrating, but Jinjin takes gentle hold of her arm and tells her 'for Wenlie's sake' not to make a scene, 'we can wait for the doctor.'

Some ten minutes later Janping sees the cheerful doctor come through the entrance, and she jumps up and walks fast towards him under the colourful lanterns, ignoring the call of the receptionist to resume her seat and wait. And when they bow to each other, she tells him that the mother and uncle of Tsai Yuling have arrived.

The Chief Doctor is concerned. He had hoped, though not entirely expected, that he would hear no more from the excitable Dongang woman. But now he can see a man and a second woman sitting waiting, and as he goes over to them, he thinks it a sad task to disappoint genuine enquirers of a lost child - from their expressions, something tells him these people are genuine. He bows and introduces himself as Professor Su.

Wenlie and Jinjin have already stood, and they bow back.

Looking from the man to the woman, he begins: 'We have a boy here who this lady saw briefly two days ago through doors from a little distance. But I fear we may have a case of mistaken identity. I don't want to disappoint you...' He is cut short by the excitable woman who begins to protest, and he listens while the man tells her to let him continue.

He looks back to his visitors. 'It has been about ten days since Yamin - that's the name we call our young patient - was found in the hills near here. He has unpleasant injuries, particularly burns to a hand, and there was also an animal bite. Unfortunately we haven't yet been able to get him out of his amnesia, though he now remembers the animal attack. But he doesn't know who he is.' He hesitates. 'How could anyone get through the wild hills from Dongang to here? Obviously...'

Jinjin breaks in: 'But my father and Yuling weren't near Dongang, Professor, they were much further into the hills.'

Professor Su is surprised. 'I see. But clearly our boy must have been taken into the hills from here, from Tuxieng or the villages, we think dumped or lured there.' He coughs to the side. 'I understand there was a gun explosion and a grandfather died. That interested me. But didn't this happen at a lake near a tea plantation at Dongang?' He looks towards the excitable woman.

'No,' Jinjin says, 'they were at the Hut, the Hut and the lake are far from Dongang, in fact they're probably closer to here.'

There is a short silence as the Chief Doctor straightens and touches his glasses. He is about to speak, when Jinjin adds: 'Can I talk with you in private? There's one thing we didn't mention to the women, and I must ask you about it.'

Wenlie looks at her brother-in-law and frowns. He turns to her. 'It won't take a minute Wenlie, this could be very important.'

The doctor beckons and leads him down the hallway to the front of the Buddha shrine with its many flowers. Janping watches them and begins talking, but Wenlie asks her to remain quiet, and looks in the other direction towards stairs. The women remain standing.

A couple of minutes later the men return. 'I'm truly amazed,' the Chief Doctor says looking at the taller fine but sad-looking woman. 'This gentleman has just given me the most startling information that would certainly confirm the identity. He says, and I am sorry to mention this, that he saw a finger on the floor.'

Janping lets out an utterance of disgust, and Wenlie gives her brother-in-law a look mixing disbelief with great disapproval.

'Well our boy *is* missing the little finger on his left hand, the hand that is badly burnt by a gun explosion I now realize. The head was much less seriously burnt, I'm glad to tell you.'

Jinjin nods but avoids Wenlie's eyes.

'May I say a word,' she says, speaking quietly towards the doctor she thinks looks intelligent and talks kindly. 'I want to believe but cannot. The boy you have, is he strong-looking? My son was tall and well-built for his age.'

'Yes, madam, we have been thinking he's thirteen but he's not yet into puberty.'

Wenlie finds that she cannot talk in the present tense as if Alinga is alive. 'My son would have been twelve a few days ago, but he looked older than his age.'

'Does he have a brother?' the doctor asks, 'he thinks he might.'

'Yes, my other son Ayi, he's nine.'

'Then let me ask you the same question I asked your friend here. Does your son have a special talent, musical, mathematics, that sort of thing? I ask you, because the boy we have definitely does, he is extraordinary in one respect, quite extraordinary.'

Wenlie searches the doctor's expression, for the first time realizing but frightened to acknowledge where the question might positively lead. But before she can answer, Jinjin jumps in again: 'He certainly does Professor, look at this!' He takes from his bag a roll of drawing paper, unfurls it and holds it up.

The doctor can hardly believe what he is looking at - a beautifully executed coloured drawing of a cabin perched on a cliff in evening sun - and he knows at once who has drawn it, the broadest smile coming over his face. 'Oh my, oh my!' he exclaims as he looks from the drawing and back to the woman he now realizes is the mother; he'd been right, the boy did come from a good family. 'Then I think you'd better meet our Yamin, he's got the whole hospital wanting to have their portraits drawn, even Tari our Mongolian over there!' He looks towards the guard's annex, and sees the big man's back.

No one in the standing group notices the surprised looks of the two receptionists listening from their stools behind the high table.

Wenlie stares at the doctor. She falls back into one of the chairs, her head lowers and she feels herself about to break down as she covers her face in her hands. 'I'm sorry,' she bursts out, 'you see, I was certain he was dead, that's what they told me, there was so much blood they said...' She stops herself. 'I've been thinking of his body in the hills, and now...' She is daring for the first time to think that the impossible could be coming true. She feels as if the chains of the very gates of death have begun to operate like the slow rising of a huge iron grill, and that her Alinga - who in her mind she still cannot see on the other side - might soon be walking through the dark towards her.

She feels Janping's arm come round her shoulders. She takes her hands from her face, whispering without looking up: 'Can we see your boy?' She dare not use her son's name, cannot tempt fate.

'You certainly can! I'm at a loss to tell you what I feel and how pleased I am. He may well not recognize you, but that should happen soon, I hope very soon. The shock has already lasted much too long. But it's good that he now recalls the animal attack, and I must talk to you later about that.' Professor Su pauses, waiting for the mother to look up. When she does, he adds: 'Please, if he doesn't recognize you, I must ask you not to be emotional. That will be hard for you, but I don't want him to be stressed or confused, I'm sure you agree. Until our good friend here identified him, not without some difficulty in getting into my hospital I might add,' he chuckles towards the Dongang woman who had failed his litmus test because she had given him some ridiculous answer about a parrot, 'we were concerned that no local family had been found. We suspected he was an abandoned, though his obvious intelligence and talent made that seem very strange.'

They go up stairs and along passages, Wenlie remaining a few steps behind the others. When she sees the doctor look into a room, she cannot bring herself to go further. 'You go in,' she whispers to Jinjin, now back with her fearful doubts, expecting to go through another heart-breaking moment in her life.

The boy has had a shocking night, waking three times from nightmares, each time certain that evil spirits were attacking him, were taking him back to the forest and the loneliness and the pain. Only the reality of Sanchi's presence stopped his cries as he clung to her. Daylight and morning could not have come too soon.

He has dressed, Sanchi has gone home, and he is thinking of going into the crowded men's ward to talk with some of the patients he has drawn; he likes it that his portraits are often pinned up by their beds. Or student Bai Yamin might challenge him to a game of chess; they are very even despite the age difference.

And he liked his name. 'Which Yamin won?' patients or family members would call out laughing towards them. 'Did you beat Yamin, Yamin!'

He is sitting on his bed with the door wide open, looking at a book on the seasons that Sanchi has given him to read, when he hears several people coming along the passage.

'It's Doctor Ya Ya again!' the Chief Doctor says with a big smile at him. 'And Yamin, I'm bringing some very important visitors, your family!'

The last word greatly surprises him, as does the entry of a woman followed by a man. He recognizes the woman as the one he saw through the glass doors when he heard her call out another name several times. Very soon afterwards, when he was drawing an eight-year-old boy visiting his sick father, he had thought of his dream at the boulder, and believed that the girl might have called him that Yuling name, though he wasn't sure. The doctors and helpers had kept on at him to tell them whenever he thought he had a recall, but he hadn't liked to mention this one.

He gets off the bed and bows. The man is immediately staring at him, and he doesn't think he knows him. He watches him eagerly calling out a name, as if to someone else who is outside the room.

A second woman comes in, she is taller and looking at him in fright; and just as he hears Doctor Ya Ya ask if he knows anyone, the woman cries out and runs to him and is touching his face and his good hand and calling him 'my darling, my darling, oh my precious Alinga,' and she is trying to hug and then kiss him though he leans back feeling very awkward and looks to the doctor, anxious that the woman doesn't touch his bad arm, especially the hand in its sling.

'Yamin, this is your mother and your uncle,' he hears the Chief Doctor say, 'your family have found you. Your real name is Yuling, Tsai Yuling.'

The girl in the boulder dream flashes into his mind. The doctor say something to the woman, and she lets go but stays very close. And when he looks at her, she has tears in her eyes though she is smiling at him, and he finds this disturbing because although he thinks she looks nice, she means nothing to him. If she really is his mother, it might not be bad. He sits back on the bed and hopes she won't try to embrace him again.

'Do you recognize any of your visitors?' Doctor Ya Ya asks.

The other man the doctor called an uncle is also smiling widely at him. Yamin gives him a friendly look back, now wondering if in fact he might have seen him before ...and with that, a small girl comes into his mind. He looks at the doctor. 'I can see a girl, very young,' he says.

'How old is she? What does she look like?' the taller woman standing close asks; she has just clutched his good hand again; her hand seems clammy and he wants to withdraw but thinks he will answer first; he doesn't have to think hard - the image remains vivid as when he draws patients.

'She's two or three, pigtails are coming over her...' He manages to withdraw his hand, and gestures to left and right how they fall in the front.

'That must be my Pin, my little one!' the man exclaims, 'she's your youngest cousin, you live with us and we have three girls.'

'Yamin,' the doctor says, 'you have remembered the high shelf in the cavern and falling into the water. Do you remember anything before that, being with your grandfather, walking with him? He was with you in the hills, his gun exploded by a lake and that's how you got these burns. Do you remember anything about the explosion? It would have been shockingly painful for you.'

As the doctor is talking, the boy feels strange, as if what he is hearing about a grandfather is not completely foreign; but he cannot connect to an explosion or to a lake, other than the terror of fleeing from the two tigers at a lake, and quickly he throws them out of his thoughts as he frowns to the doctor.

The woman so near him asks: 'Can't you remember grandfather with his drooping moustache? And he loved birds, you were often with him in the outhouse, all the stuffed birds, can't you remember them, Alinga?'

Alinga - that name again, she seems always to be calling him this; but the other woman called him the Yuling name; he's confused.

For the first time since the visitors entered his room he lets himself look into the eyes of the woman the doctor says is his mother; she seems to be trying to help him, and now their mention of a grandfather has begun flying around inside his head without him being able to catch it; and an empty k'ang appears to him and with it a feeling so unpleasant that he knows trembling is coming on.

But the man who is his uncle brings him away from the nastiness, because he is holding up a coloured drawing that immediately interests him, and the urge to tremble goes away. 'Surely you remember drawing this, Alinga,' he says.

He looks at it and thinks the composition and colours and shading are good: a small building is perched on top of what looks to him like a rock face, it stands in streaks of evening light, and a single bird is drawn in the upper left of the picture. Away in his thoughts and only half listening while the man says something to the Chief Doctor about a hut, he imagines the bird flying out of the drawing, and thinks of the buzzard he saw at the cavern opening.

A few minutes later Wenlie and the other two are asked by the Chief Doctor to leave so that her Alinga can have some treatment. But she finds it almost impossible to let go of her son's hand. She feels the doctor touch her arm; he has a few things to discuss with her, and she can visit in the afternoon.

Once outside the room, she feels in a daze walking back along the passage; and as they go down the stairs, she tells the doctor that she had had to force herself to walk into that room. 'And now I feel utter unbelievable joy,' she says, 'but I'm scared, he has this different look in his eyes.'

Professor Su stops on the landing. 'Your son suffered two horrific events, be patient. You are reunited, that's the most important thing at the moment. Just seeing you, I'm hoping inner doors are opening.'

Wenlie wants to ask about the hand, but the doctor continues: 'I find it extraordinary that he survived in the hills with those injuries, he had the Lord Buddha's own protection. Not only did he survive a gun explosion and a cat attack, he told us he saw two tigers. And the peasant woman who visits your son - her husband, I should tell you, brought him a long way on a stretcher to my friend Dr Chen - she told me that the aggressive horses where he was found would have killed him if the simpleton hadn't found him.'

'The simpleton?'

'Has Miss Luo not told you? It was in the newspaper she had. ' He takes a sideways look at Janping. 'He is often called the Imbecile, the man brought him to the peasant farmers, your boy was in a very bad state and owes his life to him first, and to them. I am feeling guilty, I was sure the man had taken him into the hills, and Dr Chen thought so too.'

When they reach his office, he tells her that her son will be able to leave the hospital within a week, but that he needs him to remain in Tuxieng for a further three weeks for observation. 'We think there is no infection from the panther bite but must make sure. I have spoken with Doctor Chen and Sanchi, she's his daughter, she's been staying near your son during the nights because of his fears and terrifying dreams. She's been wonderfully helpful to us here and they have become friends. The Chens would be happy to have him live with them for that period, and now that you have found your son, I'm sure they will extend the invitation to you as well.'

Before Wenlie leaves the hospital, she asks to meet the families of the other patients who have been sharing their meals with her son. When they hear that she is the mother, they give her very warm greetings, and show her the drawings he did of them. But they refuse to consider the idea of any payment.

She walks out of Professor Su's hospital feeling a reality both magical and frightening - her son has come back to her but does not know her. The abundant gardens she walks through and the smile of a gardener give her comforting assurances.

As she and Janping start their double-seat rickshaw journey back to the Great Mandarin, she turns to her friend, her voice emotional: 'Forgive me Janping, please forgive me, I was sure you were mistaken. I will never forget what you have done, never. And I don't care if the world sees me.' She leans over and puts her lips to Janping's cheek, keeping them there while the rickshaw puller trundles along.

Janping cannot prevent herself from smiling, and as her friend comes away she giggles: 'And you know what, Wenlie, through Yuling I've met a lovely man!'

For the first time in what seems an eternity, Wenlie can laugh within and smile without. 'Beware of men with colourful scarves!' she whispers into Janping's ear.

About half way to the hotel she calls to the rickshaw puller to let her out, and tells Janping to continue to the hotel, saying she needs to be alone for a while.

As Janping looks back, she sees Wenlie disappearing into a lane, towards what she takes to be a small temple because she can see sweeping roofs of blue and white tiles.

Wenlie knows what she has to do. She feels the spirituality of the Taoist grounds as soon as she enters; she can pray there as in a Buddhist temple.

Exquisite trees and bushes are dotted inside a walled courtyard, its October garden beautifully maintained; large tablets stand at intervals with their teachings carved on them.

Passing through richly painted doors depicting gods protecting the inner goddesses, she comes immediately to the fifth of five small chapels, one to each concubine. She knows their story well: You live and we all live, you die and we die with you, the women answered their master who had decided to die rather than submit to the new rulers of China; they had donned their elaborate robes and hanged themselves. And in one of Wenlie's worst moments a few days after returning from Dongang, she too had thought of ending her life, though she had not said anything to Fainan. Her holding of her younger son Ayi - feeling his young head, his hair - had been her saving.

She sees a tiny priest; he is elderly and sweeping leaves from the base of one of the tablets. The man looks up, and they nod to each other, faces serious.

She goes on her knees before the statue of the fifth goddess, close to a stone incense burner. A sacred lamp flickers at the deity's feet, its metal the shape of a lotus flower.

As Wenlie looks at the small flame and is about to start her prayer, all her pent-up emotions burst through and she begins to sob, sobbing with tears of relief and of guilt, guilt that she had not trusted her instinct and stood up to her father-in-law to prevent Alinga being taken into the uplands, guilt that since the terrible news that he must have died, she had abandoned her prayers and religious duties.

She never hears the priest come up behind her, or his gentle words before he retires. When she dries away her tears, she turns her thoughts to the Holy One. She tells him she is ashamed to have abandoned her prayers, to have doubted his goodness and wisdom, to have shunned the temple in Luchian since her son was lost.

She says her last prayer in a whisper looking towards the feet of the beautiful goddess; it is her gratitude and supplication to the enlightened founder of her faith:

'Lord Buddha I thank you and I thank all the gods and all the good spirits from the depths of my being for the preservation and safety of my dear Alinga in his perilous ordeal in the hills, and from an unknown grave in the forests. Help him recover his memory and heal from his injuries. Let your protection have an impression for good that will ever remain with him. And whether or not in his loneliness and suffering he asked the gods to spare him, let him always remember that they saw him into the hands of good people who saved his life. May your teachings be with him and guide him, and your guidance be with my second son Ayi, and with my beloved husband Peijinn and dear grandfather Peiheng on their continuing journeys.'

In the lane outside the temple, as Wenlie waves to draw the attention of a rickshaw puller in a connecting street, she passes a sad little man, his ankles in chains; he stands beside the reddish brown bark of a juniper tree, murmuring to himself, his upper body moving from side to side, and she wonders what he has done to deserve his punishment. Close by, an elderly beggar squats on a mat against the courtyard wall, near one of the old stone tablets; a rusty tin mug sits on the mat in front of his feet. She goes up to him, bends down and puts a coin in the mug, wishing him well, and receiving back warm gratitude as the beggar nods vigorously and looks up with white eyes.

As she enters the rickshaw, she thinks no more of either man. Wenlie, already feeling her life has returned since walking into that hospital room, does not know what the murmuring swaying man in ankle chains has done for her.

*

That afternoon she visited Yuling, this time alone. Jinjin had left to return to Luchian, and she could well imagine the rejoicing at home and in the school. Janping had excused herself and gone to send a second message to her parents: that although the reunion between mother and son had taken place, she needed a few more days in Tuxieng, although she did not say why.

Wenlie found it unnerving to be looking at her son, to adore him yet know he had no present feelings towards her. He kept giving her polite or restrained answers and only occasionally smiled. She tried to hold his hand as before, but usually he withdrew.

She spoke to him about his brother Ayi, that they were very different in character, his brother a serious boy, Yuling often happy and laughing; and about their life with his uncle and aunt and three younger girl cousins. And she talked about his father.

Trying to jog his memory, she told him about the Hut, about the journey she and his father had made there, and about the small shrine they built overlooking the escarpment.

He told her of the buzzard he'd watched from the cavern opening; and when he mentioned the green snake in the stream and told her that he followed it, she laughed and said no one else in the family liked snakes.

She told him that when she was a girl with her father in the hills near Fuzhou she had seen a tiger, hoping he would unburden himself about the tigers he saw; but he clammed up, and she wished she hadn't mentioned it, thinking better than to ask about the panther attack.

He asked her where she lived and if there was a dog with a tail that was partly cut off or small, and if she knew of a woman art teacher who had come into his mind just a few days earlier. She told him about the dog and about his teacher, and she said that she also taught at the school - drama, music and singing - and that he was becoming a good actor.

He talked to her of the peasant woman called Meibei, said what she and her husband had done for him, mentioning the large wart on her forehead and saying she had twice been to see him and that he liked her but couldn't always understand what she was saying.

Wenlie asked about the simpleton who had found him, and he told her how the man had picked him up and carried him through the horses, that he had made strange noises, and what Meibei had said about Lam.

They had been talking for some time when a girl with very short hair came into the room, bowed to her, and introduced herself as Sanchi, Doctor Chen's daughter, before greeting her son as if she was his sister or a close friend.

'I'm very pleased you've found Yamin,' the girl said smiling at her son before looking back to her, 'and my father will be too. We read together from my mother's books, and we play dominoes, he's good!'

Wenlie immediately thanked the girl for looking after her son at night and helping to feed him. She asked her to convey her deep gratitude to her father for his first treatment. But when she told her she would take over the nights, to her shock Yuling shook his head. 'Stay with me Sanchi,' he said looking at the girl.

Wenlie felt deeply hurt and troubled. The girl must have realized her pain, because she quickly changed the subject, telling her how amazed she had been when seeing 'Yamin's' early drawings. 'One of the patients is so ugly,' she said again towards Yuling, 'he didn't want to be drawn, but you'd already done one of him quietly, hadn't you, and the man liked it so much he took it round the hospital and then into the street!'

Wenlie thought Sanchi pleasant if rather forceful for a girl of only fifteen talking to an adult. When the subject of Yuling's father came up, the girl suddenly became intense, saying she'd just heard from Doctor Ya Ya that he had died in Manchuria against the Japanese. 'He was murdered! He should never have died like that. The Nationalists were really badly led, they only gave token resistance. I'm sorry for you and Yamin. Our country is rotten and divided under the Whites. Chiang Kai-shek only wants to kill Communists and intellectuals. Our poor province, it's terrible that we're now under these Nanjing murderers, he's nothing but a warlord criminal! He should be fighting the Japanese imperialist devils.'

Wenlie was taken aback by the vehemence, and for a split second saw the girl as an effective actress on the stage. But she was in no state to debate the political situation, and moved the talk to the girl's future.

Soon it was clear to her that she was in the way and thought she had better leave. Awkwardly she said her goodbyes, kissing Yuling but receiving no response. And before she had gone from the room the young ones were talking away. Once more the unpleasantness of being a stranger to her own son hit her hard.

She had, however, a good, a very good, realization: that she was out of her deep despair, that the darkness had lifted.

The rickshaw lad, rough-looking and no more than seventeen Wenlie thought, agreed to go as far as he could out of Tuxieng towards the sagging bridge. As he pulled her through the countryside on the gentle upwards incline in the late morning of a breezy day, he did not ask her why she needed to go so far, and she remained silent, still trying to take in the extraordinary events since receiving the message that Yuling was alive. She felt guilty towards the young man, because he had soon stopped to remove his shirt and tie it round his waist. He maintained a slow run, and was panting when they reached the point where the road became too bumpy. She was relieved he could go no further, and watched him park the rickshaw by an old date tree. He escorted her the rest of the way to a sagging bridge of bamboo and rope, where she paid him the fare and assured him that she had plenty of time to walk back to the town, that he was not to wait as she did not know how long she would be.

'It's Empress come to see her peasants,' Meibei quipped, as she and her husband stood near Lam's stone and watched an elegant woman with a shoulder bag coming along their path holding her hair in the breeze, 'she wants her dues an' goods!' Meibei was clutching a long-handle weeding fork, and thought what a strange couple of weeks they were having.

She began moving along the path in her waddling way, her husband following. The woman called out a greeting, and soon they were given a full bow. The farmer reciprocated, but Meibei just nodded.

Wenlie asked: 'Are you the people who took a badly injured boy to Doctor Chen?' She was pretty sure she had found the right people because the woman had a wart on her forehead.

'What if we are?' Meibei growled, looking at her husband and back. 'Is newspaper sending a woman now?'

'I'm the mother of the boy you so greatly helped. My name is Tsai Wenlie.' Wenlie gave them a smile.

The couple were taken by surprise and looked at each other, neither saying anything. The water buffalo mooed low as if mournfully; it was standing nearby, tethered through its nose to a stake. Meibei, who for days had been harbouring thoughts that the boy's family had treated him cruelly and that he might come to live with her as a substitute for the loss of her sons to the true revolution, moved a step forward, half brandishing the fork. 'You seen the boy? Do he know you?'

Wenlie felt the aggression. 'Yes of course I've seen him, so has his uncle, I've just come from him. But he doesn't recognize me yet, although Doctor...'

'Abandoned him, didn't you, threw him out!'

'No, no! Please, let me explain.' Wenlie tried to find her words. In a shaking voice she told them about her father-in-law, about the Hut and the

117

gun explosion that burnt her son's head and hand, that he had walked alone through the hills, and that was why they had found him so injured. She felt she had their attention.

But when she told them about her friend from Dongang who had heard about an article in a Tuxieng newspaper, Meibei huffed. 'The boy shouldn't have been there in the first place, lady, only hunters go up, it was dumb of you!'

Still feeling raw, Wenlie could no longer hold back her emotions, and had to turn away.

'Wife, woman's come to see us,' the farmer said quietly; he'd seen the tall woman was distressed. 'She's lad's mother, must be hospitable.'

But Meibei was already softening; she liked the manner of this woman, could see she was genuine, had tears, didn't have airs and graces but spoke to them like equals.

'Come inside then, you can see where he lay when we brought him in. Is he Yamin or what?'

Minutes later, after they told her about Lam and what he did, they went outside the mud cottage and the farmer pointed out the birch trees.

Wenlie turned to Meibei. 'My son told me that when he was on your k'ang, he thought he was leaving to the next world. But he came back to you when he heard you calling him, you were stroking his face, he said your touch was very comforting.' She felt her emotions swelling again, but tried to keep them in check. 'I have to say something to you. I cannot adequately tell you how much I feel about what you did. I lost my husband, and I was sure I'd lost my son. I'm a teacher and I haven't got much, but I am going to give you something, I don't know what, I've got to think about it.'

Meibei looked at her husband. Then she said, pointing to the buffalo: 'Lam's stone, you'll want to see him, he's normally at the temple near Zhejiang Road if he's not in the central market.'

Before she left them, Wenlie told Meibei to get a traveller's message to her at the hotel saying when she next wanted to visit her son, and she would send a rickshaw for her.

They parted in friendly bows, Wenlie walking back along the path towards the track that led down to the sagging bridge.

Meibei went inside her cottage, her husband to one of the mud embankments between paddies.

As Wenlie reached the track, she paused and looked up to the trees and the first hills behind. Soon she was walking upwards.

The farmer only spotted her after she had passed his last terrace, crossed the stream and was reaching his red warning-post, and he got a severe shock. He began shouting and waving.

Meibei re-appeared, and when they realized their visitor couldn't hear him for the breeze, he ran as quickly as he could along the mud embankment towards the track, frequently calling out, thinking that no woman, let alone a well-dressed one, had ever been that far up, and that he'd had enough of these scares and having to run up the track.

Wenlie heard one of the shouts, looking back down and seeing the farmer. She stopped; she was only a little short of the first birches where she was in any case going to turn round having seen that the track was petering out.

She watched him cross the little water, and soon he was kicking out the red post.

When he reached her, she was surprised he went a few paces in front; he was looking with fright into the trees and clutching the post in both hands.

'Can't go up there, lady,' he gasped, 'horses, got to go back!'

The dialect was strong and he was so out of breath that she wasn't sure what he'd said. But she had caught the fear, and when he repeated the word 'horses', she understood.

She looked up through the birches; they were alive in the light wind, their small leaves shimmering autumn yellow praises to the gods.

She imagined her son being carried down by the man called Lam. And she thought about her husband, and knew that he had helped guide their son to these people.

She took a pouch from her shoulder bag, untied it, and dipped her hand in, then bent down to the ground. 'This is for you,' she said softly, opening the hand. As the white rose petals left her, the spirits in the hills and in the forests accepted her homage, their messenger the breeze taking up the offering.

Half way across the sagging bridge, Wenlie was surprised to see the rickshaw lad waiting for her, and they each laughed when it was swaying under her.

When they reached the rickshaw, she asked him to take her to the temple in Zhejiang Road. He looked puzzled, and told her there wasn't one, that she must mean the one off that road in nearby Formosa Lane.

While he pulled her through the countryside, she found herself unburdening to the young stranger, telling him what had happened to her son, and that the peasant farmer's wife was an interesting character, one she might include in plays performed at her school.

She learnt that he was one of five children, they were very poor, and none could have an education; he had never even seen another town; but he liked his job, except if the wind was too strong as then he had to be careful because rickshaws could overturn.

Only as they turned from Zhejiang Road into Formosa Lane did Wenlie realize that they could be stopping at the very temple she had been to the previous day, the Temple of the Five Concubines. She thought of the blind beggar and his white eyes, and wondered if he was there every day and if other people had given him money or something small to eat.

She discharged the sweating rickshaw lad, knowing better than to offend when he declined her offer of further payment.

*

Priest Ho Chitian has nearly finished tidying a patch of garden, when he hears a woman calling to him.

'I am looking for a man called Lam,' Wenlie says going up to him, 'I understand he lives beside this temple.'

He at once recognizes the woman as the one who cried in front of the fifth goddess. He strokes his chin but does not reply, preferring silence to talking.

'He found my son, took him to peasant farmers, and I've just come from them. They said I can find the man here or maybe in the central market.'

Now he speaks. 'First tell me how is your son.'

'He's doing well, but he doesn't recognize me yet, he's still in shock.'

Ho Chitian touches the mother on an arm and indicates her to follow. He takes her to the stone bench facing the shrine to the third goddess, where they sit. He tells her that he knows about her boy. 'The police have called twice, they were not pleasant. I told them I am as certain as the Yellow River flows to the sea that Lam did not take your son to the hills, did not do him harm.'

'He certainly did not!' Wenlie exclaims in horror.

And soon she has told him the story.

When she finishes, Ho Chitian says to her, quietly looking towards the goddess: 'I am a Taoist priest, you are a mother, we are all a part of nature and so small a part, and we must all follow her ways, we must all have a sense of oneness with our surroundings. But your son has seen into her vastness as you and I shall never experience.' He turns to the mother. 'He was found and saved by a special man, with whom I am very close. Simpletons have good souls, often better than we clever folk.' He touches her arm again, and stands.

They go through a door in the courtyard wall, and a few paces away Wenlie sees to her astonishment the strange little man she passed the day before near the juniper tree; chains remain round the ankles, and he sits on a stool outside a shack, its rusty metal roof severely warped and looking about to fall.

'Lam, do you know who this woman is?' she hears the tiny priest say. 'She is the mother of the injured boy you took to Meibei, you helped carry him to the doctor.'

Wenlie watches as the simpleton moves his head, but he does not look up at them; he is silent with one hand on a knee.

'Is it alright to touch him?' she asks quietly.

'He picked up your son.'

She places her shoulder bag on the ground, and goes on one knee. Looking first at the chains and then into the simpleton's eyes - though he is looking to one side - she puts her hands on his small hand, it is bony, and to her relief he does not withdraw.

'My son is Tsai Yuling,' she begins, feeling a distinct sensation of warmth flowing into her hands from his. 'He was lost in the hills. You found him, you brought him to safety.' She looks up at the priest, wondering if her words might be too complicated. When she turns back, the simpleton is looking straight at her. She gives him a long smile that she wants to go deep. 'You have saved my son's life, and you have given me back my own. Your righteous deed will be recognised by the gods, they will fully reward you, I can assure you.' She is pleased that her voice has remained calm. 'It may be that after this life you will never have to suffer again, never be re-born into a harsh world. But if you are, your suffering will surely be less.' She takes up his hand, bends her head to it, and touches it to her forehead. When she releases it back to his knee, she asks the old priest to help her up. Once standing, she bows to the simpleton with all the reverence she can invoke.

Lam makes no move, is looking away again. She glances at the shack.

'He's happy,' Ho Chitian says as he leads her back through the door in the wall, 'listen to the slow chatter, that's his sign.'

'I must go at once to the police,' she says.

'Will they believe you?'

'When they hear what I tell them, and who my husband was, they will. They might already have heard from the hospital, and they can check right away. I won't give them peace until those things are off his ankles.'

They take two rickshaws, Wenlie in one, Ho Chitian and Lam in another. Lam with his chains has to be helped into and out of the rickshaw.

Three quarters of an hour later he is back at his shack able to walk freely.

Wenlie asks Ho Chitian what present she might give her son's rescuer. 'It can be for Lam' - now she likes calling him by his name - 'or for the temple, but I would prefer it was for him.'

'He has all he needs,' the priest replies with a serious expression.

'We shall see,' she answers with determination.

*

That night the boy - who preferred the staff and patients to keep calling him Yamin - asked for a lamp to be left on the table in his room, rather than a candle. Despite Sanchi being just outside in the passage, he always felt the terrors of the dark - any shape, all shapes, seemed to him like the beast he had seen on the rock shelf, and he kept imagining it slinking past the sleeping girl and coming round the door of his room to take him away.

In the middle of the night he dreamt he was with a boy he knew was his brother, and with three younger girls he thought he also knew. They were in the middle of the front row of a theatre, watching a play, and no one else was in the theatre. The tall woman who kept holding his hand in the hospital was one of the actors; in fact, although at first there were other performers on the stage, every important part of the play seemed to revolve around her, and she was constantly putting on and taking off frightening masks, each one causing them to cry out.

A mesmerizing cat walked up and down at the front of the stage, preventing them from running away. Sword grass with eyes in their long leaves lashed the air about them, and he tried to wake up but couldn't. From the side of the stage a violently swaying dragon of evil blue came spitting fire to burn their heads and arms. And then there was sudden darkness and a terrifying silence, they all knew the worst scene was about to be enacted and they could run nowhere, hide nowhere. The youngest girl in pigtails began whimpering, saying she could see something coming from the back of the stage, and slowly he began to realize two eyes were looking their way, eyes that were growing larger and were interchanging colours between red and green, and the others began crying out, and very soon he started shrieking as he saw the sinuous shape of a wild cat, the body moving stealthily across the stage getting ever closer and flashing its teeth, and then the cat became a tiger that started running towards them, and in the next moment the tiger changed to panther as it leapt straight out at him knocking him with tremendous force into the air and over the edge of a gigantic waterfall, and as he fell through the spray that was not unpleasant, a snake curled itself round his injured white-hot arm and bit into it and immediately the arm was cooled and comforted, and a bear held firmly but gently to his other arm, they were falling with him while he was screaming, and they were preventing him from going head over heels, the bear-figure interchanging between animal and the tall woman calling herself his mother, finally reverting to the tall woman, and in his screams he kept hearing someone calling a name he was partly familiar with, and when he began to register the breaking through into his consciousness of the girl's 'Yamin! Yamin!' and felt her hard tugs on his right shoulder, he woke to find Sanchi saying she was trying to comfort him '...you *must* let me,' he heard her say, 'you're alright, I'm here, I'm with you!'

Sanchi let her young friend cling to her as he had done several times already after his nightmares. When his hard breathing grew less, she came away and brought the lamp nearer, her face close to his.

She asked him to tell her about the dream. As he spluttered it out, she felt some atmospheric release from the room, as if bad spirits had departed. And when he finished she asked him: 'The woman in the dream, the actress with all the masks, who held onto your arm or the bear did, do you know her now?' With the light of the lamp on his face, she thought he gave her a very strange look. 'Do you know her name,' the nurse-to-be pressed, 'have you seen her recently?'

In the morning, when Professor Su came into his office he picked up a large note sitting on his desk; it was from his friend's daughter. And as soon as he read it he cried out and let it drop, and as he ran into the corridor it fell off the desk, and passing the plump helper he called without stopping: 'Shuyuan, have you heard the news, look on my desk or on the floor, I allow you!'

The Chief Doctor burst through the open door without his usual self-introduction, finding his patient standing alone at the table looking at pieces on a chessboard.

'Yamin, now do you know who you are, who your family are?' His patient gave him a faint smile, and it was worth the recoveries of a hundred old men. 'Oh praises, oh praises! And do you recall the explosion?' He saw anguish come into the eyes, and was angry with himself that he had asked so brutally. He touched the boy's good arm and invited him to join him on the bed.

'Trust me, you are now doing really well, it's all that warm sesame oil we put on your forehead!' The doctor paused and smiled reassuringly. 'When that gun went off, what happened to you? Go on, you can tell me, be brave, I'm here to help you get over it all, and then you'll begin to feel very much better.'

Yuling shook his head. Since the nightmare and the return of his memory, he did not want to be taken back to his ordeal, especially not to the start of it all, to the lake. But the doctor was urging him.

He touched the bed cover; it felt comforting, he was safe with the doctor beside him; and he was longing to see his mother. He managed to get out: 'I was on fire, I got to the water and fell in, the pain was...' but he couldn't go on.

'It must have been terrible. I hardly dare ask you, but did you see what happened to your grandfather? He wouldn't have suffered, he would have been taken from this life at once and without pain, he wouldn't have known anything about the explosion, am I right?'

Yuling looked into Doctor Ya Ya's kind eyes and found himself nodding, blurting out: 'He was lying on the ground and his shirt was burning...' He looked down to the floor, he wanted to share with the doctor the hollowed blackened face, and as the doctor was praising him for speaking, his tears began.

But just then Doctor Li came running in, and Yuling looked up; the young doctor was smiling at him and came over to the bed, and the tears stopped almost as soon as they came.

'You know what saved your life, Yamin,' Doctor Ya Ya continued, for a moment forgetting this was not the boy's real name, 'the lake, it put out the fire on you, otherwise your clothes would have caught, and it dealt immediately with your burning hand and your head. Look at me.'

Yuling turned through his sniffles.

'Don't think much about the explosion or the animals, think of all the good times you had with your grandfather. You were in the hills for two or three weeks I hear. That picture you did, what do you call it, the cabin, it's brilliant. Think of the cabin like that, in evening sunshine. And over the next few days, before you go to Sanchi's home, we're going to sit in my gardens, you, me and your mother, and you're going to tell us about those good experiences with your grandfather, I want to hear all about them, I know quite a lot about birds too, you know.' The Chief Doctor looked up to his colleague. 'We go through good times and bad times with our patients Li, don't we.' He smiled back at his unique patient. 'But this is one of the best Yuling, ha! got your name right at last!'

Strict instructions were given to the reception that when the boy's mother came, she was not to go immediately to see her son but was to wait while the Chief Doctor was found.

Meibei had decided to visit Yamin that morning and had left very early, no time to get a message to the hotel for a rickshaw; she would walk and get lifts as before. She had taken to the mother, a widow. 'Her man weren't really a White,' she said to her husband as they went back into their cottage after watching the mother go down to the sagging bamboo bridge.

When she reached the hospital and heard that the mother was expected but had not arrived, she decided to wait, and to go up to see the boy if the mother didn't soon come.

Wenlie was pleased to find the farmer's wife waiting for her, showing her pleasure by bowing twice. She introduced Janping, telling Meibei that it was Janping who had found Yuling in the hospital.

The sour receptionist had a more benevolent look as she called out: 'Doctor Ya Ya wants to speak with you right away, madam, we'll fetch him. I'm to tell you that all is well.'

Wenlie was reassured by the comment, but did not realize it might have special meaning; the image of her son's indifference to her though not to the fiery Sanchi remained strong in her mind.

While they waited, Meibei described to Janping her little tenant holding, mentioning a useless area of grassy scrub-land on the other side of the cottage, unfit for growing rice or vegetables or fruit trees, bedrock being near the surface. She had just finished when the Chief Doctor appeared.

'I have a surprise for you!' he called out to Wenlie as he came to greet them. 'Come with me but don't ask!' He led them to the top floor, Meibei having difficulty with the stairs, and Wenlie helped her. When he reached Yuling's room he looked in to find his patient and Sanchi standing at a table working on a drawing. He said nothing and allowed the three women to walk past him.

Wenlie needed only one look into her Alinga's eyes, and at the expression on his face - they told her all she wanted to know.

*

Panther Boy recovers memory headlined the second page of the Tuxieng News, giving way only to the main story of the extraordinary happenings in neighbouring Jiangsi province, where a huge convoy of Communist soldiers and civilians had smuggled through the Nationalist encirclement and were fleeing.

> *The Reds are running westwards though they will surely be stopped. They have finally left our neighbour province where for a few years as readers know they have been usurping the rights of landlords, businesses and other property-owning Chinese under a false soviet ideology of agrarian reform, an experiment that should never have been allowed to happen there or here in parts of Fujian.*

The story about Tsai Yuling was lengthy. Of his rescue it commented:

> *He was found in a very weak and injured state among the wild horses in the hills, the dangerous area where nine years ago a hunter was kicked to death by the beasts and another man was seriously injured. He had burns from the gun explosion, forest cuts all over him, and injury from the cat attack. Fang Lamgang, who lives in a shack beside the Temple of the Five Concubines and is unable to speak but is known to the market people, stumbled on the boy. Surprisingly Fang visits the animals from time to time without a gun - he would not be able to use one - and they do him no harm, though readers are strongly warned not to attempt the same. When interviewed this week, the boy told our reporter that he was lying on the ground and knew horses were near him but had no strength to move.*

The article continued. When it came to its end it said:

The mother states that Fang saved the life of her son and has vowed to restore his shack to a good condition. She is the widow of Captain Tsai Peijinn who fell in battle three years ago in Manchuria's Valley of Heroes of the Twentieth Year. Scandalously the puppet government of the Japanese in so-called Manchukuo refuse to permit families to visit where their husbands, fathers and soldier-sons died.

The story caused a sensation in Tuxieng and other Fujian towns, and before Wenlie and Yuling returned home, more reporters came to interview them at Doctor Chen's house, one from the provincial capital Fuzhou. On each occasion Wenlie asked the good doctor to be present; she was going to shield her son from all-comers, and she only allowed them interviews on condition that if he preferred not to answer a question, they had to respect that or the interview would end.

Wenlie found the doctor jovial and courteous, but very untidy in his cluttered surgery and medicine preparation rooms. She took into her storage of characters his occasional left eye twitch, and noticed that nothing much ruffled him except when Sanchi started on her politics '...she can be so hot-headed just like her mother, if she becomes active at the nursing school in Amoy it could be dangerous for her...'

A few days into their stay, she had to act concerning her finances. As she left the courtyard and went into the street, the doctor was stepping from his personal rickshaw and hailed her.

'Doctor Chen, do you know a respectable pawnbroker?' she got in first.

'Don't go near one is my advice to you.'

'But I have to,' she said embarrassed, looking from him to his servant pulling away the rickshaw, before turning back to the doctor and his warm expression. 'I must pay you for your help to Alinga, and for your hospitality, and I need to offer the hospital some reasonable payment, and I must do something for Meibei and her husband, and for Lam who badly needs...'

'The peasant farmers alright,' she heard, seeing the eye twitch, 'but me no. And Professor Su won't take much either, you have suffered already and you are a widow.'

Wenlie could not believe the kindness, and began to feel emotional.

'No woman may cry in front of me, it sets me off!' he quipped.

She checked herself. She felt in her shoulder bag, and pulled out the jade and emerald brooch wrapped in its old velvet cover. She opened the velvet.

'You mustn't take this to a pawnbroker! It's beautiful, you won't see it again, they'll charge you twenty, thirty per cent.'

Wenlie bit her lower lip.

'Please, it's none of my business, but would you tell me how much you need?'

As they went through the small courtyard, Wenlie said a prayer of thanks. In exchange for her acceptance of the loan, she extracted the doctor's agreement to let her tidy his surgery and preparation rooms, including to throw out all old papers, equipment and herbs he no longer used. When he heard this condition, he beamed.

During their final week staying at the Chens, Wenlie took Yuling back to the peasant farmers under the hills; they were pulled by the same rickshaw lad who she had befriended. At first Yuling said he would not go, had not wanted to be reminded of his rescue; but he felt something special with Meibei, and knew he must say goodbye to her, that he might never see her again.

'Can't be same boy, can't be!' the farmer kept saying with a look mixing amazement and joy as he walked round Yuling, 'you were so bad when I carried you, and look at you now!'

Yuling was interested to see that the rice had been harvested. He had already glanced up at the stream and the trees and seen the path Lam carried him down; but he blocked out memories before that.

Near the end of their morning, Wenlie asked the farmer to show her the scrub side of his mud cottage. 'Your wife told us in the hospital that you want geese but don't have the money,' she said. 'If you'll let me help, I will set you up with twenty geese, breeding birds as well as gosling. The geese could sell in the town, and you might do even better with the feathers, they bring us women good fortune if we wear them in our hair.'

They discussed figures, and she told him to collect the money from the doctor. 'This is my heartfelt thanks to you both, and to your wife for visiting my son in the hospital.'

'Don't mind admitting,' he said looking towards the scrub, 'not long ago we were at our end, rice bags ran out see, debts to landlord, even old buffalo belongs to him now. And we've lost our sons, wife's sure youngest is dead. But it's not the Chinese way, is it. We suffer our fate and keep smiling.' He looked at the tall handsome woman, the mother of the boy he helped rescue, and a twinkle came into his eye. 'Getting visitors. Two elders came last week, said they honoured us.' He grinned. 'Folk want to see where your lad were found, wife's starting to get money from them, if they can pay! Won't let them beyond red post though.'

10

During the latter part of the Spring Festival of 1935, a high-born girl of twelve, Huang Huihua, sat beside her mother on a sofa in the lady's apartments at Wuyi Court near Mingon, a semi-fortified mansion locals called the Court. She was reading aloud to three people - her mother, her seven-year-old brother Shanghan, and their Chinese governess from Hong Kong, the territory all mainland Chinese believed was forced into a lease by British imperialism. The story told of a boy who had walked alone and injured through part of the uplands. A long report had appeared in a Cantonese monthly magazine that the household received, the Editor-in-Chief stating that he had personally interviewed the mother and son, finding the boy *remarkably open and articulate for a twelve year old who has recently endured such a shocking experience.*

In the middle of Huihua's reading, her brother, sitting nearby at a table with the governess, piped up: 'I want to meet the boy who fought the panther.'

'Do you indeed!' Madame Huang chuckled, smiling at her daughter.

Huihua was not spoilt, but she had grown up in a world of servants and deference, mainly at the Court in the west of Fujian province, but also in coastal Fuzhou when her father had military or political affairs to attend to.

Her mother had had difficulties producing children; a stillborn boy came three years before Huihua arrived into the world, and then her mother had an agonizing five-year gap until brother Shanghan was born.

Her grandfather had been a warlord, fiercely proud of Fujian's independence from Chinese central government control, and jealous of his own territorial and feudal independence. He had a predilection for very young concubines, always having six living at the Court, ever changing them once they reached twenty. He had died when Huihua was very young, and her father had inherited much of the wealth and power, had attended Whampoa, the military academy for officers near Canton further south, and had seen the way the wind was blowing, deciding to back Chiang Kai-shek's bid to bring the province under Nationalist control, a bid that substantially succeeded. For his efforts, her father had been promoted to full colonel, and the feudal benefits were left untouched including the power to levy taxes and to have his own military corps of up to four thousand soldiers and officers loyal first to him.

That afternoon Colonel Huang called his private secretary to his office, a room called the Study. The secretary was elderly, and had held that position for many years with his father the old warlord.

'Lee, did you see this article? I haven't bothered to read it.' He stretched his arm across a mounted sword that lay on his large desk, giving the open magazine to the retainer.

'Yes, my lord, Mistress Huihua showed it to me yesterday evening, an astonishing story I must…'

'Contact our main agent in Luchian, find out anything interesting about the family. I know the father died in the Valley, you know the military blunder I mean. Find out if the Communist influence has got to any of them, they could be bitter you understand me. I need to know if there are any pro-Reds in the family. No need to tell him why we want this. And while you're at it, get the man to file a report on the town and its district, are any Reds left there, I want to know that too.'

A few days later the report arrived. It was from a Kuomintang policeman in Luchian. After stating that the Tsai family was *clean*, it went on:

> *The mother is a teacher thought to be non-political, is admired for her stage acting and singing, an attractive widow of two boys aged about twelve and nine. None of the family men are thought to be Red or Red-inclined. The father died three years ago against the invaders - an engineer. The grandfather helped build Sun Yat-sen Bridge and died recently in a gun accident in the uplands, and the story of the older boy who was with him has become well known. As to Reds in the Luchian area, most fled Fujian over the past year, but there are a number of peasant farmers and a handful of young men, and, we should state, young women in the town who might be supporters though we do not believe they are active partisans. Anti-government posters still crop up but are far less than in previous years. We will keep tabs on all suspects.*

'I want the names and addresses of those Reds, Lee,' Colonel Huang barked, 'and ask about known or likely ringleaders and the contents of the posters.' He'd been surprised posters were still getting up, though he could guess what they said: railing against taxes and so-called corruption.

As his secretary was leaving the Study, the colonel looked again at the police report. The agent's comment concerning the widow's appearance did not escape the attention of the son of the old warlord.

*

In Luchian, Fainan was sweeping the dusty ground outside the front of her house when a messenger came up and asked if Tsai Wenlie was at home. A policeman accompanied him, a man everyone in the town knew and many distrusted. She nodded and asked the messenger what he wanted with Wenlie.

He took an envelope from a leather satchel. 'Hand this to the woman. I've orders to wait for her confirmation.'

Wenlie was inside the house and deep in thought, reading a possible play for performance at her school, and was very surprised to be given a wax-sealed envelope and to be told there was a man waiting outside for her confirmatory answer. She could only think it must be something official relating to her late husband, from the military perhaps.

> *As Private Secretary to Colonel Huang Mingchang of Wuyi Court…*

Her heart missed a beat - the Slayer of the Reds, what could that frighteningly powerful man or his secretary possibly want with her?

> *…I am instructed to require your attendance and that of your son Tsai Yuling and other son four days hence at the Court at the specific request of Madame Huang and of my lord and my lady's two children who wish to meet your sons. Assuming you are not indisposed, you should take riverboats three days hence from Luchian to Hanyeng, stay in a respectable establishment there, and be at the West Tower at noon the following day where a carriage will arrive to bring you to Mingon. The audience will take place shortly after you arrive. You will be fed and accommodated overnight at the Court. You will leave by the carriage at eight the following morning. Your expenses will be reimbursed in full. Bring provisions for the journey. You will be provided for the return.*

The invitation ended by asking her to notify the messenger

> *…of your expected acceptance, for the sake of the noble children of my lord Colonel Huang and Madame Huang.*

Wenlie had absolutely no wish to accept. She didn't know if *noble* referred to the children's status or character, believing status. Nor did she know their ages. As she ran to the back of the house, to the wooden outhouse where her boys and Fainan's eldest daughter had been given the job of dusting and wiping down their grandfather's bird collection, she was desperately thinking how to refuse.

Yuling was looking closely at a mounted white dove when his mother came rushing in and surprised them; he had just been telling the others that he would have to apply gum paste to part of the feathers that had dropped. It was nearly four months since his rescue. The sling had long gone, and the shoulder and upper arm had healed though each bore indentations. He was able to use the left hand, new skin having covered the burnt parts; it was lined and blemished and he knew it looked very ugly despite adults telling him otherwise, but he was glad he had reasonable flexion of the thumb and three fingers. The head burn had also healed, hair having grown back except in a small patch, hardly noticeable he was assured.

After showing him the message, Wenlie said: 'I don't like this Colonel Huang, he's a cruel man Alinga, you won't want to meet his family, we must politely decline.'

Three days later, on a fresh spring morning a reluctant anxious mother, an excited twelve-year-old and a frightened younger brother began the river journeys to Hanyeng.

The following midday they were met at the tower by a small covered carriage pulled by two horses, two men in livery on top; curtains were drawn back either side. The carriage caused a stir in the town, people running alongside admiring the paintwork and the sparkling struts of the wheels.

The journey to Wuyi Court took just under three hours, the road easy on the horses, and they kept to a steady pace except on the inclines. There were occasional rests for the animals to drink, and during the first rest, Wenlie, Yuling and Ayi learnt something about the colonel's children and the interesting mansion, and Ayi's fear lessened to some extent. Nearing the end of their journey, they passed Mingon's Great Gate without going through it - an ancient three tier bastion - and proceeded along a road leading away from the town, a road with woods on the left and paddies, orchards, palm and bamboo groves on the right.

A quarter of an hour later they came to dark red walls that were long and high, and half way along the front they turned between two stone-carved chimera statues, huge lions, their heads roaring, their bodies of folded wings and serpents' tails. Flags flew above the tall wood and metal gates that they went through, and immediately soldier guards greeted the riders and the carriage stopped.

They were in a large courtyard full of bustle and noise; soldiers mingled with citizens, tradesmen carried provisions on bamboo shoulder poles, vendors stood at stalls selling wares and foods, flower pedlars mixed with palmists, and children seemed to be running everywhere. In one corner a puppet troupe caught Wenlie's eye, and she pointed it out to the boys just before they stepped from the carriage; a crowd was watching the string puppets moving across the stage. Around the sides of the courtyard, trees rose high not far from the walls, predominantly banyan but also palms of different variety.

A soldier guard met them and led them through the activities along a central flagstone path to the far end of the courtyard, where they proceeded up steps past two more guards and into another courtyard raised and smaller, also high-walled but seemingly empty of people.

To their immediate right in one corner of the courtyard stood a building against the side wall. 'Officers Building, used to be Concubines Ménage when I came as a lad,' the guard chuckled pointing, though he did not look at Wenlie. 'Girls walked in file round here.'

Lines of mature cypress and well-kept palms led the eye to the mansion. It had a distinctly red look about it, mainly from the sweeping roofs and the six wood-carved round columns along the front from the ground to the first floor, but also from a number of large lanterns hanging from first floor level. It stood three storeys, stone behind the columns to the first floor, then wood to the roofs, the magnificent tiled roofs curving down from the middle and up again at the ends. Central stone steps wide and straight led to the first floor main doors of the mansion, their greyish white marble balusters carved in pine cones.

As the visitors started up the steps, they saw an elderly gentleman in long black gown waiting for them, and Ayi immediately became scared again.

The man bowed deeply and addressed himself to Wenlie. 'I am Secretary Lee, I have the honour to be Colonel Huang's private secretary.' His officious manner alarmed her, and she glanced at Ayi who had a very worried look. 'My lord's family are pleased that you accepted, though that was expected, naturally.' The secretary turned briefly to Yuling and back, seeming to ignore Ayi. 'They look forward to meeting the young man. Follow me.'

He led them through dark-stained wooden doors opened by a male servant, and along a corridor whose walls were covered in traditional Fujian woodcarvings. Tall blue and white vases stood at intervals on the floor.

'The Reception Hall,' he said as they entered an enormous room. 'It is sometimes called the Music Chamber for obvious reasons. Kindly be seated. You will be seen shortly in the Study.' Wenlie thought he gave emphasis to the last word. 'And when you meet Madame Huang you will address her as "my lady."' He indicated chairs - they were very fine - gave a short nod, and went out.

As she and Ayi sat down, Wenlie felt more apprehensive than ever. The Study didn't sound like a place to meet children. And was there a suggestion that the Study and meeting 'my lady' would be separate? Now she definitely regretted accepting the invitation, holding one hand nervously tight over the other. But the invitation came from Madame Huang and her children, so she continued telling herself that there was a very good chance that she would not be meeting the infamous father, that he would have little or no interest in their visit.

Yuling remained standing and began looking around. The room had a wooden floor immaculately polished, and along its sides stood several clay sculptures of warriors, more ceramic vases, and many richly carved chairs. The ceiling was decorated in diagrams, and opposite them were three big windows, through which he could see some of the nearer trees they had passed under in the inner courtyard. The long wall behind them, and the far wall to their left, were each partly covered by large murals, and there was a gallery above the nearer mural. Other parts of the walls held military and civilian portraits. An ebony table stood in front of the mural at the far wall, red sandalwood chairs at each end.

He became at once fascinated with the murals. 'Come with me,' he said pulling his mother up, then leading her by the arm to the long table. Ayi did not want to be left alone in case the old man in black returned, so quickly followed. 'I've seen pictures like this in books,' Yuling said, 'but I can't believe how big they are, they must have taken the artist years.' He paused to look at the mural behind the table. 'I feel like I'm high up looking from another hill.'

'More than one artist must have done them,' Wenlie said, not feeling at all comfortable; inside she was having another conversation, that they shouldn't be there.

Yuling's eyes roamed over the work of art, over its layers of hills, the most distant he noticed being almost the same in colour as the skies they rose to. Except with Doctor Ya Ya in the hospital garden or when answering the reporters' questions, he had avoided thinking about his time with his grandfather at the Hut. But this magnificent mural: it was taking him back to the moment when he stood near the little shrine looking out over the escarpment; his grandfather had said it would be impossible to paint a picture of the scene before them; yet here he was, standing in front of a panorama not very different although the mural had a river; he couldn't believe it.

'I really like the blues and greys,' he said, releasing Wenlie's arm and walking round the table, the three unaware of movement behind a half-drawn curtain in the comparative darkness of the musicians' gallery now behind them.

'And I like the birds,' she replied, watching him go to the mural and starting to touch the painted rock face.

He walked back to his mother and brother. 'I know how the artist made it seem you're in the picture. That tree,' he pointed, 'it's coming from the side of the painting as if it's really near, and you think it's near because it's painted much bigger and thicker than the other trees.' He looked at Ayi, could tell he wasn't interested, was remaining scared.

'That's good of you to observe,' Wenlie said, 'it's a well-known trick called creating perspective.'

'I know,' he replied.

Just as she was thinking they should return to their seats, the stern-faced secretary returned. 'We will go through this other door,' he said walking towards them and pointing.

He led them out, and after a short corridor, they turned at a curving wooden staircase, finely carved, and decorated with small flags top and bottom. 'The Study,' the secretary said as he led the way up.

They were ushered through heavily embossed double-doors into another room, much smaller than the Reception Hall yet still sizeable. At the far end an officer in military uniform, a leather strap diagonal across his broad chest, stood behind a large desk, alone and clearly expecting them, and Wenlie saw to her horror that they were about to come face to face with the Slayer of the Reds who she had so keenly hoped not to meet.

While the secretary was announcing their names, the officer started moving round his desk. As they were led towards him, Wenlie saw a facially strong-featured man, physically big though not tall, the dark eyebrows particularly noticeable above what appeared to be a smirk. Immediately she felt the power.

Yuling and Ayi made their bows before she did, Yuling surprised how slow his mother was to return to the upright. Only when she did so did the colonel make a peremptory bow towards them.

Ten-year-old Ayi began to feel spirited youthful antagonism; he knew about the colonel, Uncle Jinjin had told him.

'Madam, we are grateful you have made the journey to visit us.' Colonel Huang glanced at Yuling. 'And is this the young man my children are talking about.'

Wenlie inclined her head. There was a silence. Yuling caught his brother's frown at this famous man, and could not understand why his mother did not speak, though he wasn't going to say anything himself unless asked a question.

They were shown to enormous cushioned chairs, white painted and with animal carvings at the ends of the arms; the carvings were of tigers and gave Yuling a nasty fright.

He watched the colonel dismissing the elderly man and clicking his fingers loudly at a male attendant who he had not seen when entering. The men went out. Trying to forget the tiger ends, he made himself comfortable while the colonel returned to the other side of the desk, and saw a magnificent sword mounted on the desk, nearer to his mother, brother and himself than the colonel. It was straight, dark and long, its blade blemished, its handle snaking black and gold filigree almost as long as the blade; there was no scabbard.

'I have you for half an hour,' the colonel said looking firmly at Wenlie, 'then you will be escorted to my wife's apartments. My family are going to enjoy meeting your sons, I'm sure you'll have a pleasant time with them.'

Wenlie was further shocked: half an hour seemed very long, and she gave her weakest smile, looking to one side and still not speaking.

'I know about your husband, a gallant man.' She swallowed. 'It was a tragedy that should never have happened, they were sent straight into an ambush. I am glad I was *not* involved in that fateful mistake. He has my undying respect.'

'Thank you,' she managed to whisper, finding the word 'undying' strange in the context, her eyes now on the man's thick hands that lay flat on the desk and that seemed to be pointing directly at her.

Ayi was now feeling in the presence of some powerful enemy, knowing the colonel had killed many people. But Yuling felt nothing against the colonel and no fear; he was just astonished at the world they had entered since first seeing the carriage coming towards them in Hanyeng. He had not met such a high person before. But his mother …he had never seen his lively, often firm-minded mother like this, she usually stood up to people. He realized with surprise that she was frightened, and it startled him. But he didn't have time to think more about it because the eyes had turned his way.

'How are you feeling, Tsai Yuling, recovered from your bad time, I trust?'

'Yes sir.'

'Good. You're getting more famous than me!' The colonel laughed loud towards his mother. 'And how many days were you in those hills with your uncle before the accident…'

'Grandfather' Ayi bravely interrupted under his breath and without looking up but searching the side of the desk.

Wenlie was surprised at his boldness, and nodded her appreciation. 'It was nearly three weeks sir,' she replied for Yuling, looking a little up from the powerful hands to the lower buttons of the tunic below the strap.

'I see. And how many nights did you spend on your own afterwards? The gun exploded I believe.'

Wenlie did not want Yuling to reply about the nights; she had been hoping a more gentle question might come that would be unrelated to what he went through. The colonel was looking at her again.

Yuling had been taken by surprise at the mention of an uncle and now by the bluntness of the question; the reporters had not been so direct, they had been kind and he'd had Doctor Chen by his side. But he was prepared to answer. 'Three or four nights, I'm not sure.'

There followed further questions, Wenlie sometimes thinking she would have to pluck up courage and speak again, but amazed how well Yuling was replying to questions far more penetrating than the reporters had asked. She was trying to smile at him in support, though he always looked at the colonel.

And soon to her surprise, he was even answering about first seeing the animal in the mist from the rock shelf, and she was learning things he had not divulged before: that he had held his father's knife when trying to defend himself against the panther, and that he had nearly been attacked by wild cats and shot at them.

Then the colonel asked: 'What was the worst moment of all?'

She was aghast, and saw Yuling's right hand tighten over the tiger-end of his chair; he was looking towards the sword, fear in his face. 'Forgive me sir,' she said, forced to look at the colonel, 'that's too hard a question, and...'

'The boy must face up to what happened,' he said sharply back at her, still with the hint of an underlying smile.

She had wanted to add that the question was unnecessary, and to say that Yuling continued to have nightmares; but she found she couldn't go on, she felt paralysed by some dominating force in the colonel's eyes, they had opened at her under their menacing brows, and she had already been impolite.

The gaze reverted to Yuling who was still looking at the object on the desk. 'You came through your experience well, so I want to hear, answer me!'

Wenlie looked in fright at Yuling, and hoped he would simply say it was the animal attack, so that they could move on; and if he didn't, she could make a suggestion to him so he could reply: perhaps he could say running from the tigers that he'd seen, as he'd told her what happened and the spots that blurred his vision for a while when he thought they were coming for him. But power surrounded them, it continued to bind her from speaking, and she hated not having the courage to protest a second time.

Yuling didn't want to answer, but he could feel all eyes looking towards him including Ayi's, and he knew he had to. He stared at the sword's dark blade, and some of the horrors rushed through his mind at random: the terror suddenly being confronted by the wild cat looking down at him from the rock when he couldn't get at the revolver quickly enough; his horrible fear first leaving the Hut and trying to keep the gun from shaking; the unbearable unbearable pain as he staggered away from the lake; the shivering time in the blackness on the cavern floor after he'd climbed out of the water, he'd been so cold in his body and so utterly lost in his mind that he'd expected to expire, to die, yes that was the worst …but as the sinuous shape was forcing itself onto him, he heard the colonel again ordering him to speak, and was about to say the breath-holding moments when he heard the hissing and the panther jumped onto the rock shelf and he knew he was about to be killed… 'Grandfather's face,' he cried out, jumping off the large chair to seek refuge in his mother's arms.

'Grandfather's face?'

Wenlie caught the colonel's surprise as she buried herself in Yuling's head, her hand stroking his hair, feeling her fear and impotency give way to rising anger, and catching that Ayi was also pained for his brother, he was scowling towards the colonel and it gave her courage. She looked up and almost glared into the eyes of her son's tormentor. 'Please Colonel, do not press more,' her voice was shaking, 'he saw his grandfather's body just after the gun explosion.' She turned away to remove Yuling's tears.

The Study went quiet.

The colonel stood up. 'Stop your crying,' he barked. 'When that animal attacked you, you may have wounded it with your father's knife. You were very fortunate to escape.' He coughed quickly. 'You were looking at the sword. Guess how old it is. Go on, feel it.'

Yuling wiped his eyes and left his mother. He moved a finger along the top of the blade; it was smoother than he expected, but he had no idea what to say, his only thought being that it was too big for anyone but a giant to hold, or maybe a man as strong as the colonel. 'Fifty years.'

Ayi thought it must be older and that the colonel would often use it to kill people.

'Ha! Well over three hundred years, from near the end of the Ming Dynasty. Pick up the handle but don't drop it, use both hands.'

Wenlie and Ayi watched as Yuling took hold of the long handle and tried to move it up from its mount. Wenlie allowed herself a smile, unintentionally glancing at the colonel and meeting eyes of triumph, an expression she greatly distrusted.

'Ah, Lee!' the colonel was calling as the black-gowned secretary returned and bowed from the embossed doors. 'Are the family waiting to meet our young friends?'

'They are, my lord.'

Wenlie felt a great release of fear, and she was about to stand when the colonel waved his hand in a firm downward gesture for her to remain in her chair. 'Stay seated woman!' he commanded.

She was shocked, another sinking feeling overcoming her, her courage leaving again as the man was moving round the desk towards them. She looked at Yuling.

'Tsai Yuling and brother, go with my secretary,' the colonel ordered, 'he'll take you to meet the children, I wish to speak with your mother first.' He turned to Wenlie. 'You will follow shortly. I'm sure your sons will like my children, my boy Shanghan has an interesting collection of toy soldiers.'

She watched him nod curtly for Yuling and Ayi to leave. The Slayer was now almost standing over her. 'I have something private to say to you,' he added with what looked like a smile of military and male domination.

She was gripped with fear again. 'Go along,' she found herself saying to the boys, 'I'll come very soon.'

Yuling and Ayi bowed to the colonel. Yuling smiled at his mother and then strode towards the secretary, Ayi walking behind him feeling worried for his mother. Yuling was relieved his grilling by the colonel was over, and he was now looking forward to the next episode in their Mingon adventure.

Wenlie followed her sons with her eyes.

When Colonel Huang Mingchang had first looked down from the gallery curtain, he thought that the mother looked distinctly promising, that the Luchian agent might be pleasingly right in his report.

Half an hour earlier, a Red partisan who had not fled west with the Communists the previous October had been brought in, and the man's defiance had made the colonel live up to his reputation: he'd shot him himself. And not many minutes later, he'd learnt of the Tsai woman's arrival; one of the guards at the main gates told him through the intercom system. He'd leaned back from the curtain so not to be seen, and had keenly listened to the quiet voice, it seemed charming and musical, could perhaps whisper things into his ear …on a sofa …he loved those moments, because with such whispers came promising sins. He'd told Lee to bring the visitors to him after fifteen minutes, but he hadn't waited that long, he'd returned to the Study and ordered them brought to him at once.

Only when he'd moved round his large desk to welcome them had he realized just how handsome the woman was, and what a divine figure she displayed, longish and full in the right places, taller than he was, taller than any of his conquests. And the wide eyes, the cheekbones that could carry sweet-smelling powder, the lips …early thirties, perfect, she fitted his greatest fantasy: a strikingly good-looking woman, she would be experienced, she was a widow, and she lived far enough away from the suspicious eyes of his wife.

Up to his late teens he'd lusted after some of his father's young concubines who lived in the Concubines Ménage, the corner-building in the inner courtyard that was now the Officers Building, he'd flirted with them though never dared touch lest they squealed to his father; he knew how frightened they were of his father, as he had been, and that they were loyal only to their master, their owner until they were twenty and sent away with a little money to help them marry. Then at nineteen came a great change in his worldly experience and appetite, a change brought about by a seductive woman in her early thirties who had at first enthralled him by her huge breasts and soon captured him for two years and taught him much about love-making. From then on, including after his pre-arranged marriage, an older full-bodied woman became for him much more exciting a challenge than a frightened compliant slim girl; she knew better how to play difficult to catch, could be more artful; but once she succumbed, his power over her was absolute as it was over the husbands, it was intoxicating; and the skin of an older woman could be just as soft, or well soft enough; she would know how to tease, play games, go slow, please a man like him...

From the moment he'd returned to his father's high chair after greeting the mother and her two sons, he'd felt the exciting stir; and within a few seconds of sitting down, an unstoppable thrill had overcome him as he looked at the woman.

The chase was on. Yes, the Luchian agent could be *very* useful. While the twelve-year-old had been answering his questions, the colonel's eyes had been mostly on the adorable mother sitting on the other side of his fine desk. He'd thought about visits he could make to the Luchian area, imagining her being prepared with fragrances by a paid local 'helper', before being brought to his quarters.

He'd given her his best smile mixed with authority, a combination that invariably reaped its reward. But during the interview, he'd noticed she wasn't looking at him nearly enough, not in the way to give him recurring thrills, and he'd told himself she'd soon learn who had the might and who must submit. He'd expected her to be deferential, so had been surprised that between the meekness and silences she'd been gutsy and at one point even hostile, it seemed. Clearly she was afraid of him. Good. He was going to press the advantages that went with the position and power; they were his birthright, as they had been his warlord father's.

And now that he was alone with the widow and standing so near her that she could not get up, he breathed her in and imagined what he could not see, particularly her legs that must be long because she was tall, they could wrap themselves round him, hold him...

The door has just closed, there is a disturbing quiet. Wenlie is vulnerable and doesn't know what to do or what will happen next, only that she is being controlled as everybody else must be who comes into contact with this odious man. She wants to rise from the chair and ask permission to follow Yuling and Ayi, can say she's suddenly feeling unwell after the journey and needs to rest in Madame Huang's apartments. But the colonel is far too close, he is looking down at her and his legs are apart like some of the ancient warriors in the Reception Hall.

The silence continues. Fear grows by the second, so she concentrates on an ancient helmet in a niche in the wall.

She is about to make her excuse to leave, when he speaks. 'You have an extraordinary older son, madam.' Now it is madam again, no doubt with a purpose. She inclines her head but dares not look up at the man, or at his breeches. 'I would like to help him.' She is startled, searches for an answer. 'You shall allow me to become guardian to your boys, I intend putting money their way, helping their later studies, my privilege.'

She is dumbfounded, finds it incredible what he has said, and said as a fait accompli not a request. Wretchedly her mind goes blank, she can't think what to say, knows she remains under the power of the man's presence.

But if somehow she can stand, risk the command to remain seated, as she wouldn't be seeking permission - she is a woman and in his mansion - she will at least have made a move, might feel braver on her feet and could give herself a little time to think.

Starting to feel physically sick, she pushes backwards, and miraculously the large white chair moves on the polished floor. Quickly she stands and takes a step to her right and then another one back, feeling horribly awkward and sensing the colonel's surprise.

But no command has yet been given. She glances towards him and sees the look has changed to a leer, reading he's perhaps excited by her brave move, and it brings clearance as she realizes the frightening situation she is in: being offered by the most feared man in southern China the possibility of money for her children's future. Why? She knows the answer; he'd given her that look in the talk with Yuling; the evil in the lecher's proposal is obvious. And from this man of all people.

She turns her head to one side and blurts out: 'Your offer is most unexpected, sir. Of course it is generous, but it is so sudden, I must have time to consider.' No! Why has she said that!

'Take all the time you need.'

Seducer! He is moving close again and she's horrified because she's beginning to pant, she can't hide her breathlessness and it's making her lips stay open and she can tell he's looking at them. Still trapped. She sees him pushing her onto a bed, unbuttoning her robe, her desperate cries to her husband but calls in the wind. She must act quickly or he'll overwhelm her and she might say something that will have dreadful consequences.

She takes another step back and looks fully into the eyes: they are expectant, and they revolt her.

'My sons have their uncles as guardians, Colonel Huang...' she has to take another breath, '...my late husband told me that this should be so if anything happened to him....' she narrows her eyes, the panting is less and she sees she has surprised him again and looks from one powerful shoulder to the other, '...but I am grateful for your offer, sir, now may I be taken to meet your wife and children.'

'Not so fast ...please!'

The last word, spoken sickly, sounds to Wenlie like an afterthought with clamps attached. He is leering again, the eyes have moved to her breasts, but at least he hasn't taken a step nearer. She stares at him and forces him to look back to her face.

He says: 'If you will not let me give you ...help your sons I mean, you will allow that we meet and become friends when I visit the Luchian area with my soldiers, which I do from time to time, it would be so pleasant, and then you can tell me if there is any small way I can help your sons, whose father...'

'That would not be proper,' she gets in quickly before he goes any further, not adding colonel or sir, knowing exactly where he is leading. Her strength of mind has at last returned, her own mention of her husband seems to be helping her. She wishes she could add that she is still in her period of mourning, but that long since passed. Guessing he might be about to come close again, she indicates with her right hand the direction of the doors that the boys and the secretary used, bows, half turns and adds severely: 'I must go to your wife, she is expecting me.'

She is now looking towards the embossed doors, and when the colonel makes no move on her - she'd thought he might order her to stay, or might even try to grab and hold her to his body with threats if she struggled - she steels herself, turns further and starts walking, willing the secretary or attendant or anybody to enter, at every step expecting the command to stop, not knowing what she would then do, aware of her highly disrespectful conduct, fearful what might happen next or what she would do once she reaches the doors and goes through.

But Colonel Huang's fire is fast dampening. With the woman daring to stand and then to excuse herself without his say-so, and now walking to the doors, the unexpected challenge of impropriety and the awareness that she is about to be talking with his wife brings him back to reality. This tall widow with the delicious figure might be awkward, she has just rejected his advances, and his offer; he cannot allow a scene to develop.

Wenlie hears a name barked out, and almost immediately the attendant enters from the doors she is approaching. She stops in relief as she hears the colonel ordering the man to escort her to the lady's apartments. She turns and looks back without making eye contact, bowing faster than normally she would. But she sees that a finger is up indicating he wants to say something, and her fear returns as he begins walking towards her. She looks towards the attendant.

The colonel reaches her and speaks close into her left ear though she tries to lean away. 'I hope we can meet again ...very soon,' she hears, and at once she walks to the attendant.

The thin girl who met Wenlie could hardly have been fourteen; the servant spoke with a strong dialect and said her name was Yiying and that she was the personal maid to Mistress Huihua.

Soon she was ushered into one of the rooms in the lady's apartments, where she saw Yuling and Ayi standing at a trestle-table with a girl she took to be the colonel's daughter - the Mistress - but what a contrast. Looking innocent and pretty and nothing like her father, the girl was Yuling's age or younger, wore a high velvet robe of light green embroidered with yellow floral sprigs, her shining black hair swept behind her and held in a flower-clip matching the robe's colour. They were looking at some book, and behind them two other women watched from chairs, one clearly Madame Huang, also richly dressed though in a much deeper green - it was springtime - with immaculate hair tied in a bow on the top of her head, the other woman in her early twenties wearing a western-style lady's white shirt and a long grey dress.

As Madame Huang walked towards her, Wenlie saw from her short steps that she had the stunted feet of a girl foot-bound in childhood, and she knew how alluring that must have been to her betrothed, as it was not so many years back to many men in their country.

She bowed, and was greeted with an expression and a bow that was reserved but not cold. She was first introduced to the girl Huihua - while bowing, surprised to see bare feet under her floral robe - and then to the governess.

From Yuling's big smile at her she could tell that he at least was enjoying the visit, and guessed that the women hosts had been delicate in not asking uncomfortable questions.

'My son Shanghan is pony riding, he will join us later,' the lady said.

Very soon Wenlie found she could be reasonably at ease with the colonel's wife; she was not made to feel inferior, and they could talk the Mandarin each had spoken growing up in Fuzhou, although the lady spoke more formally. It was helpful that the Hong Kong governess was with them, and Wenlie noticed that although there was clear deference from the younger woman, there was no condescension from her employer. She felt immensely relieved to be with the women, and wondered how the lady dealt with her husband's power, and whether she had found it strange that Yuling and Ayi were brought to them first, leaving the mother with her husband; she hoped no question would be asked.

While the boys, the girl and the governess talked at the table, Wenlie was led to an area of sofas through two wooden columns beautifully carved in plant motifs. She was invited to sit at one of the sofas, and the lady placed herself on another, though close.

Madame Huang asked: 'Have you and your children been able to get back to a normal life after your son's experience? I realize, of course, that you lost your father-in-law in a shocking way.'

'More or less, my lady,' she replied, 'though the letters we receive have become a burden and I've given up replying. We've had letters from almost every southern and central province. Often we can't read the writing or understand them, and many are from children. Only the other day a child wrote asking what it was like being brought up by tigers!'

The lady allowed herself a smile, but very soon became serious again. 'And no serious after-effects?'

Was there something behind the question? 'He still has his nightmares, though much less, so I sleep near him in his brother's bed.'

'I see.' The lady paused, and then held up a magazine article. 'You probably will not have seen this.'

Wenlie recognized the Cantonese magazine, and said: 'The Editor recently sent us a copy. We liked him, he is an elderly gentleman and he sent me a courteous letter of introduction and then called on us after travelling for two weeks in Jiangsi. He told me he'd been finding out first-hand what the people feel there after their time under the Reds, and how the Nationalists are handling the vacuum now they've gone. He gave my son a book on the emperors which he'd carried on his travels.'

Madame Huang let the magazine down. 'That was kind. As I am sure you know, my husband has been heavily involved against the Reds, he regards the government's handling of the Communist threat abysmal, and our generals not much better. They had them trapped, and allowed them to get away. He believes their escape means a great opportunity has been thrown away, and China will suffer for it.'

They took bowls of tea brought on silver trays by the thin maid Yiying and by another older female servant. Afterwards, the lady asked Wenlie if she would like to see the gardens, expressing pride in them. It was suggested that the three young ones draw under the supervision of the governess, though Wenlie knew that Yuling would need no guidance.

In the gardens, she was introduced to two gardeners, an older man and his son. Then the lady led her through to early lily ponds. As they stopped before an arched bridge, Wenlie was suddenly given an odd look, and she wondered what was coming, expecting a question concerning the colonel's talk alone with her.

'Mrs Tsai, I ought to appraise you, and I mention this without serious criticism you understand me, that when the maid brought your sons to my apartments, at first your older boy acted most peculiarly, almost as if in a trance, completely forgetting himself and where he was. He did not bow to me, though his brother did, he did not even acknowledge me, or the governess for that matter. It was strange. He just stared at my daughter with his mouth open. He had his hands together like this...' the lady clasped her hands low down '...as if he intended to raise them to show respect to my daughter and then did not know how to complete his duty. I immediately wondered if the shock we had read about in the magazine was persisting, and that we had made a mistake to invite him. Was it perhaps wrong of my husband to have separated the three of you?'

Wenlie was horrified, and she caught the innuendo in the separation question, which she hoped was said more as a comment than a rebuke. 'That's extraordinary,' she replied acutely embarrassed, 'I'm ashamed to hear this, my lady. He bowed properly to your husband, I'm relieved to say. Sometimes he has his bad moments, but he's always well-mannered, and I've never seen him as you describe.' She looked anxiously into the aristocratic eyes. 'I deeply apologize, and I will talk to him, of course. Occasionally he drifts off in his thoughts, something he never did before the gun accident.'

'That would be for his good, naturally. But I repeat, we do not hold it against him, and we soon found that he is a fine boy.' Madame Huang began touching a green shoot in a hanging basket. 'You know, my daughter has a lively spirit, and she is rather good at putting people at ease, servants, townsfolk and the like. After her initial surprise when she looked towards me, she went up to your son and put her arm in his, which I thought very nice, and as soon as this happened his face completely changed and he smiled shyly, it was delightful to see. She told him she and her brother had been looking forward to meeting your boys, and by the time she brought him over to us, he seemed to have left his thoughts, and from that moment on he was perfectly content to be with us, and was courteous and respectful, I am pleased to tell you, as was your other son.' The lady's face remained stern. 'However, he never did bow.'

As they walked over the curving bridge, Wenlie remained puzzled and silent. She knew she would have to talk about it to Yuling; but she was greatly relieved that no offence had been taken, and that he had pulled himself together.

When they came to a young rose garden, the lady stopped. 'These are cuttings from a new rose we cultivated a few years ago,' she said, pointing out several new stems low in the soil. 'They become substantial bushes, and the gardeners are proud of them and named them after my late father-in-law. They are prolific in the flowers they produce.' The lady paused, just as Wenlie was glancing at the flower bed aware she was receiving another odd look. 'Aptly named, he had concubines, mistresses and some offspring from them, it was hard for my mother-in-law as you can imagine.' The lady began moving away, adding: 'My husband rather likes the bushes, but I prefer a more dependable upright rose plant.'

It took Wenlie only a few steps to realize that she had been given a message, and a warning about the colonel.

When they returned to the lady's apartments, they found seven-year-old Shanghan had appeared. He bowed earnestly to Wenlie, a nice upright-looking boy, she thought, though she could see he was the son of the father.

'My lady, you must look at these,' the governess said, showing two pictures that Yuling had drawn and one by Ayi, 'Tsai Yuling is excellent and so quick.'

'Don't you ever use a rubber eraser?' Huihua asked him. Her visitor shook his head with a wide smile at her, no usual deference but as though they had been long-term friends.

Madame Huang was very surprised at the quality of the older boy's pictures, and asked without looking up: 'Can you draw people, faces?'

'Yes, I drew some of the patients in the hospital.'

'He can draw from memory,' Ayi added.

The lady gave a short laugh. 'Then do a picture of my husband.' She turned to her children. 'All of you, I give you fifteen minutes.'

'Of father!' Huihua protested, 'that's impossible if we don't have him here.' But her little brother Shanghan said firmly that he could draw his father, and the governess was instructed to put them to it.

Huihua hated her part drawing, soon tearing it up and watching with excitement as her interesting, nice-looking visitor (except for the horrid left hand), who to her surprise was nine months younger than she was, worked on his own. She was intrigued that he occasionally stopped to close his eyes.

When the drawings were produced, Madame Huang was stunned as she glanced at the older brother's drawing, but she did not show her feelings, commenting first on her own son's picture, praising him although the likeness to her husband was very poor, and then making a generous remark about the younger brother Ayi's attempt.

She turned to Yuling's drawing. 'It is a remarkable likeness, my husband must see this. You have a great talent young man.'

Wenlie also thought it good, though there was an integrity shown in the face that the man certainly did not deserve.

That evening she, Yuling and Ayi dined with the governess and the children, and spent the night in rooms in the lady's apartments; they had been placed elsewhere in the mansion in two separate rooms that were reserved for the colonel's visitors, but the lady had made it clear to Wenlie that she had decided they might be more comfortably accommodated '...within my own apartments, nearer my children, you are really our guests...'

'My husband regrets' Madame Huang said the next morning, 'that he is unable to express his gratitude in person for your visit, he has military affairs to attend to. He has seen your drawing,' she was now looking at Yuling, 'and it gave him great pleasure. Might we keep it?'

'He has already given it to me, mother,' Huihua said quickly, looking from her mother to the visitor who she hoped would remember her partly because she had dressed in her favourite special robe.

'I see, then we shall be able to look at it from time to time,' the lady said.

As Secretary Lee led them along the last corridor towards the main doors, Wenlie found that the elderly retainer had mellowed. 'News about you, Tsai Yuling, has spread,' the secretary said. 'Expect some of the staff to be waiting to see you off.'

Wenlie guessed what might be coming. In Luchian, he had become the figure of attention since they had returned from Doctor Chen's Tuxieng house; people he did not know hailed him and often wanted to talk.

When they went through the doors, a crowd of servants stood waiting at the bottom of the marble steps. The secretary handed them over to the same soldier guard who had greeted them at the main gates the previous afternoon.

At first there was murmuring among the staff, but as they began to walk down the steps, the servants started clapping.

They reached the bottom and walked through the group, Ayi recognizing and giving a quick acknowledgement to Huihua's personal maid while Yuling heard their mother thanking people. The clapping only ended when they had gone some way along the central path through the cypress and palm trees, and only after Wenlie had turned and clasped her hands in grateful salute. Ayi only half turned; he was enjoying the accolade for his brother or for the three of them, but he was glad to be out of the rich man's mansion.

If Yuling had looked back, up to the Reception Hall's large middle window above one of the external hanging lanterns, he would have seen the Mistress also waving. 'Why are you wearing one of your best robes?' her mother had asked her before the breakfast with the visitors. Huihua had shrugged. 'I don't know, I just like its rich red,' she had replied.

The reception they received in the outer courtyard was of a different order. Civilians, soldiers and children were looking their way, and this time Wenlie felt apprehensive, for cheering, shouting and clapping soon greeted them. People began patting her sons on the back, children of all ages were calling out to them.

Ayi now did not enjoy the attention, but it was an exciting experience for Yuling. The guard kept ordering people to move aside. 'Let the woman and lads get to the carriage, move away I say!' One or two soldiers on horseback raised their caps. 'A thousand years of life to you!' an old man shouted, his face wrinkled and dark from the sun. As Yuling stepped into the carriage, he heard a woman call out: 'Respect to you, Tsai Yuling!'

They were driven away from the main gates by the same two drivers of the previous day, though Yuling noticed that the horses had been changed. They pulled the curtains as far back as they could to see out, and Wenlie breathed deeply the fresh air of a morning in spring. She was relieved that her unexpected ordeal with the colonel was now behind her; it had left a nasty feeling of shock, and she had slept very badly. She was pleased for Yuling who had obviously enjoyed the unique visit, more so than Ayi, though she would very soon have to talk to Yuling about his strange unacceptable behaviour in failing to greet the two ladies and the girl correctly.

In the peace of the countryside on the road back to Mingon, Yuling asked her while he looked out to rice paddies in water: 'You know I told you about my dream, not one of the bad ones, the one I had at the boulder before Lam found me, the girl in the dream kept telling me not to give up, to keep walking, and we were in a colourful stream? You said I shouldn't tell the newspaper men about it.'

Wenlie and Ayi looked at him, Wenlie wondering why he'd suddenly mentioned the boulder dream, and waited. But he turned his head further away, and seemed to study hills in the distance as though he'd gone into one of his drifts. She and Ayi looked at each other, and she was about to ask Yuling what he wanted to say, when one of the men on her side of the carriage called down asking if they wanted to spend a few minutes inside Mingon. She called back that she preferred to keep going, to get to Hanyeng. And when she turned to Yuling, he had closed his eyes, and she thought she would leave him - maybe he too had not slept well in the ancestral home of the Slayer of the Reds.

She rested her head back. The colonel's leer came into her thoughts, and quickly she put him away and conjured up the daughter, especially her rich clothes, the *noble* girl who to her amusement had worn no shoes or sandals in the mansion.

At the first stop to give the horses water, she was surprised when one of the riders handed her a small wooden box saying: 'Instructions are you're not to open it until after we leave you.'

'From Madame Huang?' she asked, puzzled why the lady had not given it to her in person.

'Don't know, Secretary Lee said to give it to you once we're on the journey.'

That it came to her via the colonel's elderly secretary worried Wenlie, and on the first river voyage by sampan back to Luchian, she decided to open the box, though under the cover of a shawl as there were a few other passengers.

Yuling had his arm in hers. 'Madame Huang liked you, I could tell,' he said. 'Maybe it's a large brooch.'

Inside she was amazed to see newly minted silver dollar coins, well packed under a hand-written note, and she heard Ayi letting out an exclamation. She became immediately frightened, getting free of Yuling's arm. 'Let me read this alone,' she said to the boys, 'turn away.'

The note was addressed to no one and was unsigned.

I beg you to think of suitable presents, for yourself particularly, and for the boys.

She folded the note and looked quickly at the money, guessing it could be five years of her wages as an inland female teacher.

Yuling looked again at her. 'Is it from the Colonel?' She closed the box. 'You mustn't ask me any more about this.'

That night Colonel Huang paid a visit to his wife. She found him more than usually energetic, and thought of the tall, striking-looking mother, and the unexplained minutes when her husband had the woman alone.

*

On an unpleasantly humid morning some two months after the Wuyi Court visit, a running messenger came to Wenlie's school. She was with young boys in a garden at the back of the building. The head teacher - the only person she had allowed to come to her in her collapsed state after Yuling was thought dead in the hills - was teaching inside a front classroom with its shutters open. He went out to meet the man. The runner asked if teacher Tsai Wenlie was at the school, and on being told she was, handed him an envelope making it clear 'the woman is to be given it at once.' The messenger bowed and ran off.

The head teacher went quickly to the back of the school. Telling the outdoor class to remain quiet, he took Wenlie aside and handed her the envelope, asking her to let him know if he could be of any assistance should it be something important.

'I have no idea what it can be,' she said, 'maybe the Manchurian puppet government will let me visit the Valley.' He knew she was referring to the place where her husband had lost his life.

He remained nearby, and soon heard her gasp.

> *Am in Kwehang only two hours south of you, a delightful ancient town if you do not know it. It would be the greatest honour if you would accept my invitation to be my guest for three days. Coaches can use the new road between us. One of my officers has business in Luchian tomorrow afternoon, he will be going there with a mounted escort and will be available to collect you in the main street at the end of your lane at about four. I believe other adults live with you, so you will not turn this down by reason of having to make arrangements concerning your sons, who I continue to wish to help materially.*

Wenlie sat down on a low wall. Feeling in immediate need of support from somebody she could trust, she gave the note to the head teacher, telling him it was from the Slayer of the Reds himself, she was certain of that even though it was not signed.

On returning from Mingon she had asked the head's advice about the silver coins, telling him her instinct was to return them, she did not want to be in any way beholden to the colonel. But he had replied that Yuling and Ayi must have impressed at Wuyi Court, and that she could regard the gift as welcome recompense for all her Tuxieng expenses, and could easily repay the doctor's interest-free loan she had mentioned. It was hardly likely the colonel would continue such benevolence. She had replied she was far less sure, but had not mentioned being alone with the colonel in the Study.

With Doctor Chen's loan, she had paid the hospital (Professor Su had more than halved the bill), settled with the hotel, rebuilt Lam's shack, given a donation to the Temple of the Five Concubines, and set up Meibei's husband with the geese; and to her surprise and delight, Doctor Chen had given the farmers a young nanny goat.

The colonel's bribe money was tempting, and she had foolishly kept it until she would decide when and how to return it. But the argument had run ever stronger in her head that her husband had died through Nationalist negligence, the family income had thus been severely affected forever, and she might regard the money partly as recompense, albeit directly from a senior officer rather than through the military. Now she bitterly regretted her inaction and failure to send back the coins.

'I'm lost for words!' the head teacher said after reading the note and returning it. 'Surely you won't accept?'

She pursed her lips. 'I'd rather trust a snake! Please don't mention this to anyone, I'll have to think how to deal with it.'

She felt sick, just as she had done when the colonel stood over her. She knew she was still attractive to men, but it was her worst possible luck to find herself pursued by such a powerful and nasty man, whose largesse was not meant benevolently. At such a moment she missed her husband terribly, yearned for those arms she would never feel again.

But she had no means to send a refusal, and did not know where the colonel could be contacted in Kwehang. She was sorely tempted to leave Luchian the next morning, with or without the boys, for a few days in a town high in the hills, where she might at least get some relief from the humidity. It would be no use going to the other family house in Luchian where another of her brothers-in-law lived, as she would be found - the KMT police would soon track her down.

The next morning, all through her teaching she felt very apprehensive. But she recalled the warning Madame Huang had given her in the gardens, and it seemed to tell her to stand firm. She decided not to run. When the coach arrived, she would inform the officer or whoever came to her door - she wasn't going to the end of her lane to wait - that she had school duties to attend to, and the person was to take back her message that she was unable to come and that she asked to be left alone, and she wouldn't state any regret.

As the afternoon hour drew closer she felt ever more nervous, and suspected that her intended message would not stop the colonel. With her husband, she had occasionally drunk wine although she had no head for alcohol. She had taken none since his death. Now she found herself drinking her late father-in-law's rice wine, first one glass, then another, and finally a third, all against Fainan's growing warnings.

*

The black-curtained military coach being driven through Luchian's old walls and along one of the two main streets stops at the end of the lane where the large corner shrine stands bedecked with flower ornamentation and candles. The small coach has a number of mounted soldiers front and back, and has already attracted many townsfolk and children. A coachman - a soldier in the uniform of the Huang corps - has been sent on foot down the lane, and with him walks the policeman whose report went to Wuyi Court. As the coachman approaches the house, the policeman stays back.

When Wenlie hears loud banging at the courtyard entrance, she is already

150

light-headed. She is still anxious, but less so than in the morning. The banging makes her leap out of the chair, and she gestures to Fainan to deal it, glad that none of the children are around.

'Are you Tsai Wenlie?' the man asks Fainan.

'I am,' Wenlie calls out walking towards them and not catching Fainan's look of concern.

'Lady, you ready to take the coach? We're at the end of the lane. I can carry any case you've got, or bag.'

'I will *not* be going,' she begins, aware her voice sounds shaky. 'My children need me, my school too, so does...' she stops, unable to think what else she can add. 'Tell the officer I don't wish to receive...' she waits to exhale the wine air, but it won't come up, '...I don't wish to receive any further invitations from the...' she nearly says Slayer but manages to hold back '...would you make this clear?' She looks at the soldier and gives a decisive head nod, and as she adds 'thank you' the wine air comes up.

She is surprised to see how ill at ease the man has become, he's moving from one foot to the other, and for a short moment she wonders if there could be another man just behind him.

'I can't say that!' she hears as she is turning round to go back towards the house and beginning to feel pleased with herself, 'sorry lady, but I've my orders, they're to bring you to the coach, so please help me and come, much obliged to you.'

Wenlie's fears vanish. Seeing Fainan she turns to the man. 'No I won't come and that's that! Inform Colonel ...inform Colonel...' she wants to say Slayer again, 'Huang,' Fainan says, 'Huang, yes, that's right, when you reach Kwehang will you...' Fainan is speaking under her breath 'Wenlie, he's got to give your message to the officer in the coach.' Wenlie has to think. 'The officer, yes, the officer, tell him I'm staying here with my children if that makes it any easier for you.' She has to swallow because she thinks the wine itself could now be coming up.

'I can't say that either, I'd lose my post!' Fright is in the voice.

'Post! Course you wouldn't!' Wenlie watches him shake his head, and this makes her bold. 'Then I will!' She looks semi-triumphantly to Fainan, and sees fear. 'I *will*!' she repeats, giving her a smile as she strides past the soldier ...or two ...and begins walking down the lane as quickly as she can manage, wondering why it seems to be waving, thinking it must be to do with the humidity.

The soldier beside her starts crying out 'Woman stop! Stop! What are you going to do?' Fainan is also calling to her from behind 'Wenlie, come back!'

She passes the policeman who she knows about and dislikes, catching the look of surprise, and hears the soldier's further plea but ignores it; he is now running a little in front of her, like fellow actors sometimes do in her theatre, only this is real life and more exciting, except that on the stage she is usually in control of herself unless having to improvise, but now…

She can see townsfolk at the end of the lane, they are milling around mounted soldiers, and she catches sight of the back of a small coach; the corner shrine hides the front of the coach and forward soldiers.

She reaches the shrine and bows towards it, her large red candle still burning …or is it someone else's, there are so many…

Pushing her way through the crowd, she comes to the coach and finds that a dark curtain is hiding the occupant.

She is now playing the central role, her audience all around her; she feels so bold she could bellow at Chiang Kai-shek himself.

She slaps a hand against the curtain, expecting it to be pulled back. 'Tell your Colonel he can't buy me!' she shouts.

The curtain moves, it is drawn half way, and part of the face of an officer becomes visible, but he is in shadow and the curtain obscures the rest.

Some greeting ushers from within, and the coach door comes slowly towards her, clearly inviting her.

If Colonel Huang intends to step out to be greeted by his future mistress, he soon discovers he is not to get the opportunity; or if he thinks Tsai Wenlie will do his bidding and at once enter his private world, he is soon disabused. Using the force of both hands, Wenlie flings the door forward so that it slams against the latch and comes hard back at her and starts to flap, and while it flaps she catches a better view of the man inside and it gives her a shock - the officer looks like the colonel, only the man seems smaller than she remembers him when she sat in that white chair with the ogre standing so close.

Wine and stage have already taken over. Hiccuping for the first time, she points down the street. 'Be on your way whoever you are!' She bends nearer the curtain and pulls it right back, looking the man fully in the face, now definitely seeing who it is, and noticing him wince as the head tries to draw away. 'How dare you come to seduce …to seduce the widow of a Valley hero!'

A sudden fainting feeling comes over her, but she is glad to have reached the end of that part of her impromptu speech, though she realizes she might not know the next lines and Fainan is tugging at her arm as she hears 'Wenlie, come away, come away!'

A deathly hush has fallen over the crowd and the mounted soldiers. The rustle of a horse's harness breaks the silence, at once followed by Wenlie. 'I will *not* be bought,' she cries as a thought occurs: she will make her move to checkmate, like Alinga is always doing to her. She tries to glare at the colonel, though some of him seems to have disappeared into a darker recess. 'Do you want me to tell your wife Madame …Madame …Madame Mingon,' she knows the name is wrong, but it will do, 'that fine woman?'

She just finishes and is standing upright again when she feels a draining of blood from her head and her legs give way.

Fainan tries to hold Wenlie from falling but fails, catching a momentary view of a bully stung beyond the ability to reply.

As three male citizens carry unconscious Wenlie back along the lane, Fainan keeps looking round, terrified she will hear horse soldiers coming after them, imagining they'll be stopped before they reach the house. She keeps urging the men to hurry.

But Colonel Huang had rapidly closed the curtain, and after several seconds of internal alarm turning to horror and then panic, he had barked out an order and the coach was rolling.

The man is smarting, smarting badly. Women have been angry with him before, even very occasionally thrown things at him, but only in private, never in front of others let alone his own soldiers, and in such a public, shocking manner. This is far worse than losing face, unpleasant though that was on the times in his life he can count on one hand that occurred long, long ago.

He had felt impotent and helpless. Those full lips that he'd relished and been certain of kissing within a very few hours - if not within the coach itself - had become the thin lips of a laughing witch; and in the eyes he had seen hatred, and worse, derision. His power and his spirit had melted in a furnace.

He feels deeply humiliated. His mind goes back to the public thrashing his father gave him in front of the staff when he was ten, at the bottom of the marble steps in the inner courtyard. He hadn't meant for the pistol he'd aimed from a window to go off, he thought the catch was on, but the bullet had somehow by sheer bad luck hit a woodcutter who was trimming branches, and the man had been killed. He'd felt guilty about it; the beating had been justified, he'd always accepted his punishment.

On the journey to Kwehang, all sorts of revenges pass through his mind. But when the coach reaches its destination and the soldiers dismount, he orders them to stay with their horses while he takes aside the junior officer in charge of the escort. He trusts and admires the young man, who he knows did well at the military academy; he has been grooming him for a higher position in his corps.

'Ma, you must order the men not to divulge what they saw and heard, not to any other soldier or to their families or to anybody at all. Warn them that if they do and I find out, I'll throw them out and pursue them and their families. Make this absolutely clear to the men.' The young officer nods, and can see that his colonel hasn't finished. 'Be frank, tell me what you thought of the incident.

I shouldn't be asking you, but you see how upset I am, I'm not thinking clearly. Speak plainly, I won't hold it against you.'

Lieutenant Ma does not hesitate. 'You should dismiss the occurrence from your mind, Colonel, especially the woman, it's completely trivial in the context of our task to secure the south from the Communists ever returning. Our job is to hunt down any Red partisans left behind and snuff out their cells. And we've got the Japanese in Manchuria, they could come south or they could invade again from their islands and seize our coastal cities, we've got to build up our defences. What's happened was a private matter, sir, of no consequence. Anyway, she was drunk, I could see that, she's not worth it.' The officer does not add that he'd been amazed: for a woman, rather a tall and appealing one he couldn't help notice, to dare to shout at any man like that, and especially at the colonel knowing his reputation ...well it had been unbelievable.

Colonel Huang feels immediate relief at the young man's comments, and recalls how mature beyond his own age he himself had been as a young officer out of Whampoa.

That evening, against his earlier expectations, he dines with some of his officers including Lieutenant Ma. He drinks heavily and asks if there is any bordello in town. At first there is a hush, before someone replies that none are known. He is desperately frustrated.

Alone in his bed, he hardly sleeps. He thinks again of the thrashing he received as a boy; it was no more than fathers did to sons. But what this woman had done to him in front of the men - it makes him break out in sweats.

Early in the humid night, he is forced to throw off the sheet and lie naked ...without a woman.

The wounding humiliation took long to recede. But the important business of purging the south of the Reds, and the enjoyment that went with the company of existing and new mistresses, eventually allowed it to vanish ...almost, or to be buried deep. Colonel Huang's silver bribe-coins were not returned, and rich man that he was, he gave them no thought. He never again saw the Tsai woman as available let alone a continuing challenge. He didn't know that the story was soon round all his troops and reached the Wuyi Court servants, and that Lee his private secretary heard about it. Lee thought about the coins, but felt it best not to make any mention of them.

Madame Huang had her own ways of being informed of events or goings on that concerned her. She had liked the Tsai mother's transparent decency and intelligence. Now she felt very grateful to her, indeed admired her, though she found the coach story astonishing.

She and her daughter never forgot the interesting visit of the two boys and their mother. Huihua kept the drawing of her father. She did not have it framed because she wanted it to be just as her visitor had given her. She marked on the back:

> Drawn here at the Court during the Spring Festival in the Twenty-fourth year of the Republic, by Tsai Yuling of Luchian, nine months younger than me though he is much bigger. He was lost for days in the uplands and survived a panther attack and has a horrible looking hand without a little finger. He was not shy and I think one day he will become a famous painter. I wish he lived nearer. I really liked him.
> HH.

For several months it sat on her table beside a bowl filled often with lotus blossom from the water garden. Then it went into her desk.

11

Six years later, 1941, a university evacuated to a wartime campus in the unoccupied west part of Fujian province, Imperial Japan having occupied much of China's coastal east and south since 1937/38.

Several weeks before the end of Yuling's first year at university, a letter awaited him one evening on his return to his lodgings; it was from his mother.

> *My precious Alinga,*
> *A terrible thing has happened - Lam is in prison accused of murdering a woman, the trial has been fixed very fast but why we don't know, in about four weeks, with Magistrate Liao of all people, you will know his name as No Mercy. Our lovely Lam is incapable of such a thing, but he was seen in the canal area where the body was found, two women saying he acted suspiciously. Your stepfather is going to try to represent him with a town elder who I don't think you know, and they will tell the story of his rescuing you. Ayi says he'll organize a march on the court so No Mercy knows the people's feelings. Lam's mother will beg for him - you know the woman who is with him sometimes at the temple - and I've just come back from talking with the old priest Ho Chitian who is very upset and says he wants to speak as well, brave of him as you know how timid he is. No Mercy won't be able to stop Meibei, I've sent her a message telling her where Lam is being held and that I will let her know when the trial is starting. Go to the Temple of the Stars, Alinga, Ho Chitian says it is beautiful, your prayers above everyone's may be answered, please go there my sweet. I will get a message to you as soon as there is more information. Ever your loving but anxious mother.*

The next morning Yuling was hardly able to concentrate at the first lecture on early eastern drawings of trees and flowers given by Professor Koo Guanglu the senior art professor. At the end, as soon he and the other students had bowed to the professor, he ran up to him and showed him the letter, telling him it was Lam who saved his life and asking permission to take one week off once he heard from his mother when the trial would be.

He liked and admired the professor, so was surprised and concerned when the answer was to ask again when he knew the date, and not necessarily to expect a favourable answer, as 'the tests are coming up, and others can no doubt tell the court your story.'

At once he wrote back to his mother that he was determined to be at the trial whether he got permission to be absent or not.

But four days later he received a longer even more distressing letter.

> My Alinga,
> This will cause you more pain than I dare to think. The court sent a message this morning to your stepfather while I was at school, the trial was being brought forward to this afternoon, no reason given, Chennie had to abandon his work and come for me.
> He did his best in front of Liao, gave your rescue story, and he talked about Lam's gentle character, but he wasn't allowed to question the two women, one was clearly a whore. Lam sat there hands bound, not looking his usual smiling self, often muttering in his way, I'm sure he knew something bad was going on. The elder couldn't come, and Ayi couldn't find the mother. I had no time to alert Meibei. We just managed to get the old priest, who did his best when speaking though he had to go on his knees begging to be allowed to talk, and as soon as he told No mercy that the lights of heaven were being shut out from the court, he wasn't allowed to say another word.
> Our worst fears have come, I can hardly write the word to you, our dear man of the horses is to die, and for a crime we all know in our bones he couldn't have committed. I'm having to keep away the tears as I write. There was an outcry when No Mercy gave the verdict, and when he stated execution would take place in twenty four hours, I lost myself for all of us but for you especially, I screamed at him telling him I'd met Governor Huang and his lady concerning your ordeal and Lam finding you, and we'd immediately be contacting them about the terrible injustice. The man screamed back at me and told me to sit down and hold my tongue, but I shouted that we'd be warning the general loud and

clear that the citizens of Tuxieng support Lam and that if he's executed before a petition is heard, there would be bad trouble. You should have seen the man's face, he shrieked at me and then tried to hurry out, but Ayi sprang up and barred the way, and the attendants didn't dare touch your fine brother, they refused to obey the screeches to remove him. I went up to the man and said that the general would have to divert troops to the town because all the market folk and angry farmers and temple priests would descend on No Mercy and his life would be in danger, and if he fled he'd have no grace and favour residence or court left in the town to return to, they'd be burnt to cinders.

Your stepfather was the complete opposite to me, very cool and authoritative, how much I admire him. He demanded: 'In the name of the people of Tuxieng, return to your seat Magistrate Liao, and do not leave this court until we the people have a stay of execution signed by your own hand, pending the hearing of a petition to General Huang.'

With lots of people shouting at him, No Mercy eventually returned to his chair. I glared at him while Chennie wrote out a paper, it's in front of me as I write, and it states: 'A petition for clemency or for a proper re-trial will be delivered to the governor's mansion at Mingon as soon as ever possible and definitely within seven days. Meanwhile the citizens and farmers of Tuxieng and district demand as a right of the people of Fujian province, and are hereby granted, a stay of execution of the death penalty against Fang Lamgang until the governor has informed the petitioners and court of his decision.'

No Mercy signed it, grudgingly I must say, and Chennie required an attendant to wax it and the magistrate to stamp his seal. The man then angrily stood up and dismissed us, saying if he didn't hear from the governor by the very same hour in fourteen days, the execution would proceed.

Alinga, at least we have a short reprieve. Chennie and Ayi are drafting the petition in the surgery as I write. Ayi will get it signed this evening and tomorrow by as many people as he can get hold of.

Ho Chitian is going to seek an audience, though he is loath to do it, he'll set off the day after tomorrow, and as none of us think he's the right person to speak, can you leave Suodin at once and meet him at the East Gate Monastery. I know it might take you a day and a half to reach Mingon, but he'll wait for you, and if *you don't appear by next Monday he'll deliver the petition the following day.*

You remember our visit to Wuyi Court and meeting the Huang family. The general is a horrible and powerful man, Ayi and I both hate him for our different reasons. Be careful. If he bullies you, act cleverly, use your charm, appeal to his better nature if there is any, use the bended knee if you have to, invoke the name of your father, and if it is going badly, show him your worth, stand up to him and act like you did at school as the brave mandarin in Koxinga's Life.

Write at once or send a telegram that you'll do this, I'm certain you will. Chennie is writing to Huang informing him that a People's petition for clemency will be presented very soon by the priest and hopefully by you who were rescued, but he'll avoid mentioning my name - you know those awful moments I had with the man. I am writing to Madame Huang, so when you get there, don't mention to the general about my letter to his wife, as that could be disastrous.

Did you go to the temple? It's so important.

I embrace you and send you your mother's dearest love.

Yuling read the letter with horror, and thought about poor Lam in prison being harmed by guards or criminals. And he feared for another reason - having to plead before Nationalist General Huang. The man's reputation against the Reds in the southern provinces was bad enough. But unofficial smuggled reports of the Whites' ambush of fellow Chinese of the Communist New Fourth Army leaving Anhui had shocked him and many of his student friends, as well as some of the teachers prepared to listen. Since the Japanese occupation of the east, the two Chinese factions (the Nationalists and Communists) were supposed to be joined in the Second United Front in the War of Resistance against Japan. Instead (the reports said) the Nationalists had demanded that the Reds leave under threat they would be forced out by battle if necessary; and when they went peacefully under the belief there was tacit agreement they would not be attacked, they were massacred with huge casualties, and many of the Reds were young. Yuling's younger brother Ayi had been so incensed that he'd applied to join the Chinese Communist Party, as did two of Yuling's university friends.

He showed his mother's letter to his landlord and said he had to leave at once, asking him to send her a telegram that he was going to Mingon. Then he ran to a friend's house, gave him the letter and told him to show it to Professor Koo as soon as he could. On it Yuling wrote his apologies, saying he hoped to be back within a week or a little more, depending on the audience date with the governor, and begging to be allowed back to continue his studies and take the tests; he added that he had an absolute duty to try to save his friend who was unable to speak so had not been able to defend himself in the court.

'As if I could refuse to take him back, one of the most outstanding talents we've ever had,' Professor Koo commented to a colleague later that day. 'May the gods be with him and with the man he wants to save. You know, I talk and advise all the other students while they're drawing or painting, help them along. But with Tsai Yuling...' he shook his head '...I cannot interrupt a genius. That painting of the peasant woman and her wart, it's unbelievably powerful, the judges couldn't have given the prize to anyone else.' He was referring to Yuling's tempera painting of Meibei standing in a narrow paddy of well-growing rice, she appeared to have been weeding and was half way to coming upright again, she was looking to where her husband was pointing towards birch trees higher up below dark green hills. The two judges had been sure there was a message, a yearning for a brighter future for the Chinese people, and they had not minded the political tone. But they did not know what Professor Koo knew, that the young artist had reconstructed something altogether more personal, from an extraordinary and shocking childhood experience.

By the early afternoon Yuling sat in a sampan going up a tributary of a larger river in the direction of Mingon. He and a handful of other passengers were warned that Japanese planes sometimes came from the Amoy area and strafed; the captain would be hugging the banks as long as the water was deep enough, and all had to watch the skies and for submerged mud banks, or worse old tree stumps.

It was a relief when the captain said at dusk that they should be free from attack that day, that planes rarely came after dark unless the sky was clear and the moon strong. An hour later they moored at the landing of a small town.

In the late afternoon of the following day they arrived at Mingon without incident, and Yuling went straight to the East Gate Monastery, where he was greeted almost as a son by the tiny old priest Ho Chitian, and was introduced to a number of the Buddhist monks; they had welcomed the Taoist priest as a spiritual brother.

'I went to the main gates of Wuyi Court,' Ho Chitian told him, 'the guards spoke with the secretary and said we've got to be there tomorrow one hour after sunset. The governor will only allow us ten minutes, we're the last petition before he goes travelling.'

Yuling was given a guest room and ate alone, his evening meal presented to him by a novice. Afterwards Ho Chitian took him to an underground corridor, turned up the wick of a lamp, and showed him the People's petition.

The deep echo of an old gong rang out, and they joined the monks in their temple. But there were no candles, lamps or burning urns, though incense sticks were allowed; the only light came from the stars - Mingon was under blackout orders.

He slipped away in the middle of the chanting. He had been told when the monastery would be locked, and had obtained a key to a side entrance. Until near midnight when the town gates would also be closed preventing him returning to the monastery if he was inside the town, he walked the dark streets in the warmth of the early night, from gate to gate on all four points of the compass. No moon was in the night sky, but the stars between clouds enabled him to see enough not to stumble. The absence of light in homes and shrines made him fear for what the next day would bring. He thought again of Lam in the prison at Tuxieng, and of Meibei, knowing how worried she would be, how much love and compassion she felt for their smiling friend.

He slept through the first early-morning sounds of the old gong, and through the next strikes. When he awoke and sought fresh air, making exercises under the large green fronds of a truncated palm, he saw hobbling towards him an old monk, severely bent, who he had not met the previous evening; a stick was in one hand, and what looked like rolled parchment in the other.

The monk gave a greeting and tried to look up. 'My son, you are welcome in our earthly home. I am Zen Yahan, and I know something of your story from priest Ho Chitian. He says you are a remarkable artist.' The bare head went down again. Looking to the ground but holding out his hand, he continued: 'Allow me to present you with this, you may think it is special, you could use it as a petition for your own personal entreaty. We used to have close connections to Wuyi Court. If you mention this somewhere in the petition, perhaps it could help.'

Yuling took what he saw was a scroll. He was at once impressed by the quality, undid two white binds top and bottom, and as he unfurled it he realized he was looking at something of great age and beauty, a parchment of light yellow hue, clear and waiting for character script, the edges embroidered in blue silk, and pale uneven grooves in the parchment gave him the faintest impression of hills and trees.

'You may sit in my ground floor room for as long as you need, my old brush pens and new black ink are on the desk, you will not be disturbed. When you hear our ancient gong calling us to meditation and prayer, you must continue your work knowing we are praying for your success.'

During that clammy morning, at a desk looking through open windows towards the ochre-coloured side wall of the monastery temple, Yuling harnessed his greatest powers under the deepest emotions. Before each dip in the ink, he thought of the points he had scribbled when on the sampan, of every word, of the ancient characters he would use taken from his country's natural beauty.

Holding the brush vertically, he invoked the spirit of China's great masters of calligraphy.

And in his script he also used guile - against the man he had to impress.

He took no lunch, and after he had finished in the early part of the afternoon, he went outside the room and along a corridor, finding the old monk dozing on a bamboo double chair. As he passed to go into the open air, Zen Yahan stirred and called him, asking if he had finished.

Soon the monk was at the window ringing a small bell as high as he could without being able to look up. When he stopped he said: 'With your talent your future will be bright, especially if you learn to combine self-discipline with a degree of inner mastery over yourself, as we monks seek for ourselves but do not always achieve.'

Several monks and novices appeared outside the window.

'Hold it up,' he told Yuling, 'I want them to see.'

The monks and novices came closer. There was a silence as they read. Then some of them burst into applause.

The old man spoke to them. 'This parchment has been waiting for its moment for over a hundred years. It belonged to my mentor, Master Jian. May his spirit guide Ho Chitian and our young friend to success this evening.'

One of the monks was looking with particular care at the scroll. 'Your handwork is beautiful,' he said. 'I see the curves of eagles' wings in flight, and crescent moons over fine temples, it is the best standard of our art that I have ever seen at our monastery.'

The old monk smiled and whispered towards the floor. 'This is the highest accolade, my friend, it comes from our most accomplished calligrapher.'

But Yuling hardly accepted the praise; he was feeling very nervous about the task ahead, and was frightened that his part in student street theatre - the acting of scenes depicting the Whites' corruption and cruelty and their ineffectiveness against the invaders - could have been reported and had reached the Slayer of the Reds. He was also very worried that the general-cum-governor might hold against them the coach incident with his mother, though he hoped it was sufficiently in the past not to affect the audience, or that the man was somehow 'big enough' to regard the petition and the incident as separate matters.

Madame Huang had been interested to receive a letter from the fine-looking widow who she well remembered had visited six years earlier with her interesting boys - the woman who had bravely stopped her husband's advances. She noted the concern expressed in the letter *...I beg you to bring whatever indirect help you can, madam...* and knew why she had been written to and not her husband; indeed the Tsai mother expressly asked her not to mention the letter to her husband. Above all, she was gratified to hear that she had remarried. She noticed that the letter did not say what had become of the older boy, but that the mother expected him to be with the priest when the petition was presented.

She spoke to her thirteen-year-old son Shanghan shortly before he was to join his father and other officers for a lunch separate from the ladies. 'I hope you are having some interesting audiences beside father, my dear. I am sure you learn a great deal from him, and it is really a very good way for you to master one of the arts of leadership, which includes handling poor or afflicted people in a compassionate way, do you not agree?' She looked keenly at her fine son, was so proud of him. 'Something I most detest is to hear that an innocent person has been condemned because of false or suspicious evidence. If you get such a case, I know your father will warn you to be careful, not to condemn a person to be flogged or put in prison, and especially not to die, unless the evidence is clear.'

Her son gave her back a responsible look. 'He is very good with me, mother, we sometimes go into the annex and he asks what I think, and then we return to the Study and he tells the people his decision. He likes me to tell him afterwards if I don't agree any decision, and we then discuss it.'

'Well just remember, simpletons and retarded folk, people like that, always treat them decently when you see them, or when someone petitions on their behalf if they are not able to speak for themselves. If they are accused of something, they could well be innocent, it is often other mean people who try to get rid of them by making them look guilty of something they have not done.'

A few minutes later, at lunch with her daughter, she asked Huihua if she recalled the visit of a Mrs Tsai and her two sons.

'Of course, very well,' Huihua replied with surprise and feeling, 'Tsai Yuling was an amazing drawer, do you remember? I've still got his picture of father in my desk, I was looking at it only the other day.'

'It is possible, but please on no account tell your father or Shanghan, that the young man may be coming this evening or tomorrow to petition for the life of the simpleton who rescued him. I have heard from the mother. Apparently the man has been condemned to death for a murder he may not have committed. She says he would not be capable of such a thing as he is a gentle soul. The problem is he cannot speak. I repeat, Hua, do not mention this to your father or Lee, or to Shanghan, or you might make things worse for the young man, or more importantly for the simpleton. If Tsai Yuling comes, it will be with a priest.'

In the late afternoon, a troop of foot soldiers and an officer escorted the ladies to Mingon; they were carried in separate sedan chairs handled by bearers.

They were being taken along a wide path through woods that made snake-like turns. The woods began after a clearing of about two hundred paces from Wuyi Court, and ended at a clearing before the town's ancient Great Gate. Each lady had the curtains drawn back and was using a fan (before reaching the town, the curtains would be closed). Clouds covered the sky, though no rain threatened. The ladies had several matters to attend to, and this longer route, taking three-quarters of an hour instead of fifteen minutes by the road, meant that they could not be spotted from the air and exposed to attack by trigger-happy Japanese pilots. The road would have been dangerous to take during the day, even in cloudy weather.

Daylight had well gone when their business was finished. They did not have to ask the officer's opinion if it was safe to take the shorter route by road back to their home, because there were no stars or moon showing through the cloudy early night.

As they came to the first of the chimera lion statues at the main gates of their ancestral home, each of them heard the officer shouting at monks to make way, to get off the road. Madame Huang was startled, wondering what on earth monks were doing there, thinking they must be a travelling group who were seeking permission to sleep within the outer courtyard for protection from robbers, without knowing robbers never dared come near the mansion for fear of the military patrols.

No lamps were burning when she and Huihua alighted in the dark just inside the gates. She tried to make out the group, and asked the officer what was happening. He was unable to tell her, so she walked with him outside, and noticed a taller figure in the group.

'What are you doing, why are you here?' the officer called out.

The tall figure started walking towards them, followed by what they soon saw was a very little man, and the officer immediately held up his revolver. 'Halt where you stand!'

The figures stopped, the tall one calling back: 'We've come to petition the governor.'

Over the officer's shoulder Madame Huang said: 'I am the governor's wife. Do we know you?'

'Yes my lady, from some years ago, my name is Tsai Yuling, I came here with my mother when I was twelve. My companion is Ho Chitian, priest of the Temple of the Five Concubines in Tuxieng.'

Huihua had approached and was now standing behind her mother. 'Ah yes,' her mother said, 'good, it's alright Lieutenant, these people are genuine, you may put down the gun, and thank you for escorting us.'

Yuling saw the figure of Madame Huang come from round the officer, and as she walked in short steps towards him he clasped his hands and bowed.

'I am most interested to meet you again, Tsai Yuling, please come into the Guard House so I can see you properly, it is so dark now we are not allowed to light the courtyards. I am afraid you find us in an unhappy state, a wartime reduced staff, and having to dodge planes. I know you want to see my husband as soon as possible, so I will not detain you long.'

As she turned to go back through the gates, she called to the group of monks: 'Zen Yahan is not among you, is he? I cannot make any of you out.'

'No,' she heard back, 'he's in the temple praying for the success of the audience.'

'Then kindly convey Madame Huang's most respectful regards for his health and well being,' she said loudly, 'I want to visit him soon.'

Yuling followed the lady, unexpectedly coming to another person he had not seen behind the challenging soldier, a young woman though he could not see her face well. Quickly he bowed, receiving a more dignified one back, and realized she could well be the daughter he had met six years earlier. If so, she was now a little taller than her mother. They were not introduced, and the young woman said nothing.

The large gates closed behind them.

'Lieutenant, would you and the guards wait outside,' the lady said. She went inside the Guard House followed by the younger woman, and Yuling followed old Ho Chitian in and had to duck the entrance.

The first part of the room was almost as dark as outside, despite a wall lamp dimly glowing in the far corner. Once the door was shut, the lady asked him to turn up the wick. 'There are no windows, so we cannot be seen from the air,' she said.

In the darkness outside the gates, Huihua had been struck by Tsai Yuling's height; but now she was surprised how broad and strong he looked, at once remembering that she had been impressed by his size even when he was a boy; she wondered if his hand still looked bad.

Madame Huang said: 'I have just received a letter from your mother saying you might be coming. She will be pleased you are here. I realize how important this matter is to you. Convey my regards to her. And I am pleased to hear she remarried.' Yuling gave a short nod. 'A word of advice. Speak firmly by all means, but without too much emotion, my husband does not take to over displays. And make no mention of your mother's letter, we do not want him to feel ...well you understand me, I am sure. Now tell me, what are you doing with your life?'

'I am at the temporary campus in Suodin, studying Art and Japanese.'

'Japanese? Do you enjoy it?'

'Very much.'

'Why are you learning the enemy's language?'

'I like it, and the culture interests me, and I have a feeling I might be able to put it to use in our cause against them, I don't know.'

'A fair answer, but never go over to them will you.' It was a rhetorical question, and before she allowed an answer she added: 'Do you get to paint or is the art more in the line of history and drawing?'

'Yes, in different media, we do landscape, also experimental work, at the moment we have portraiture.'

'Perhaps one day, when this wretched war is over, you might visit us and show what you can do, or we might see your work in a gallery, that would be good.'

Yuling inclined his head in a polite smile.

'Well, good luck with the petition. Kindly turn down the wick,' she directed.

Throughout the brief exchange, Huihua noticed that the tiny priest never looked up, and the student looked only at her mother, though their eyes did once meet, when she detected his recognition and interest and sensed his nervousness.

A guard told them to wait just inside the main gates, beside a door in one of them. A few minutes later they were following two soldiers through the outer courtyard, and Yuling could not help recall that sunny day in spring when he, Ayi and their mother had visited and seen the bustle and activity of the courtyard; and the following day he had walked through the cheering crowd. The contrast now with the dark empty courtyard was stark.

They were handed to other guards who appeared out of nowhere, and led through the inner courtyard to the steps of the mansion, its huge lanterns cold and lifeless. One of the men ushered them through the main doors into a low lit corridor, and took them along passages now bare of the vases that Yuling recalled, and soon up the curving staircase to a side room where they were told to take seats and wait.

A weak lamp on a table cast a miserable light. Their door to the staircase was left open, the guard standing just outside. Yuling could hear the general's voice - how could he forget it - something about the cause of flooding and crops destroyed; the Slayer was asking questions in an unpleasant tone. But he could not make out the replies, only that a peasant man was answering quietly.

After very little time, he heard a peremptory dismissal, and soon a door was opened and a shaft of light came partly across their floor as they watched an elderly couple shuffle out, the woman crying and holding her husband's arm, followed by a soldier and an old man darkly dressed, who Yuling recognised as the secretary.

The secretary introduced himself. They were to follow 'into my lord's Study.' They went through the embossed door into the larger room, curtains hanging down before windows that Yuling guessed would also be shuttered.

General Huang was sitting in his high-backed chair behind the large desk, looking stern towards them. A cadet in uniform sat beside him on his right, and two armed soldiers stood behind.

As they were being led quickly forward, Yuling saw on the desk the long Ming sword he had never forgotten.

They were stopped a few steps from the desk at a line showing dark orange in the lamplight, and they made their bows.

The general neither stood nor bowed, though the cadet did both, and Yuling realized the boy was the son Shanghan, decent-looking and about thirteen, he guessed.

The secretary went to a chair and a small table to one side of the desk, and sat down with a sigh.

Yuling thought the general looked older but otherwise hadn't changed much; he'd seen his picture often in the newspapers. He expected to have to explain himself early on over his anti-government street-acting, and had prepared his answer based on his hatred of the Japanese who had killed his father, and his belief that more should be done to fight them; he sincerely hoped they would not know that he was partly responsible for the designs and wording of some of the posters placed secretly around Suodin and smuggled to other towns.

'So we meet again Tsai Yuling,' General Huang said brusquely, 'you've grown up. And you are?'

'Ho Chitian, your excellency,' the old priest answered very quietly and looking down.

'Speak up! Which temple?'

'Five Concubines, Formosa Lane, Tuxieng,' he said almost under his breath.

Yuling wished his companion would speak louder.

'And I see you want to plead for someone who has murdered a woman. I have a letter from a Doctor Chen of Tuxieng saying you'd be coming. Well, you address me Tsai, I can hardly hear the priest.'

'Yes sir.' Yuling looked directly at the general, feeling very uncomfortable in the presence of such coldness. The few lamps in the room were less strong than he'd first thought, their shadows and the two soldiers behind the general adding to the threatening atmosphere. He took one of the petitions from his grandfather's leather bag. 'Here first is the People's petition, drawn up immediately after Magistrate Liao pronounced Fang Lamgang guilty and ordered the death penalty. You will see it has been signed by many citizens, some could write themselves, and others have written names for those who couldn't. Three elders have also signed.' He began to move towards the desk to hand the petition to the general.

'To me first, student,' the secretary called out, hastily trying to stand. Yuling turned, waited, and handed it to the secretary, who delivered it over the desk to the general and moved back to the side. Yuling resumed his place beside Ho Chitian.

All went quiet as Yuling watched the general's head moving up and down the petition. He wondered if he was looking for specific names, perhaps of known Reds, or merely skimming it while waiting for him to speak. He decided to start his address.

'It makes a number of points, sir.' He was surprised the general did not immediately look up to hear him. 'First, the evidence of one of the two women witnesses should have been treated as completely unsatisfactory. She's a common prostitute and a known liar in the town. Secondly...'

'Silence!' The general had practically growled to the petition, and now looked at him.

Yuling was taken aback to meet such early anger in the eyes. He waited for the general to speak, and was very relieved when the man returned to the petition, though he noticed he only seemed to be reading the top of it.

At last the general spoke, but again without looking up. 'Anything else?'

'The people's second point is that Doctor Chen was not permitted...'

'Yes, yes, I've read it. Is this all?'

Yuling looked at Ho Chitian, but his companion's head remained lowered, and he knew he was on his own.

'No, sir, here is my own petition prepared at the East Gate Monastery.' (After what old monk Zen Yahan had said about the monastery's connection with Wuyi Court, he thought that might impress). The general made no comment. He removed the scroll from his bag and went to the secretary, handing it to him, aware the general's eyes were following.

The old man stood up carefully, and looked surprised as he untied the white binds, his head coming more upright when he opened the scroll and saw what he was holding. He walked to the desk and passed it open to the general.

The cadet caught a glimpse of the character script, letting out a small exclamation, but the scroll curled in his father's hands.

The general half opened it again, looked at it for several seconds, and let it curl up on the desk.

Yuling thought this indicated he could continue, which he needed to do. 'In my petition...'

'Quiet!' the general called out looking up fiercely at him. 'Murder is murder! The magistrate heard the evidence. No witnesses were called to say the man was somewhere else when the woman was murdered. And why do you write about being found in the uplands? What relevance is it that the man might have helped you?'

'He didn't just help me, he brought me to safety, I would have died or been killed if he hadn't found me.' Yuling was glad he had answered quickly, but his voice had shaken too much when thinking of the rescue. He looked quickly to the cadet, then back to the general. 'The farmers didn't know what Lam ...Fang Lamgang...' he corrected himself '...was trying to tell them, he came back for me. And he can't talk. Some of the newspapers called him a hero and he was. He couldn't have committed murder, it's not in his...'

'Someone would have found you no doubt.'

'No sir, I was where no one...'

'That's enough I say! I'm not going to allow irrelevant argument.'

'But sir, why aren't you taking into acc...'

'Don't be insolent student!' the general shouted, leaping up and thumping the desk causing the long sword to vibrate on its mounts. 'Remember who you're addressing! Be careful Tsai, I warn you!' Eyes blazed under thick eyebrows, and the celestial warrior's fierce countenance on the escarpment door of the Hut flashed into Yuling's mind, as he saw the cadet look at his father and knew the moment for the bended knee was inappropriate.

'Please General Huang,' he braved, speaking as decently as he could, 'I am not being disrespectful, I am trying to explain that Fang Lamgang has only ever been a gentle person, as the first petition says and all those signatures testify. They include tenant farmers, elders, shopkeepers, good citizens of Tuxieng...' the back of his mouth was starting to dry up '...he doesn't have it in him to be violent, he wouldn't know how to hurt somebody let alone commit murder.'

The general remained standing glaring, but Yuling sensed that his words had calmed him somewhat, though the fists stayed clenched on the desk.

The general snapped: 'Has the man got family?' and pushed the furled scroll towards his son.

'He has a mother, hers is the first signature on the People's petition,' Yuling replied watching the cadet open his scroll, the boy placing a glass paper weight at the top.

'She is an old woman,' Ho Chitian said quietly without taking his eyes from the floor, 'she would be distraught.'

Yuling was relieved his companion had spoken, and believed the general would have heard him.

'Huh! And the father, is he alive?' The general lent over to his son and looked towards the top of the scroll. 'Is the second name yours, priest?'

There was an unpleasant silence.

'I have never heard of a father,' Yuling replied, and looked enquiringly to Ho Chitian.

'I asked this man two questions, not you,' the general was now pointing, 'let *him* answer me! Do you know who the father is, priest, or was? Speak up!'

Yuling watched Ho Chitian, waiting for him to answer; but the face looked a picture of despair, and the head dropped further.

'I thought so!'

Yuling was thunderstruck, and turned to the general; the Slayer with a smirk on his face was staring at Ho Chitian.

'The name of your temple suits you priest, five concubines, huh! Who are the other four?' He smirked some more towards his private secretary, sat down at his high-backed chair, and looked at Yuling. 'Tell me then, who is this Doctor Chen?'

Yuling was still reeling from the discovery of Lam's father, and answered as best he could: 'He's my stepfather.' Now it was too late, he had introduced his mother, the very thing he had hoped to avoid. 'You may recall my father was killed in the north ten years ago. My mother married Doctor Chen a few years later.'

'Did she indeed!' The smirk had become a sneer.

Yuling tried to keep his own expression bland; he knew the audience was going disastrously, but said to himself that he had to keep going. 'My own petition begs that you exercise the great Chinese quality of...'

'That is *all!*' the general thundered, jumping up once more. 'I've heard and seen enough I tell you! The audience is at an end! Lee, these people will be informed of my decision shortly. They're dismissed!' The right hand shot out and he pointed to the far doors. Loudly he clicked his fingers, and the two soldiers started moving.

Yuling felt sick to the stomach. 'General, how will you know where to contact us?' he blurted out. 'We'll be at the monastery near...'

'Out! Out!' The face was puce as the soldiers came round the large desk towards them, bayoneted rifles held diagonally, Yuling turning fast and catching sight of the cadet holding the open scroll looking astonished towards his father.

'You have been dismissed,' the secretary said calmly as if unaffected by the bleak atmosphere. 'Go at once with the soldiers.'

Rifle butts prodded them none too gently. The moment was as dark, Yuling thought, as the blackout curtains they were pushed past.

A few minutes later they reached the main gates and heard the monks - still chanting prayers - waiting for them in the dark on the other side of the road. They were instructed to go through the door in one of the gates.

Once outside, the door was closed firmly, and they heard it being braced.

A wooden aperture opened behind a metal grill in the upper part of the door, and a guard's rough voice called out: 'I'm ordered to inform you, petition denied.'

The aperture slammed shut.

12

He stands rooted to the spot on paving stones just outside the main gates, hears the tiny priest's cry of despair and watches him fall to his knees. At first he disbelieves; the decision is so sudden, the guard is being mischievous or has made a mistake. But the words 'ordered' and 'denied' echo in his head, and a terrifying cold enters him, such as he has not felt since being lost in the hills.

Ho Chitian starts to weep. The monks have stopped their chanting.

Outrage wells up in Tsai Yuling, old monk Zen Yahan's recommendation that he seek a degree of mastery over himself having no place in his thoughts. He bangs the door with his fists as hard as he can and several times, then shouts: 'Open up, let me in again, I demand to see the General! Open up, guards!'

He stops the banging. Soon he hears laughter, it is near him on the other side of the gates. 'Go back to your books, scholar!' More laughter.

He looks around him through the dark, cannot see anything to help him, and walks fast along the high walls past the serpent tail of one of the chimera stone lions. A few paces further on and he feels with his foot some rock, it is partly embedded in the ground, and soon he is kicking and pulling at it, and it comes loose, is not too heavy.

He returns to the gates, and for all he is worth he bangs the chunk of rock against the door just below the closed aperture, then does it again, and a third time, each attack causing the door to shudder though he can tell it is too strong, he may only dent the wood.

He lets the rock fall to one side, goes back past the dark figure of Ho Chitian who is now standing, and runs at the door, hurling himself sideways causing a tremendous noise in one of the main gates as his shoulder and body crash into it.

He picks up the rock again regardless of the immediate pain and without seeing two monks taking the old priest back to their huddled group. 'Open up or I'll tear the door down!' he screams, knowing he has lost control, that what he is doing is a hopeless display of fury ...and very dangerous.

'Ha, you try!' comes the reply.

He smashes the rock against the door, again just below the grilled aperture, and continues to hit the wood with such force that splinters start appearing.

'Stop student or we'll shoot the lot of you!' he hears as he pauses for breath, letting the rock down on paving stones to give his arms a rest. The shoulder no longer hurts.

He can just see the biggest splinter, takes two long breaths, picks up the rock again, and aims in that area of the door, putting all his strength behind the blow and making another great noise, and the next moment the aperture is opening and a bayonet soon pokes through the grill.

'We'll shoot!'

'Move away, get down!' he shouts back to the group whose resumed chanting is noticeably louder. 'So you'd shoot monks and priests would you?' he yells towards the aperture before smashing the rock against the bayonet causing the gun to move violently and the guard to swear.

The bayonet is retracted, the aperture left open, and between his continuing strikes at the door where he thinks a hole might soon be appearing he can hear sharp talking.

Now bars are being removed. He moves a few steps to the side and bends low, rock still in hands. The door is pulled open, and through the dark comes first one guard and then a second and their heads are moving to search him out.

They see him and as they run at him, he is about to throw the rock at the legs of the first soldier when the man hits his left elbow with the flat side of a bayonet, causing him to cry out and let go of the rock which falls harmlessly onto the paving stones. He sees the bayonet of the second soldier coming straight for his middle, leaps to his right and manages to grab the gun, then knees the man in the groin making him cry out and double up, and as the guard loosens his grip on the rifle, Yuling wrenches it from him. The first soldier is doing something with his own rifle clearly intending to fire, but he smashes it with the rifle he has taken, lets the rifle fall and punches the soldier in the stomach, then hand chops at the neck, and as the man yells and collapses, he picks up both rifles and runs through the opening and slams the door.

No other soldiers come at him from the Guard House. Quickly he puts the rifles on the ground, finds a horizontal metal bar at the back of one of the main gates, and pulls it across the door, leaving the aperture open.

One of the guards outside the gates is cursing and calling out to be let in, and starts hitting the door, and between the bangs Yuling can hear continual cries of pain from the other man.

He checks one of the rifles and feels for a bullet; the safety catch is off, he aims into the night and fires, the gun vibrating in his hands.

A guard is calling out again and shouting that his colleague is injured, but Yuling doesn't wait, he runs with both rifles towards the only light there is - the inside of the Guard House still dimly lit by its corner lamp. He ducks to go in, pulls the door with his foot kicking it shut, leans the guns against a wall, feels a top bolt and pulls it over, and finds a bottom one, doing the same though it jams part way and he can't push it further.

He is well past the point of no return; his father was killed through the negligence of a Nationalist general, and now he has very likely signed his own death warrant, carried out by another White general.

He turns up the lamp, discovers a stack of bullets in a large wooden box on the floor, and as he checks which rifle needs reloading, he hears shouting and running feet and soon the bar is being removed from across the door in the gate.

More shouting ensues, it is coming nearer, the handle of his Guard House door is being rattled and someone is kicking the door.

'This is Captain Ma, what the devil do you think you're doing, student, unbolt this door at once, are you mad!'

Yuling's heart is pounding. 'I will *not*!' he shouts back holding one of the rifles. 'I'll shoot anyone who tries to come through.' Gritting his teeth, he aims at the base of the door and fires. His ears shatter, and he never hears the commotion on the other side as officer and soldiers leap away.

A few seconds later: 'You stupid idiot! Why are you doing this? We'll break the door down and you'll be killed.'

'Try me! Some of you will die as well.' He seeks for more breath. 'The General won't listen, tell him I *demand* to see him!' His voice echoes in the little room, and he can hardly believe his own words, it is as though someone else is shouting. 'He's condemned an innocent man, that's why. And tell Madame Huang before we all die, she'll be shocked.' He's glad he thought of her.

As soon as the audience had ended, and while the soldiers were escorting the student and old priest from the Study, the cadet had looked with concern at his father pacing up and down the side wall, but had not dared to speak. The secretary had resumed his position at the small table but had remained standing. Shanghan had been surprised at the harshness towards the elderly peasants, and frightened how angry his father had been with the student and priest. He remembered a little of the visit of Tsai Yuling six years earlier; seeing him again as a strong young man had impressed him, though he'd thought the talking back to his father had been very disrespectful and foolish.

When his father had picked up the inner telephone and ordered a guard to say that the petition was denied, he'd been shocked. And his father hadn't taken him into the annex and asked for his views as he usually did. 'Father...'

he'd begun, but a hand had flapped at him to stay silent, something that never happened before.

The boy knew he could say nothing more; he had looked down at the scroll starting to read the script more carefully. He was deeply affected by it. It begged for his father's wisdom and magnanimity, it said that many people in Tuxieng loved the simpleton, and it stated the petitioner's deepest belief that the gods had been with the simpleton when the man rescued him *from under the hooves of wild horses*. Holding the scroll open, the boy had then stood up and taken it to Secretary Lee whose face had remained impassive. 'Look at this, Lee,' he'd whispered hoping he wouldn't further anger his father who was continuing to pace the wall. The old retainer had taken hold of the scroll and studied it, and at one point the boy saw the eyes open wide, and guessed he'd reached the part that called his father *a great patriot for the motherland in the defence of Zhongguo against the Japanese*. After finishing reading, Lee had let the scroll furl, and placed it on his table but said nothing.

'Come! It's time to visit the ladies for a short while,' his father had finally said. Shanghan had followed him out, picking up the scroll from the table, guessing the secretary would not seek to stop him.

As father and son entered the lady's apartments, Madame Huang and the Mistress caught at once the serious expressions on their faces. 'Hua and I met Tsai Yuling and a number of East Gate monks at the main gates,' the lady said going towards them and addressing her husband. 'Do you remember him, my dear? A fine young man he has turned out to be. He told us why they have come. I trust they conducted themselves well?' But her husband's face turned to anger that sent a shiver of fear through her.

'On the contrary, the student was forward and insolent.' The general looked towards his daughter and back to his wife. 'He kept interrupting me, would you believe, and he said nothing to suggest I should overrule the magistrate.'

As his father spoke, Shanghan handed the scroll to Huihua, who unfurled it and turned aside.

For a brief moment the lady was taken aback, and wondered if she dare ask more. But remembering the mother's letter, she plucked up courage. 'I am truly sorry and very surprised to hear of insolence, most wrong of him, students can be so passionate.' She paused, but only for a second, and tried to smile at her husband, masking her anxiety to know the outcome. 'Nevertheless, I am sure you had the nobility of spirit to allow the man to live. Saving that boy's life was indeed an extraordinary act for a simpleton, much of southern China talked about it for months, and you will remember our children were thrilled to meet him.' She looked at Shanghan but thought about the Tsai mother, wondering if the woman's rebuff of her husband's advances had played a negative decisive part in his thoughts during the audience.

Huihua was so struck by the fine quality of the brushwork and the worthiness of its script that at first she did not take in her father's reply '…that the priest and student have already been informed, Magistrate Liao's verdict and sentence stand.' But she felt the atmosphere, soon realized what had been said, and looked up to see her mother's hand raised to her mouth. Huihua too was shocked; she was about to ask if her father had not been impressed by Tsai Yuling's petition, when they were startled to hear a single gunshot echoing through the night around the courtyard walls.

'Hurry, servants main staircase!' the general said giving his wife a short look, then turning and walking quickly out.

When the general reached the Study, he took up a loaded revolver and semi ran to the main doors of his mansion.

For emergencies, the ladies and Shanghan had practised going down to one of the basement rooms, where soldiers would guard them in case of assassination or kidnap attempt; they too had hurriedly made for the door.

'Don't know what's happening, General,' one of two guards answers, crouching at the top of the steps, rifles aimed into the blackness, 'the shots seemed to come from the outer courtyard or from outside the main gates.'

'Shots?'

'We've heard two, sir, the second was distant or muted, maybe a guard at the gates has seen someone suspicious and fired and been fired back at.'

There is quiet, and General Huang senses that the situation is not too serious or that the matter has been brought under control. He orders one of the guards to accompany him, and walks carefully in the dark down the wide marble steps thinking their pine cones black and rather forbidding. They pass through the inner courtyard and are about to descend the steps into the outer, when he sees two figures running towards them, one whose voice he recognises as that of his captain.

Though relieved to hear no Japanese spy has penetrated the grounds or Red partisans were trying something on, the general can hardly believe what the captain is telling him: that the shots and commotion were caused by the student, that the young man had attacked and overpowered two of his trained guards, taken their guns, locked them out of the sturdy gates, and seemed ready to commit suicide in the Guard House '…something about an innocent man having to die,' the captain adds, 'he's threatening to shoot if we break the door down, he's already fired one shot at us, and he's got ammunition in there, he's demanding to see you, and Madame Huang as well.'

'My wife! This is all I need just before I go off to the military council. Come Ma, we'll soon sort this out.'

As they march through the outer courtyard, the general thinks: How about this, I've unexpectedly got the witch, couldn't open her legs but I'll have the son, then how'll she feel? She's going to regret what she did...

On reaching the door of the Guard House he bangs with his fist. 'This is General Huang. Come out you scoundrel, unbolt or we'll break this door down and I'll personally shoot you!' He hears groaning somewhere behind him, looks back and can make out several soldiers; one on the ground seems to be holding his head. 'And I'll shoot you too!'

'General, please come away from the door,' his captain pleads from the side.

The general is not going to move.

'And I am the elder son of Captain Tsai Peijinn. My father and another man died carrying a wounded comrade, and I'm not afraid to die trying to save a man who carried me to safety and is wrongly accused. He is like a brother to me, General. If you storm this door, you'll have dead men around you.'

'You impudent devil! You'll be the dead one if you don't come to your senses, you hear me! Open up at once!' He bangs more.

'Slayer! Murderer of innocents, I'll shoot!'

'He's got two rifles, you must be prudent General, I urge you to move to the side, we can't have your life sacrificed for nothing, and as I assess the situation, he's a hot-headed student and right now he's willing to die and take you or me or any of us with him.'

Wise Ma. The general hesitates; if a bullet from the witch's son hits him, kills him... But nobody has ever dared call him that name, and if he hears that a captured Red has used it, the man has breathed his last. He moves only partly to the side, nearer to his best officer.

'What's that droning noise?'

'He's come with half a dozen monks from the East Gate Monastery.'

'Monks!'

'I don't think they'll leave until they know what's happened to him.'

General Huang thinks of the coach scene at Luchian; the woman's face was at the curtain, she was screaming at him in front of his men and all those people, her snake-like tongue lashing him when he should have been savouring the kisses... 'Why have you attacked my men and holed yourself up? Answer me! When I make decisions, everyone must accept them.'

The voice comes back a little resonating: 'Because for reasons I don't understand, General, you didn't give priest Ho Chitian and me a fair hearing, you wouldn't let me speak and you never read my petition.'

The general looks towards his captain. It was Ma, then a lieutenant, who

176

witnessed his humiliation at the coach; and here they are, Ma now a captain and he a general, and he is again being tested in front of the very same officer and in front of soldiers in his corps, not by the woman but by the son; the irony strikes him as worthy of a story from one of the classics. He hears: 'I need to impress on you not just the strength of our feelings for our friend that he was falsely accused, but the feelings of many in Tuxieng. If Fang Lamgang, he never hurt anybody and is mute, he can't speak General, couldn't defend himself in the court, don't you understand that, if he's executed there'll be an outcry. And because he rescued me and I have a duty to save his life. Wouldn't you fight for a man who saved your life? I'm sure your son would when he is older.'

Clever bastard.

He's not just recklessly brave, Captain Ma thinks, he's eloquent.

General Huang feels his captain's eyes on him. He hears his wife's words, her expectation of nobility of spirit. 'Is there anything else you want to say before my captain has this door broken down?'

'No General, you've now heard my points, a rifle's trained on the door and another's beside me.'

'*Don't* threaten me student!' He collects himself, anxious not to lose face in front of his men. 'I give you one last warning, Tsai. Put the rifles on the floor and surrender yourself.' The general hears his captain cough, and quickly looks his way. 'I'll decide what punishment is appropriate for your outrageous attack on my guards, and you'll be informed very shortly whether there is any change in my decision about this worthless man. You have ten seconds from now to obey or I'll have the door bashed in and you'll be dead.' As he nods to the captain and turns to the door, a vision of the witch comes to him - she is lying on the ground beating the earth in agonies of grief, beside the body of her son...

The voice comes back: 'I take that as your agreement as an officer, in front of your captain, to reconsider your decision, is that correct General?'

'You've had my last word, student.' The general clicks his fingers. 'One, two, three...' He is standing to one side of the door, his revolver pointing, he can hear Ma ordering soldiers to beat down the door, from the sides if possible, others to train their rifles '...eight, nine, ten...' He stops counting. Only the chanting of the monks can be heard. He holds up his left hand in the ready position and knows Ma can see it.

A bolt is being pulled, then a second making a clang, the door soon swings inwards, and Tsai Yuling's large figure, empty handed and partly lit by lamplight, ducks the door and comes out of the Guard House.

In the basement room, there was nothing for the family to do but wait until the all-clear sounded or a soldier came to tell them they could leave; the servants had gathered in a room nearby; one of them, head domestic Wang who had been a soldier, had a revolver.

In other emergencies Shanghan had noticed how calm his mother appeared, and tried to emulate her. His father allowed him to keep a loaded pistol in a niche in the wall, and the cadet had placed it beside himself on a nearby table.

'You must see this,' Huihua said, handing her mother the scroll. 'The quality of the parchment and the character script, it's beautiful and so powerful.'

The lady made no comment but began looking, and very soon she too felt its strength. When Shanghan thought she was finishing, he pointed to the part near the end ...*if not for your humble petitioner or the good citizens and peasantry of Tuxieng and districts, then for the spirit of your petitioner's father, who lies under wild violets in the Valley of the Heroes of the Twentieth Year...*

'What did your father say about this?' she asked him.

'He hardly unfurled it, I don't think he was reading it.'

She handed the scroll back to Huihua. Some ten minutes later the all-clear sounded, and they were relieved to return to the lady's apartments.

'The student!' exclaimed Madame Huang in disbelief when Huihua's maid began to tell them what she had heard, 'you mean Tsai Yuling! Where is he now?'

Huihua was also aghast, and wondered how her initial judgement of the student had been so wrong, and if he had become a Red.

'Been taken to cells, my lady.'

'Are the guards badly injured?'

'Heard one of them can't hold head up.'

The lady looked very unhappy. 'You must take a note at once to Lee, he is to hand it to my lord at the earliest opportunity, you understand Yiying, the earliest opportunity.' She moved to a table and began to write, her children watching without speaking.

Secretary Lee received back the scroll with the lady's note tucked under one of the white binds. He had learnt what had happened, and although very little surprised him any more, he admitted to himself that it was a most unusual occurrence, and feared to meet the general at that moment, knowing the Huang temper and thinking of his master's conduct at the audience with the Tuxieng petitioners. But the old retainer never dared disappoint the lady, often thinking she was more cunning than her husband.

He was therefore relieved when the general hailed him from the foot of the curving staircase leading to the Study, and he found him in a better frame of mind than he had expected.

'Thank you, Lee,' General Huang said receiving the scroll with its note which the secretary pointed out. 'I have told Ma to replace and discipline those guards, our training was faulty. If a student can entice soldiers out and beat them up...' He shook his head. 'We'll change our procedures. I'm angry with those men.'

'Naturally you are right to be, my lord. But in one sense, as you perhaps indicate, the young man has served a useful purpose?' Secretary Lee looked a little down and let a brief moment pass, feeling the general's eyes on him, before, without making eye contact again, he asked: 'Shall I now inform the magistrate of your decision against the petition, sir?'

General Huang did not reply. He removed his wife's note and went under a nearby oil lamp. He read it, and then untied the scroll's binds, fully unfurling the old parchment. He took in the exquisite brushwork and the graceful prose. He thought of his love of his province Fujian and his love and pride for his vast country, of its mountains and great rivers, its trees in blossom and rich silk gowns, its poets and temples, its fine women, yes its fine women - the student's mother did not come into his mind - and of its suffering, its fallen heroes, and its humiliation at the hands of foreigners...

> ...this scroll is fit for an Emperor, it calls you a great patriot, it says the people look to you my worthy husband to help throw out the invaders one day. It was for the generosity of your mind and the wisdom of a good governor that they asked for mercy for a simpleton, and so now do I, your most dutiful wife...

Secretary Lee waited.
'Has Wang my clothes ready for the journey?'
'I believe he has, my lord, three trunks.'

When the general handed back the petition, the note fell to the floor and he started up the stairs to the Study. His secretary bent down with difficulty and picked it up, none the wiser if the decision stood, though he expected it did. He would wait to ask again in the morning, at the latest shortly before his master left.

Shanghan, still wearing his cadet uniform, went to see his father, entering not through the embossed doors but the side door not far from the large desk. He found him deep in thought, elbows on the desk. He knew he was leaving them for many weeks, possibly even months, and each time they wondered if they would see him again if hostilities restarted.

'Ah, Shanghan!' the general said, 'I'm off to a military council and then exercises and further travel. The imperialists could be planning to grab more, though hopefully not in the immediate future.' He sighed. 'They are bad enough, but I loathe the Reds more, feeding the people with propaganda and false hopes. I've done my best to get rid of them and we've had much success, but they're entrenched in the mountains. Getting recruits from peasants and citizens is becoming more difficult.'

'We hate it when you go, father.'

General Huang looked anxiously at his son and thought of Japanese invincibility. 'You know what to do if it looks you're going to be attacked. The corps will fight where we're sent, and soldiers will escort you to the hills. You'll have an officer who you must obey, you should be safe there as it's not an area of any use to the enemy.'

The boy said nothing but felt apprehensive and sad. 'That wretched student's scroll,' his father continued, 'it makes me think what we have to fight for. In three years, when you're soldier age, may our fortunes be restored.'

'What is going to happen to the student?'

The Sung: short whip, back and front, upper and lower body, not head or privates, thirty lashes max, five mins duration.

The Mongol: long whip, whole body, fifty lashes max, ten mins duration, avoid death or pay docked.

Captain Ma, having seen soldier even officer material in the tall student, found himself very reluctant to carry out the general's order, and was relieved the category had not been stated. 'Sung,' he said, 'and don't overdo it, Guo.'

Corporal Guo, a pock-faced man, was not particularly disappointed. He didn't regard himself a cruel person when performing his task in the underground cells near the main gates - this happened to be one of his jobs in the general's corps. He was used to inflicting more Sungs than Mongols, though the Reds always got Mongols unless they immediately agreed to join the Whites. Many did and avoided their flogging; others cried out in the middle and agreed to join; and those who refused got their deserts. Occasionally he allowed himself to feel sorry for the victims, as some were only lads, and in those cases he let up a little, sometimes.

The first lash hit de-shirted Yuling in the middle of the back; it was so shockingly stinging that his left wrist jerked on the rope binding him to a ring in a damp crumbling wall; and when the next stroke came in the same area, it forced his lungs to empty; but before he could draw breath or collect any thought, the third hit further up between the shoulders near the neck and he yelled out.

More strokes landed, and soon it felt as if the whole of his back was alight; he could think of nothing but the firing pains or where the next stroke would come; he didn't think of his mother or his family or Lam or even the general, and crying out at each stroke was unavoidable.

But as further strokes came, he focussed on the flames of two flickering candles burning on the floor, and found his mind taken away, he was back at the lake, staggering from his grandfather's body, remembering the agonies of his burnt hand and his white-hot scalp ...and now in the cell he knew he had endured worse than the lashes. 'Go higher!' his grandfather called as the flogger turned to the backside and legs. He saw the black kites, their long wing-end feathers, and stopped his yelling, holding the birds in his mind, soaring with them and diving and rising again, never letting them out of his sight as he cried inwardly, silently, from the onslaught.

He was hardly aware that two soldiers had come into the cell, only that the beatings had stopped and that his hands were being released from the rings. Gasping, he tried not to fall lest they kick him. Manhandled up steps and into the open, he felt the night air against his face and realized they were taking him towards the main gates. When they reached the door that he had battered, he was pushed through and fell onto the paving stones.

A soldier shouted: 'That'll teach you student, good riddance!' The splintered door was shut, bars applied.

Monks ran over to him and began talking among themselves. Priest Ho Chitian tried to comfort him, and someone put a water flask to his mouth.

A few seconds later they heard: 'Monks, quiet!' It was a well-spoken voice calling through the aperture's grill. There was a hush.

'I'm sorry, the decision hasn't altered, the sentence stands.' A collective gasp went up. 'Tell the student that Captain Ma hopes he recovers soon.'

Yuling, on the ground, his body burning, heard the captain's words and heard the aperture being closed. Nobody moved. 'Ho Chitian,' he whispered '...can't get up, you've got to get to Tuxieng...' he tried to take in more air but the chest felt as if it was tightened by rope '...tell my brother Ayi ...chance you'll get there before No Mercy acts...'

'I'll go,' someone said quietly, 'I can run well and I know the roads and ways.'

Yuling could not turn over to see the young novice. And the smarting in his eyes had become full tears, for Lam more than the pain.

*

'I am going to the East Gate Monastery this morning,' Madame Huang said to her daughter in her deliberate way of talking, before sitting down to breakfast. It was two weeks after her husband had left them. 'We seem to have a welcome fresher day. Do you want to come with me, dear, and look at the gardens? I need to speak with Zen Yahan, I have not seen him recently, and he is getting very old. I want to pray with him for your father and for our country.' Before Huihua's birth, and then in the long five years before Shanghan arrived, the

Buddhist monk had been a tower of strength to her when she had despaired of having children and especially a boy ...I'll have a son elsewhere, her husband had threatened.

'Definitely I'll come,' Huihua answered, at once thinking of the student; she'd been overwhelmingly relieved to hear that he hadn't been shot - in fact the force of her feelings had surprised her. Captain Ma had assured her that the young man would recover from the flogging; and two days after it, she had sent her personal maid Yiying to enquire about him at the monastery without mention to her mother, and had sent her again a few days later.

Her mother caught the thought. 'If the unfortunate student has now departed, I would like to hear that he was not too seriously hurt and that he is recovering. I have been thinking of writing to his mother to let her know that I tried to get a reprieve for the simpleton. Maybe I shall also express my regret at the beating, I am not sure. He was most insolent to your father, and what happened afterwards to the guards was utterly unpardonable, however strong his feelings.'

'It was a good thing he was in the monastery and not taken back to Tuxieng,' Huihua said, thinking of Magistrate Liao's untimely death in the rioting reported a few days earlier, and also thinking that her father, or in his absence other KMT authorities, would have treated the student as a ringleader had he been with the rioters. She had asked the captain what had become of the simpleton, but he could not tell her because he had not heard.

Escorted by foot soldiers, they took sedan chairs through the woods and arrived in the middle of the morning. At the entrance to the monastery, the lady asked that Zen Yahan, her former confidant, be informed of their presence, and when the old man came shuffling along, she was shocked to see how much more bent he had become.

'You have aged, my dear counsellor, how *are* you these days?' she asked.

Zen Yahan tried to keep his head up but it soon dropped. 'It is so good to see you, my lady, a great honour that you should call on us. And to see Mistress Huihua, I rejoice, I rejoice! I am afraid I can hardly look at either of you for more than a second, let alone pay my respects with bows. But I am doing as well as the gods permit, and no day passes when I have not prayed for you all.'

'Do you still use the outer garden? You remember how much I love gardens, we used to sit and you listened and gave me your wisdom. Could we go there now? I would like my daughter to see the flowers at this lovely time of the year.'

The old monk smiled to the ground. 'It would be a pleasure.'

Slowly they went through an area of well-tendered palms, with water channelled to the base of the trees on either side of the path. He led them through an arch, and they came to the outer garden where he invited them to sit on seats in the shade of a bower.

'Has student Tsai Yuling left you?' the lady asked at once. 'We hope he recovered. It is sad to say, but he deserved his punishment, one of our guards is still seriously hurt at the neck.'

'That is bad to hear. Such violence can never be condoned, may the poor guard fully heal.' Zen Yahan moved his upper body from side to side, trying to get a better look at his important visitors. 'The student leaves us soon, he will be alright, his wounds are healing but they need more time.'

The lady looked at Huihua, and was about to say she was relieved, when he asked her: 'Did you see the scroll presented to your husband at the audience?'

'We did,' she replied with feeling, 'it was quite excellently done, and now you ask, I realize where it came from. We congratulate one of your colleagues for so wonderfully handling the brushes.' She knew the scroll had not worked to change her husband's decision, nor had her note to him, but the beauty and strength of the petition had greatly impressed her and her children.

The old monk craned his neck long enough to look up, and Huihua caught the twinkle and guessed.

'Aha, my gracious ladies! Then you have not realized, there has been the flogging of a young master of our ancient art.'

'The student!' the lady exclaimed as Huihua felt a strange joy and could not prevent a smile. 'I am truly astonished!'

'Not even our best calligrapher could have worked that parchment as Tsai Yuling did. Over one hundred years old, and it is as if the scroll has been waiting all these years for such a talent to appear, and for such a purpose, though alas it did not succeed.'

'I must say, mother, I wondered,' Huihua said, 'he was already a brilliant drawer as a boy.'

'Had it worked,' the old monk added, 'there would have been no loss of life. But at least the riots were short and I hear are over.'

'So the news travels through your monastery walls,' the lady said.

'All Mingon knows about it, I believe,' he replied, looking to the ground and thinking of the young novice, recently returned from Tuxieng with the student's mother, the information first hand.

Huihua wanted to ask about the fate of the simpleton, but her mother started talking about the past. Soon she was invited to leave them so that the two could speak privately. The old monk suggested she take a stroll through the lower garden and return in half an hour, after which they would enter the temple.

She wandered into the lower garden; it adjoined one side of the monastery. As she was admiring a trellis creeper of red trumpet flowers with long heart-shaped leaves, trying to name it, she heard what sounded like window glass being firmly tapped as if for attention. She looked up to the first floor from some thirty paces, and was taken aback to see the student behind one of the few windows with glass, a breathtaking smile flying towards her. Although hugely embarrassed and wondering how long he had been looking out - she had already been in that area about a minute - she found herself returning the smile, and her next thought was how he could smile at her like that when it was her own father who had ordered his punishment.

She composed herself, bowed short and quick, and turned round to the trumpet flowers, pretending to study the whitish stamen in one of the larger ones, while she tried to decide if to walk fast away the shortest route to be out of sight, or to continue meandering through the lower garden, if possible away from the view from the window. She knew he would not tap again, and sincerely hoped that he would not presume on her awkward position by following with his eyes. She decided on the casual departure. What she could *not* contemplate was to look up again at the building.

Why she *had* looked she could not explain to herself in her bed that night. But after just a few steps she had stopped, and she *did* look back up, and felt transfixed by another extraordinary smile, and she knew there and then that she could not have walked on even if she had told her legs to do so. For a brief moment, she had even imagined herself hovering close to the window pane. She had been unable, utterly unable, to divert her gaze when he mouthed some words, words she had not been able to make out.

Before screwing down the wick of her lamp, Huihua turned to the old wooden ceiling with its carvings of swans. He could easily have spoken loudly enough for her to hear. Why hadn't he done so if he was unable to open the window because of his wounds? She'd been brave, she thought, shaking her head to tell him she didn't understand. And then he'd turned away as if someone had come into his room, but while turning he'd looked back a last time and attempted what she took to be a bow, and only when he'd disappeared had the spell on her been broken.

Morning glory! The name of the trumpet flowers finally came to her as she tried in vain to sleep.

13

More than a year later

'Mother you'll hate it, it's really bad!' fourteen-year-old Shanghan exclaimed before going to meet his tutor. 'I look like a baby with hair. He's strange, I think he was frightened, he hardly spoke to me, it was so boring just sitting staring at the wall.'

A few minutes later Madame Huang took one look at the small portrait and bowed to the little artist without giving away her feelings. She signalled to Secretary Lee to follow her out, telling him to close the door. In the corridor she spoke quietly but firmly: 'That is not our good-looking young Master, is it? I am really disappointed I must say. We will need to think of something else for my husband. Kindly inform the man his work is unacceptable, it is not to my liking. Pay him a token and show him the door whether he complains or not.' She half turned. 'And Lee, it must be destroyed immediately.'

Huihua outright laughed when she saw the small painting the secretary was carrying, and quipped: 'My father would have put the Ming sword through this!'

That night she woke to a moment of artistic enlightenment. She loved to experience such feelings when they came, which she considered was not nearly often enough, and she always grasped them. In the darkness of her room with her window black-curtained against the escape of light, she felt animated - a poem about walking beside a lake, one she had given up months earlier as poorly constructed, began to reshape in her mind; words she had striven for now came easily. She lit a candle - she preferred its light to lamplight when in one of these moods - and grabbed the notebook.

Well after she blew out the candle a bird started singing; and although she peered behind the curtain and through the shutter to find it remained dark outside, the pleasure she felt from her success and the continuing racing of her poetic mind meant that she did not get to sleep again. As more birds began their pre-dawn songs, she knew she would soon submit her poem to Mr Shehan, the enthusiastic chairman of the Fujian Poetry Society. And she had a suggestion for her mother about the portrait idea - a thought that had come to her as she penned new lines describing the colours in the water near wild lilies overhanging from a riverbank. She did not expect her mother to take up the idea, but it was worth a try.

'Look at this, mother, do you remember, why don't we ask the art student Tsai Yuling?'

Huihua was standing at the breakfast swivel table handing her mother the drawing that had lain in her desk since she was twelve. 'He told us he studied portraiture. This drawing of father, it's still amazing, and he's bound to be even better now.' She sat on her stool, moved the swivel table so that the fruit bowl came round to her, and awaited the negative response.

'Ha! He is hardly likely to come after last year's drama and punishment, is he! Anyway, we need an artist of repute.' The lady looked at the drawing and placed it upright against a silver tray filled with dried lavender and late-flowering roses. She poured green tea into her tea bowl, and stared again at the drawing: yes, her husband was strong of mind and powerful-looking, though he had aged the last few years with the stress of wars; but the Tsai boy had caught him brilliantly.

She turned to her daughter. 'That scroll was inspired, I must admit. Well, maybe the idea is worth exploring, provided the university has full confidence in him and he comes quickly. Even better, perhaps they can recommend a portrait painter from the staff. But whoever comes must brave the planes, it is getting worse.'

When Shanghan came from an early clean of the horses and heard his sister's idea, he said: 'Father won't mind who the artist is so long as the portrait is good, unless Tsai Yuling is a Communist of course. He'll be surprised, that's for sure, but I heard Captain Ma talking with father saying he'd be a good soldier, so if he comes, maybe they can recruit him!'

'And all would be forgiven,' his mother replied without a smile, 'that would be a turnabout.'

Huihua said nothing. She couldn't forget what happened to her in the monastery garden, the bodily sensations she had experienced for many days afterwards, though once they stopped she put them from her mind. When her maid had informed her that Tsai Yuling had finally left the monastery, she regretted not having had the courage to try to see him, or at least to have written him a note to say she felt sorry about the flogging. And she certainly hadn't forgotten his childhood story.

She couldn't hide from herself that she would have been interested to talk with him about what was denied her in her restricted life. As a young woman there was no place at the few colleges operating inland away from the Japanese; and even if there had been, as the daughter of a Nationalist general - particularly her father's daughter - she would have been an obvious kidnap target, or worse, one for Red revenge.

She also felt that the student had unknowingly helped her in an agonizingly difficult decision. Eight years earlier, her future marriage into the influential Yang family, to the eldest boy, had been arranged. Yang had become a newly-commissioned officer though not in her father's corps; and when the families had met at the Court just two months before the monastery garden incident, she hadn't at all taken to her husband-to-be, he seemed arrogant and condescending, she was not impressed by his looks, and she had as tactfully as possible made her feelings known to him, though she thought he might not have understood her.

But her parents had seemed as keen as ever, and before the young man and his parents had left the mansion on the understanding that the families would shortly start to make the wedding arrangements despite war-time conditions, she told her parents that she was unhappy and not ready or ever likely to proceed with the commitment. Perfunctorily her father had replied: 'Daughter, you will do your filial duty, you could not have a better marriage, and your mother and I will be speaking shortly to the Yangs about the details. Only a Japanese attack coming this way can prevent the union.' Just a few weeks after the monastery garden incident, she had summoned enough courage to tell her parents that she could no longer agree to marry the officer. 'I simply do not like him,' she said. When each parent became angry, she'd cried out to them: 'I don't care how old a family the Yangs are or how many presents we've exchanged.' Then, horribly, her father had struck her, shouting that she was '...a headstrong, disobedient, disloyal girl, an unworthy daughter...' and she had fled the room.

The student had helped her because, during that heart-searching period before telling her parents, she had sometimes thought of his astonishing smile at her from the monastery window. Not because she yearned to meet him again - she did not, she had later felt some surprise at his presumption, although she admitted to herself that she'd been in a flutter at the time - but because it helped her to realize that she could only accept a husband who she knew she loved or felt she could come to love, and most importantly could trust. She admired her father for many reasons, but not the philandering she heard about through different sources; she was not going to suffer as she knew her mother had suffered. In any case, Yang was not one of the three men she might have considered as marriage partners, names she was eventually forced to divulge. She was at once informed that none of those three were acceptable, that they did not come from a comparable family.

*

'No! He killed my friend, never!' Yuling was standing in a corridor at his college, rudely shaking his head, knowing he'd gone much too far, had virtually shouted into the face of his favourite professor while other students looked on astonished. But to return to Wuyi Court would be a betrayal of Lam, shot by one of the prison guards in No Mercy's presence within a minute of the crowd reaching the Tuxieng prison. And the magistrate and two guards had been hacked to death. Yuling's fiery brother Ayi had been in the thick of the riots, rallying citizens and peasant farmers, though luckily had not been at the storming of the prison. When their mother had come to the monastery to help Yuling recover and to break the news, he'd wept in her arms, at one point hearing her crying back '...I'm to blame Alinga, I've caused Lam's death by standing up to Huang at the coach, and he saved my own son's life...' At that moment he'd never held to his mother so tight, despite the discomfort of some of the lacerations, for he loved and admired her above all others. Later she'd said: 'You're my gentle giant, happy and calm unless roused beyond endurance. How could you two be so different. Ayi's so fervent and excitable, he worries me terribly.'

Professor Koo Guanglu, a small man with a grey goatee, looked hard at his student, had never seen him like this before, only knew him as a respectful, warm-hearted young man though he knew there was steel under the quiet exterior and that he went his own way artistically.

He kept his own composure. 'Your friend's death was dreadful, but you must put that behind you. It says the General's on exercises, he won't be there, he'll...'

'He's a tyrant, he's got with more Chinese blood on his hands than the Japanese dogs themselves.'

'Tsai Yuling, I can't let you turn this invitation down. Do it for the honour of the university, and think about the money, it could make your repu...'

'No, no! You forget he had me flogged!' Part of Yuling still felt crushed from the flogging, scarred inwardly and not just on his body.

The senior art professor started to feel anger, partly at the unexpected interruptions and disrespect and in front of other students nearby, but also at the student's blindness.

'I do *not* forget. The Principal has received this letter, we will not let Madame Huang down, she has asked for you personally and I can hazard a guess why, some feeling of guilt no doubt, and if you're so stupid not to do it, one of my staff will.'

Silence.

Professor Koo waved at the students to go away, and they turned. He softened his tone. 'Did you meet the boy?'

'The boy? Not meet but I saw him.'

'And would he make an interesting subject?'

Yuling's mind took him back to the audience the previous year, picturing the cadet sitting beside his father, and also to the brief meeting with the ladies beforehand in the Guard House. 'Yes, so would his sister...' He checked himself, had not meant to mention Huang Huihua.

'His sister!' The professor detected something in the eyes. He placed a hand on the young man's shoulder. 'Then go and do the portrait and do one of her on the side! And you're not going to be meeting the man, that's the main thing. You would be a real real fool not to accept, it's the biggest opportunity I've ever known come a student's way.' He stroked his goatee and giggled. 'And do it a little for me, I would be so proud. You can have my best oils and brushes and repay me from your commission. If you go immediately, you'll be back in three weeks, and I've already spoken with Lecturer Yin, he's very excited for you and says you must grasp the opportunity. We're early into the academic year, he says you should take the main Japanese textbook with you, and he can soon bring you up to date on what you've missed.'

Yuling thought of the commission he would earn, and remembered the colonel's silver coins in the small box opened on the sampan; they had greatly helped his mother; she had eventually told the family that she treated the colonel's *benevolence* as the military repaying her for the loss of her husband, and the horrible man for what he put her through.

He thought again of the sister. Since the flogging and her sprite-like appearance below him in the monastery garden, he had often found himself thinking of her, usually when he was with female company near the campus at Suodin, and had wondered to which lucky officer or rich family she was promised. He knew the reality was that he would never be able to get near her, and in any case he wouldn't want to for long, it was unimaginable, she had the Slayer's blood in her.

But he could dream, and had done so many times after that fateful audience trying to save Lam. When he was about to go to sleep, sometimes he imagined himself in the middle of a line of fine young men, some extremely handsome and all in military uniform except himself. She was moving slowly and stopping at each man, looking into the eyes to choose which one to take with her; and when she looked into his, it was as if she knew him of old yet was insisting on searching his inner thoughts, demanding his submission before she moved on;

and as she came back along the line, he already knew two or three officers away that she would be stopping at him, she always stopped in front of him, and put her gentle beautiful hand on his shoulder...

He felt the professor's firm hand still on his shoulder. 'You will do it, my best student, you must delight Madame Huang with a western-style portrait, and you won't make the paint too thick, will you, because don't forget you've got to varnish, and you can't wait too long for the paint to dry as you must come back to us. I am going to lend you my light-red Japanese sash, I bought it in Tokyo years ago, that'll make you feel good and it will impress Madame Huang. I have the fullest confidence in you, Tsai Yuling. And think of your mother, she'll be so...'

'My mother!' He'd interrupted again, though in a different mood. 'She'll be shocked if I go back to the Huang mansion, and my brother will say I'm turning into a White. I must think about this, I'm not saying I'll do it.'

Sixteen months after leaving Wuyi Court on the monks' stretcher, Yuling made the journey back to Mingon, this time taking boats at night, as day boats were rare, the enemy having shot up and sunk a number though they had not wasted bombs. It was late September 1942. There was distaste in his mouth at what he was doing, and not a little fear; he would get the job done to the best of his ability, and leave fast.

On reaching the town he went straight to the East Gate Monastery, where he was warmly greeted, but sad to be told that old Zen Yahan who gave him the scroll had journeyed to the next world. He remained for an hour.

In a sombre mood matching the dark clouds of the early afternoon, and deciding to risk walking in the open knowing no planes would fly in such weather, he made his way through Mingon's ancient Great Gate, and started along the road.

Half way to the mansion the heavens opened. He tried to seek shelter in a wayside shack, but found parts of the roof broken and he was drenched in no time, the rain pouring over his doli as he huddled in a corner. He knew that the few clothes and sandals in his heavy sack would get wet, though the brushes, his name chop and its little paste box would be safe, as would be the paint tins. He keenly hoped that the Japanese textbook in a towel, and the inside pages of an old drawing pad he had wrapped in a small bag at the bottom of the clothes, would avoid getting soaked. He had flicked through a number of his old drawing books, and did not know why he had picked up the very pad he'd used in Doctor Ya Ya's hospital, except that it still held some clear pages which he thought he could fill; he'd rarely looked into it, as the panther drawing remained an unpleasant reminder, though he hadn't torn it out.

The hard rains abated to a drizzle, and he walked the rest of the way in the steamy atmosphere of a sodden landscape.

Approaching the large winged lions, he felt very uncomfortable, less from his soaked state than from the thought that the two guards who had rushed at him might be there. He prayed they were not on duty. It had been dark on the previous year's visit, and the fight with the two men had happened so quickly that he was sure he wouldn't recognise them, though they would know him because he was big.

The piece of rock he'd hurled at the door still lay on the ground some way along the wall, a high wall dripping dark red streaks from the rains.

He knocked hard on a new door in one of the gates, and after calling out, he was very relieved when the guard who peered through the grill did not recognize him. But probably because he looked wet, he had difficulty persuading the man that he had been invited, and a call had to be made before he was allowed through.

'So you're one of the elite then, are you student,' joked one of the guards, 'come along professor!'

'The General's not here is he?' he asked low-keyed as they walked along the middle path of the outer courtyard. 'Nay,' was all he got, but it was enough. He engaged the man in a little talk, and learnt that somewhere in the nearby woods was a military camp, hidden, about twenty minutes from the Court.

Yuling's journey fears back to Mingon seemed to disappear on reaching the inner courtyard and seeing the mansion again with its red tiled roofs that he thought resembled the wings of a great bird. He knew that in accepting the commission he was seriously challenging himself; and if he succeeded ...the remuneration ...the start of a career as the professor had said. The palms and especially the fine dark-leaved cypress trees he recalled from his childhood visit still looked magnificent even in their wet state. Huh, he thought, these don't reflect the man; he knew that for the ancient Chinese, cypress trees on a person's property were symbols of the owner's high principles and sublime spiritual power.

He was escorted to the basement, where a middle-aged man in servant's apparel met him and introduced himself as Wang the head domestic, leading him to a room that he was informed was to be his sleeping room for his stay. 'I'm the valet, waiter, now dogsbody since the invasion when half the servants were dismissed,' the unsmiling man said opening the bedroom door, 'surprised you're here after what I heard. Did they forgive you then?'

He didn't think he had to answer. 'All my clothes are soaked, do you have a warming room, please? And if I could have a spare pair of old trousers and a shirt until my clothes dry...' He didn't finish because the head domestic was looking him up and down.

'You're tall but I'll see what we have. You've got yourself a task, student, Madame Huang's hard to please.' The man nodded and left.

Yuling unpacked, relieved to find that the inner pages of his hospital drawing book had not been damaged, though there was dampness along the edges of the cover.

He heard feminine chatter coming along the passage, and soon there was knocking at his door. He opened it to find two maids giving short bows and then staring at him; one was quite pretty, who he guessed might be in her late twenties, the other younger and thin and he thought he recognized her from his visit as a boy.

'Oooh,' the older one exclaimed with a twinkle, 'have we been in the Pearl River!' The thin maid put a hand to her mouth to suppress giggles. 'Here,' the first one said handing him some clothes, 'head domestic Wang has found these for you, do you think they'll be large enough? Let's have your wet things then.'

He caught their mood, smiled back and took the clothes, glad to feel dry material. Without speaking, he raised his eyebrows in expectation they leave, and when they made no move, he indicated with a hand and slowly closed the door. No sooner had it shut than the older maid called out: 'Be quick about it painter, we haven't got all day.' When they departed there was more giggling.

The dry clothes were short and tight and he had difficulty getting them on. He wondered if to ask for larger ones, but decided not to risk more ribaldry. When they came back and he opened the door to hand over his damp clothes including the spares he'd brought, both maids looked wide-eyed before shrieking at each other.

'My, those bulges!' the older one exclaimed taking hold of the clothes. They giggled again, he closed the door firmly on them feeling distinctly self-conscious, and as they started back along the corridor, he heard: 'We'll return before supper, or you can keep the new clothes, painter, if they don't pop!'

In the late afternoon and wearing again his own clothes, he was taken into an annex of the kitchens and given a bowl of black tea. He was told that the incident the previous year had caused a great stir, and the two guards had been sent to defensive duties not far from the enemy, inland of Amoy. He was to present himself to Secretary Lee, and Wang the head domestic would take him there. No one mentioned the general's daughter, and he was too nervous to think much about her, other than to hope she might pass his way during his time there, if she hadn't married and gone elsewhere.

The secretary gave a quick bow and greeted him coldly. 'Good thing you were not involved in those riots, young man, or you would not be here, or in this world for that matter. If Tuxieng had not been an important recruiting area, there would have been serious reprisals.'

Yuling's culture and upbringing made him want to show unquestioning respect to the old man; but he was incensed at the comment, though had half expected something of the sort from the Slayer's private secretary.

'My friend was completely innocent,' he replied with feeling. 'Is it Nationalist policy to condemn an innocent and handicapped person?'

Eyebrows rose, and Yuling awaited the angry rebuke.

'You had better not repeat that here, or you will be sent away faster than you can run. You could not have expected the governor to change his decision, not after your outrageous conduct.' The brows returned to normal, and the man cleared his throat. 'Be that as it may, it is behind you. Now, as to why you are here, I trust a much better portrait of Master Shanghan will be produced this time, as the previous artist's work was lamentable, I had to burn it.' The old retainer then paid Yuling a compliment. 'If you reach the same standard as that scroll you produced,' he pointed to shelves containing many papers and scrolls, 'you should have a chance of satisfying her Ladyship.'

Evening had come early, though there was still light outside. The heavy clouds had gone leaving a thinner cloud cover. But the window in the room the secretary took him to called the Painting Room seemed small, and the furniture consisted of only a single chair and a low table. There was a good-sized easel, and a small canvas leaning nearby against the wall.

As Yuling was turning the canvas round, the secretary asked: 'Is there anything else you need? The young Master will attend in the morning for one hour at ten, between tutorials. Be sure he is released, otherwise Tutor will be angry with you.'

'I will need him for two or three sittings,' he replied. 'And there's only this little window, it's going to be too dark for me in here. Is there another room I could have?' The old man in his black gown looked startled, so Yuling added: 'Please could you ask Madame Huang. And I will need a much higher table for Huang Shanghan to sit on, or a very tall chair, and a much bigger canvas, three times the size of this.' He nodded to the small canvas.

The secretary frowned. 'I feel obliged to point out, young man, that in all my fifty-six years of dutiful service to the Huang family, this has always been the Painting Room, and no doubt shall ever remain so. You are the first to complain, and it will not be taken well.'

Yuling was receiving a look expecting him to retract. 'It's important to me,' he said.

The frown changed to mild surprise. 'Very well. Remain here. I will return, but it will not be the news you want.'

'Another room, Lee!' the lady said, calling down the inner telephone that hung from her wall. 'Certainly not! You can no doubt arrange a different table and a canvas, I like the idea of a bigger picture, that horrid one was on the small side. My husband will appreciate a bold one to hang up, if the student can produce something good that is.' She listened, then spoke louder into the mouthpiece. 'I said tell him *No*.'

Ten minutes later Secretary Lee had to use the telephone again. 'I am afraid, my lady, he is insistent about changing the room. Might I disturb by requesting that your Ladyship speaks with him yourself, he would naturally take a No from you.'

Yuling felt nervous again. He had been surprised when the secretary came back with the lady's refusal, and from what the man said, it was clear he'd immediately made himself unpopular. A nasty feeling of inferiority overcame him, so he thought of his father and grandfather, each loved and admired. He looked out of the small window, remembering the last time he was in the mansion. He pictured the old couple coming from the audience room, the woman crying, just before he and priest Ho Chitian were led into the Study by the secretary to petition the general.

He heard the steps outside the room, turned, and saw first Madame Huang and then Secretary Lee enter.

'Ah, Tsai Yuling,' the lady called out, 'we meet again, in happier circumstances I trust.' As he made his bow, she walked in little steps towards him, and when she stopped she gave him hers before saying: 'I tell you at once, we will not refer to last year. I am grateful that you have come, and speedily. I hope the journey was uneventful.'

'Thank you, my lady, it was, except for the rain on the last part.' He was glad she did not want to talk about the audience with her terrifying husband, or about what followed especially in Tuxieng, as he might not have been able to hold back his pain over Lam.

The lady seemed not to hear him. 'I am told you are asking for a different room, is that right? Surely not necessary, this *is* the Painting Room.'

'I know. But if I'm to give of my best, I must have a bigger window that allows me more light.' He conjured up little Professor Koo standing beside him and felt bolder, was on his own artistic ground. He turned towards the window. 'I can paint a portrait in a room with no window, only lamplight, but the one I have in mind will use natural light, which for a young face is much the best.' Now he felt he had her attention. 'Can you please give me a two-window room, or one with a much larger one? I know it's evening now, but I still think this room will be too dark in the morning, and I believe it faces north.'

Madame Huang found herself admiring the young man's points and strength of purpose; he had already shown his will the previous year though in quite the wrong way. And yes, her excellent son should be painted in the light of the day. She looked closely up at the tall broad student. 'So you think you can do a suitable painting of my son, a family present for my husband?'

Quickly he put the general from his mind. 'I believe I can. I remember your son has youthful nobility in his face. But I must be given the right conditions to work in, because if I feel unhappy I might fail and then I would be unhappy for you. I don't want it to be an old-fashioned picture where the light is dim and the background dark.'

Madame Huang maintained her gaze. 'You use the "must" word too often!' She looked at the secretary, guessing his thoughts but knowing he would do her bidding. 'Lee, the window is rather small for this room, I must agree.' She allowed herself a wry smile at her own unintended use of the word. 'Can we show our visitor the empty guest rooms overlooking the water garden, they do not face north do they? Let our friend choose, then he will have no excuse if he produces poor work, which we earnestly hope he does not.' She came back to the student. 'One thing. Your Principal categorically states you are not a Red, a member of the Communist Party, is that right? I require a truthful answer.'

Yuling had prepared for such a question, intending to mix truth with evasive assurance: he was in a potentially dangerous place in a Nationalist general's ex-warlord mansion. 'My sympathies are with them, but no I'm not a party member, you have my word.'

The lady pursed her lips. 'What is there to sympathize about? They espouse disorder leading to anarchy under the guise of helping the proletariat, a horrid word, and they call for revolution, we certainly do not want that.'

Yuling managed to keep eye contact despite feeling he was looking feudalism in the face. 'Their aims are the right ones, to save the nation from the Japanese, never to be humiliated by foreign powers again, and to help the masses to a better living, especially the peasants.' He thought surely she couldn't object to what he had said, though he didn't dare add that the Whites lined their own pockets and were the last people to help the poor of the countryside and in the towns; nor could he tell her his hatred of the generalissimo Chiang Kai-shek, who he considered had betrayed Sun Yat-sen's revolutionary principles.

'I understand you take part in anti-government street acting. This greatly surprised me I must say, and I tell you it nearly made me change my mind about offering you this commission.'

So they knew about him. The university must have passed on the information, though he couldn't believe Professor Koo would have volunteered any; or maybe she had contacted the Kuomintang police. What else was she going to ask? Surely they couldn't know about his poster-writing activities, the posters put up secretly by friends, often at night, around Suodin, the town housing his wartime campus; the posters railed against the corruption of the

Nationalist government in non-occupied China, and against Chinese quislings running eastern cities under the Japanese including Amoy. Did she know about his brother Ayi's even stronger pro-Communist views, from Kuomintang police or agents in Tuxieng?

But she hadn't asked a question, so he inclined his head and tried to smile innocently into the white-powdered face of wealth and power and, so far as the lady's husband was concerned, oppression.

'Many of us think of the poor, the masses as you call them,' she continued, 'we help them more than you realize.' The lady put firmness back into her voice. 'I trust they told you my condition, do not break it. You must not in any way discuss the political or military situation with my son. Do you accept that?'

'Certainly,' he replied giving a nodding assent, greatly relieved the conversation could be ending. 'I have come to paint.'

'Very well.' She turned. 'Lee, make sure you show our no-more-than-sympathizer friend the servants main staircase to the basement, in case the air alarm sounds.'

'We did have fun with painter, and he's so big!' thin maid Yiying with the strong accent told her Mistress that same evening. 'Came all soaked, looked like bedraggled hen! Spare clothes didn't fit, they were far too small, we thought they were going to burst all over him!'

Huihua laughed. She had felt enormously pleased and surprised to hear that Tsai Yuling had come back; she had been almost sure he would not, that an art teacher from his college would be sent, someone she would be keen to talk to about him - her short prayer had been answered. Now she much looked forward to meeting him, to finding out what his life was like, to talk with him about his studies. And she wanted to ask about the simpleton, though she had not decided how to do it; she knew that the magistrate had been killed in the riots, but her mother did not know about the simpleton; and in front of Captain Ma her father had abruptly stopped her further enquiry, telling her the matter was closed, best not looked into by ladies, and she was not to refer to it again.

The following morning, half an hour before Shanghan was due to appear, Yuling set up the room he had chosen. Good daylight though not sunlight came through the two windows. He felt some surprise that he was beginning to enjoy the experience of being in a Nationalist mansion, and the staff had told him that their master would not be returning while he was there.

And he was pleased with the height of the sturdy pear-wood table the secretary had arranged, and with the size of the larger canvas.

He placed his palette board, oils tins, brushes and rags on the smaller table, and began to think about some of the portraits he most admired in his studies.

When the fourteen-year-old was brought to him by the tutor, he was even more pleased to find that his subject had retained what he had seen at the previous year's audience: an aura of youthful self-assurance, a promise of potential fine manhood; the lad was already beginning to look quite sturdy like the father, and Yuling thought he was sure to follow into the military. The tutor, a man in middle age, gave a firm directive to release the young Master after an hour.

He instructed him to sit towards the end of the table. 'I want you to look out of the nearest window, not down to the garden but a little upwards towards the higher branches of the tree.'

'Don't you want me to face you?' Shanghan asked with surprise. 'That's what the other man did.'

'Not square on. What I want is to paint you looking to your future, it will be good hanging on a wall, believe me.'

Yuling immediately set to work. 'We can talk, it doesn't disturb me, just don't move your head much unless you have to, and tell me any time you want a break. Sometimes I'll ask you not to move your eyes or your mouth. And for the next session, could you bring that tunic you were wearing when I came last year.'

'My cadet uniform? Yes, good! I'm glad we can talk, the other man didn't want me to.'

With thinned blue paint mixed in turpentine, Yuling was soon mapping out the position of the head and its main features, while the boy talked about his love of horses and how his favourite had just become lame in a leg.

Early on he was asked about his bad time in the hills, but he skated over it, telling him only about the two snakes he had seen, the curled cobra and the green snake he had followed by a stream; and about Meibei, though he couldn't talk about Lam.

'My sister says you became famous because of your adventure,' the boy said.

'It was no adventure,' he replied applying brush strokes in the area of the chin, picking up at once that the sister might well be in the building. 'My grandfather died and I nearly did too.' He came away from the canvas and looked up. 'I prefer not to think of it, you're putting me off, we must talk about something else, what other interests do you have?'

*

She walks quickly towards the old guest rooms, stopping at the one Secretary Lee said had become the temporary painting room. She listens but hears nothing, wondering if the old man gave her the wrong room. She opens the squeaking door to half way, and is pleased to find her brother sitting on a high table with his back to her; she sees the profile of the right side of his face, and he is looking out of the window.

'Do I disturb?' she asks, opening the door fully, then closing it as it squeaks more, and taking in that the student is standing somewhat bent on the other side of an easel, the back of a sizeable canvas facing her at an angle.

'Hua, come and join us,' her brother calls without looking round. 'It's so much better! I can look outside at the tree and the sky and see part of the walls, and we can talk though we're not doing so at the moment.'

Huihua stays near the door, at first startled that the student has not looked up and acknowledged her presence with an immediate bow, or at least with a short greeting. He appears engrossed, no doubt applying paint with a brush she cannot see because the canvas is in the way. She cannot help notice the broadness of the shoulders and the thickness of the open lips.

'That's good!' she hears him exclaim while still not looking up, as he moves back a step and seems to examine the upper part of the canvas. She becomes alarmed; this is appalling etiquette, or lack of it, she feels really disappointed to find that the student is ill-mannered. Is he coarse as well?

When he looks over his painting, she lifts her head and waits for the bow before she will give hers - their different positions in society. But he is looking at her as if dazed or dazzled and in a manner quite outside her experience. It doesn't come into her mind that he also failed to bow when he visited as a boy, because the look she is now receiving is altogether different. Occasionally she has been gaped at before, but never in this way; officers nearly always conduct themselves properly, knowing whose daughter she is; and civilians are respectful, aware of her standing, her family. When a man looks at her - especially the first look - she can usually tell if he likes her appearance and will conduct himself correctly, or if something presumptuous is going through the mind, when she might need to ignore or even rebuff (she can do either) or retire. The student is not a man of standing, yet he dares to stare in a way that tells her she has greatly impressed. Obviously he has never met a young lady in her position; and sadly (she thinks) they have grown far apart since their enjoyable meeting as twelve-year-olds.

Why won't he give her a respectful bow? And Shanghan has now turned his head to her. Well, she will show Tsai Yuling. Still near the door, she makes a dignified bow, and immediately there flows into his face that broad smile she saw from the monastery garden, so warm and natural, and again it takes her breath away.

Yuling's eyes had been fixed on his canvas when he heard the door being opened. He'd been thinking he would soon tell his fine-looking subject about his best friend at college, a cartographer student. He had moved from the mouth to the front hair, and hadn't realized who had appeared in the room, was determined not to be deflected from the next few strokes, not by any member of staff including the tutor or officious old secretary.

But the instant he heard the voice an overpowering feeling of wonder and joy passed through him …don't stop even if she's the angel, got to get this quiff right, it's so unusual, *got* to before looking at her, this side of the head is so fantastic in the light, specially the forehead, don't look up… He was holding his breath as he applied the brush, two short careful strokes.

He breathed out and looked over the easel and felt immediately in awe, whose daughter she was never entering his mind: loveliness, aristocracy, character shown in face and bearing, only an actress playing a court role came near. He took in the head held with authority but dignity, marvelled at the shiny yellow robe, neck-clinging and buttoned down the left side, and loved the dangling turquoise earrings and a silver white broach at the collar. The light from one of the windows was catching the hair in a sheen on one side of her head, the hair turned up at the sides and the back to be held in clasps the form of flower-motifs at the top of the head, though a curling strand fell enticingly down the left cheek, reaching slightly over the collar. He felt like pinching himself that he was looking at her, and knew she *had* to stay in the room: the student, the painter, the boy who dreamed at the boulder, each now thanked the gods that he'd come back, that the professor and cartographer friend had persuaded him. 'Hua' her brother had called her; the name was perfect, she was indeed a flower.

'Oh what magic!' she hears him say when he moves to the side of the canvas. He is wearing a faded red sash round his waist, one she has never seen on a working man, and she doesn't think it is Chinese; very becoming she admits to herself as she tries to ignore the comment, the compliment maybe. She walks towards him feeling relief when he begins his bow to her; it is unusually slow, and she finds herself inwardly smiling, seeing a palette board in the left hand and a brush in the right descend with the upper body and wondering if the oil paints she can smell might drop from the board.

And two other thoughts come: that the student's unusual boldness is novel, his initial stare not meant rudely, and that a man's smile, no the whole face, can sometimes be beautiful, a theme perhaps for a new poem.

'We are pleased you have come, Tsai Yuling, I fully expected you to decline, so did our mother.'

'We'd have understood,' Shanghan chips in.

The smile vanishes. 'It was too good a challenge,' he replies looking to her brother. 'And what happened is in the past, or that's what Secretary Lee said, and that's how I must try to think of it.'

'Ah yes, I was going to ask you,' her brother says, 'we never heard about the man you were pleading for, I hope he lived.'

Huihua sees sadness come into the eyes, and as the student looks down she guesses the worst - had long done so after her father's words - and regrets the timing and bluntness of her brother's question. She is about to say that he need not answer, when he says to the floor: 'He was killed.'

'Oh no!' Shanghan exclaims, Huihua feeling a stab of pain.

'Murdered by guards in the prison on No Mercy's order.'

'Murdered!' The boy looks horror-struck.

The student adds: 'They got their just deserts, including the magistrate.'

Huihua catches her brother's eye in an unpleasant silence. She sees the student turn to his canvas as if in pain and anger.

'I'm truly sorry,' she says quietly in his direction, knowing what he must have felt for the simpleton, and what he would think of their father. She wonders whether the time is right to tell him that she had so wanted the petition to succeed, and especially that she hated he was flogged. For months afterwards, she had felt that what had happened to him had somehow hurt her too; she could not explain the feeling, other than to think that his childhood story was so extraordinary, and that in some way she had participated in it or rather had been affected by it through his visit as a boy. But she adds nothing more, not wanting to cause further pain and awkwardness.

Her brother moves the subject. 'My sister had the idea to invite you to paint me.'

The student comes away from his thoughts, and gives her a rueful smile, in which she wants to read some gratitude but she is uncertain. She says: 'Please do continue, I would like to watch for a few minutes. I have never seen a portrait artist actually at work.' She begins moving towards the easel, but to her surprise the expression turns to one of fright, and he comes forward as if to bar the way.

'I'm sorry,' she hears, agitation in the voice, 'I never like to be watched from behind or the side.'

Huihua is astonished. The simpleton and her sympathy leave her, the student is being strange, difficult again, she finds his directness or whatever it is no longer novel - people are dutiful and respectful to her, she's not used to being told she cannot do something, except by her parents, certainly not something perfectly normal and in her own home. Her mood changes and she is about to protest, when he adds still looking worried towards her: 'But I want you to stay, your presence will inspire me.'

Now he's gone way above himself, has become much too forward in speaking to her in that manner and in front of her brother. She feels unhappy at the sudden turn of events.

Shanghan says enthusiastically: 'Come and sit with me Hua, the table's strong.'

'Excellent idea, it'll hold you both,' she hears with further surprise as she throws her head back and half laughs towards her brother, knowing it will be very difficult in her tight-fitting robe to get herself up onto such a high table. Was the student somehow challenging her? She glances at him. He is looking with that disturbing full smile again, the smile that lacks any deference let alone proper thought towards a woman's feelings. Then he says to her: 'The three of us can talk together though not about politics, and please, not when I ask for quiet.'

She watches with apprehension as he puts down the palette board and brush, wipes his hands on a cloth and gestures her to the table. Her brother is looking at her expectantly, and the next moment she finds herself walking towards Shanghan past the back of the easel with the strangest sensation that someone else is propelling her.

She puts a hand on top of the table and knows at once with relief that she cannot jump up and that they would realize it. But before she can move to the side, the student is in front of her, much too close, she cannot believe it but his hands are going round her waist, and now she is rising to the table as if effortlessly, and her left hand is holding his bare forearm to balance though she doesn't need to.

A great flush comes over her as she removes her hand. She sees her brother's expression turn from surprise to sheepish pleasure, and tries to smile back at him but can't. There is a short silence with the student still in front of her, looking at her though she isn't looking at him.

'Now you can include my sister in the painting, Tsai Yuling!' her brother is saying while her inner turmoil gives her away; she had caught the student's amused expression as he was lifting her. 'That would surprise our mother and please father even more!'

'The naked feet would be another challenge,' she hears the brazen artist joke or half joke as he returns to the far side of his wretched easel.

Stupid, stupid, stupid! She should never have walked to the table …and why hadn't she worn those shoes, she had so nearly put them on…

Lips tighten, she looks defiantly at the student who needs to be taught a lesson, she'll jump down there and then and leave without speaking whatever her brother says, and she will await an apology, no, she will *demand* one through Lee.

But her defiance is being ignored. He is not looking back to her, his face has become serious and he is studying her brother who has resumed his pose looking away from her.

She fumes but she does not jump.

'Don't move your head, don't think of your sister,' she hears with more alarm, 'forget the view from the window for a while, imagine there are wild lilies just in front of you at eye level, they're in full bloom and you're studying them with interest and pleasure but with only the smallest of smiles on your face. That's what I want to capture in your eyes and your expression.'

The indignity and helplessness grows on the Mistress; she feels like a hen in the garden huts, perched at the edge of a ledge thinking if to drop to the ground. She is shocked to be treated so casually and to be expected to remain where she is. And her feet - it is excruciatingly embarrassing, he can look at them, probably will do he's so shameless. This cocksure student doesn't have proper regard to their respective status however decent he might be, though she doesn't know what he is *really* like. It is inconceivable that a man would get so close to a woman, and to her especially, yet he'd presumed to do so. No man apart from her father helping her down from a horse has ever touched her like that, neither Head Groom nor the officers she has occasionally taken picnics with in the presence of her family - she mounts and dismounts on her own.

She steels herself and moves forward to jump despite the height from the table. But Shanghan's left hand has come over her lap and is searching for hers though he is not looking round. 'Hua, what's the tree outside?'

She takes hold of the hand and looks out of the nearer window. 'Pagoda, you know that.'

'Let's name every tree we can think of!'

Huihua doesn't want to do this, doesn't want to stay cooped up on her perch for the artist to make comments, or worse ogle. But her brother's fingers are squeezing hers. After a couple of seconds and with great reluctance she gets free of him and wriggles herself back. 'Including fruit trees?' she asks without keenness, taking hold of the hand again.

'Yes.'

'But not bushes,' she states.

'Alright. I'll start. Pagoda, palm, banyan…'

Soon she is joining in, beginning with fruit trees, sister and brother complementing each other, until Shanghan runs out of names and Huihua continues on her own, always looking out of the window or towards her brother so close.

After Yuling lifted the fragrant young lady onto the table and returned to the canvas, his spirit flew round the room, and he took up the palette board and mixed as if directed by some higher force. He hid from himself that he had

202

gone way beyond the boundary of correct conduct. Telling the boy to think of the lilies, he observed his subject as never before, while another part of him laid spiritual flowers all around the sister, on the table, on the floor, in her lap, in her hair, between her toes of each beautiful foot...

And one of Professor Koo's thinner brushes is soon dipping in the paint and moving to the left eye, the one most prominent in the picture. As its holder listens to tree after tree and allows himself occasionally to look up, the sister's voice fills him with such happiness that he knows something powerful is working in his art, that the brushes can do no wrong, that perfect tones are being created.

And all the time he is holding back his own tree, longing for the sister not to think of it, longing to impress. And when it seems she has run out of names, he looks over the canvas and calls: 'Scholar tree!' and beams at her although she isn't looking towards him, as again he takes in the profile, the figure, the left earring ...so he can recapture her forever.

'Is there such a tree, Hua?' the boy asks maintaining his pose. She accepts it, though only reluctantly Yuling thinks, expecting her to turn to him and acknowledge, but she does neither. 'Excellent!' the boy says.

He goes back to his work in the new silence of the room.

Many seconds later she says: 'Almond.'

'Good!' Shanghan says.

Yuling looks up; the lovely head remains turned away.

Another tree comes to him, the one his grandfather is buried at near the lake. 'Hemlock!' he calls out feeling triumphant.

'We've had that!' the boy exclaims.

'It was one of the first,' the sister adds pointedly, looking coolly his way but only very briefly.

'Really?'

He thinks again what fine siblings they are, that a painting of them together would indeed turn heads.

Huihua knows where the eyes might sometimes be, but keeps her gaze at the old pagoda tree's upper parts, keenly going again through the conifers to see if she has missed any.

'Mulberry!' she suddenly hears, the painter almost shouting in self-applause. She is surprised, annoyed to have missed it.

'Very good!' Shanghan says laughing. 'About thirty I think!'

'Silkworms love them,' Yuling adds towards the pair on the table, 'and so do I, to look at and the fruit.' At once he realizes the risqué double meaning that could be taken - he hadn't consciously intended such. But he feels too pleased with himself to linger over any embarrassment, and he thinks he catches the tinge of a smile in the cheeks of the divine.

Huihua is not going to give the satisfaction of any assent, and has decided to jump down very soon ...once she can find another tree, asking the pagoda's twisting branches to help her; she doesn't want the student's mulberry to be the last, not after her hard thinking and long list.

Yuling returns to his work. Half a minute goes by in more silence. He assumes the game is over and wishes the painting session could continue well past the tutor's allotted hour, wondering if he dare risk the man's anger.

'Dove tree,' Huihua says almost in a whisper, turning towards the student, opening her eyes at him. The student's head stays buried in his artwork, and she allows a pause as she listens to her brother's pleasure, before adding, louder, challengingly, 'and lacquer tree.'

She gives Shanghan's hand a squeeze, and watches a smile wing towards the canvas from her brother's insolent but singular painter; perhaps she will stay and talk with her brother a little more; the hour must soon be up.

Yuling does not participate in the next conversations between the two on the table. He praises the cadet for holding his pose, and reminds him not to turn towards his sister. And although he is always keenly observing his subject and never for some minutes looks at the other person on the table, and although he tries not to allow his conscious mind to think of that person, he feels the effect she is having on his painting, and keeps inwardly blessing her.

Before the sister came into the room, twice in the session he closed his eyes, asking himself what was special or interesting about the boy's head and about his spirit. Whether painting landscapes or portraits, sometimes he found this enabled him to see more clearly the essence of his subject, so he could tell what needed more emphasis or less.

But now, with the sister sitting on the table, the third time he closes his eyes he finds he can no longer concentrate. Two conversations are going on in his head, one concerning the portrait, the other...

And when he opens them, she is looking straight at him.

'We had hilarious lunch, Mistress,' the thin maid said, 'painter entertained us with mimicking, said his mother's even better.'

'Really Yiying? What sort of mimicking?'

'People, animals, one I liked best was donkey, lips and nose were moving up and down like this.' The maid vigorously moved her mouth and jaw. 'And his crying, we...'

'His crying!'

'Yes, we all burst out, even head domestic Wang, and you don't see that often! Says he learnt it in street theatre, he asked me to slap his face. First time I did, he smiled and told me harder, so I did, really hard, everyone gasped and you should have seen him, face changed completely and he began to cry, honest

Mistress, tears came down his cheeks. I was stunned at first and then we died laughing, and he began smiling again! He says it only comes with practice.'

'He's very full of himself, don't you think?'

'Not really, he's lovely, treats us normal. And he's so good-looking and so strong! Dajuan's ten years older and she can't take her eyes off him, I think he gets embarrassed.'

That afternoon Yuling walked to Mingon's Great Gate taking the snaking path through the woods as the secretary suggested. When he came through the final trees, he found himself at a clearing, with the ancient fortified entrance about two hundred paces ahead of him.

Half way across the clearing fear gripped as he heard the noise of plane engines, and looking up to his right he spotted several Japanese planes coming out of the sky. He began running towards the town walls, seeing other people doing the same.

Soon he was racing along a wall in the direction of the bastion entrance, but he had not reached it when he heard the planes coming, and dived to the ground between a bush and the wall.

Six passed over very low, they were fighters, and he got up and ran into the comparative safety of the huge stone and brick edifice. He heard them circling the town, and watched as they headed away. He thought of his father, and wondered if China would ever be rid of the invaders.

He had not come to visit the East Gate Monastery but a furniture maker's shop he had noticed on his moonless night walk the day before the audience the previous year.

Several children were playing outside the shop, and as he entered, one of them, a clear faced girl of about twelve, her hair in plaits and wearing a festival fragrance pouch round her waist, followed and began talking with him.

He asked if her father was the owner and if he was about, and she told him he was in the backyard and that she would fetch him.

The shop was narrow with a central passage, light coming in places through the roof; it was crowded with what looked like old and new furniture, whole and bits, mainly bamboo but other woods as well.

He was moving a hand over the top of a dark table he guessed was teak, when a man came running along in short quick steps. The man bowed deeply. 'Welcome sir, welcome.'

Yuling made his bow. 'I admire your work,' he said, 'but I'm only looking for something very small to take to my mother, a little box perhaps, something I can carry in a sack.'

'Please follow me, sir,' the man replied smiling, and led the way to the back of the shop, the girl between them.

He was shown four small boxes. 'Each can be used for jewellery or trinkets or whatever a woman desires,' the man said.

'Which do you like?' Yuling asked the girl, and caught the man's surprise.

She looked them over and put her finger on a lid with a bird inlay, and Yuling nodded as the girl looked up at him.

'Ashenga, it is for the gentleman to decide.' Turning to him, the man said: 'That is a little more expensive, sir.'

'But I agree with your daughter.' He smiled at the girl. 'You probably like the turned up tail, and I like wrens, small birds with big songs.' He looked at the furniture maker. 'I'm working at Wuyi Court and won't be able to pay for this until I get my commission, I hope in about ten days.'

'Then I'll reserve it for you, sir.' The man hesitated. 'May I ask the nature of your work at the Court?'

'I'm painting the portrait of a boy,' he replied with discretion, just as a woman he thought must be the man's wife came up. They bowed to each other.

The man looked at his wife and then back. 'We are honoured to have you in our shop. It would be a further honour if you would take tea with us. Our name is Wu, and this young lady is our helpful daughter Ashenga.' He began fondling one of the girl's plaits.

Yuling was happy to accept, especially after seeing those planes; and in a room beside the shop, he had a natural and enjoyable hour, tasting a dark green tea he found good, and being entertained by a number of boys from nine downwards who went in and out. 'I've lost count how many children you have!' he said at one stage.

'Four are ours and two we look after,' the father replied. 'We're very grateful to have Ashenga as the eldest, she's good at keeping them under control and semi-clean.'

He learnt from Mrs Wu that the elderly cook he had met at Wuyi Court was her aunt, who had been in service for over forty years including during the old warlord period.

They were getting on so well that at the end Yuling asked if the furniture maker would consider taking him on as a very short-term apprentice for a few days, perhaps ten or twelve, before he varnished the portrait and returned to his college. He said he could start in two days once the portrait was complete, adding that he would pay for the privilege. He told them he had always thought a carpenter or a furniture maker's job would be fulfilling.

No figure was discussed, but it was agreed he could start as soon as he liked.

'We're poor,' the man said, escorting him back through the passage to the street. 'When the invaders came my contacts in the east dried up. Nobody around here can afford anything, so my shop is full of unwanted furniture as you see.'

'How do you live?' Yuling felt able to ask, coming onto the pavement and thinking of the mouths to feed.

'People want their chairs mending and sometimes parts of their houses, and if they can't pay me they give rice or vegetables. And we rent a piece of land a few minutes away outside the walls, that's our main source of food as well as the river fish, and we've hens. But it's not easy. Sometimes I have luck when one of the officers at the camp wants a piece of furniture.'

After leaving the shop, Yuling went to an inn on another street not far away and secured a first floor room, telling the innkeeper that he would need it in two days. He negotiated what he considered a cheap daily rate, and only then did he mention, when pressed, that he was soon to finish a job at the mansion. As he left he wondered if he should have looked at other inns; he didn't take to the nosy man.

'We will see about that!' the lady stated that evening when Shanghan surprised her by saying the student had stopped Huihua looking at the canvas. 'Let him know who is paying whom! We shall have some sport!'

Shanghan frowned. She looked at her son. 'He did not give you any propaganda, I trust? Did he talk any politics, did he say anything about the government or the Reds, or anything about street theatre?'

The next morning at the same hour as before, the young Master was brought to the temporary painting room, this time not by his tutor but by his mother and sister.

'Good morning, Tsai Yuling,' Madame Huang said as she entered followed by her son and daughter.

They found the student standing with a rag by the easel, removing a brush from a tin. Immediately he placed the brush and rag on the small table and bowed gravely.

Huihua merely nodded, looking keenly at him, assertively she hoped he would see. It had been bad enough being manhandled onto the table, but to have seen the cocky smile on the student's face when she and Shanghan jumped down at the session end was further confirmation that he needed to understand his place and be taught how to act in the presence of a lady. Now he was about to find out where matters stood.

Madame Huang stopped a few steps from the easel, Huihua beside her. Shanghan went to the table though did not jump up.

'I trust you are comfortable in your room in the servants quarters and are being fed,' she said in a matter-of-fact way, 'and that you have everything you need for your painting?' She had turned her eyes from the student to the back of the canvas.

'I'm very pleased, thank you my lady,' she heard him reply, 'my subject is a good sitter.' He was smiling at her son.

'Excellent. Now move aside would you, and let me see how you are getting along.' She began taking short steps towards the student's side of the easel, saw a look of horror come over the face, and was shocked when he jumped between her and her objective.

'No,' he burst out at her, 'I can't have that, please respect my wish that you only see my work when I'm happy with it.'

'Can't have that!' She was now very close to the student and gave him her sternest look. 'You forget to whom you are speaking, young man, *and* where you are! Do not be ridiculous, of course I can see how you are doing, I have commissioned you, have I not!' She gave a short laugh in her daughter's direction. 'And if you are worried what I might think, I can agree to say nothing, unless of course it is clearly bad, when I will tell you to stop, as I should have done with the last man. That would be in your interest.'

She expected him at once to make way, and when to her surprise he maintained his look of fright, she started to walk round him, but he leapt back and pulled the easel away from her, and she saw that he struggled to hold the sizeable canvas from tipping.

'No! No!' he said in quick breaths, 'if you insist on looking at my uncompleted work I must leave.'

Huihua was appalled. Madame Huang was astonished, and he'd used the 'must' word again. She thought this a most unusual reaction. Maybe he knew his picture was already not working. He certainly was strange, and he knew his mind, was again showing remarkable courage, or obstinacy - the Guard House incident, a different painting room, and now this.

'If you look and I continue,' he added with emotion, 'I can't guarantee I'll succeed, it's something to do with remaining all the time focussed on my own aims, using my own intuitions, connecting alone with my subject until completion, no outside influence. I can't explain it better. My professors respect this, they only look and criticize afterwards.'

Shanghan was now standing beside his artist. 'Mother, we must let Tsai Yuling work his own way, it is his painting and he is different from the last man, and I respect him.'

There was a hush. The lady could well see how troubled the student had become. She looked at her son and thought how impressive he was. She frowned to Huihua, then looked back at the student, knowing he would catch her disapproval.

'As you wish. But I will expect you to show my son's admirable character, and if I do not like your work, I tell you now, it will be destroyed like the last horrible one, and you will be lucky to receive your travel costs.'

She turned and walked to the door as briskly as she could, given her feet, followed by Huihua, each leaving without looking back.

The lady's surprise and initial anger soon turned to wry amusement. 'Our student has too strong a head,' she said to Huihua as they returned along the passages towards her apartments. 'We should have known that from last year's performance. I am afraid we have made a big mistake, my dear. I ought to have made it clearer that my preference was for a staff member of their art department to come, or a portrait painter from Suodin if they knew of a good one.'

'He acted disgracefully,' Huihua replied, 'I certainly won't be joining Shanghan this time.'

'We have been thwarted, and I am not looking forward to the viewing, and disappointing Shanghan again.' Turning to her daughter, she added: 'Do not fall for him, Hua, he has a charming smile like the mother, and he clearly has determination.'

'Of course I won't! Anyway, he's far too direct, in fact insolent at times.'

'*And* he is a Red sympathizer, we had better keep *that* from your father.' The lady did not add that the student reminded her of her husband before their marriage, very well built only much taller. As a girl of fifteen she had admired her betrothed's physique when meeting the warlord's son for the second time. Now she certainly hoped that her own daughter would not think the same way about the student; she was confident she would not allow any such thoughts to take her far - Huihua knew her duty towards her parents.

Shanghan gave Yuling a smile through gritted teeth. 'You shouldn't have put my sister on here,' he said from his position on the pear-wood table early in the second session, 'you shouldn't have touched her, she's a lady, she didn't like that, she nearly hit me afterwards in the corridor.'

'Hit you!' Yuling stared at his youthful quite strong-looking subject.

'Men shouldn't touch women in that way,' the boy pronounced, 'unless they are married of course, I told her not to tell our mother.'

Yuling became worried, and had to think before replying. 'That is the custom, I agree. But I know a number of young men and even women who don't strictly hold to that these days, and sometimes I'm one of them. We think it's good to be natural to our feelings.' He wished he'd stopped short of that last part, didn't want to invite a question and be reported back to the haughty sister. The last thing he wanted was for Huang Huihua to be angry towards him and to remain so, to dislike him even; he was keenly hoping he might see her again

209

while he was painting or sealing. Raising her onto the table had happened so quickly, and at the time he hadn't been able to stop himself, in fact touching her waist had been magical, as had every single minute afterwards until the session ended.

'Should I express my regret for offending, say I meant none? I have an impetuous streak that sometimes lands me in trouble. I wouldn't want her to think badly of me.'

Shanghan shook his head. 'I'll tell my sister what you've said, and that you are sorry. I'll tell her I'm partly to blame, because I could have helped her up or got her a chair.'

Yuling resumed his painting with a slight frown on his face. But soon he was working at his best again despite the sister not being there. He marvelled at the quality of Professor Koo's oils; they seemed to mix on the palette to produce the best colours he had ever applied. He knew he was painting the head well, capturing the strength in that adolescent chin, showing the bright future in the pose, and in the eyes that looked a little up towards the source of natural light painted coming in on the left side of the canvas onto parts of the face. Now he had to concentrate on the skin tones in the left cheek, and finish the dramatic youthful forehead and the left ear. He would come back later to make the last strokes to the hair.

And the collar: he was pleased that Huang Shanghan was now wearing the uniform, it added greatly to the boy's presence in the picture, its light blue an excellent colour to work with, one to contrast with the subtle tones and shadows in the face.

Although he wondered if the sister might look in again, he knew that that would be highly unlikely: he had improperly touched her, and he had a near disastrous meeting with the mother over seeing the incomplete portrait. He was more than sorry she would not be there, but it did not affect his painting; her spirit had already worked its power onto the canvas.

Early in the second session the boy invited him to look afterwards at his lame horse, saying his tutor was ill in bed and that he could attend to his studies later.

When the hour came to an end, Yuling told him that it was unlikely he would need him to sit again, that he had mainly to finish the background and hoped to complete the portrait before the servants lunch hour or in the early afternoon. He said he would get a message to the secretary once he had finished, so that the viewing could be arranged. 'Aren't you keen to see your portrait first?' he teased.

'No,' the boy answered emphatically, 'I'd rather see it only when my mother does.'

They went to the stables, where he was introduced to someone called simply Head Groom. The man showed him the leg of the boy's horse, saying it was a bad muscle sprain, and that had it been a breakage it would have been terminal. Yuling thought the horses very fine, and learnt with surprise that the sister was also a keen rider, not something he associated with a woman in their province.

Back at the easel he worked to complete the background, and decided to miss lunch as he knew the final brush strokes would soon be coming. He would walk among the trees of the inner courtyard before returning for a last analysis, and would then report to the secretary.

Madame Huang and her children were in her rooms when Secretary Lee telephoned to say that the portrait could be viewed whenever was convenient. In answer to her question, the old retainer replied that he had not seen it, and said that the student was asking permission to spend an hour in the Reception Hall after the viewing, to study the two murals he remembered from his childhood visit.

'We will come straight away,' she called down the mouthpiece. 'And if we dislike it, which I expect, the student must leave at once, though you can perhaps give him a bit more than the other man, he came a long way and had to interrupt his studies.'

The family found the secretary waiting outside the temporary painting room. He opened the door for them.

Yuling had been looking out at the pagoda tree, visualizing that two or three of the twisting branches would make a good painting, or a drawing at least. Quickly he bowed, and went to the easel, his expression serious, the back of the canvas facing his visitors.

Madame Huang was looking sternly at him. 'The moment has arrived, Tsai Yuling, kindly turn your painting round.'

He did so. There was a short silence, followed by gasps, and he watched the mother's look of surprise, and the daughter had wide eyes and an expression that filled him with pleasure as he read what she was thinking.

'I like it very much mother, really I do!' Shanghan said going up to the canvas, Yuling quickly warning him against touching wet paint. 'My uniform and the collar, it looks so good.'

'It certainly does, my dear,' his mother replied turning to the secretary. 'Oh this is splendid Lee, what do you say!'

'I think my lord will be most gratified with such a present,' the old man answered with a tilt of the head to her, before he gave what Yuling took to be an attempt at a smile at him.

'You have portrayed my son's character *very* well,' she continued while Yuling was looking back at the portrait, 'and the light, it is just right, not too strong here,' she was pointing to the light source, the window not seen in the painting. 'I particularly like the way you have done the pose.' She turned to him. 'You must be heartily congratulated.'

He gave a dignified nod but remained thoughtful. 'I must come back in about eight days to seal with a varnish so long as the paint has dried, so I respectfully suggest that a framer is only instructed after that. When I return, may I take a photograph, my lady? I would like to show my professor and have a record.'

The mother looked to her son and back. 'Certainly, so long as you do not distribute copies or disclose who the subject is. May I have your word on that?'

'Yes my lady, I would never do that, not in these difficult times.'

'Good. And are *you* pleased with your work?'

Yuling could not suppress a smile; he meant to answer to the mother and then turn to the son, but found himself nodding to the sister, into her wonderful eyes.

It was the presumptuous look towards her daughter that Madame Huang caught with surprise and immediate concern.

14

Over-the-moon Yuling returned to his basement room to ponder and marvel. Lying on his bed and closing his eyes, his mind roamed from what he had achieved, to the heavenly being of the sister. She would not be far from him in the mansion, could steal down to his room where there were no good-looking military officers in the passage longing for her favours as in his pre-sleep reveries; this time he dreamt on, she would be whispering for him outside his door, and when he opened it her eyes would say all, no hand on his shoulder, he would pull her to him and close the door quietly and take hold of the waist - oh that waist - and shower her with kisses...

It mattered nothing that she was not beautiful in the classical sense; she was so lovely he could have cried *Huihua* from the top of the escarpment and the wind would carry it over the hills and valleys to his home, to the college, to wherever he was...

When he'd looked up in the first painting session and seen her at the door, she had more than taken his breath away; and when she sat on the table with her brother, dangling those earrings, speaking into his heart with every tree she named, he'd never seen any girl, any woman, so alluring. And at the viewing, her expression of wonder at his work had made him want to fall at those beautiful feet, to proclaim veneration with his spiritual flowers ...if only the others hadn't been there.

Everything about her overwhelmed him: from the way she walked with her head held high, to the intelligence he saw in her face, to the cheeks he could kiss to eternity, to the scent he caught when placing her on the table. And her figure! She seemed to be the only slim one in the Huang family; even her brother had the stockiness of the parents.

He pictured himself painting her portrait: he couldn't decide which would be best, a portrait of her head and neck, or the whole adorable person; perhaps she would be sitting in a chair in dignified pose befitting her status; better than standing - too masculine. He'd show the eyes that mixed admiration and challenge, as she'd last looked at him. And the hair would be curled up as it had been when he had looked over the canvas, so promising of falling like the strand she allowed to drop. She would have to be in Chinese robe, though he could imagine her looking wonderful in chiffon in the western fashion that Professor Koo had lectured on. And would her garment be the magical shining yellow of that silk robe she had worn at the painting session, or white, such an effective colour of purity in a young woman - yellow, the colourist in him guessed.

And he knew that only an oil painting could do justice to her face and her presence; the paint with its rich and subtle tones, with his different brush strokes, would make the imagination work; it would be more three-dimensional than a watercolour or a drawing or photograph, more immediately real and intimate.

He went into a deep sleep. When he woke, the afternoon had moved on and he felt hungry having skipped lunch; so he asked at the kitchens if they could spare him some cooked rice. The two cooks welcomed him, telling him that everyone had been upstairs to admire the portrait. He told the elderly cook called Xuiey that he had met her niece Mrs Wu at the shop. They insisted on sitting him down to sesame rice, star fruit, and sweet warm kumquat tea.

He found Secretary Lee in a benevolent mood, and was informed that Madame Huang had given permission for him to study the murals. He told the secretary that he would spend the next hour or so in the Reception Hall, and then walk into town the safer way through the woods, saying he might visit the furniture maker with whom he was shortly to serve a few days apprenticeship. He would be returning to Wuyi Court later that evening for his final night, and had secured lodgings at an inn; when the time came to varnish in a little over a week, he would present himself a last time.

The old retainer told him to appear at nine the following morning to be paid the commission; no mention was made of the amount, and he did not think he should ask.

He walked along the corridors, bare of the tall blue and white vases that had so impressed him on his visit as a boy, though the superb Fujian wall woodcarvings remained; this was wartime, valuable objects had been stored away. A guard greeted him from the base of the stairs leading up to the Study, the general's office.

Coming into the Reception Hall, he found it dark, curtains hanging down over the large windows, blocking out much of the evening light. All the clay warriors and richly carved chairs he remembered were gone, as had the vases and portraits and ebony table, leaving only the murals and two ordinary chairs to one side of the middle window.

As he pulled apart that window's curtains half way, the late sun beamed into the great room and onto the old floor, giving lustre to the polish and bringing to life a substantial part of the mural on the opposite wall. The other

214

mural at the far end to his right - the one he had looked at with his mother - remained in shadow.

He sat down with his old pad and began to study the panorama. His elation over the portrait's success made him imagine himself being accepted into the company of the mural masters; soon he was drawing a close copy, absorbed in the drama of grand nature.

'Good evening Maestro Tsai!'

...oh heavens be, she's come to me, the Mistress is calling me from the far door, a miracle's happening, I'm going to be talking with the sister, alone... Quickly he stands. 'These are the best murals I've ever seen,' he calls back, 'they're really magnificent!' - and so are you, he wishes he could add as his trumpets sound through the mansion. She is in a robe of quiet blue, loose fitting, no brooches or earrings, and he thinks she looks sensational, there flashing through his mind that her portrait might be even better without the distraction of jewellery.

Huihua walks gracefully as comes naturally, her simple robe brushing the floor. She feels a pleasure almost tangible: the portrait of her beloved brother has worked brilliantly and will be the best possible present for their father's birthday.

And while riding that afternoon, she had realized that her earlier anger at the student's impudence and forwardness in the table incident, and her shock at his defiance of her mother over the unfinished canvas, had each dissolved. Somewhat to her surprise, she now saw him as an extremely talented and interesting young man, and, though she tried not to let herself get carried away, rather too good-looking. She sensed something special about him, quite apart from his physique or the extraordinary childhood history. And when at the painting session he had closed his eyes, she had not admitted to herself then but she did later, his face and head and the whole being seemed to hold sincerity and strength of character; and he was refreshingly open - too direct sometimes - and there was no arrogance over his talent, and no fawning from his lower status; he seemed to be blessed with both a happy and a serious disposition. She was glad, very glad, that her idea to suggest him had turned out so well. She believed she could like him even if he was a Red sympathizer, so long as it was nothing seriously more, and she had already wondered if they could perhaps be friends by correspondence; they might write to each other about their different lives and artistic endeavours, his in colour on canvas, hers literary on paper.

'I was told you might be here. Would you like to know the history of the murals?'

'Very much. I can see they're by separate hands, the styles are different.'

'You are right.' She gestures him to his chair, and sits down first.

'Still no sandals or shoes, and in a mansion!' Yuling says unable to stop himself, and with a smile he knows he ought to curb in the presence of a high-born lady.

Huihua wants to gently rebuke, but instead finds herself returning the smile as she moves her feet under the pleat of her robe. She had, of course, thought about wearing shoes this time, but preferred to remain natural. She clasps her hands and decides to begin the history.

But he speaks first. 'You must forgive me, sometimes a moment …the light on your hair and your shoulders …it would make a lovely painting.'

She does not take the comment amiss, being struck by the genuine expression on his face, and the well-meaning of his creative mind, and by the fact he has paid her a compliment without flirting.

She looks towards the two walls and gives the names of the masters of each mural, telling him that they were executed shortly after the middle of the previous century, some fifty years before the end of the Qing dynasty.

'My Huang great grandfather was a rough man, I have to admit, a landowner who early on took to a form of banditry. But he did something good with his money, marrying my great grandmother, a lady banished from the Emperor's court. She came south, and she loved all the arts particularly painting. And soon after their marriage they built this mansion including the part we are now in, though it was smaller in those days. She was very energetic…' Huihua stops, is looking straight into the eyes that are so attractive, and they are making her concentration waver.

She straightens, knows she must look away but doesn't want to, so keeps talking. 'Well, there was much entertainment for some years, but she was struck with illness in her middle thirties and tragically died. My great grandfather carried out her last wish, that their children would have…' she stops again, he is looking at her with greater intensity, and it makes her frown to the sunlit floor and unclasp her hands '…that they would have the beauty and greatness of China's landscapes in their home, to inspire them in their lives and to remember their mother by. I particularly like the one we are looking at.' She continues searching the floor.

'Why?' she hears, and the bluntness makes her think of her father. This is ridiculous, of course she can have a conversation with a handsome man without getting flustered like this …if only he wouldn't be so direct and look at her so keenly, yes he's an artist, but why can't he be more humble or considerate…

She looks back to the panorama; describing it might take her mind off him, might help her concentrate. 'It has so much activity don't you think, the hills and clouds and rocks. There are ravines rising steeply up with conifers, and look at the birds far off in the sky and the bigger ones on the dead branches to the right,' she points, 'and the river, it is almost emerald, and that longboat, and the waterfall...' she hesitates, but this time is determined not to lose herself again, '...and can you see two people, Tsai Yuling, they are tiny, you have to look for them, treading up that path...' again she points, '...towards the small cabin, I think they are carrying some provisions on shoulder poles.'

She is pleased to have finished, to have described the scene rather well. But there is a silence, and she becomes disturbed, feeling the gaze still on her. She looks back to him but is mistaken, he is no longer looking at her but at the mural, clearly studying it, his face serious.

And she studies his profile.

When she thinks he is about to turn to her, she adds, hastily looking back to the panorama: 'Do you agree with me? What do *you* see as an artist?' But she feels her mind and emotions are no longer hers entirely to command.

'I see something altogether lovely,' she hears him say as her heart leaps up though she doesn't want it to, certain he isn't referring only to the landscape.

An inner voice speaks ...what on earth's happening, Hua, perhaps you'd better leave, control yourself, you're a Huang, a general's daughter...

...that's right, another one mocks, don't go near those eyes again my girl, but what are you going to do about that smile eh, you were captured in the monastery garden, you were in a little heaven for days, don't deny it, you were touching yourself, you remember alright, if he gives you that look again you'll swoon, you won't be able to ride away on Ajin, don't look I say ...ah, but you can't stop yourself can you, no you can't... And unable to hold herself back, the Mistress of Wuyi Court leaves the waterfall and the river and the mountains and the sky to meet the face of her brother's painter, to meet an expression that tells of adoration ...of adoration for her. She cannot prevent herself from searching those eyes, and inexorably she loses herself in that strong but gentle face, and having succumbed, Huihua is overwhelmed by a sudden, unexpected and delicious arousal.

Just looking at the sister and being so close to her, it takes Yuling several seconds to come out of his own reverie, actual this time, not pre-dream. And when he pulls himself away from the bewitching strand of hair falling in curls down her soft cheek, back to the masterpiece on the wall, he needs more time to move his mind from one wonder to another, and in the movement of his thoughts he knows he is as near heaven in life as he could ever be.

'I am inside the painting, I love its vastness, its grandeur, those great boulders, the overhanging rocks, I am in the rolling mists, I am on the branches with the birds, the scene fills me with awe and with a sense of beauty.' He pauses. 'But also of loneliness, of our smallness in the immenseness of things. And I feel the poet's rhythms of nature speaking to me. If you look closely, Huihua, you will see that Master Chang delineated nothing too strongly except for the foreground rocks. The change of tones is often subtle, so that the whole has a dreamlike quality helped by the presence of the mists. It is like a poem of the mountains, where great men disappeared for years at a time to be in the beauty and the wild, and then they composed their verse.'

Although Huihua heard every word, she says nothing because she still cannot believe what she so powerfully feels, and she easily lets through that he has used familiarity in her name. But to prevent herself from daring to be captured again, and partly because she is so impressed with the answer, she stands up intending to go closer to the mural.

He does not stand, which surprises her - she is getting used to being surprised by Tsai Yuling - and begins walking to the opposite wall, wondering if he will follow or follow only with his eyes.

She reaches the mural knowing he has not moved, and after pretending to study the paintwork in the grey and white waterfall, she calls back without turning: 'You love art. I do too, but I love poetry more...' ...aren't you going to go back to him, you might never have another chance... 'Our great poets were not only men, you know. Sometimes I send in my poems...' ...go on, turn... She glances back, how *good* he looks, and turns fully. 'I won a prize last June, and the Fujian Poetry Society found me out, discovered where I live, and they insisted I use my true name.' The arousal is as strong as ever, and she is loving talking from afar yet straight at him, letting herself invite him with her eyes and with her voice, she wants him to come over to her, to join her at the mural, she wants to feel her pull of him. 'I had a pseudonym at first, but if you'll allow me to mention...' ...why are you talking like this, he's not coming to you is he, he's not moving from the chair, and you want to be close to him again, so go back, you want to lose yourself, go and stand over him and look down, he'll love that, it's more exciting than sitting together, you can open your eyes at him and make him stand, you want him to touch you, he might put his hands on your waist and lift you up to his amazing face and hold you there so you can feel his strong arm again or maybe both and then anything can happen... '... Mr Shehan, he's the Chairman, he wrote me a letter saying they were deeply honoured and had made me a free life member.' With all her feminine power Huihua smiles at her admirer.

Yuling is spellbound, taking in her every word and every movement, wondering how he is going to hold himself back from touching her beautiful tender face when he is near her again. 'I would like to see some of your work. We love poetry in my family. What's the title of your winning poem?'

She starts walking. ...that's it, well done, soon beside him... 'I called it "Falling feathers". It came to me in the middle of the night or rather the main idea did and some of the verse. I strived for many weeks to make it as perfect as

I could. And I've just finished another...' She stops in mid-sentence just as she reaches him, because the air-raid siren has begun its fast ascending wail.

Yuling leaps up, his pad and pencil falling to the floor, and the next moment they hear the sound of a plane or planes flying towards the mansion.

'Quick! Got to get to the basement,' she cries as he reads her fear. She begins running to the nearest door, Yuling following. 'No time to get to the servants main staircase,' she shouts, 'could be bombing, Lee's showed me another way.'

Huihua runs fast along the corridor and into a narrower passage, Yuling having difficulty keeping up. The alarm has grown to its loudest, but he can still hear the planes, two have just flown directly over them.

At the end she stops by a small door. The door goes inwards into what he sees is a spiral wooden staircase, some daylight coming from below, and immediately he realizes the danger of descending by what could be a stairwell partly jutting out of the mansion. But he knows they will quickly reach the comparative safety of the basement, so says nothing except 'Hurry, hurry!' as he pushes her.

Huihua goes down several turning steps before stopping at a vertical glassless window long and narrow. The alarm's wailing is dying, and Yuling can hear again the sound of engines and knows the aircraft are circling.

'Keep going!' he cries as he pushes her again. But she has spotted a plane with the Rising Sun markings, it is near the end of its curve and will soon be coming directly towards them, not much higher, she thinks, than the courtyard walls, and she has the sudden thought that the basement is still many steps down, and that it might be safer to return to the passage to seek shelter further into the building.

From his higher step Yuling cannot see the plane, but he grabs her shoulders, pushes her against the opening and squeezes round her, momentarily catching a view of what is coming, and stumbling on steps that change from wood to stone, nearly falling. He is now just below the window and pulls hard on her arms, forcing her to fall towards him just as a burst of bullets comes crashing into the walls of the mansion.

'Hold onto me!' he yells through the deafening sound, not hearing his own voice or her scream as he puts one arm round her and picks her up, starting downwards through the crescendo, having to keep his balance by using his other hand against the underparts of the stone steps.

Hardly has he gone down three or four when he hears the roar of the plane flying away, followed almost immediately by a further ear-splitting burst of firing hitting the building around them as another plane attacks, instinct making him duck as he feels Huihua grabbing him tighter, he terrified the bullets will tear through the walls before he can reach below ground level, or they might come through the long narrow opening and ricochet down.

The second firing ends just as the spiralling steps bring him into semi-darkness, Yuling realizing that they are below ground and hearing the plane going over. A few more curving steps and he reaches a stone floor.

'We're in the basement,' he gasps as he lets her down, noticing for the first time nasty stinging in the neck area on the right side. 'Are you alright?' he asks her as he checks and comes to a little blood; but he can't find a wound.

She gives him no reply. He touches a door, it is metal, cold, and when he moves the handle the door won't open and he thinks it must be locked. He searches for bolts but there are none, and starts banging and shouting, wanting servants to hear, rattling the handle more.

Nobody comes. He tells Huihua to go up a step, but she doesn't move. He has to push her firmly to one side. Bracing his back against the wall under the stone stairs, he pushes the door with all his might, then kicks it several times.

It hardly moves. 'It's bolted on the other side,' he says panting.

'They're coming again!' Huihua cries just as Yuling also hears them.

'Crouch!' he shouts, pulling her into the narrow corner at the base of the stairwell, putting his hands on her shoulders and kneeling down with her. They are opposite each other and close, though he can hardly see her in the semi-dark; his back faces the last few curving steps.

Almost the next moment more bullets come thundering into the mansion and very near he believes, and at once he puts his arms round her as he feels a great shudder run through her; and while the walls of the mansion erupt above them, it comes to him that they might not be in the basement proper, not far enough below ground level, that if bullets get to them and hit him in the back, he will die younger than his father; and with that thought and Huihua's continuing trembling, his own shaking starts, and try as he does, he cannot stop himself.

'I'm sorry!' he shouts through the colossal din as he buries the side of his face into the top of her head and tries to hold her tighter despite his own shaking, thinking the firing going on forever, begging it to stop.

Huihua has never felt such terror and also expects to die at any moment, her mind full of the evil of the aircraft she saw coming and the goggles of its pilot. But the student's shaking brings her to act. Her trembling miraculously stops, she removes her hands from her ears, struggles to get free of his hold, and puts her arms round him so that they are now holding to each other for their lives as the second plane ends its murderous fire.

Some seconds later, Yuling's shaking ends, and he hears the fading roar of the plane. 'Thank you, thank you!' he gasps, head still buried in hers.

They remain in their terrified embrace, neither saying anything, Yuling waiting to see if the attack will continue.

Soon he is squeezing her gently to give comfort, and stroking her hair, his fingers sometimes touching above her eyes; but she does not react and he stops.

A minute or so later he raises his head. 'We've got to get out. If no one comes we'll have to go back up.' He removes his arms from around her.

She slurs some words he doesn't catch. He is about to get her to release him when he hears '...feel terrible...' she is trembling again, and her head is dropping '...keep holding me, don't let me go...' her voice seems alarmingly weak as the horror occurs to him that she could have received a bullet and might be dying. 'Huihua, you've not been hit have you, tell me?'

She doesn't answer him, and he repeats the question and starts feeling her back, terrified his hands will touch blood. Her head gives a small shake and he hears a weak 'No', and breathes a great sigh of relief that they have survived. And in the silence he is relieved on another count: the attack seems not to be the beginning of a Japanese assault on the mansion, something he earlier feared.

He doesn't want to stay in that place a moment longer. 'Do you feel able to get up? Let go so I can bang the door again.'

She does so with a gasp that suggests she could be fainting. He touches one of her arms and finds it limp. He sways her. 'Angel?' The word just comes out of him.

Slowly the top of her head comes up and touches his chin. '...can't...can't stand...' She shudders in his arms and lets out a guttural sound.

He holds her tighter. 'We're safe now, they've gone, I didn't know you get attacked.' But the head is dropping again, and he puts a hand firmly under her chin and tries to raise it, feeling her short breaths.

One of her hands moves up and cups his. Her spasmodic trembling continues, and as he tries to comfort her with more gentle strokes of her head, he knows he must soon act, that if she faints, he will let go of her so he can bang the door for attention, or he might have to pick her up and go back up the stairwell, if it is not in ruins.

She raises her head and does something that startles him, just as he realizes too late that the air has become thick with dust, that there is the new danger of suffocation.

'We've got to get out fast, I can hardly breathe,' he says, coughing and having to release her knowing she might collapse.

He begins bashing the metal door, shouting as best he can with the dust now in his nose and mouth, banging and listening and banging again. And almost at once, to his colossal relief, he hears voices from the other side and the door is being unbolted.

'Mistress Hua!' Xuiey the elderly cook cries out as dust comes towards her and she and head domestic Wang take in the scene: the Mistress is kneeling under the stairwell, and the student is standing and spluttering, his hands covering his face, there is debris on the steps and grey dust on the hair and shoulders of the young man.

'Oh my poor girl!' she exclaims when Wang and Yuling help Huihua to her feet and out into the passage.

The head domestic slams the door. 'Are you alright?' he asks Yuling.

'I think so,' he says, blinking and wiping his eyes, then putting a hand to his neck. 'Have I been hit? There's some blood isn't there, it's stinging.'

The man takes a look. 'Something's grazed you at the base of your neck, but it doesn't seem bad. Bathe it, and come and see me if you need to.'

The cook begins leading Huihua away. 'You're shaking like a leaf, pet, you come with Xuiey, we'll tidy you up and give you something calming in the kitchens.'

'The Mistress looks really dazed,' Wang whispers to Yuling as they follow along the passage.

'I didn't know you get fired on,' he replies, brushing some thin particles of stone from the front of his shirt. He looks at the head domestic. 'I thought they might be going to bomb the mansion.'

The man is shaking his head. 'I'm really surprised we were attacked, and they wouldn't bomb the Court, but they could the military camp in the woods. We've checked the building, and there's no fire, thank heavens.'

Yuling went straight to his room and washed in a bowl of cold water, dabbing slightly swollen areas that had appeared in a short bloodied line between his neck and right shoulder; there was stinging but hardly pain, and he guessed that bullets must have shattered the wall of the stairwell causing chips to hit him in a series of minor cuts.

He decided he would still go to Mingon to see the furniture maker's family. After such a terrifying incident, he needed to be in the open air and in the company of good folk.

On the path through the woods, he knew he had experienced within a matter of minutes the bliss of early love and the hell of near death. He walked slowly, deep in his random thoughts, one ear still singing from the deafening attacks.

The evening sun rays came low through the trees, adding to his pensive mood, and as he looked at the long shadows and thought how fortunate he was to be alive, he wondered what his chances would be if the Japanese moved into more of southern China - he would try to flee westward, might seek out whatever Chinese force he could find including the Communists further north, he could train with the Reds, their guerilla tactics might be more effective than the greater forces of the Nationalists.

And the other thought that filled his mind was of the sister, not of his wonder in the temporary painting room and in the Reception Hall (those feelings had for the present been eclipsed by their shocking baptism of fire), but about her near collapse and her earlier holding of him when his shaking wouldn't stop, when she calmed him in that terrifying space by the metal door as bullets crashed into the walls above them. He was seriously worried about her; he too had seen the bewildered vacant look on her face.

15

Huihua, lively and robust, proud of the families she came from, and proud to be the daughter of a general, felt panicky, really very disturbed, very confused, and hated it. She couldn't stop trembling from the memory of the plane firings, and from her certainty that her life had been about to end. She had always considered herself quite strong of mind, but now she kept bursting into tears.

'I feel ghastly,' she said, fear in her eyes, back in her rooms as she garbled out to her mother and brother what had happened. 'Please, one of you *must* stay with me.' Then she began sobbing.

'Shanghan, get a rider,' Madame Huang said, 'Head Groom, anyone, he's to use the road and risk planes, I want Linnie to come at once, and *he's* to use the road too, hurry!'

Over the hour and a bit that it took Doctor Lin to arrive, the mother sat on the bed under the wood-carved swans, stroking her daughter's hand and talking with her (she had never ever seen her like this) and calling up cook Xuiey and the maids Yiying and Dajuan to comfort her.

When the doctor came running into the Mistress' bedroom and saw her state - in Mingon he had heard the planes and the attack - he was very relieved to find she was not injured, and he soon knew from what she suffered.

'I suddenly start shaking and crying,' she told him, 'I can't stop myself, can't describe how I feel, just really unwell, I want to be sick but can't be. I feel strange as though I'm not myself, I've lost all my confidence, Doctor Linnie, it's horrible!'

'This spasmodic shaking, your feeling sometimes sick and the occasional weeps, they are perfectly normal Mistress Huihua, perfectly normal in the circumstances,' the elderly doctor with high eyebrows replied as he touched her forehead and felt her hands, her fingers, 'and I'll tell you why.'

He smiled down at the girl who, as a newborn babe, he had seen just a few seconds after she was helped into the world by the two midwives. This was the girl whose hymen had inexplicably broken at sixteen, causing her and even more her suspicious parents very considerable anguish, and for a short time he had been most worried. The preservation of her chastity was vital in their patriarchal society, a pre-condition of marriage, especially considering the lofty family she came from. The breaking of the hymen placed the arranged marriage into the old Yang family in serious doubt, and threatened family shame and her future prospects. He did not know of any other woman who rode in their part of the province, but he had soon wondered if the girl's love of horses was connected; he had looked into a translated western medical book that he hardly ever turned to, and it had given him the likely answer: excessive riding. His relief and that of the girl was great; that of non-riding Madame Huang had been even greater, though she later told him of the difficulty she had trying to educate and reassure the mother of the boy.

He let go of her hand. 'It is no more than some soldiers experience the first time they have been under fire. You have had a bad shock to your brain, but it will pass, you will be alright, I can assure you. Your father would confirm the phenomenon were he here. But I want you to take a medicinal extract I have brought with me, it will help you and calm you. You are to take it every two hours. I will look in again later, and I will stay here tonight if your Ladyship will permit,' he gave a quick look towards the mother, 'and we will see how you feel in the morning.'

Huihua felt better for the visit and gentle touching of the avuncular doctor and hearing she would get better and that he was staying on. But she continued to feel very insecure, powerless to prevent herself trembling in front of him and in front of her family and the maids.

He told her that she should visit the horses, and when he had left to a guest room, Shanghan took her to the stables. There, between sudden bursts of crying, she stroked Ajin's head and sat outside in the yard with her brother while they watched Head Groom and his new young assistant give the horses a last walk of the day.

Secretary Lee and Captain Ma were summoned to the lady's apartments, deliberately together, and found Madame Huang in an angry mood, each knowing the different reason.

She turned first to the officer. 'Why did we not have even ten seconds warning, Captain, when we always had at least fifteen minutes?'

'I am already investigating this, madam. One or more of the observation posts must be to blame, unless they were attacked before they could tell us, which is possible. The enemy have mastery of the skies and can cause surprise by flying very low, or sometimes they use cloud cover to avoid detection, though they should have been heard. I will report to you as soon as possible, and of course to General Huang.'

'Do you think this was a prelude for what is to come, bombing maybe? Did they fire on the town? They have hit boats and people on the roads before, but never come for the Court or the town.'

'They didn't strafe Mingon. They've been in the east four years and we've been spared. If they come this way the Court could be useful to them, they might want to preserve it as a headquarters. I suspect the pilots were ordered to give us a shock, to warn us not to use this place for holding troops. But if the strafing continues, you will have to move to the basement or evacuate for your family's safety.'

'Moved from my home, that would be terrible.' She turned on the old retainer. 'Lee, my daughter is in some sort of shock, and Linnie is here.' The voice had risen to a high pitch of accusation. 'She is shaking like a leaf and crying, and she says the student helped her down those narrow spiral stairs as the planes started shooting, but at the bottom the door was bolted on the servants' side, scandalously bolted!' She glared. 'It appears he tried to shield her. What is your explanation? I am very displeased, the Mistress' life was almost lost because, it seems, you failed to ensure that the door could be used in such an emergency, though you told her about it.'

The old man looked mortified. He stammered: 'I have no answer yet, my lady. I knew it was an escape route as did the servants, so why it was bolted and by whom I cannot understand though I am endeavouring to find out. I am deeply distressed to hear about the Mistress. I offer you my sincerest apologies and naturally will do so to my master.'

Madame Huang caught the my master innuendo when he always said my lord. 'You had better offer those to my daughter when she gets better! And to Tsai Yuling. If I had had to write to his mother …I do not like to think of it, and after what he went through as a child.'

The secretary was stunned, unable to reply, he was particularly wounded losing face before the captain. But the officer had also been challenged. And the lady was not entitled to receive his resignation; besides, he knew he was too valuable to her husband.

The lady read the thought. It always irked her that Secretary Lee was safe in his position; no doubt he was privy to some of her husband's secrets concerning other ladies. Tersely she asked: 'When are we to pay the student?'

'Tomorrow morning, my lady, at nine.'

'You know what you and I agreed to pay the other man if his picture had worked. Pay the same, and I think it would be appropriate if you add a substantial sum of your own for the student's help to my daughter, don't you? He must also be shaken by the experience.' She looked from the secretary to the captain. 'That is all, I will now return to my trembling girl.'

The next morning, as Yuling walked along one of the mansion's corridors towards the secretary's office, he passed the same guard he had seen the previous day.

'Glad Mistress and you weren't hurt,' the man said. 'Sorry she's taken it badly.'

'Do you know how she is?' he asked.

'Cook told me she's not good.'

When he reached the office, the old man was back to his usual coldness, and gave him a perfunctory nod.

'You are to be well paid, and there is something extra for your help yesterday.'

For his *help*! He was surprised at the low-key gratitude, and assumed the something extra must come from the lady. But no apology was proffered, and he was not asked about his own welfare following the air attack. He watched the secretary open an iron safe in the wall and remove a leather pouch.

'How is Huang Huihua?' he asked as the man placed the pouch on the desk.

'This is your commission and more, be careful with it young man, use it wisely. Take it!'

Yuling picked it up; it was heavy. The pouch was tied at the top by a green ribbon, so he could not immediately look inside, but he could tell that it contained many coins, clearly silver. He thanked the secretary and put it into his sack. 'The Mistress?'

The secretary scowled. 'I understand Mistress Huihua remains in her bed, but she is expected to recover. You are to go to the Reception Hall and wait for Madame Huang, she wishes to speak with you before you leave.'

He was startled, and assumed the lady might want to see that he was alright and thank him for helping her daughter. At least he would be able to find out how Huihua was, and thank the lady for the payment.

Light streamed through the still partly-drawn middle curtains of the Reception Hall, and Yuling at once found his drawing pad and pencil on the floor.

He was standing near the second mural without much interest, the one he and Huihua had not examined, when the far door opened and a purposeful Madame Huang entered. He bowed to her from the mural, but only received back the faintest movement of the head.

'Come over here, would you,' she said, voice commanding, without the politeness of using his name, and she began walking very slowly towards him. When he reached her he received a strange look and felt yet more worried.

'We are it seems even more indebted to you, first the painting and now this. My daughter tells me you took her, no, in fact you carried her down the stairwell away from the narrow window, is that correct?'

'Yes, my lady, I did what anybody would have done, the planes came suddenly and then they were firing, they seemed to come straight at us.' He realized she was not going to ask how he was feeling.

'I am sure it was terrifying. We were in the basement, we heard the bullets hitting the walls. We were worried where my daughter was, so two of the servants went up the main staircase to look for her, brave of them, do you not think?' The lady paused. 'My daughter is very unwell and remains distressed, most unlike her, she has the family courage, you see.'

Yuling was now distinctly apprehensive, finding it difficult to continue meeting the gaze. 'I'm very sorry to hear that, but I'm not surprised. I can't get the terrible event out of my head, and one of my ears is still affected. If the planes had attacked a day or two earlier, I could never have produced your son's portrait.' Why he had added that last point he couldn't think, except to bring the lady back to how she felt at its success. He decided not to mention the small cuts near his neck that Mrs Wu the furniture maker's wife had attended to; they stung when he turned his head, no more.

'Quite so.'

There was an awkward silence, Yuling looking to one side, waiting.

'Doctor Lin is with her as we speak. He came yesterday and stayed overnight, very good of him.'

'Oh dear!' he exclaimed, unable to think what more to say.

'How long were you by that door?'

He was taken aback and looked at her. 'How long? A minute or two, I don't know.'

'My daughter is too shaken to recall properly, but from what I gather, it seems about five minutes. You were shielding her, is that correct?'

A question and an implied accusation? He felt extremely uncomfortable and wanted to avoid further talk about the time element. 'I thought bullets could reach us, so I made your daughter crouch, and I tried to put myself between her and the stairs so she'd have less chance being hit.'

'Praiseworthy, naturally. But you held her, did you not?'

He swallowed. 'Yes, she was shaking. I needed to keep her from moving. I'd already tried to get the door open but it was barred on the other side. I banged the metal thinking servants would hear me.'

'My daughter tells me that she was forced to hold you because you were also shaking. That seems to me, her mother, most strange.'

'She must have done it to stop me, and it worked because...'

'Did you do anything more than hold her, you know what I mean I am sure?'

'No!' He was shocked where she was leading, and gave a pained look, wondering what the daughter had said.

'So you did not touch her head?'

He hesitated, was looking straight at eyes of suspicion. 'I held her head, yes, I was worried she could faint.'

'She says you stroked her hair.'

This was getting dreadful. 'I tried to comfort her, was that wrong?' Immediately he regretted his challenge.

'That was impertinent, kindly retract.' Madame Huang turned her head to one side but continued strong eye contact.

'Forgive me,' he blurted, 'but...'

'And nothing else occurred? I want the truth Tsai Yuling, it will not lessen my family's gratitude towards you for trying to help my daughter.'

'No, I hope and believe I acted properly.' He dreaded whatever the next question would be, was concerned what the distressed daughter might have said, no doubt under her mother's direct or subtle interrogation: had he not buried his face in her hair (amazingly scented he couldn't help recall); had his hands not felt her back and sides to search for a wound; had he not held and caressed her chin when he thought her head was dropping and she might collapse; had she not cupped her hand to his; and worst of all, had she not done that other thing - it had been gentle and beautiful - that so surprised him just before he became aware that they could suffocate from the particles and dust in the air...

He maintained his expression of hurt. But she seemed to have run her course of questions. 'I understand you will be returning in a few days, but only for a short visit, half an hour or so, no more will be necessary I trust. After that I hope you will have a trouble-free return to your university. Now please see me out.'

This time she bowed, and he did so again. He walked awkwardly beside her as she took her short foot-bound steps, and he wondered whether to thank for the payment. She had left open the door, and when they reached it, she gave him a cool searching look, said nothing more, and went out.

Secretary Lee's letter sent to the university on Madame Huang's behalf was equally cool, a fact not lost on the Principal. But he was relieved to hear that the portrait had been accepted and their talented student paid. The Principal was not to know that in an earlier letter written by the general's wife in her own hand, she had called the portrait *brilliant*, and had expressed her pleasure at the student's success. But it had not been sent from the Court before the air attack, not before the mother had seen her daughter and heard part of the story and sensed what *more* might have happened at the bottom of the stairwell, enough to make her most fearful.

*

'You have your position to consider, my dear, and that of your father and me,' Madame Huang said to her daughter two days after the nasty event. She saw Huihua was struggling to embroider, something she normally performed excellently, and knew she was in no condition to talk back. 'We are your parents to whom, I do not need to remind you, you owe certain duties. It was, as you must now realize, very wrong and foolish of you to have repudiated the Yang marriage agreement. I hear he is betrothed again. And one day, hopefully not long from now, you will marry into the right family, one that your father and I shall approve, naturally. You had a bad fright with those planes, and cannot be seeing things clearly at the moment. But I do for you, and I can assure you, you will soon be back to your usual self.'

After the air attack, Huihua had at first been consumed by its horror, and kept imagining that the student had been killed as he was carrying her, and that she had fallen down the last few steps and was lying badly injured, though not from the bullets, they had embedded themselves in the walls just above her. She could not get out of her mind what she saw coming towards her through that long window opening, and the horrendous noise that made her scream. She thought much about the suddenness of death, and about her fear of expiring by that immovable door as she and the student clung to each other.

Such horrors and fantasy images pushed from her mind any possibility of dwelling on the comforting things each had done to help the other. And her unsettled thoughts never took her back to the emotional and physical excitements she experienced in the Reception Hall when she looked with the student at one of the murals.

The next day, when her mother insisted that they take a morning walk in the gardens and brave being caught out if the air-raid siren sounded late again, Huihua found herself looking indifferently at the flowers and the fruits. She was not able to hold a conversation with the father and son gardeners as she usually did. And she hardly felt better, though she realized that the uncontrollable trembles had much lessened and the weeps seemed to have ended, and she did not mind that Doctor Linnie had returned to Mingon.

After the walk she went to the stables. Head Groom and the new assistant were not around as she entered Ajin's stall. The horse was standing and gave a nudge to her shoulder, but Huihua did not pat or stroke as she normally would. She sat on a stool in one corner and watched the horse look out to the yard, wondering what he was thinking, and if he sensed that she still felt unwell, and if he had been affected by the noise of the planes and bullets. She closed her eyes, and a few seconds later, just as the horse bent his knees to lie down, her head dropped.

Several minutes later she was roused from her doze by a woman giggling in the stall beside her that she knew was empty. Soon it was followed by male chuckles, and she thought that one of the stable-gate guards must have let in a peasant girl.

Unsure what to do, she was very soon brought to act when the titters became horseplay. Making a sizeable cough, she had just stood up when the head of the new assistant groom looked over the wooden partition, shock on his face. Ajin also rose.

As Huihua walked past the empty stall, she turned and saw Dajuan, her mother's personal maid, crouching and looking towards her in alarm. She walked on without saying a word, surprised that the thirty-year-old was with such a young fellow and that they had dared to risk what they were doing within the grounds of the Court, amorous conduct by staff being strictly forbidden.

During the rest of that day, she had no desire to go riding or to work her embroidery or to read poetry let alone create verse. She was experiencing dramatic mood swings, from panic to numbness, from nasty fantasy thoughts to bursts of elation.

Waking up the next morning, she felt bad, refusing to be coaxed from her rooms by her mother or by Yiying. But as the morning progressed, she began to feel better, and by the middle of the day she told her maid she felt good. In the early afternoon she was feeling positively euphoric, that if she had survived the air attack she could survive anything. She told her mother that she wanted to go riding *straight away*.

Madame Huang was unconvinced, finding her daughter had become light-headed, the pendulum of her psychological health swinging alarmingly. But she knew the powerful effect horses played in Huihua's life, so did not discourage the idea. Besides, a good-looking cavalry officer whose fiancée had died in some accident, a Lieutenant Chu, had arrived to serve in her husband's corps, and she was aware of the good repute of his family, albeit he came from Guangdong, the province to the south; she thought he looked distinctly promising.

Soon into the ride, Head Groom realized that the Mistress was not practising her usual excellent horsemanship; she was trotting too quickly, and when she suddenly challenged him and the lieutenant to a race through part of the woods, she was off into a dangerous gallop without waiting for them to answer, was racing along the wide but frequently curving path, and they had no option but to chase after her.

'Not the Mistress I know,' Head Groom shouted to his companion, 'got to stop her before she gets injured or knocks someone over or we'll be in trouble.'

The men had dangerous rides trying to catch her, each nearly hitting branches, and when the lieutenant finally caught hold of Ajin's reins and pulled the horse up just as the path was narrowing into a single track, Head Groom came up calling out breathlessly: 'That wasn't good, Mistress! You're in our care, we'll turn round.'

He received a defiant look and was shocked to see the fire in her eyes.

Huihua had never felt better; she had no intention to go back. 'We'll canter to the rocks, Head Groom,' she proclaimed.

'No we won't, pardon me.' Head Groom turned his horse. 'It's back to the Court and we'll clear this up with her Ladyship, your father not being here.' He nodded to the officer.

The lieutenant began pulling the horses round, but Huihua kicked Ajin and whacked her crop against the horse's side, then tried to do the same to one of the officer's hands, but he saw it coming and stopped the crop with his arm just as her horse tried to go. 'Keep hold of her man!' Head Groom shouted. 'None of this, Mistress, what's come over you! We'll return now at a dignified trot, General put me in charge and I'll do my duty by him.'

As they started back, the men were very relieved that the Mistress was making no further protest and had gone quiet; and by the time they were approaching the high walls and side gates into the stables, Head Groom noticed that the eyes had lost their fire, in fact now seemed dull. And when they dismounted, he was surprised that she showed no interest in cooling Ajin and wiping him, something she normally loved to do. He went at once to Secretary Lee to get a message to Madame Huang that he was concerned for the Mistress' health, she was clearly unwell, had acted so out of character, impulsively and dangerously.

Back in her rooms to wash and change, the euphoric emotions Huihua had experienced while galloping along the twisting path had turned into an apathetic confusion, and she sat at her dressing table head in hands still in her riding clothes.

Her mother had been taken by escort to talk with the colonel in charge of the nearby military camp in the woods, and maid Yiying was elsewhere in the mansion, not expecting her Mistress to return early from the ride.

Several minutes later she stood up cursing her lot. A strong new emotion had arisen - anger. At first she thought it was annoyance at life's difficulties, at being trussed up in a mansion and having undesirable suitors thrust at her.

She was staring from one of her windows, looking towards the old pagoda tree that had been in late bloom only a few weeks earlier. Near the upper branches, her eyes took her to a window of one of the old guest rooms, where the painting of her brother had taken place, and a sense of outrage overcame her.

...he had the gall to physically touch me, *me* my father's daughter, a lady of the Huang family, he actually put his hands on my waist and he's a nimmeny-pimmeny student yet he placed me on that awful high table and laughed ... and during the planes, how *dare* he put his arms round me ...he had no need to do that, *no* ...I didn't ask him to hold me, more like it he asked me to hold *him*, which I did to stop his shaking ...yes the whole thing was terrifying and he carried me away from that horrible window, though again he took a mighty liberty and I would no doubt have got down on my own and survived somehow ...and I did *not* do that thing to him, no, no, I won't even think about it because it never happened, it must have been something I've later imagined, not being well...

Her mother was right. She was born into a top family, and naturally she should only ever have close physical contact with a man of similar position, and only when married, someone like the fairly handsome officer who accompanied her with Head Groom on her fast ride, a captain or lieutenant or whatever he was, whoever he was...

Now she remembered the Reception Hall ...he flirted with me, scandalously flirted ...just because his portrait is good, it gave him no licence to act so audaciously, not with me ...and my father had him flogged only last year, I can't believe his impudence...

She was now more sure than ever that the student had gone much too far with her at the first painting session and then later at the bottom of the stairwell by that basement door. 'My dear, that was *very* wrong of him! Held you tight! Stroked your hair when the planes went!' Her mother had kept giving her horrified looks. 'I never heard such a thing, shameless rascal! What else did he do to you?'

The more she considered it all, the more she could see that the student had acted completely out of order. She felt incensed, defiled almost, and by an underling.

At the meal-table that evening - her brother was absent - Huihua's forceful emotions had partly subsided, but she mentioned some of her thoughts, though not all.

'I praise you for seeing the matter in its proper light,' her mother replied, taking two white coconut slivers from the blue china plate. 'It is absolutely clear he took gross liberties. A pity, his work was very good.' She turned to her daughter. 'But we ladies must be careful, Hua. Especially at your age, you must guard against forward men, lechers and the like...' She paused, thinking briefly of her own husband. 'By the way, did you actually thank him at least, for trying to help you?'

Huihua looked up, surprised by the question, and tried to remember. 'I'm not sure, I don't think so, it was all so frightening, I felt numb.' She needed to think. 'Should I? I can send Yiying with a note, or could speak to him when he comes back, he's coming back isn't he, to do something?'

The mother gave her daughter a trusting smile. 'Well now, why don't you come into town with me in the morning, I have a few matters to attend to, we can call on Linnie because you are not right yet, I can tell that. And the sedans can stop at the shop, Lee says it is a furniture maker, and you can deliver short thanks, if he is there that is.'

'Excellent idea!' Huihua replied, glad her mother knew she was not feeling right, not her normal self, glad she would be seeing the old doctor again. 'I can't put it any other way, I still feel somewhat unwell.'

The mother changed her expression to serious. 'Naturally, you must also inform him...' she had lowered her voice two notches to the level she knew people feared including her own children, '...very firmly, using your authority as the daughter from our high family, that the nature of the protection the two of you appear to have given each other must and shall be completely forgotten by him. He clearly overstepped the mark, and you never know what ideas above their station young men have in their excitable heads, *especially* students.' She waited for her words to sink in. 'Did I tell you? The guards say that he was here yesterday enquiring after you. One must assume his enquiry was honourable, but...?' She gave her daughter a look of uncertainty.

The Wu family made their working guest very welcome in their home, but the parents were shocked to hear his story of the air attack. What they liked about the young man was his unaffected manner with them, and his good spirits; he gave all the children lessons in drawing and crayoning, including the youngest boy of two and a half.

Mr Wu told Yuling that his coming to learn for a few days was giving him a boost of spirits, he was going to put him to working on one or two pieces left unfinished just a few years earlier. And if no one wanted them, the furniture maker would simply look at them with pride. 'One day things might change,' the man said wistfully.

Yuling paid for his mother's present, and gave generously to the furniture maker for the ten-day apprenticeship. And when early on Mr Wu asked him why his name seemed familiar, the story of his boyhood flight in the hills came out, and they said that they felt even more privileged to have him with them.

But he did not tell them what was going on inside him. He could not put out of his mind Huihua's looks at him in the Reception Hall. The smell of her hair would not leave him, nor would the smile or the voice that made him worship. 'Mistress is still not well,' was all the guards could tell him at the main gates. He longed to know that she was recovering, and desperately hoped that when he went to varnish, she would be better and that he would be able to see and talk with her again.

As each day passed it became an agony not knowing how she was and whether she was at all thinking about him. He kept asking Mrs Wu if she had heard from her aunt at the Court - the old cook called Xuiey - but no news came.

'You're a natural with wood,' the furniture maker told him while he was helping create the legs of a large table. 'I could soon teach you many of the skills.'

*

A few days into Yuling's help at the shop, while he is carefully using a plane to level the top of a poplar table the Wu girl comes running through the hens in the backyard, to tell him that a well-dressed woman is inside the shop asking to speak with him.

'For me Ashenga, are you sure?' Yuling does not think of Huihua; he would never expect her to come there. And it couldn't be his own mother because she doesn't know he is in Mingon - he isn't going to tell her about the portrait commission until after he returns to university, as she will be shocked to hear he has gone back to the Slayer of the Reds' mansion.

When he sees Huihua standing in the middle of the passage, his surprise and joy are such that all he can do is smile at her as he starts to walk between the furniture. But very quickly he takes in the serious look, and when he reaches her and they bow, he sees with fright that this is a different young lady, far removed from the glorious person who came to talk with him about the murals. His heart sinks, his expression turning into a half smile of fear. He wants to ask how she is feeling, but she gets in first.

'May I speak with you alone?'

Yuling looks at the girl who has followed him. 'Leave us please, Ashenga, and ask your parents and the boys not to disturb us for a few minutes, Mistress Huang Huihua has come to speak with me.'

For a second the girl stands open-mouthed; then she runs off to the back.

He waits.

Huihua has a task to fulfil, and her private training in handling people takes over. She feels resolute, reasonably; her mother is outside in one of the single sedans.

'Tsai Yuling, I'm not sure that I thanked you after that horrid door was opened, or before perhaps, I just don't remember, it will always be a very unpleasant memory as you know. You helped me down those stairs and I think you tried to protect me. Please accept my gratitude.' She is glad to have had the courage to look straight at him and to state her gratitude in a firm and decent manner.

A chill runs through Yuling; it is like a speech, could have been the mother. He only just manages to hold his part smile. 'There is no need for this between us, but of course I accept your gratitude as you put it. It was a terrible experience for both of us, and you placed your arms round me when I couldn't stop shaking, that comforted me more than I can tell you in words.' He sees her unhappy expression and hesitates - her eyes are so different to those that searched his in the Reception Hall. 'And you thanked me in the most precious way.'

Huihua frowns and looks to one side, not wanting to be reminded of anything that happened in the stairwell.

There is an unpleasant silence. Without looking up she invokes her mother's words. 'You must be referring to the few moments we shared. They were necessary for me as I believe they were for you. I was as scared as you were. But I ask you, no I require you to forget those moments as I will …have…' she corrects herself. 'It is clear that when trying to shield me you overstepped the bounds of proper behaviour, but in the frightening circumstances I am prepared to forgive you.' She makes a short nod to the floor. 'No, I *do* forgive you.' Good, she has said the right thing.

She feels his eyes on her and can well imagine his face.

Yuling's part smile has vanished; he is too stunned to speak. Something like the cold metal of that door has barred him and then pushed him hard away, something killing and final to his soul. He keeps on looking at her, and realizes that this will be the last time he will ever see her …and to end like this.

Huihua needs to continue, finish what she has come to do; she keeps looking to the floor. 'And if I overreacted, and I do not say that I did, it must have been because of my fright. But such moments must be removed from your mind,' she pauses, 'as they have been from mine, definitely,' and nods.

He stares at her. From somewhere he finds a voice. 'Look at me.' He moves closer, bending his head towards hers.

Hurriedly she steps back. 'Keep your proper distance.' She realizes her words sound harsh, but she is not going to look up.

'How can I forget the help and comfort we gave each other?' he says. 'We nearly died. We all know when those rare special moments come in our lives. I had such a moment when you sat beside your brother and I painted, I blessed you a thousand times, you were my inspiration. And I had another at the murals, I thought you were so lovely…' He stops himself, he's gone too far again, and now she'll admonish him and he'll die. 'I cannot put these moments out of my mind even if I want to, I cannot forget them, I cannot forget you. Yes I can live with them as memory, but don't ask me to remove them, your kiss in my palm...' he sees Huihua start '...will stay with me for as long as I draw breath.'

Her eyes search the floor. Why oh why did she go so far? It must have been the shock Doctor Linnie talked about. She decides to end what has become a deeply unhappy visit. 'Very well, I have given you my gratitude, and I repeat it. Now my mother awaits me in the street.' She looks up at last, sees the pain, and bows quickly. When he does not reciprocate, she turns and begins walking along the passage between cupboards, tables and bamboo chairs.

'Huihua' she hears when she is near the entrance. She half turns, and is surprised that he is running towards her, and wonders what now might be coming. 'Accept this at least, as a token of my ...as a gift to remember me by.' She receives some small scrappy piece of brown paper, multi-folded, and thinks he must have had it in a pocket. 'It's a Japanese prose poem I translated at college. You told me you love poetry.'

He bows to her. Huihua meets the eyes; they are a picture of defeat and sadness. Still holding the folded paper, she brings her hands together in a slower courteous farewell, and goes out through the entrance to the waiting chairs and the escort. From one of the sedans, she sees that between foot soldiers her mother is looking at her through a slit in a curtain.

Once inside her own chair, she pulls the curtain to, the bearers pick her up, and they start along the street towards the doctor's house.

She opens the folded paper. Sufficient light comes into her private world for her to read.

> As rising floods from spring waters cover the earth and all the animals therein perish and the world is dark, then dies my soul...
> Until the day when the waters have gone, and radiant flowers in Heaven's every colour cover the earth again, and wild orchids smile to the skies.

She puts the paper on her lap and moves the left-hand curtain back a little. They are passing Elder Han's house. Over the entrance, its colourful dragons are spitting fire as they always have. She reads the poem again.

16

The furniture maker very soon noticed how unhappy his excellent short-term apprentice had become, following the extraordinary visit to his shop of the general's daughter. He had not seen the young lady, but Ashenga told him about her. He mentioned his concern to his wife, saying that the lively spontaneity and interest of the student seemed to have vanished, that he looked forlorn and no longer had his mind on the tasks he gave him. They concluded that perhaps General Huang had returned and not liked the portrait of his son - Mrs Wu's aunt Xuiey the cook had told them whose portrait it was.

The student had just helped him place a half-finished table onto a workbench when Mr Wu felt bold enough to speak. 'Forgive me Tsai Yuling, you look very unhappy, you haven't had bad news, have you?'

His helper turned to him and sighed. 'I'm sorry, but I can't go on working today.'

'Is there anything we can do to help, you're not feeling ill are you?'

'Not ill, just very low, I've never felt so...'

Tears seemed to be coming, and the furniture maker was shocked. He heard the student mumble another apology, and watched him wipe dirty fingers under an eye. 'Did the General reject the portrait? I can give you your money back, don't worry.'

'No, nothing like that.'

Mr Wu waited. The student was giving him a pathetic look.

'I've just felt an angel's coldness.'

The furniture maker was astonished. 'You mean the lady who came here! The Mistress!'

The student nodded. For a short while the furniture maker was lost for words. But again he plucked up courage. 'Surely you're not saying you have feelings for the lady, she's the General's daughter! You can't possibly...' He stopped himself, waited, and when the student said nothing, he asked: 'Does she know how you feel? You can't have known her for long?' The young man seemed unable to answer. Mr Wu could hold himself back no longer. 'It's not my place to say, but aren't you playing with fire?'

As Yuling entered the inn, it was all he could do to raise his clasped hands in polite greeting to the inquisitive innkeeper. 'Why you back so early?' the man asked. But he just shook his head and went through the hanging beads that were a colourful barrier against insects.

He climbed up the stairs and collapsed onto the bed in his first-floor room. Lying on one side and looking at the miserable grey wall, he pictured the cold Mistress in the shop passage as she looked towards the floor, talking as if he was an unwelcome intrusion into her life. What really hurt was the comment of overstepping, and her delivery of those icy words so unjust: 'No, I *do* forgive you.'

Yet she had given him such looks in the Reception Hall that he *knew* she had felt something special between them; there was searching and wonder and longing ...wasn't there ...or was he mistaken, had he simply been dazzled by her and by her position of privilege, and lost his head?

To be rejected, and in that manner ...to long for her because he knew he already loved her even though he'd spent so little time with her ...and she had stopped it at the start. He felt sick. It happened to others and now it was happening to him.

He heard again the furniture maker's playing with fire comment. Oh why did she have to come from such a family? Almost any other girl. But an old warlord family now Nationalist, and the daughter of one of the worst, this was his terrible misfortune.

And he had to return to varnish in a very few days. He might not see her. Almost certainly she wouldn't appear - why should she after her shut-out words? He would be leaving the mansion for the last time, never to see her again, never to look into her eyes or hear her voice, only to have the memory of seeing the heavenly being at the door of his painting room and then before the planes came.

And whenever he would look at another woman, how could he not be reminded of her? Yes he could lose himself in other women, but how could he ever feel for another the same way, she would always be between them, her kiss in his hand a reminder, never to release him.

He felt wretched, wished he had never accepted the commission; he should have heeded his all-powerful feeling that he could never go back to Mingon to do something for the man whose evil power led to Lam's death. Why had he done so! Now he was horribly wounded, not by the father but the daughter who, though she did not know it and he never sentimentally dwelt on it, had been part of him since that night when he dreamt, the night before his rescue.

*

The following afternoon Huihua went riding, assuring her mother and Head Groom that as each day passed she was 'feeling more myself' - and it was true - she would not gallop off, she added. Another soldier, not Lieutenant Chu, escorted her with Head Groom.

She rode intelligently enough but did not enjoy it, and when they returned to the stables, this time she attended to the wiping down of her horse. As she looked at the large dark eyes, she felt reproached; was Ajin telling her that he behaved naturally but she did not?

That night she kept waking, each time with one thought only: that of the student's deeply unhappy looks at her in the shop passage, pain she had caused.

Her mind wandered back to the Reception Hall, to her incredible emotions as she talked with him. She had been excited before by a man, but never anything to that extent. She thought of Yang, the unattractive arrogant officer she had been meant to marry, and thanked her stars she was not lying beside him or worse under him.

Was Tsai Yuling simply a cocksure student who had got above his station and flirted? His looks towards her - and she had liked them hugely - told otherwise, that he allowed himself to feel for her in an almost reverential way. And his decency was transparent; yes he could be much too direct, but he was a young man of great courage, and he was a superb artist.

In the darkness of her room, for the first time since the horrible disturbance to her mind had gone, she took herself back to what actually occurred by that basement door, and thought about his gentleness; his arms round her and his stroking her head kept her from fainting. She recalled the terrible point when she thought she could actually be dying from shock of the noise of the bullets; his firmer hold of her at that moment, and the hand under her chin, had felt life-saving.

And he was as terrified as she was, why shouldn't he have held to her? He didn't take advantage in the least way, quite the opposite.

In truth, he had probably saved her from the planes and from suffocating ...and in the shop she had said those things to him.

Without moving from her bed, she lit one of the candles and lay back, looking up at the old wooden ceiling of carved swans, from which she reaped such imaginative ideas for her poetry.

Poetry. His scrappy translated Japanese poem was on the table beside her.

She re-read it, and then stared at one of the swans; its curved neck and beak pointed to the door; a long crack in the carving showed black in the candlelight, enhancing the length of the neck.

For some time she stayed awake, until eventually sleep came.

When finally she woke, it was with the memory of a strange dream she had, and she didn't know whether it was pleasing or not. She was chasing a young man she didn't think she knew, whose face she couldn't see, though why she was chasing him she also didn't know. And as she was about to catch him, the man turned round but the face was in full shadow, though somehow she knew there was a beseeching look in the eyes as if he meant to love her, possess her, something she wasn't prepared for. And then she was fleeing and looking back, he was running after her, the smile was slowing her as if by magnetic force that was by no means unpleasant, and when she came to a division of the path into two, she saw that one way was a cul-de-sac bordered by high side walls and a high barrier not far ahead, the other had no walls or barrier and gave her a clear run to a wood she could hide in. And she chose the first path, immediately knowing she shouldn't have, and as she came to the high barrier feeling excited, she turned and her father stood before her with a great frown, the pursuer nowhere.

That morning at the swivel breakfast table, her mother asked her: 'Are you riding today, Hua? You are looking a lot better.'

'I prefer not to,' she replied, 'I think I'll stay quiet for a few days, as in June.'

Madame Huang understood, knowing that occasionally her daughter needed to rest for womanly reasons; she was glad to hear she was reading again.

But Huihua's monthly was not affecting her. She did indeed now feel much better; the mood swings had completely gone, and she felt stronger in mind. And since seeing the student in the furniture shop, she found herself thinking in equal measure of his amazing looks at her in the Reception Hall, and of the agony on his face in the shop passage; they spoke to her of something deep, something special.

That same day Yuling sealed the painting. Afterwards, when leaving Wuyi Court, he had the heaviest of hearts saying goodbye in the outer courtyard to the impressive boy whose portrait was now complete and ready for framing. Walking through the main gates for the last time, he thought of the sister's terrifying haughtiness - so like the mother - and of her brush-off words that continued to cast a dark shadow over him. And now, with every step he took past the main gates - gates he hated for good reason - he was living the very moment when his expulsion forever from her life was reality.

241

He passed one of the roaring winged lions, and started back in sunshine towards Mingon. A guard called after him, pointing upwards: 'Don't take the road, student, use the woods.'

But he didn't heed the warning. ...you idiot, his brother Ayi was saying as he left the dark red walls behind ...you were mad, how could you even *think* of letting yourself fall for her, she's the tyrant's daughter for god's sake, don't forget I went with you and mother to that awful place of oppression and power when we were young... His mother was looking at him and shaking her head ...you *can't* love that ogre's daughter, Alinga, you *can't!* ...His stepfather was taking him into the orchard ...shake her off, face reality, you've got to get on with your life, your studies ...it was unwise, the man's not pleasant, I don't need to remind you of that, it might be worse than a flogging next time, put her behind you Yuling, put it all behind you...

The road took him through a palm plantation, trees young and old, some straight, others blown half over by winds, trees that he knew gave no shelter against planes. As he stopped to look at the blackened husks of coconuts rotting on the ground, feelings of thwarted early love and of self-pity welled up to overwhelm, and soon he was weeping against one of the palms. No one was on the road to see him; only a mangy dog lay curled up nearby, and it did not stir.

Why hadn't he stopped himself thinking about her like that? Why did he sometimes get so bold? Maybe when he painted he just felt free. But to have touched her, held her... No! He had to stop thinking of her that way, it was finished, in fact it never got started, she'd crushed him, she didn't think of him as he thought of her. So he had to try to forget her. Maybe he'd feel better with distance and time, they were supposed to be healers the writers said, didn't they...

By the time he reached the Great Gate his mind had partly cleared; the fresh air had done him good. He wandered into the bustle of the small town, and thought about the Wu family not far away. He loved learning the carpentry skills and being among them, but he could never remain in Mingon knowing she was only a short walk away; now he couldn't even say her name to himself. He must leave very soon, get back to Suodin, studies, his friends.

And there was a serious matter to attend to three months later when he would be returning home to Tuxieng for the Chinese New Year. He needed to talk again with Ayi, to impress on him to go to college and become an engineer like their father and grandfather, not to do anything so foolish and dangerous as to join the few Red partisan groups still known to be in Fujian (which Ayi had told him he was thinking he might do); if Ayi was caught, the Nationalists could well kill him.

When Huihua's brother came to see her that afternoon in her self-imposed retirement in her rooms, she had great difficulty keeping her emotions hidden. She was embroidering and sitting cross-legged on the floor. Even though he was still only fourteen, she could sometimes talk with him and confide her thoughts, as she had the previous year over her decision not to marry Yang.

'How did he seem, was he pleased to be finishing it?' she asked, trying not to seem too interested.

Shanghan stood looking down at her. 'I'm not sure, he was quiet, but father will love it. He took a photograph and then added the varnish, it brings it more to life, he says it preserves the paint. It's amazing Hua, my picture's going to last for many generations after my life ends, think of that!' He grinned at her. 'I really like him, I took him to near the main gates and told him the framer's coming tomorrow, and he said he hopes we choose a good one.'

'Is he enjoying working at the furniture shop?'

'He didn't say anything about that, but he's leaving Mingon and going back to his college, and it was strange, when he said that, he looked really unhappy and I thought he was going to cry.'

'Cry?' Huihua placed her needlework on the floor and looked closely up at her brother.

'Yes, I asked him why he had tears in his eyes, he said he couldn't talk about it, so I asked him if it was about someone in his family, and he said something like...' Shanghan blinked, 'something like: "It's a weakness" or...'

'Did he say: "Call it an artist's weakness for beauty"?'

'That's it! I suppose he must be pleased with the portrait, so perhaps he was sad to be leaving it. He was looking out of the window at the tree, and I actually saw a tear fall, is that what artists do when finishing a painting, cry sometimes?'

The following morning Huihua's mother asked her: 'Hua, the framer is coming this afternoon with samples, do you want to have a say in the one we choose? Shanghan is leaving it to us. The man told Lee he can make the frame in less than a day, and we are allowing him to use the workshops.'

'Not particularly,' she replied, 'you'll choose well I know. But it must be worthy of the portrait, it is a very fine one.' She ignored the look her mother gave her.

Later that day, when they met the secretary and the framer in the temporary painting room, Huihua looked briefly at the samples and two photographs the framer had brought of other framed portraits, and said nothing by way of approval or choice.

While her mother was talking with the man, she walked over to the easel where sunlight was catching the canvas front on. She marvelled at the portrait's vitality now sealed, and saw at once the artist's signature in red paste, imprinted by his personal name chop. The chop was stunning, and she guessed he had carved it himself. With his amazing talent, he would do well in life. She thought it extraordinary that a piece of primed stretched cloth could be turned into a majestic painting of such strength and beauty.

She felt in two minds about often seeing the portrait. It would remind her of a man of special ability, with whom she had shared some terrifying minutes that neither could ever forget, and with whom she had experienced a special feeling in the Reception Hall. But their paths would not cross again, and this thought was now making her feel distinctly sad ...different destinies for every human being...

She had already decided she must write to him at his university, to say ... she was undecided how to express her thoughts, except that she needed to tell him that she hadn't meant all her words in the shop passage as he must have understood them, and she wanted to thank him for the poem, and maybe to hint that she would like to stay in touch. She could send a poem of her own ... or would she dare before knowing his reaction?

She walked round the easel to the brown unprimed back of the portrait. She heard old Lee answering her mother, and she was about to walk away when something caught her eye; it was on the left side of the stretched cloth about half way up and camouflaging well.

Was she imagining, or was there some script? She looked closer and took in the flourish of faint brushwork, soon startled to see the word *Inspired*. And the next moment she realized there was other script below. At first she couldn't make out the characters as they were opaque, almost hidden. But just as she was giving up and straightening, all the words flew out at her: *Inspired by an angel in crimson.*

She stared. She could hear the talk behind her but wasn't listening. The words referred to her, she was certain. Or did they? Why the colour? She had worn her shiny yellow robe when visiting the painting session, and the simple light blue one at the viewing and the murals. In the session, he had told her that he wanted her to stay in the room, and in the shop he said she had been his inspiration. And by the bolted door at the bottom of the stairwell he had called her 'angel' sometime after the planes had gone; at the time the word seemed to have magical properties, it brought her back to his presence and the protection from fainting she felt in his arms.

Huihua dragged herself away from the easel and went to the window, to look out at the broad old pagoda tree with its twisting branches and pointed leaves. She was standing in the very room where the student had varnished and had talked with her brother, and now she knew that he had shed the tear for her.

She looked down to the gardens, picturing herself leaning against the furrowed bark of the tree and looking up to the artist in his light-filled temporary painting room, just as she had found herself looking up to him from the monastery garden the previous year when she had been captured by that joy flying towards her.

What kind of a man could smile like that so soon after such a cruel beating - and at her, whose father had ordered it? What kind of a man could hand a poem to a girl just after being so harshly spoken to, so wrongly she had come to realize?

She walked to the front of the canvas, and as she looked once more at the painting of her fine brother and thought of the brilliance of the artist who portrayed his character so well, she began to yearn.

That evening she played the Truth Game, solo in her bedroom without her few intimate and trustworthy young lady friends. She knew that she would have difficulty applying the strict rules of the Yes or No answers required, and that she must try to keep to the very short time limits. She was aware that to play the game was a dangerous road to travel, knowing only too well what her parents conjugally expected of her.

She thought hard about the ten questions. Then she took up her ink-dipped pen and wrote them down. Among others, she asked whether a daughter's filial duty to her parents - to accept their decision on who she should marry - overrode every other consideration including the girl's deepest desire for another. And whether a man's family status, if lower, was too serious an impediment to an intimate relationship for a person from her standing. And whether she would ever be prepared to marry someone she did not love, even if she liked and respected him.

She finished the questions and began to answer them. Usually she had little trouble writing down her answers with the immediacy required by the rules. But to her fifth question: *Could it be that I might be falling for him?* (she had been careful not to write his name), she intended to write *No*, but before she knew it her pen had written *Yes* ...Oh dear! I should never have asked this question, perhaps I'd better stop, it's impossible, some of the answers aren't coming out as I want, and I'm not allowed to alter them...

She looked up at the swan carvings, and urged herself to think more clearly and be more truthful. She thought about breaching the rules and striking out her answer to question five and putting ...*it's too early to say*... or ...*not yet*... or ...*not sure*... or ...*I fear maybe yes*... After all, why shouldn't she change her answers, she was on her own, she didn't *have* to write Yes or No, there was no money penalty to pay because there were no other participants.

But she managed to keep her self-promise to abide by the rules, and moved quickly to answer question six. When she finished, she lay back on her pillows without looking again at her answers, and closed her eyes. Soon her horse came into her mind, she was galloping Ajin in the open, no danger of branches, and when she came back to the stables and thrust the reins into the hands of the new assistant groom, she was running up to the Reception Hall and bursting in, her brother's artist was waiting for her, she was living again the overwhelming feelings she'd experienced with the student before the air-raid siren had sounded, he was putting his strong arms round her and she was letting him because she wanted to be very close to him again, cultural taboos or no. In the comfort of her own bed she didn't care that her imagination was running free.

A few minutes later she sat up and looked at her answers. She saw what she already knew, that she was on the path towards loving Tsai Yuling.

Now she began to fear. When had he written that faint script on the back of the canvas? She desperately hoped he had done so at the time he varnished, as that could mean he had not changed his feelings for her despite her shop-passage words, words she now realized had been suggested to her by her mother. But if he now hated her, and if he had left Mingon...

Strangely, despite her fear, she began to feel the muse on her shoulder, and soon was composing a poem, one coming from deep within her.

*

The hand lamp shines in Huihua's eyes; she has just woken from her mother's touch. 'We are going in a few minutes, Hua. Are you sure you do not mind us leaving you? We can postpone it until next week.'

Huihua moves her pillows and sits up in the bed, giving a short smile away from the light. 'No, you must go. Take care, I'll be fine, I just want to stay quiet.' She yawns and rubs her eyes. 'Don't think I'll ride though. I might get back to some verse.'

She sees her mother looking at the table on the other side of her bed where Tsai Yuling's translated Japanese poem and her own new one lie together upside down with the Truth Game writing.

'You have been busy already, I see. Go back to sleep, my dear. We will be home two or three nights from now.' Her mother bends down and kisses her, and Huihua returns a kiss into the air.

Madame Huang and Shanghan are about to make a short journey by river to two of the four estates the family own, a visit made every six months to discuss taxes and rents of money and kind, and to settle disputes between their peasants. Lieutenant Chu and six soldiers will be escorting them, because small bandit groups remain a possible threat, not in the vicinity of the mansion but much further along the river. The other danger comes from trigger-happy

Japanese planes; hence they are setting off well before dawn in order to reach the first estate shortly after daybreak.

'Is there anything you need in town, Mistress?' maid Yiying says when coming with breakfast into Huihua's writing room. 'You haven't forgot it's my day off? I can bring back some apples, or ya pears if there are any left.'

'That would be nice, thank you Yiying. No I hadn't forgotten.'

The maid puts the tray down.

Huihua speaks sternly: 'Tell everyone that I don't want to be disturbed, not at all, *all day* you understand. I'm in the middle of some difficult composition. And tell Xuiey I don't want any lunch brought up either, as I've got fruits here, but I'll need a small supper later.' She moves a tea bowl from the tray to the table. 'Are you going right away? You'll take the path through the woods, won't you?'

'Yes Mistress. It's beautiful day, you should go for short walks in gardens, in between writing I mean.'

Huihua thanks her for the suggestion. 'And please, no one to disturb me or I'll lose my concentration.' The thin maid bows before leaving the room.

Half an hour later Huihua changes into the worker clothes that she wears when occasionally helping the father and son gardeners, puts on old sandals, and takes up the doli her governess gave her five years earlier - the hat that protects against the sun - not wearing it but letting it hang on her back with its strap round her neck.

Quietly moving from her room, she makes her way along the passages, relieved no servant appears; if one comes she is ready to say she is going to the gardens. On reaching two linen rooms in a short corridor, she takes an iron key from her pocket (her mother and brother each have a similar key), listens, looks both ways and unlocks a third door to the right, the noise of the lock making her wince.

Quickly entering the small empty room, carefully she closes the door and places the key on the floor without re-locking. Daylight comes through a tiny window showing her the ring on the floor. She listens again for footsteps, and then pulls up a hinged trapdoor.

Only once before has she descended the internal wooden stairs leading to the underground passage; three years earlier she had a practice run with her parents and brother against the possibility of a commando assault on the mansion. Her father told them that none of the servants knew of the passage except Secretary Lee, and she and Shanghan were never to mention it.

A lamp stands on the third step with a small matchbox beside it, and soon she has it working. A powerful stick lies on the next step, propped against the wall. She leaves the trapdoor open and starts down, unable to use the rope railing as she has the lamp in one hand and stick in the other. The straight stairs creak and seem to have no end, but when she reaches level ground, she sees the passage go into darkness, and begins the long walk, slightly bent though there is reasonable headroom, and immediately feeling the cool.

Rats run from lamplight her father had said on the practice run when he wielded the stick in front of him. She knows the passage stretches a good two hundred paces, and that at the end it comes to a few steps leading up to another trapdoor inside the White Pavilion, the single-storey summerhouse outside the walls near the edge of the woods and strictly out of bounds to all but family.

The air is dank and unpleasant. She counts each step, and at about half way she hears scurrying noises ahead followed by high-pitched squeaking as she beats the stick against the walls and holds the lamp as far out as she can, pushing herself on.

She never sees the rats, and is hugely relieved when the noise abruptly stops, though she wonders where they have gone and prays they are not following.

The last part is uneventful except for water on the floor that soaks her sandals and the bottom of her worker trousers.

She comes to the first step and moves up, guessing the unpleasant ordeal hasn't taken more than two to three minutes. She places the lamp and stick on one of the steps, braces herself on another and pushes at the trapdoor, and as it opens, a light carpet slides off and chains prevent the cover from tilting back. Warmer air at once hits her. Still on the upper steps, she removes her sandals, leaves them there and extinguishes the lamp.

She takes up the stick, moves onto the floor of the pavilion, and looks round at the octagonal room with its narrow supports, the summerhouse her great grandfather built that enjoyed times of high entertainment in days long gone. Old bamboo furniture under dusty lanterns stand in various parts of the room, and enough sunlight comes through cracks in the walls for her to see well enough.

Moving to the central doors, she pulls back a wooden brace. She takes from a pocket a brown linen cloth and places it over her head to hide her face, before putting on the doli.

She half opens one of the doors, looks out and squeezes through, then looks again and listens for a patrol. She is now well outside the grounds, facing a path leading back through sparse trees towards the high dark red walls of her mansion home.

She walks down the veranda steps and turns the other way, moving round to the back of the pavilion. The air under the October morning sun is pleasingly fresh as she makes her way on a sunlit track that soon takes her to the main path through the woods towards Mingon.

Once on the path she goes quickly, the ground firm under her feet, good to walk on; going barefoot has been one of Huihua's loves since a young girl. Several people come towards her including soldiers from her father's corps going to the military camp or the Court; but she doesn't look up, holds the head-cloth to cover much of her face, and is very relieved each time when no one stops to talk.

As she comes near the clearing before the town walls, she hears horses trotting up behind her and moves smartly to the side; and when the riders pass her, she looks up and sees to her fright Head Groom and the new young assistant. Luckily neither is riding Ajin or Peony; if they had been, the horses could well have smelt or somehow known her and stopped of their own accord; she could then have been in serious trouble, would have had to pretend her recent illness from shock had returned.

She places the stick behind a curling pine that makes her think of a dragon searching her out, and quickly walks out from the trees and into the open. Soon she reaches the ancient entrance of the town, going through it and into the street. Although fearful, she feels reasonably confident that she cannot be recognised; she looks like a peasant.

Before deciding to use the secret passage, she had agonized whether to try to speak with Tsai Yuling if he was still there, to tell him how much she had come to regret her words in the shop, especially her comment of overstepping. Her natural courage told her to face him and be honest, to say she was sorry and that she admired him, his talent, though she wouldn't dare say more. And if he then asked her to leave… Perhaps the most she could hope for would be for him to say he forgave her and would like to remain friends.

As she crosses an undulating pavement by a narrow alley, an ugly old man is scraping his tongue and stands in her way, eyeing her, his face and actions telling her that she has no place to be there, in disguise, chasing a mirage. She has to step into the street to get round him, and when she does so, two men pulling an empty wagon pass from behind and look back at her and she feels growing alarm. …mustn't question what I'm doing, just hand it over, to anyone who's there, or put it down in an obvious place, then leave quickly and await events, though nothing's going to happen if he's not in town any more, or at least not for weeks, and only then if I'm lucky…

She passes a fruit-seller, thinks of Yiying, and prays her personal maid is not nearby and spots her. But she doesn't have time to think what she would say because a man has hailed her; he is squatting between his sacks of different rice, sample bowls in front on the ground. She looks away and hurries on.

…shouldn't be doing this, Hua …what was I thinking, composing such feelings in a poem, on paper …turn round …go back… She wonders if her mind is still unsettled despite her feeling better; it is not for any Chinese woman to seek out a man, and certainly not like this. But she's not seeking him out, is she?

She just needs to put things right, wants only to explain, let him know a little how she feels. And she couldn't entrust her maid to deliver the poem because her mother controls both maids.

More doubts crowd in. Suppose she is mistaken, that *Inspired by an angel in crimson* on the back of the canvas doesn't refer to her at all, has some other meaning, suppose the sadness Shanghan saw was unrelated, suppose Tsai Yuling now thinks of her as the arrogant cold daughter of the man who had him flogged.

The worst thought returns: if he has already left Mingon, she will never again receive those looks he gave her in the Reception Hall, she will forever have a terrible taste in her mouth at what she has done, and any letter she might find the courage to send could go unanswered, or worse could be replied with abruptness or even real unpleasantness.

As she makes her way along the street beside the continually rising and dropping pavements, the general's daughter now knows that she more than admires the art student she suggested to her mother, everything about him. The thought that in the very next minute she will discover he has gone, gone completely from her life, fills her with anxiety more fearful than the thought she might meet him.

Several times she has to force herself on, to do what she has taken this great risk to do - turning back would be so easy. She tries to invoke the adoring looks he gave her at the murals, but the hurt on his face in the shop - the shop she is about to reach - keeps imposing itself. She is in turmoil, can feel her heart beating as she sees the entrance, at once concerned that no member of the family is outside. And if he is there and comes out, will she disclose herself and face him, or panic and walk on?

She hears the Sage of Changlu speaking to her: 'The coward creeps away like a cur, the brave rides the wings of eagles.'

Huihua enters the shop. No one is around. She calls out, but there is no answer and nobody comes. She walks slowly through the passage, passing the spot where she delivered her 'gratitude,' telling herself she must put her envelope down, anywhere conspicuous, and get out quickly. She stops and calls again, desperately hoping that somebody will hear, though please not the person she is thinking about.

To her immense relief a little boy she takes to be about three appears from the side of some furniture a few paces ahead of her; he is deep in his own world, holding something in his hands, and he almost reaches her before looking up.

'Has Tsai Yuling gone away or is he still here?' she asks quietly. 'Or you might call him Yuling, he's the student.'

The little boy doesn't seem to understand. He says slowly: 'Do you want Papi?'

She takes out a folded envelope. 'I want you to give this to your mother or your father, would you do this for me, right away.' She helps him place the envelope behind what he is holding, a toy wooden chariot without its horse. Then she turns him round. 'Run along now, take this to your parents as quickly as you can.'

She watches the boy walking towards the end of the passage, fearful he might put the envelope down somewhere or drop and forget it. 'Or give it to your sister,' she calls out though not too loudly, after remembering the older girl with the plaits.

She returns to the noisy street, feeling more relief that the student has not suddenly appeared, but wondering if he will ever receive her envelope. She is now sure that he must have left Mingon; already there seems a great distance between them.

She begins to make her way slowly towards the Great Gate, her head-cloth well protecting from prying eyes. She visualizes herself walking back through the woods, crestfallen with what might have been, her guilt remaining, her rooms and her parent-pressure life at the Court awaiting her. She thinks of Ajin; when alone with her horse she will whisper her regrets, her sorrow.

Yuling stands under a wooden canopy at the far end of the backyard. He is bent over a sandalwood table, chiselling out a groove, when he hears Mr Wu calling him from the back of the shop. Just two days earlier, the furniture maker had come to fetch him from the inn, telling him that the best remedy 'for that sort of pain' was work. So he had agreed to help until the table was complete.

There is paper in the man's hand; he is calling out that one of the boys has received an envelope for him. He walks over through hens dozing on the ground. To his surprise he sees that it is a fine envelope with his name written stylishly, and he thinks first of the old secretary at the Huang mansion and then of Shanghan's tutor.

Intrigued and still holding the chisel with Mr Wu standing beside him, he opens the envelope with his thumb; and as soon as he sees poetry, he is astonished and knows who the sender is. And his next thought is that Huihua is responding to the Japanese poem he gave her; it was a spur of the moment act when she was going from him forever, when he wanted her to have something of his, even something so scrappy and small. He thinks maybe she is sending him a farewell poem, perhaps as a way to say she bears him no ill will; it might even be one of her own. His eyes fly over the words.

I see in every orchid the radiant colours of Heaven, and as an arrow you pin me to the truth;

I behold your eyes in the hall of landscapes, and in the misty hills
you place me;
I glimpse the sprite's shadow in the shallows of the water, and bells
ring out through the depths of the soul.
But I feel your pain, and my blood runs cold.
Oh victor of forests and victor of canvas, forgive me I beg,
And if you choose to see this 'angel' no more, know that a heart
was touched for always by a smile.

He stands motionless. He reads the poem a second time, more slowly, still only partly able to take it in. The furniture maker shuffles. He looks at the man, then down to the ground shaking his head. He stammers: 'I think she's sent me a goodbye poem, or a love poem, I don't know which.'

He doesn't see the worried look Mr Wu gives him. He turns and begins walking back through the yard, and when he reaches the table, he puts the envelope and the poem on the top in the middle. He looks at the poem for a few seconds, then starts chiselling again, more carefully than ever.

The sweet smell of the sandalwood comes to him, and with it the thought that the table is much lower than the one he raised her onto so she could sit beside her brother. He cuts two more grooves, pushes away the chippings and looks down the yard, and the next moment he has grabbed the poem and is running through squawking hens towards the furniture maker who has resumed measuring a table top.

'Forgive me I beg!' he cries without realizing he is quoting from the poem, thrusting the chisel's sharp end into the man's hand and running into the shop still clutching the paper, nearly knocking over Mrs Wu and having to catch her by the shoulders to stop her from falling, apologising as he sees her astonished look.

'Don't do anything foolish!' her husband calls out.

But Yuling doesn't hear him, he's running between the furniture in the passage and soon out into the street, he's looking in all directions searching for Huihua or for a sedan chair and bearers or for a servant from Wuyi Court, one of the maids perhaps...

Many people are passing to and fro but nobody catches his attention. He starts running towards the bastion entrance, praying he might see someone he recognizes, even a guard, so that he can at least deliver a verbal message, though what he would say...

Without realizing, he brushes past Huihua as she inches her way in front of a metalworker's open shed.

She sees him and stops, her mind in panic as quickly she covers more of her face and doesn't know what to do: dare she call to him, would he hear her, carts are rumbling past, townsfolk are walking in the street and on the pavements, people are standing about talking or doing nothing ...but if she doesn't call out... Too late, through the edges of the head-cloth she watches him disappear into the ancient three-layered gate.

The moment is slipping away, it might already have slipped away; if he goes down the outer street that follows the old wall, they will never meet, and if he runs all the way to the Court and asks for her there, her mother will find out when returning from the estates.

More than anything ever mattered to her, Huihua now realizes she wants to meet the student so she can unburden herself ...and see what he feels. She steps from the pavement onto the street, and as she starts again towards the gate, he comes running back through it and she catches his frantic look.

He stops about twenty paces from her. She is unable to take another step despite her desperation they meet. She watches through the head-cloth; he is clutching what she takes to be her poem, and he is staring at people.

She sees him look towards her. She turns half away, flips the doli from her head to her back, and keeps the brown cloth over her but pulls one side, the side facing him, more open. She looks upwards. There she catches a glimpse of the moon, hazy in the morning's cloudless sky. Riveted to the spot, she seeks in vain the craters of earth's pale sister, before whispering his full name through the noises around her as her inner voice begs him to come to her.

A few seconds later he is before her, searching into her face, soon wonder coming into his eyes, her doubts evaporating, and before she can stop him she is being whisked off the ground and hears him say 'the loveliest peasant in all Fujian,' and she's gasping and being carried in those strong arms, she's experiencing feelings far beyond the words of her poetry; the thrill, the unexpectedness of what is happening to her, and her amazement at his courage (both towards her and in a public place) take her breath away; he is breaching all the norms of their society, where even the holding of hands is a rare sight.

'Put me down,' she whispers as she realizes he is carrying her into the narrow alley that she passed on the way to the shop. A few steps on and she feels again the ground under her feet; she is between a small palm and a house shrine burning two red candles, and quickly she looks both ways though she cannot see properly through the fronds of the palm.

'There's no one here,' he says into her eyes, pushing her poem into his working man's shirt pocket, then removing the strap from under her chin, letting the doli fall to the ground.

Part of her wants to draw away, she feels hot, needs to talk, but he's taking the head-cloth off her and dropping that too, he isn't going to kiss her is he, their culture, her position... 'Tsai Yuling...' she begins, about to step back though she knows she might not be able to move far because of the wall of the house. But his looks at her are so beautiful, full of longing, his hands seem to be searching for hers, she feels breathless at what is happening and she cannot finish what she wants to say because he's smiling in a way she finds irresistible while the tips of her fingers are now being fondled, she's fighting with herself whether to pull free and step to the side or take hold of the hands. And the next moment the fingers of her left hand are intertwining with his, she is letting herself be pulled, his other arm has come round her and he is burying his head in her hair as she gasps more and can smell his woodwork, her right hand is now holding him and feeling the strength of his body as she did in the stairwell, only this time there is no terror of planes, there are no bullets, just submission to the tenderness of the young man who is overwhelming her.

Her left cheek feels the first kiss gentle and quick, too fast for her to demur, and when the lips touch the other cheek and linger, for a moment her eyes close.

'Not here,' she whispers though she meant to say he must stop, but the third kiss touches her forehead, also lingering, forcing her to close her eyes for longer and to hold her breath, and when he comes away she looks up at him and soon is drinking deeply of the love of her brother's painter, knowing she wants to be conquered. And now his nose is touching the tip of hers and it is making her smile, but the immediacy of his lips on hers blows the smile away as she puts her free hand round his glorious head to keep him there, never noticing the moon curving round a roof to one side of the alley, or the house martins flying just above their heads …though her greatest admirer has heard them.

17

They walked along the street several paces apart, Huihua in front so not to arouse suspicion - a woman beside a man, or more usually following shortly behind, could be taken to be his wife and might draw attention.

She was in a daze, could still feel the lips on hers, wondering how she would ever stop herself wanting more kisses, the sheer physical pleasure all-consuming. She had never been kissed, and the sensation was far greater than she had ever imagined. Several times in the last three or four years she had hoped a young officer would be brave, but etiquette and whose daughter she was seemed to work against her. Though often full of fun and against her nature to be too shy, she had always conducted herself properly where men and possible suitors (Yang agreement notwithstanding) were concerned, acting in the reserved manner required of a young woman.

At a vacant patch between two dwellings, a storyteller with a long beard squatted on the ground some paces back from the street. A crowd was listening, those nearer the man also squatting. Huihua stopped and lowered her head; she had caught the name of Qu Yuan and heard the man talking about the early poet-patriot who had thrown himself into the river after his king failed to heed his advice for defending the capital, and it had fallen.

Yuling kept well back from the crowd; he couldn't hear the story because of the noises of the town, and was willing her to keep going. Very soon she did, and as they passed the front of the monastery after going through the East Gate, he gave a wry smile towards the barefoot peasant so wonderfully leading him, the aristocratic girl who came to talk with him in the Reception Hall.

They reached the first of tall willows by Mingon's curving river, and he took her to the secluded spot where he had enjoyed a late afternoon with the Wu family the day before the incident in the shop passage. He helped her down through bushes between the willows, into shade by a grassy short riverbank.

She removed her doli and head-cloth and placed them on the grass, thinking to herself that from the moment she had gone down those creaking stairs to the underground passage, she was already leading another life; she tingled with anticipation, and some fear.

But almost at once he was taking her face in his hands and playfully rubbing his nose with hers; and when he put his arms round her waist and gently swayed her, not kissing, just looking at her and showing much more than admiration, the fear went.

'I'm in heaven again,' he said quietly as they stood at the water's edge in the warmth of the middle morning. 'You're beautiful and brave, Huihua, brave to come to the shop and brave to let me hold you like this.'

At first she did not reply, but took her eyes from his and looked past him at palms and more willows on the far bank. 'I'm not beautiful,' she said, face serious, 'I may be quite pretty to some men...'

Yuling stopped her with a finger, feeling the softness of her lips. 'When I saw you with your brother as I was painting, I thought I had never seen any girl so lovely, not in real life, not in a portrait, you were a princess.' She was looking at him again, and he sighed. 'And now you're a peasant girl and I'm still in raptures. You're a jewel, a pearl, you're a lovely poetess, I will always lie at your feet and worship you,' he couldn't prevent himself from smiling, 'whether they're clean or dirty!'

She felt near heaven at his smile. 'They're dirty at the moment!' she laughed, looking down. He continued to sway her, now in silence, eyes to eyes, Huihua in his arms also in raptures.

When he released her, he kicked off his sandals and put a foot in the river. 'Quick!' he said, scooping up water with both hands. She bent forward, put her hands under his and drank. He scooped up more, drank some himself, and threw the rest in the air over her, droplets running down her face.

He pulled her to sit with him on the bank, and pressed the back of her hand to his cheek. 'I can't believe I'm touching you,' he said.

Huihua was looking at his every feature, just as she had done in a very different mood perched on the table in the temporary painting room, when his eyes were closed. But now she was filled with awe, couldn't believe the power of her emotions, was telling herself she could never imagine feeling such intensity with another man.

She started saying: 'I feel so bad about my words in the shop...' but he shushed her. She searched his eyes and read his thoughts.

She pulled her hand away from his face, and took his right hand in both of hers. 'This is for carrying me down that awful stairwell and protecting me from the planes.' Bending her head, she held her lips firmly against his palm, before coming away with a gentle just audible kiss. 'Let me have the other.' Still she did not look at him. 'This is to tell you how I feel at the moment.' She did the same into the other palm, and a second time near the place of the missing finger, and a weight of guilt left her.

When she looked up, such love was flowing towards her that she had no choice but to receive his embrace. 'I adore you,' she heard him whisper into her ear. 'Would you let down your hair for me, it's so beautiful.'

She pulled away, turned her head towards the bushes that secluded them, removed two clasps and shook her head as her hair unravelled. Soon he was touching it and she was smiling coyly and thinking what she would have missed had the bullets hit them or had she not been brave to seek him out. 'If we'd been killed or wounded...' she began.

'But I *was* wounded!' he exclaimed playing with her hair, marvelling, unable to stop stroking it, his fingers running through.

'You were wounded?' She was startled, surprised his eyes seemed to be dancing; she frowned at him.

'See!' He pulled down his collar to expose the base of his neck. 'You held me too tight! At first I thought the wall must have shattered and fragments had hit me.'

Huihua let out a gasp as she saw a purple line of healed marks from two or three of her fingernails that cut into him as she screamed while he carried her down the stairwell.

They stayed undisturbed among the riverside bushes, partly shielded from the sun by the willows behind them. While they watched two fishermen near the far bank working lines in the water, and identified a few birds including two blue-orange kingfishers that flew several times across them skimming over the river fast and low, they talked about their different lives, including Yuling's time at the university and his hopes for an artistic future combining painting and teaching.

He asked her to recite a favourite poem of hers from the classics. When she finished, he surprised her by jumping up. 'We're going into the river,' he said, bending down and taking both her hands and pulling her up as her eyes widened, 'just the edge, it's not deep and it's not cold.' He laughed. 'I did this with Ashenga and one of the boys, they liked it.'

She watched him roll his trousers to his knees, and thought again how powerful he looked. She did the same with her worker trousers, took up her doli and put it over her hair that now hung down, and they walked into the river arm in arm.

'The mud's lovely and so soft,' she said as they trod through the water, Huihua nearest the bank. She saw the fishermen looking their way; one of them started waving, then seemed to giggle to his companion before they resumed their work; no peasant had ever dared do that to her, a lady; but she wasn't a lady that morning, and the feeling was liberating.

Under a palm hanging well over the water Yuling felt playful, grabbing her shoulders from behind, tilting her towards the middle of the river calling 'Can you swim?' as she let out a cry of 'No!'

'I can't either!' he laughed, bringing her back, his nose close to the side of her head, a slave to her fragrance.

Huihua experienced more feelings of liberation; she had frolicked with her brother when he was younger, and with a few other friends - all girls - when she was a girl; but otherwise her sense of fun enjoyed little outlet, especially now she was a young woman. She was loving every moment since they had found each other near the Great Gate. It was far more amazing than a wonderful dream.

She wanted to kick or splash water at her admirer, but he was pressing her arm again and giving her little space. 'When I was in the monastery garden last year,' she said, still under the leaning palm and looking at her legs in the water, 'and you tapped the window, you mouthed something, do you remember? What did you say?'

'How can I forget? I said "Come back to me sometime, *please*", though I never expected in a million years that I'd see you again, not after I returned to my college in Suodin.'

She looked across the river. The fishermen had their backs to them, and there was no one else near the river. Huihua well knew that a woman should never make a first or impulsive move with a man, must hold back outward expressions of inner feelings; but these things had melted beside Tsai Yuling's refreshing naturalness. The spontaneity in her character that had sometimes helped her poetry now came to the fore; she did what she had yearned to do one day to the man she would love (if she was lucky enough to love and be loved): to kiss before being kissed. She flipped back her doli, leaned up and put her lips to his cheek, feeling his masculinity, incredibly exciting for her, only very slowly coming away. Something had told her that making such a gesture would strengthen her determination never again to be forced into a marriage she did not want; that if what was happening on this fairy-tale morning did not for whatever reason lead to her happiness, she would forever remember the deepest joy she was now feeling with this truly remarkable lovely man.

Yuling was taken by surprise; her seeking him out in peasant clothes and her kisses in his palms had already told him what an exceptional girl she was. He too looked to the other bank and then along their own. 'Do it again,' he said trying not to grin, closing his eyes, looking upwards.

He felt her hands on his left arm pulling him down towards her, and the next moment the smoothness of her mouth touched his face and he was taking a full breath and holding it as the water half way to his knees gently tugged him the other way and his feet sank further into the comforting mud.

He put his arm round her shoulders and pressed her to him, and when she came away they looked long at each other. At last he whispered: 'You *are* courageous and you *are* lovely.'

They walked on until they came to a bend in the river, where he suggested they turn back. As they did so she asked: 'You never said if you liked my poem?' She felt another arm squeeze. 'It's beautiful,' he said, 'if you dedicate it to me, I will love you forever.' She smiled across the water, to the two kingfishers now patrolling the far side.

Sitting back at their spot on the riverbank, he took her poem from his pocket and read it aloud with both her hands resting on his forearm. Then he asked: 'What made you change your mind about me?'

She looked at him with unhappy eyes. 'Once I began to feel better and could think clearly, I hated myself for even suggesting you might have gone too far when you were trying to help me. I hated the feeling that I'd hurt you, and I longed to tell you. But the idea you might have gone already, that I'd not see you again, it was horrible.' She paused. 'I was thinking of writing to you. Shanghan told me how sad you were, and I can't put out of my mind what you did for me, what we went through together. How could I let you leave with my awful words.' Her head dropped. He was lifting it up and she could tell he was about to say something, but she needed to finish. 'And your painting, it spoke to me Yuling, it catches Shanghan superbly. I could never compose as well as you paint.' It was the first time she had called him by his personal name without the preceding family name. She looked at his broad left shoulder and put a hand inside his shirt sleeve, beginning gently to feel his upper arm, stroking it.

He gave her a look of admiration. 'Oh yes you can, "I see in every orchid the radiant colours of Heaven". You're a thinker and a romantic, the best combination. You must show me more of your poems.'

Her hand kept stroking the arm, feeling his strength, and her mind took her to the emptiness she had felt in the temporary painting room when the framer was with her mother and Secretary Lee. She gave him an enquiring look. 'I saw the back of the portrait.' She waited for him to speak, but he said nothing. 'Am I the angel?' When composing her poem she had been certain, but afterwards doubts had crowded in.

He nodded with that quiet trusting smile at her that she was coming to love just as much as the smiting broad one. His confirmation of what she had felt gave her now a powerful feeling of attachment to him, as if something deep within her had stirred.

'But why the colour? Do you imagine me looking good in red?'

Unexpectedly he turned his face away and became serious, unhappy almost she read as she realized something else was in his mind, something perhaps she should not pursue.

Yuling was looking at the fishermen; they had moved out of the water and were standing on the far bank by small baskets. He could not suppress a slight frown, and looked back to the person he had always thought of as the girl who came to help him in the boulder dream. 'I'll tell you sometime, not now,' he said, not wanting to take himself back to his ordeal, not during present moments of incredible happiness when he had never felt so alive, and thinking to add that anyway she wouldn't believe him. He wanted to return to his feelings of wonder about her, so he could take that wonder back with him to his college until he next saw her.

He searched again Huihua's face, his fingers caressing her cheek, and soon he was touching the strand of her hair. 'When I was in the monastery and saw you below in the garden,' he said, 'that look you gave me, you helped me get better, all the time I imagined you cradling me in your arms, it was lovely!'

They talked about horses, she telling him how sensitive and perceptive they were, that sometimes, when she talked to them, she felt she was having a conversation.

Before he could stop himself and against his earlier wish to avoid going back to his bad time, he told her of the moment he lay on the ground, all strength gone and knowing a wild horse was virtually over him because there was pawing of the ground near his head and he expected to be stamped or bitten. He said that before the miracle happened with Lam looking down at him, he had felt a horse's warm snorts on his head, and whiskers even touched his face. He told her that he had never mentioned this to anyone before including his mother.

Huihua was looking keenly at him. She said she thought the horse would have known he was injured, and the pawing of the ground was not to hurt him but more an expression of its fear.

Fear - the word brought Yuling back to the present, or perhaps mentioning Lam had. He looked at the general's daughter. 'What are we going to do? How can I keep seeing you? It's obvious your father won't accept me, not after what happened last year. And anyway he'll never accept anyone from my position, I'm a student and I don't like the Nationalists. And there's something else...' He stopped himself.

'Tell me,' she said, feeling worried again.

He was about to mention his mother's dramatic rejection of her father's advances a few years earlier, but he couldn't, didn't want the coach incident to affect their young love, didn't know how she would take it. He thought she would be so horrified that she might allow it to dampen or even extinguish her feelings towards him, too awful to contemplate. And he imagined again his mother's shock at being told who he had fallen in love with.

'Your mother questioned me about the planes,' he said, 'she seemed suspicious. I think she understood why we held each other, but she didn't like it at all that I stroked your hair, she thought more had gone on. I'm afraid I was disrespectful, it was very awkward.' He saw the worry come into Huihua's face and tightened his lips. 'Your parents must have a high family in mind for you.'

'I was to be married to a man I didn't like, and I finally told them I couldn't go through with it, they were very angry.' She took one of his hands and pressed it in both of hers. 'There's something I have to ask you, and please, you must be honest with me, you will be I know.'

Yuling expected a question about female friends.

'Don't tell me you're a Communist, I couldn't bear it. My mother calls you a Red sympathizer.'

He laughed, and the kindness in his eyes gave her some relief.

'I'm not a Red, I told her so. But would it make a difference if I was or if I become one?' He was being naughty; teasing was not Chinese, but Lecturer Yin did it and he had started to follow.

'Of *course* it would!' She gave him an imploring look, not releasing his hand. 'You won't become one will you?'

The smile left his face. 'I can't see that happening, unless... What do we do if the Japanese come further? The Whites could withdraw and not fight unless the Americans help us more, and what do we do if the Reds keep fighting, they might be our only hope? They get behind the enemy and engage them and capture their weapons so they can keep fighting. I might try to get to them, I don't know.'

'No you mustn't!' Huihua was shaking her head and looking to the grass slope. 'You shouldn't sympathize with them, they caused the civil war. I've seen them brought in, they're nothing but deluded brainwashed peasants. I can't understand you! They're out to change everything, they go far further than Sun Yat-sen's Three Principles.' She looked up at him. 'And they can't win against Imperial Japan, can they? They'll be wiped out and you'd be killed if you joined them.'

'Not at the moment they can't. But if they are the only effective force, what then?' He shrugged. 'Some of my friends might try to get to them.'

'But they won't be the only force, we've got better armies than the Reds, the Nationalists will fight, they won't all be crushed, Chiang Kai-shek's too clever for that.'

'Clever! I don't think so. He's been waging war for years against his own people. He'll never work with the Communists. He agreed to, but only after

261

his own officers kidnapped him and forced him to join a united front, but it came to nothing.'

They were not quarrelling, and Yuling felt no chill between them, in fact he admired Huihua's spirit. But he saw her concern, and for some reason he suddenly imagined being with her at the Hut above the escarpment, alone, looking out over the forests and the valleys, unseen and untouched by a world on fire.

He came back to their talk. 'I know that the Reds will never be strong enough as a political force, but they have idealism and a vision for our poor land, to get rid of the Japanese and all foreigners and to end the corruption and the landlords' stranglehold and the crippling taxes, and to put food into the mouths of the peasants.' He was almost quoting from some of his anti-government posters he had created in Suodin.

Huihua made no reply. He realized he was probably giving her a new view on things. He thought about his brief meeting with the captain between the courtyards. 'Captain Ma would like me to become an officer.'

'A soldier!'

'I was shocked. He asked me to think about it.'

'What did you say?'

'I told him I've never thought of myself as a military type, and I didn't like the idea. My father wasn't one really, he was an engineer and they put him into uniform. I still don't like it. He said he's sure the invaders will push for more of China. But I want to finish my studies, and I said I'd absolutely refuse to be put against my own countrymen if the civil war breaks out again.' Yuling was careful not to add that he'd also told the captain he could never serve in the Huang corps, never under the general.

'And do you really take part in marches and political plays?'

'Not processions or protests, but street acting, yes.' He huffed in amusement. 'My theatre friends get me to take the part of Japanese brutes because I speak some of the language. But I'm too big, I wear their soldiers' berets and they're much too small, so the crowd often laugh, though they don't at the nasty bits when the acting becomes serious, then they shout at me!' He saw that Huihua couldn't contain a smile. 'Street theatre is fun, it can be planned or spontaneous. We show the people that our own administrators are corrupt, including those working in the occupied areas. In Amoy they are in cahoots with the invaders and getting rich.'

He thought he would see how much she knew. 'And you know what the Whites did in Nanjing when we were young, before the Japanese massacre? And what happened recently to the Reds in Anhui?' He was surprised when she shook her head. He told her about the capital Nanjing in the civil war years before the government had to flee to Chongqing when the Japanese came, how Chiang Kai-shek's Kuomintang killed thousands of intellectuals and Communists.

And he told her about the horror felt at his university only the previous year, at the Whites' deception and ambush of Red forces in Anhui. He was careful not to mention Huihua's father - his appalling cruelty to Communists in the south - thinking it possible she might only know her father was strongly anti-Red and might not even know the name given to him. 'Our recent history is very dark,' he ended, 'but don't worry, although I have strong views, I'm not too serious an activist and definitely not a partisan.'

Huihua had picked up straight away that there was more than a veiled criticism of her father as a Nationalist. She was well aware of his reputation for dealing firmly with captured Reds, and she knew the Slayer name which she thought was horrible. But she was relieved beyond belief to find that she had not fallen for a man seriously involved with the very people she considered were as dangerous to their country's future as the invaders.

Yuling watched her looking at her feet, dark brown from the river mud as his were. 'You want to say something, I can feel it,' he said, leaning over and pecking her cheek. 'I hope it's not unpleasant, I haven't alarmed you have I?'

'No,' she said still gazing at her feet. 'Yuling, try not to hate my father, because if you do, you hurt me. I can guess what you think of him after what happened to you. But take *me*, be friends with *me*, do you understand what I'm trying to say?'

He saw her pained expression, one he was getting to know; it was almost as alluring as her adorable smiles. 'This is my answer to you,' he said, turning her head towards him, putting his lips gently on hers, soon feeling her short but tender response.

She came away maintaining her sad look. 'When are you leaving? Please, please don't go for a while, I'm just getting to know you.'

'I'd decided to leave after the varnishing, but Mr Wu asked me to help him. Perhaps the day after tomorrow...'

'No you can't! Stay for two more weeks, I'll get messages to you at the shop or your inn.' She looked eagerly at him. 'There's a place I want to show you.'

Now he was the one to be alarmed. 'Don't send anything to the inn, I don't like the man.' He hesitated. 'I can't stay more than six days at the most, I've got to get back or my professors will be worried. But Mr Wu will be pleased, and I'll definitely come to see you sometime during the New Year period when I'm going home to Tuxieng.'

'Where can I write to you?'

'Send messages to Lee Dingchang, he's a friend of mine at college, a good cartographer. And whatever you do, don't put my name on envelopes or in your letters, don't give anything away, and don't sign them. You can call me Yamin if you like, that was my hospital name. And don't write to me at home, that would be too obvious and dangerous, could be intercepted.' He paused. 'It's going to be more difficult for me to write to you, anything sent to Wuyi Court could be opened.'

'Not to the Court. Write or send messages to the furniture man. Maybe I can collect from there.'

'Mrs Wu has an aunt at the Court, the one who rescued us...'

'Xuiey?'

He nodded.

'She could be very useful,' Huihua said thinking of the elderly cook, the only servant she could fully trust. A slight tremble came into her voice. 'I'm overwhelmed with feelings about you. We've got to keep our meetings absolutely secret. We don't know how the future will turn out, but somehow we'll find a way to see more of each other, however impossible you might think that will be. And don't think I will ever take another man and marry, I won't.' She shook her head again, she'd had to say that, to let him know how strongly she felt. 'And if I'm questioned or you're questioned, we must deny ever seeing each other except when you were painting. But we can say we have struck up a friendship, an artistic bond. I'll be careful, and hopefully an opportunity will come when I can mention you to my parents or one of them.' Anxiety came back into her expression. 'I'll always be patient, it's one of the great virtues of our people. But will *you* always be patient? You must meet young women, you'll be greatly admired.'

'Will I be patient? No words can describe what I feel for you, Huihua, and if I tried to paint you, I could never come near the truth of who I see in front of me. But it would be the greatest portrait of a young lady China has ever seen, men would flock to your door, then I'd have no chance!'

While Huihua stayed hidden by the bushes, Yuling ran back into Mingon. The storyteller with the long beard was now standing, his audience mainly children, and they were often laughing.

Within twenty minutes he had returned with two pomegranates and a bag of pumpkin seeds sweetened in honey; he'd had no money on him but promised the woman to pay later, and she knew the Wu family.

They ate the seeds and the fruit while dangling their feet in the water. Later, as they walked further beside the river among the tall willows in the pleasant warmth of the day, Huihua felt safe enough to dispense with the head-cloth, not even looking down under her doli when they came near a man sitting against a tree.

They found another spot where ivy covered the ground and dog rose grew over an abandoned shack, and there they sheltered and talked and held hands well into the middle of the afternoon.

Twice Huihua told herself she would have to return to the Court, but only on the third occasion, after Yuling pulled her up to ask if part of the ruin would make a good drawing, did she force herself to speak. He had earlier asked if she wouldn't be missed at the Court, and she had told him of her ruse with the staff. 'Come with me through the woods,' she said, 'planes won't see us. You'll have to stay some way behind me. You'll see fairly soon a larger path going off to the left, but don't take it as it goes to the military camp. Just follow and I'll stop before we get near the walls.'

They walked back to Mingon and went through the town towards the Great Gate, this time on opposite sides of the street. As Yuling was coming near to the ancient portal, Huihua quickened her pace and went over to him through other pedestrians, one hand clutching the head-cloth that again covered her face. 'Come!' she whispered just in front of him, turning into the narrow alley. She was relieved to see it was still empty of people, though she noticed the ugly old man now asleep against the corner, no longer tongue-scraping.

She stopped at the far side of the small palm, and he came up to her. 'I can't resist you any longer,' she said going up on her toes and putting her hands against his cheeks.

Ever brave, he thought, if someone comes along... but her mouth was nearly touching his, and he pulled her closer to the fronds...

When he drew away and her eyes opened, he said: 'The house martins are blessing us, I can almost catch them!' She had still not noticed them, but now she did.

They went separately through the town's main entrance and started across the wide clearing towards the first trees, Huihua in front. She reached the woods, and Yuling saw her collect a stick from the side of a severely twisted old pine. He noticed how well she hid her face and how she walked a little bent - quite an actress as well as a poet, he said to himself halfway across the clearing while looking up listening for planes.

He stayed well back as they walked along the path; he was tall and well-built and Court staff or guards would recognize him and might want to talk. He tried to keep her in sight, but she went quickly and the path curved many times, and when occasionally he lost her, he had to run to check that she hadn't left the path for another. He remembered how fast she had run along the passages in the mansion when the planes were circling to attack.

A few people came towards him, though none he recognised; one or two greeted him and he replied but did not stop. The last time he had passed through the woods, after the varnishing, he had felt miserable. Now he was longing to hold Huihua again, feel her softness, lose himself in her hair, if only she would stop!

When eventually she turned onto a narrow track at a stone tablet that stood beside the path, he followed and soon could see through the trees a low grey-white building, many sided, with small concave roofs, and guessed they were not far from the walls of the mansion.

He found that the track was well hidden from the main path, and could see Huihua a little ahead looking towards him. She was keeping her face hidden, leaning enticingly against a long tree trunk that lay on the ground among soft ferns, the type of ferns without spikes, many of their fronds browned by the sun through the pines; her stick was against the trunk.

She unveiled, wiped her face and started fanning herself with the doli. 'It's alright,' she said as he came up to her, 'nobody comes here, there's...' But before she could say more he was *doing it again*, raising her, was placing her on the tree trunk close to a sizeable cap-shaped mushroom.

He caught her look of surprise, and it soon turned to joyful expectancy as she put her doli on top of the mushroom, her head now well above his.

'You walked fast!' he said smiling up at her. 'This is how I want to think of you until I see you again, as my Empress, order me!'

She felt his hands pressing against her hips. She put on a haughty expression, one that came naturally. 'When you receive my messages, read and obey!' Her voice was commanding, and some alarm came over Yuling, seeing the mother in the daughter.

'Anything else, my lady?' He'd meant to say 'Mistress'.

'I thought I was an Empress!' Her head went up with a sudden start and her eyes widened. 'People are coming!' she said in fright and pointing behind him.

Soldiers! he thought with fear as quickly he took his hands away and turned.

With both feet she pushed him hard forcing him to step away, swung her legs over the top of the tree trunk - her toes just missing the mushroom with its hat - and called out: 'Catch me, painter!' jumping down the other side into ferns chest high.

As she ran through the undergrowth she looked back and saw him leaping over what she guessed were dead branches on the far side of the fallen tree, and realized he was trying to get to the narrower end to jump over it.

She crouched beside a pine. Soon he'd leapt over the tree and was moving through the ferns towards her, she could hear them being kicked and beaten, but when again she looked up, he was nowhere near her. She made a squeak. He came close, and before she could stop herself - fearful he might knock into her - she let out a stifled giggle and in no time he was holding her shoulders and going on his knees as the ferns moved around them, he was taking her in his arms, pressing her to his chest, soon toppling over - deliberately she knew - keeping her above him as she saw the yearning in his eyes, her face close to his...

Sometime later she pushed free, knelt beside looking down at him, and began smoothing her hair, clasping it back. 'I've got to be going, really,' she said. 'Up you get Tsai Yuling, carry me to the tree trunk, my doli...' As he took her through the undergrowth she studied his face. 'Your nose is big,' she said, touching it up and down with a finger and making him smile though he continued to look ahead, was not replying.

With her feet brushing the soft ferns, a thrill ran through her as it had briefly in the painting room when he'd placed her onto the table to sit with her brother; except now it lasted, where then she hadn't allowed herself to enjoy the feeling, her honour had taken instant control to make her angry at his unforgivable impudence.

She whispered into his ear, and he stopped. She felt the kiss on her neck, and as he moved round the hollow in the ground made by large roots thrown up when the tree fell, all the time she was either stroking the back of his head or pinching his shoulders, and her mind took her to the Truth Game, she was striking out the side questions, and in immediate answer to question five: *Could it be that I might be falling for him*, her pen was covering the paper with *yes, yes, yes* from top to bottom, from right to left, and doing the same all over the back of her brother's portrait.

When he put her on the ground she said: 'I must show myself to the staff.' She saw him look round and read his thoughts. 'Patrols don't come here often, and there's no danger of robbers or bandits day or night, they know they'll be shot on sight, the army camp is not far. I come riding everywhere around here and we never have any problem.' She picked her doli off the mushroom. Not wanting to risk more time in an embrace, she gave his arm a quick touch, and put the cloth over her head. 'Now turn and don't look round, and promise me never go near that building. Go Yuling!'

She watched him to the tablet by the main path. Then she walked round the roots of the tree in the opposite direction, towards the White Pavilion, looking about her as she came into the open.

Standing at the trapdoor inside the old summerhouse, Huihua felt deliriously happy, and remembered how differently she felt only a few hours earlier walking into Mingon. But as she sat on the top step and moved a finger slowly over her lips, she got a shock: the matchbox! She had left it on the steps in the mansion, no means to light the lamp. She knew she might not have time to return to town to beg for matches; if she ran all the way, people might be suspicious, she could come to Yuling still on the path, she would not get back for well over an hour, meanwhile some servants might look for her in her rooms or elsewhere in the Court. But if she started along the underground passage without light - the rats - she could be horribly bitten, or worse might fall.

...only three minutes or less and I'll be there, got to do it, just keep going and use the stick, yes use the stick... After putting on her sandals, she moved lower and pulled the trapdoor over her, not thinking to pull down the carpet with it. She fumbled for the lamp and then the stick, but the stick fell and clattered down the steps.

The blackness was so threatening, that for several seconds she lost heart. She pushed against the trapdoor thinking of the relief to have some light. But the thought returned that her absence could be discovered - she would have to lie, could say she'd been in the temporary painting room getting inspiration from the old pagoda tree; but would she be believed, someone might have looked for her there.

She steeled herself, groped for the lamp and moved down the steps. At the bottom she felt for the stick with her foot and picked it up. Very slowly she began walking, but a few steps into the ever cooler damp passage and she knew she was in a position far worse than a nightmare: there was real physical danger; she could not wake up.

...I'm walking too timidly, got to quicken my steps, and lengthen them... Her feet were now getting wet. Although she knew there was no obstacle to hit her, she had a horror that she might have disturbed the ceiling on her morning walk through the passage; part could be hanging down and smash into her face.

...have more courage, hit the wall harder and start counting in my head ...good idea, eighteen, nineteen, twenty...

Soon she was actually whispering words '...twenty nine, thirty, thirty one...' finding a degree of comfort in her voice and telling herself she would be at fifty very shortly, then a hundred and about half way...

As she reached each count of ten and realized she was through the wet patch, she felt more exposed than ever, straining to hear any noise other than the stick, several times finding it almost impossible to urge herself on.

Coming into the eighties she heard rats and nearly cried out. At once she stopped. And they weren't squeaking as in the morning under lamplight, but screeching, and she was sure they were near. Her head went into her shoulders ...must, must keep going... Frantically she beat the stick against each side wall and kicked out and took another step and then another, the counting going clear out of her head as she thought several rats could be following behind her, so she began kicking backwards as well, telling herself that if she was bitten she would have to drop the useless lamp and run with the stick using her free hand against the wall for balance. But which way, back to the White Pavilion or keep going?

She thrashed the stick low down and started hissing as loud as she could to drown out the noise and partly to take her mind off her shaking, conjuring up her father in front and Shanghan behind, each kicking away the rats.

The counting came back into her head, she might be past half way ... don't kick so much ...be there in a minute or more if only they don't attack me... Sometimes she turned and hit the stick behind her, all the time ready to scream.

Just as she realized she was breathing too fast and had reached the one hundred and forties, the screeching abruptly ended. She quickened her pace, stopped hitting the walls, held out the stick against imaginary obstacles, and said to herself that if what she was doing was for love, and if life was about kisses, there was always a price to pay. ...seventy eight, seventy nine, a hundred and eighty, a hundred and eighty one, eighty two...

She knew that the bottom step was coming, walked a little slower, and started pushing the stick along the uneven floor. The steps seemed never to arrive, and then at last she saw the third or fourth step in the faintest light.

As she tiptoed up the wooden stairs, each seemed to creak louder than the last. She put the lamp and the stick near the top step, cursed the matchbox, and stood in the little room, listening. She closed the trapdoor as quietly as she could, heard no noise from the corridor, removed her damp sandals, dried her feet on the head-cloth, and shook down her worker clothes.

Less than a minute later back in her rooms undetected, Huihua collapsed onto her bed, and looked out of the open window at the weakening sun in the late afternoon. She would stay in her worker clothes, show herself down at the kitchens, and see that the horses were well watered; she might even speak with the father and son gardeners if their work hadn't finished. If any servant asked her where she had been, saying they had been looking for her, she would now reply that she had found a private hideaway in the grounds where she was able to compose undisturbed.

She wanted to shout her joy. She turned on her back, rested her head on the pillows and looked up at the swans. She thought first of the rats - their screeches - and then of her beautiful student and the passion in his eyes. She longed to be with him again, was going to be very shortly as they had arranged, longed to feel his strength that took her breath away, to feel his fingers caressing her...

Not once had she thought he was going to ask for more than she was prepared to give, even though in the ferns she had abandoned herself to his kisses. Already she had a complete trust in his goodness, had read it in his eyes and in his gentleness and his talking, feeling his respect for her.

She re-lived the moment when they were walking in the river and had nearly returned to their spot at the tall willows. The fishermen had disappeared. He'd stopped her and was fondling her cheeks, and she could have died of bliss standing in that warm mud and being touched like that.

The ceiling woodcarvings took her back to her poetry. She recalled the inspiration at night not three weeks earlier, when the words flowed and the idea came to suggest the art student to her mother. She marvelled at what she now felt, and knew she would brave the underground passage again ...with lamplight.

Still looking at the swans, she took up her notebook and rested it on her middle, as sometimes she did during the night, writing without seeing.

> *He's pierced me and there's nothing I can do about it. He's magnificent in every way - well not the politics maybe - and I'm well and truly captured. This is as it should be, the greatest moment of my life, can anything compare? And I hear a voice deep within me saying he will never feel for another woman as he does for me, I don't know why, I just know this to be true - beyond words, unbelievably wonderful. How did the gods conjure such feelings for mortals, for me?*

18

'You accepted his resignation!' Madame Huang was astonished. She was sitting on one of her sofas looking up at the rueful expression on her husband's face. He had returned to Wuyi Court earlier than expected, at first able only to pay her a short visit to her apartments, as he needed to attend to urgent military matters at the camp in the woods.

'I should have dealt with it long ago,' he said standing beside one of the columns with their plant motifs, lighting a cheroot, inhaling and puffing several times. 'Lee is really much too old we all agree, he's become badly forgetful as you know. But I've told him gently, and it is not because of Hua getting caught by the planes. He'll stay on for the next three months, or two if he prefers. I want him to help train someone to my ways. I'm already considering his replacement, what do you think about Wang?'

'Wang!' She was further amazed.

'He hinted at it not long ago, told me he was well-educated in Tianjin, keeps up with what's happening in the war. He was a sergeant, do you remember, one of my best too, we took him into service after his accident. He told me he felt grateful to become head domestic but sad, sad that he couldn't use his intelligence more. I know he'd be another unsmiling secretary.'

'Well!' She hesitated, knowing Wang had done her bidding for some years, that he might be useful to her in such a position of trust to her roaming husband. 'Interesting! He's certainly intelligent, he could learn quickly, with or without Lee.'

'That's what I think, though Ma is not keen at all, but I think he could be good in no time, and time's precious.' General Huang sat down in the sofa near his wife and rubbed his eyes.

'You look exhausted,' she said, 'I have told the cooks to think of more energy-providing meals for you.' He gave her no reply, but looked wearily towards a small vase. She asked: 'Did Lee or Ma tell you who was with Hua during the attack?'

This brought him fast out of his thoughts. 'They did indeed, I meant to ask you. He's got a nerve coming back! Apparently you invited him, I couldn't believe it. They begged my forgiveness and said you would tell me yourself, that you ordered them not to say anything but it was to do with something pleasing. All very strange I must say. I heard he somehow protected Hua by pulling her away from a window.' The heavy eyebrows rose. 'Well?'

'Good! Your children and I have a surprise for your recent birthday, but you must trust us a little longer. When Shanghan comes back you will know.' Her husband frowned. 'The student has gone,' she added, 'we will not see him again.'

He shook his head, wasn't thinking any more about the student, he needed to sort out some jealousies among lower ranks concerning recent promotions.

When General Huang returned from the camp, he was pleased to find his family waiting for him on the top step outside the mansion doors, to show him his present they said.

'Your uniform suits you,' he called forward to his son as they took him along the passage of wall woodcarvings, among Fujian's finest. 'This is mysterious!' he exclaimed entering the Reception Hall.

They led him to the far side of the nearest mural. Some large picture was hanging on the wall with a cloth draped over it, placed where an oil painting had been removed against bombing. Evening light came through one of the large windows and cast a yellow hue over the floor and much of the cloth.

'Take off the cover, father, and see!' Shanghan said, pointing.

'Another painting? Not of me, surely. Intriguing!' The general pulled away the cloth and stared, unaware his daughter was keenly looking at him. He took a step forward and burst into applause. 'First class, first class!' he said turning to his son and patting him on the arm, then looking again to the painting. 'Excellent that you wore the uniform, A wonderful present!' He paused. 'One of the best portraits we've ever had at the Court. Reminds me of the Generalissimo's portrait in his bunker at Chongqing, only this is far better. I didn't think his was a good likeness, it showed him with too strong a smile.'

Madame Huang looked at Huihua and back to her husband. 'We are glad you like it, my dear, but we ask you not to be displeased when we tell you that the artist was the student Tsai Yuling, he was highly recommended by his university.'

General Huang was stunned. 'Tsai Yuling?' he exclaimed feeling disbelief, turning to his wife.

'Yes, we only thought of him after another man came and produced a horrid little portrait,' she said, 'we did not have much time to…'

'Lee burnt it, father,' Huihua jumped in, 'and you remember the excellent drawing Tsai Yuling did of you when he came here as a b…'

'But it was because of him and that dreadful little priest that Tuxieng had the riots!' He scowled at his daughter. 'How could you even *think* of inviting him back after what he did here?'

There was a hush. He looked again at his wife, but she also seemed unable to answer him.

Huihua was about to say that Yuling had not been involved in the riots, had been recovering in the monastery, when Shanghan asked in dismay: 'So you don't like my portrait now, you don't think our present is wonderful any more?'

The general looked hard at his son, then back to the painting. He began rubbing his chin; a soldier-barber would shortly be removing the stubble of five days travel, and later he would be taking his wife to his bed, in his rooms; she was the first woman in his life, though the mistresses were his greater pleasure.

An expression of surprise replaced the scowl. 'I accept he's done a remarkable portrait.' He looked at his daughter. 'Strange that he dared to come back. He helped you I hear in that attack. Lee took it badly what happened to you, he blames himself.'

'Tsai Yuling saved Hua's life, father,' Shanghan said firmly, very relieved his father still liked the portrait. 'We found many bullets, and the walls and stairs were in a terrible mess.'

Huihua added: 'We'd both be dead if he hadn't got me down those stairs into the basement.'

'Carried you,' her mother said coolly gazing at her.

The general looked at his wife. 'There was no air-raid warning because they took out the observers, but we've new posts in place and better camouflaged. What's the other thing you wanted to mention?'

'I'll tell you privately,' she replied.

'More mystery.' He looked again at the painting. 'I'll have to forget the artist and ignore the name chop. We'll store it in case of a more serious attack.'

'Won't you have it in the Study?' Shanghan asked. 'It would look good behind grandfather's chair.'

The general caught his wife's nod. 'Alright, for a few weeks, then best kept safe.'

That evening Madame Huang had her husband to herself, and told him more about their daughter's medical shock from her baptism of fire, how unwell she became and her strange behaviour. The general listened to what might have gone on at the bottom of the stairwell. 'Poor Hua,' he replied, 'but he would never have dared go far with our daughter, and she would not have let him.' He paused. 'I'm still astonished you thought of the fellow to do the portrait.'

She dodged the rebuke. 'He stroked her hair, they were huddled together

273

for several minutes after the planes went away, and I prefer not to think what else happened. Afterwards she became quite agitated as though she wanted to blot it out, and she agreed with me he must have gone too far, even if he had been trying to comfort her. She saw him in town...'

'In town! You mean *spoke* with him?'

'We were visiting Linnie, so we called on the shop where he was working and she thanked him for helping her. She told him clearly, at least I believe she did, I was outside in a sedan chair, that he had overstepped what was proper when giving his protection, and that he must forget whatever happened between them.'

'Absolutely! And I'm glad you called in Linnie. But she has recovered well, she's looking very good at the moment, I must say. I've never seen her so pretty.' The general looked at his wife, could see she remained concerned, and thought about his young-bodied mistress in Jinyang and her firmer, riper breasts. He shook his head. 'No cause for continuing worry about the wretched student, Hua knows her privileged position and our expectations of her. It's over, he's gone away you say.' He read his wife's thoughts. 'I know she's strong-minded and stubborn, but we'll find the right man for her. By the way, I'm doing as you want about Chu, making discreet enquiries with the family though I haven't approached him yet. I'll talk to you when some checks have been made. The family goes back longer than ours.'

'Good,' she said as he slowly inhaled.

*

Perfect! Chose well, too windy maybe but bless Xuiey! The old cook has managed to get Huihua's sealed message to the furniture shop, and the Mistress now sits in her bed, knees up under the quilt, already dressed in her worker clothes and waiting; this is her last opportunity to see Yuling before he returns to Suodin.

Thirty minutes before midnight, she steals out of the mansion while her brother sleeps a few doors away and their parents lie together in her father's rooms in another wing.

This time she wears her riding boots, having brought them up from the stables. At the start of the underground passage she turns up the lamp, takes a few deep breaths, and begins walking. Not until about half way does she get the fright she has been waiting for, but the noise of the rats is nothing to the screeches they made just a few days earlier. And although soon she sees a rat in front and is horrified by its size, it scurries away out of sight as she beats the ground and repeats in her head her father's words that rats hate light. She pushes on, and the noise stops abruptly as before.

274

Standing once more on the floor of the White Pavilion, she listens to the wind rattling the shutters, and thinks of the secrets the summerhouse possesses, amused she is adding to them. Removing a tiny bottle from her pocket, she dabs her wrists and each side of her neck, and touches around her hair, before leaving the bottle by the trapdoor.

The strength of the night wind hits her as she walks along the path towards the tree trunk. But although the air is cool it is not cold, and her view under a waning moon is good, the sky showing intermittent clouds moving quickly below a heaven of indistinct stars.

She reaches the fallen tree well before midnight, sees Yuling has not arrived, and goes round the end of the big upturned roots. She knows she will not hear him through the noise of the pines, so keeps looking out between two of the roots.

The fourth or fifth time she does so she sees a figure, and inwardly trembles from twin thoughts that it is her lover but could be somebody else. But soon she makes out Yuling's large frame, and with a feeling of intense excitement she crouches and waits.

When she believes he has stopped, she moves round the hollow in the ground. He is a few paces from her, has placed something down and is looking the other way. She creeps up and pounces.

Yuling lets out a cry that is blown to the heavens, then takes her arm and swings her to him as his stick falls. He holds her tight with one arm round the lower part of her back, the other pulling her head towards him as he catches the perfume.

Only her persistent jabs in his middle a minute or so later bring him to release her, partly.

The wind fluctuates in strength during the twenty minutes it takes them to reach the valley, and when it is strong Huihua has to leave Yuling's arm to hold her hair. 'You sure it's safe?' he calls into her ear as the trees sway around them. 'I don't like walking here at night.'

She leans over. 'Promise you, there'll be no one around, we'll be away from the wind soon. And I can defend myself if I have to...' He doesn't catch the '... and you.'

During a lull she tells him that her father has returned and admired the portrait, though she keeps back the reaction to the artist's name. Yuling surprises her by making no comment; he is looking anxiously about, and she says no more.

'I can't get back to the inn,' he says, 'the town gates closed at quarter to midnight. I paid the innkeeper and told him I'm studying stars, but I don't think he believed me. I said I wouldn't be back, that I am catching the first boat. I've left my sack under a tree near the clearing. I don't trust the man, I let out…well it doesn't matter.' He had wondered if to tell Huihua that a friend of the innkeeper had seen him carrying her into the alley, though the man hadn't identified her, and Yuling knew the man would never have thought of the general's daughter; Huihua's face had been partly covered, and he himself at first thought it was a peasant with a likeness until he was actually in front of her.

They come out of the trees and soon reach the edge of a valley that looks to him narrow and deep, the wind having again strengthened to the extent that they can hardly hear each other and have to shout. 'Ninety eight,' she calls out as she leads him down pebble steps with short wooden uprights.

Soon they are in relative calm as the wind skims over the valley. The steps end at a path that gently descends and hugs the valley wall. Moonlight is strong enough to give them little difficulty seeing their way, though they have to watch for tree roots that occasionally surface.

'Don't fall down there,' Huihua calls back pointing into the valley, 'it's not too steep but the undergrowth could hurt you.'

Yuling touches the rock face on his immediate right, thinks of the terrible shelf above the water in his childhood night ordeal in the cave, and swiftly buries the thought. He is surprised how smooth it seems. 'This was created by river, thousands of years ago,' he says, feeling the wave-like undulations as a long creeper strokes his face from some rock hold above.

'There's a small river at the bottom,' she says without turning. 'We'll be going there.'

They walk for several minutes along the narrow path, and then she stops and he comes up behind her. 'See!' she says. He has already spotted the red and yellow glows of flickering candles somewhere ahead; they take him straight back to the fireflies at the cavern opening when he was lost to the world and to himself; in his shock and confusion in that lonely inhospitable place, he hadn't known what they were; though since his ordeal he had often seen the night-flashing beetles.

The path leads upwards again, and soon they reach the shrine, Yuling at once feeling its atmosphere. He has been in temples and evening processions in the dark before, but always with his family or others around, never alone and well into the night.

They come towards the first urn. It has a reassuring smell of incense wafting around them, and they can see the large Buddha statue carved in a sizeable cavity in the valley wall; it is fully garlanded, and is guarded by several small deities.

Huihua stands on the step looking into the shrine, Yuling behind her having placed the stick on the step. He puts his arms round her and she leans back.

'I must have been six when I first came here,' she says loudly as the wind above them seems to call briefly into the valley, 'in daylight of course, the Hong Kong governess brought me, you met her.' She breathes in. 'Isn't it spiritual and other-worldly!'

Yuling doesn't answer; his cheek is touching hers, and her hand has come to hold his head - her skin, her perfume, the incense, and the gods are working their different spells.

She leads him to the bottom of the valley, through short grasses to a small river. There they sit against a stone facing back to the glow of the shrine that is now well above them, Yuling with an arm round Huihua's shoulders and noticing that the sounds of the river are greater than the wind sweeping over the valley.

'Do you think there are snakes here, near us?' she asks.

'Bound to be,' he answers matter-of-fact, 'but they won't disturb us, they'll have felt us through the ground and will keep away. Don't you like snakes?'

'No I don't! A snake killed one of the young horses last year. Why? You don't do you?'

'Certainly, they're a treasure of nature,' and playfully he bites into her shoulder.

Quickly she pinches his upper leg in imitation, and as she does so she feels his mouth warm on her neck; the kiss is long, but she manages to hold her squeeze until he comes away.

'I've brought you a present,' she says, taking out folded paper from her pocket and handing it to him, 'they are three of my better poems including the one I wrote when I thought of you to paint Shanghan.' He holds up the first sheet, but the light of the moon is not enough for him to read. 'Be truthful. When you've read them, tell me what you think, but be kind.'

They talk of their favourite books, especially of the classics, Yuling soon discovering that Huihua's knowledge of their country's literature is much wider than his, and that she admires certain modern Chinese poets of whom he knows little.

Later he says: 'I wonder if I'd ever have got close to you if the planes hadn't attacked, I wouldn't have had an opportunity, your high family would have got in the way if I'd tried.' Her head has come to rest on his chest, and he blows inside her hair making her wriggle.

'When I see Lee,' she says, 'I'm specially nice to him, he doesn't know why. I'm always thanking him in my mind, because if that door hadn't been bolted...' she pauses, '...I think we'd have become friends, I was going to write to you.'

That cursed metal door, cold as death ...it wouldn't budge, and they had nearly suffocated ...and here he is, holding the girl in a valley at night, she's so lovely, full of life, it's incredible...

She frees herself and sits facing him and asks him to do some of the mimics her maid Yiying told her about. 'Do the crying one first.'

'I can't,' he laughs, 'I've got to have an audience for that!'

She presses, but still he refuses, though he stands up. 'I'm not mocking her, I really love her, she saved me,' he says of Meibei as he tells Huihua about the woman with the wart on her forehead, his peasant friend under the hills near Tuxieng. And soon he is imitating her waddle and dialect, and Huihua is captivated. When he moves to animals and makes the face and noise of a donkey and seems to walk like one, she kicks out in her joy, feels like pinching herself that such a talented but unaffected and interestingly different man has come into her life, just as she was again despairing from further parental pressure.

They lie on their backs in the grass, her head resting on his upper arm. He talks about his family and about his Uncle Jinjin and the three younger girl cousins he grew up with until his mother remarried and moved to Tuxieng.

Looking up to fast-moving clouds silhouetted against a moon beginning to disappear behind the rim of the valley, he says: 'After we heard of my father's death, my mother was very brave, but I'd just turned nine and was completely lost, and for a long time I felt cut off from my earlier years. My brother was two years younger but didn't seem too affected.'

He tells her more about Ayi, about his fiery character and their worry that he might leave home; but before he mentions the family fear that he could join the Reds and get himself killed, he makes Huihua promise to keep to herself what he discloses; in his love for her he is sure she will.

They cuddle for a minute or two in their separate thoughts, listening to the river and the wind above. Suddenly she asks: 'Do you have women friends? At university?'

'Yes. Well not in the college, there aren't any. In town.'

'Do you hold them like you're holding me?'

She gets no answer, then feels him ruffling her hair. Freeing herself, she kneels and looks down to him with a hand on his chest. 'Is there one girl in particular? Tell me.'

'There might be.' His head comes off the grass, his lips touch her forehead, and he lies back.

She catches the inflection in his voice, and can make out his smile in the semi-dark, each so alluring that she can't resist bending close to his face. 'And?' She tries to search his eyes but her own shadow makes them unreadable.

'And what?'

'Tell me her name you buzzard!'

'Well now, let's think. There's Ashenga, she's young and attractive and whenever I see her she always has her hair in plaits just for me, and she wears a fragrance pouch because she knows I like that. But she's not the only one. Sanchi, oh, she's strong-minded, politically intense, and Fainan...' He bursts out laughing, clutches her shoulders and pulls her down to one side as she cries out in surprise.

Now Yuling has her on the ground on her back, and he is kneeling astride her adorable slim waist, leaning slightly to one side to let the moonlight catch her face. 'Say Fuzhou,' he demands, surprising her further.

'Fuzhou? Why do you want me to...' But before she can finish her question, a hand is behind her head and he has leaned right down and is kissing her very slowly, first her lower lip, then both lips, and his tongue begins searching for hers.

And when he comes away, her head is spinning and his hand is still holding her. 'It's the way your lips move,' she hears as she looks up into his dark face and begins to hear the river again, 'they drive me crazy.'

Fingers touch her mouth and start squeezing her cheeks firmly, then releasing. 'Say it!' It is like a command. She holds back, is not going to obey. 'Say it!' The voice is gravely, legs either side of her are pressing. She is about to try to move her head from his hand when her cheeks are again squeezed, and before she can stop herself, she is repeating the word and almost at once is taken back into their intimate world, a world so amazing that when he comes away from her she is quivering with desire and soon leaning up on her elbows and repeating the name of the provincial capital, sure of the effect.

Time and intimacies pass.

They are lying side by side on the grass holding hands, Huihua on his right, when Yuling starts talking about the Hut. 'When I went there the first time, my grandfather pointed out two birds, they were black kites soaring high above us. He loved birds, and we'd watch them through his long glass. He'd talk to them as if I wasn't there, tell them how magnificent they were and ask them where their young ones had gone. I surprised him one evening when he was sitting with his back to the shrine. He was telling them how much he missed my grandmother and my father. I came round the Hut and when he saw me he laughed and said I should talk to them as well, but I didn't.' Yuling smiles up to the fleeing clouds. 'I might now, if I was alone.'

'How often have you been there, since your nasty experiences I mean?'

'Three times, two years ago was the last.' He thinks back to his visit to Wuyi Court as a boy. 'I went up to the Hut with my mother and others when I was twelve and a half, shortly after I met you. You were very nice to me and Ayi, we thought you were very pretty!' He nudges her, pulling up her hand and holding it close to his lips. 'We had to leave Ayi behind because the walk is hard. He was ten and it takes six hours, though less coming down. Three priests came with us, and they chanted most of the way banging drums and cymbals. There must have been thirty or more people, family and friends, and we had tents. My uncles went up two or three days before to clean up...' He stopped himself, had never liked to think in what state they found the Hut, they had never spoken to him about it.

'Go on.' Her tender fingers have just touched his mouth, comforting to him.

'At first I refused to go, but my mother forced me, she was determined to have a service by the high lake, and one of the priests told me that if I didn't go, my grandfather's spirit would be troubled on his journey. And when I got there, I wouldn't let them take me inside the Hut, I stayed the night with Uncle Jinjin in a tent near the shrine. We painted the Buddha in gold again. And I couldn't go along the path either, to the lake, that's where it happened. All the others went to the grave, but Janping stayed behind with me, and...'

'Janping?'

'She's our tea plantation friend in Dongang, she found me in the hospital. We watched the procession go off, and I can still see them disappearing through the trees. I burst into tears, and she held me, and then she burst into tears, and I think I stopped before she did!'

'You can go inside the Hut now, can't you? And to the lake?'

'Yes. But going back to Janping, this is as extraordinary and as true as we're touching. The family never saw more than two black kites over the escarpment unless the adults had young ones. But eight adult birds appeared right over us, I counted them with her, they were making a great noise and circling, and then they came low just above us and flew off towards the lake, and Janping said they were paying homage to my grandfather and telling us to follow. A lot of my fear disappeared then, and when I saw the group by the hemlock tree, it wasn't bad at all, my mother came to greet me, there were masses of flowers on the grave, people must have carried them up and also picked wild ones. I told this to a bird expert in Suodin, and he said he didn't want to disbelieve my story, but kites can gather in numbers and they take fish. I still like to think they were paying homage. At any rate, all of them being there just at that moment was a big coincidence.'

He puts an arm round her, bringing her head to rest on his chest. Huihua can hear his heartbeat rhythmical and strong, and wonders how she is going to cope having to wait three months before she's next in his arms. She is absolutely sure that he loves her; and although he joked about women friends, she is as certain as she can be that he is not a womaniser - he hasn't taken advantage of her in that way.

She wants him to hold her always in his thoughts until they meet in the New Year. Hearing again the Sage of Changlu to be brave - to ride the wings of eagles - she feels for his right hand and puts it to her breast, holding the hand firmly, pushing her head against his chin and feeling his mouth comes softly again into her hair. 'I'm totally in love with you Yuling,' she whispers loud enough for him to hear above the water. 'I can't believe how happy I feel.'

They stay that way for a short while, in silence. When she releases her firmness over the hand, she feels the fingers caressing her breast, never thinking she is taking too great a risk, but prepared to stop him going further if she is wrong. And as she breathes deeply of the cool night air, she experiences her own wondrous excitement.

'What was that?' he suddenly asks in alarm, her head still on his chest, as a rasping bark of some distant animal makes him remove his hand.

'I don't know, but there's nothing to worry about, there's nothing dangerous here, no big cats or anything like that.' She takes his hand and entwines her fingers to comfort. 'I promise you, lots of people come walking here from Mingon in the evening and at weekends.'

Yuling feels greatly reassured. Soon he is asking her what else she is good at or likes doing apart from her poetry and riding. She mentions embroidery, and that she can run fast. 'I can outrun you,' she adds.

She catches the shake of the head.

'Up!' she orders as she gets free of the hand and scrambles to her feet. She begins taking off her boots. 'I'm better without them.' He stands up with a challenging laugh, though he already knows she is quick.

She leads him a few paces away from the river, to a path she knows to be reasonably straight that follows the floor of the valley.

'Stay here, put the stick down, and when I say Go, run as fast as you can.' She points along the path, much of which is caught in the light of the part moon now swimming in a dip in the rim of the valley. 'Go on, stick down!'

She walks twenty paces back. 'Ready?'

Yuling places his right foot behind him; his left leg is poised as he looks down the path; he can see a surprisingly long way.

'Run!' he hears her call, but she hasn't said Go as he takes off with the smile that won't leave. And when he is running as fast as he can, he looks half back and is amazed to see Huihua already closing, her hair flying to the side. He tries to go quicker, but his inner laughter gets the better of him; and not many strides further along the path he feels the hard pull on his shoulder and stops.

She is looking triumphant, doesn't seem to him too much out of breath. He scoops her up and holds her above him round the back of her legs, the tips of her hair touching his face. 'You're so heavenly,' he pants, 'I could shout to the stars!'

'No don't!' she exclaims.

'You're my Chang-o, my swift goddess of the moon.'

She puts her arms over his shoulders. But soon she feels herself slipping in the relaxation of his hold, and when she comes head to head and his arms tighten behind her back, Chang-o, feet still off the ground, gives herself up to her victor of the forests and victor of the canvas.

19

The university teachers were very pleased to see the black and white photograph their most talented art student showed them as he explained the colours he had used. They thought his portrait of the fourteen-year-old looked excellent, showing the subject's early strength of character. It was much better than they had expected after hearing about Madame Huang's cool letter to the Principal. But they were shocked to hear that the student and the general's daughter were caught in an air attack and had nearly lost their lives.

'I want no payment.' Professor Koo told Yuling outside the main art room. 'I'll take back the sash and the remains of the oils, but you must keep the brushes, they're my present to you, I'm so pleased.' He giggled. 'And did you do a picture of the sister on the side?'

Back in Mingon, every night before turning down the wick of her lamp or blowing out the candles, and often during the day, Huihua would open a large book on flowers and take out two pictures she had hidden. She still much liked the drawing of her father that Yuling had given her as a boy. But the one he handed her just before they parted on the windy night by the tree trunk was special - it spoke to her like a poem. Often she thought of that moment after coming back from the valley, when she tiptoed to her rooms and untied his drawing for the first time. 'It's an exact copy,' he'd called into her ear as he held her tight and the night howled around them, 'for you alone angel, I drew the original in hospital when I couldn't remember anything, not even who I was.' He'd put his lips to her brow, a gesture she'd come to know meant his complete and special love for her. 'This drawing means more to me than any other. Now we've each got one. I thought about making amendments to better it, but decided against, I prefer to keep it as originally drawn.' Despite the wind, Huihua had caught the emotion in his voice.

When she had first looked at the drawing under the flickering light of a single candle, she had seen a night scene of a crescent moon, the faint outline of the whole circle of the moon depicted against slanting dark pencil-work.

Below the moon, a girl and a boy were drawn, the girl's robe the only colour in the picture; she appeared to be bending down with a hand outstretched to the boy who was crouching under a large rock looking frightened, his figure much less strongly defined though the rock around him was powerfully shaded. Huihua at once thought that the boy resembled twelve-year-old Yuling when he had visited them at the Court. And the girl in a robe like the rich red silk her governess had brought her from Hong Kong...she moved the drawing closer to the flame.

*

'My dear, we are inviting Lieutenant Chu shortly,' her mother said as Huihua sat down on one of the sofas opposite her father in the main room of her mother's apartments. When she had entered the room, she had already sensed something unpleasant might be coming, as it was strange that her father was there in the middle of the afternoon. Her mother's words hit her like a blast of cold air.

Her father saw the frown and was surprised. He said: 'He can tell us about Guangdong and his family, they go back a long way, you can get to know him better. Head Groom told me that Chu helped bring Ajin to a stop when you were riding too fast,' his eyed widened under the thick eyebrows, 'or the horse took off perhaps.'

'Your father thinks he is a promising officer,' her mother quickly added looking from daughter to husband and back, 'and he is handsome and comes from an excellent family. We are sure you agree he would be a very good prospect for a young lady.'

'No I don't!' Huihua said, wishing she could be more diplomatic but unable to stop herself answering with feeling. 'I'm in no condition to meet men right now. Do you forget, it's only a few weeks since I was nearly killed!' She knew her excuse was weak, that she had completely recovered from the planes after only a few days. She turned to her father. 'All I want at the moment is a quiet life father, without pressures of this sort, and I certainly don't want the lieutenant being my escort so often, I'm embarrassed. He's polite of course, a bit too much I must say. But if I'm pressured in this way I might be hard on him.' She was telling herself it was best to try to nip this one in the bud if at all possible, though she knew it could be a forlorn hope.

Her mother gave her a strange look, but she was hoping her answer had worked on her father.

'Hua, I've already invited him...' he said.

'Father!'

'...and he's accepted to come tomorrow afternoon at four.'

'Well I don't want to be here! I'm not in the mood for that sort of thing, you must think of my feelings too!' She began shaking her head, looking down to the Persian carpet on which she played so often as a girl.

'Not to worry, treat him like a friend, see how it goes. His betrothed died of some accident, that's why he came to us as you know, wanted to get right away from Guangdong.' Her father's voice became firmer. 'But he's coming, and we must show Huang hospitality, naturally.'

'That went fairly well I thought,' the general said to his wife without conviction after the young officer had taken his leave and their daughter and son had gone their ways and they were alone. 'He clearly likes Hua, and he dealt with Shanghan's comment about the Communists rather well, "in every way dangerous to the nation" were the right words.'

'Of course he likes her! But you saw how cool she was towards him, I felt most awkward, she seemed to be challenging him. And where did she get those ideas about the Reds leaving Anhui? She called it "a massacre of young innocent Chinese", I'm glad you put her right.'

'I know, I was as surprised as you. Look, let's play this carefully, not rush her. And if I can put him in her way, not when she rides perhaps, but make him work here rather than in the Officers Building, he could be in the map room below the Study stairs, maybe they'll see more of each other.'

'He picked her up! Carried his sister! I didn't think he had one.' Madame Huang's face was one of astonishment towards the innkeeper she had summoned to the Court. She stood up from her chair wondering if the art student had acquired a stepsister when his mother married the Tuxieng doctor.

'That's what he told me, my lady, I didn't believe him, told him so. It was strange, the first time he came and asked for a room he was all happy, and not long after that he was looking really miserable, and a few days later it was all smiles again. I guessed he'd woman trouble, beg pardon my lady, when he was looking so bad, I told him that too and he sort of admitted it. My friend says he'd never seen a man holding a woman like that unless they'd just married or it was in theatre. And the way he carried her off the street, he says it didn't look like what a brother does.'

'How long was he with you?'

The innkeeper scratched his head with the hand holding a cap. 'Two weeks maybe, but he wasn't there the last night, said he was going star-watching, didn't believe that neither.'

'Would your friend recognize the woman if he saw her again?'

'Don't know, my lady, he thought maybe she was a peasant from outside town.'

'Peasant!'

'Yes ma'am, she was barefoot.'

Madame Huang stared at the man and thought of her daughter often walking in the mansion without shoes, even now she was a young woman. He shuffled under her gaze. 'Would your friend know my daughter if he saw her?'

'Your daughter, my lady?'

'Yes, the Mistress.'

'I'm not sure, don't think so, not sure I would, I haven't seen her for some years. Sedan chairs from the Court always have their curtains closed.'

She paused. 'I will try to bring a young woman with me tomorrow at about ten, I need to discuss next February's night festival with Elder Han. You are to be with your friend near the Han entrance, the one with the dragons. If he recognizes her as the girl he saw with the student, he must nod fully. Have you understood that? I will be looking towards you. Tell him to look down to the ground if he does not recognize her.'

The innkeeper gave a low bow.

'And I require you to keep a lookout for the student just in case he returns.'

The following morning Huihua was happy to accompany her mother to Elder Han, so she could bring the benefit of her literary and creative mind to the meeting, one of the events to be poetry reading; the readings were to take place under lantern light in the courtyard of the East Gate Monastery. Her father had given permission for the town elders to hold a four hour festival starting at seven in the evening, part of the wartime muted celebrations to take place three months later during the New Year. The enemy had never bombed Mingon, and it seemed the Japanese regarded the inland town as strategically unimportant. The elders had reported to her father that the townsfolk wanted to continue their traditions despite the risk. The only place off-limits to the organizers was Wuyi Court itself, for the obvious reason that it had recently been strafed and posed a bombing target, being owned by a Nationalist general.

As they passed the furniture maker's shop in their separate sedan chairs carried by bearers and guarded by military escort, Huihua pulled briefly back the curtain and quietly blessed the Wu family for befriending her beautiful student, and Mrs Wu for being the niece of Xuiey the cook, her means of communication with Yuling in Suodin. She imagined Yuling as he must have worked in the shop - at a bench, her hand on his strong arm, moving with him as he sawed.

At the house with the spitting red and green dragons, Elder Han and his wife and two maids were waiting for them in the road, their heads bowed.

When Huihua's chair was placed on the ground and she stepped out, she saw the usual crowd of inquisitive people, but took little notice.

Madame Huang also saw the onlookers. Between the formal greetings, she kept looking their way. What's that supposed to mean, that's not nodding, and he's not looking down. Stupid man! But Elder Han was gesturing for her to enter his courtyard, and she could not keep him waiting any longer.

Huihua thought the meeting went well, Elder Han much pleasing her by saying he would come to the reading if she honoured them with two of her own poems. But walking back through the courtyard, she sensed that her mother was less happy, and when she asked her if something was wrong, her mother just shook her head but said nothing.

That evening when Huihua paid a call to the kitchens, Xuiey pushed paper into her hand while the second cook was in the Storeroom. 'New Year, first week,' she heard the old cook whisper. It was the information she had been longing for.

In her bedroom she scrutinized every word of the message.

> Chang-o, dove trees, willows, riverbanks, palm kisses, kingfishers, soft muds, honey seeds, tree roots, empresses, ferns, noses, winds, perfumes, moons, candles, donkey noises, black kites, running catch-you's, Fuzhous, Fuzhous, Fuzhous, Buzzard.

*

In middle of the afternoon of a cloudy day in early February 1943 during the Chinese New Year festival, Yuling was on a dark green brown-camouflaged sampan as it drew close to one of Mingon's river landings. He had never felt more extraordinarily excited. It was coming up to three and a half months since he had left Huihua and Mingon to return to his final year studies. He had been lucky to find a captain and crew prepared at double price to travel up river in daylight, taking him and three other passengers also keen to reach Mingon. No planes had appeared, and in little over a day, if he could get a message to Huihua, he would soon be holding her, looking into her eyes, touching her magical face, her amazingly soft skin, her fingers, smelling her scent, caressing her neck, listening to her voice in his ear, losing himself in her embraces...

During the journey he had found it hard to take his mind off her, except if he was on watch for planes or bandits. When he tried to count the number of swans in a large colony - some in the river, others on the riverbank - before long his mind had completely forgotten the counting and he was making love to her again at the ferns. And as he tried to identify the different trees they passed, determined not to think of her, soon she was among them calling to him to remember the night valley. He even closed his eyes and promised himself in the name of his father and grandfather that he would not open them until he had remembered, in sequence if possible, every important drawing and painting he'd done at the university. But he hadn't reached the middle of his first year before she was jumping in front of the pictures, telling him that whatever he did to recall them, she would always be in the way, he couldn't resist her. And when he surrendered and opened his eyes to the flowing water and the lush vegetation on the riverbanks, he was as high as Fuzhou's Blue Pagoda.

Her single letter that reached him via his college friend had awakened his senses like no other. And he thought often about his cryptic Chang-o message that crossed with her letter, chuckling at the idea of someone intercepting it or seeing it and trying to decipher; and he knew how much she would have loved it.

Stepping onto the moving landing stage, everything looked to him fascinating, from a grey heron that let itself fall off its perch on a nearby poplar and rose slowly up as it flapped its long wings, to the frail shacks that lined the riverside, some overhanging the water, their dull red tiles parched and cracked.

When he made his way through the bustle of the town to the Wu family shop, his mind kept racing, wondering if somehow Huihua had guessed his exact arrival and had managed to get out of the mansion and would suddenly pounce on him from a street corner as she had at the fallen tree. He was looking at every young-looking peasant woman.

The Wu parents gave him a guarded welcome, and he read their thoughts: that they hoped he was not pursuing his feelings for the general's daughter. He drank a bowl of tea with them and promised to return to a wine supper; he had brought the rice wine with him. He told them he needed first to book himself into the Ten Lanterns Tavern just outside the South Gate, and that he was glad not to be going back to the nosy innkeeper.

'Tree trunk,' cook Xuiey said to Huihua under her breath in the late morning, just after head domestic Wang had left the kitchens, 'and I won't ask questions nor answer any.'

The old servant watched as the Mistress looked around, and was startled to receive a peck on her cheek, the first time since formal etiquette had taken hold of her darling girl some years earlier. She was so surprised that she began to chortle, but soon stopped when the Mistress put up a finger of silence.

For the rest of that day Huihua had difficulty keeping herself focussed on whatever she was doing; even the horse riding seemed to be taking too long. And as she wiped Ajin down, she could have sworn his eyes knew her secret.

Having dinner alone with her mother was particularly trying; her father and brother were dining elsewhere in the mansion with officers.

But the hour came, Huihua had long ago retired to her bedroom, and her mother's bedroom was in the opposite direction to the linen rooms.

This time she was not going to risk a candle, but would feel her way along the corridor. She did not at all like the idea of using the underground passage, but the thought of soon being in Yuling's arms easily conquered that fear, and she wished she could move the clock forward to the very moment when she would be feeling the strength and tenderness of his body.

The iron key worried her. If she was heard by her mother, she would have to say she had had a fright from a recurring nightmare of a Japanese assault on their home, and that for peace of mind, she needed to check that the door to the emergency passage worked.

...but why are you wearing worker clothes and boots and why are you in the dark...

...merely I wanted to see, mother, how long it would take to get dressed from my bed in an emergency, no time to light a lamp or candle...

She reached the door beside the two linen rooms, unheard she was reasonably confident. There was complete silence. She felt for the lock, surprised by the roughness of the surrounding wood, and carefully wriggled in the key, grimacing at the sound of metal against metal, sure it had not been as loud on the two previous occasions.

She began to turn the key, visualizing Yuling half way through the woods to the tree trunk.

The lock did not respond. She pushed the key further and tried again, then pulled it a little back and tried turning, each time to no effect as her heart sank further.

She touched the area surrounding the lock, and from the irregularity of the door's surface she realized with horror that the lock had been changed, and went into panic ...one more try, mustn't give up, might be imagining it ...oh no, it's not working ...what's she know, she can't have guessed ...he'll be waiting...

She stopped breathing and made a final effort, but this time the noise caused her to gasp.

The night was cold, Yuling soon shivering on the frightening walk through the woods. It was much darker than under the part moon those three months earlier, though now at least there was little wind.

The pines had their strange noises, and as he walked cautiously along the

289

snaking path, he thought of robbers and prepared himself despite Huihua's assurance there were none near the Court.

He was longing for her as he came towards the fallen tree, and this time he would catch her before she pounced.

But she wasn't there. And she wasn't behind the upturned roots, and he even made a little call of her name into the hollow in the ground in case she was hiding there or had fallen.

Leaning against the trunk, he began to think the message had not reached her, and thought about her comment that it might sometimes be impossible for her to get out of the mansion. He wrapped his arms round himself, willing her figure to appear.

Some time later, he made his long unhappy way back to the tavern outside the gate.

When morning came he helped in the furniture maker's shop, and waited.

He waited all the next day, and was tidying the backyard in the evening when a young fellow handed a sealed envelope to Mrs Wu, who was sitting at the entrance onto the street. The young fellow immediately left without speaking or answering her question. It was addressed 'For Buzzard,' she guessed who was meant, and handed it over with a look of concern.

The following afternoon Huihua told her mother and brother that she was going riding even though the weather remained unusually cold; she loved the cold air she said. She knew that they would be occupied with Lee and Wang on matters concerning the estates, and had been very surprised to hear that her father was making the head domestic his private secretary. She also knew that Head Groom had left the Court a few days earlier with her father's permission, to attend to a dying relative in the town.

When she appeared at the stables in her riding outfit, she caught the assistant groom by surprise and saw at once his embarrassment. 'You delivered it?' He nodded. 'Then saddle up. You'll escort me for a two hour ride. No need to ask a soldier to accompany us.'

She received a worried look, but the use of her voice of authority, or her hold over him, worked, and he moved off to another stall while she went to saddle Ajin. First hurdle jumped. She recalled the look of anguish on Dajuan's face '...her Ladyship don't allow any canoodling,' her mother's personal maid had said, 'least not in the Court, please Mistress, please don't report us, I'll lose my position...'

As they rode up to the stable gates, one of the two guards called to the assistant groom: 'Shouldn't Mistress be having a military rider?'

'Completely unnecessary!' Huihua said, looking down at the man and gently tapping her crop against the assistant groom's revolver. 'In many years of riding there's never been any problem, never, you know how safe it is around here. Anyway, we'll be back soon.' She gave the soldier a wide-eyed smile, but was thinking that everything depended on the very next moment - if the guards used their intercom to speak to an officer in the Officers Building, her plan would fail. 'Open one of the gates, I want a good short ride,' she ordered.

She saw the hesitation and kept her smile at the man. 'Go on! I need some cool air touching my face.' She nodded to him and began stroking her cheek, holding his attention. The guard looked at her in surprise, turned to his companion and signalled, and soon a heavy wooden bar was being pulled back.

'Bit chilly Mistress, don't be too long,' he said, as Ajin went through the gate without her command or heel.

'Come! Hurry up!' she called to the assistant groom not looking round. ... phew, main one jumped... She could almost *feel* Yuling's caresses.

'What a smile at you, take that to your k'ang!' the other guard joked as they watched the riders trotting off towards the woods.

'We'll ride the northern path for a while,' Huihua said to the assistant, looking back for the first time; he was two horse-lengths behind and remained silent.

A few minutes later they came to a clearing among the trees, where often the horses rested after exercise, where a stream ran and the grass was good. She turned Ajin to face the assistant. 'Dismount. Stay here and let Peony rest, I'm riding on for a while.'

The young man looked startled and made no move.

She gestured him. 'Go ahead, dismount! I'll be back with you in an hour or so, you just wait for me here, and don't panic if I'm a bit longer.'

Still he hesitated, and she could see that he was trying to pluck up courage to speak. 'Your secret is safe with me,' she said, 'you won't lose your post, I've told Dajuan that, neither of you will lose your posts so long as you do as I say. Now dismount, that's an order, and wait for me.'

He got off the horse looking worried as before.

'No need for Head Groom to know about this, or anyone else,' she added. 'If planes come, tie Peony to a tree, you understand me?'

She didn't wait any longer, turned Ajin and kicked. Final jump taken, Huihua was in a state of elation as she cantered away from the clearing, heading along a path that after a few minutes would take her to an area of giant rocks. She couldn't have cared less that it was cold.

When she reached the first of the rocks, she had to lead the horse on foot as some of them were overhanging.

Yuling had arrived several minutes earlier having run part of the way, so was not particularly feeling the cold. It was his first time there, and he had discovered that a main track wound through the rocks, though how far the rocks extended he did not know or feel he had time to explore. Smaller tracks deviated round some of the rocks and seemed to link up again.

He had placed himself down a gentle incline on a straighter part of the main track with massive rocks on either side of him. His view was good, and he was leaning against a head-high chunk of granite, chewing on melon seeds, when he saw Huihua leading a fine light brown horse.

He spat out the seeds, she hadn't spotted him, and he moved to the middle of the path, placing fists against hips, elbows outwards in mock waiting, holding a look of displeasure.

Some thirty paces away Huihua saw him, let go of the reins and ran, releasing her hair as she did so.

He held his stance and his expression. She registered the posture and his look, knew he was not going to move, and when she reached him she launched herself, his arms moving out to catch her as she saw the smile come flowing over his face. Her arms went round his neck, her legs either side of him, she was crying out in her longing, at once showering him with kisses.

Yuling swayed with the impact, had to move a leg back to keep balance, and reverted to acting-mode displeasure.

It took her a little while to realize he wasn't responding to her kisses or even holding her; she'd expected to feel his arms round her and his fingers in her hair, before being devoured.

She pulled her head back, caught the frown, looked searchingly into his eyes, and put her lips very close to his without touching, holding them there, challenging him, feeling the warmth of his breath in the cold air.

A second or two later she was still clinging to him and still he hadn't kissed her or held her though the frown had gone. She pulled back again. He was looking at her lips. She mouthed the name of the provincial capital, and instantly she knew she had won as his hands came round her and she felt the first wonderful kiss.

No words were spoken. When he released her, he led her into a narrow side track, a secluded spot between the rocks. She let him pull her to him on the ground, and with the faintest of smiles on her face she watched him as he began undoing the buttons of her tunic. Since their time in the night valley, she had so often thought about this moment; she was going to allow him her breasts, fully, it was a further act sealing their love.

And soon Huihua was sighing to the heavens. But she was not giving everything, and Yuling was not asking it; his respect for her and whose daughter she was would not allow him to contemplate such a thing.

It was Ajin's whinny that brought them back to the world they had forgotten. Yuling looked up to see the head of the animal round one of the rocks; the horse had entered the narrow side track and was not far from them, his head lowered.

'We mustn't let him come further,' Huihua said as Yuling pulled her up, 'we can't turn him.'

They went to the horse, and as Huihua stroked him, she whispered into one of the upright ears: 'You won't let on handsome, will you!'

'Did you have a good ride, dear?' Madame Huang asked her daughter at their light evening meal. 'It must have been very cold.'

'Yes, and I like the cold sometimes.'

'So you said. Were you lucky enough to have Lieutenant Chu, or shouldn't I ask?'

'No you shouldn't! By the way, Shanghan says his horse's leg problem has come back again.'

Madame Huang could tell that her daughter was trying to put her off speaking about the lieutenant. She sensed she did not want to talk more about the ride, and did not press.

Afterwards, she called her maid to her rooms. 'Dajuan, find out from Head Groom, this evening if possible, who was escorting the Mistress on her ride today, and ask him if he thinks she is alright at the moment, he will understand what I mean. She seems to be occupied in her own thoughts, hardly talks to me at mealtimes.'

The maid nodded respectfully without speaking, and went out.

'She went off *alone!* Without you, for more than an *hour!* And you didn't have an escort!' Dajuan looked horrified at her young lover.

'You can't tell her that!' the assistant groom cried, 'I'll be thrown out.'

'You fool, you fool!' she shouted, striking his shoulder and making him flinch. 'I'll have to tell her that Head Groom's not back and that the Mistress ordered you to go riding without a soldier, she'll find out anyway from the guards.'

'Don't tell her the Mistress went off alone, they'll flog me, and you'll be in trouble if she tells her mother what we were doing in the horse stall.'

Dajuan hit him again.

Madame Huang very quickly noticed there was agitation behind her maid's seemingly matter-of-fact report. She was surprised to hear that Head Groom was still away, and shocked and suspicious that her daughter had said it was not necessary for a military rider to accompany her. When her maid added that she hoped the assistant groom would not be punished, that he was fairly new to the job, she coldly thanked her and reminded her that if the matter of *that* drawing and *those* papers came up, it was she, Dajuan, who had spotted them while tidying the Mistress' room. 'Now bring the young man to me at once,' she ordered. 'What is his name, Feng, Fong?'

When the assistant groom's presence was announced, she told the maid to remain with them. 'That's enough bowing,' she said from her chair. 'I want to hear, Feng, you knew that my son and my daughter are not to go riding except with a military man present, did you not?'

The young fellow swallowed and was slow to answer her. 'No,' he got out as his eyes started blinking.

'But you have been here four months or so! You have seen them leave the stables, they have always had Head Groom and an officer or a soldier riding with them.'

'Yes.'

'Where did you go?'

'Beg pardon?' The blinking was as bad as ever, and the young man had turned his head to her maid. Nor was he addressing her properly.

'You heard me, look at me when you answer! Where did you and the Mistress ride to? Which route did you take?'

'I don't know all the routes yet, I'm getting to learn them. We stopped at a stream, the horse could graze there.'

'Of course you know the routes, you have been here long enough for that! And what do you mean "the horse?"'

The young man shuffled. 'Horses.'

The lady felt very uneasy at what she was learning or not learning. 'Well did you go towards town or to the valley, or to the river maybe or the rocks, or did you stay all the time in the woods?'

He was swallowing again. 'I don't know, we rode for a bit, it was along paths in the woods, and then we just stopped and rested the horses as I said...' - he was hesitating she thought - 'and then we came back, I think it may be the way to the river, I've not been in that part before.'

She gave him an angry look, would tell her husband he seemed no good. 'Did you meet anyone?'

'Meet anybody?'

'Answer me!'

'No, we...' He stopped.

His nervousness made her yet more suspicious.

'Are you sure?'

'Positive.'

He was looking directly at her, wouldn't dare lie to her. She felt a measure of relief. 'And you were with the Mistress all the time of course?'

Again he looked sideways towards her maid.

'Yes,' he said, soon turning back to her.

Before wanting to talk to her daughter, Madame Huang hoped to speak first with her husband that same evening. But he sent a verbal message through Wang that there were so many matters to attend to, he would be staying in his own rooms and could not be with her until the following morning shortly after eleven, and then only for about fifteen minutes between military meetings. She was disappointed, but took the opportunity to tell Wang that she heard he was handling himself well as the deputy secretary, and that she thought he would make a good private secretary when he took over from Lee in the next few days.

'Mistress, your father requires you to come with me immediately to the Study.'

Huihua was startled. 'Do you know the purpose of this requirement, Wang?'

The man shook his head and merely said 'please' with an outstretched hand.

As they walked along the corridors, Huihua suspected it might be to question her about her ride without a military man, and had prepared her answer. She told herself that Yuling's presence in town, if noticed by anyone with Wuyi Court connections, would not have been considered significant or important enough to report to her father; Yuling was not an actual Red though he supported their aims, not a member of the Communist Party, and he had not taken part in the Tuxieng riots.

They reached the top step of the curving staircase. One of the embossed doors was open, and her heart missed a beat as she entered the Study to see both her parents standing talking near the far desk. She was announced by Wang, unnecessarily she thought, and the door was shut behind her.

As she walked over to her parents, her father's face was stern and her mother's posture firmly erect; Huihua had already had breakfast with her mother, and nothing had been said to warn of such a meeting.

'My daughter, I trust none of us have told untruths between us in the family?'

'Of course we haven't father!' she replied fearful what was to come, there flashing through her mind that her father would have kept many secrets from her mother about parts of his 'other' private life.

'And you know well your duty of loyalty to us your parents.'

It was not a question. She felt her mother's eyes on her, and gave a nod to her father.

'A strange report, though I don't believe it, has come to your mother that you could have been seen in town last October with that student, the Tsai fellow. This can't be true, relieve me on this would you.'

A shock ran through Huihua. And she was going to have to lie to her parents which she would hate.

'Tsai Yuling? You mean the artist?' She felt herself redden, waited, and received her father's curt nod. She looked at her mother. 'I saw him in the furniture shop as you know.' She turned back to her father. 'Who says they could have seen me?'

'One of my agents is an innkeeper, the student was staying at the inn, a friend of the agent says the student was seen with a peasant girl who bore some resemblance to you, though I hear he was unsure.'

'To me! A peasant! Then he must be mistaken. Does he know me this man? Anyway, we never go to town unless escorted.'

Her mother asked: 'So you have not used the emergency passage?'

Huihua pretended fright and thought about the new lock. 'The horrid damp underground passage! We'd never go down there unless we were being attacked, would we, there are horrible rats aren't there?' She feigned a shiver, not difficult.

Her father said: 'And when the student worked here, nothing started between you, you know what I mean.'

'Started!' She acted offended, could tell there was no conviction in the question.

'I regret asking you this, Hua,' her father continued, 'but it's a fact you were drawn close together in that air attack.'

'No, nothing "started" as you say, except a friendship.' She was going to admit to a "friendship" and risk more questions. She looked again at her mother. 'Mother, you've been far too suspicious, you greatly exaggerated, we only gave each other the comfort of ordinary human beings in peril, we were terrified we were going to die, if you remember!' She looked at them both. 'You're not fair to Tsai Yuling, he's a very decent man.'

'Very decent!' her mother said with indignation. 'I thought you were upset he overstepped the mark, and how! I'm talking about *after* his protection, when the planes had gone.'

'He certainly did not go in any way too far. A day or two later I thought he might have, I accept that. But I was ill, confused at the time, and when the shock wore off and Shanghan told me of all the bullets, I realized he'd probably saved my life.' She gave her father a pleading look, had seen him place a hand on the desk near the ancient sword. 'He was a gentleman, father, very much.'

Her mother said: 'So you now regard him as a friend, and you even admire him. How are you friends?'

'Yes I do admire him, Shanghan and I both like him.' Come what may, she was going to use the present tense as her mother had. 'His character is excellent and his portrait is brilliant, we all think that.' She looked towards the painting still on the wall behind her father's desk, and kept her head high. 'I hope to correspond with him, we share artistic interests.'

'Correspond!' her father said in his own shock, 'you shall *not*! he's been a troublemaker, Hua, you mustn't be in touch with him.' He paused, his face seemed to her to soften. 'So you can assure us that nothing untoward happened between you. Your mother...'

'Father! That is not good to ask me! Yes I can. He protected me, shielded me, and that's *all* he did!' She hoped her mother wouldn't start on hair-stroking or whatever, adding: 'And you my parents should be incredibly grateful to him for that, as Shanghan is.' She had now gone too far, but didn't regret her boldness. The unsure sighting of her in Mingon was a great blow, but if she could make a start to swing them just a little way towards recognizing what Yuling had done in saving her life, and that he was a good man...

'What were you doing riding yesterday without one of my cavalrymen?' Her father removed his hand from the desk. 'That must not happen again, Hua. Feng is completely inexperienced, I'm angry with Head Groom, he should have instructed the lad, they'll both be disciplined. It's not a risk I'm prepared for you or Shanghan to take.'

Before she could answer, her mother jumped in: 'Why did you not ask for Lieutenant Chu or some other horse soldier to accompany you as usual?'

'Because I didn't want to bother any of them, it was rather cold so I thought I would spare the escort. And it's completely safe, ask Head Groom when he comes back.' More bravery. But underneath, Huihua felt horribly uncomfortable.

She saw her mother's face take on that strange look she feared.

'Which route did you take? Towards the river? To look at riverbanks, willows and kingfishers?'

Huihua's eyes narrowed. So her mother had searched her bedroom and found Yuling's beautiful Chang-o message in the flower book. Well she couldn't learn anything from it. She would refuse to explain private matters, though she could pretend that it was sent to her through the Poetry Society as ideas. 'No, we went towards the rocks, but we stopped well short at the grassy clearing with the stream, you know the place.'

She felt her mother probing her thoughts. 'And you promise us you did not meet anyone, the student has not come back?'

'Mother, I went out to give the horses exercise and to let them graze, speak to Feng if you like, though I expect you've done that already.' She locked eyes, wishing she had added - to try to put them off - that anyway Tsai Yuling lived and studied far away.

She was surprised her mother didn't scold her, but there was the continuing look of suspicion.

'There is a picture,' her mother went on, 'partly red coloured, it was in one of your books when Dajuan cleaned your rooms, is this something the student gave you?'

'How *dare* she go through my things!' Huihua well knew her mother had made Dajuan do it.

'She wanted to tidy, it fell out, nothing more, Yiying being ill as you know.'

'That's a beautiful drawing, Tsai Yuling gave it to me before he left, because I told him I admired his work.'

Her father seemed about to say something, when her mother jumped in again: 'With whom did you play the Truth Game? Who is the man you have fallen for? We have a right to know.'

Huihua gasped. She gave her mother a look mixing fury with contempt.

'Hua, your mother and I...' But she was already turning, gave her father a short bow, and began walking to the far doors. Obedience or no, filial piety or no, she would not answer more, and if all the Emperors of China called her back, she would walk on until restrained, though she wished she had gone for the nearer door to one side of the desk.

Shanghan entered before his sister reached the embossed doors, at once catching the bad atmosphere. 'Forgive me for disturbing, father, but you asked me to see you.' He looked at his watch. 'We're to have a meeting with Captain Ma and the officers.' His sister walked past him without a look and went out.

The Wu family and their guest had been laughing round the lunch table. Yuling sat between Ashenga and one of the older boys, helping him name the dynasties; the rest of the family were told by Mrs Wu to remain quiet and listen.

The boy mentioned six though not in historical order and one was wrongly pronounced. Yuling was saying '...not Jiang...' when they were startled to hear a violent bang from the direction of the yard as if the gate had crashed to the ground, followed by the sound of running boots and squawking hens and other running was coming from along the shop passage.

Yuling's shocked reaction was that Japanese troops had somehow silently invaded the town, and he leapt off his stool knocking Ashenga over. Just as he was trying to help her and had seen Mr Wu move towards the door that led to the yard, men rushed into the room from the passage, and he saw they were Kuomintang soldiers of the general's corps.

One man had a revolver pointing at him and was shouting that he was not to move, and as some of the children screamed, more men came in from the yard and pushed their father to the floor, soldiers now coming at Yuling from both ends of the table.

Amid the cries, three or four grabbed him, the gun was near his head, and he was ordered to put his hands behind him. He shouted at the soldiers not to hurt the family, and while his wrists were being tied he watched Mrs Wu bending down and helping her husband up. Apart from his fears as to what was going to happen to him, he felt desperately guilty towards the family.

'Will you come quiet' the soldier holding the gun said loud into his face 'or shall we tie your feet and drag you?'

Soon he was being pushed into the backyard, there racing through his mind that he was being press-ganged by the Whites - he'd heard they forced young men into their armies. A few further steps and he was asking the soldier with the pistol why they were doing this and where they were taking him. But as soon as he'd finished his question, another soldier came from the side, he was holding the nozzle of a rifle and swinging the butt, and it hit him on his right side below the ribs making him yell and double up.

There was shouting among the soldiers around him as he was pulled up, and they began pushing and kicking him through the yard - the hens had previously scattered - though he could hardly walk.

As they went along the street with citizens looking at him, one of the soldiers - the soldier who struck him - called out: 'Hey swine, remember me?' The man gave a nasty grin, and Yuling was taken back to the two guards who rushed at him through the door of Wuyi Court's main gates after he'd pounded it with the chunk of rock, after he'd heard that the petition for Lam had failed. It had been very dark, but he guessed the man who had just called out could have been one of them, probably the one he'd hand-chopped at the neck.

Staggering along, he thought of Huihua and the general and that his presence in Mingon had clearly been reported by someone. But when they reached the woods and the path to the army camp and the mansion, he remained in denial that what was happening concerned Huihua. Even if the parents had found out from her that they were seeing each other, he couldn't believe they would be treating him this way, not after the success of the portrait, unless the general was going to take it out on him for the Tuxieng riots; but he could have done that much earlier in the twenty or so months since the death of the magistrate and two prison guards. He still held to the press-gang idea, though he didn't believe that decent Captain Ma, who asked him to consider becoming an officer, would be part of it; he thought they must be taking him to the army camp which was somewhere in the woods.

He began to feel sick but dared not vomit as his right side was excruciating every step. He begged the soldier who had the revolver to loosen his hands, saying he could hardly feel one of them.

'Pull another one, student!' the man replied hoarsely, 'General wants you brought in roped, you're to be watched so you don't run.'

So now he knew: it was to do with Huihua or the riots or possibly both; either way, he dreaded what the Slayer of the Reds would do to him; he could be killed, the man was ruthless. He thought of the man's humiliation at the hand of his mother when he was a colonel. And the new lock: Huihua had told him about it at the rocks. He wondered how much if anything they might have got out of her - if it was to do with her.

What he did not know was that when he had been recovering in the monastery (after the flogging and after the novice monk had returned with the news of the Tuxieng riots), old monk Zen Yahan had sent a written plea to Secretary Lee to inform General Huang at once that

> *the student acted honourably in trying to plead for the simpleton who saved his life, and he took no part in the disturbances, he still recovers in our monastery. For the prayers we always say and shall continue for your welfare, we beg that you take no reprisal against him. Let not what would be a deep injustice stain the illustrious name of your family.*

They passed through the main gates less than an hour later, and he was taken down to the terrifying cells. A door was opened, he was pushed hard in the back, and as he fell onto the stone floor, some protrusion in the wall nicked the side of his head.

He could not easily sit up against the wall because of the pain in his middle, so he lay where he fell, a trickle of blood snaking down one side of his face.

*

General Huang is in bad humour, he is going to be disciplining three soldiers being brought from the camp; they were found in a new opium den in the town, and he's very disappointed with one of them, a man recently promoted to corporal.

And what is the student who beat up his guards doing back in Mingon? It couldn't have anything to do with Hua, though her wanting to correspond with him was singular, something to do with artistic interests. Yes she'd been difficult, but she'd given them the assurance he had expected from her, though who she might love he had no idea, clearly not Lieutenant Chu to whom she seemed so cool. He intended to find out by a more subtle approach, catch his daughter when they were alone and more at ease with each other, ask her about the sort of family the man comes from, get her to open up by telling her he is prepared to lower his sights just a little. Certainly his wife was making much too much of the planes and what went on in the stairwell, though for her sake he agreed to test it. The new lock had not been necessary; Hua would never have gone down into the underground escape route, she made that clear, it was indeed an unpleasant passage and he hoped never to be forced to use it.

He sits at his desk recalling the student's scroll concerning that simpleton; the beautiful script of the petition, and his own wife's note, had nearly swayed him to leniency; but the man was called the Imbecile and might not have known he had murdered; he was best out of the way, though not the way it happened.

The sergeant comes in and salutes from the far doors. 'We've got the student, General, he's at the bottom of the stairs.'

'His hands are tied I trust.'

'Yes General.'

'I don't expect to click, but if I do, you know the procedure. And there are two civilians in the servants quarters, get them here right away, they're to wait outside the doors.' He beckons the soldier to bring up the charge.

When two soldiers pull the student into his office, General Huang is greatly surprised. He remembers a tall, strong-looking young man, and when the student came out of the Guard House to surrender himself in that near darkness, he'd seemed almost proud of his dangerous stand. But now he is hunched and has some sort of head wound.

'What's happened here? I didn't order him roughed up.'

'Liu took revenge General with a rifle swipe before we could stop him.'

'Retribution, eh!'

He watches as the soldiers lead the student to the mark in the floor four paces from his desk.

Yuling sees the general glaring at him from a high-backed chair, a thick finger tapping the desk. He feels the sergeant's closeness. He is very frightened, loathes the feeling of being at the mercy of another human being. And he is incensed; he wants to protest at being brought in, and in such a manner; but speaking will not be easy, his chest hurts with every breath. He blurts out: 'Why have you...'

'Tsai! You and your family have caused me more trouble than I care to think.' The general is aware he has obliquely referred to the viper of the mother whom he wished long gone from his memory. He speaks coldly and without thought to the student's portrait of Shanghan hanging behind him or to the protection given to his daughter in the air attack. 'You're back in Mingon for some reason and I want to know why.'

Big relief, it may not be about the Tuxieng riots. 'I came to see a family ... do some work...'

'Liar! You came to see a woman, didn't you?'

More relief, probably not about Huihua.

The general often admires peasant women in Mingon and elsewhere; he cannot dangle with them because they are lowly, but he never misses an alluring face or an enticing body, and sometimes he flirts with the ones who are a little older - late twenties early thirties, his favourite age for a woman - telling them with his eyes that he can have them if he wants.

He waits, can see the student is thinking up some reply.

'Do you have a sister?'

'Sister? ...have a stepsister.'

'She's not been in town, has she? She's not the woman you carried in the street? You were seen when you were here last.'

The fright returns as Yuling thinks of the innkeeper questioning him three months earlier, now worried the man's friend might have identified Huihua though he still doubts it. 'Don't know what you're referring to,' he manages to say.

General Huang raises his voice. 'Did you have a woman in town when you were here, yes or no? Have you come back to see her? Answer me!' He fully expects an affirmative reply - nothing wrong in having a woman friend, natural at the young man's age ...and later in life.

'No, wasn't here long, came to paint your son...' Yuling draws in what breath he can '...only come for few days...'

'Liar again!' The general is angry at the denial, quickly standing, staring at the fellow in the way he knows frightens. The agent's friend definitely saw this student carrying a young woman, and nobody does that unless a woman is owned or is being retrieved or abducted. He walks slowly to a nearby window and looks out.

'When did you get here?' he barks without turning.

'Three days ago. I protest...'

'Shut up!'

The general allows a short silence.

'Where were you yesterday afternoon?'

'Afternoon?' Yuling lets out a stifled cry as his ribs catch him and he thinks of the rocks. '...walking by the river ...other side of town...' he needs to bend '...can I sit...'

'Stay standing in the presence of the General,' the sergeant close to him calls in a rough voice.

General Huang keeps his back to the student. 'Have you given my daughter a present?'

Yuling needs to think.

The general turns. 'I just asked you a question!'

Yuling is wondering if Huihua has shown his boulder picture to her parents; it was hardly a present in the normal sense. Looking half at the Slayer and half at the floor, he gets out '...gave your daughter a drawing if that's what you mean ...said she liked it...'

General Huang thinks it strange that the student has unnecessarily lied about having a woman, and further strange that there was no expressed surprise at the sudden question about his daughter, though he hadn't agreed with his wife there was anything ominous in the giving of the present, only 'artistic interests.'

'Madame Huang says the girl in the picture, I haven't seen it, is our daughter when she was young, and the boy looks like you.' He sniggers. 'That can't be the case, can it? Feminine imagination.'

Yuling is stunned, unable to think how he can possibly explain the history of the drawing.

'Well?' The eyes continue to stare.

'No' is all he dare say.

'You expect me to believe you haven't a woman friend here?'

Yuling is about to deny again when the general calls out a name he recognizes. As he half turns, he sees the innkeeper entering from the far doors, followed by another man he had occasionally seen outside the inn. The men are brought to stand near him. The innkeeper isn't looking at him but at the general.

'Have you seen this student before?' General Huang asks the other man.

He gives Yuling a glance. 'Yes sir, he was at the inn.'

'And? And what did you see?'

'I saw him running and picking up a peasant girl, she was in his arms, I never saw anything like it, he was carrying her in the street twelve weeks back or more.'

'You didn't recognize the woman?'

'No sir, I only got a look at the side of her face 'cos some of it was covered.'

'Have you seen her since?'

'Don't think so, the young woman with her Ladyship outside the doctor's courtyard, well she was a lady so it couldn't been her though she might have looked quite like the peasant, that why I didn't know what to do, see, nod or look down.' The man shakes his head and turns towards his innkeeper friend.

General Huang knows very well that the peasant girl was not his daughter, but he is not going to be blocked by this bastard of a student. He goes close and pokes a finger in the big chest.

Yuling flinches but tries to stand straighter.

'So, Tsai, who's the pretty peasant then? Tell me or say where we can check her out, then you'll be in the clear, won't you, and we'll see and hear no more of you finally.'

Again Yuling doesn't know what to answer, he's in a nightmare situation, the general's face so near and he's 'guilty'; but he isn't going to let Huihua down - they'd agreed only to admit seeing each other when he'd been painting; he could try to bluff that he'd never known the full name of the girl or where she lived, though he would have to invent some name. After Huihua's rejection in the shop passage, when he'd felt so miserable, he'd admitted to the innkeeper that he had woman trouble. But apart from the other man's uncertain sighting, he believed the parents would have no reason to suspect his meetings with her, and he knew she wouldn't have given anything away.

His courage partly returns, he will not succumb to the bully, not in front of the innkeeper or the others. He looks back into the cold eyes.

'Every man's private life is his own.'

The general starts, his head goes back just a little, and he pokes again.

'My wife thinks you've been seeing our daughter outside the Court, what have you to say to that?'

It is the question Yuling most fears; and while he hesitates, the general takes a step back, clicks fingers, and before Yuling knows what's happening, the sergeant's fist hits him in the solar plexus and he cries out as he crumples to the floor.

'I want an answer,' he hears, his ribcage an agony, breathing almost impossible. 'You've nothing to hide, so who's the girl, student? What's her name?'

His head is practically touching the floor, and he never registers the commotion and shouts of women coming up the curving staircase, nor sees Huihua rushing into the Study followed shortly afterwards by her mother.

Huihua stops open-mouthed inside the embossed doors, trying to take in the scene: all sorts of people, soldiers and civilians, are in the Study, and she sees Yuling immediately, his broad back, he is on the floor with a sergeant who she knows standing over him, the man's fist clenched and her father nearby.

Her mother grabs her shoulder but she jerks the hand away and runs towards the main group, catching her father's astonishment.

'Hua!' But before he can say more, she is pushing the sergeant hard away - the fist had been lowered - and Yuling is struggling to his feet, and to her fright she sees blood on his face.

'What are you *doing*!' she screams towards her father as she tries to help Yuling up. 'How could you *do* this to a good man!'

But Yuling is starting to totter, he is too heavy for her, and he falls back with a thud.

Her father takes a step forward. 'Get away!' she cries, lashing out as he arches and her hand waves in the air between them.

'Leave us *at once* Hua!' the general commands, realizing the worst as he watches his daughter kneel to help the student.

Huihua looks quickly up at her mother. 'Fetch clean water if you have *any* humanity in you!'

For a moment Madame Huang, now quite close to them, stands as if horror-struck. The sergeant and two soldiers have retreated to the side door not far from the desk intent on keeping some distance; the innkeeper and his companion are standing awkwardly near the opposite wall; and Shanghan and Lieutenant Chu have just entered, they were in the map room near the bottom of the staircase, the boy having been shocked to hear his mother's cries as she tried with her restricted feet to follow his sister up the stairs.

General Huang sees them all; he is being ignored in front of everybody in his own office. 'Out girl, out!' he shouts pointing to the far doors. 'Leave the Study *at once* I tell you!'

Huihua catches her mother's anguish, and has also seen her brother. 'Yes Shanghan, our father did this, our brutal father!'

The general turns to the two civilians. 'Go!' he orders, waving an arm and deciding immediate action necessary. He moves closer to his out-of-control daughter, is going to pick her up and carry her to the side door, and he'll order the sergeant to take and keep her away and everyone else to leave except his wife and the wretched student.

Huihua, still kneeling, feels the grip on her arm, and strikes with her right hand in a flat slicing chop that hits the upper part of her father's left boot, causing him to yelp and step back as her mother cries out.

'Leave the room boy!' her father shouts, 'Chu, here!'

Shanghan in cadet uniform looks towards his father, immediately turning and going out though he stays on the top stair. At the same time his mother leaves by the side door.

After hearing his daughter using astonishingly warm words to the student, the general goes to the lieutenant who has only come half way into the room. He speaks more quietly.

Huihua hears the word 'Mongol' and knows what it means; after Yuling was flogged, her brother had told her it could have been a worse one.

'If you hurt Tsai Yuling any more, father, I will leave with him.'

'You shall *not*! You shall be confined to your rooms for as long as is necessary until you come to your *senses*.' He practically shrieks the last word.

'You've cruelly hurt my friend, Shanghan's friend, and a brilliant artist. I hate you, I really *hate* you!'

Shanghan, from his position on the other side of the carved doors, hears his sister's every word.

The general bellows: 'Get up girl and go to your room *now*!' before pointing to the person on the floor, 'traitor! deceiver! my family foolishly commissioned you to paint my son, and you go and abuse my daughter, a Huang lady you upstart, now you'll really suffer!'

'I will *not* leave!' Huihua shouts back without looking up, kneeling behind Yuling and desperately trying to loosen the rope from hands that seem both purple and white.

General Huang runs back to his daughter, picks her up from behind, holds her tight while she begins yelling and kicking out, struggles the few paces along the front of his long desk, and thrusts her into the arms of his unsuspecting sergeant.

'Take her out and keep her out man!' he cries panting.

No sooner has the soldier taken hold of his unique prisoner, than he feels fingers hard on his cheek and immediately releases the Mistress just as the mother returns through the side door, a bowl in one hand and cloth in the other.

Madame Huang sees Huihua run back to the student, and follows as quickly as she can, then kneels with her.

On seeing his wife return, the general's fury is checked. But not for long. As soon as he catches the looks of his soldiers that tell him his authority has been challenged, that the scene will be round the corps in no time, fury bursts out again and he moves towards his daughter.

Huihua sees the intent, darts to the desk, grasps the filigree handle in both hands, heaves the sword off its mount, and begins cutting the air not once but three or four times in the manner of the swords woman she has been trained to be against a Japanese commando assault, sharp edge ever facing the approaching danger.

Madame Huang, dipping the cloth in water, feels the brushes of air. 'Hua! Hua!' she cries out as the dark blade swings in the space between daughter and husband.

'Hua stop, please stop!' Shanghan is shouting from the far doors.

The general backs off heart pounding, hears his son but doesn't turn, he's looking at the flames in his daughter's eyes and watching the tip of the Ming sword falling with a clang to the floor.

Shanghan calls again. 'Father, why is Tsai Yuling on the floor, why is he being treated like this, he saved Hua's life, have you forgotten?'

Huihua is now crouching looking at her father, face resolute and hands still firmly round the handle.

Momentarily the general marvels that a woman is able to pick up the ancient weapon let alone wield it. And there comes to him that yet again the Tsai family is showing him up before others; though this time it is less a humiliating loss of face as in the coach incident, more a feeling that everything important in his life is going badly wrong.

He looks at his wife; she has started dabbing the side of the student's head.

'We have our answer, you were right,' he says, voice lower.

He turns to the lieutenant whose embarrassment he sees. 'All out!' he barks as he walks away towards the officer, beckoning the soldiers to follow.

Shanghan, sensing his father might tell him to go to his room for insubordination, or require him to be away from whatever happens next, runs down the stairs and into the map room, staying behind the half-open door.

Soon he hears several people coming down towards him, and his father begins addressing the lieutenant close to the door. 'The soldiers are to remain at the marble steps outside. Add four more to the others, and I'll get my wife to leave. And Chu, you're to storm in and disarm my deranged daughter, and if she threatens with the sword, the men must use gun butts to parry, but get it off her, then escort her back to her rooms with force if necessary, and if she causes trouble, you have my order to bind her hands if you have to, gag her, do whatever, but get her there and add guards to the corridor so she can't leave, got that? Any guard who lets her through will be heavily dealt with I can assure you, and I'll be severely disappointed in you. When you've got her away, throw him out, he's too hurt to give you trouble. And he will never return to Mingon, that's an ord...' General Huang stops because he wonders if he has seen a shadow behind the map room door, then dismisses the idea but grabs the handle, closing the door hard. He speaks more quietly. 'Tell him he's got twenty-four hours to leave town, and if he's found here after that, or if he ever comes back, he'll be shot and I'll do it myself.'

Shanghan is very relieved that his father hadn't looked into the room, but he heard nothing after the door was shut.

General Huang treads wearily up the staircase towards his office, often holding onto the wooden balustrade. When he comes through the doors, he sees his daughter and the student kneeling; one of the fellow's hands is in hers, rope is on the floor, and his wife is bending down trying to pick up the sword and failing.

'Come!' he calls to her. 'I'll deal with that. Stop whatever you're doing, leave them.'

His wife straightens, her expression still fearful. 'I beg you, no more harm to come to Tsai Yuling.'

He stares at her before giving a nod, then looks at the young man having decided against a further flogging; the death order will certainly be effective. 'He'll be taken to the main gates. He's banned from returning to Mingon.'

'And Hua?' his wife asks him.

'You will be escorted to your rooms,' he says coldly towards his daughter, 'where you will remain until I say otherwise. Do not cause difficulty with the soldiers, they have their orders.'

'No father,' Huihua is looking only at Yuling, 'I will stay with Tsai Yuling until I know he is being treated properly.'

The general gives his daughter a long look, during which she turns briefly, defiantly, to him. He raises his large eyebrows to his wife, and walks out.

'Go *mother*!' Huihua says, 'you've done enough harm, go!'

Madame Huang catches the contempt. And in the student's expression towards her disloyal daughter, she reads his feelings and thinks back to the moment the two looked at each other at the portrait viewing. She leaves the bowl on the floor with the cloth on its rim, and walks slowly to the far doors. From there she turns back to the couple still on the floor, and knows she has lost the battle for a desirable marriage, for the union of the best families …at least for a long time.

When both his parents have gone and there is silence, Shanghan runs up to the Study and is very surprised to find his sister and the student standing in an embrace. His sister looks towards him; she has tears in her eyes.

'Soldiers are coming very soon, Hua, don't put up any resistance, that would be stupid.' He goes over to them, bends down and takes the sword's handle in both hands near where it meets the blade, heaving it onto the desk; then he puts it on the mounts and turns to Tsai Yuling.

'You're not going to be flogged, but you are banned from Mingon.'

He walks past them and takes up a position half way in the room facing the embossed doors.

Huihua is stroking one of Yuling's hands when they hear running in the corridor and soon on the stairs.

Lieutenant Chu bursts through the doors followed by his soldiers with guns, and is taken aback to see the cadet standing with both hands held high in the stop sign. At once he understands that there is unlikely to be resistance from the Mistress, and he notices with relief that the sword is back in its place. He orders the soldiers to halt, and as they do so, their gun butts clatter to the floor.

Out of breath he says to Shanghan: 'I've your father's orders to escort Mistress Huihua to her rooms, and the student to the main gates.' He looks towards the couple. 'Would you please come with my men, Mistress, peacefully.'

'My sister is not to be tied or gagged,' Shanghan says lowering only the left hand, 'and as a lady she will go quietly and I will be with her. You can see Tsai Yuling has been injured, he will be feeling shaky, so let him walk slowly and he must not be hit any more.' The right hand now comes down, the thumb going into a small pocket at the front of the cadet uniform.

Yet again Lieutenant Chu feels admiration for the young Master, now fifteen, one day he could be a great leader.

'Go Huihua,' Yuling says, cupping a hand to her ear and whispering 'You've pulled me up again!'

Huihua nearly cries out in her anguish. She thinks he is referring to the moment she pulled him up in the night valley when she challenged him she could run faster, could catch him. She wants to smile but cannot. She whispers something out of the hearing of the others, and releases his hands.

To the lieutenant's intense relief, the Mistress looks from the student to her brother and then walks slowly towards him. He sees the tears running and feels very awkward. There is no need to order the men to part, they do so automatically.

Huihua does not look round as she goes out of her father's office.

As soon as Shanghan has escorted his weeping sister to her rooms - without words, not knowing how to comfort her - he runs back through the corridors and passages and out of the main doors, and sees through some of the tall green cypress trees that the lieutenant's party has reached half way across the inner courtyard.

He catches them up, glad that his portrait artist has been allowed to walk freely and seems not to have too much trouble.

He walks in silence beside him through the outer courtyard, until they come to the main gates. A guard salutes him and the lieutenant, and pulls back the new door.

The lieutenant indicates with a hand for Yuling to go through, and gives him a peremptory nod but says nothing. As Yuling does so, the officer turns back and gives some order to his men.

Shanghan goes with Yuling to the right side winged lion. There he stops. 'I hope we meet again sometime. My portrait will remind me of you. Good luck Tsai Yuling.' With hands together, the cadet bows fully, then gives a salute.

'I am glad to have captured your spirit, Huang Shanghan,' Yuling replies, one hand clasped over the other in the gesture of respect; he is unable to reciprocate a full bow, but gives a dignified incline of the head.

20

Exploding fireworks lit up the mid-February night sky around Mingon's Great Gate; not many, there would be more on the last day of the festival period, but enough to delight the two older Wu children as they walked with their mother along the main street back towards their home, seeing over roofs towards the upper tier of the ancient gate; ghosts lurking in the town, spirits around their home, they were being thrown out, their mother told them.

They were returning from the poetry reading, passing street and house shrines where candles glowed and oil lamps burned.

Mrs Wu had been saying to herself that life, though hard and insecure, was not all bad so long as the Japanese came no further and their horrible planes did no harm to her unimportant town, though she hadn't got over the shock of the Huang corps soldiers coming into her house not many days earlier.

'She's really pretty, she knew who I was,' thirteen-year-old Ashenga called out in delight.

'You shouldn't have run up to her like that! You must be more respectful, she's the General's daughter, she's a lady.' The mother's smile was one of embarrassment. 'What was she saying to you?'

The girl did a once-round twirl as they passed by a series of dark blue lanterns under candle-light.

'She said she was very pleased to see me, she asked the poem I liked the most, I said the frog poem and she said that was her favourite too, she liked the monk pushing out his chest, he was pretending to jump wasn't he, just like a frog, you laughed too, it was so funny.'

'I've never seen you laughing so much! Did she say anything about your drawing?'

'Oh yes, "It's lovely" she said, she liked the hills, I've given it to her and she'll put it up in her room in the Court, my picture! She asked me if Yuling helped me, I said only the shadows, well a bit.'

'Did she turn it over?'

The girl looked at her mother. 'Of course, I told her to, she saw what he wrote to me, didn't you see her smiling? And she kissed me, oh she's so nice.'

'She kissed you!'

'She did! She asked me when did he write it on the back, it was just before he left for the boat when he wasn't walking very well. And Elder Han came up, he's very bald isn't he, and she showed him the drawing and he said it was really good.'

'He's a very wise gentleman, so if he said it is good, you can take that as high praise.'

'I know.' Ashenga twirled again.

After some dreadful hours of intermittent sobbing in her bedroom following Yuling's departure - when she had let herself go and barred the door and shouted several times to her mother and to her maid Yiying to leave her alone, telling Yiying to '...keep Dajuan away or I'll strike her...' - Huihua had begun to feel better almost from the moment Ajin's head kept ruffling the side of her hair. Thankfully her mother had told the two guards that they were no longer needed outside the rooms. As she led the horse round and round the stable yard, she talked to him, blessing him for taking her to the rocks, to her man. 'Every time I come to you,' she said into one of the ears talking above a whisper, 'it will be as though he's walking with us or holding onto me as we ride.'

The following day her father had sent for her, and Wang came again to escort her to the Study. But she had refused to go, told him that her father picking her up and her mother spying in her rooms gave her justification for her refusal, that each of her parents had for the present forfeited their right to her obedience. Then, with stated regret, she had closed her door on him, though not rudely.

She knew her remarks would be passed on, and if her father was going to come to her rooms in a state of further anger, possibly demanding answers concerning her seeing Yuling, she had told herself she would try to remain calm, refuse to talk about her private life, and stand her ground, if need be challenge him against striking her or even physically abusing her again, though she was reasonably confident the moment had passed and he would do neither. She even imagined there might be some contrition on his part; but then there might not. Naturally she had been frightened of such a meeting, of his authority, of having another storm.

He had not come, or sent another order or message; and when later they met in the passage, she had given a respectful bow of the head while passing, and he had merely told her '...the day is good, go riding with Shanghan for the fresh air...'

On her way back to her rooms, she had met her mother's maid who tried to use words of regret; but she had cut her short, telling her she was '...never again under any circumstances to enter my rooms even if my mother orders you to, or I'll beat you black and blue, and although you don't deserve it, Dajuan, your secret is safe with me, for the time being.' Before turning and walking away, she had seen the anguish.

The day after reading her two poems at the night festival, she enlisted cook Xuiey's help, and had the assistant groom and one of the stable-gate guards bring her brother's portrait to her rooms. As soon as Yuling had been thrown out, her father had consigned it to underground storage, away from the mansion itself but within the grounds. She did not ask permission from her parents or her brother to remove it to her rooms, though she would tell Shanghan later and ask him to confirm that he did not mind.

As the men carried the painting up the servants staircase, they were met by Wang who asked what they were doing; then he accompanied them to the Mistress' rooms.

Huihua assured Wang she would not be keeping the portrait for long (though she fully intended to). The men placed it against her wall, and on her instructions they turned it to face her desk, the desk that looked out towards the old pagoda tree in the middle distance.

Wang said: 'It's a very good painting Mistress, by a young man whom I'm sorry...' he stopped himself, putting up a hand to a little cough '...who I had the pleasure to meet.' He gave a short bow with a rare part smile, and signalled authoritatively to the other two who also bowed.

'Thank you, Wang.' She looked the ex-head domestic in the eye, feeling he had grown in stature in his new position. She had always sensed there could be cunning in him, that she wouldn't be able to trust him as she had sometimes old Lee. 'Tsai Yuling is the finest man I have ever met, and I *shall* meet him again.' She nodded for them to leave.

She had meals as usual with her mother, joined sometimes by her brother when he was not with the officers - always a big relief to her when they were three. Yuling was never mentioned. With her mother alone, she kept her talk tight, and felt strength of mind surprising to herself, imagining Yuling often by her side standing tall and determined as he'd acted on that path when she ran to him through the rocks.

She thought it strange that Shanghan hadn't asked her anything about her relationship with Yuling; he'd simply told her what Yuling had said about the portrait when they said goodbye at the main gates, and that they parted as friends. Later, while they rode together with Head Groom and two soldiers though not Lieutenant Chu, her brother suddenly called out to her to stop, and when she pulled Ajin over, he asked her if she loved Tsai Yuling, and she answered quietly that she did, very much. She looked at him, expecting another question or comment, possibly even a small rebuke, but he merely raised his eyebrows as their father sometimes did, and trotted on.

Often she looked at Yuling's drawing that he said had meant more to him than any other - of the girl in the red robe bending to a boy crouching at a rock at night - the drawing she no longer hid in her flower book but left facing her on her desk. And Ashenga's picture she kept holding to her breasts until she realized it was becoming crinkled, when she placed it taped to the front of a book standing beside her bed. On the back of the girl's drawing he had written:

> *Ashenga of the fragrance pouch - Only if you want to, please give this excellent drawing of yours to Huang Huihua at the monastery poetry readings. She will love your flowers and the hills behind them that remind me of those near Fuzhou. Your good friend, Tsai Yuling.*

Many times she looked at his calligraphic writing, especially the name of the provincial capital. And she wrote two letters, one that spoke her heart poetically, giving it secretly to Xuiey, addressed to Yuling's cartographer friend in Suodin. The other was very difficult to compose, which she handed to her mother in an envelope after a near silent lunch.

It told her parents that, after some days of reflection, she wanted them to know her mind

> *...namely that I and Tsai Yuling love each other, that our love will always last, that he is a very good, kind, educated and wonderfully talented man from a respectable family, that I can never love another the same way, and that on no account will I be pressured any more into a marriage, military or otherwise.*

She stated that naturally she loved her parents, and she asked for forgiveness for her disobedience in the matter of her future. But she said that she was a modern woman with a life she was entitled to choose herself. Finally she wrote:

> *If the man I love is killed on whoever's orders, I will end my own life. I copy this to Shanghan so he will throughout his life know what his sister's deepest feelings were should you my parents cause the worst to happen. Believe me, your distressed but very determined daughter, Hua.*

She had given her brother his copy before the lunch with her mother, asking him not to talk about it to their parents unless they spoke to him.

*

It took Yuling five days instead of the normal two to reach the outlying villages near Tuxieng, partly by river but mainly on foot; he could only walk slowly, and needed several stops for rests, including at inns.

Although he often felt like crying - not from the pain but the hopelessness of his situation - the tears seemed blocked. At least the discomfort below the right side of his lower ribs grew less each day, and by the time he was clambering over the sagging bamboo and rope bridge to see Meibei and her husband before going on further to his home, he was feeling much better physically.

But not in spirits. Desperately unhappy, he found himself repeating the words she had whispered into his ear: 'Patience my sweet, I love you more than I can say, and I'll wait for you or I'll come to you, I will, patience my Yuling.' But the words did not help, did not comfort; he saw no possibility of a future with Huihua, she was bound to her parents, bound to the power of her father; there was no chance he could ever see her again, and it tore deep into him, was far worse than the feelings he had experienced after her rejection in the Wu shop passage. He could never return to Mingon; he would be killed under the general's orders given to him by the lieutenant just before Huihua's brother joined them in the inner courtyard.

He sat on the track at Meibei's end of the bridge in the middle of a dull but warm afternoon, his head in his hands. He couldn't go straight to Meibei, though she was less than two minutes away, not immediately, he'd break down, and he didn't want to tell her where he'd been, who he loved, what had happened. Why was it that at the great emotional moments in his life, it seemed to be a woman's tenderness he sought? He knew that his peasant friend, whose hand against his cheek and joke about her wart had so comforted him on their k'ang when he'd nearly died ...he knew she would embrace him. And at that thought the tears came, and soon they would not stop. He tried to conjure Huihua's face in the Reception Hall before the air attack, when he'd lost himself just looking at her and hearing her voice, and he tried to think of her at the willows standing in the warm river mud. But she would not come, his despair would not allow it as he told himself their love had been crushed under the feet of the Wuyi Court roaring lions.

A few minutes later the tears stopped, and he looked to the top of the track, to where it disappeared into the birch wood. Somewhere higher up was the boulder that protected him on that night by the stream, a shelter he would never see again, a great chunk of rock where he had terribly feared, and had dreamed.

He thought about Lam and pictured his spirit with the wild horses. He remembered his little friend near the mud cottage trying in vain to keep away the chicks from drying rice using the long bamboo pole with feathers. A brief smile came back into his heart, and it made him stand.

Soon he was turning off the track and onto the cottage path, raising a hand to the farmer who was waving enthusiastically towards him from near Lam's stone; he could hear him calling out to Meibei. The contrast between the tiny cottage and Wuyi Court hit him hard.

Meibei could now hardly walk as she came out to greet him, but her head went firmly against his chest, her arms holding him too tight though he managed not to say anything as he looked towards her grinning husband.

In the mud cottage, she told him she could no longer help her husband in the rice terraces. 'So what you been doing with yourself Yuling, still education?' but before he could answer, she added 'you got two mothers an' I'm one.' He saw the warmth in her worn-out face, and thought of the coldness in the general's eyes.

Although he longed to open his heart about Huihua, all he said was that he had a good friend, a young woman, and he loved her deeply. 'What's she look like?' Meibei asked. As he was describing her, her face and hair, her figure and clothes - though he did not mention the earrings and brooches - he found himself talking about Huihua with pride, as if somehow she would always belong to him although he would never see her again, and he felt the emotions releasing. And when he said that she often walked without sandals, the farmer laughed. 'Get woman here, I'll soon have her working in rice fields!'

The next morning, before he left them, Meibei said to him: 'If she's what you want Yuling, if she's got any money, get her,' she beamed, 'bring her to Meibei.'

*

Eighteen-year-old Ayi tried to take it in, tried to accept the words just spoken by his older brother, but he couldn't, and began shaking his head.

'Huang's daughter! The Huang girl we met when we went there with mother? I ...I don't believe you Alinga, what are you telling me? You're joking with me.'

He stared at Yuling, and when he registered his brother was serious, all he could say was: 'Oh no! Oh no!' He looked towards the orchard. 'My own brother unbelievably goes to paint the Slayer's son, and ends up cavorting with the daughter!'

He turned back, saw his words had caused anger but no matter, he wasn't done whether his brother liked it or not. 'You stupid, stupid idiot!' he shouted into Yuling's face. 'The Whites will be crawling all over us. I've got to go, and just when I was about to join the cause in this area...' He stopped. 'And ...and what'll happen to mother you dumb fool, you didn't think of her, did you?'

'They won't touch mother as long as I stay away from Mingon. And Huihua...'

'Oh yeh, oh yeh, princess high and mighty Huihua!' Ayi was starting to hyperventilate, finding it difficult to speak. 'You think he'll drop it do you ... he'll ...he'll take his revenge alright, you wait ...you'd better clear out too, go! go for all our sakes...' Now he could hardly breathe. 'Where ...where ...where am I going...' he looked to the ground, 'dreadful ...dreadful!'

Yuling had only just managed not to smack Ayi's face at the slur to Huihua, but he knew well his brother's excitable and zealous nature, and that there was indeed danger, though he hoped it was nothing like as serious as his brother was making out. Certainly the thought of possible revenge by the general had been on his mind the past few days since he'd arrived home to find his brother away. But there had been no nasty visitors, and the stern letter Madame Huang had sent to their mother showed him and his stepfather that she at least treated the matter as absolutely closed.

His mother had been very upset with him when he'd told her about the painting commission he'd done four months earlier in October, and who he'd come to love and some of what occurred. His stepfather had been able to calm her after a time, but her outbursts had wounded him deeply. She kept giving him severe looks of disapproval and disappointment, as though he had betrayed her, ones she had never given him before. It made him feel guilty towards the mother he loved, except he knew the coming together with Huihua had been beautiful.

It was only when his mother had told him again what she thought about the general - her hatred and his cruelty - and asked him to confirm '...for my sake Alinga, in fact for Chennie and my sakes as well as for your own, that your shockingly irresponsible affair with this girl is well and truly over...' that he felt at a loss how to answer her, and had looked in anguish to his stepfather, before she ran from the room leaving him with inner pain greater than ever.

And now he was trying to calm his volatile idealistic brother. He adopted a gentler tone. 'Ayi, you've just got back here, this has given you a shock, I know, and I'm...'

'A shock!'

'I'm sorry for that, but I don't think you need fear so much, nothing's happened to us, specially not to mother, the letter from Madame Huang says it's closed, and anyway I'll be away from here in three days.' He wanted to touch his brother's arm but thought the better of it. 'But what are *you* thinking of, you mustn't become a partisan, you'd be crazy. Does mother know and Chennie? This is what I've been wanting to talk to you about, you'd be putting yourself in great danger and mother too, isn't that going too far? You...'

' "and mother too!" ' Ayi sought for more breath. 'You can talk! Crazy is it ...to serve the cause, fight for our people ...for freedom from tyranny.' He sneered. 'I suppose you're a half White ...or are you all White now, being with that girl!'

Yuling took the further insult, and thought it ironic that their father had died with the Nationalists, and yet both his sons were more in the opposite camp, one about to become an underground Communist.

'Not at all,' he replied, 'you know that I've always been against this terrible government, and it might interest you to know...'

'I don't want to hear *any more*.'

Their stepfather appeared from the back door of his medicine preparation room. Doctor Chen had realized there was an argument, and knew what it would be about, relieved Wenlie was at her school.

Ayi ran towards him. 'I've got to leave fast,' he blurted out as he passed, 'don't know if I'll be back...'

'Oh no!' the doctor exclaimed, 'please, Ayi...'

From inside the door Ayi shouted: 'Tell mother and thank her for everything.'

'Ayi!' Yuling cried out, but his brother had disappeared into the house.

Yuling ran towards his stepfather. 'We've got to stop him Chennie, the situation's not as bad as he thinks.'

'I'm afraid it is,' the doctor said, his left eye twitching as he put a restraining hand on Yuling's arm. Yuling saw his stepfather's sadness, a look almost of resignation; the doctor's jovial nature had deserted him. 'I lost Sanchi to politics, Meibei lost a son, and now I fear we'll lose Ayi. I did my part in saving you, but now you've gone and put your life and ours in great danger because of this very unwise affair. You must give the girl up, I'm sorry Yuling, you must, for your mother's sake as well as your own.'

But Yuling was waiting no longer; he was thinking of his brother and ran inside the house calling out his name. He continued shouting as he ran through the preparation room and the surgery and up the stairs.

Ayi had already fled.

Both Yuling and Wenlie made a number of overt and discreet enquiries in Tuxieng as to Ayi's whereabouts, but drew a blank. Yuling again visited Meibei and her husband, this time to find out if they knew anything about the Red underground movement in the province, but they didn't. They told him they occasionally received a visit from a CCP official and what good people they were; there were some pockets of Reds somewhere in the south of the province as well as still in Jiangsi over the border. And they had finally heard from one of the officials that their younger son had died some years earlier at the hands of the Whites in Guangdong.

When the farmer asked him why Ayi had suddenly left home, he talked of his brother's political passion for the Communists, which they already knew and partly admired, but he made no mention of his own part in causing the flight.

He felt even more guilty towards his mother after Ayi left. She accused him of 'splitting the family' and bringing about the loss 'probably forever' of his brother. And when he tried to argue that Ayi would likely have left anyway to join the Reds, she would have none of it. She remained distinctly cool for his last three days at home. Twice he said that if only she could meet Huihua... but each time she stopped him, making it clear the idea was absurd, as was his thinking there could be any future with the Slayer's daughter. 'You mustn't write or have any messages with her,' she said, 'none you hear me, you'd be asking for bad trouble and bringing it on us, the man's ruthless.'

But Yuling had already sent an unsigned note to Mrs Wu on the very day he had reached home, knowing Huihua would be very concerned for him. *Please get a verbal message, through you know who, to my friend that I am fine and will always be patient.* He'd asked a merchant going some of the way towards Mingon to pass it to any traveller going there. He hoped, but was not at all sure, that Mrs Wu would pass it on to her aunt the old cook. He would wait until another time to write and tell Huihua in a coded way how much he loved her and that he thought about her all the time.

Not quite two weeks after leaving Mingon, he kissed his tearful mother, embraced his stepfather, and began the return journey to Suodin for his final few months at university. When he reached his student lodgings, a note from his cartographer friend awaited him. It made his spirits leap, telling him an envelope had arrived, that his friend had looked inside and knew who it was for, and he'd gone away on a field trip for two days, the envelope was under the chart he was working on ...*and Yuling, good pal, you've got to see Yin at once, but don't rush away, I must see you.*

He didn't understand the 'rush away' comment. Nor did he immediately look inside the envelope. It was a glorious late February evening as he walked to his favourite spot among the drooping hair branches of a huge banyan tree, one of the many trees dotting the wartime campus requisitioned from Christian missionaries. Some of the banyan's branches had rooted in the ground. Shafts of yellow and light red sunlight streaked across the grasses and paths, creating the effect of a skewed domino set.

In semi-shade he opened the envelope. It was a prose poem from Huihua. In the Wu backyard he had received her earlier poem and hadn't at first known if it was a farewell message or more. But now, as he put the paper to his nose, he was sure of her love, and when he read the first words, an inner cry of joy ran through him despite never being able to return to Mingon.

You beautiful beautiful drawer, for one who has a heart so full of
the strongest love for you she could die;
You beautiful beautiful painter of my brother so noble and dear;
I want to call you my own but I dare not, I cannot, though you
say I must.
I, who am filled with joy and sorrow,
with the greatest deepest joy a human can have,
with the greatest deepest sorrow that harm befell you on my
account,
with the greatest deepest joy for heaven's precious moments together,
with the greatest deepest sorrow that I cannot for the present see
your lovely face nor read the thoughts of your mind -
I, yes I, adore you.
The eyes of my horse shall ever haunt you,
The pull of the wind shall ever remind you,
The moon in the night shall ever shine on you,
The heat of my feelings shall ever embrace you.

He read and re-read it, and as he did so he was with her among the rocks, he was with her at the murals, he was with her in the valley on the moonlit grass, he was with her in the soft moving ferns, he was with her in their alley between the palm and the house shrine, he was with her in the painting room...

He didn't go to see the lecturer of Japanese Studies - that could wait until the morning. As someone called his name through the rays of the evening sun, once more he put the poem to his face and closed his eyes. Something would happen, sometime, to help them come together...

'Ah, Tsai Yuling,' Lecturer Yin called from the corridor near a lecture hall as Yuling went towards him, 'let us go over here, we shan't be heard.' The man indicated a corner window. Above it a sizeable crucifix with the nailed Christ was still attached to the wall.

Yuling followed and began to feel anxious; the lecturer, who could be a teaser, had a serious expression, sad almost.

'I have some very bad news for you,' he said, at first looking out of the window, 'and it distresses us all.' He turned. 'Or do you know by any chance what I have to say?'

Yuling frowned, wondering if his brother had been arrested - that would be bad enough, though hopefully it would not be worse. He merely shook his head and waited, now seriously worried, visualizing a KMT raid at his home and his mother in prison because of him.

'You are dismissed from this university, I am most sorry, you must leave us by midday.' The lecturer cleared his throat. 'News came through that you dishonoured yourself in Mingon, and I'm afraid us. We've got the gist of it, but I don't want to talk about it if you don't mind. We have received a letter from a man called Wang, General Huang's private secretary, and we have no alternative. And the Principal has asked me to state that on no account will he see you, and that naturally an appeal cannot be entertained.'

Yuling stared at Lecturer Yin. All his hard work, so close to being recognised, was being tossed out of the window as if worthless, by the university he'd been proud to belong to. And worse, he was instantly branded a disgrace by the institution, and would forever be regarded there as an outcast. The general was taking more revenge.

The man continued: 'I must say I am personally most upset for you, and my wife is shocked and says she will miss you, she asks to be remembered. I have enjoyed teaching you, and you have done very well. You would have been given the highest degree, it's a great shame.'

Shame, like a criminal exposed to public ridicule, was how Yuling felt - he was shattered.

'Your art teachers want to see you, please go there at once. I'm afraid I must be going. Well, good luck, let us know what becomes of you.' The man bowed.

Yuling gave a forced one back, and followed with his eyes as the teacher walked towards the lecture hall.

Three students about to enter the lecture came up to commiserate, said they had heard the news, and asked what he would do. He couldn't give much of an answer. Nor could he face going into the art department.

'Where is he?' Professor Koo Guanglu was standing at the outer door of a students lodging house, asking an elderly woman who had a toothless grin.

She led the senior art professor along a ground floor passage, past other student rooms, and signalled him to a door half open.

'Yuling,' the little professor called as he pushed the door fully and went in; he hardly ever used a student's personal name, but this moment was different. He found his final-year student removing drawings off a wall; some of them he recognised from their practical work.

Yuling turned, a drawing in hand, bowed a little but said nothing.

The professor found it difficult to smile, one hand nervously holding his goatee. 'I am desperately sad. But do not think this is the end of the world for you, it is not.' He moved his hand to the student's wrist, which he found himself holding firmly, not wanting him to leave. 'Am I a little responsible, my mentioning the sister? I feel very bad.'

Yuling looked at his pencil drawing - a junk passing river cliffs - and remembered the finger smudges he applied to good effect in the cliffs. 'No, of course not' he sighed, letting it fall to the bed where it lay face down.

Professor Koo said: 'You know the proverb: "The door that swings, swings two ways, shows two ways." You haven't lost anything by this, your excellence will shine through, I know it will, believe me, don't be too despondent.' He softened his hold of the wrist. 'You were about to finish here anyway in a few months, weeks really, and my department could have taught you nothing more.'

Yuling pursed his lips, then said. 'If there's one thing I hate more than anything, it's power, the use of power. I hate the invaders, I hate the Generalissimo, I hate the Slayer of...' He stopped himself, remembering Huihua's plea that he would be hurting her if he hated her father.

'Power is a fact of life, my friend, like evil and love and infidelity, they hit us, affect each of us, and we can only react in whatever way we can at the time, and sometimes we fall to the ground. But we can always try to rise, can't we? Never forget that.'

The professor took his hand away and began fumbling in his jacket, pulling out an envelope. 'You remember I've talked about my time in Tokyo. My best friend there wasn't Chinese, though I was in a group of Chinese students. He was Japanese, a fun-loving friend who didn't look down on us Chinese like most of the other students. He even invited me to his home several times, his parents were very kind.' He forced a giggle. 'His younger brother was a live-wire, the parents couldn't control him. And the mother was a wonderful cook. Now, have a look at this and tell me what you think.' He took a piece of paper from the envelope and gave it to the big student who he would so greatly miss.

Yuling was surprised to see writing in Japanese. 'I know it is poor Japanese' he heard the professor add as he tried to read it, curiosity temporarily eclipsing sorrow, 'but my old friend will understand me. I am asking him to see you, his name is Takashi Hijiya, he is somewhere high up in the imperialist education system in Amoy, that is if you're prepared to go into the occupied area and see him, of course. Maybe he can find you a teaching post, you could be useful teaching Japanese to Chinese officials, or art in a school, or even both I should think. And you'd be earning yens.'

Yuling read on, mixed feelings of gratitude and concern coming over him as his favourite teacher added: 'I've tried to explain that you have been one of my very best students in twenty-five years of teaching, that will impress him, I know it will. He is an enthusiastic man, you would like him unless he has changed now he's a conqueror. A couple of years ago he wrote to me, asked me to meet him but I refused. I wrote him my angriest letter in terrible Japanese...' the professor chuckled '...I told him his countrymen had no right being in China, and I wouldn't meet him unless they were leaving. He replied he was sad, and that if he could help me in any way I was to ask. Well, here's an opportunity, no? You'll have to stay here until he replies, I'll speak with the Principal, I'm sure he'll let you. And I'll ask my old friend to get you a pass, you can't risk going there at night between border posts.'

21

'Dongang! She's at Dongang!' The doctor looks horrified. 'You'd better not send a message to Yuling, and you'd better send her back to Wuyi Court fast or we'll all be in real trouble.'

'Don't worry Chennie,' Wenlie replies, tearing the message into tiny pieces, 'I'll send her packing however high she thinks she is. But it seems Alinga knows. I don't deserve this,' she laments.

It is mid-June, four months since Ayi fled and Yuling returned to Suodin and his expulsion. Tan Zhiyong's message, delivered in the evening, is been strange to say the least, but Wenlie at once understands the meaning.

Help. She's here, what do we do? And He may get here too very soon, Tea Z.

'Shall I come with you?' the doctor asks. 'I'd rather not, but if I can help save at least one of our straying children...'

*

Very early the following morning, Wenlie is on a sampan travelling against the flow of the river much too slowly for her liking. She is glad of her fan because the humidity is already unpleasant. The captain hugs the riverbank as much as he can despite the possibility of bandit ambush; at least there is no longer much risk from Japanese planes - planes now simply flew over and away.

When they finally tie up at the Sun Yat-sen Bridge that her father-in-law helped build, she does not wait the near six hours for the next boat to Dongang, but starts straight away along the damp road to the Luos, one that has seen much recent rain. Old Luo the plantation owner has died, but his wife is still alive, and Janping's husband Tan Zhiyong, ever silk scarfed, has taken over the plantation. Although Wenlie decidedly is not looking forward to meeting the daughter of the terrifying general, she tells herself there is possibly one huge consolation: if Yuling comes from Amoy, she will see him for the first time since February, though she will be very worried for his safety.

Five and a half hours later she stands exhausted and wet - from perspiration, not rain, no more has fallen - in front of the door in the wall outside the Luo-Tan courtyard. It is the middle of the afternoon. She bangs several times, looking up to the branches of the old gum tree inside the courtyard, and at once hears dangerous Genghis squawking from not far away.

A subdued female servant answers her banging, letting her through the heavy door. 'Where is the lady visitor?' she asks as soon as she is in the courtyard. 'And my son, he hasn't arrived?'

'No Mrs Tsai, well, I mean the young woman has been put in the cottage on the other side of the Zass River, Mr Tan might be with her, he's over in the plantation. I don't know anything about your son.'

'And Mrs Tan?'

'She's out with the children, they're coming back soon.'

Wenlie thinks for a second. 'I can't wait. I'll pay my respects to Mrs Luo, and change quickly. Tell them I'm going over the river if I can get the ferry.'

Huihua sits in the shade outside the cottage, in an old wicker rocking chair; she is wearing black trousers and a smock in colourful reds and yellows that is loose at the neck and short-sleeved. She is feeling good her fourth day out of the Court, always fascinated by the rising hillsides of tea bushes, and by the forests she can see above them that are part of the valleys and hills containing the place called the Hut that Yuling has told her so much about.

If he comes to her from Amoy - she knows he works at a Japanese school, and she is sure he will try to get to her provided he receives her coded message sent within half an hour of getting past the guards, or receives the one Tan Zhiyong carefully sent at her request - it will be heaven, at last alone with him for a decent period, hopefully a few days.

She had smuggled out of the Court in disguise wearing worker clothes, with the help of visiting food merchants who she handsomely bribed; she had not taken Xuiey into her confidence, as she did not want to implicate her favourite servant. The smock and black trousers had been in her small sack.

But would Yuling be upset with her? She realized only too well that he would be worried what she had done - the world could be searching for her if her note to her mother had not worked. And her dread was that her father's Nationalist contacts in Amoy might also take Yuling (they were sure to know where he lived and worked), or his men could catch him before he reached her. Her horror thought was that he could again be physically beaten or worse. Hopefully the note to her mother (her father was away) would put them off her trail.

I need a change of scenery for a while, may go to Fuzhou but not
to the cousins, will be back within two to four weeks, that is a

promise so there is no need to involve Father or distract him from
military matters. Please try not to be concerned. I have promised
to come back soon.
Hua.

It was hard deciding not to mention Yuling in the note; her first draft
had added: *I'm not going to be seeing Tsai Yuling so please leave him alone, he is*
innocent in my leaving... But that was a lie if her hope was to be realized, and
she had reasoned she would not be believed, and that it would put her in yet
a worse light if either they were discovered or, on her return, she decided to
divulge that they had met. She had also thought of involving Shanghan in the
note, but didn't want her excellent brother to be a part of her deception.

She would return home in her own time without being found, within the
two to four weeks she had stated. And probably - she would decide when the
time arrived - she would openly admit that she had seen him, try to make her
mother finally understand that she could not be kept away from the man she
loved and who loved her; if necessary she would restate her life threat.

After the clearly unwelcome surprise she gave the Tans when turning up
on their doorstep explaining who she was, they were considerate, Mr Tan in
particular, and it was he who told her that the cottage would be a better place
for her to stay than the inn she meant to go to. She has now slept alone at the
cottage for three nights, cut off from the world on the far side of a river, an
interesting but not frightening experience. She had books in the cottage to
read, and plenty of time to start composing a short story, though she had not
got further than three pages. Only the humidity and the night mosquitoes
troubled. Mr Tan brought her food and water and some wine, and spoke nicely
with her, amusingly sometimes. And she enjoyed watching the ferry and the
birds and speaking occasionally to some of the plantation women, whose faces
she thought very burnt from the sun.

She has just picked up her pad from the ground and begun to write, when
she hears footsteps coming towards her on the other side of the cottage, glad
Mr Tan is visiting again. But as she stands, a tall woman comes round the
corner, partly looking down under a doli, and when the woman looks up and
their eyes meet, it does not take Huihua long to feel shock as her childhood
memory takes her back to the good-looking mother who came with Yuling
and his brother to the Court when she was twelve. She realizes at once that
Mr Tan must have sent a message to the mother, or perhaps his emotionally
strange wife had.

Wenlie stops a few paces from the young woman who is looking at her in
surprise from old Luo's rocking chair. Quickly she puts her hands together

and bows, recognizing in the grown-up person the girl she saw eight years previously.

'Huang Huihua?' The respect she would always have shown such a person is set aside by her fear and her resolve, fear that took hold when Tan Zhiyong's message arrived at her and the doctor's home.

'Yes.' Huihua bows more slowly, unable to manage even half a smile, while she waits for the mother to continue.

Wenlie comes closer. 'You know who I am?' She watches the young woman give a nod. 'What are you thinking coming here?' She has prepared that short second question and is not too keen to hear the answer, giving out her coldest look. She receives back a searching not unfriendly one.

'I've come to see Yuling, and I hope...'

'Whatever you hope you will not achieve! Does your family know you are here?'

'No, but I...'

'Then it's my duty to tell them.'

Huihua's eyes widen, she feels the enmity and lowers her gaze to the path as she seeks for a reply.

'Oh you may well look to the ground! You are standing near where I lay prostrate after being told my elder son was *dead*.' Wenlie watches the general's daughter bite her lower lip. She can see she is lost for words. 'And do you imagine I am going to go through that a second time because of *you*? You will come back with me now, this instant, gather up whatever you've brought, we will stay with the Tans, and tomorrow first thing we will go to the police so that you are escorted back, they can arrange for you to be met at the Sun Bridge or Hanyeng or wherever is best, they will tell us.'

Huihua looks up. 'Mrs Tsai, I...'

'I am not interested in whatever you want to say. You haven't thought about the dangers you are putting my son to, have you?'

'Yes I have and I do, but I've promised my mother I'll be back soon, and we can overcome the dangers if...'

'Overcome them! You're from an old warlord family, your parents are not going to let you marry an art student, are they? Well he *was* a student until your father had him kicked out of the university, that's one of the things you've done for my son!' She gives the daughter a fearful look. 'You know what your father is called? I don't want my family to be another of his victims.' She stares at her son's lover, trying to put from her mind that the young girl of twelve has become an attractive woman whose face and figure bear no resemblance to the ogre her father. She changes her tone from accusatory to factual. 'Anyway, it's impossible, your father will still hate me, he won't have forgotten...' She stops herself; the daughter is shaking her head.

'Hate you? Forgotten? What do you mean, I don't understand this talk about my father. How can he hate you, he doesn't know you does he?' A shock-thought occurs to Huihua that her father might somehow have had a secret 'friendship' with Yuling's mother.

'Ha! I knew my son hadn't told you!'

Wenlie takes a step back, removes her doli and begins fanning herself in the humid air; she forgot her fan at the Tans' house.

Huihua waits, dismisses her thought, and has no idea what to expect.

'I refuse to go into detail, but your father and I had words in two horrible encounters some years ago, that is all I will say,' Wenlie hesitates, 'except he probably won't want to talk about it, so do not ask him, it would only make things a lot worse, a *lot* worse.'

Huihua is stunned. Yuling has said nothing of this to her, only that his brother could well become a Red which she was never to mention.

'Why did you have words with my father? Was he unpleasant to you? He can be very abrupt. You mean when you came to the Court?' Her inner strength is returning; she stands straighter. 'If it affects me, this whatever happened, I have a right to know, kindly tell me.' There is now firmness in the voice, authority she means the mother to feel despite the respect she wants to show towards the older generation; she is now giving back the same firm look she has been receiving, though not an angry one.

'No, I don't think it's in anybody's interest to open old wounds, you must not press. Now bring whatever you have, we must wait for the ferry to...'

'Mrs Tsai, you *must* tell me.'

'No.'

'Well if you refuse, I must find out another way. And please, I will stay here until...'

'No again.'

'If Yuling comes and you stay with Mr and Mrs Tan, we can both see him and talk, I would like that so m...'

'Do you realize your father has ordered my son be killed?' Wenlie has returned to her fierce look. 'Have you grasped that, or have your clutches gone so deep you won't see reality and let him go?' She conveniently fails to mention that it would only happen if he went back to Mingon.

'Killed! Clutches! I love Yuling and...'

'Impossible! It's impossible, it's got to stop.' Wenlie gives the general's daughter a scornful look, and places the doli back on her head. 'You are going back to your parents whether you like it or not ...and ...and go and find another man to make...'

'What do you mean my father ordered him killed? He banned him from returning to Mingon, that's all, and he won't, I won't let him until my parents...'

'You naïve girl! Didn't they tell you?'

Wenlie moves very close and grasps Huihua's left arm. 'You are coming with me, his life's in danger because you are here, so is my other son's life.' She begins pulling her.

Huihua only partly resists, taking a couple of short steps. She could easily throw off the grasp, but this is her Yuling's mother who she so wanted to meet again and like, acting with frightening emotion, and the words '...ordered my son be killed...' are echoing in her head. She knows she could never think of fighting off the mother. But why has her father, and especially Shanghan if he knew, not mentioned the death threat? She is now more than ever glad that she warned her parents of the consequences of such harm befalling Yuling. 'Please, my things, my sandals...' and pulls gently back.

Wenlie, tight lipped, releases her but says nothing more.

Huihua turns and walks past the wicker chair into the cottage, trying to think how she can somehow prolong staying at the Tans or stay undetected somewhere else in Dongang. She certainly is not going to be made to give herself to the police, and if the mother tries to force her, she will have to run from her, which she knows she can do.

She has been inside for little more than a minute when she hears a man calling the mother - Mr Tan's voice she realizes with enormous relief. She has put on her sandals, and has her bag over her shoulder. She looks back to the small room with its tasselled lantern, thanks the cottage, and is about to go out of the door when she catches her breath, hearing the call for her, the voice she has for four long months so wanted to hear.

Almost the next moment Yuling is before her in the doorway, he is flinging his arms round her just inside the palm-leaf mat, kissing her cheek hard and then looking into her eyes as he tousles her hair and tells her he loves her smock; and she is gasping and grasping him though she feels clammy and unclean and very embarrassed with the mother so near.

And soon he is pulling her outside and she catches his beam to his mother and the return look of anxiety, and sees the smile over the tea planter's perspiring face as several egrets fly overhead, their wings beating the oppressive air.

They went back over the river in Tan Zhiyong's boat, spending the evening in the house, its insect-netted windows wide open for cooler air.

Huihua enjoyed a half hour with the young children, and when they were taken to bed she tried her hardest to be pleasant to Yuling's mother, mixing courtesy with a friendliness that was not reciprocated, and never interrupting; he did not need to, Yuling did that on several occasions, heatedly twice which made her feel most awkward and she had to ask him not to get upset. When he went on his knees to his mother in front of them all and begged her to let him take her to the Hut '...for just a few days...', the firm refusal caused his head to drop and she could see he nearly cried.

Before Wenlie retired to bed, hardly more reconciled to the unhappy and dangerous situation, Yuling had forced an agreement from her that the following day, for one day only, he could have Huihua to himself, while Wenlie rushed back to Tuxieng in case the town police called at her home and found her absent. And she had insisted that the day after, Huihua would return to Mingon by boat and he would return to Amoy, and that there would be no subsequent escaping by the general's daughter, though to Wenlie's consternation Yuling would not let Huihua give a promise on that last point.

As to the future, Wenlie looked despairingly at her son; she had tried to persuade the two of them that their friendship - 'deep love' he interrupted her - could not be taken any further. At least she was gratified to see that his short explanation to the girl about what had occurred with her father when he was a colonel at the coach scene in Luchian had hit home; a look of horror had come over her face, and it remained for some minutes.

But Wenlie was surprised when Tan Zhiyong, supported by Janping and her old mother, said he strongly agreed with Yuling that while he and Huihua had to remain very careful, they must also in the name of their '...true feelings for each other...' remain resolute, to hope that one day a way could open for them to be together. 'Your romanticism, Zhiyong,' she said sharply to the tea planter, 'befits the flamboyant clothes you wear, but beware the reality and coldness of steel and bullet.'

'Oh, it's so exciting,' Janping had twittered, to Wenlie's intense annoyance, 'you two together, Genghis approves you know.'

As she turned restlessly under the bed-netting through the ever humid night, often she thought the worst, that soon she could be living alone with the good doctor, her elder son dead, her younger boy far away in some Communist pocket, her family shattered.

And when in the darkness of the room she felt weepy, she tried to find comfort from the memory of one of the greatest moments of her life: with her husband alone as they built the small shrine by the Hut, the music of the wind and the call of the birds their company; since his going away from her forever, the recollection of that time - whenever she tapped into it - gave her a feeling of inner warmth that nothing and nobody could take from her ...But her Alinga was so like his father, and now to lose him as well as Ayi, the idea was terrifying.

Early the next morning she felt exhausted and very distressed. Though Yuling and the general's daughter were in separate rooms, she had seen how much the girl loved him, even though she sometimes pulled away or had a word with him. And he ...to her continuing fear he was clearly deliriously happy to be with her, to the extent he seemed to make light of the great danger he faced.

There was no possibility she could warm to the daughter. But she could see why he had fallen for her. She was certainly pretty, she was intelligent, and naturally she spoke well. That she was a young lady obviously excited him; she had a presence only to be expected considering whose family she came from, and Wenlie could imagine her looking very good dressed up.

At an early breakfast she said: 'None of us must say that we met here in Dongang, for your sake Zhiyong as well as for Alinga's.'

Afterwards, she told Huihua to remain in the house, that she wanted to walk alone with her son to catch the boat. In front of Yuling, she added looking firmly into the eyes of the general's daughter: 'It is no exaggeration to say that my son's life is in your hands. Be very careful. As you care for him...' - she wasn't going to use the love word - 'always think of him before yourself. What each of us does has consequences for others, sometimes grave, you *must* remember that.' Now she gave her an imploring look, she had to make her understand. 'I lost my husband, and my son's life is too precious for us all, so never run away again, ever.'

She made a short bow to the girl, one that was returned with a respectful smile that she preferred not to receive, and went out of the house and down into the luxuriant courtyard of bougainvillea and palms, seeing the colourful parrot preening itself in its cage under the pealing gum tree.

'It'll be alright mother,' Yuling said, his arm in hers, after they had walked in silence a short distance along the winding street.

'Will it? What if the Whites come for you in Amoy, silently, kill you?'

'That's not going to happen, I've been there four months and I'm always careful. I'm not important to them.'

Wenlie looked ahead and made no reply. As they walked past a half empty fruit cart and turned the corner towards the river, she said: 'Get her to tell her parents she's no longer interested in going further with you, then at least there's a chance they'll leave you alone. I know what you're going to say, you love her and you intend seeing each other from time to time, somehow, and you'll say they'll pressure her into marrying some officer. But she can refuse, can't she? I can see she is strong-willed, so why can't she tell them she needs to wait a while after what's happened with you?'

Yuling thought the idea possibly good, but wondered how it would help him ever to be accepted. 'I'll talk to her,' he said. 'Mother, do you like Huihua? You've been very cool, that's not nice for me to see.'

Wenlie gave a wan smile towards her son; she tightened his arm in hers and looked away, preferring not to answer, and was thankful he did not press.

Soon they came to the top of wooden steps above a landing where a sampan waited. Her eyes began to fill as she caught sight of the rickety ferry moored upstream. 'This is an awful moment,' she said looking at him. 'We've lost Ayi. He came a few weeks ago but didn't stay for more than ten minutes. He said he's likely to be going far away, possibly Yan'an, and didn't think he'd be back for a very long time. I've only got you and Chennie, and if something happens to you...' She found it hard to continue. 'I love you so much, I only want you to be safe.' She gave him a desperate look and tried to sniff away her sadness and fear.

'You two coming?' one of the boatmen called up.

'Just my mother.'

Wenlie looked across the Zass River to the hillsides, to the tea bushes rising above the palms that stood haphazard and angled covering the far bank. She took her son in her arms and held her cheek to his, feeling his firm embrace. In the embrace she was with her first born and with her husband.

She moved a hand to his head and stroked his hair. 'Go on then precious,' she sniffled, 'but don't have more than two days up there.' She came away and looked into his eyes. 'Three at the most, *please* Alinga, she's got to go back, every day's a danger for you. And be honourable, respectful to her...' she couldn't go on.

She saw his gratitude and love, but this didn't lessen the fear inside her. She felt in a pocket and handed him a small white candle. 'Light this when you get up there, and pray for us all. Ask the spirits of the hills to look after you Alinga as they did before.'

She held back her tears as he led her down the steps to the boat. There, on the floating platform, they embraced a last time.

Five minutes later, as the swollen brown river took the sampan along with it and they rounded a corner away from the bank, Wenlie lost sight of her beloved son. Soon she was openly crying as she tried to look out through a wide slit in the sampan's arch covering. Two male passengers sitting opposite glanced at each other but said nothing.

*

'I like Tan Zhiyong,' Huihua says, back in her worker clothes, as they tramp up the hunters track in the first steep part of the forest, 'he's very good to his wife. When he gave you his rifle, he took me into another room and insisted on me having his pistol, "the best for the best" he said. He's a character.'

They walk for several hours, the hills and valleys steamy and sometimes

331

noisy from insects and birds, the sky above - when they see it through the thickness of the forest canopy - for the most part covered in cloud that is not thick or rain threatening.

Often they stop to refresh themselves in the streams and pools they come to. 'You know it's strange,' Yuling says at one of the rests, 'but having to leave Suodin without the degree hasn't turned out badly at all.' He catches Huihua's look of concern. 'No really, I'm happy in the job. Mr Hijiya, Professor Koo's friend, was extremely helpful, and at the school my Japanese is coming along well.'

By early afternoon they are half way along the plateau lakes, and already the air feels much clearer and fresher. Two hunters Tan Zhiyong told them about had gone into the hills only a few days earlier. They were not at the first or the second hut; Yuling has been hoping they were at one of those in case Huihua wanted to rest the night at the third.

But as they come past a clump of rocks and see the third hut and the small lake beside it, they spot the men squatting on the ground, their guns leaning against the wooden wall.

The men wave and stand and give them generous bows and greetings, inviting them to take green leaf tea. 'Much better up here, not humid,' one of them says.

They sit on the ground and talk. When Huihua asks them to confirm there are no tigers, both men laugh and shake their heads. 'No tigers round here miss,' one of them says, 'and you won't find them where you're going, they were killed off years ago. We've been up there, cleared some of the path below the ravine.'

They stay only a short while before Yuling winks at Huihua and nods towards the track and the forest she can see. The sun now breaks through, its direct heat making them wear the dolis that they had on their backs during the walk up to the lakes.

As they pick their way through the ravine, Yuling points to the Buddha boulder, and when they reach the top and follow the stream and can see the Hut for the first time, they stop and wash themselves in the cool water.

Yuling looks at the Hut - about a hundred paces away - and back to the girl bending down splashing herself, and is filled with an overwhelming feeling of happiness; he is living what in Amoy seemed an impossible dream.

They put their sacks and Tan Zhiyong's rifle against the wall of the Hut by the main door facing the wood, and Yuling turns to Huihua. 'Come and look at the escarpment first.'

He takes her hand and leads her past the little shrine his parents built, to the back of the building. The hot sun to their right is still some way above the furthest row of hills. 'It's beautiful,' she says gazing out as he pulls her to sit beside him on the old cedar wood bench under the shutters. Close by, the eyes of the celestial warrior blaze out from the door under the little portico, his sword defying evil spirits to come near, as it always has.

They stretch their legs, and Yuling moves closer so their sides touch. 'It reminds me of the murals,' she adds, 'there's no waterfall or path or little men, but I'm going to get inspiration here. First the Tan cottage and now this, I've never felt so free.' His lips press her cheek, but she doesn't at first turn to him; she is looking out over the forests towards the hills. 'You've opened my cage,' she says coming away from him and studying his expression. 'I just had to leave the Court, Yuling, it terrified me I'd never see you again, I don't know what I'd have done...' She stops because he is pressing her hand and looking pensive. She asks: 'Are you too exhausted you can't walk any further?'

Yuling says quietly: 'Don't leave again, my mother is right. You urged me to be patient and I will be.' He draws in his legs. 'No, I don't feel too bad, better than last time I came, I'm in good shape at the moment.' She is smiling at him in a way he can hardly resist. 'It's like the river and willows again,' he says back into her eyes, 'I'm buzzing!' and he leans towards her.

They kiss, and for a long time are lost in each other. When she pushes gently on his chest and he finally comes away, she asks: 'Would you take me to the lake you told me about, before we open up the Hut?'

A bird's shrill call comes to Yuling's ears and he looks up. 'See! Hear that, I told you! They know we're here, and look at those wings!' Two black kites have flown from behind and are circling high above the escarpment, calling to each other every few seconds. 'I remember sitting on this bench with my grandfather, they weren't higher than eye level and not far from us, they were enjoying the uplifts, it was fantastic.' He goes quiet, and they watch the birds.

Soon he is pulling her up, and twenty minutes later they come through the wood to the lake, and see the lonely tree at the far end. 'Wasn't that one of the trees I got wrong, the hemlock?' he says, squeezing her arm as he leads her towards the left side of the water. 'The lake's full because of the rains. I'll teach you to fish.'

They reach the grave, and she asks him to hold her; she nestles in his arms facing the stones. 'It's not just grandfather I think of when I'm here,' he says, his head touching the side of hers, 'but my father. Mr Hijiya says he can get us passes for mother and me to visit the Valley, but Manchuria is so far away, and we'd have to travel through all the occupied areas. I forgot to mention this to mother, you took my mind away! Anyway, she wouldn't want to go, not with the Japanese around.'

Huihua says nothing; she is looking at the wild flowers among the stones; Yuling has gone silent and she knows he is with his thoughts.

After a while he says: 'Sometimes I really think my grandfather has been helping me in my life. When the soldier was flogging me...' He stops, realizing who caused the flogging. 'I'm sorry,' he says as her head tilts to his. 'In the middle of it, I began thinking of the birds, I imagined I was flying with them, I'm sure it was grandfather who put them into my mind, and honestly, from that moment on, it wasn't so bad.' He hugs her tighter.

He leads her onto the promontory, and when he lets go of her hand and places the rifle on the ground, he stands silently beside her looking down. She feels the emotion coming over him, and guesses. 'The lake saved me,' he says as she turns to him and sees his tears. 'I'm so glad you're here...' He can't say more, and she takes him into her arms.

When he looks at her again, she receives his quiet smile that tells her what he feels for her at the deepest level.

Well after the sun went down behind the far hills, they light Wenlie's white candle at the small shrine and make a fire nearby, facing out over the escarpment, eating and talking and embracing through the twilight and well into the appearance of the stars.

He tells her about his visit to his stepsister Sanchi in Amoy, tells her again what Sanchi did for him in Doctor Ya Ya's hospital. 'She was like a mother and a sister to me, and she held me after my nightmares. And now we have so little in common, she's so strident, I really don't like it. She married secretly and then wrote and told my stepfather. But I like her husband, he speaks quietly and intelligently, he says he's a Red because it's the best chance for a better life for everybody especially the peasants, if only the Japanese could be pushed out. He told me he pins his hopes on the Americans, their long-range bombers. And he said that if the Soviets can one day turn against Japan - they are beating the Germans at the moment - we would have another powerful ally. But he's sure there's no chance Nationalist and Communist armies can beat the Japanese without foreign help, even if they combine which they won't because the Generalissimo hates Communists.'

'Do Sanchi and her husband know about me, about us?'

'No. That was my main worry, that Ayi might have got a message to them. But they didn't say anything and I didn't mention you, though I was prepared to be open.'

He talks of life in the city '...a hotbed of factions, the invaders are all-powerful, they treat us with contempt, we're often having to fawn and bow down very low, specially when a soldier comes along the pavement, we have to step off onto the street. I've been hit several times, they hit you for nothing and me because I'm much bigger. And our own administrators and police are pretty bad too. And then you've got the underground movements.'

His job comes to his mind. 'At first I didn't want to work in a Japanese school, and I asked Sanchi's husband what he thought. I told him I just have this feeling that one day my Japanese might be useful, perhaps in the Resistance, though I don't know how. He seemed to understand, said that as long as I stop short of collaborating or helping the devils lord it over us Chinese, I should take the job, if I could stand being among people who have an overbearing sense of superiority.' Yuling pauses. 'The Japanese intelligence man who interviewed me is a nasty piece of work. He wanted to know everything about your family and everybody I met at Wuyi Court. He scares me, I didn't like him at all, you can hardly see his eyes.'

That night Huihua slept in the small room with the two k'angs, Yuling on the long k'ang in the larger room, the room with the single red column and the two hanging lanterns; between them hung the curtain of phoenixes. He had seen how exhausted she was from the trek to the Hut and to the lake, as he was; and he could not presume on her.

Refreshed the following morning, they return to the lake, and he teaches her how to fish. On the way back through the wood she says: 'The drawing you gave me, I love it, and I know it has a meaning for you because you said so and I feel it.' She is holding a bucket of two fish, and lets it to the ground. 'The boy and the girl, they look quite like you and me when we were young. My mother's maid spied in my bedroom and found it. My mother was certain it's us, but...' she hesitates, 'you told me you drew it in the hospital before you came the first time to the Court, so it can't be me.'

Yuling looks seriously at his girl; the curling strand of hair he loves has fallen down one side of her cheek almost to her shoulder. He cups her face in his hands, something he loves to do. 'It *is* us, but I don't expect you to believe this. When I was lost and alone in these hills, I thought I was the only person in the world, just me and nature and tigers, I told you about the two I saw at a lake. I had a powerful dream sleeping under a boulder, you came to me or that's what I will always think.' Huihua's eyes are searching his, and he tries to put on a smile but cannot hold it. 'A girl my age seemed to come from the moon, it was night at the start of the dream, and she pulled me up and took me into a stream, and suddenly it was a sunny day and we walked in the water. And when I saw you the first time at Wuyi Court in your mother's rooms, I couldn't believe it, there you were, the girl in my dream! When I woke it was still night, and I was terrified the tigers would find me. But the girl's presence seemed to stay with me as though she was protecting me until I went back to sleep, a guarding friendly spirit is all I can describe it, very very comforting.'

Huihua thinks of the simpleton but doesn't know what to call him. 'How long after that were you found by the man?'

He comes away from the boulder, the softness of her skin a wonder as he continues to cup her. 'There was a silver mist when I woke up. A few hours maybe, I don't know.' He pauses. 'Don't move.' He takes his hands from her face, goes partly round her, and Huihua feels several playful taps on the back of her head. 'I've been owing you that for years,' he says smiling at her and doing it again on her upper back as she laughs. 'The girl kept cuffing me when we were walking in the stream, she was telling me not to give up, to keep going. She wore a beautiful crimson robe, and I'll never forget the reflections in the water. Ever since then, I often think it's my favourite colour. Sometimes, when I was working on a canvas or a drawing that needed colour - I'm talking about when I was a teenager and in my first year at college - if I wanted inspiration I'd let myself go back to the girl, and it always had a good effect on my work. Now I only have to think of you when you came into the painting room, and I'm away!'

Later, as Huihua sits near the end of the cedar bench wearing again her colourful smock, with Yuling squatting at her feet looking up at her, she reads to him from one of his grandmother's books she found in the Hut - Excerpts from Chinese and Translated Japanese Classics. She has just finished two passages from Chinese stories when he rubs his hand at the back of her leg and asks if the book includes anything from Lady Murasaki's Tale of Genji, a nine hundred-year-old Japanese classic, one she has heard of but never read.

She finds it does, and soon is reading again. When she comes to the lines

> ...there was a wattle fence over which some ivy-like creeper spread
> its cool green leaves, and among the leaves were white flowers
> with petals half unfolded like the lips of people smiling at their
> own thoughts...

she exclaims: 'That's so poetic! You've not only opened my cage, you're opening another literary door for me.' She gives him a short nod and smiles. 'Told you, women can write beautifully too!'

As she reads on, a strange noise comes to Yuling's ears from somewhere below in the forest, a noise that he soon realizes is growing. 'Shush!' He squeezes her leg and turns to look out over the escarpment. 'Listen!'

Huihua stops and at once picks up the noise.

'Bees I think!' he calls, 'look!' She sees the rising cloud just as he points; it covers a quarter of the near forest and seems to be moving in their direction. 'Into the Hut, fast!' he shouts as he scrambles up and grabs her hand, Huihua dropping the book on the bench.

They run in through the portico, Yuling crying out 'Do the other doors, I'll do the shutters!'

The noise grows ever louder, and shortly after the second shutter is closed, greyness envelopes the little building as a gigantic swarm comes up and over the edge of the escarpment, making it impossible for them to speak as they cling to each other and wait anxiously.

Yuling knows there are several slits in the shutter edges as well as higher up in the old wooden walls, and wonders how they are going to deal with the danger if many bees land and enter.

After an unpleasant time approaching half a minute, the end of the swarm passes over and the noise very soon fades, until they are in silence again.

'Phew, I've never experienced that before!' he says releasing himself from her. He goes into the tiny cooking area and cautiously opens the door to the outside, Huihua staying under an unlit lantern in the room with the red column. From the door, he looks for signs of remnant bees along the outside wall that partly faces the stream. He calls back: 'Can't see any, but we'd better not open the shutters for a while just in case. I'll go out later and inspect.' He closes the door.

'Yuling.' He catches the emotion in Huihua's voice. 'Hold me, kiss me, I love it.' He goes back to her. She is standing barefoot as usual, some sunlight coming through one of the warped shutters onto the back of her head; the rest of the room is in semi-darkness. He puts his arms over her shoulders, and as he begins pecking her his left hand feels the warmth of the sunbeams.

When he turns her, a ray catches the upper part of her face and shows the painted flower motifs running up the red column nearby. 'You're delicious,' he says, looking closely at one eye and then at the other. 'Do you know, right now your pupils are bigger than usual, and your eyes are saying different things to me.' He gazes at the right eye. 'This eye is definitely larger than the left, it's challenging me to look away from you,' he starts shaking his head, 'but I can't, it's mesmerizing me as if for something bigger,' he keeps looking at the right eye, 'and all the time I can feel, I can actually feel the power of your other eye, it's incredible, I'm trying not to be pulled away but it's forcing me over.' He moves to the left eye and wants to fall to his knees and hug her round the legs. 'Now you've got me! It's almost quivering, it's narrower and it's very inviting, it's telling me "I'm even more sensual than my partner, and we've caught you, you're coming in whether you want to resist us or not, and if you try, we'll open wide and flicker and the next moment you'll be out of control."'

He runs a fingernail up one side of her face, Huihua loving the touch, and as he comes over her brow and down the other cheek, she reaches up on her toes and feels his arms tighten round her waist as she loses herself in their kiss.

When he comes away he says: 'I love you Huihua, I really love you. When I heard your voice before I even looked up from the canvas, I...'

She stops him with a finger, pressing it to his mouth. 'I came to the old guest room to see *you*.' For many weeks she has thought of the words she wants to say to him if she could somehow see him alone, obviously away from the Court. And now the time has come. How he would react she would leave to the gods. She would not mention some of the other thoughts that so much troubled: her terrible worry about the long periods they were likely to be apart, that they might make him change his mind about her, especially when he met other women in Amoy; and that after his mother's revelation about her father's despicable behaviour, she would never be able to get her father to accept him.

She removes her finger from his lips and feels behind for his hands. 'Yuling, just as I'm touching you now in this truly lovely place, I will always hold you as my own. From this precious moment I want you to know that I'm yours if you want me, if you'll have me, whenever, do you understand, even though I must go back.' There, she has said it and it came out more or less as she hoped. She gives him a certain look.

Her wait is very short. Soon he is carrying her past the phoenix curtain, through the alcove and into the room she slept in, thrills and trepidations racing through her as she knows his answer. Overwhelmed by her emotions and the goodness and the strength of her young man, Huihua has already accepted what is to come, their culture notwithstanding - it is what she wants more than anything, come whatever.

In the morning they decide to have a final day and one more blissful night in their isolation at the edge of the escarpment. Yuling draws a small portrait of Huihua down to the base of her neck, using crayons he had left at the Hut four years earlier; little knowing, he said, '...that these pastels would be used for such a magical time.' She sits inside the Hut in front of one of the open shutters, not looking out but towards his right and a little down - that is the way he wants, not like her brother who posed looking upwards to the left of the viewer. 'I'll show part of the shutter and maybe hint at the distant hills,' he says, 'but I'm not including the birds, I don't want any distraction from my lovely subject.'

In the early afternoon he takes her to the second ravine, the route he wrongly took when he became lost the morning after the gun explosion. As they stand by the divided stream near the top of the ravine, he tells her how he kept looking for the path, even down in the forest at the end of the rocks, and that he has never been down there again.

He places his rifle on the ground and puts his arms round her. 'My mother says the celestial warrior and other spirits saved me, and who am I to say she's wrong. But I prefer to think you and Lam did.' He begins swaying her the way she loves, the way she will remember when back alone in her rooms at the Court.

...gliding from one ravine to the other and then away, two great birds of prey call to each other as they look down at humans with long sticks and become fearful of bangs that might come...

Barefoot and carrying their sandals, they retrace their steps on the left side of the stream, each sometimes going into the water, Yuling having to be careful not to slip as the rifle is strapped to his back.

When Huihua can see the Hut again, she feels playful, play that has a purpose. They are both near the water's edge and she is looking a little ahead, asking him to pick up a small stone for her as a keepsake. She lets go of his hand and points. 'See, that one with the water flowing over it, yes that one there!'

The stream sparkles in the afternoon sun, and he puts the rifle against a small rock and goes back into the water.

'Catch me if you can!' she cries as he bends down and she starts running, sandals in hand.

He laughs. 'Don't think I can,' he calls as he treads quickly over submerged pebbles.

Half way to the Hut she slows and looks back, twice waving a sandal in the hurry-up gesture, as she sees him running with the rifle and knows he must have left his sandals at the stream.

Coming to the small shrine, she has a quick decision to make: to go round the outside of the Hut and keep running away from him as he comes to each corner, or to run in through the door to the alcove, which would probably mean she'd be trapped, unless she could get through one of the other doors before he caught her.

She goes for the door, a few seconds later pushing it open and rushing in and slamming it, breathing hard in the semi-darkness, a smile of longing over her face, she is going to let herself be caught, definitely, she can hardly *wait* for his arms again, to make beautiful full love with her artist...

A curtain rail or some protrusion from the door touches her hair. She is about to move away when hard metal presses against her head and the horror of a gun flashes into her mind, and as she quarter turns, a hand grabs her mouth and someone is pulling her round and she cannot see the person because she's just come from strong sunshine. And now she is being dragged through the phoenix curtain into the room with the red column where shafts of light come glancing through the closed shutters striking the lanterns; and as she struggles and kicks out, she hears Yuling fling the door open and call her name in the way that would thrill but now terrifies, and the next moment a sharp voice is telling him to raise his hands fast or he'll be dead.

What ensues in the alcove behind the phoenixes she cannot tell because she is pushed onto the floor face down, the hand releases her so she can breathe, and her arms are being forced behind her and her hands are being tied.

'Yuling!' she manages to cry though rather weakly, registering no struggle is going on behind the curtain. But a gag is soon being tied round her mouth, its smell sickening, and she is being left on the floor.

'Don't hurt the girl,' she hears Yuling plead as a gruff voice tells him to go outside. And the next moment there is much shouting and she can tell that a struggle is taking place.

She rolls onto her side, but when she tries to get to her feet a gun explodes and she wants to cry out but cannot, and she cannot get up either. She hears more shouting, the wall of the Hut is being banged, and while she is wriggling across the floor towards the curtain, there is another shot and she hears Yuling scream in agony, her mind going into shock as the screams turn to groans and she knows her father's men have found them and he could be dying.

Her head is now pushing against the bottom corner of the curtain. She hears a soldier running back towards the door, and tries to move into a position so she can kick, whether he is a Huang corps soldier or not. Very soon sunlight is streaming through the door into the alcove, and then the phoenixes are being flung back on the curtain rings, and Yuling is looking down at her, he has a revolver in his hand and his hair and shirt are severely messed.

Her relief at seeing him is overwhelming. 'Only two of them,' he says panting as he kneels and feels her head, 'one's run away, I've got the guns.' He unties the gag.

'Oh ...oh ...I thought the soldiers had shot you,' she cries.

'Not soldiers...' he's shaking his head and starting to unbind her hands, '...not hunters either, must be bandits, first time, one's shot himself in the leg, he's outside.' She wants to hug him but her hands are not yet free. She can hear the man's loud groaning.

The last part of the cord comes loose, and he helps her up. 'Are you alright, not hurt?' he asks with a worried look.

'Come!' she says not answering. 'Where's the other gone?'

'Ran towards the wood...' but already Huihua is moving outside and he is following and sees her looking towards the man lying on the ground a few paces away; he is gripping his upper leg, his head shaking.

Yuling hands her the revolver. 'Hold on,' he says as he grabs a bandit's rifle lying on the ground.

But she is going up to the man while Yuling is inspecting the rifle. 'How many are you?' she shouts. The fellow grimaces; he's looking through his trousers at a bleeding wound above the knee. She waits, and when he gives her no reply, she hits the barrel of the revolver against the shin of the other leg, making him yell out and soon cry for mercy. 'You'll get a bullet through your head next time,' she shouts between his cries as she wields the gun near his face. 'How many?'

'Three ...two...' he calls through his pain '...two,' he repeats.

'What do you mean three?'

The man looks towards the path leading to the wood. 'Just him,' he gasps.

Yuling comes up and shouts: 'What you doing here? You come all this way to rob us, we haven't anything.'

The man is groaning too much to answer.

'Maybe they were scouting to set up a camp,' she says.

'Your pal's going to have to get you down to Dongang,' Yuling adds, 'and that's a long way.' He turns to Huihua and whispers: 'We've got to get out of here fast in case he comes back,' he nods towards the wood, 'could still have a knife.'

'Bandits work in groups,' she whispers back, 'more could be around or coming up.'

'We'll see them before they see us if we're careful, plenty of rocks to hide behind. And there's the forest, they won't be thinking of us coming down alone, won't be expecting us. We'll get to the two hunters, and if they're still there, we'll have some protection for the night.'

He pulls her away, each looking towards the trees. 'Grab our things,' he says, 'I'll deal with the revolver and guns, I know a place to hide them. Close the shutters, and don't worry if you hear a shot or two, it'll be me.'

Hardly more than four or five minutes later (after Huihua has seen Yuling pulling up floorboards in the tiny cooking area and heard two shots ringing out and has gone to check he was alright and to look towards the wood) they are ready to leave.

Yuling flings the old tin medical box on the ground near the injured man, and puts a water jug beside him but says nothing.

'Got the drawing?' She nods. 'And Tan Zhiyong's pistol?' She taps her sack. 'Safety catch on?' She gives him a quick smile.

They walk fast away looking back several times to the wood, Yuling carrying too much: a bandit's rifle strapped to his back, his sack over a shoulder, and Tan Zhiyong's rifle in his hand ready to fire if they see the second man or anyone else.

The black kites are nowhere to be seen.

He puts on his sandals left at the stream. Soon over the water, they make their way towards the first of the huge rocks that leads into the ravine. It is not easy for either of them to get down through the rocks, especially for Yuling so burdened, and twice he has to ask Huihua to wait for him. All the time they look out for other bandits below them and to the sides of the ravine.

They get about three-quarters down when Huihua, once more well in front, thinks she sees movement behind a rock about thirty or forty paces below her on the path near the tumbling water. She stops and crouches and releases her sack from round her neck. She cannot signal to Yuling because a few rocks separate their view of each other. While he is edging down to her, she takes out the pistol.

He reaches her, bends low, and she points and whispers: 'There's either a man or an animal behind that rock.'

He sees several rocks, some higher and wider than a human, others smaller, and makes her identify the exact one; and when he is satisfied, he tells her to cover her ears.

Still crouching, he takes aim at one side of the rock and fires, then fires at the other, and almost at once in the echoing around them they catch a glimpse of the back of a man, he is wearing a headband and jumping down through the rocks in the direction of the end of the ravine and the forest that starts further on.

Yuling stands and fires again just as the head disappears, the bullet ricocheting off a boulder. As he is taking bullets from a pocket, Huihua starts running with pistol in hand; she has removed the safety catch, kicked off her sandals and left her sack.

'Huihua, stop!' he shouts, pointing his rifle away, 'Huihua!' But she is ignoring him, and he watches in fear as she tears down the path that wriggles its way through the ravine.

He pushes the sandals into her sack, picks up both sacks and starts down as best as he can, frequently looking to see where she has got to and calling out to her.

By the time the bandit reaches the bottom of the ravine, Huihua reckons she is within about twenty strides of catching him. But she still has to get past some smaller rocks, and he has already looked round once and knows he is being chased.

Suddenly he stops and turns and shakes a handgun towards her, and she jumps behind one of the rocks, feeling surprise he hasn't fired because for a moment he had a clear view of her; she is also surprised how young he seems.

She listens to frantic shouting that he'll shoot her if she comes any nearer.

In the ensuing silence she waits only a very short time before looking round the side of the rock; he is now running along the path towards the forest where she knows he can easily hide, from which to attack them.

As she weaves through the last of the rocks, she catches Yuling's cries but not his words, and soon she is chasing the fellow along the clearer straighter path, gaining all the time and ready to bend low and fire if he turns again, determined to wound not kill because she wants to find out if there are other bandits to deal with; the return trek to the tea plantation at the river is long.

The man is half way to the forest and Huihua only a few strides from catching him, when the ground erupts to one side of him as the noise of rifle shot shatters the air and echoes through the ravine.

Shocked that Yuling has risked firing so close to her, Huihua stops and crouches, aiming the pistol at the bandit's legs, thinking to shoot, when another shot rings out. This time she doesn't see the ground explode, but the fellow is falling to his knees, his back is turned to her and she thinks Yuling's second bullet has hit him.

Quickly she looks back. She can see Yuling still among the bigger rocks, rifle dangerously aimed towards them, and prays he won't risk a third shot. She turns fast back to the bandit, shouting: 'Put your gun on the ground where I can see it or I'll kill you.'

She watches him lay down his revolver. 'Push it away to the side,' she calls, still crouching with her finger on the trigger of Tan Zhiyong's pistol.

He does so and he's panting. She runs up to him and puts the pistol hard on the back of the headband - rolls reversed she tells herself, thinking of the gun metal against her head in the Hut's alcove. Almost at once there's another shot and then a fourth, they echo around her and she thinks they come from Yuling in the ravine but isn't at all sure, and wonders if other bandits could be firing at her, though she hasn't felt the rush of bullets or seen the ground disturbed.

She half turns, can see Yuling waving a rifle above his head, her first thought being that he doesn't want her to take the bandit's life - which now she's not going to - her next that he has seen others and is trying to warn her.

She presses her gun harder against the headband, and looks all around her, but sees nobody.

Her captive's head is dropping. With her foot she pushes away his revolver, picks it up, takes two steps from him so he can't lunge, then looks for signs of blood but sees none.

The head is now close to the ground, hands covering the face, and the body has begun trembling.

'Are you hit?' she asks fiercely. He doesn't answer. 'Are there any more of you?' The head shakes as if to say No.

She sees Yuling is nearing the end of the ravine. It takes him another couple of minutes to reach her, and as he approaches, she can tell he isn't only struggling with his load but seems visibly shaken.

'I've got his gun,' she calls to him, thinking he's giving the bandit a strange look. 'He says there aren't any others, but after the last man, can we believe him?' She watches him put down his burden. He seems to be waiting to get his breath back. She hands him the bandit's revolver. 'We can't afford to walk into an ambu...'

'Betrayer!' he screams towards the bandit, letting the revolver drop to the ground on its barrel head.

She gasps. 'You know this man?' Fury is in Yuling's eyes, frenzy almost, a look that hugely frightens her - a new and unpleasant side to her lover. She watches him go up to the bandit and take the back of his shirt, physically hauling him up and turning him round.

'My own brother! Betrayer!' Yuling pulls off the headband and thrashes the back of his hand across Ayi's face, causing him to shriek and reel back as Huihua cries out 'Your brother!'

'They're not bandits,' Yuling shouts again, 'they're Reds, and that he could do this to *me*, and mother let us come...'

'We could have killed him,' she cries recalling the ten-year-old boy who accompanied Yuling to the Court when she was a girl. She is finding it hard to take in, her pistol now pointing to the ground. The brother is semi-bent, a hand covering the front of his face against further strike. She realizes that the intelligence she sensed in that moment when he brandished the handgun and she leapt behind the rock might have told her this was no bandit - that might have been why he hadn't fired, couldn't bring himself to kill his brother's girl. And once, in the outer courtyard, she had witnessed captured Reds adopting the same kneeling, head-low position.

Yuling, his breathing hardly easier, ignores Ayi's raised hand, and grabs his brother's shirt now from the front. 'Are others waiting to kill us? Tell me or I'll lose myself,' he shouts.

'Don't hit him again, *please*,' Huihua beseeches.

Yuling is glaring at Ayi. 'One's wounded up there, another's hidden himself in the wood. So?'

Ayi looks away. He says quietly: 'Just us, no one else, you weren't going to be harmed, neither of you.'

'How did you know we were here, or did you go home and ask Chennie who'd have trusted you?'

Ayi nods to the ground.

Yuling lets go of the shirt but stays very close. 'What were you going to do with her, eh?'

The head comes slowly up, and there is a different look that Huihua sees at once and she's worried what Yuling might do.

Ayi's shame at an early mission failure and at being found out and nearly killed by his own brother or by the Slayer's daughter has given way to other emotions. He doesn't believe Yuling will seriously hurt him, and as for the girl - the girl he despises for the family she comes from, for the wealth and power he remembers from their childhood visit - he hates her, the hatred festering over recent months since his brother terrified him with the name of his lover.

Despite his brother standing so near, Ayi turns his head towards the girl and imagines the father.

Yuling catches the defiance, and when he sees his brother is not going to answer and feels rage swelling up again and is about to hit him, Huihua is pushing him hard with both hands, her right still holding Tan Zhiyong's pistol. 'No Yuling, don't, not for me, not to your brother, they wanted to kidnap me, not kill me.' He has to step away for balance, and she keeps pushing him, he letting her do so, until he pulls her firmly aside.

'Mother let us come here,' he repeats towards Ayi, relieved to feel more in control of himself, 'she and father built the shrine, and now you've defiled our lovely Hut.'

Huihua sees the brother stand straighter, and notices he is not nearly as tall or broad but has a family similarity in the shape of the head

'The shrine!' Ayi sneers, glancing at the girl. 'Religion's finished. She's the one who's defiled it.'

Huihua jumps in front of Yuling, her left hand pushing at his shoulder.

'I've lost a brother,' he says over her head. 'You've become a tool of the Reds.' He nods towards the ravine. 'You'd better go up there and give your comrade some help. How you'll get the bullet out and get him down...' He shakes his head. 'It'll take you days, and don't bother looking for the guns, I've thrown the ammunition over the escarpment.' He looks at Huihua, her anxious face. 'Let's go.'

He picks up the Communist military revolver, puts it in his sack and pulls out Huihua's sandals. 'Scorpions' is all he says as he hands them to her. This time he gives her a sad look, then bends down and picks up his own sack and the two rifles, and begins walking away, signalling her to follow.

Huihua takes a final look at the brother.

'You're lucky there aren't tigers,' Yuling calls back without turning as she runs to him.

When they come to the forest, they hear the shout: 'You're the betrayer, Slayer lover! Concubine trash!'

'Don't look round,' Huihua implores, 'leave him.'

*

Two days later, when the June sun was going down, Huihua left the Mingon woods and approached the dark red walls of her family mansion, the part of the walls guarding the granary and stables. It was some thirteen days after she had stolen out in disguise. The fear she had been trying to suppress came

345

powerfully back; she feared her mother, but she knew her father had the real power over her, and desperately hoped that he had not returned because of her absence, though what she feared most was what would happen to Yuling if they caught him.

She banged on the familiar stable gates, the gates she loved going through when riding out on Ajin. She was longing to be with her horse again, before she went up to the confrontation there was sure to be.

One of the guards called out asking her to identify herself.

'The Mistress,' she called back.

There was a silence. She heard the guards talking; she was puzzled, the talking seemed to go on for far too long. She banged again, surprised the bar wasn't being pulled back, and heard someone running up the stone steps to one side of the gates.

She was about to call out when a head appeared above the gates; it was the guard who she had smiled at when she ordered they be opened so she could ride to Yuling at the rocks; he was looking down giving a couple of nods of respect.

'Beg pardon, Mistress, orders are not to let you in.'

Huihua felt shock.

'They'll tell you what to do at the main gates, sorry Mistress, wish we could open up.' The man nodded again and disappeared, and she heard him going back down the steps.

She stood there for a few seconds, unable to believe her mother or her parents were shutting her out; they had always drilled into her the danger of being outside the Court unescorted.

She walked quickly along the side walls of the inner and the outer courtyards, turned at the front corner, and soon came to one of the stone chimera lions; its roar now frightened her where it had never done before, even when she was a little girl.

As she banged on the door, she could hear guards running from the Guard House. The grill opened, and she saw a soldier she did not recognize. 'It's the Mistress, Huang Huihua,' she said for effect, 'open the door.'

'Can't do that, her Ladyship's orders.'

She heard another guard whispering to the man.

'Yes. You're to go to the East Gate Monastery, take the road Mistress before it gets too dark, shouldn't be planes, hurry mind as they could shut soon.'

Huihua knew better than to beg to be allowed through. But this was a huge blow, not only because she felt exhausted but because she had no idea what was now to happen to her. Was she actually been thrown out? She found that hard to accept, but feared such a reality; her mother could be hard and unforgiving.

She made her way towards the town in the gathering darkness. It didn't take her long to decide that if she really was being thrown out, she would leave Mingon the next morning and make her way somehow to Amoy, and get a message to Yuling where she could be found; she would have to smuggle between Japanese border posts. And there was always a possibility to go to Fuzhou, to cousins on her mother's side, unless they had been warned and poisoned.

She had just gone through the town's Great Gate when she heard riders coming up fast behind her. She leapt onto the pavement beside the first dwellings, suspecting they were looking for her and that there might be a sedan coming along behind on the road. The riders went slowly by her as she nipped into the small alley that was especially hers and Yuling's. She waited several minutes by the unlit house shrine, telling herself that she was not going to give her mother the satisfaction of fetching her home that night. Her recent freedom was having its effect.

When she reached Elder Han's house in the darkness, she tugged at the long tassel leading to a bell hanging under one of the fire-breathing dragons; she could make them out, but not their colours.

'Get a message to my husband that she is back. And beg him, from me you understand Wang, make this clear, to call off the hunt for Tsai Yuling. I wish he were out of our lives, but I definitely do not want him killed, I am sure you get my meaning after what I divulged the other day in distress. It is very important that my husband understands my concern about our daughter, she is too headstrong for her own good, and love-blind. And also...' Madame Huang gave her husband's private secretary a more gentle look, '...you must forgive whatever emotion you saw from me, my harsh words, they were a mother's concern, you realize. I regret my decision last night. My idea to shock her and your idea of the monastery did not work. Well, maybe it did partly, maybe she *was* shocked, but she is not saying.' The private secretary, previously head domestic, now tilted his head and held his hands clasped together, sensing the lady had not finished. 'Soon you and I must put on our thinking caps and see what more we can do to prevent another, shall we say, escape.'

'Has the Mistress said where she has been, ma'am, and if I may ask, anything about the student?'

'She refuses to talk.' But Madame Huang knew that to be untrue; she had had a blazing row with her daughter, had to shout at her to try to get her to say where she had been and if she had met him and if he had *made love* to her, and having to hear back that she wouldn't answer such questions and that '...I worship him, no other word can I use...' and that '...I would die for him...' and having to listen to part of the reason why her husband was so dead against the

347

fellow '...because of his appalling, appalling advances on Tsai Yuling's mother, shame, shame on my own father...'

'Wang, she will not tell me anything, a most unhappy situation between mother and daughter, as you can imagine. We might have known more if my son was here and not with his father. Perhaps she might give *you* some idea, if you tell her that the staff were very worried about her. You could ask her innocently if it was easy for a woman alone without papers to get in and out of Fuzhou, see what she says, though I suspect she never went there at all.'

On returning to Tuxieng after her tearful boat departure from Dongang, Wenlie had been mightily relieved to hear that there had been no callers from the authorities in the two days she had been away. If there had been, she would have been in trouble, as the lie she had asked her husband to give - that she was visiting family in Luchian - would have been disbelieved and soon exposed.

But the very next day two Kuomintang policemen called at her house. They were aggressive, demanding to know where her elder son was living - they said they had details of his address in Amoy but required her to confirm them - and what she knew of his whereabouts over the previous few days 'as he has disappeared', and when had she last seen him and where, and what had been the last communication between them.

At the beginning she played mild and innocent, with the doctor and a medical apprentice by her side. But as soon as one of the policemen accused her of lying, she began to act *the main role*, rising a little on her feet and becoming taller than either policeman, looking from one to the other and telling them forcefully that she was not a liar, that was against her Buddhist religion, and that her husband 'the respected Doctor Chen', she gave a short smile in her husband's direction, 'would absolutely confirm that we have not seen my son here for months, or anywhere else in Tuxieng, or nearby for that matter, not since the New Year period.' She was relieved when her husband began nodding to the men, though the eye was twitching.

She was also relieved no mention was made of the general's daughter, or worse some question raised. When they asked her what family she had in Fuzhou, at first she expressed surprise, her son was in Amoy she said, he wouldn't have gone to Fuzhou. But on being pressed, she divulged her two sisters' addresses, reluctantly she added, but believing the information gave the men something for them to report back, so they might think she had not been entirely difficult or evasive.

As they were leaving she played the dead-hero card, reminding them who her first husband had been.

'I was waiting for them to start on Ayi,' the doctor said going back into his surgery when they had gone. 'I need a stiff drink.'

Three weeks later, a near neighbour came to their house. He had received a written message, and only after reading it a second time had he understood that it was intended for the doctor and his wife. The names meant nothing to him, he had realized they might be coded, and Tsai Yuling had spoken to him back in February when, against his better judgement, he had agreed to receive the odd letter or message but only if it was absolutely essential and could not be sent direct to Doctor Chen's house. He had been told no reason why this service was being asked of him, and he preferred not to know.

It was indeed from Yuling, his name and the others were disguised, and it put Wenlie and the doctor into shock, Wenlie at once beginning to cry. In between her outbursts at the general '...and his wretched daughter...' she said how much she regretted letting the lovers go to the Hut '...because then Ayi's horrible horrible action would never have happened,' she sobbed.

The doctor also berated himself for telling his younger stepson that his mother had gone to Dongang and why. But Ayi had suddenly appeared at the house and caught him by surprise. 'It's more my fault, Wenlie, much more my fault than yours.'

'We'll never see Ayi again,' she cried out. 'Oh Ayi ...oh this is terrible Chennie, I can't live like this...'

It was the fifteenth day of the month, the day of spiritual duty that Wenlie never missed. 'I can't go to the temple,' she said, wiping her eyes.

22

'Head Teacher praises you and that pleases me,' Japanese education administrator Takashi Hijiya said, standing just inside the entrance to the school grounds on a breezy mid-morning in early September 1943, the Japanese flag waving strongly on its pole nearby. He handed Yuling back his black and white photograph of the Chinese cadet. 'My brother thought the portrait you did looked very good, wondered what colours you'd used. I mentioned you preferred not to say who the boy was and he was intrigued.' Professor Koo's friend from Tokyo student days gave him an enquiring look, but Yuling said nothing. 'I told him what Koo Guanglu wrote about you. My brother requires you to paint him on the basis no payment if not liked, otherwise good money and maybe other commissions from the military. Do you agree to that, Tsai Yuling?'

'Yes, thank you Mr Hijiya, thank you very much.' Yuling kept his expression serious despite feeling very pleased, and made a good bow. Coming back to the upright he added: 'I've got the professor's brushes, a present...'

'Excellent, I'll tell him, and I look forward to seeing the end result.' The education administrator gave a quick laugh. 'We're different my brother and me, I'm taller and married with children, he's smaller and a bachelor with lady friends. I'm a bookworm, he never reads except newspapers and magazines. I've put on weight over the years, he's stayed more or less the same, must be the military! And he's more outgoing, in fact very, you'll need to catch his exuberance, though we both enjoy life.' He chuckled.

'He is in the military?'

A no-nonsense look came over the administrator's face. 'Can't tell you anything, security, but you'll find out. Now, I must praise you for your Japanese, you've improved greatly in only a few months. When did I meet you first, March was it?'

Now Yuling couldn't suppress a smile. He knew that working in the art and music department at the small Japanese junior school in Amoy's eastern district had helped him speak the invaders' language much better, particularly as he had to talk with the children and answer their fast questions. At the start, it had been made clear by the Head Teacher and the three Japanese women teachers - as a group in the Head's office - that he had not been the preferred choice and was an inferior and had to be respectful at all times or faced immediate loss of the job and appropriate disciplining. And some of the children had been arrogant and rude towards him. But after about four weeks, a change had taken place and he was treated with more courtesy, and soon there was friendliness and even joking with him.

That afternoon he waited nervously on the street outside the school gates as instructed, with a bag over one shoulder that contained his drawing pad and pencils.

It was not long before a black car pulled up sharply, two military policemen jumping out, one barking in a Japanese dialect he found difficult to understand, asking, it seemed, if he was the art teacher.

They signalled him to the car. The one who had spoken gave him a minor prod into the back seat and followed him in.

Nothing was said to him. The men talked away to the driver who was also in uniform, and Yuling caught only parts of what they were saying. As they sped through the streets at alarming speed - this was his first time in an automobile and he was sure they would crash and was bracing himself - he imagined his father asking him what he was doing in a vehicle of the enemy. He'd already imagined his father and grandfather asking a similar question about his working in a Japanese school, answering them to his own satisfaction that he was learning a useful language and it was not a job that oppressed his own people.

After about twenty minutes, including leaving the city and speeding along flat countryside, they came to a checkpoint with a large military board announcing the Japanese Army Air Force. As he watched the driver being signalled through an opening barrier, the man beside him told him they were blindfolding him.

The car gathered speed, and soon they seemed to be racing again, and he guessed they were travelling along a runway with no traffic or pedestrians. Not more than a minute later he heard the sound of what he took to be a plane engine.

The car came to a halt, and he was helped out still blindfolded. Each arm was firmly held, and he was walked along a hard surface - an unnerving experience, he kept wanting to pull back. Soon he was being led into some building and taken through passages and round corners.

He was finally brought to a stop and the blindfold removed. The large room he found himself in had inner blinds hanging down before windows, the light coming only from electric ceiling bulbs spaced between stationary fans. The two military policemen he had been with in the car left him, and another nodded at him and told him he must remain standing. The man went to the door and called down the passage.

Barely a minute later he heard quick footsteps, and soon a senior air officer, a short man, walked in. Yuling leapt up feeling very nervous, and gave the deep bow required of every Chinese in the presence of a Japanese.

The officer came straight over, smiling generously which greatly surprised him. He had some folder in his hand, and Yuling saw at once a likeness to Mr Takashi Hijiya.

'This is going to be interesting! You've painted in General Huang's mansion, I'm told. I've flown over it. And now here you are about to do a portrait of *me*! Your life-story will be even more interesting than I hear it is already! Come, sit.' Colonel Hijiya drew up another chair, Yuling waiting until the officer sat down.

'My brother showed me the photograph, it's the general's boy I have discovered, we can find out most things! Now. Can you make me a drawing first, I'll show you what I want, and then do the painting?'

'Yes, sir.'

'Can you draw aeroplanes?'

Yuling was taken aback; he'd hardly ever drawn one, and then only years ago at school out of a book, a bi-plane. 'Yes sir. I can draw most things.' The nerves were leaving.

'Good!' The colonel handed him a piece of paper from the folder. 'This is what I have in mind.'

Yuling was yet more surprised, seeing a rough sketch of a human figure full length with crude facial features, and directly above the figure a plane was drawn large and badly. 'Can you do it?' he heard, already thinking of the problem of harmony, there being three or possibly four elements: man, machine, sky and background. 'This is the plane I want,' the colonel added, handing him a coloured drawing that Yuling thought good, and several black and white photographs. 'My fighter, a beautiful Ki 60, they won't let me fly the 61, they say I'm too old at forty seven, nonsense!'

Yuling did not look up; he felt honoured that the colonel was sitting with him, it seemed to give him the confidence to speak.

'*You* must be the main feature sir, not the plane. A portrait succeeds only if the distinguished face is properly shown. I see two possibilities, either a bust-like portrait from here up...' he put his arm across his upper chest, 'your head and face would then be the main feature, or a full body-length portrait, and in either picture your plane would be top left, not directly above your head. If I make the plane too big, unreality comes in.' He looked at the colonel and guessed he would like a brisk recommendation. 'I suggest the first, but can do either.'

The air officer laughed. 'Huh! You mean I'm too short for a full-length picture! Alright, do it chest up, but don't make the plane too small.' He gave a curt nod and promptly stood.

Yuling wanted to jump up, but was fumbling with the drawing and the photographs on his lap. 'We'll be in this briefing room,' he heard as he was getting to his feet, 'it's not in use at the moment. You'll have to accept the light, and don't you look past the blinds or you'll be in deep trouble. Let me see your rough drawing in half an hour, then we'll discuss size and money.'

Two days after his first meeting with the artist, Colonel Hijiya felt in a very good mood. His request to remain as Senior Operational Air Officer Southern China, not to be promoted and posted back to Staff HQ in Nanjing, had just been approved.

'We know a lot about you from Koo Guanglu,' he said early on in the first session to the young man who impressed him. 'My brother said you became famous from some childhood accident, and you've been expelled from university for making love to Huang's daughter. Now that must have been exciting, not the expulsion, the love-making!' He smiled broadly; the thought he was talking to a young Chinese, a large and virile one at that, who had succeeded in seducing such a girl - he was sure she must be very pretty - was clearly an invitation for amusement. He'd already had a very good laugh about it over drinks with some of his pilots. 'Tell me about her, what's she look like, not her father I hope!' He roared with laughter.

Yuling found the exuberance distracting, a serious nuisance. The colonel would not hold his head position for long, or his expression, and was frequently talking.

'She's high-born, literary and determined,' he replied, putting one brush into a tall wide-rimmed bottle and picking up another, not wanting to describe Huihua's physical attributes.

'Do you like women?'

The abruptness of such a question took him by surprise and he didn't know what to answer, though he was glad the colonel hadn't pressed about her. He thought about Huihua's come-on smile in the Hut, the expectant eyes, when he took her to the room with the two k'angs and they loved and loved to distraction, to eventual sleep in each other's arms.

His sitter saw the embarrassment. 'Course you do!'

'Please sir,' he braved, looking more at the canvas than the airman, 'I need you to keep your pose for just a few minutes at a time.'

The colonel resumed his position. 'They're the greatest spice given to man,' he said loudly just after some engine began revving not far away, at a hangar or runway Yuling thought; on several occasions he had already heard planes taxiing or flying past.

He did not reply, was embarrassed to be talking about women as if they were playthings, and to a foreigner more than twice his age. He started mixing paints for the tone under the lips; the colonel had a good chin, and an interesting darkish complexion from a strong close-shaved beard.

But the officer seemed to have gone into his own thoughts (of women no doubt), and there was a welcome silence.

Though not for long enough. 'I remember Koo Guanglu, small like me, used to come to my parents' home. He was rather shy, unlike me! I haven't seen him since then, is he still shy?'

'I didn't find him shy, sir, but quiet, and I liked him the most.'

'He wrote to my brother that my pilots nearly killed you.' The air officer turned his head. 'I'm glad they didn't or you wouldn't be here!' The tone changed abruptly. 'I want to know what happened.'

Japanese arrogance had come into the voice, Yuling thought as he heard 'That was a mistake by the lead pilot, he was disciplined. Well?'

Yuling was being made to relate the horror of the air attack. 'I was in a large hall of murals, wall paintings, talking with the young lady,' he preferred not to mention Huihua by name, 'when the air-raid siren began and at the same time we heard planes.' He hesitated.

'Yes?'

'We tried to get down to the basement, I caught a glimpse of a plane coming towards us very low, but before we got there the firing started and bullets came crashing into our part of the building.'

'Nasty. You were behind a metal door, it was jammed or something, like me being nearly roasted in my damned cockpit when my plane was on fire over the sea.'

Yuling was at once startled to hear that his subject had had an escape from a burning aeroplane, and put down his palette board, aware of the strangeness of talking to a Japanese airman about each of them nearly dying.

But he could tell the colonel was waiting to hear more. 'I was terrified the first bullets would hit us through a window or the walls, and when there was more firing I thought we could still be killed, and then the air got thick with dust and I realized much too late that we could suffocate, but luckily servants came and rescued us. Somebody had fitted the bolts on the other side of the door by mistake. At one stage I was frightened we might be bombed. I think when the alarm sounded, my friend mentioned something about bombing being possible.'

'They were fighter aircraft not bombers, and we wouldn't have done that to the place, much more important targets further west. You and the girl were lucky.' Yuling now felt he was being talked to almost as an equal. 'And I know the fear. When my engine caught fire and I couldn't get the hatch open, I was sure my time had come.' The airman gave a short chuckle.

Yuling wanted to know how his subject escaped; it made him bold enough to ask: 'What happened next, sir?'

'Got up more speed, a bad few seconds, if the flames had come through the cockpit I'd have been roasted, history. Brought the plane hard up like that...' the hand was pointing near vertical '...the hatch shot open and I bailed out somehow, should have caught fire which was a second miracle, landed in the sea, plane came down before me not far away, very lucky escape.'

The colonel had begun smiling half way through his story and was now openly laughing - a strange reaction, these Japanese were cocky and seemed to take a light view of death, traits he did not associate with his own countrymen.

The first sitting was only allowed to last forty minutes, so Yuling had to work fast. But as happened sometimes before, he found that speed could work to the advantage of a painting.

He was pleased to receive a clear 'alright' when he asked the colonel not to see the painting until completion, telling him why: that he did not like to be influenced. If the man had objected, he would have had to accept the situation; in any case, he knew the officer could easily peep between sessions, as the easel and canvas remained in the room.

When the colonel left him to paint on, the military policeman remained nearby. At first the man was silent, but for a short time Yuling engaged him in conversation, and they talked about the man's family.

The next session three days later was hardly longer than the first, and at the start the colonel caught him by surprise. 'Go and get her! You're clearly in love with her, I can tell. I'll get her a pass and you can bring her to Amoy, I can arrange a secure place for her to live, then you can be with her, marry her if you're a fool!'

Yuling looked over the easel but couldn't think what to reply. The thought of having Huihua with him was staggering, but he knew the reality would be very different in the occupied zone - she could be a pawn in the hands of the quisling Chinese administration, or subject to another Red attempt on her, or most likely would be smuggled back to Mingon by Nationalists, and he well knew what they would then do to him.

'Oh, of course, the parents don't want you then?'

Yuling nodded, and had to ask his subject as politely as he could to keep his mouth gently closed for just a couple of minutes while he worked on that area.

By the end of the session he told the air officer he would not need him to sit again, explaining that he had been blessed with an eye for facial memory, and that he would soon be working on the plane, which he was looking forward to. He didn't add that at the school, after the children had gone home, he'd been practising painting the plane.

He was satisfied that the unusual combination of man and aircraft would work, and he believed that he had already captured the adventurous look of his subject, partly helped by the trick of painting the man's right collar turned up as if loose, imaginatively caught perhaps by the wind from the plane's spinning propeller yet to be painted.

He needed two longer visits to the airfield before he had completed the work, the canvas being larger than the Huang Shanghan portrait; at neither visit did the colonel come along the passage to disturb him.

Then he had to wait more than two weeks for the airman to return from somewhere, during which he pressed his red signature name chop at the bottom left of the canvas, and near the end of the period he sealed with a varnish.

When Colonel Hijiya came back and went into the briefing room with another officer to see the portrait, he was ecstatic, sending a car at once to the school to collect the painter, with a note that they had a top-class artist. The Head felt honour and pleasure, releasing his teacher immediately.

Yuling sat waiting in the briefing room still with its blinds down, talking with the same military policeman as before. A few minutes later he heard the colonel striding down the passage and soon calling his name, and at once he stood. When the airman came into the room, Yuling barely had time to bow before he was being clapped several times on his upper arm, and the colonel was looking at the painting and telling him how pleased he was and was asking the policeman what he thought of it but not waiting for a reply.

'My Kawasaki, you've got it perfectly, curving, port wing low, pointing towards my head, prop whirling, my markings, excellent!'

Yuling made another short bow, but the colonel was already walking back to the door and calling out a name, and he heard him ordering drinks. The officer was beaming as he returned to the canvas.

They talked about framing, and soon a butler arrived with a tray of bottles, placing the tray on a nearby table. 'A choice of three, Colonel, sake and wines, different potencies.'

The colonel pointed to one of them. 'My favourite, delicious, have you ever had our plum wine?'

Yuling shook his head, and he watched the butler pour the first drink. He was about to say he could not take much alcohol, when a full glass was thrust into his hand.

'Kanpai!' the Japanese airman called out, before savouring the wine and swallowing.

'Kanpai!' the polite Chinese artist replied without conviction.

*

'Oooh, can I have him?' The Japanese girl has just parted two of the vertical strips making up the ceiling-to-floor blind hanging between the girls' viewing room and the clients' plush reception area. 'He's young, and look at that face!' She thinks he isn't much older than she is.

Some of the other girls twitter.

'It's not your turn,' another girl snaps who has also taken a peep.

Madam puffs at the end of a cigarette, long ash about to fall, then stubs it into a dish. 'You take the soldier,' she says to the second girl; she lets out a stifled cry of dismay. 'Yes, he's yours Nanako, and don't forget, Colonel Hijiya's paying, so don't ask for money.'

Nanako feels an early pleasure unusual in her admittedly short experience at Geisha Plus. She had seen the tall man being greeted, being taken to one of the deep chairs, and had thought that whichever of the five girls he was given to could be in for a treat. Her own countrymen, and the Chinese officials they sometimes brought with them, were always older and smaller, and they were usually married, though the army air colonel was an exception.

She goes to the partition, slides it back, steps through in her kimono and closes it again. Gliding silently past a middle-aged army man and inclining her head without making eye contact, she comes to the Chinaman. He has a hand over his forehead partly hiding the eyes, and isn't looking at all happy. She kneels and bows right down to the floor in respect and humility, the floor she helped polish that very morning - Madam insisted that the girls gave the same respect to their Chinese clients. And when she comes up, she catches the bemused look at her, and smiles shyly before gracefully standing again.

She tells him her name, and with hands by her side says: 'Do you know any Japanese, sir? I can try a little Mandarin if you like but I don't know very much.' Without waiting for an answer - Chinese officials she entertains do not speak her language and it never matters - she adds: 'Please to follow Nanako.' She half turns, raises her arm towards him, and is relieved when his hand comes down from his head and he leans forward in the plush chair and hauls himself up.

And how large he is, though not plump like some of the other guests. 'Please sir, take my arm.' She looks a little less shyly into the eyes of the Chinaman, and sees she is beside one of the best-looking men she has come across in her five months since the stormy crossing from Nagoya.

He is now staring at her. She gives him her gentle smile, and to her pleasure his hand comes to rest on her sleeve. She bends her head the other way, takes a short step and then another, and starts to move a little faster as the hand on her arm becomes heavier. She suspects he has been drinking, though it is only the middle of the afternoon - she hopes not too much, it doesn't seem too much, he is walking without difficulty, unlike some clients.

When they reach the end of the passage, slowly she lowers her arm, the hand leaves her, and she pulls aside another partition and beckons him to enter.

'Please to mind,' she says almost in a whisper in her own language, pointing down to the partition rail in the floor, knowing he wouldn't understand her. She holds under one of his arms and lifts him over, before following and quietly closing the partition behind her.

During Yuling's journey by military car out of the airfield and back into Amoy proper, his head had felt ever lighter, and the erection he hadn't been able to stop coming had made him keep his hands above his lap; he needed to hide it from the military policeman sitting beside him. He didn't feel sick from the plum wine, and hoped his excitement - clearly brought on by two full glasses and by elation that the painting had been so well approved - would disappear before they reached the school.

When the car screeched to a halt the policemen were laughing, and one of them told him to 'take your time'. He had been puzzled where they were, not recognising the buildings, there seemed to be only houses; where was his school and its flag?

'Here's the money, very well deserved,' Colonel Hijiya had earlier said to him, handing over a wad of yen notes. 'My officers are jealous of my portrait, some might ask you themselves to do one, but don't do any as good as mine!' The airman had as always laughed loud at his own joke. 'It will hang in my office wherever I am, and I'm giving you a little present, enjoy it to the full.'

'No, this is not my school!' Yuling had exclaimed in Japanese to one of the policemen as he was being pushed forward and a door was being knocked and the man was telling him he should have a good time courtesy of the colonel '... you must not refuse our hospitality, Chinaman, that would be offensive coming from you.'

A stout Japanese woman well into middle age had opened the door; she was in a heavy kimono and had thick white make-up, and there had been some fast talk between her and the military policeman, Yuling hearing the words 'kindness' and 'Colonel Hijiya.'

And the next thing he knew, the woman was pulling him inside the house and the door was being shut hard, and soon he was smelling perfume that took him straight to Huihua, and the woman was saying something about his height or body, he wasn't sure, and was leading him too firmly by his elbow, and when she released it she was telling him to '...sit in the most comfortable chair in all Amoy, my esteemed new client...'

He had obeyed because, although he'd just been in a large car, his head told him he must quickly sit again; and when he did so, the leather chair felt very welcoming as he sank into it, a contrast to the bumpy car-ride and to the hard stool he'd had in the briefing room where he'd painted.

Almost at once a relaxing sensation had come over him, he seemed no longer so worried that he was not back at the school helping the children tidy the art room, or so concerned as to what was happening to him care of the senior airman. The stout woman's words '...welcome to Geisha Plus...' told him that he was in some form of Japanese house of genteel entertainment, where cultured young women would talk with him, he could enjoy their tea and confectionery and maybe there might be some quiet singing and spoken poetry; he had read about the Geisha culture.

'A good establishment if you can afford it, very.' A gruff Japanese man had suddenly spoken. Yuling had turned in fright to see a middle-aged officer lounging in another chair, and had been about to leap up and bow, but the downward wave of the man's hand had told him this was not required - a unique and strange feeling not to have to bow in the presence of the invader. He had sunk back into his own pleasurable chair.

The girl is small and well endowed and knows that her face and young body are pleasing to most men. She wears a light kimono without any of the usual Geisha undergarments; it is patterned with red and white roses, lines of sequin running in curves from her breasts down to the floor. She is wearing her favourite pink sash, its bow tied at the front. Her hair is raised and ivory-pinned across, her face white-powdered though lightly and not immediately under the line of the hair or at the nape of the neck.

Now standing close to the tall young man, she looks up at him, feels she catches his eyes, and steps out of her high shoes. Speaking musically in a way she hopes he will find alluring even though he won't understand her language, she says: 'Let Nanako take away your cares and worries, sir, and when you leave us you can go back to your work or your family and you will feel much much better, much happier.' She holds his look, something telling her this one might have got the gist of her comment because he has an intelligent face.

In Chinese that she knows is badly pronounced she asks him his name. He seems not to understand her, then gives it but she cannot take it in and forgets it at once. She reverts to Japanese, telling him, and gesturing, to take off his shirt and his sandals but not his trousers.

As she walks slowly to a table, she sees in a long mirror at the wall that before he starts removing his shirt, he is still looking at her, and this pleases her. She bends over the table, lights two joss sticks, and places them in a narrow bowl painted with petals, making sure that the back of her kimono comes up just enough to expose ankles she knows men find irresistible.

When she turns round, she is stunned to see such a beautiful well-built body, and thinks how jealous the others girls will be, before a sudden fear comes that he might be too big for her.

She takes him to a hand bowl where she asks him to wash his face, handing him a towel and again gesturing what she means. When he has finished, she throws the water into a basin and pours fresh warm water from a jug into the bowl. 'Let me,' she says taking one of his hands to wash with sweet-smelling lilac soap, sure he will enjoy the experience. But she is startled to see that the hand is deformed or has somehow been injured; there are only three fingers with the thumb, and the skin on the upper side is taut and lined. She does not recoil or make any comment, and when she has dried the hand, she does the same to the other.

She points to a wide mattress on the floor, asking him to lie on his back, his body in the middle, his head on the cushion two hand-lengths from the end. She is just about to lead him to the mattress to show him the correct position, when he does exactly as she has instructed, unlike any of her first-time Chinese clients. 'Oh, you can understand me!' she exclaims, now looking down at him and knowing her treatment could be even more effective - and more pleasurable for herself. 'Can you speak my language?'

He doesn't answer her, but she receives his first smile and thinks it lovely. 'Then please close your eyes, sir, empty your mind, and let Nanako take your troubles away by my touch.'

The eyes close, and the face becomes serious again.

The room is light from a single upper window open to the sky, and is warm from the warmth outside.

The girl kneels on the floor at the end of the mattress and starts to sing a lullaby she learnt as a little girl from her mother, her hands caressing the underparts and the upper parts of one of the feet, from above the ankle to the tips of the toes, sure that a first thrill is going through her client.

A bowl of lavender oil is beside her with water and towels, and after the caressing, she begins to wash the foot. When she has dried it, her fingers dip in the oil, and she starts massaging in a gentle touching of the whole foot, not the hard knuckle-pressure she has heard the Chinese practise on the underparts, but a soft circling and quiet pressing in places she knows gives pleasure.

Still quietly singing - enticingly she hopes - she turns to the other foot, and as she washes it, she recalls how she felt not six months earlier, how she cried for days and days when blackmailed by the army captain to come to his posting city in south China, how much she had feared him, fear that soon turned to hatred after the worst three weeks of her life, how he threw her out into the foreign city without money, with no means to return to Japan, and she found herself at the door of Geisha Plus.

And now here she is, enjoying what she is doing to this magnificent foreigner, and telling herself she would remember him.

As her touch comes to the back of the foot and she fondles in and around the ankle, pressing her fingers on either side of the strong muscle and holding her touch and pressing and stroking again, she notices that his breathing has grown deeper, his chest moving more slowly. He says something in Chinese that she doesn't understand, but guesses that he likes it.

She finishes the feet, stands, kneels on the mattress on his right side and takes up his hand, very softly rubbing up and down and underneath and gently pulling on each finger as she looks long at the young man's face and studies the broad forehead, the nose, the mouth, the strong hair...

Soon she can feel his arm and shoulder relaxing, and she watches the head tilting towards her, to rest as if in slumber light but aware. And when she finishes, she gives his fingers a last slow touch of hers, before placing the hand on the mattress.

She stands again, removes the ivory pins from her lightly creamed hair - the hair stays in place - and goes to his left side. As she kneels, she sees again the strange left hand, and begins to give it the same treatment though now without singing, just a humming of her favourite song she used to sing with her pilot lover before his death against the American warship, before the horrible captain came into her life.

She is very pleased that her client isn't rushing her. Many of her own countrymen want quick action, unless they are too drunk, when her lullaby and immediate head massage sometimes makes them sleep, and she can afterwards con them into thinking they have been manly with her, 'as strong as lions' she would tell them.

She notices that the upper part of the injured hand has no hair, and when she is circling the underside and massaging the fingers with the scented oil and looking again at the chest, the head tilts towards her, and quickly she looks back to the hand.

Soon she realizes hers are not the only eyes open. Keeping her gaze on the hand, she lets a quiet smile come into her cheeks, and opens her mouth a touch.

Yuling has never felt so relaxed, and now that he is looking again at the Japanese girl touching his ugly hand so delicately, he finds he cannot take his eyes off her, especially the red lips, the lower one noticeably less red, a geisha look he believes. Like a lover and like an artist he begins to study her ...and her thin kimono, letting his mind imagine what he cannot see, knowing he doesn't love her but loves her exotic look, loves what she is doing to him, loves the tenderness...

Nanako finishes caressing the hand. She looks at her client though not for long. She asks him to close his eyes again, and when he fails to do so, she smiles wider and tells him he is naughty, before bending and putting her open wrists carefully over each eyelid and closing them down. 'Let Nanako do everything slowly, slowly,' she says quietly. 'I like you,' she whispers before she can stop herself but pleased she has said it.

Yuling hears her. A few seconds later he becomes entranced; she has begun to sing again, the voice is so alluring, and he loves it that he can understand her. And he can tell she has gone behind him as there is a long rustle of the kimono, and through the mattress he feels her kneeling by his head cushion.

Her voice now seems near his head, her song about the three virtues of a rose: beauty and colour and scent. Scent! The girl's sensational perfume envelops him, and as her fingers start circling one of his temples and very softly press, he is back to the first holding of Huihua as he smothered himself in her scented hair, holding to her in that terrifying stairwell when the planes came.

And the planes take him to the army air colonel; the officer's frequent movements in that first painting sitting three weeks earlier caused him great difficulty as he applied the brushes; the airman was talking about Professor Koo and mentioned that wretched metal door, the door he never liked to recall except that it was where Huihua, who he thought might be collapsing or even dying, had amazed him by kissing into his palm.

And much as he loves what the girl with the red lips is doing to him, he wants her to stop caressing his temple, to stop touching him altogether so that he can capture a very strange thought coming to him about that cold door bolted against them.

But the girl's fingers are now wonderfully touching the other temple, and at the same time they are stroking the hair at the side of his neck, and his mind takes him to the Hut and to Huihua's look in those sunbeams through the shutters, the look that led to their abandonment on the k'ang and his thrusts when she kept crying out and he'd felt his power over her, knew it was ecstasy for her as it was for him, knew she was unsurpassable and utterly his in their seclusion high above the world.

And Nanako is loving what she is doing, she has stopped her singing and is bending near the left ear and warmly blowing onto the side of the head, knowing her power over men from that point on was absolute.

And the terrible door comes back to haunt, it won't go away, nor will the astonishing thought about the Huang servant. And partly to stop himself thinking more of the air attack, and partly because his excitement is as strong as ever, he takes his hands from his chest and puts them up behind him to touch the girl's kimono at the shoulders, or to touch the face, his way to thank her for her so gentle treatment of him, for her femininity ...and he finds he is touching bare shoulders and that some of the hair has fallen, and as he keeps his hands on the miracle of the girl's skin, Huihua and the door vanish, and he is moving to feel the girl's head, it is almost touching his, her hair is so soft and has a different scent to the massage oil, she is fondling his ears, she is probing, soon he can feel a light tugging of his lobes, and when she leaves them and moves to his cheeks she is cooing, and now she is caressing his chin and the tender hands are coming back and fingers are stroking his lower lip, and he is letting go of her head and rolling over...

23

'Here's the pass. And you're not going to be seeing the girl, as well as your mother I mean? She's not going to escape again I hope!' The Head Teacher smiled half-expectantly. He'd been riveted on hearing something about the romance - it had not been difficult to get his art teacher to open up, the young man was clearly head over heels with the girl, the daughter of a Nationalist general of all people. And somehow the death order imposed by the father if he went back to Mingon, the drama of the daughter's short elopement in June, and the young man's profoundly apologetic refusal to disclose where they had met (he would only say '...a lovely place high in the hills...') increased the Head Teacher's enjoyment of the story. And he had done as instructed by Intelligence, had passed on everything he'd learnt.

'No I'm certainly not going to get a message to her that my mother is ill and that I am visiting home,' his teacher replied, 'I don't want to give her ideas, she knows she mustn't leave her parents again, her father would have me killed, he hates me and my family.'

The Japanese sentries at one of their border posts well outside Amoy between occupied and free China were not too inquisitive, although they required Yuling to state when he would be returning. They studied the pass and made a telephone call, and within ten minutes he was waved through, together with two Fujian merchants who told him they were going part of his way.

'Arrogant foreign devils!' one of the merchants said aloud when they were well out of hearing.

Yuling reached Suodin a day and a half later. He no longer felt too awkward about his university disgrace eight months earlier. And he *had* to see Professor Koo about the extraordinary revelatory thought he'd had at that house of entertainment. He knew his art professor would be very welcoming, would want to hear about the Hijiya brothers.

He felt immeasurably happier than on that fateful day in late February when he'd been shattered at the news of his expulsion. Later he had taken

Huihua to the Hut where their love had been sealed, although his brother's kidnap attempt on her had been a shocker. And from the moment he had met education administrator Takashi Hijiya, life had been good to him in Amoy.

He was carrying a present for the art professor (the person who helped him find the job): a late nineteenth century Japanese watercolour painted on rice paper, one he admired in a shop and bought with some of the yens he'd earned.

It was only his longing to see Huihua - to be with her again - and the danger that went with the longing that sometimes tore at him; though most of the time he could live with being apart, sure of their feelings for one another. But her coded letter dated late August - smuggled out and reaching him through the Amoy shopkeeper whose address he'd given her - told him she had not been feeling well, and it had been worrying him.

'One of the guards has brought this in, it's marked strictly private, for you Captain. He said a messenger delivered it.'

It was first thing in the morning and Captain Ma had only just sat at his desk in the Officers Building within the inner courtyard. He thanked the soldier, looked at the grubby envelope, and opened it.

> *Have been with a senior enemy airman. Of vital importance we meet at once, and that you come to me. You must tell nobody of my presence, I repeat nobody, especially not General Huang. I say this not for my own sake but for that of our country. You must believe me Captain. Will remain at the only inn in Beilu. If you don't come in the next two days, I will have to decide if to risk coming to you and being shot under present orders before being able to impart my information, or getting the message to you some other way. From the person you spoke with in the General's office last year.*

The captain was astonished, finding it difficult to take in: somebody in Beilu twelve li east of Mingon wanted to meet him, claiming to have been with a senior Japanese airman, and this person had some vital information and the general was not to be told - it was unbelievable! And the person says he could be shot.

He couldn't connect who the sender might be; he was often in the Study speaking with the general and other officers and occasionally with civilians.

He sat down and re-read it; he didn't think it was some madman's note, the writing was excellent.

It was the words ...*risk coming to you and being shot under present orders...*

365

and the calligraphic nature of the writing that made him think of the tall artist, the impressive young man who had caused and continued to cause such distress to the general and his wife. He was not certain it came from him, but now thought it likely; he'd heard that the young man had gone to the occupied east.

He decided to act at once. As he put the note in a pocket, he informed a junior officer that some startling information had reached him that needed looking into in Beilu; that he might not be back before the afternoon.

When he reached the inn in the middle morning, he asked the innkeeper's wife who she had staying, and was told there was only one young man. Her description of the artist confirmed his guess, somewhat relieving him.

But Captain Ma felt very uncomfortable meeting with a man his general had ordered be shot if he came back. The note left him little choice, except to have gone there with men and taken the artist prisoner, something he preferred not to do; he did not want him killed.

Yuling had told the innkeeper and his wife who to expect, and was reading on his bed when the woman called at his door to say that the captain was below asking for him. 'Does he have soldiers?' he asked as he leapt off the bed, and she replied she hadn't seen any. He put on his sandals, went quickly downstairs, and when he walked into the tacky dining area he saw the captain waiting, hand on a revolver on the table.

Quickly he bowed. 'Thank you Cap...'

'Are you mad! You shouldn't be here! And this is a big risk to me, a real nuisance. Well, what do you want to say that's so vital, what information have you got?'

'I'm sorry I called you, but I had to with this death threat over me.' Yuling hesitated. 'Captain, will you give me your word not to mention my presence to anyone except General Huang? This is very important.'

'Depends what you have to say, and I thought you didn't want General Huang to know you're here.'

Yuling let the comment pass. 'Last week I was painting a portrait of Colonel Hijiya at his air base just outside Amoy...' he caught Captain Ma's look of surprise '...and from our conversations, I believe I have information that I must give only to the General with no one else present except you. Is he at Wuyi Court at the moment?'

'That's none of your business. And the General's not going to see you except with a bullet in your head. You'd better tell me.'

Yuling looked long at the unfriendly captain, for whom he'd previously felt a liking. He shook his head. 'No, I'm sorry Captain, I must talk with General Huang himself, it's too important. But I'll only do so if he guarantees the death threat is lifted.'

'He's certainly not going to do that after all you've done.'

'I'm prepared to take a gamble he will when he hears what I can tell him.' He gave the captain a pleading half smile. 'Look, I've come all this way from Amoy, I've had to lie to my Japanese employers why I need a few days away. They've only released me because they think my mother is ill and they're pleased the portrait of Colonel Hijiya was liked. I realize this seems mysterious and I'm asking you to trust me,' he paused, 'you must, please, you don't realize what I have.'

Captain Ma was again astonished. The note had amazed him, and now this young man was telling him that he'd been with the enemy's operational air chief, and was acting with a self-confidence he could only admire given the danger of his coming so near Mingon. He looked hard at him, and realized the artist wasn't going to divulge whatever he had.

'Well if you're prepared to put your own life at risk that's your decision. If you come back with me, I'll put you in one of the cells, and I can't speak for what the General will do to you, though it's pretty clear. Your death would not be on my conscience.'

Yuling did not have to think. 'I'll come. But you *must* make sure you are alone when you speak to the General, and it's vital he doesn't tell anyone else that I'm here and you don't either, especially not the secretary, and not his wife either, or other officers, the guards, the staff, no one....' he hesitated, 'not even Huang Huihua, she must not know I'm here Captain, the General and you will soon understand why this is essential.'

*

'He's *here?*' exclaims General Huang without letting Captain Ma say more, leaping up from his desk and finding his captain's quiet tone most strange, believing the Tsai fellow's appearance must concern his daughter. 'You've brought him in and he wants to see me! You should have shot him Ma, you'd have done Madame Huang and myself a great service.'

The general walks round his large desk with its Ming sword, recalling the appalling incident with Tsai Yuling and his daughter earlier in the year. He snatches at the note in the captain's hand, while the officer continues speaking quietly. He begins reading it; it is not to do with his daughter; he stares at the paper.

'Hijiya you say! Hijiya! How's he been allowed to get near him?'

'He's done the Colonel's portrait. I'm sorry General, he refuses to tell me anything, except he has something vital he can only say to you personally, and you mustn't tell anyone that he's here, he's very insistent on that, not even the Mistress.' Captain Ma feels foolish saying all this. 'He didn't even want to be

367

seen by the guards, I had to make them go into the Guard House and close the door, and he had his doli covering his face. And he says no one must be close to us in the cells, no one must hear him.'

'He's not armed?'

'No.'

'Then his end will come!' General Huang gives a quick shake of the head. 'What a nerve and what a fool!'

As he goes with his captain down the wide marble steps from the mansion doors and moves onto the front path of the inner courtyard, the memory of his childhood humiliation at that spot - when his father thrashed him in front of the staff after his gun had accidentally killed a tree worker - comes powerfully into his mind. And half way across the courtyard on the path between the cypress and the palm trees he thinks of the alarming talks he has had with his disobedient daughter. The first was on his return to the ancestral home in hot humid early July. He ordered her to say where she had been when she absconded for several days, and if she had met the student; he'd shouted at her when she admitted seeing him but refused to say where, and he had to listen to her threat that they would lose her if anything happened to the fellow, she would give up her life, she had made it coldly without cries or emotion, a threat he never wanted to take as seriously as his wife, but...

And only a few days later, she had been in his arms and told him through tears that he was ruining her happiness and was being unfair to the man she loved; that he her father should look at the fellow's qualities, and that whatever happened with the Tsai mother was well past all of them. They had talked, she was clearly besotted, and he'd been unable to make her realize that she had to end it and seek a far better match; that anyway, he and her mother could never consider such a man, a troublemaker.

And now as he and Ma are going past the guards at the doors between the courtyards and down into the outer courtyard, his beloved daughter's recent 'announcement' reverberates in his ears: she is carrying a baby. The scandalous news had shocked him to the core, and his wife's head had dropped - something he hardly ever saw - at the defiant look of their disloyal daughter who was disgracing herself and bringing deep shame on the family, unless it could be hushed up and the baby placed elsewhere.

Oh yes, the wretch has been treacherous and will die! General Huang is carrying his revolver and will use it himself, or he might get his captain to do the necessary. His daughter's suicide threat now does not enter his mind.

But it is incredible he has come back, he must have lost his head in some fantasy about the enemy. And does he know the catastrophic news of the pregnancy, has she somehow got a message to him? Well he the father, the head of the old Huang family and a Nationalist general, he will do what is necessary to protect his wayward daughter from herself, and more importantly protect family honour. He will not tell her that Tsai has come and what they will do to him (though the fellow's instruction that she is not to know he is there is most peculiar). He and his wife will solve this shocking *little problem* their daughter has given them.

'Have your revolver ready and pointing Ma, and if I tell you to shoot, kill him though I might do so myself.' They are going down into the cells. 'Which one?'

The captain points to the third door along, goes in front and pulls back an iron brace. When they enter they see the large figure of Tsai Yuling standing against the back wall, with not much daylight coming from an opening high up.

They are immediately given an unusually deep bow - he's clearly been living with the enemy, the general thinks, now pointing his gun at the wide chest which he cannot miss.

'My Captain has orders to shoot you dead student if you move one step, and so will I, one step you hear! You've got a hell of a nerve coming back after ruining my daughter's life. What's so important you've got to tell me?'

Yuling lets the remark about Huihua go, believing it refers to her love for him that she must have expressed to her parents.

'General, I've been with Colonel Hijiya...'

'So I've heard. Quisling are you?'

'Not at all, I've been working in a Japanese school and I painted his portrait, no more. But I have always had a feeling that learning their language could come in useful. If my information proves correct, will you end your threat on my life, and allow your daughter and me to see each other from time to time?'

'You will *not* see my daughter.' General Huang has almost shouted, is brandishing his revolver and nearly losing control, finger firmly on the trigger. 'And I won't bargain with the likes of you, you seducer! What's the information?' The general is getting used to the poor light, and watches the student turn towards his captain and then back. 'Speak or I'll shoot!' he cries out, not caring if his guards hear.

'No General, you will thank me when you know what I can tell you, it may well affect you militarily, and once before in the name of my father I asked you to re-consider your decision on Fang Lamgang who saved my life, you didn't, and the consequences were disastrous for you as well as for me. Now I'm asking you again, in fact...' Yuling hesitates '...I'm begging you to act honourably, and I did not seduce your daughter...'

'Honourably! You should speak, ruining the prospects of a Huang lady! I've just told you I won't bargain, two bullets are coming your way unless you out with it, ready Ma?'

369

Yuling is back at the audience for Lam in the presence of power, back to that feeling of fear and impotence; but this time he is not going to be silenced. 'We love each other and if you shoot me,' he turns to the gun in the captain's hand, 'you kill us both and you lose information that could be vital for China.'

'General...' the captain says quietly, caution urged in the voice.

The general looks to his officer and hesitates.

'Alright Ma, once we hear what this bastard's got to say, and you think I should reconsider,' he nods, 'I will, on the death order if the information is worth it, not on his seeing my daughter, absolutely not.'

The two officers eye the tall figure in front of them, Captain Ma desperately hoping he won't be ordered to shoot, thinking he'll go for an arm. 'Out with it!' he calls, his patience also spent.

Yuling is thinking of the general's ban, that he will probably never see Huihua again unless she absconds as before or even flees... 'Shoot him!' the general shouts.

'You have a spy here.'

'What!' the captain exclaims, 'a spy?'

General Huang feels disbelief fast turning to shock. 'Who's a spy? How do you know? For the Reds?'

'No, the Japanese.'

'The imperialist dogs?'

'Yes General. I'm in your hands. Now will you act decently towards me? Will you end the death order if I tell you what I know and am proved right about an enemy here? I've risked my life coming to you, can't you understand that?'

The general looks again at his most trusted officer, and gives a curt nod.

Yuling coughs; there is a nasty dampness in the cell, an unpleasant smell.

'I've just come from seeing Professor Koo Guanglu, my art professor in Suodin. When I left the university, he gave me a letter of introduction to Colonel Hijiya's brother, he's an education administrator in Amoy. I read it and it didn't say much, but it did say that I painted here, and it told him that if he would meet me he should look at the photograph I made of the painting of your son. Mr Hijiya was very helpful, he soon found me a job, and he wrote to my professor, I should have said they were student friends in Tokyo, and he asked for more information about me. Professor Koo wrote and told him a few things, that I had nearly been killed with your daughter during the air attack a year ago, you were away at the time.' He coughs again. 'When I was working on the air Colonel's portrait, he told me they knew a lot about me from the professor, including that we were trapped by a metal door in an air attack by his own pilots. The point is General, I never told Professor Koo what happened in the air attack, only that I'd tried to protect Huihua,' Yuling deliberately speaks her name, challenging a rebuke, 'and that we could have died from bullets or dust. He never knew about the door. Somebody from here must have told enemy intelligence how we were caught, for them to know about the door and that it is made of metal.'

The general still feels some shock but less so. 'You must have told the professor and forgotten.' The captain adds: 'And you would have definitely told your college friends, one of them obviously told the professor.'

'No. I only told my friends we were caught in the spray of bullets by enemy planes, I very well remember I didn't like to talk about it, it was a really nasty event. And I've just come from seeing Professor Koo. I asked him what details he knew of the attack, and he didn't know anything except that we'd nearly died, he didn't know that we were in the stairwell or trapped in the basement by the door. He's got a very good memory, so I asked him if he recalled what he wrote about me to his friend Mr Hijiya, and he surprised me by going straight to his desk and bringing out an exact copy of his letter. He's a meticulous man. He told me he makes copies of anything he regards as interesting or important, and he holds all the correspondence with his friend going back thirty years. The letter only mentioned the air attack in general terms, not...'

Captain Ma interrupts: 'You yourself might have told the administrator brother about the attack, and he passed it on to Colonel Hijiya.'

The general thinks that is another good point and nods, but is surprised to see the student shaking his head.

'No, I never spoke to him about it, that's certain. And I haven't to anybody else in Amoy for that matter, including my fellow teachers at the Japanese school, though they know why I had to leave the university.'

'So who is this supposed spy who told them all about you?' the general says allowing a smirk, now reasonably confident the student has got something badly wrong. He takes a step forward to get a better look at the face, wondering how he is going to despatch the seducer ...yes, he'll leave it to Ma. 'Tutor? Head Groom? Chu, Lieutenant Chu?' - though why he mentions the young officer he cannot think, except he is not from Fujian.

'I could be mistaken and you'll have to catch him out, your private secretary.'

'Old Lee! Don't be absurd...'

'I think he means Wang, General.'

'Wang! Wang!' Again the general hesitates, stunned a second time. 'What on earth makes you accuse him?' He is more shocked than ever, thinking of all the military messages passing between himself whenever he is there at the Court, and Chiang Kai-shek and his staff at Allied HQ in Chongqing, as well as the military throughout the south.

'Because he is now your secretary and close to your papers, and it's hardly likely to be a serving officer. When he was head domestic, did he have access to your office? And...' Yuling pauses, has their full attention, '...because when he opened that door and saved us from suffocating, I told him I'd been frightened they might have bombed us, and he said they'd never do that to Wuyi Court but they might bomb the camp in the woods, or words to that effect. I think he also said he was surprised at the attack, though I'm not sure of my memory as I was shaken up. And Colonel Hijiya said practically the same thing to me when I was doing the portrait, that it was a pilot mistake to attack here. I agree it could be only a coincidence of words, but it fits that they wouldn't bomb this place when they've someone very useful working for them. As I say, I could be wrong who it is, but I'm sure you have a spy here. The Japanese knew about that metal door, and I very much doubt they got the information from an agent in Mingon who just might have heard every detail from a person working here. You can send someone to speak with Professor Koo if you need his verification of what he knew.' He waits, expecting another question, and when none comes he adds: 'And General, I have another reason to suspect Wang. The opening of that door was the prominent part of what happened so far as he was concerned, it was he who opened it, he must have included it in his report about me to his masters. I never mentioned it when they grilled me...'

'Who grilled you? When?' The general is trying to hide his enormous concern. While the student was talking, he has also realized that Wang became privy to the underground passage, that if enemy troops assault the mansion, they would know where it ended in the White Pavilion outside the walls.

'A nasty man from Japanese intelligence, he had a Chinese official with him and they weren't friendly, especially the intelligence officer. It was when they were thinking of giving me the job a few weeks after I got to Amoy in March. I was required to go to the Central Intelligence Building and tell them everything about myself, mainly in Japanese but sometimes I was told to repeat it in Chinese to the official. Mr Hijiya told them I had done a portrait here, and they asked me about you, and who I met here, and about your daughter and the air attack. I told them we were holding each other for our lives, but I didn't go into any details about exactly where we were in the building during the attack, and I definitely didn't mention the door. They were surprised when I told them about the death order.'

'Did they mention Wang?' the captain asks.

'No, but I listed Wang as one of the servants here, I had to say who everyone was.'

There is another silence, General Huang looking down at the stone floor, starting to think of tests to see if his new secretary of a few months could really be a traitor as this other treacherous fellow is claiming.

He hears his captain ask: 'Are you certain Hijiya mentioned the metal quality of the door?'

'Yes, absolutely. But it didn't hit me until three weeks later when I realized what he'd said. I knew I hadn't talked about it to Professor Koo or anyone else except my family. And I was sure the letter Wang wrote to the university to expel me would not have gone into such details. Anyway, as I say, the professor showed me his letters.'

'Come, Ma,' the general says turning to the door.

'General, you understand why no one must know I'm here. If it gets to Wang, or whoever, that you're holding me, the person will wonder what I'm doing here with a death order against me. And the Amoy authorities will wonder too when he tells them, as they think I'm in Tuxieng. He could lie low.'

The general gives him a short look and goes out, followed by the captain. Yuling hears the door being barred. He is very relieved to have delivered his information, as it has weighed heavily on him for many days since he asked the Head Teacher to get him a pass. But is his life still under imminent threat? Or will they keep him until they know if it is Wang or another? He has to get back to Amoy in a few days or the Japanese will become suspicious, and he needs to pay a quick call on his *ill* mother.

All the time on his journey towards Mingon he'd thought of Huihua, knowing he wouldn't be able to see her, though he had with him a present to be smuggled if possible. And now, in one of the nasty cells where he was flogged, it is a different 'agony' being so near her. He wonders what she is doing at this moment. She will not even find out he's been there unless he is allowed to leave and can get a message through; her father certainly won't tell her, for personal and security reasons.

Some minutes later he hears footsteps and the fear returns. When the door opens and the general and captain enter, only the general is holding a handgun, and it is by his side.

'Tsai.' The general comes closer. 'Captain Ma thinks you've been courageous coming here. You're lucky you're not a dead man. But I am not convinced. I've heard what you say but you're likely mistaken, maybe you misheard what Hijiya said, you were concentrating on your painting or whatever. We're going to test your theory, and we may not know for a little while.' The general clears his throat. 'You're free to leave, but the death order will not be rescinded unless you are right about a spy, and even then, if you come back near Mingon I'll clap you in irons for life and far away. So don't you hang around now.' The gun waves by the general's side but is not being pointed. 'I want you out of our lives, you've already caused me and my wife big trouble, very big.'

Yuling feels tremendously relieved, and for the first time since he met the general two and a half years earlier at the dreadful audience to save Lam, he thinks the man has started to speak to him with at least some degree of consideration, perhaps because of the good captain's presence. He is about to protest his and Huihua's feelings for each other when the general continues: 'A ban can't be a problem, you've the rest of the province to live in.'

'General, I...'

'I can guess what you're going to say, I'm coming to my daughter.' General Huang is glad that Ma is there to hear him. 'You will not see her again, ever. You have taken her future away which I her father must try to give her back. You mention your own father, huh! you're not a worthy son. From this moment on you will regard the friendship or whatever it is as at an end.' He gives one of his short nods to Ma and turns back to this troublesome student. 'You will write and tell her so for everybody's sake, especially her own. I make no unjust comment on your family background, but my daughter's future shall be in a marriage with a family similar to our own. She will need a decent property to live at, and as good an income as is possible in these harsh times, which hopefully one day will pass. You shall let her go, release her.' He catches the look of anguish. 'Look, you're in Amoy, plenty of suitable women there, plenty of pretty ones. You can be happy with another woman, very.' He makes the last word definite, giving yet another nod.

Yuling lets out a short gasp and looks away from the eyes that he is less than fond of. 'What can I say, wealth hasn't entered our thoughts, we are like one, I adore her and just want to be with her. We think alike, she...'

'Enough!' General Huang wants to avoid any more sentimental talk. 'Where did you meet in June? You weren't in Fuzhou I'll bet.'

Yuling has for days expected the question, deciding he had to stand his ground. 'We made a promise to each other to keep such matters to ourselves. Forgive me, I cannot break your daughter's trust. If she tells you...' he shrugs, '...but I'm not wishing to be disrespectful, I understand what you're telling me, in fact it was one of the first things I mentioned to her, that you would find me unsuitable. But neither of us believes this should be a bar, Huihua...' again he is using her name '...was more definite on this than me.' He half expects thunder. But the general is silent, gazing at him. 'Could you tell me how she is, I've been very worried about her.'

General Huang frowns, does not want to answer, now fairly sure the fellow doesn't know about the pregnancy. 'She'll be alright,' he says frostily.

'But she's not been seriously ill? She's not still ill is she?'

'She's alright I said, don't ask more or I'll become angry. Now, I require to hear from you in my captain's presence that you'll release her, let her have the life Madame Huang and I have been expecting since she was a girl.'

Yuling's head drops.

'What does your family say? I believe you have a stepfather, he wouldn't agree to this, surely?' The general cannot bring himself to mention the mother.

Yuling is taken aback, and lets out: 'They think it should stop, but that's imposs...'

'And so it must. It *will* stop I tell you, or...' The gun again points, this time at the lower regions.

*

Old cook Xuiey smiled naughtily as she handed the Mistress a deep basket half filled with Chinese apples. 'Dig,' she whispered into her ear in the corridor near the kitchens, 'it was delivered to my niece yesterday by some passer-by who she didn't know, it's got your name on it, it could be from *him*, couldn't it?'

Something told Huihua it must be from Yuling, but she was by no means sure. She returned to her rooms, thankful she had not met her mother, and went into her bedroom and pulled the old wooden lock into place - an original lock, her rooms were in the oldest part of the mansion. If her mother or maid called at the door, she would say she was composing and wanted no disturbance, the locking to feel alone for inspiration, strange though that reason would seem.

Standing by her bed, she tried not to feel too excited when finding the small parcel at the bottom of the apples and starting to unwrap rough paper; only her name was on it, in writing certainly not Yuling's. But as soon as she saw that inside was better quality wrapping paper covering a small cardboard box tied four sides by string, her hopes dramatically rose, and when she came to folded writing paper and a small jade figure, she knew.

She took the object into her hands; it was exquisitely carved and highly polished, the figure of a courtly lady of old China about twice the length of her index finger, and she realized at once that the jade had a meaning: it was his commitment to her, just as couples going back to the early dynasties committed themselves to each other with a gift of the precious stone that was hewn in the mountain rivers of their beautiful land.

The letter was dated the previous day.

My lovely angel, it has been necessary for me to meet your father here today...

She caught her breath, couldn't believe what she was reading, that he'd been there, a panic running through her (despite the jade and the first three words) that he'd bravely returned to tell her father it was over with her, though...

...for a very important reason to do with our country, completely unconnected with you and me or our future.

She breathed a huge sigh of relief.

I know this will seem incredible to you and you will not understand and will wonder how I dared come and why I didn't get a message to you that I was coming so we could try somehow to meet. But if you truly love me as I know you did 'when the bees passed over' - as I loved you then and love you now more than ever - you will obey, yes obey my instruction that you tell nobody you have learnt from me that I was here. I have not been into Mingon, and only your father and Captain Ma know, and I ask you not to speak to them. But if you do, do so only if they are absolutely alone. They will be able to explain, though they may prefer not to for the time being, in which case you must respect that.

Your father has rescinded the death order in view of certain information I have given him that could be vitally useful, but he still imposes the ban on me coming near Mingon. He wanted me to say that I release you for another and better future. But I couldn't, it is impossible for me to do that, you would have to tell me yourself that that is what you want, though I would hardly believe you. And how can I now 'release' you after finding out today your incredible news.

Huihua gasped.

Oh how I wish with all my heart I could be with you to share your growing burden.

She stopped reading, lay on the bed and placed the letter on her tummy, pressing it there. 'Thank you,' she whispered up towards the swans, 'he knows, oh he knows!' But for her condition, she could have stood on her bed and jumped to the ceiling to kiss those long necks. Release him! She could no more do that than give birth to a panda. With her head on the pillows she read on.

This carving is my gift to you, bought a few days ago shortly after finishing a portrait, and in my heart now more than ever I want you to have it.

At the end of our meeting, your father mentioned that I should consider taking a commission though in another province - Captain Ma's idea last year, do you remember, I told you at the river. I don't feel a military type, but if you think it is the route I should take to give me a chance one day to be accepted by your parents, I would do so, though your father made it clear they will always be opposed to me and I must never return to Mingon. Let me know your feelings on this, coded. I will not take this course if they continue to reject the very idea of us being married.

And whatever you do, don't mention in your communications to me anything about my visiting Wuyi Court or Mingon, or that you wish you'd seen me, or anything about you being pleased that I know about your condition - I'm sure you are - because any one of those comments would put me in the greatest peril with my masters in Amoy.

Be very careful about all this. When you next write, make it that you are telling me for the first time that you are carrying our baby, how excited you are, how you want to see me again and that you will work on your father to try to get him to accept me and to rescind the death order so I can visit. Your letter, if the Japanese intercept it, or if I need to show to my Head Teacher, should put them off thinking I have just been to Mingon - I don't want them to wonder if I had anything to do with giving your father the information I have just given him.

And there is something else. In coming here, what I have tried to do for our country means your father may soon have it in his power to leak to the enemy about me and so end my life. That is a risk I have had to take. I anxiously hope he would not be so base - he should soon be very grateful to me - but when you find out why I came here, you may need to appeal to him, his honour, perhaps invoke the help of your brother for whom I hold a respect amounting to real fondness.

I go now to see my mother for a very short visit before returning to Amoy. In every hour of every day I think of you and hold you in my arms, though as you know I prefer to think of you holding me in yours! Often I imagine sitting at your feet and gazing up into your lovely face as you read to me over the escarpment. Look after yourself in the coming weeks and months, thinking of me always with you in spirit. Somehow we will find a way to come together. Your news fills me with so much love and warmth that I feel an unbreakable cord has always bound me to you, from seeing you as a girl at Wuyi Court (a moment I can never forget), to catching sight of you, a young lady, among the bushes in the monastery garden, from beholding you in the painting room, to carrying my peasant girl into the alley (the greatest moment of my life to that point), from the willows to the ferns to the night valley, from Ajin's rocks to the Hut and our bliss.

Your Yuling.

Memorize this, then I beg that you burn it, do not hide it.

24

'Regret the long wait General, you are now to go in.' The Nationalist major left the door slightly open, was looking down at the man sitting so awkwardly half on, half off the chair, who at that moment was not too popular in Chongqing - in fact the major had never seen his Commander-in-Chief so angry when the news of the Huang spy disaster came through a few days earlier. 'There's an American liaison officer here, Lieutenant Colonel Ivans, he speaks Mandarin and is rather forthright.'

Huang stood quickly, alarmed there would be a witness to the moment he had been dreading. The door was further opened for him, and as he entered, he saw the Generalissimo sitting behind a desk, and a tall foreigner in United States Air Force uniform standing at the side of the desk to the Generalissimo's left. Immediately he felt the cool atmosphere as the door closed behind him.

He saluted his Chief. To his surprise the American reciprocated though seemed to be frowning, Huang deciding not to give a second salute to the officer who was lower in rank, but courteously bowing to the man. Chiang Kai-shek returned no salute, nor gave even a head bow, but rose slowly, his face grave.

'Sit down, Huang.'

He was not introduced to the straight-standing foreigner, and the Nationalist leader stayed on his feet looking across his desk, unpleasantly Huang thought.

'My best culler of Reds in the south, my worst leaker of information to the Japs.' Chiang Kai-shek liked to use the shortened English word the Allies had for the enemy often spoken derogatorily; he knew his general would know the word. He allowed a further pause as he glared at the son of the difficult old warlord from Fujian, who in the twenties he had tried unsuccessfully to get under his control.

He could see his barb was hurting. 'The man's been shot?'

'Not yet, we think we could turn him to use, feed them counter-intelligence...'

'No!' the Generalissimo thundered, startling Huang who had been keenly hoping to redeem himself in the eyes of his superiors at Allied HQ and the military generally.

'You want him dealt with then.' There was hardly a question in his voice. He watched his Commander-in-Chief turn to the American and give a firm nod, before he was fixed again with angry eyes, by each.

'You have your own corps and officers, yet you allow civilians access to military information and documents. We clearly failed you at Whampoa and later, or you weren't learning elementary, rudimentary military ways there.' The Generalissimo spoke with scorn. 'It must concern you as it does my friend here, our so valued ally, that information was passed to the enemy for so long.'

'It couldn't have been for long, one trusted civilian in service...'

'Two,' the Generalissimo barked, 'there was another man before him, was there not?'

Huang was shocked at the accusatory tone, feeling horrible loss of face.

'Lee, yes, my father's private secr...'

'Exactly! And he was *your* secretary too Huang, so a second civilian saw military papers.'

'Lee was utterly trustworthy, and the new man had access to very little of importance.' He wished he hadn't used that last word. 'He certainly couldn't have seen much,' he lied, 'most of my orders were directly to my officers.' Cool sticky sweat was now dripping from his armpits into his uniform, making him very uncomfortable. 'And he wasn't there for long, considering I was more often away, I only appointed him in...'

'That's incorrect,' the American colonel interrupted in rather too good Chinese. Huang was shocked at the rudeness considering their respective ranks and that he hadn't finished speaking, this was worse that his father's public thrashing, the officer was treating him like a junior officer. He guessed what was coming, hating the humiliation of having to reply to an accusing foreigner. But his Commander-in-Chief was there, what could he do except try to defend himself, diffuse the situation if possible. 'He was a servant before you foolishly made him your secretary,' the American continued, 'so he must have been operating under your very nose and almost as far back as the invasion.' ...under your very nose...how dare he! Huang swallowed, wanted to answer but the man added in a peremptory manner: 'United States intelligence require to know how they recruited him.'

At least he could answer that point. 'He used to work in the Japanese Concession in Tianjin, and still has family there I understand.' Huang was trying to keep his voice from faltering. 'He said they found out that he'd become a soldier in my corps, that was before his accident when we took him into service as head domestic. They threatened his family if he didn't agree...' He preferred not to go on.

'What's the position in Mingon?' the American asked. 'Any other collaborators or spies you've missed under Jap control? Anyone who splashes out, seems to have money when nobody else does?'

...spies you've missed... this was appalling, Huang shook his head. 'Definitely not, I have lots of agents, we know everything and everybody there, and in many other places.' He hoped his tone would satisfy the arrogant foreigner as well as the Commander-in-Chief whose eyes remained uncomfortably fixed on him.

The Generalissimo asked abruptly: 'Madame Chiang has sent a message to your wife. Did she get it?'

He was taken by surprise. 'My wife! Not that I've been told. Ought I to enquire the nature of the message?'

'She heard, independent of me I might add, she has excellent feelers,' Chiang Kai-shek allowed a slight smile towards Ivans, before reverting to coldness towards his disastrous general, 'that someone called Tsai...' he paused and looked at a note on his desk, '...Tsai Yuling...' and the next few words he spoke deliberately loudly '...exposed the traitor in your household, Huang.' He allowed a moment to pass, and lowered his voice again. 'In so doing, he took great personal risk to himself because you were threatening to kill him. The name rings a bell with my wife, there may be many called that name, but she says that if this is the same person who was a boy lost in Fujian's tiger-infested hills, she would be very interested.'

Huang said to himself that at least they'd got off talking about his appointment of Wang, though he hardly felt more comfortable having to talk about his daughter's lover. 'Yes, that's him.' The picture came of the Tsai mother spitting words at him into his coach. 'Something happened and it became a news story for a short time some years ago.' His shirt was now horribly wet including at the back where it it was sticking, as he sat being accused in the Commander-in-Chief's Chongqing bunker. 'And the fellow had a stroke of luck, Hijiya let out something. That was while he was doing a portrait, he's an artist...'

'You mean *you* Huang had a mighty stroke of luck!' Chiang Kai-shek thundered a second time.

'Jeepers,' Colonel Ivans said aloud in American slang Huang didn't understand though the Commander-in-Chief did, before adding in Chinese with emotion, 'so did we all! Back in the States we'd be giving the guy a top civil medal. How old is he?'

Huang had to think. 'Twenty two, something like that.'

'Remarkable what he did,' the American exclaimed, '*and* he speaks Japanese. We've lots of west coast Japanese Americans, but hardly any speak Chinese as well. Sounds very useful, so why aren't you recruiting him?'

Another accusation. 'I'm actively trying to,' he lied again, stopping himself because he could tell that the Generalissimo was about to speak.

'As it is the person my wife has in mind, she'll want to see you. You'd better watch out, she wants to know why you had that death order on the young man. He's the son of a Valley hero. Explain yourself to us first, and then tell me what I am to say to Mr Roosevelt and Mr Churchill when they ask me to my face about this appalling Chinese embarrassment. The British leader can be very direct. Well Huang?'

*

'No my lady, I'm not able to recommend or administer anything to terminate, and the apothecary's suggestion would be much too dangerous for her. The baby is already seventeen or eighteen weeks in the womb.' Madame Huang could see concern written all over Doctor Lin's face, as he stood on the top step outside the main doors of her mansion. She received a deferential nod, knowing he disapproved of her idea. 'The Mistress is in rude health and spirits,' he added, 'very good to see, long may that continue, though naturally I hope a solution can be found for the family predicament.'

The lady said nothing more, received the bow, gestured back, and watched the old man move slowly down the marble steps.

She turned into her home. So... giving it up, or rather removing it was the only alternative. She knew her daughter would never agree to the first, so the baby would have to be whisked away to a pre-arranged home as far from Mingon as possible, and the seismic reaction would have to be faced and dealt with ...somehow.

Everything seemed to her topsy-turvy.

Because of the Wang disaster, her husband had warned her that he could lose the corps, that it would no longer have his name. And if he did not offer to resign, he might even lose his rank - almost unprecedented at the level of a general he told her. In trepidation she awaited his return from Chongqing.

And although she had tried to hush up the delicate matter of her daughter's condition, the news had somehow spread through high circles, the family was disgraced and their daughter could forever remain unmarried.

She simply did not believe her. '...I did *not* set out to have a child, I did *not* run away in June with that intention, there was *no* trap to force your hand ... this child comes out of our love, yes *love* mother, I prefer not to have a nasty scheming mind...' her daughter had disgracefully added.

And because of a surprising and awkward letter from Madame Chiang seeking information about Huihua and the artist, she had had a most difficult time composing the reply.

And even her beloved fifteen-year-old Shanghan, so upright and self-assured, had wounded her, saying he saw no reason why his sister and Tsai

Yuling should not marry. Never had he spoken to her, his own mother, so forcefully '...I was really shocked when Hua told me. He's a very good man, mother. I knew he was banned from returning to Mingon, but not that his life would be taken just because he's fallen in love with her and she loves him back, that's a terrible thought! It would have made me never want to see my portrait again, even if she'd hung it up in grief...'

And the estates: they were badly failing, now producing a quarter of the income and well less than half the produce they had ten years earlier.

And most frightening of all, if the Japanese moved to take more of eastern China including Mingon, what would happen to her and her children? She could lose her home, everything.

Her life was topsy-turvy indeed.

She had wondered whether to call in the Tsai mother to whom she had written. Between them they could try to persuade the lovers to part, and her daughter to give the baby up as soon as born. Or the Tsai mother might take the baby herself, or have it looked after in Tuxieng, perhaps until the son was in a position with another woman to take over the child. But she saw major problems, not least her daughter's infatuation with the artist, and the mother's changed view. In a recent reply, Mrs Chen Tsai Wenlie said that early on she had tried her hardest to persuade her son to break off the affair, but the pregnancy had changed everything, her view now was that the couple ...*should be allowed to enjoy their love in proper marriage and with their child, it is clearly genuine and deep...*

Madame Huang felt cold towards the baby in the womb. That it was half Huang counted nothing with her.

Her husband returned one night a few weeks later, and did not come to her as he usually did. When she saw him in the morning, he looked distressed and chastened.

'It could have been worse,' he told her. 'If the fellow hadn't been lucky enough to find out about Wang, I'd have really been for it. We're sure the Japanese are going to push soon, and Wang could have given them very damaging information. He's been executed, Chiang's order.' (Huang wasn't going to tell his wife that he'd done the deed himself.) 'The staff have been told by Ma that he took his own life for reasons unknown.' He put on a look of some disbelief. 'Huh! I've been forbidden to communicate or send military messages from here, only from the camp.'

'Is that all?' she asked with concern.

'I've kept the corps, but Chiang requires us to move west, I may not be able to get back for a long time. At least he paid me one compliment, said he didn't want to lose a fighting general. Ma and nearly all the officers will be with me.'

'Will we have any protection?'

'Only a few men under a junior officer, I can't spare more.' Her husband sighed. 'And there will be nothing to stop them if they come via Mingon, you'll have to flee into the hills. We think they're preparing a major offensive to take the allied bomber bases, and if we can't prevent them it'll be bad.'

His wife looked long at him, imagining having to live in huts in the hills, and thinking of the horror of more of China being under the boot of the despicable enemy. She came back to her daughter. 'And Hua?'

He gave her a resigned look. 'I've given up on her, she'll have to suffer the consequences of what she's done, and we'll have to accept him though I'll have nothing to do with the fellow.'

'Given up! Accept him!' The lady was shocked to hear her normally firm-minded husband speaking such defeatist language. 'We can try to persuade her to let go of the baby to another family, surely? And if she won't agree, we will have to force the issue, if necessary I can have the infant taken away.'

She expected her husband to agree the first idea even if he jibbed at the second, and was further surprised when he did not seem to take more interest. She thought of her idea of the Tsai mother taking charge of the baby, but decided she had better not raise it - her husband had never once mentioned the woman since the coach incident in Luchian. But the idea could be useful, for another time perhaps.

'In Chongqing Madame Chiang asked me what we were going to do about Hua and him. I thought she was still in America, but no, she insisted on seeing me, it was very difficult. She's so forceful in her cunning charming way. She kept saying "love is beautiful love" and told me to my face "in America parents would be proud to have a son-in-law like him, so why aren't you?" She seemed well-informed, knew about Hua getting out of here, and now being pregnant, and she asked me what we'd got against him. You must have a friend who is also a confidant of hers. She had the gall to say she didn't consider we should feel any shame, "that's old China!" she said.'

The lady was stunned. 'What did you reply? I hope you told her he took her purity away, and that he is practically a Red, and he has a hopelessly insecure future?'

'Of course. I reminded her that families like ours require our daughters to be chaste, that we *do* feel the shame, that a young lady out of marriage should never allow herself to become a mother. She huffed, was scornful, she's been tainted by the West, she said "So let them get married, we're living in the middle of the twentieth century not the Qing dynasty!" I was almost speechless.'

'I can guess who her contact is,' the lady said. 'And Madame Chiang wrote to me, she asked me detailed questions.' She paused. 'Look, suppose we get him here, try to talk reason into him, get him to see that this is just not practical, and then you can offer him that carrot, get him trained and commissioned and then posted to a dangerous area with fighting. Meanwhile we will have to force the issue with Hua, and if necessary prepare to get the baby taken elsewhere ...if we have time and survive the Japanese,' she added.

'If any of us survive.' Her husband was looking into his cheroot box. 'I've got to call him in soon anyway, to hand over Chiang's bauble. He wants him recruited. We can get him trained somewhere else, Ma's going to get a message to him.'

*

The driver of the old Japanese bus taking Yuling in the evening along one of the main streets of Amoy was frequently ringing its bell. It was already dark, and light rain was falling, the first for several weeks. A few other people had entered with him into the gloom of the near-empty bus. He was going from his rented room to meet up with a friend in the middle of the city at a particular tea house they frequented two or three times a month.

Sitting alone by a window in the back seat and looking out at the street scene, he thought everything seemed dismal: gas lamps low-lit, pavements wet, rickshaw pullers in plastic against the rain, people scurrying along, some with umbrellas. At such moments he liked to imagine himself with Huihua in the sunshine at the sparkling stream near the Hut, holding her hand to his face, kissing every finger, taking the little one in his mouth, challenging her with his eyes, feeling her other hand in his hair...

Away in his delicious thoughts, he little noticed that the bus had stopped, or that it had begun to move again, hardly registered its bell, or that one of the passengers who had entered with him into the semi-dark of the bus had moved from the front and come to the back seat and was sitting close by.

'Don't look at me, Tsai,' he suddenly heard, and immediately turned, elbow ready to hit out hard. The man had spoken not much louder than the noise of the bus, his head looking towards the front. Yuling didn't say anything. 'Don't look at me, turn away, I'm not a collaborator, I've a message for you from high up.'

He felt some relief but checked for gun or knife; he found it hard to see, but the hands seemed empty. He looked only partly away.

'You were right about the man.'

He was puzzled. 'What man?'

'Wuyi Court.'

Wang! So it was him, he'd been pretty sure. He kept his guard up - this could be a Japanese trick to see if he'd been implicated. 'I don't know what you're talking about.'

'He's been killed.'

He looked at the man. 'Who's been killed?'

The driver started sounding the bell again, and Yuling couldn't hear the first part of the reply, though he caught the word 'commander' and General Huang coming into his mind, and he thought the man said something about a medal but the bell kept ringing and he wasn't sure.

When it stopped, he was about to ask the man to repeat himself, but he had stood and was walking towards the front.

Wang dead. He thought of that moment of unbelievable relief after the air attack, when he'd heard the door being unbolted on the other side, and soon through the dust in his eyes he caught the looks of astonishment on the faces of the old cook and the head domestic. And now the man who had rescued them was dead because he'd exposed him.

He watched trickles of rain running in curves down the window.

A few days later, on a cool late-November morning after drawing class Yuling went to see the Head Teacher with the letter in his hand that he had been longing for. He put on a disbelieving smile when asking to speak with him, and showed Huihua's letter, though he knew the man could not read Chinese.

'I'm to be a father!' he said in pretended surprise, 'and the General has ended the death order and wants to see me in two to three weeks. And Huang Huihua is fine! I can't believe it!' He kept shaking his head, his acting abilities to the fore learnt from his mother and in the street.

The man smiled back and gave a short nod. 'Are the parents accepting you now?'

'It doesn't say that. If you'll allow me and can get me a pass, I'll leave here about the middle of December, what will that make her, six months with our child, I think.' He let his face become serious. 'Did you have this feeling when you first heard your wife was carrying a baby?'

The Head Teacher laughed. 'Yes, it's one of life's best moments, but then you worry how it will go. But I was married, you are not. You're not going to be leaving us, I trust?'

'No, no. If you're prepared to keep me, I would like to continue working here and make occasional visits to...'

'If they let you visit. They might not.'

Yuling sighed. 'If it is still bad news with the parents, I don't know what we'll do. She is very strong-willed.'

The poorly coded part of Huihua's letter had told Yuling the answer to his question whether he should join the military.

I was talking to a girl the other day and she made me laugh when

386

*she said she wants to marry a bird-seller or a puppeteer, not a
farmer, soldier or gardener. I expect your engineer grandfather
might have said the same when he was a boy, putting bird-seller
first.*

Shortly after Yuling left the school that afternoon, a scruffy man stopped
him at a street corner and said under his breath that he had a message from
a Major Ma. Yuling was beginning to feel his life in Amoy was becoming
disrupted by sudden messages from strangers who were possibly dangerous. But
he had lived important moments with the captain - now apparently promoted -
and he respected him. He sensed that the scruffy man was genuine.

After the cell meeting with the general, the captain had escorted Yuling
alone to one of the roads leading away from Wuyi Court and Mingon. Just
before they had parted, Yuling begged him to tell the truth about Huihua's
health, saying it gave him much worry in Amoy. The officer had replied: 'You
haven't seen or heard this from me,' before demonstrating with his hands the
bulge of a pregnant woman, and telling him she was in excellent health. It was
a moment of exquisite joy and happiness for Yuling.

The scruffy man hailed a rickshaw and invited him to enter first, telling the
puller to take them to one of the larger temples. They had no difficulty talking
through the noise of the traffic without the puller hearing. When Yuling was
told the military were keen to recruit him into the officer class, he replied that
he was not interested in becoming a soldier, adding sarcastically '...not even a
Nationalist officer with all the perks.'

He was then invited to join the underground in Amoy against the
imperialists, the man being enthusiastic about the use he could be put to in the
Resistance with his knowledge of Japanese. Yuling replied that he was already
thinking he might do so at some future stage.

'We know the service you've already rendered,' the man said before asking
him to memorize an address near the large bamboo groves in the southern
outskirts of Amoy. 'Contact us as soon as you feel able. We need you.'

'Would I have to give up my teaching job?'

'Not immediately, we might prefer you to stay there, but it depends on
the work we would have for you.' The scruffy man leaned over. 'I nearly forgot,
you're to go to Mingon before the end of December at the latest, General
Huang requires to see you.'

*

'Tsai Yuling, the Head Teacher wants you in his office right away.' One of
the Japanese women teachers has just called into his art room, and her usual

warm expression towards him is not there, she looks serious, in fact cold. He is standing among a dozen children, demonstrating wet on wet watercolour. The unmarried woman in her mid-thirties has often tried to flirt, but he always looked away. He had made an excuse when she asked him to escort her home one day, and at another time had declined to join her at a tea house.

It is less than a week since showing Huihua's letter to the Head Teacher.

As soon as he enters the office, he receives a shock, seeing the same Japanese intelligence officer who interrogated him and took his photograph before the school employed him, the man whose narrow eyes he thinks so sinister. The officer wears a dark suit and ugly grey tie, and sits in the Head Teacher's chair behind the desk, a cigarette in the left hand, a brown folder in front displaying the Rising Sun. The Head Teacher stands nearby like a frightened subordinate.

He bows low to the officer first, then to the Head. But the officer doesn't look up, and the Head Teacher barely nods.

'Intelligence require you to answer questions.' The Head Teacher has spoken rather quietly in a tone Yuling finds ominous.

He waits for the officer to speak. The man says nothing. When he finally speaks, the eyes remain on the folder.

'You want to go to Mingon, that's a turnaround.'

Yuling doesn't know if to reply. A question has not been asked, and the greatest respect must be shown to the invader at all times. He is about to say that he will be a father, when the man taps the cigarette over an ashtray and adds, still not looking at him: 'You can't go unless I say so, and right now I do not.'

He is deeply dismayed, has been counting down the days to the mid-December departure, imagining soon holding Huihua's face in his hands as she puts her swelling between them so long as the parents allow him near her, alone.

'When were you last there?'

The question terrifies. Were they somehow onto him. Has General Huang tipped them off. 'Mingon? Nine months ago,' he lies feeling hot, 'when I was kicked out of the mansion.'

'When did you last see your lady friend?'

'In June,' Yuling says looking to the Head Teacher, 'she ran away and we had a few days together as you know, sir.'

Still the officer has not looked at him. 'Didn't you see her when visiting your mother some weeks back? Didn't you get her a message and she came to you again?'

'No,' he answers pretending surprise, relieved to be able to say truthfully that she did not abscond a second time (and he had not seen her when he went to Mingon to expose Wang). He senses they probably haven't checked up on his mother's *illness*, although a question could still be coming. He already knows what illness to give her: he mentioned it to her in his short visit after Mingon, in case she was asked questions by some stranger, or enquiries were made about her in Tuxieng by some Japanese agent or collaborator working there. 'I told Huang Huihua never to run away again, it would put me in great danger with her father, the Whites know I work here. Anyway, she wouldn't leave, she's now carrying our baby.'

'So you didn't go to Wuyi Court or nearby?'

'No, of course not.' A horrible thought comes to Yuling that Wang might have been working with another agent or had some accomplice in Mingon, the nasty innkeeper for instance, that his presence at the mansion or on the roads was detected.

The intelligence officer at last looks up, and Yuling sees eyes extremely narrow and threatening.

'Why has General Huang suddenly ended the death order? Odd don't you think? And they're now prepared to see you, the lover, the very person they didn't want for their daughter.'

Yuling watches the man inhale, and before he answers, smoke is blown directly into his face and the tobacco smells foul and he wishes he could blow it away. 'Well they must want to talk to me about the future, I hope.' His throat is going dry.

'No. They'll want to get rid of the baby, they're not going to accept you.'

Yuling knows the truth of the second comment, though the unpleasant first one comes as a shock as it hasn't occurred to him before. He frowns. There is further silence. He moves his look away from the officer to the Head Teacher and then down to the desk. And when he cannot stand the gaze and doesn't want to be seen to be hiding anything, he looks at the officer as innocently as he can. But still the man stares through narrow eyes as if probing his mind.

'Who do you know at Wuyi Court?'

Immediately he thinks of Wang. 'I don't know anybody except the general's daughter.'

'Yes you do, don't play games with me.'

'Games? I...'

'You told me in March that you lived in the basement for nearly a week when you were painting. Who did you meet there?' The voice has risen.

He tries to put on an expression of decency. 'I believe I mentioned this when you interviewed me before the school took me on. I met some maids, one of them spied on my lady friend, I think her name was Dajuan, and there was a groom called Head Groom...' he looks half to the ceiling pretending to recall, '...and an elderly gentleman called Lee who was the private secretary, I met the tutor a few times but only briefly, and the head domestic, and one of the cooks,' he pauses, 'no, two cooks. And some of the guards were friendly.' He stops, intensely hoping there won't be a question about Wang.

The intelligence officer gets up, comes round the desk and stands close, holding up the cigarette near Yuling's chin.

He thinks how small the officer is, like fellow countryman Colonel Hijiya, though anything but friendly, unlike the exuberant airman. The eyes widen at him; the pupils are the smallest of any person Yuling has ever looked at closely when painting.

'The name of the head domestic?'

'The head domestic?' he repeats into the man's face, 'I think it was Wang.' He holds his innocent look and waits, can hardly breathe, dreads other questions about their spy he was told on the bus is dead.

'You know very well it was Wang, and you know that he became the private secretary to the general, don't you.'

'Wang! Became the general's private secretary? No I didn't know that.' He raises his shoulders. 'Why are you asking me about him?'

A smirk comes over the face, the nasty eyes remaining wide. 'So at your June hideaway she didn't talk about him, between you making love?'

'About the head domestic, I mean the private secretary?' Yuling shakes his head. 'Why should she?'

'Because he rescued you lovers, didn't he.'

Yuling wants to swallow but can't. Another silence. He is about to admit Wang's involvement with unbolting the door, when he is asked: 'Where's the love nest in the hills?'

He hesitates, but only for a very short moment, instinct telling him to be open, that they haven't found out he was at Wuyi Court. He *has* to make the man think he is being truthful.

'It's on the other side of the Zass River, high above Dongang, but the General doesn't know that, you're the first person I'm telling this to. There's no road there, only a difficult path.'

The smirk disappears and the eyes narrow again. The cigarette moves menacingly in the hand. 'You can chose to do as I say, or you can lose your life for nothing.'

Yuling's eyebrows rise and he knows he is unable to hide the fear - the conquerors count Chinese lives for nothing.

'You will go immediately to Mingon, you will not wait, and you will report back to me within one week what has happened to Wang, and I want details.'

'I don't understand, what do you mean "what has happened to Wang"? Why is he of interest to you?'

'He's dead by his own hand, that's what Huang wants us to believe.'

'Dead!' The acting is of life-saving importance.

'You will tell me if that is true or how he died. If he's dead, find out why. If he's alive, I want to know where he is.' The man pauses. 'If you don't come back, we will come for you and your end will be agony. And if you double-cross me...' The man does not end his threat, but Yuling's throat is being pressed with the thumb of the hand holding the cigarette, and for a second he feels the heat against his neck and expects to be burnt at any moment, expects to cry out.

'But if the General isn't there until after mid-December, I'll have to wait to see him.'

The intelligence officer narrows his eyes. 'Be back by the twentieth, or else.'

His smoke breath is very unpleasant.

'Strange he didn't mention Wang first,' the intelligence officer says from the chair, looking up at the Head Teacher just a short silent moment after the Chinaman has been dismissed, 'the very person who saved his life, and the girl's. He talked about him early on in the job interview as though he'd got to know him quite well and was very grateful he'd rescued them. Weeks back he asks for immediate leave to visit his sick mother, goes off, and not long afterwards we get no more reports from Wang, and the next thing we hear, our agent is supposed to have killed himself.' The intelligence officer taps a finger on his folder on the Head Teacher's desk. 'We've been watching your painter. You say he's clean and trustworthy. I'm not so sure. When he comes back, *if* he comes back, you tell me everything he says to you or your women, and anything that strikes you as odd, anything. Get him to talk. And it's none of your business which one, but a teacher here is our agent. I shall be instructing her to make greater efforts to lure him, and she will be watching more closely how you handle him.'

*

Yuling reached Mingon four days later, at first by boat through the occupied zone, and then mainly on foot.

As he approached the large stone lions that had twice witnessed bad moments in his life, he wondered what lay in store for him: would the parents allow him to see Huihua, surely they must, he would try to insist; the possibility of repeating a visit and not seeing her was unthinkable, especially now he knew her condition since the decent captain - now major - had disclosed it.

He was searched, and a soldier came to collect him from the Guard House. 'The old cook still here?' he asked innocently as they walked through the outer courtyard. He received a Yes. 'Could you get this to her, she's expecting it,' he lied, handing over a small envelope he had addressed to Xuiey. The soldier took it and Yuling thanked him. Inside was a note.

Chang-o, am here expecting to meet with your father right now.

As he was taken into the Study - the general's office where he had crumpled to the floor nine months earlier when the sergeant punched him - he could see Huihua's parents standing talking quietly by the large desk.

'Ah, Tsai,' the general called out, surprising Yuling by the semi-friendly manner of the greeting.

He bowed from the embossed doors, and walked nervously towards them. When he came close he received short bows from each of them, and gave his again. But there was no polite thanking him for making the journey, and the general began at once.

'First things first. I am instructed by the Commander-in-Chief to present you with his medal and his personal letter. He requires me to thank you on behalf of the military for your part in the Wang affair.' The general gave a curt nod, turned and picked up a small hard-leather case and an envelope, red sealed, offering them over.

Yuling was taken aback. 'From Chiang Kai-shek!' he exclaimed, keeping his arms by his side and starting to shake his head, looking from the general's outstretched hands to Madame Huang.

'Yes, take them man.'

'I don't want anything from the Generalissimo!'

'I beg your pardon?' General Huang couldn't believe what he had heard, his face one of astonishment as he continued holding out the medal case and envelope. 'You don't want our leader's personal medal? You'd better think again Tsai, this is a great honour.'

'Please,' the lady said in a quiet tone, 'in memory of your father. And your mother would be proud. The respect of a nation.' Madame Huang did not regret mentioning the mother in her husband's presence.

Yuling caught the intelligence behind the plea. Yet still he felt very reluctant to receive the objects. Since the incident in the semi-dark bus (when he'd wondered if the general might be awarding him some wretched medal), he'd told himself he would never receive any such thing from the Slayer of the Reds, the man who had treated him so badly and condemned dear Lam to die. Deep down, despite Huihua being the daughter, despite her imploring him not to hate her father, he did, for the brutal history and abuse of power.

'You *must* accept these,' General Huang said, not prepared to take such disrespect, pushing them against the young man's left hand. 'Don't open them now if you don't want to, talk with your stepfather and open them later. Just don't take them back to Amoy for obvious reasons, leave them at your home.'

Yuling felt he had little choice, and took hold of what was touching him, though he said nothing. He thought it strange that the general wasn't himself thanking him for exposing Wang, or at least giving him some acknowledgement. Little did he realize that General Huang had nearly lost his rank and his corps because of him, that he had arrived back at his old warlord mansion tail between legs.

'Ironic, no?' the general continued. 'You obviously don't like our nation's leader, and here he is, bestowing his highest civil award on you, a Red supporter I hear, even if you're not a Communist Party member.'

Yuling would not be drawn. He was talking with his lovely girl's antagonistic parents, and wanted to know what they would now say to him about the baby and the future. And he desperately wanted to see Huihua …and he had to find out more about Wang, to report back to the terrifying intelligence officer.

'Well, let us move on,' General Huang added, half looking at his wife, feeling stronger in mind since his return to her; he now agreed with her, they must continue to resist the fellow despite the pregnancy, and despite Madame Chiang's *modern* thinking, her western ways. 'Now what are we going to do about our daughter's future in the right marriage?'

'General,' Yuling was determined to speak before the father could continue, 'my lady,' he turned quickly to the mother to speak into her eyes, 'I must see Huihua.'

'Yes, yes, you will,' the general replied, Yuling's heart leaping up. But the general was now feeling considerable irritation at the demanding tone of the fellow who had caused him so much trouble: loss of respect within the military, family shame in social circles. 'But first you will agree with us what you must say to her…'

'…for a final farewell,' the lady added, 'then she must rest you understand, she is not always well.'

He was about to protest, but the general's hand came up to silence him. 'This extremely unfortunate occurrence, it is our belief and firm intention that in everybody's interest, not least your own, you end the matter, and the baby must go to another family as soon after birth as possible.'

He went into disbelief, was again shaking his head and catching the lady's looks at him.

'My wife has found two families, each very suitable, the child would be well cared for and the family paid, you would have no financial responsibilities, you must think of that.'

'But this is *our* child,' he blurted out, looking at the lady's opal neck-brooch, 'we love each other, your daughter and I love each other,' he hotly repeated, 'the child will be your grandchild.'

'I have told you before' General Huang reverted to an authoritative tone

393

that could lead to anger, 'that our daughter must marry into a similar family, families at our level have positions to maintain…'

'…estates to run,' the lady interjected in a more moderate voice, 'talk it through with her,' she went on before her husband lost his patience with the young man, 'act like the brave person you are, we all have to make difficult decisions in our lives, but they almost always turn out for the best if wisdom guides. And here wisdom dictates, we assure you, that our family will be most unhappily affected if you do not break this off.'

'And the child's future?' Yuling asked her with incredulity.

'It could have a good life,' she replied, 'yes, with the right family.'

The general came back into the conversation: 'This is not just in our own interest, our daughter's husband should be in the military and from a high family, you do not…'

'With respect,' he firmly interrupted, aware this was a pivotal moment in his life and thinking how it would be without his girl, 'have you asked what Huihua wants?' He looked squarely at the father. 'Do her views not count the most? And am I so unacceptable in your eyes because I'm not rich or an officer and have different views of the way forward for our country?'

He could see his comments had some impact, because neither parent was rushing to answer; the general even seemed to be trying to smile towards him or rather towards his chest, a first time.

'If you wanted to be an officer,' General Huang said, 'after a suitable period of time things might change, we would have to see. But I hear you do not.' He stopped and turned. Huihua had just come through the side door near the desk. She was with them in a trice.

The general was very disappointed to see his daughter; he hadn't wanted her brought into the discussion until things were agreed with the artist or teacher or whatever he was.

Huihua had not received the Chang-o message; she had told the soldiers at the main gates that they were to get a message to her via the servants or other guards the moment her close friend, the tall artist, arrived to see her father, though she hadn't expected to see him so soon and guessed his longing to see her after her letter, and his natural exuberance, had made him come early.

She was wearing a velvet robe of off-white, loose-fitting suitable to her condition, and gave him a shy smile with her bow. He hardly bowed back, his face a picture of wonder at her as she read his thoughts, and she was very pleased he was not afraid to display his feelings in front of the parents she knew remained as hostile as ever. She saw there were things in his hands, and her mother was standing close to him, no doubt to intimidate or for her own cunning reasons.

'It is wonderful to see you,' she said quietly as if speaking to him alone.

Yuling was transfixed. How different, how marvellous Huihua looked, womanhood at one of its greatest moments he said to himself, and she was his woman whatever the future, *his*. He wished he could hold her again.

'We have been discussing the way forward,' her father said to her as she turned, 'and as you know, your mother and I, much as we understand our friend's feelings, are certain it is in your own interest and ours that the matter goes no further. I make no...'

'Father, we are having our baby and we shall marry, that is our wish, we...'

'Marry!' The general was horrified at the word, shocked at his daughter's firmness of purpose; she seemed often now to startle him; he must force parental authority onto the scene, though if possible keep anger at bay. 'No, Hua, you may not get married in this instance, as I have told you many times. Your mother and I do not give our consent, and Tsai Yuling knows our reasons,' he gave the young man a quick look that he hoped was firm but not fierce, 'and I'm sure he understands them even if they cause him pain, only natural.' He continued to address his difficult daughter. 'When you have the child it will be best if...'

'When I have my child it will be Tsai Yuling's child,' Huihua looked quickly at Yuling and back to her father, 'we will become a family of three, and if I have to run away to protect...'

'Run away!' he exclaimed, 'that shall *not* happen again!'

'...to protect our child, I will go straight to Chongqing and...'

'Chongqing!' the lady said in her own shock.

'Yes mother, Madame Chiang Kai-shek will give us shelter if needs be, those are her own words to me.'

There was a hush. Yuling looked at Huihua, astonished at what he'd heard and at her strength and the clarity of her voice; she was dealing her parents a severe blow, and he waited the retorts. But Huihua was now in full swing.

'And it's no use talking to us about another family having our baby, because I will never agree, *never!*' She gave another quick look at Yuling. 'We will never agree. And to take our baby away by force or do something worse will lead to disaster for all of us, you including me, and Shanghan will be horribly affected.' She leaned towards her father, his concern impossible to miss. 'The Chiangs will be the first to hear, father, I have contacts who will instantly relay messages.'

The general's eye caught a view of the Ming sword. Underneath his shock and outrage at the disloyalty, he couldn't help admire his first child, a Huang through and through, as strong in character as any of them. The sight of his daughter crouching where he now stood came powerfully back to him, her hands round the filigree handle, Huang eyes challenging him to test her resolve. He looked to the young man and found himself partly understanding why his daughter had fallen for the fellow, physically powerful like himself, even more so perhaps - well he was younger - and yes, Ma was right, he did have courage.

The near empty room they were permitted to have for half an hour '...to talk things through and come to the only right decision for all ...to give more consideration to our family name and our parental rights and feelings...' had nothing but a single chair near the door; everything else had long ago been stored underground for safety against bombing.

When the door closed behind them, they waited until they could hear Huihua's mother returning along the passage, and then the Mistress looked enquiringly up at her brother's artist, took one of his hands and placed it against her tummy, opening her eyes to catch his every emotion.

'This is an extraordinary moment,' Yuling said thinking he might feel some kicks though he didn't. 'I can almost hear the bees!'

He took his hand away, cupped her face, her head went back, and they began kissing, passionately.

When they stopped, he said: 'You were magnificent, the Madame Chiang thing, is it really true?'

Huihua needed time to bring herself from his physical wonder, torn between her abandonment and the question. But he'd expressed some disbelief.

'Absolutely. Dajuan kept trying to make up with me, and said I might want to take a look at a letter on my mother's dressing table, she wouldn't say why except that it concerned you. I couldn't believe it, there was a letter from Chiang Kai-shek's wife telling her what she'd told my father, that you were exceptional and asking why my parents were so against, especially as you were to receive her husband's personal medal. When I read that I was so proud, and I knew why, because Major Ma told me in great confidence what you did. I smuggled out a long letter to her telling her everything, and about your character and my fears, and I got her reply just a few days ago.'

She was looking at the medal case and the envelope that Yuling had placed on the chair. 'May I?' Her father's parting words as they left the Study were that she should '...persuade Tsai Yuling to open the honour bestowed...'

She saw Yuling's expression of some distaste, took up the envelope and looked into his eyes. 'Please let me open them. Think of it as our country's appreciation.'

Like mother like daughter; he rubbed the back of his hand up and down her miraculous cheek, and she pressed against it. 'My lovely girl, you can ask me anything and I'm likely to agree!'

Carefully she broke the flap round the seal and removed a yellow-tinted card, at once seeing excellent handwriting. She turned the card towards him.

To Tsai Yuling, citizen of Tuxieng, Fujian province:
I write this to pay honour to you, that in our mighty struggle in
the War of Resistance Against Japan, you exposed a great danger
to our efforts without regard to the order standing against you on
your own life. In a nation's gratitude.
Chiang Kai-shek,
Allied Commander-in-Chief,
Chongqing.
20th October 1943, the 32nd Year of the Republic.

On the left side of the handwriting was the official stamp of the Commander-in-Chief. Huihua looked at Yuling, read it quickly again, and put it back in the envelope, handing it to him. She took up the small hard-leather case, pushed up the clasp and opened it, and was looking down at a silk band of white and blue attached to a silver coin depicting the head of the Generalissimo.

'I give it to you,' he said quietly.

She took the envelope from him and put it on the chair with the medal case, leaving it open. 'Sway me,' she said, turning her back on him. She felt his arms come round her and his lips touch her right cheek, and she let herself go in his arms, being gently moved from side to side and imagining they were three.

Yuling did not want to let go of his radiant and brave girl carrying their love, but something else was pressing on his mind. After a while he took his hands away and turned her round.

'Huihua,' he said, suddenly frightening her with his look and tone, 'you mustn't ask me why I have to find out, but do you know what happened to Wang? Some man from your father or at any rate the Nationalists came and sat beside me in a dark bus and whispered he'd been killed. If he's dead, it may be he killed himself? If you know but can't tell me because you're not allowed to, I'll have to speak to your father again or to Captain Ma,' he corrected himself 'Major Ma. But it's vital you tell me if you can, vital for my sake.'

Huihua was looking closely at him. 'Of course I'll tell you, and I do know but it's not pleasant. My father was so angry when he got back from Chongqing that he took him to the woods and shot him himself. He doesn't know I know this. The guards were told Wang committed suicide but not why, and not why he'd been locked up. I'm sure my father feels shame about it all.' She continued to search him. 'You're not in danger because of this, are you? My father hasn't…'

He shook his head. 'How was he found out?'

'Dummy reconnaissance bunkers were built in forest clearings far apart, somewhere east and south of here, well camouflaged Major Ma said. Then he let Wang see the information about the positions, and within two days planes were buzzing all over the two areas trying to find them, and soon the bunkers were bombed. He was immediately arrested, and they found radio transmitting equipment in his office behind lots of books. Apparently Wang had always locked his bedroom when he was head domestic, and when he took over Lee's office he used to lock that too and didn't let the cleaners in. Major Ma had already been having suspicions by the time you came along and exposed him, because some of my father's orders or messages from the Study were taking too long to reach the Officers Building. It's strange, but honestly I never entirely trusted Wang.'

Yuling had listened carefully, but now he was putting a finger firmly to her mouth. 'I don't want to talk about it any more,' he said eyes sparkling at her, 'you look ravishing! I'm so happy just looking at you!' He took the medal case and envelope off the chair and placed them on the floor, and sat and pulled her sideways onto his lap.

'I love this,' he said, his left hand stroking her velvet robe above her knees, his right caressing her back and moving up to her collar and hair. 'I think of you so much.'

She pulled his hand to feel her middle again, becoming coy, her nose touching his. 'What would you like?'

She smelt delicious, as she had at the Hut. 'Boys keep the line going,' he said, 'and they're more useful, girls are more trouble and cost a lot, so I'll have a boy.' He touched the tip of her nose. 'Then again, two of you would be double bliss, you can pamper me, so I'll have a girl.' He tickled near her ear, teasing her until her shoulder moved up in delight.

'Let's walk in the gardens,' she said, 'and if my mother comes I'll tell her we still need time to talk about what they were saying.'

A few minutes later they came to the old pagoda tree, Huihua running a finger along its furrowed bark and looking up towards the two windows of Yuling's painting room.

'That's where it began for me,' she said, 'you captured me with your smile, and then when I saw the portrait I knew you were special.' She rose on her toes - she'd already checked that the father and son gardeners were elsewhere - and pressed her lips to his cheek, knowing how much he loved it, inwardly laughing at herself at the anger she had felt when sitting on that table after he wouldn't let her see how the painting was coming along. 'Shanghan wants to see you, he's joined the corps as an ordinary soldier under Lieutenant Chu, he'll become an officer later. He's fully for us coming together.'

'Maybe you can get him to work on your parents, so nothing bad happens about the baby,' he said, 'and we've got to decide what we'll now say to them. Being with you makes me feel braver, I can tell them we simply can't give each other up. But I cannot go against their authority, I cannot insist we...' He stopped; she was shaking her head at him in her determined way.

'I will tell them we wish to be married one day, and to live together as soon as conditions permit, nothing less, and that if they wish me to move away, I will do so, with our child of course. The baby will be yours and mine not theirs.'

He gave her a pensive look; his lovely girl was so purposeful. But he couldn't see her leaving, couldn't imagine them living together if the parents with the father's power were dead against. He came back to the reality of his own position.

'I may not be able to come back for some time after the birth, it depends on the school and the authorities, it's no longer easy to get a pass, things are tense. But you will always know that I am thinking of you the whole time and will get back whenever I can.'

He couldn't tell her what was also on his mind, about the talk in the rickshaw with the scruffy man and possible recruitment into the Resistance inside the Japanese area. He'd agonized about telling her, but didn't want to frighten, especially not in her condition, and the less she knew the better for the security of each of them. He had told himself that if he went underground, he would be able to get back to her occasionally, hopefully for decent spells - that had to be a condition of his joining the Resistance.

Huihua said: 'And I shall tell them again that my future has to be mine in the end to decide. Leave any threats to me if I'm forced to make them.'

Between curtains from a window far away, a mother watched with a sinking feeling.

*

Nerve-racking though it was reporting back to the intelligence officer, it went better than Yuling could have hoped for. Almost the worst part was having to go through the doors of the Central Intelligence Building, knowing its reputation and that if he made a wrong step or if they had found out more on him, his life would be threatened.

He felt very scared as he stood in front of the desk. The same Chinese official, the collaborator who had attended the pre-job first interview, was again present.

As soon as he told the Japanese officer that Wang was definitely dead, repeating it in Chinese to the official, and how he had died - not by suicide but at General Huang's own hand in the woods - and that his source of information was the daughter, and how Major Ma had become suspicious and discovered Wang's equipment, the Japanese officer's tone turned to a sickly friendliness.

'So now you know why we required you to find out about him,' he said with the smirk Yuling loathed.

'Yes. I couldn't believe it when Huang Huihua told me he'd been found out as an agent.' He was trying to prevent his knees from shaking, and returned to the truth of how the major had set up Wang to catch him. And when he told him that no one else knew what happened to the man, not even Wuyi Court staff or the guards, because the general seemed to feel shame, and when he deliberately disclosed that the general and part of the corps were shortly to depart west to Hunan province - possibly new information for the Japanese which they would anyway very soon find out for themselves to corroborate his evidence and point to his honesty - he felt the man was believing him, that hopefully he'd done enough to put them off suspecting, if they had such thoughts, that he'd had anything to do with Wang's discovery. But he didn't say the whole corps was leaving, certainly didn't want the enemy to think of mounting some quick assault on the mansion.

'Will you now be taken into the family?' the evil-looking officer asked with eyes more open than usual.

Yuling suddenly imagined being a possible Japanese recruitment target as their next agent. He put on a deep frown. 'No, they won't have me, and they're threatening to give the baby away. But we don't think they'll dare, the consequences would be very bad, they could lose their daughter, she'll try to come to me. I hinted we could live in Tuxieng with the baby near my mother and stepfather, but the General said that was out of the question. Our position is very difficult, they simply refuse to accept me. The Major wanted me to join the army, but I'm an artist not a soldier and I told the General I wouldn't. Anyway, I'm very happy here in Amoy at the school with the excellent children...' - your own Japanese children, to end with a compliment he hoped would be swallowed - 'except that I can't be near my girl.'

The interview soon came to an end, the intelligence officer offering no words of appreciation, the face resorting to cold disdain. 'That's all, go.' A hand waved.

The spy-exposer bowed extra low and avoided all eye contact.

'We may call you in at any time,' he heard as he was going out of the room, longing to step into the street, longing to be away from the building.

A few weeks later he was hailed from a rickshaw and recognized the passenger. He joined the scruffy man, listened to the question, and replied that he was ready to help the Resistance, telling him about the interviews with the intelligence officer.

The position inside China was clear: there was little realistic possibility the enemy could ever be pushed out, made to leave. Yet Yuling felt more and more that the time had arrived - despite Huihua and the coming baby - when he should offer his services, to put his knowledge of Japanese at the disposal of his country. The news he had for long been hearing in Amoy's tea houses showed that the war in Eastern Europe and North Africa had turned against Germany, and that Japan's *great victories* heralded in the invader's newspapers masked the truth: that the Japanese were stretched everywhere they had conquered in South-East Asia, they had suffered a severe naval defeat against the United States a year and a half earlier opening up the Pacific, and American bombers from western Chinese bases were a threat to their islands.

The scruffy man told him to remain at the school, adding he would be contacted 'when the time was right,' and giving him an address near the southern bamboo groves in case he thought the Japanese were onto him, telling him to ask for 'Chang.' They parted on either side of the rickshaw in the thick of the thoroughfare's traffic.

Mid-March 1944 soon came - the predicted time for the birth - and Yuling went every day to the shop to ask if any letter had come for him, and each time he went away disappointed, getting more and more worried as the second and then the third week passed. His morbid self-pitying imagination came back to haunt; he saw Huihua dead on her bed, the baby sent away for adoption.

He was not to know that Madame Huang had discovered Huihua's use of the old cook to get messages to him via Mrs Wu to the Amoy shopkeeper, and had put an end to it on pain of Xuiey losing her position. Nor did he know that the baby came two weeks early, and that Huihua had had a long hard birth and been weak for many days after.

Her daughter's worrying state, coupled with the wonder of a baby that she and the two maids crowed over, were major reasons why Madame Huang put aside for the time being further thought of removing the child to the family she had chosen; her own hardships as a young woman - trying to conceive, having a stillborn, and the long wait for Shanghan - came strongly back to her.

Yuling's teachers knew he was suffering and why. He was on the point of asking for leave when news that he'd had a daughter reached him unexpectedly by way of a few words scribbled on an empty envelope with his name on. It was left between path-stones just inside the school gate, was in an unknown hand, unsigned and with no date, and it told him nothing about Huihua or when the birth occurred. It was handed to him by one of the women teachers who had picked it up, and he took it at once to the Head Teacher, feeling a mixture of excitement and concern, asking permission to take immediate temporary leave.

'If it was up to me you could go,' the man replied. 'I'll see what I can do, but under present circumstances it is unlikely the authorities will give you a pass.'

Yuling knew what he referred to: strong rumours had been circulating through Amoy that after several years occupying China's coastal regions, a major Japanese offensive to take more of the country was imminent. Great ships had been entering the eastern harbours, and in Amoy vast numbers of transport vehicles had been seen passing through, including many horses and mules.

Two days later, as Yuling came out from his art room, the Head Teacher said: 'I'm sorry, the answer is No, and you are not to ask again.' The man looked kindly at him. 'In time I'm sure you'll be able to see your lady friend, and your child of course.'

The next few weeks were filled with worry, no further message let alone letter reaching him. He weighed up the dangers of abandoning his job. He was an employee of the invaders; they could treat him very badly, and they would shoot him if he was caught trying to get through strengthened Japanese border positions to reach Huihua.

Yet again he thought of her as mentally the stronger. 'Yuling, promise me you will never act impetuously on my behalf if it puts you in danger,' she had said shortly before they parted after the second difficult almost hopeless meeting with her parents, 'and always think for the longer term, I will wait for you however long it takes, *we* can wait for you,' she'd added. 'I know that I shouldn't have absconded from the Court and gone to wait for you at Dongang, but it turned out wonderfully. I don't want to lose you now. You *must* take care.'

25

'We've got to leave at once, they could be coming this way.' Lieutenant Xi stopped to catch his breath. 'Please be ready in ten minutes, main gates.' He had run from the wall doors between the courtyards, and was standing at the entrance to the Officers Building; Madame Huang thought he looked frightened and too young to be an officer.

She had moved into the building shortly after her husband and corps, including Shanghan, had departed two provinces west, as it had been considered too risky to remain in the mansion itself.

'How far are they away?'

'A few hours, it depends how they come, but they could bomb first.'

She realized the worst moment of her life was upon her, and had visions of being imprisoned by the enemy or worse. But she had no time to ask or say anything more, as the greenling had turned and was running back.

In Mingon pandemonium had broken out after the few citizens with radio sets picked up the transmission from Nationalist Chongqing that a major Japanese offensive had started and that any town attacked from the air or in the line of an advance should at once evacuate unless protected by a substantial force.

Soon the streets were full of people rushing to leave, going in every direction except east, carrying what rice and other meagre foods they could as well as blankets. People were crying out, some of the women hugging menfolk who were going to take up positions in futile attempts to slow whatever force came their way.

A few weeks earlier, when it was realized Mingon could be in the path of a new push, there had been heated debate. Those advocating nothing be done to hinder the enemy lest they raze the town were well outvoted after wise Elder Han pointed out that just a few years earlier the Japanese sometimes burnt towns whether resisted or not, and that the absolute priority was to give the citizens as much time as possible to get into the forests and hills to hide.

'What'll happen to me if they catch us?' one of the younger boys cried out to his father the furniture maker, just after the large Wu family had managed to get through the congested Great Gate and were in the clearing heading into the woods, to take a track leading to hills. He watched his parents look at each other in fear, and felt his mother's hand pushing him in the back to keep going. His father gave him no reply. Nor did his sister, fifteen-year-old Ashenga, when he repeated his question, though he saw how scared she looked.

Ten interchanging soldiers, left by the general to guard his family under the lieutenant, carried Madame Huang in a single sedan chair for the nearly five hours it took the small group to reach the pre-determined village in the hills, hours that included frequent stops. Sometimes she held the six-weeks-old baby in her arms, sometimes it lay beside her. The lady had to be carried because she could not have walked quickly or far enough with her severely shortened feet. She knew that some of the bearers wanted to be with their families, but she had made them promise to remain with her in such an emergency, under threat of severe punishment from her husband on his eventual return.

Huihua had completely recovered from the trial of the birth and walked the whole way, unwilling to ask some of the soldiers to bring a second chair. She had released her maid Yiying to run to her own family, but Dajuan was also with them, having refused to leave the lady's side. Although Huihua had dearly wanted to see Ajin and Peony before fleeing - they were the only horses left by her father when the corps had departed - she had at once realized the correctness of her mother's urgent statement to think only of the baby, and she knew that Head Groom would get them away into hiding as previously arranged.

In Amoy, Yuling very quickly realized that the major offensive so long rumoured had begun, many planes flying over as he made his way on foot to the school. There seemed to be fewer people in the streets and buses. Fellow Chinese huddled in twos and threes looking concerned, hardly talking. Rickshaws that passed, usually with Japanese passengers, were far fewer than normal.

He turned a corner at a closed day market just as an open truck of Japanese soldiers hooted and passed in front. Quickly he stopped and bowed his head. Several more came behind the first, and he waited until the last truck had gone well past before looking up, not wanting to risk a casual bullet for perceived insubordination.

'Devils! They'll take more, they'll spill more blood,' an elderly man with a long grey beard said in his direction, standing outside a fish shop holding a mop.

When he went into the school gate and saw the Head Teacher - a benign man he had come to like - standing under the Japanese flag and looking pensive, he asked him: 'Do you know what your military are doing?' After a year at the school, he felt able to talk reasonably freely to his foreign employer.

'I have no idea,' came back the reply without a look towards him.

The air was still, the flag motionless.

As soon as school finished and his art-room was clean, he went straight to the southern bamboo groves near the outskirts of the city, and sought the address he'd memorized; it was a shabby little eating place, closed for the afternoon or because of the military situation. He'd been careful to check that he'd not been followed, and sometimes had stopped to observe people; collaborators abounded.

'We're closed,' a middle-aged woman called out from a decrepit chair as he was about to press a bell.

'I'm trying to find a man called Chang, is he here?'

The woman looked hard at him, then said: 'See that lane,' she indicated with her head, 'walk up and down, and in about twenty minutes he might come to you. If he doesn't, come back when we open at five, if we open.'

An hour later he was sitting at a table with three men. One was the scruffy man now identifying himself as Chang. He was in his late thirties and had brought Yuling to whatever building he was in - he'd had to look down all the way and had no idea what streets they had passed along. The second man was a crisp intellectual-looking man with glasses, somewhat younger, and the third a very small fellow of indeterminate age, with bulging eyes and shaved head.

He learnt at once that they knew no more than he did what the enemy intended, though the one with glasses said he suspected they could be aiming to capture the airfields in western China that the Americans were using.

He asked them if they had any news about Mingon or Tuxieng, but they said they did not.

They told him they wanted him to listen to enemy broadcasts, and to translate whatever enemy papers they gave him. When he asked where he would be working, they said they lived there together, and that one of them, they would not yet say which one, was the leader and that discipline had to be strictly kept; what the leader said went.

'Am I going to be asked to take part in anything active?' he asked. 'I can handle guns if I have to.'

'That's not likely,' the little bald one replied, 'I need you below.'

'Your code name will be heron,' Chang said, 'we all have code names, and although we know who you are, you will never know our real names.'

'And there's a problem,' the crisp one with glasses said, 'you're unusually big, you'll stand out. We'll have to be specially careful with you and can't let you outside. You must agree to this or we can't have you.'

Yuling did not like that idea but saw the sense. 'I haven't seen my girl for a few months, and she's had our baby daughter some weeks ago. I'm going to leave the school any day now and try to make it out on my own to see them, and then I'll join you in about four weeks.'

'Crazy,' Chang said, 'anyone out after nine is shot, you know that, never been tighter, don't do it, not right now.'

'Two us have families inland,' the one with glasses said, 'we can't go to them either, far too dangerous. If our loved ones hear that the enemy is getting near they'll flee. There'll be others to help your lady friend, specially seeing who she is. All we can do is hope they get away safely.'

'We won't let you try to see them until *we* say so,' Chang said. 'This is another condition. If you left us even for a short time and got captured, it puts us in big danger, you know roughly where we are.'

The one with glasses seemed to sneer. 'Doesn't it concern you that we're Whites?'

'Why do you ask?' he answered suspiciously.

'We've been told you don't like us, though you're not a full-blooded Red like your brother.' The man sniggered.

'What do you know about my brother?'

'He went to the Reds, nothing more.'

'Do you know where he is? Do you know if he's still alive?' Yuling didn't expect much of an answer but had to ask.

The man shrugged and said nothing.

Yuling had already summed them up; he didn't like the idea of being with them, but given his decision to help the Resistance, and knowing the Nationalist underground was the most active in the eastern cities, he felt it would be a start.

'Come with me,' the little bald man said. He was taken down through a trapdoor and into a cellar, where radio equipment stood on a table. Earphones were put on him, and the man began turning a knob. Very soon he was surprised to hear a Japanese broadcasting station, and began listening closely.

For the next few days he continued going to the school, growing angrier by the day at every piece of military news made public. He read the Japanese newspapers that reached Amoy, and felt crushed; they trumpeted the advances already being made further inland. And he realized he could not risk trying to smuggle through the occupied zone to reach Mingon. What he did not know was that the town and Wuyi Court had already been evacuated, that Huihua and the baby were in the hills.

On the fifth day after meeting with the underground cell, he felt afraid and emotional at the close of the school day, and hoped no one would notice. He bowed a last time to the children, received their usual ones back, and gave his deeper bows to the women teachers and the Head Teacher, as he always had.

'Anything wrong?' the woman asked him who recently had been trying to flirt more and more. She had just run up as he was through the school gate. (The previous day, alone with him in the art room, she had suddenly run her hand along his forearm, and he had had to ask her please not to do that; she had then opened the top button of her dress that was already quite low, and he had fled the room). 'Come with me to my flat, we're friends,' she was smiling invitingly, 'you can confide in me, come Tsai Yuling, it's not far.' But he was already on his way to do what he had to do, gave her a firm 'I'm alright' and turned, walking on faster, soon extremely relieved when she did not pursue him along the pavement, though he wondered if she might ask for him at his accommodation because the school knew his address.

Light rain was falling in the middle of the afternoon when he opened the side door to the house where he rented a room; he was going out a last time.

'What have you in your sack, you'll get wet,' the landlord called down the stairs. 'And make sure you're in by eight thirty for safety.'

'Will do,' he called back about to shut the door, 'hope to sell a few things at the evening market, if it's open that is.' He didn't wait for any further remark telling him it would not be.

The note he'd left under his pillow rather than on the table was addressed to the Head Teacher:

> In view of this further invasion into the heart of my country and the certain loss of life and misery for our soldiers and civilians, I can no longer continue to work at the school. I thank you and the staff and the children for the courtesy that has been shown me. Tsai Yuling.

The lady's group stayed nearly three weeks in the hills, in various peasant dwellings and in tents that some of the soldiers had carried on their backs. And when a runner came in the evening with news that the enemy had not in fact gone near Mingon but had been advancing through provinces further north, everyone felt very relieved, and the group prepared to make the return journey the following day.

News soon came to Yuling - now working with his three underground companions - that Mingon and Tuxieng were not attacked or in the line of advances, and he also breathed sighs of relief. It seemed to soothe much of his concern at the lack of any knowledge about Huihua and the child; he felt she must be alright, knowing the inner strength she possessed. If something terrible had happened to her, someone would surely have got a message to him;

except that no one but his companions, and presumably someone higher up in the military to whom the cell supplied information, knew what he was doing and where they were. Neither Huihua nor his own mother and stepfather knew that he had joined the Resistance; he had deliberately kept it from them.

Weeks passed, during which he was aware from the military situation and the tighter border areas that it would still be too risky to try to make it out of the Amoy zone to Huihua.

The leader of the cell, the intellectual bespectacled man, seemed unbending and had curtness in manner he thoroughly disliked. When Yuling challenged him that he must be a Special Forces officer and could without much difficulty get a message to Huihua at the mansion and retrieve her reply, the man said coolly across the table: 'All family and emotional ties have to be put firmly aside for the foreseeable future, you will do as I say.' This made Yuling angry, and he leant over and grabbed the man's collar. 'You get her a message from me or I'll leave,' he shouted. 'You can't,' the man said, seemingly without emotion with his collar still held. 'We'd have to shoot you. Orders.' Yuling was so incensed he hit him hard on the chin with the back of his hand, making the man fall off his stool, the glasses also falling; and a worse scene was only prevented by the other two holding him, the scruffy man called Chang telling him to calm down, that they would try to think of some way to get his message through.

A day later he received the leader's assurance that a coded radio message had been sent to Wuyi Court. The man said: 'Your lady friend could now know you left the school and are working elsewhere and that you'll try to see her when security allows.' He added: 'She can't get messages to you, it is not possible for her to use military equipment for personal purposes.' Yuling did not like the 'could' word, but this was war, he had to accept the situation.

*

The weeks passed into months, and whenever and wherever the enemy made fresh pushes, they seemed to triumph despite the fighting, so that further large areas of central and southern China were occupied.

Yuling found his life unpleasant and lonely. He missed the settled life of the school, and thought about particular children he liked; and he missed the fun and creativity in the classroom.

He was not allowed to leave the building. The others did, and for his own safety they refused to talk about what they were doing. But it was obvious they were not passive in the Resistance as he was; sometimes they came back exhausted, dirty and strained, the little bald one throwing down one of his numerous wigs of disguise.

When Yuling told them that their activities were a bigger danger to him -

their coming back to the building - than he going occasionally outside and into Amoy would be to them, they still required him to remain hidden. 'Out of the question,' Chang said, 'the police will soon spot you, they'll continue to look out for you, the place is swarming with agents and collaborators.'

He thought all the time about Huihua, and longed to see his daughter and to know what name had been given her. Again and again he turned over in his mind all the precious moments he'd had with his fun-loving, fast-running poetess. In the nights, many nights, he was back with her at the Hut, devouring her, being in her arms, blanking out the horrible intrusion of the two men and his own brother. And during the day, if he wasn't working but dozing, he would put her on top of him and order her to kiss him very slowly, never to stop...

Many times he thought of defying the three men, getting away when they were not there; only for a short period, he would leave a message that he'd return. This was particularly tempting when they were on one of their activities, their 'missions' as they called them. But he knew his work was appreciated, they kept assuring him of that. And a fourth man smuggled into the building for a day had been much more open, had told him that a number of the enemy documents he had translated had given invaluable information to the military, that the usefulness of '...our best operatives in Amoy...' had been noticed at Allied HQ.

Sometimes he thought about Huihua's implacable parents. Should he have taken the suggestion of a commission and joined the army (away from the general's corps naturally, as he could never have served under the Slayer of the Reds)? It might have made them change their minds about him, once they'd seen him in uniform. But whether such a meeting with the father could ever have happened, now that the man and corps were much further west, seemed to him very unlikely.

Occasionally he turned over in his mind the shocking event with his brother below the ravine. He wondered where Ayi was, picturing him somewhere in mountains with the Communists, possibly fighting the Japanese in the lower hills and valleys. In his stepfather's garden he had tried to play down Ayi's huge fear. But now, well over a year later, he understood that fear, and part of him admired his brother's idealism. He wished he could make up with him, fearing he might never see him again.

And he thought about his mother and stepfather, longed also to see them, though his guilt towards his mother remained - his falling in love with Huihua had precipitated Ayi's flight. When he had quickly visited them after exposing Wang, and had told them Huihua was three months carrying their child, his mother had looked at him in shock and shaken her head saying she was totally lost for words.

As to his job, often he was translating from documents taken by force or stealth. Every day he had to listen to Japanese broadcasts, for short spells only to avoid detection. The picture of what the enemy intended had soon become clear, the earlier guesses correct: to seize the western airfields, to prevent bombing of their homeland islands from China, and to link up with Japanese forces in Indo-China.

Then one day he picked up a transmission that ...*our ever victorious Imperial Army is engaged in a glorious battle, certain of early victory against Nationalist forces under the command of General Huang Mingchang. The Chinese are surrounded, holed up with tens of thousands of troops, surrender sure to come in a matter of days...*

A week went by, then another, and still the broadcasts remained the same, and it became clear to Yuling and his companions that the Chinese were fiercely resisting.

*

The bombers came without warning almost as soon as the sun had risen, no sirens sounding over Wuyi Court or in Mingon; observation posts had been taken out.

Huihua and her eight-month-old daughter were in the basement of the Officers Building at the corner of the inner courtyard, seventy paces or so from the mansion, the old dwelling that once, not so long ago, housed her warlord grandfather's very young concubines. She had been up three times in the night to comfort her teething girl; deep in sleep, she never heard the drone of the planes.

The first colossal explosion woke her to a terrible fright so that she nearly screamed as she fell from the bed. A broad candle on the table was still burning, its flame now wavering. She picked herself up, but such were the wall vibrations that her first thought was that the building was collapsing on them. She hardly had time to touch the child when another bomb exploded shattering her thoughts, though she realized it was very near and if they were not crushed they could be burnt alive. She tried to cover the girl's ears, her own feeling horrible.

Her daughter began crying out. She picked her up just as her mother rushed into the room in nightdress, her hair long.

Then a third exploded, shutting out their cries.

They huddled in a corner and waited. They could do nothing else, Huihua remembering Yuling's comfort at the bottom of the stairwell, now dreadfully missing his arms. She felt again that panic, but was able to control it holding the little one's head against her breasts.

Shanghan's portrait had crashed to the floor and was lying against the bed

410

end, one corner of the frame completely broken off. An armorial china water jug and two glasses had also fallen from the table, pieces scattered across the floor.

Dajuan called from outside the room; she and Yiying had hurriedly dressed and come down to the basement. The lady went out to the maids.

Two minutes later Dajuan unbarred the ground floor door to the courtyard, and she, Madame Huang and Huihua were staring at the horror: through the palms and the cypress trees, some of which were fiercely burning, fire and smoke belched out of the middle and right side of the mansion, including through two of the Reception Hall windows and the sweeping roof on that side. Many of the front wooden columns were either burning or had disappeared altogether, as had most of the large old lanterns.

Another conflagration came from the direction of the gardens, its light catching the higher parts of the walls of the courtyard to their right. And they could hear though not see a third conflagration coming from somewhere behind them, probably in the outer courtyard.

Two guards stood on a side path gaping at the burning spectacle, and as the lady was about to go to them - she had wrapped a coat round herself - Lieutenant Xi came running up just as he had months earlier, and she fully expected him to tell them again that they had to flee to the hills, that the dreaded Japanese were close.

'My lady, you must come with us to the woods right away in case there's more bombing.'

'Are troops coming?'

'We don't think so.'

'Then we must try to put out the flames.'

The young officer turned towards the building and back, shaking his head. 'It's not possible. Please come with me for your safety.' He looked pleadingly to Huihua, who had left the little one with Yiying and had quickly put on worker clothes and sandals. 'There's nothing we can do, the fire's too great. Please,' he repeated to the lady.

Huihua took a couple of steps along the path, her eyes now in the direction of the gardens. She heard her mother say 'This is revenge isn't it, for my husband's stand?' Then she was off, running through the nearer trees that were not burning, running towards the right side courtyard walls that led to the gate into the first part of the gardens. Her mother was calling out to her, and she shouted back that she would follow them to the woods; she'd known at once that nothing could be done to save their home.

As she drew close to the gate into the gardens, she began to feel the heat of the blaze. Racing through the first garden but as far away as she could from the burning mansion, she had just reached the top of the little bridge over the lily ponds when she let out a cry of fear, seeing vast plumes of black smoke coming from the area of the stables and the granary.

She came through the opening from the second garden into the stable yard, and the sight and noise were sickening: the granary at the far end seemed untouched, but part of the stables, the important part, had collapsed, its far end burning beside a huge crater in the ground; masonry and wood covered much of the rest of the yard; and at the rim of the crater stood the figure of Head Groom, head in hands.

She didn't see the revolver at his feet, or wait to call him, but began clambering over a stable door that had fallen outwards and was lying at an awkward angle on top of debris.

A pitiful part whinny came to her ears just as she caught the shocking sight of Peony's dark hindquarters; they were separated from the rest of the body, body she could not see, and there was much blood. She realized Ajin must still be alive in his stall under the collapsed roof. A blaze burned from two flattened stalls further on.

She scrambled over the rubble calling his name, and came to a mound of beams and masonry covering what she knew was her horse trapped on his side. At first she was even unsure where the head lay. But very soon, after nastily splintering herself in a hand as she pulled away pieces of wood, she found the muzzle and tore at tiles and rubble, shouting to Head Groom to help her, as eventually she exposed the head up to the forelock and an ear.

She was half kneeling, panting, could tell the horse was in shock and going to die - the eye had an unworldly look, it did not move, did not acknowledge her.

She shouted again, not realizing the man was trying to reach her, his gun in hand. 'Please leave him, Mistress,' she caught over the sound of burning timber. She was stroking the horse's cheek, tears now coursing down her face. A woman's agitated voice was shouting for her. 'Head Groom, where is she?' 'Xuiey, over here, over here!' he was calling back.

A few seconds later the old cook stood in the rubble of the yard, her chest heaving. 'Mistress …Mistress Hua …got to hurry …got to go pet at once … case they come back…'

Huihua tried to stand but had to catch her balance on a fallen beam, the splintered hand sharply hurting. She turned and began scrambling towards her beloved servant. 'Please go, for the little one's sake,' she heard Head Groom say as she took his outstretched hand, seeing his distress and noticing for the first time the handgun as he helped her over the ruins.

She said nothing. The cook put an arm round her and pulled her away.

Well before they reached the water garden they heard a shot. Half way through the next garden a second shot rang out to pierce the loud crackling of the burning mansion.

26

The Japanese general sat hunched at a collapsible table in a large military tent outside the city his troops had finally taken at heavy cost. He was weary and very angry, his only consolation a feeling of gratification to have just received from High Command their confirmation that the Chinese general standing before him, who had caused them so much trouble and loss of life, should forfeit his own.

'I gave you not one but two opportunities to stop the fighting,' he shouted to the prisoner who stood between soldiers, a Japanese translator from Manchukuo trying to keep up. 'I told you, and we wrote it in Chinese, that you could save thousands of men on both sides. Why didn't you accept my offer, why?'

Huang stood straight. He listened to the translation but kept his eyes firmly on the victor. 'Tell General Toyamo that the Chinese army will never surrender to a nation that invades our country and tries to colonize us and control the rest of Asia. Tell him we curse his nation for the misery it has brought us. Tell him your countrymen are arrogant foreign dogs who have no right...'

The translator reached the curse. 'Shut up! Shut up!' screamed the Japanese general, leaping up and grabbing a baton, running round the table and thrashing the stick across the Chinaman's face.

Huang's head jerked to the side as he gritted his teeth against the shocking sting. He stared back at the man, tried to remain still, and thought that his nose could be broken though no blood had yet fallen.

The victor's eyes blazed. He walked back to the table, threw down the baton and picked up the message. 'You will die,' he cried, flapping the paper towards Huang, 'you will die by your own hand or by ours.'

Huang listened to the translator.

A Japanese officer spoke briskly to his general. General Toyamo huffed and saw another piece of paper, then turned to his unrepentant, abusive opponent, voice trembling: 'You will answer my Major's questions.' He sat down and looked at his officer. 'Don't take any nonsense from him Umizu.'

The major went up to Huang. 'We had an agent who was your private secretary, his name was Wang. Did you shoot him?'

Huang listened to the translation, and was surprised at the question, wondering where it could lead. 'Yes.'

'How did you find out about him?'

Why were they wanting to know about Wang? He was utterly exhausted, shattered at the defeat, and his face continued mightily to sting. He found it hard to recall. 'My officers discovered transmitting equipment.'

'What made them look?'

The shock came back to him of the moment in the cell, when the Tsai student told him and Ma that they had a spy at the Court and that it was likely to be Wang. He hesitated. 'My orders, communiques, they were taking a long time to reach my staff. They searched his office, I was away at the time.'

'Were you tipped off?'

After hearing the translation, he did not reply because he was not going to make it easy for them, was not going to give him away; the student had been trying to help the cause, he was Chinese.

'Answer my Major!' General Toyamo shouted again, banging his fist on the collapsible table; it shook so much that a rolled-up map fell off the front as the translator was giving the order to answer.

Huang opened his eyes at his opposite number, but remained silent.

The major came close. 'Who is Tsai Yuling?'

So they were onto him. He might be forced to admit the fellow's part. 'Tsai? A student or an artist, teacher, one of those.'

'He's your daughter's lover, isn't he? She's had his baby, no?'

The translator was doing his best to keep up.

'He was her lover, against my order. I trust he's gone away.'

'He tipped you off, didn't he? How did he know about Wang?'

When Huang heard the last question, he remembered that Hua and Tsai had been caught by the basement door during the air attack, and a professor somehow came into it, but it was all a jumble in his mind and long ago an irrelevance, he'd wanted the Wang catastrophe well and truly buried ...with the traitor. He looked at the major, unsure what to answer.

The officer took a step back and shouted something in Japanese. As he did so, Huang recalled that the student had painted Colonel Hijiya who had given something away.

Behind him, soldiers were pushing three battle-weary Chinese into the tent, their hands bound in front. Huang heard people entering, but did not look round.

General Toyamo thought the wretches had clearly been fighting for weeks due to his opponent's criminal obstinacy; one soldier seemed only a lad. He looked back to the man he despised.

The major asked: 'Are these men from your own corps?'

Huang heard the translation and turned, to his horror seeing Shanghan in the middle in torn battledress and looking dreadful, very dark around the eyes. But at least he was still alive. He hadn't seen his son for perhaps twelve days despite the frequent visits he'd made round the city to keep the units fighting. One of the other men, a corporal, he also knew. 'Yes,' he replied.

'What are their names?'

'He is Yen,' he said pointing to the corporal who stood on Shanghan's right. 'I don't know the other two.' His son was avoiding eye contact. As the translation proceeded, Huang turned back to face the major. 'I can't be expected to know all four thousand in my corps.'

'There were four thousand!' General Toyamo screamed in outrage after the translation. 'And how many men on both sides have you allowed to be killed in this futile siege? Ten times that number!'

The translator looked at the major and thought he wasn't meant to translate that outburst. Huang had no idea what had been shouted.

'We are going to shoot these men,' the major continued, 'and then three more every five minutes if you don't answer my question. Now, I ask you again, how did Tsai Yuling know about Wang?'

*

Yuling heard of the death of Huihua's father while listening to a Japanese broadcast proclaiming the end of the siege, the male broadcaster adding that General Huang Mingchang had been required to take his own life. He was shocked, thought of Huihua and her mother at Wuyi Court who might not have heard the news, and desperately hoped that Huang Shanghan, the impressive younger brother, had survived.

It galvanized him. He'd had enough being cooped up for too many months. When he gave his companions the news and said he had to go to Mingon and the cell leader refused, another scene developed. They were in the basement listening room. He shouted that they would have to kill or cripple him to stop him. The leader became equally agitated, telling him he would be putting their lives in danger if seen in the street. But Yuling told them that he was only asking for four weeks, that the war was bound to go on for a long time, and his mind was made up, he would be leaving that afternoon to get out of Amoy well before the night curfew. He shouted into their faces that if they resisted him, they would have to shoot him, and if they doubted his resolve, they were to think how he gained the Generalissimo's personal medal. Not even the leader spoke at that point. He continued that once out of the city, he would lie low until nightfall, and then make his way between the fortified outposts and pill-boxes, though it would take him a day or more to reach the border zone and smuggle himself through; it was difficult but achievable, resistance fighters and others did it.

In the end it was agreed he would be blindfolded and taken in a vegetable cart as far away from their building as possible.

With relief at their agreement, he told them that the last time he was blindfolded, he'd been given a Japanese limousine on his way to paint the air colonel. But they did not see amusement in the remark, and they made him agree where and when he would be met on his return. If for some reason the rendezvous failed, he had to present himself to the priests at the shrine in the middle of the bamboo groves, and would be collected.

Elsewhere in Amoy, a man with narrow eyes was raging, for the first time was feeling defeated, revenge of the nastiest kind on his mind; he'd been deceived by an inferior, an artful Chinese. He now thought it likely the tall teacher might all along have been working for the underground, despite their watching him until he had disappeared. When he was caught - unless he'd left the zone and gone far away - his end would be very unpleasant.

And the intelligence officer was angry with the Chinese official, and with the woman agent at the school, and with the Head Teacher; they had failed him badly, should have spotted the man's duplicity.

He looked at his notes of the three interviews. He saw his handwritten summary of the first ...*seems upright young man, should give us no trouble ... artist and teacher, ok for school job ...possibly useful to us in some way, consider later...*

He turned to the third interview....*am surprised, good info' gathered by Chinaman Tsai, threat paid off ...Wang caught as too slow in delivering General Huang's orders...* Yet at that interview, in his own intelligence building, he'd been spun a great yarn: the teacher had said brazenly to his face that he couldn't believe it when told at the mansion that Wang was a spy. And he, an intelligence officer - well trained, experienced, very astute - had fallen for it. He, who had been expecting promotion to the top position in Intelligence in their east coast sector, had been severely reprimanded for being too free with information to Colonel Hijiya, and for letting himself be hoodwinked by a mere art teacher of children.

As the ash of his cigarette grew long in the tray, the intelligence officer studied more carefully the second interview. He could see his wretched errors of judgement: he had thought too much about the death order, about Tsai never daring to go back to Mingon, and about the lovers in their June elopement at their love nest in the hills. And the man had said he was terrified of being assassinated by the Whites if the general's daughter absconded a second time.

That so-called illness of the mother! He hadn't checked up on it - a disaster. In that second interview he should have trusted to his instinct that all was not what it seemed. One moment there was a death order on the teacher, then he went to visit an ill mother and said he could never return to Mingon, and then Wang's reports stopped coming, and lo and behold the parents who hated him wanted to talk about a baby and the future.

'Why is Wang of interest to you?' the fox had asked him. Oh the man had made him look a fool! His colleagues in Intelligence were distinctly less respectful, and it hurt badly. He had written ...*Think he tells us the truth, but not sure, await results....* His chief had scribbled an angry wavy red line through those words.

A few days later, the intelligence officer was fuming even more. After the teacher's note had been found under the pillow, he had guessed there was more than a reasonable chance he'd gone to his lover and child, that he wasn't hiding somewhere in the city. But now, with the information that came through after the general's capture, his request for a commando raid on the ruined mansion or on Mingon itself, to capture the teacher or his lover if he wasn't there, had been turned down ...*Of no further relevance, not the resources, all available forces are engaged or must be kept strictly for military purposes...*

Once more he railed against the army air colonel - it was the airman's desire to have his portrait painted that had led to this disastrous situation, vain, naïve man!

Alone in his office, he stamped the floor in impotent fury.

*

Yuling walked through Mingon's great bastion gate on a warm late afternoon four days after leaving the underground cell, pausing at the special alley recalling the first incredible kissing of Huihua between the small palm and the house shrine after he'd swept her off her beautiful bare feet. But there seemed fewer people in the town, there was no usual bustle; an atmosphere of gloom pervaded and he knew why - the men of the Huang corps had been in the fighting.

Soon he was standing in the Wu family backyard receiving attention from the boys, and more shyly from Ashenga who he thought had grown into a fine-looking girl. But the furniture maker and his wife seemed worried at his sudden appearance, even though they knew that the death order had been lifted.

'Should you be here?' Mr Wu said. 'You won't be staying long will you?'

'You've heard about the General?' Yuling asked without answering the concern. He didn't mention that the Japanese broadcast had said Huang had committed suicide, as Ashenga and the boys were around him, the youngest, now six, playing with his fingers. The furniture maker nodded. 'I didn't want to have to break it to Huihua and her mother,' Yuling added, catching a strange look Mrs Wu was giving him; a hand had gone to her mouth, and he wondered if they had more bad news, suddenly fearing for Huihua and the child he was hoping to see for the first time in the very next hour.

'The son's also dead,' Mr Wu said.

'Dead!' Yuling felt a terrible wound to the heart; he'd realized Shanghan would likely have been caught in the siege, but had hoped...

'He's not on the list of survivors, it's just come through, they're far away in a camp. We're all mourning, we've lost half our able-bodied men.'

'Awful blows for such a family,' Mrs Wu said. 'What will the ladies do without their men and the Court burnt down?'

Yuling's mind was already reeling at the news of Huihua's brother, and this further news about the mansion made him open-mouthed, speechless.

The boy playing with his fingers said: 'I heard the bombs, they woke me up, they were great bangs.'

'You didn't know then?' the furniture maker added. 'It was bombed three weeks ago, everyone's alright except Head Groom, he couldn't take it, the horses...'

'Aunt Xuiey is heartbroken,' his wife added.

There was a silence, Yuling breathing inner sighs of relief that Huihua and the child were not injured or worse, and trying to imagine the horror they must have gone through. He realized at once that the bombing would have been reprisal for the general's staunch resistance against the further phase in the offensive.

He looked at Ashenga; the girl was biting her lip. He was now more than ever glad he'd made the journey, that he'd been insistent with his cell companions. 'Where are they living? Have you seen my daughter?' he asked Mrs Wu.

A faint smile came into the woman's face, but Ashenga spoke first. 'She's sweet, the Mistress has brought her here three times, the last time was a few weeks ago.' Mrs Wu added: 'They're all in the Officers Building.' 'She's wonderful,' the girl went on, 'she's got thick hair already. Do you know her name?' Mrs Wu jumped in: 'That's for the Mistress to tell Yuling.'

'But of course I want to know her name, tell me at once Ashenga.' He looked into an eager face that struck him as a brilliant pose for the portrait of a girl on the threshold of womanhood.

'Jia,' she replied eyes wide at him.
'Jia,' he repeated in wonder at her, 'Jia.'

He took the quicker road route to the Court, as Mrs Wu told him that planes no longer flew low or strafed, and he knew why - the Japanese were fighting in various operations of war far removed from Mingon. He ran most of the way in the evening light.

As he came towards the dark red walls of the outer courtyard, he was astonished to see that the first of the great lions on the left of the gates had completely broken in two, its fierce head lying nose-down in the ground, the winged torso heavily pockmarked and blackened from explosion.

Even more surprising was the state of the main gates when he reached them; the once awesome wooden and metal gates were hardly recognizable, parts charred, parts blown outwards, pieces of thick wood jutting at different angles, strips of metal twisted. The wall nearest the broken statue had completely collapsed outwards exposing a crater where the Guard House had stood. And through the gaping hole he could see two banyan trees had broken and been burnt; one had collapsed against the left walls. On the right side of the gates the front wall still stood.

No repairs, not even temporary, seemed to have been attempted at the gates. Anyone, he thought, could walk into the mess of the first part of the outer courtyard. And so he did.

An elderly soldier dozed on a stool under a makeshift wooden canopy in front of the crater, a bayoneted rifle between his legs. Well before reaching him, Yuling kicked away some rubble to wake the fellow. 'I'm a friend of the Mistress,' he said quickly as the man fumbled with the gun and stood up, challenging him pathetically, 'friend of Huang Huihua, I'm not armed, don't point that thing at me.' He looked around him. 'This is terrible.' He guessed the man had been left behind as too old or quality too poor to fight. The rifle was still pointing his way. 'Please get a message to Mistress Huihua that her friend Buzzard is here at the main gates, she'll understand.'

'Buzzard! That's no name! Madame and Mistress are grieving, General and son are dead, they'll not want to see you.'

'I know the news. She'll definitely want to see me, I'm her friend I tell you, I've come from Amoy, I can comfort her...' He stopped himself, thought better than to add that he was the father of the child. He hoped Huihua would come, worried that if she was not in the Officers Building, was perhaps doing something with their child elsewhere in an undamaged part of the grounds, her mother might receive the message and guess who it was or ask for further information, and might order him away.

The old soldier looked him up and down, placed the rifle on the stool, took up a small gong and banged three times.

Soon Yuling could see another soldier coming slowly through the courtyard; he was well into middle age. When the man reached them and Yuling repeated his message, the soldier turned without comment and went back, none too fast he thought; there was a feeling of resignation and depression in the mood of the two men.

A few agonizingly slow minutes passed before he spotted Huihua, his heart leaping up although he could see she was in black. She had come through the wall door between the two courtyards, and was talking to a guard and looking his way; but she wasn't waving.

As she came down the steps and began walking along the side path, he could tell that her mood mirrored that of the men. 'I'm going to her,' he said to the old soldier, and began walking away, hoping he wouldn't be challenged again, not with Huihua coming towards them.

They met near the middle of the courtyard. She gave him a gentle smile and bowed, and he saw the sadness in her eyes. He opened his arms to her, wanting to embrace her, guards looking on or not. But she did not come into them; instead she looked to the ground, and he felt an intruder into her grief, wondering if her sorrow, or even his long absence perhaps, might have made her have different feelings towards him despite the child. His arms went back to his sides.

'It's wonderful you've come,' she said, still looking half down, 'you don't know how much this means to me.'

She had answered his doubts, and he longed to hug her, to comfort her. As she looked up, he said: 'I heard the news in Amoy, your father was a very brave man.' Yuling couldn't bring himself to mention the brother; he was choked by the news.

She knew what he was thinking. 'We've lost Shanghan,' her expression was pitiful, 'my handsome brother, so much promise, so much to live for. He wasn't on the prisoner list, and the casualties were huge, no one escaped the siege. I've cried so much I don't think I've got much more.' She paused. 'Major Ma's dead.' Yuling's head dropped, himself now feeling tearful. 'He was killed near the beginning, he was such a good man. I feel really broken at the moment, but now you're here...'

She came a little nearer and smiled up at him. And the next moment she was resting her head against his chest and he was putting his arms round her and gently holding her head, his eyes closing to hold back the wet forcing its way.

They stayed like that for a short time, but he was not swaying her.

When she pulled back, some of her sadness seemed to have gone, and he guessed she was reading his mind again. She said softly: 'Come and meet your daughter, she'll be going to bed soon.' A thrill ran through him.

As they began walking towards the inner courtyard, he felt her arm come into his. 'How long can you stay?'

'Three and a half weeks, then I must return.' He saw her surprise and knew she was pleased.

Huihua was already feeling an uplift of spirits - twenty four days or so, watching him getting to know his daughter, it would hugely help her deal with the twin tragedies. They walked up the steps towards the middle-aged guard. 'This is my man, Tsai Yuling, Jia's father,' she said, Yuling now the one to be surprised at her openness and the greater strength in her voice. Huihua took a sideways look at him, catching the anticipation in his eyes, thinking he was hearing the name for the first time.

She led him towards the Officers Building, and he saw more of the disastrous effect of the bombing. Very little of the mansion's lovely red columns, lanterns and roofs were to be seen, just two columns surviving on the left side. The middle part of the mansion, including the side facing the gardens, was burnt to the ground, leaving only blackened parts of the front walls. The left side of the building still stood, though it looked dark, and its roof too had partly fallen in. The Reception Hall and its murals were no more; Yuling thought about them, knew he could closely reproduce them if ever given the opportunity there or elsewhere; they were stored in his memory, right down to the birds in each painting. The top part of the marble steps looked badly damaged and were missing their cones. Rubble stretched well into the inner courtyard. A number of the trees nearer the ruins had been severely burnt, some no more than stumps, others leaning precariously.

'My mother's not receiving callers since we heard the news three days ago. Elder Han and his wife came yesterday morning with others, but she was too upset to see them.' His hand felt her squeeze. 'Don't worry if she doesn't want to see you.'

'How did you learn about your father?' he asked as they came to the door of the Officers Building.

'Xi has radio contact with Chongqing in code. You don't know him, he's rather a weak officer, and he's only got ten men to guard us. He had to radio back to get them to answer his direct question about it, as he couldn't believe their first message, and then he came to us. He was shaking poor man, and I knew at once.'

The moment had arrived - Yuling's longing to see his child after all those months was about to be satisfied. But Huihua's sadness, the news that Shanghan must have died, the sight of the Huang home in ruins, and the awkwardness he felt of intruding - he of all people - into the grief of the antagonistic mother, these all put a dampener on his emotions, though they could not stop a tingling feeling of anticipation.

He followed Huihua down into a basement room, and when he saw his eight-month-old daughter for the first time - she was playing on the floor with the maid Yiying - wonder and pride swelled in him.

Huihua picked Jia up and handed her to him, telling her he was her father. He couldn't stop smiling as he held her and searched for likenesses, thinking of himself and Huihua and his own mother. But the little girl became agitated, and as he handed her back, Madame Huang entered the room. He turned and saw a distraught woman in black, and bowed.

She clasped her hands and inclined her head. 'You know our news?' Her voice seemed weak.

'Yes my lady, I heard it in Amoy four days ago'.

'Oh!' There was a short silence. 'How did you hear?'

'On a radio transmission. I listen to enemy broadcasts and make reports.' He paused. 'In my petition three years ago I called your husband a great patriot of Zhongguo, and now his name will be glorious in the history of Chinese resistance to foreigners.' He looked from the mother to Huihua.

'Will it?' The lady turned with dark eyes to the child. The innate authority that had previously so frightened Yuling seemed to have gone from her.

'Then you're not at the school any more?' Huihua asked in surprise.

Yuling was shocked. 'Didn't you get the message?' The cold bespectacled leader of the cell came to his mind; so the man had deceived him; well he'd have to settle scores when he returned. 'I left to become a translator,' he said which was partly true, hoping Huihua wouldn't press, but she was looking hard at him.

'Is the job dangerous?'

He pushed out his lips, frowned and shook his head, but felt he wasn't being believed. He wondered if to change the subject and mention also his terrible sorrow about Shanghan, but the lady looked too sad, and he said nothing more.

He thought of the hour; he would need to return to the town to find a hostel or inn, probably the one with the lanterns outside the South Gate, definitely not the one with the nasty innkeeper.

'I must be going, I need to...'

'You will be staying here,' Huihua got in quickly, 'our poor home is your home for as long as you are with us, there is room, and Yiying...' she turned to the maid, 'will make one of the upper rooms comfortable for you.'

The lady said nothing.

During a light meal prepared by the old cook, at which Yuling saw that Huihua's mother seemed only to peck, the lady turned to him. 'Your mother visited us a few weeks after Jia's arrival.'

'My mother!' he exclaimed, unable to hold back his surprise, aware his tone had been impolite.

'It was good,' she continued, 'Hua sent her a message. She was determined to see her grandchild, and you had fully recovered from the birth,' she said in Huihua's direction. 'It was not long after she left that we thought troops were coming our way and we had to flee into the hills.'

Yuling felt delight that his mother had been there, and was also pleased that the lady had used Huihua's shortened name to him.

'We got on very well,' Huihua said, recalling how Mrs Chen Tsai Wenlie had completely changed towards her, shown genuine warmth and concern, attentive to her health as well as to the baby's. And Huihua had quietly told her not to fall for any suggestion that the baby should go to Tuxieng or elsewhere.

She had found Yuling's mother still good-looking, and knew she was an excellent singer, actress and mimic. Huihua had come to like her; their confrontation at the cottage by the Zass River had been put behind them.

'She's utterly beautiful! I keep wanting to say Jia, Jia, Jia, all the time!' Yuling said, walking with Huihua arm in arm in the first darkness through the middle undamaged parts of the inner courtyard.

Huihua smiled up at him, still pinching herself that she was holding him. 'Yuling my strong man, your coming at this terrible time, it feels like a miracle to me, and I'm sure my mother feels some comfort. When you start doing all these tasks you're talking about, could you also mend Shanghan's portrait, the frame? I just feel that if we hang it up again, it gives us a tiny hope. And just seeing your lovely painting whole, it will help me, but leaving it as it is, it could make me despair more.'

The next morning Yuling asked grieving Madame Huang for permission to inspect the grounds. In Huihua's presence, he told her that he was surprised so much rubble had been left for so long in the two courtyards and outside the main gates, and that he thought '...as a mark of respect to your husband...' - again he did not mention Shanghan, he too did not want to accept the horror of his death - she should authorize him to organize a rebuilding of the area at the main gates, and a general clear-up operation, though not of the mansion itself, that was at present impossibly large. 'Security is all important,' he said, 'it can't wait any longer.' By which he meant (though he couldn't easily say it) that the works should not be delayed until after any funeral; he was very concerned for Huihua's and little Jia's safety, they were so exposed.

He made his inspection with timid Lieutenant Xi who seemed to him in very low spirits. He was shocked to find that the stables had not been touched, horse cadavers still visible that Huihua had warned him about. Much of the yard that had not gone down the bomb hole was deep in rubble, though luckily the yard's high walls and the stable gates were intact, the latter remaining strongly barred. Head Groom's body had been removed by his family within hours of his suicide; but otherwise the soldiers who had guarded the stable gates had cleared no more than a small path through the debris. As far as he could judge, only the two gardeners had attempted any serious clearing works near the burnt right side of the mansion that had collapsed into part of the gardens.

When they returned to the Officers Building, he asked the lieutenant to be with him as he spoke with Madame Huang, which he did just outside the door. He told her - thinking Huihua was in the basement with their daughter but unaware she was listening from the stairs - that the first priority was security against robbers or bandit groups who could return to the area to loot, the intact granary being especially at risk, he pointed out. The officer had ten soldiers, and until Chongqing ordered otherwise, they should remain to guard the ladies. He praised the lieutenant to the lady for billeting the men in the undamaged basement of the left side of the ruined mansion, so to be close, rather than at the military ghost-camp in the woods. And he asked for and received his permission to use the soldiers for the clearing and building works he had in mind, if they were not actually on duty.

The first job he suggested be tackled was the area of the main gates. He asked the lady whether she was able to pay for a dozen workmen, if they could be found after Mingon's losses, to be supervised by himself and Mr Wu the furniture maker. And he suggested that the soldiers should also receive payment while they worked on non-guarding tasks.

When she replied that she believed she could find the money, he outlined the tasks and rough timetable he had in mind. He said he had already spoken to the father and son gardeners, they were happy to do anything he asked; winter approached, so the gardens could look after themselves.

Huihua heard everything before tiptoeing back to her little girl. Despite her grief and despite her concern that Yuling's work in Amoy could be dangerous, there was pride in her heart - she had chosen the right man, and she would become his wife.

When her mother and Dajuan came down the stairs to spend time with them, she could tell straight away that her mother had perked up. Huihua had known for many months that her mother had abandoned any idea of adoption. Early on, Jia had worked her magic, and the visit of Yuling's mother had also greatly helped.

The procession and service for Huihua's father took place three days after Yuling's arrival, because Madame Huang had not been able to contemplate having it earlier. General Huang's body - though they did not know it - had been spat upon by many enemy soldiers including officers, before being flung into one of the pits for the Chinese fallen, such was Japanese anger at their own losses.

The noisy procession with funereal trumpets began on the road outside the shattered main gates, took the snaking path through the woods, went into the town through the Great Gate, and ended at the temple of the East Gate Monastery. While walking beside Huihua, Yuling knew that she and her mother were thinking not only of the general but of Shanghan. Afterwards he told Huihua that upwards of a thousand people had taken part, reflecting the anguish and grief of the citizens in their own losses.

Soon he sent a message home to Tuxieng, and shortly after the start of his second week at Wuyi Court, his mother and stepfather arrived. To see his mother and jovial Chennie enjoying themselves with Huihua and the child gave him enormous pleasure; it was the first time Huihua and his stepfather had met. The lady had begun her long period of mourning. There was little room left for the visitors in the Officers Building, so Huihua arranged for them to stay in Mingon with Elder Han and his family.

With Huihua present, Yuling talked to his mother about his brother Ayi, though no mention was made of him in front of the lady who, thankfully, did not ask. No word had come from Ayi for well over a year, since Yuling and Huihua had left him in the hills after the kidnap attempt. Now that it had been reported through non-occupied China that the general was dead, and now that Yuling was being accepted by Huihua's mother, he told himself there was no reason for his brother to be concerned about possible consequences of him and Huihua being together, a couple with their child. But he also knew that as his brother had joined either Red partisans or one of the Communist armies, Ayi would always be exposing himself to danger from capture by Nationalists.

Without the customary procession and without trumpets and drums, Yuling and Huihua were married at Elder Han's house by licence under wartime dispensation. It relieved and pleased Wenlie that the couple agreed first to have a temple service at the monastery. Apart from Wenlie and Doctor Chen, only the Han and Wu families and old cook Xuiey were present in the temple and at the Han house. Madame Huang declined to attend, saying the procession and service for her husband had taken too much out of her, she would help the maids look after the little one. But all the monks and novices were in their temple, surrounding the small group at the prayer stools before the multi-garlanded Buddha; they were duty-bound to honour and pray for the Huang family that had been munificent to them over the years, that now was in deep mourning; and they held a particular affection for the young artist who had tried to save the simpleton's life.

Huihua, out of respect to her mother, and because she herself mourned her father and brother, did not move into a bedroom with her husband, though they went on long evening walks together after Yuling's heavy work was done, walks that lasted into the early nights despite the growing cold.

And sometimes they did what most lovers do, though Huihua did not feel able to give all of herself.

And sometimes they carried Jia with them.

And once they went to the Wu family, when the little one wanted to be held only by Ashenga.

Just short of three weeks after Yuling and Mr Wu had first discussed what could be done, Shanghan's portrait was back on the basement wall, the ruined part of the front walls of the outer courtyard had been rebuilt, and the main gates had been repaired with new pieces of wood and metal. And while those major works had proceeded, Yuling helped the soldiers and the gardeners clear away the cadavers and debris in the stables area, though the two craters near the main gates and in the stable yard were left for later filling. Then they tackled the rubble and damaged trees in the outer courtyard, and entirely removed the severely damaged chimera statue, leaving the right side lion to roar on its own.

With just two days to go before Yuling had to make his way back to Amoy, Lieutenant Xi came to him while he was toiling with some of the soldiers cutting down the worst affected palms in the inner courtyard. 'I need to talk to you alone,' the officer said.

Hot and sweating, Yuling wondered what was coming as they walked beside a line of undamaged trees. He and Huihua had noticed that Xi had grown in stature, was more positive. Lieutenant Xi stopped. 'I didn't know you are in the underground.' Yuling looked at him in surprise but said nothing. 'You can't go back, not for a while, there are posters all over Amoy offering a reward for you, and if alive the reward is doubled. How did they get your photograph?'

Immediate fear came. Either the cell had been rumbled and his companions caught and made to talk, or the Japanese had discovered his involvement in exposing their agent Wang. 'They took my picture when giving me the school job. Do you know if my colleagues are alright? They haven't been taken?'

The officer shook his head. 'I've been given no more information, but the message says you mustn't go back for the time being, you'll be contacted here through me.'

'Please don't mention what you know to the Mistress,' Yuling said, not yet referring to Huihua as his wife.

Huihua was ecstatic to hear that Yuling had to remain longer with them, though she did not like it that he would not tell her the reason. He himself felt great relief, mixed with the pleasure of knowing that he could be longer with his new family, and he could continue the help at the Court where there was still much work to be done. But behind it all lay his fear.

He had decided that other men needed to be trained as guards, because Xi and his ten soldiers could be called away at any time leaving the family completely exposed. The officer had already agreed to train civilian guards, and now Yuling would be able to help him.

Early in February 1945, after Yuling had been at Wuyi Court for over three months, Madame Huang asked him to walk with her to the water garden; he realized his mother-in-law must have something important to say. Huihua was in the outer courtyard with their daughter of nearly a year and with older children, being entertained by a travelling hand-puppet troupe.

They walked more or less in silence, except for the odd comment she made. When she stopped near the little bridge, she said: 'I need to say something to you, and I also want your help.' She was looking towards the older gardener; he was out of earshot, bending down clearing winter foliage from one of the ponds. 'I am more than grateful for all your hard work and for your good practical sense. We were in despair when you arrived as you remember. I am still in despair not knowing what happened to my son.' She looked up to the charred ruins of her home. 'You have been the main source of our strength, and without you and Xi and splendid Mr Wu, I do not know how we could have coped.'

Yuling said nothing; he had already known that he was accepted.

'As you know, we have estates, they are now our only income.' The lady turned and looked directly at him. 'If I send you to the first two, would you meet with the tenants for me?'

Yuling was horrified and stared back. But she continued: 'It is not something I can do for a while, you understand. You would have my written authority, and it will impress them to know that my messenger holds the Chiang Kai-shek personal medal of honour. I will give you the list of the taxes and what each holding must produce. You would take some of the soldiers and go by boat. I have spoken to Xi, they can help on the security side and bring back the money and provisions.'

He remained shocked; that she should think he, whose political colour she well knew, would undertake such a thing was incredible, when it was the last thing he would ever do. Emotion took over and he shook his head because he hated the semi-feudal system, believing all tenants should be given their lands, that the vast majority of landlords had abused their position of power for centuries, that the time had come for them to seek other ways to make their money. If the war ever ended, he hoped for a new China, both in the free areas and those retained by the Japanese; he would never serve the old system, not in the future and certainly not at the present.

'I don't think this is the time to ask people to pay or produce anything,' he said with feeling before looking slightly away. 'There's terrible poverty everywhere, I saw it on the way here, the peasants haven't got any money, or what they've got isn't worth anything.' He thought of Meibei and her farmer husband in their tenant smallholding under the hills; his mother had told him that they were really struggling again. He looked firmly back at his broken aristocratic mother-in-law.

There was an awkward silence, during which he understood that she had come to rely on him and had expected him to help her in that way, which he could well see would also help Huihua. But he hadn't married a daughter of wealth in order to continue or be part of an unjust system that fed off others by power and privilege.

A few weeks later, Huihua heard from Yuling the news she had been dreading. He had been with them more than four precious months; and as soon as the grief had eased, they had come together for the nights. She utterly adored him, the devotion he always showed her, his humour, the organizing ability, his gentle strength. And she loved watching him holding and playing with their daughter.

But now the lieutenant was in Major Ma's old office (turned into a living room) in the Officers Building and had a piece of paper in his hand, was showing it to Yuling in her presence and asking if he understood it, and Yuling was grimacing.

Heron to be at the shop next Tuesday 2 to 3.

'I have to leave tomorrow morning,' he said looking at Huihua, knowing what she would feel, knowing which small shop was referred to, the one agreed with the cell leader.

Though the urge was great and she sensed the danger, Huihua knew better than to persuade Yuling against going. But when the officer left the room and she asked Yuling to promise to return to her '...within two months if possible, as long as it doesn't put you in greater danger...' she listened with alarm as he held her face in his hands and replied that he would try to get back within six months '...but I can't promise, and you won't be able to contact me, the job doesn't allow that, though I'll try to make sure this time that messages get to you...'

The next morning she walked alone with him to the riverboats, accompanied from a distance by two of the elderly soldiers. Near one of the wooden landings and on the other side of a large willow away from the view of the soldiers and others - an open display of love being unseemly even between a young married couple - they embraced a last time, cheek to cheek.

Huihua, facing the river, said: 'Be careful Yuling, please don't take risks, I love you so much.' She felt her eyes moisten. He was clinging tightly to her, and as she looked at the flowing water, she imagined what it would be like no more to feel his physical strength or to look into the eyes that showed his great love for her.

'I'll be careful,' she heard him whisper, 'and if it's some comfort for you to know, I'm not being asked to take part in any active operations.' He looked at her, and she felt his hand in her hair and at the back of her neck. 'Now I must tell you something. Despite the sadness in the family and the daily reminder of the bombing, these months have been the happiest of my life.'

Yuling rubbed his cheek on Huihua's a last time, then he kissed her mouth very gently, and turned; he did not want to see the tears falling.

As the sampan floated out with the current, he called back: 'Think of us at the Hut, just after the bees.' He tried to smile. 'I love you Huihua, and I love our Jia, we'll take her there, I'll carry her.'

But his heart was heavy, his mind anxious.

27

'They took the posters away after about two months,' the cell leader tells Yuling, 'but there's still a large one outside the Central Intelligence Building. We didn't call you earlier because the Japanese and collaborators were crawling all over the city looking for you. They must have found out about you.'

Yuling thinks of the general, or maybe word of his role in exposing Wang had somehow got out into Mingon and come to enemy ears.

The cell companions are very keen to put him to work at once; two despatch riders have been ambushed, there are military papers to be translated, the contents to be sent on to the Generalissimo's headquarters.

But Yuling, angry and distrustful of the leader, accuses him of double-crossing him for not getting the previous year's message to Wuyi Court to tell Huihua that he had left the school and was alright. He tells the man he is not prepared to start work until his occasional message '...to my wife...' will be sent.

Another bad argument ensues, though this time without blows. The outcome is an agreement that after six weeks he can, through the leader, send a one line message which will require Wuyi Court to reply with a password that only he and Huihua understand, so he will know she received the message. He is satisfied, his main worry being that if in the meantime Lieutenant Xi and his men are called away, there will be no chance that a message can be radioed to reach Huihua.

They bring him up to date with the war situation, Germany on its knees and Japan being steadily pushed back in the Pacific.

For the next few months he never leaves the building - it is forbidden - though he is allowed to exercise at the back whenever he needs, as it is not overlooked by windows or from a street.

His single message to Huihua says: *Chang-o, am well, who am I, reply one word.* Within two days he has the answer he wants, and he loves it: *Buzzard, Fuzhous.* It is two words, and the kisses warm his heart and soul. After that, his relations with the cell leader become better, though he still does not like the man.

What is clear is that his work is more than ever appreciated. The scruffy one called Chang tells him they have orders to keep him away from operations, that their lives are expendable but his is not, that if they are killed, he will be transferred to another cell.

On the day they hear of Germany's surrender, another man joins them to make five. The news gives them a badly needed morale booster, but they do not drink to any hoped for end of the war with Japan, because they know that should the enemy seek a peace with the western allies, it could leave the Japanese with part of Manchuria and perhaps even a Chinese eastern or southern port or two. If peace eventually comes, Yuling believes he and Huihua might have to move further west, far away from any continuing Japanese influence and possible revenge for exposing their agent.

As before, he is often left alone in the building, sometimes for a few days. He still does not know exactly where he is and he does not want to know. But he worries that if the others are caught on one of their operations and his position given away, he could be trapped. So he makes a makeshift ladder that he keeps hidden at the back, and he has a loaded revolver near him most of the time.

Every day during moments of relaxation he thinks of Huihua and Jia, picturing them in scenes he makes real by using his innate artistic ability to conjure people vividly in his mind.

And when after being back in the Resistance cell for four months he tells himself that he will soon seek permission to visit his little family again, the ever-growing demand for his work and its evident importance keeps stopping him from asking. From the greater stridency in enemy broadcasts, he can tell they are becoming frantic.

Often he sleeps badly, lying awake and fearing; he fears for himself, for Huihua and Jia's safety, and for his mother and Chennie; and sometimes he thinks about his brother Ayi.

One day in the middle of the hot summer, when his basement listening room is the coolest place to be, his companions fail to return for three days beyond the time expected, and he becomes very worried that they have been captured or something bad has happened. Just as he thinks he should leave and get back to Mingon for a while, three of them finally return to tell him that the newest member has been killed and that they will have to lie low. This makes him even more worried that the cell will be found.

Two weeks later he has a recurrence of his childhood nightmare, being attacked by animals real and legendary. As he wakes he cries out, is panting and sweating, and the hand of one of the men comes hard over his mouth.

'Don't scream like that,' the leader says a couple of seconds later after removing the hand, 'or we'll have to make you sleep with something round your mouth. You're an adult, why do you do it? Think of Chang for heaven sake.' The leader is referring to their companion in the nearby bed who is being frequently sick through the night.

'It hardly ever happens,' Yuling replies truthfully, without mentioning his past. The rest of that night he can hardly sleep, and it does not help that the room smells bad.

In the morning a messenger comes and speaks with the leader and the little bald man. Yuling is in the listening room, and Chang remains ill in bed.

The leader comes down the steps from the trapdoor. 'We've orders for an urgent operation, Chang's too ill, you must take his place. We need you and have got permission. We're prepared to smuggle you out and risk you won't be recognized, and once we get into the countryside it should be alright. I'll tell you about it on the way.'

A hot day and a warm night later - after a rickshaw ride, a short journey in a river fishing boat, and a rendezvous with two other men who handed over handguns and equipment, and after much walking along little trampled paths and beside paddy fields of young rice - Yuling finds himself crouching with his two companions in head-high undergrowth below a railway embankment of tracks for single trains.

They are well out of Amoy, but still within the occupied zone. It is early August, the sun has been up two hours, and the relative warmth of the night is turning to the first heat of the day. The village they passed the previous evening without going through now stands a few hundred paces behind them.

Under starlight in the early hours, they had laid the charges some fifty paces ahead. It took longer than they had expected as they were anxious to conceal the charges, and they also had to cover detonator wires that lay between the tracks and the shorter scrub at the rim of the embankment. Yuling had felt exhausted and fearful, unable even to doze while the sun was rising. Like the other two, he had no doli protecting against the sun, though the little man was wearing one of his wigs.

And now the first train will be passing within a few minutes, and half an hour later the target: an expected Japanese troop carrier. The enemy has for days been transporting troops through different parts of China to the coastal ports, men returning to defend their homeland.

The leader climbs up the embankment and kneels, looking often to his right where, some three hundred paces along the rails, the track curves to the right and out of sight being the direction from which the trains will be coming. To the left, the track goes as straight as a die for as far as the eye can see, though already the heat from the rails creates a minor mirage.

Soon they hear the first train, the leader rejoining them well before it comes round the curve. Yuling has crouched curled up as best he can, and as it passes above them - it seems to take a long time - his heart is thumping.

A minute later the leader resumes his position near the embankment rim, Yuling and his companion having a clear view of him. The little man has his hands close to the detonator.

Time passes terribly slowly. Yuling knows the drill. As soon as the charges explode, they are to run to the paddy and scurry behind the nearest mud embankment out of sight, then make their way past the village and back along the paths towards one of the river tributaries that feed the main river to Amoy; if anything goes wrong and they are discovered before reaching the mud embankment, it is each man for himself; and if any of them is about to be captured, he must shoot himself in the head rather than risk giving the others away who might have escaped.

He makes himself study a dog rose that brushes his shoulder, thinks of the miracles of nature, and wonders how long he has in the present world. Then he hears the leader give a stifled cry, and the next moment the man is scrambling down to them and thrusting his glasses in a pocket.

'A pull-push trolley's coming,' he says breathlessly, 'soldiers!'

'How many?' the little man asks with a look of fright.

'Two or three, and Chinese railmen.'

'If they find the charges we're done for, we'll have to run,' the little man says.

Yuling stares at the leader, his hand and gun are slightly shaking; without the glasses he is not so intellectual-looking, more a fighter.

'No, we'll take them on.' The leader points to the detonator. 'Leave it. We'll get closer and shoot the soldiers before they see us. They won't know where we're coming from or how many we are.'

'They'll find the wires and the direction,' Yuling says, 'they'll have rifles to our revolvers.'

The man turns to him as if to tell him to have more courage. 'We'll get ahead of the charges and surprise them, hit them in the back.' He looks to the little man. 'We're both good shots.'

Yuling begins to hear noises in the rails, and at the same time the leader adds: 'Hopefully they won't see the charges, come!'

They scramble through the undergrowth below the rail embankment, Yuling just behind the leader, his legs receiving scratches, one a thorn above the left knee immediately painful, and the fear of the sword grass in his childhood ordeal below the ravine flies through his mind.

The noise of the trolley grows ever louder. Soon it will be passing over them. But they have only just reached a position directly below the charges. The leader stops and they crouch very low in the undergrowth.

The trolley comes towards them and continues past. Yuling feels enormous relief, his next thought being that it is going to be dangerous running away from the scene once the charges explode under the troop train; he will suggest to the leader that one of them alone handles the detonator while the other two stay well behind at the mud embankment in the rice paddies.

The brakes of the trolley begin screeching, and Yuling's heart goes into his mouth. The noise of the wheels seems to go on forever, and when it stops he hears men shouting, and soon there is running along the rails towards them, and he can hear Japanese and knows the moment is upon them, that the charges and wires will be found.

His revolver is fully loaded. They are crouching beside the wire leading to the detonator that is now well behind them. He looks at the leader whose lips are tight. In a few seconds the soldiers will be immediately above them, and in a flash he realizes it would have been better to have stayed by the detonator and exploded the charges to kill the trolley men and soldiers at least, and bust the track, rather than to have waited for the bigger prize of the train; troops would not have been killed, but the train could not have gone on, although the troops could still have marched to the port.

The shouting continues above them, and suddenly the leader is moving up the embankment and Yuling is following, and the next moment they are in shorter undergrowth and the leader is jumping out and firing and Yuling is leaping over the rim, he sees a Japanese soldier less than four paces away, body facing him, the man has a rifle with fixed bayonet and is bending down looking at the area where one of the charges is hidden. Yuling fires, the man collapses between the rails as further gunfire explodes around him, and the next instant he is grappling with another soldier and the revolver is falling from his hand as he catches the glimpse of a man in early middle age, eyes full of terror, the two of them are stumbling across the far rail, and the little man with the wig is crashing a gun against the soldier's head as another shot deafens the ears.

Yuling jumps up to see three soldiers on the ground, one groaning, the other two including the one he grappled with probably dead, and two Chinese railmen are running away through the undergrowth below the embankment on the other side.

Then they hear the troop train. They look along the track and see the engine coming in the curve; it will reach them in less than thirty seconds.

'Scatter!' the leader shouts, jumping over the rails as if heading down the far side, surprising Yuling for following the direction of the railmen.

Not waiting to pick up his revolver, he runs back down the incline thinking to reach the detonator, and where the little man is going he doesn't see. And he hasn't gone far through the trampled undergrowth when he hears the brakes of the train, and knows that all is up, that very soon many soldiers could be shooting at him or coming for him.

He turns and makes for one of the mud embankments between two rice paddies, though not the one they had originally intended to hide behind.

He reaches the embankment just as the train stops, and scrambles out of sight wondering if he's been seen.

Now running in shallow water that splashes his ankles and lower legs, he comes to a man-length break between embankments. Carefully he looks through, and sees that the engine has stopped well short of the trolley at roughly the position of the charges, and soldiers are pouring out of carriages, some at the front already heading towards the trolley.

He leaps across the void, and continues running behind the next embankment. And just as he sees two frightened farmers looking towards him from a nearby shack, a terrific explosion rents the air, and he knows that the little man with the wig has been braver, went back to the detonator and waited for the train.

Now he runs along the edge of the paddy field, catching second sight of the farmers who are racing towards the village, but he is making for the small undulating hills they came through in the night, the ones behind the village; he has to get as far away as possible and try to hide.

He comes to the road out of the village and stops exhausted behind a clump of bamboo. Looking through the slender stems, he can see in the distance that the engine has been derailed; it leans at an angle away from his side of the track; but all the carriages remain on the track, and hundreds of soldiers are standing along the length of the train.

He is now near the twisting path they came down, and soon he is running up it, keeping as low as he can, his knees aching, aware an observant soldier with binoculars might pick him out; he fears gunshot, it would tell him he's been spotted.

But as he runs on upwards, some different noise comes to his ears that he has not expected: the sound of motorcycle engine. He is so out of breath that he has to stop and bend to get air into his lungs, and all the time the noise is growing.

The beginning of an unkempt cemetery comes on his left, and a few more faltering steps and he jumps into it and looks back down the path. Three motorcyclists are revving at the junction of the road and the path, their heads with goggles looking his way, he can see rifles strapped to their backs, and one of the men is pointing towards him.

He ducks behind a large grave carved from stone in the shape of an oyster shell, it is high in grasses. There is more revving and he thinks they are starting up the path though it won't be easy for them as it is full of dry holes.

Frantic, he looks where else he might run, and sees an old man and a young woman standing further up by newer graves, and the woman is looking at him in fear and holds a very young girl in her arms. Some of the graves remain decorated with faded red strips.

There is nowhere for him to run - those rifles - and the noise of the machines is getting closer much faster than he expects. He is wriggling on his stomach through more grasses past two graves in the abandoned part of the cemetery, when a shot from close-range makes him stop, and almost at once it is followed by a scream from the woman.

Yuling's arms on the ground start to tremble; the screaming continues. Another shot makes his body jerk as he hears a bullet ricochet off some gravestone in the direction, he guesses, of the little group.

He jumps up. 'Don't shoot them!' he shouts in Japanese, putting his hands high as two of the soldiers, now off their machines, turn rifles on him. He glances towards the family expecting immediately to be killed, and sees the woman is kneeling, hearing her cries for help; the little girl is standing beside her looking stunned holding wild flowers, and he realizes with horror that the old man could be dead or dying as he can no longer see him.

The soldiers are shouting as they run towards him, one stumbling over a small grave hidden by the grasses. Very soon a revolver is waving at him and close. 'How do you know Japanese?' the man shouts into his face, the two rifles trained.

Yuling can hardly speak for fear '...studied...' he's trying to get saliva down his throat knowing his only chance is to keep talking '...taught ...taught in your school ...Amoy...' the flirting teacher jumps into his mind '...many Japanese friends...'

The soldiers stare at him. The woman is still crying out, and he's frightened that one of them could turn on her. He wants to look towards her again but manages to keep eye contact with the man so close. 'Don't shoot the woman,' he pleads, 'she's got a child, they're visiting their burial grounds, ancestors.'

The man yells 'Move! Move!' indicating the direction with his head.

He lurches forward across an abandoned grave, keeping his hands high and realizing he is not going to be killed straight away.

They make him go down the path in front of their machines, and when he comes to the road, he is ordered to run towards the village. He can only half run as his lungs and chest hurt badly.

He reaches the first of the village shacks and sees a face looking towards him from the shadows of a glassless window, but he cannot tell if it is a man or woman. Slowing to a walk, he calls out over the noise of the engines that an old man is in the cemetery, shot, needs immediate help. He is about to mention the woman and child, when there is more soldier-shouting and one of the motorcyclists comes up on his bike and a fist hits him in the middle of the back.

Somehow he keeps going. A squawking cockerel crosses his path, a dog slinks away behind a primitive house, but otherwise there is no sign of human life in the seemingly deserted village.

A couple of minutes later and they are on a dry path through paddies of small rice, coming towards the rear end of the train. Many soldiers are standing near it, some looking his way.

*

Weeks earlier, Lieutenant Xi and his ten soldiers had finally been called away, leaving Madame Huang to arrange for six of the newly trained citizens to guard them. None of the recruited guards were Communist-inclined, they had each assured her (though she was not so sure, feeling uneasy about three of them). She and Huihua had hoped to have eight guards, but two had run away, and the lady was worried about the cost; even she could see that the time might not be far off when she would have to consider - a first time for her family - the need to raise money in Mingon from one of the two pawnbrokers.

Following Yuling's refusal to be her rent and tax collector, she had sent a Mingon rice merchant and three of the civilian guards to the two nearest estates, under an agreement they prized from her that they would receive half of the produce collected and half of any money they brought back, though they told her they did not expect to collect much money. The merchant took her written sealed authority to flaunt, but they each knew that hardly any of the peasants could read. This left the family more exposed than ever for the four days the men were expected to be away; only the three remaining civilians plus the father and son gardeners would be in attendance to guard them.

The collectors failed in their mission, and twice nearly lost their lives. On the first Huang estate, a group of angry tenants from a number of smallholdings gathered at one of the farms and chased them away with gunfire in the air and stones thrown their way. After that, they dared not go to the second estate. And on the return river journey, they were fired on from behind rocks. Fortunately they had the current with them and were able to go past fairly quickly; they never saw those who were firing, bandits they thought. They were back at the Court the morning following their departure.

After the lieutenant and his soldiers had left, Huihua very soon noticed a change in the manner of the civilian guards towards her and her mother: her father was dead, Yuling away, male authority absent. The men were less immediately biddable than the soldiers, and less trustworthy. Although they were usually respectful, the deference from some of them had gone, their faces surly.

When Elder Han visited a second time after the general's death, he told Madame Huang that a mood of anger had grown among many in Mingon, anger that so many lives had been lost in the siege and that many loved ones remained prisoners of war. 'More people seem to have become politicised,' he said ominously, 'they are agitating against the government and espousing Red causes. A new wind is blowing, my lady.'

With Lieutenant Xi gone, Huihua had no ability to receive Yuling's messages, and was feeling very anxious, having had no word for months since the first cryptic message that he was well.

She began to feel a foreboding that something bad had happened to him.

28

Inside the filthy, stinking, airless room only seven paces by five, eighteen Chinese prisoners, men of all ages except the very old, squat or lie curled up or sit half-stretched with their backs against the walls.

Two latrine buckets near the door have overflowed with urine and faeces.

'I thought they were going to finish me off, we'd killed two of them, or three,' Yuling whispers to his thin companion, sixteen-year-old Fuguang who sits beside him careful not to touch because of the beating and arm wounds. 'They dragged me along the track, and I had to identify my companion, he shot himself. Every time I said their names weren't their real names, they beat and kicked me on the ground, just behind the engine. We'd derailed it.'

'Did the others get away?'

'There was only the leader, I don't know.' Yuling was hoping against hope that somehow, sometime, Huihua and his mother would learn what had happened to him; though if the leader had managed to escape, he wouldn't have trusted him to get any message to either. 'I couldn't tell them where our cell was, only the district, that's when they did this.' He looks at the open gash in his right forearm. 'I gave a false name, but an officer recognised me from posters, he must have been in Amoy when my picture was up. He told them it must be me because I'm big, and I had to admit it or they'd have shot me.'

'Yes, that's him, Tsai's a hefty swine,' the intelligence officer called down the phone to the commandant of the prison camp. 'I'm very relieved they've delivered him to you, and don't you go and kill him, you leave him to me. I'm phoning from Shanghai and I'll be back in a few days unless...' he paused, 'you've heard the news?'

The commandant knew what was coming. 'It's terrible,' he answered, 'terrible.' He'd been told that the Chinese had broadcast from Chongqing about a special bomb dropped on a Japanese city. They said that the devastation to the population would have been total, and that it was only a matter of time before Japan had to make peace. Some Chinese near his camp had let off firecrackers, and when he first heard them, he assumed there was some festival going on. But Number Two, his grey-haired camp officer who had been a teacher back home, told him they were celebrating the news of the bomb and cocking a snook. With the Soviets now rolling through Manchukuo in the north, he was a very worried man, frightened for his own life and for his family living near the camp, and fearful for his country, it could be obliterated. Mankind had entered a new and terrifying period in history.

'Well you just keep him, you hear me, I *must* have him.' The intelligence officer couldn't bring himself to admit that the prisoner was the only Chinese who had got the better of him, but he couldn't stop himself adding 'He's going to suffer.'

Some days later, the commandant received a telephone order from Nanjing that all remaining resistance fighters were 'to be dealt with at once and in the usual way.'

He had just put down the telephone when a hand-written memorandum was handed to him by Number Two. 'From Army Air Force, top brass.'

'Army Air Force!' The commandant could not recall ever receiving a communication from the air arm.

It was addressed to the Commandant, Southern Prison Camp, Amoy District, and was brief:

> *Intelligence say I made a mistake when talking to your prisoner*
> *Tsai Yuling, giving away some information. In my judgement he*
> *is innocent, was not seeking information, not spying. I invited*
> *him to paint my portrait - he is a brilliant artist. He told me he*
> *has admiration for our country's language and culture. I am told*
> *he has a lady and now a child. This tragic war must be ending*
> *imminently. Let him live.*
> *Hiromichi Hijiya, Major General, JAAF.*

They hear them coming about an hour after sunrise. Orders are barked, soldier-guards call to each other, a bar to the door is being removed. All but one of the prisoners is sitting or curled up; the man who stands has been scratching something with a nail as high as he can on the wall.

'This is it,' Fuguang whispers into the big one's ear, crouching behind him in a corner and trying to make himself as small as possible, terrified.

The door swings fully inwards and knocks against one of the prisoners.

'Out! Out!' a guard cries before holding his nose against the stench and vigorously waving the other hand.

Another guard rushes in and begins wielding a club, shouting oaths only

Yuling can understand as he scrambles to his feet and raises his left arm to protect himself (he cannot move the right arm).

'Not you, ugly,' the guard from the door calls to him. He guesses why they are not taking him: torture has been constantly on his mind, though he desperately hopes they will shoot him instead ...but if Japanese intelligence want to interrogate him...

He lowers his arm. He can feel Fuguang clutching part of his trousers, knows he is trying to hide, so tries to widen himself by slightly parting his legs and moving out the arm a touch.

As the last prisoner is pushed out, Number Two stands in the doorway. 'You've got friends in high places.' The camp's second officer is looking in disgust at the excrement by the buckets. He turns to Yuling. 'Commandant has just had a Major General's request to spare you, but it won't work.' Yuling is slow to understand, stares back. 'Army Air Force,' the man adds. Now he realizes - Colonel Hijiya, the swash-buckling airman. He doesn't reply, wants the officer to leave so he doesn't see who is behind him. Number Two grunts, turns away, and the door is slammed.

Sometime afterwards, with Fuguang still behind Yuling who is sitting again, they hear a series of shootings that last several minutes. The two sit in silence, remaining that way after the firing stops.

Yuling thinks of the sad-looking little guard who seems often to be just outside their door, who knows he speaks Japanese, the man who whispered to him the previous day that he was sorry for what was coming to them, when Yuling asked his name.

With difficulty he stands, Fuguang helping him, and goes to the door, tapping gently.

'Shuzo, you there?'

He waits.

'What you want?'

'What's happening? When they coming?'

The guard doesn't reply.

'Do they put you in the firing squad?'

'No.'

'Shuzo, you got children?'

Another silence. Then: 'Too many.'

But for his dire situation, Yuling wants to smile. 'When it's over, will you think of my little girl, her name is Jia, if I think of your children, hope for a better future for them?'

He cannot see the guard sitting on the other side of the door shaking his head in bewilderment, and the man gives him no answer.

'How many children?'

'Eight.'

Yuling's eyes widen. He turns and goes to cowering Fuguang and whispers what he has learnt. But the lad is trembling again and says nothing.

No water, no tiny amounts even of watered rice were given them the previous day, and all the prisoners knew why. Thirst as well as fear now tears at Yuling, as does his absolute horror to be leaving Huihua without so much as a message of his love. And he will never see his daughter again, never see her grow up. He'd asked to be allowed to write, but had been angrily shouted at.

The previous day, Fuguang's older brother had been in another cell, and the kindly little guard had told Yuling that the end had come instantly without further suffering. He'd relayed this to his companion, but the thin lad looked numb.

The commandant sat at his desk exhausted, having hardly slept for days. He'd been agonizing with his wife if she and the two teenage children should try to take immediate ship back to Japan, though it would be a very dangerous voyage with the war going so badly.

News of a colossal second bomb dropped six days earlier on the homeland seemed to have affected him even more than the first shocking one; and in the north the position looked already lost to the Soviets.

The dispatching of the last prisoner but one had taken place, a job he suddenly found much more unpleasant than before.

He looked wearily at Number Two standing on the other side of the desk. 'No, we're to finish the job, clear the lot.'

'But Intelligence want the man.'

'We can't wait. HQ have just said immediate and no exceptions. Get on the phone to Intelligence and say we have our orders, and if they want to stop us, they'll have to contact Nanjing.'

Number Two went out, closing the door. The commandant's head went into his hands.

Around midday, several hours after the shootings, Yuling and Fuguang hear the footsteps again and the calling between soldiers. They get to their feet, Fuguang once more trying to stand behind his big companion. And soon the door opens, and two guards with little Shuzo are looking towards them.

Yuling catches their surprise - they have clearly seen Fuguang - and immediately calls to them not to hurt the lad. 'You're going to kill us anyway,' he shouts, raising his left hand and quickly telling Fuguang to put his hands behind his head and to follow him.

Yuling goes towards the guards, but Fuguang doesn't move. Yuling turns to see he is petrified just as a guard leaps past and starts hitting the lad with a club. Yuling shouts again, but as Fuguang cries out, there is nothing Yuling can do to stop the blows.

Fuguang is hauled to his feet whimpering, and they are pushed along a passage. Soon they are outside. After days in the hot stinking room, Yuling thinks the air wonderful to breathe and wonderful on his face, and it makes him think first of the hills - the uplands - and then of Ayi who might be in the mountains with Communist forces. He is going to die before making up with his brother; and will Ayi ever meet Huihua and Jia, he doubts it, not after what happened on the path to the forest below the ravine.

He can see a long mound with a ditch at one end. The ditch is not far from one of the camp buildings, thirty paces or so. Chinese workmen stand with shovels to one side of the mound, looking their way, expressionless.

They go past the firing squad of six soldiers, rifles by their side.

Yuling sees the commandant and the grey-haired officer coming towards them from the end of the building.

'Who's the second fellow?' he hears the commandant ask in surprise.

But he cannot catch the reply because, from the building, loud crackling is coming from a wireless set. And soon he can hear strange Japanese being broadcast. The sound is coming from some lower window; it continues for some seconds before the set goes silent.

They are made to stand near the edge of the ditch, and Yuling's right ankle is tied with thin rope to Fuguang's left. They are an arm's length apart, and ordered to face the ditch with their hands by their sides, Yuling translating for his co-doomed companion.

'You tricked us,' the commandant barks at him from near Fuguang, 'Intelligence say you must pay the price, clever painter! They wanted to get at you first, so you're lucky.'

Yuling sees the commandant nod perfunctorily to someone, and the next moment a hood is placed over his head, the immediate darkness stunning him, and he knows his end is very near.

He hears the commandant stamp away just as the wireless set comes back to life.

'What you thinking?' Fuguang calls through the crackling, his voice as if from a cave.

The question brings him away from his blankness. 'I wish this would be over,' he calls back, the little girl in the cemetery coming vividly into his mind as a shudder running through him; he can see the posy of wild flowers in her hand, and he is about to go the same way as the old man whose death he is sure he caused, her grandfather, great grandfather...

'That place you told me about in the hills...' But he listens to his companion no more, because an order he understands has just been barked, and next he hears the clicks of rifles.

He takes himself to the edge of the escarpment, turns a last time towards Huihua and Jia; they are standing by the cedar bench at the back of the Hut, the bench from which he and his grandfather looked at the birds of prey gliding above them or sometimes at eye-level; Huihua's expression is serious. The forest below beckons as once before it nearly took him to itself.

The wireless set begins blaring again, and he believes it is to drown out the shots. Some man is broadcasting in high-pitched Japanese, but he is not taking much of it in.

His mother's face flashes before him and quickly goes.

A few seconds later he is surprised still to be standing, still alive. And through the static he catches the words for *China* and the *Soviet Union*, and begins to understand that someone is speaking in archaic Japanese: Lecturer Yin at the college in Suodin had occasionally spoken it to test what Yuling and his fellow students could understand.

Now he believes the transmission must be something important to the commandant, that it might not be to drown out the shots; perhaps the man is waiting to its end before giving the order.

More words he catches or guesses at ...*the war has developed not to Japan's advantage...* Something is said about a terrible weapon, and Fuguang is crying out 'What's happening?' but he doesn't know and cannot answer ...*we have ordered the acceptance of the joint declaration of the...* He tries to get at the next words and they only come to him seconds later ...*allied powers...* Further words he fails to catch from the bad quality broadcast and from the language that seems so old-fashioned.

When are they going to fire, end it all? He wants to conjure up Huihua a last time, but in the din she won't come. It is the words ...*have resolved to pave the way to a grand peace...* that brings Yuling's mind to register the unbelievable meaning of the transmission, that the Japanese are announcing an intention to end the war.

Again he goes blank.

But not for long. He realizes that if the order to fire is given in the very next seconds, he is going to die just a few weeks, days maybe, before some form of peace.

He cannot see the ashen faces of the commandant and the grey-haired officer, doesn't know that Number Two, once a teacher of old Japanese, has started crying and has just confirmed what his superior thinks has been broadcast, that the government is to communicate to the governments of the United States, Great Britain, China and the Soviet Union, Japan's acceptance of the terms of their joint declaration for unconditional surrender.

He does not know that the voice is that of the one hundred and twenty-fourth Emperor himself, recorded the night before. But he hears the warning against any outbursts of emotion, and the words ...*devoting strength to the construction for the future*... a future he will not live to see.

Nor can he see that the commandant, who is standing close to the firing squad, has fallen to his knees, that his head is dropping, or that one or two of the guns are lowering, that there are looks of consternation and fear on the faces of the soldiers.

Then the wireless set goes quiet.

Yuling listens. The moment is too personally terrifying for him to think of his companion to tell him the news. He can hear low talking, and soon he realizes that some of the soldiers have not understood the archaic language. Someone behind him is shouting in anguish, saying there is to be a surrender, and as the word is repeated, he hears soldiers starting to cry out, they are invoking the name of their Emperor.

Soon the cries are those of men in torment.

More seconds pass in his fearful hooded darkness, the commotion behind him now so great that even if Fuguang asked again what was happening, he could not have told him above the wailing.

A shot splits the air, the noise tremendous, and to his horror the rope pulls hard at his right leg and he knows his companion has been killed. At once he starts trembling.

Another shot rings out and the head explodes as the soul registers its end in the body of Tsai Yuling, who goes into oblivion.

29

In different parts of Mingon, a few of the citizens who had wireless sets and happened to be listening became aware of the stupendous news about an hour after midday, when a Chinese station calling itself *the station of the victorious Chinese Nationalists* began transmitting from Fuzhou.

They did not rush into the streets to proclaim, but stayed by their sets listening with incredulity, or ran into each other's houses to listen ...and disbelieve. They heard the male announcer talking of terrible bombs dropped on the enemy's homeland, and of pandemonium in the occupied areas of Fujian province especially in Amoy. And when the man kept invoking the greatness of the Chinese peoples, and excitedly repeated that the Emperor had ordered his nation to surrender, and when he added that *the Japanese dogs* would be leaving China, still some of the listeners of Mingon could not take it in. They ran to Elder Han's house; he had a receiver but had not heard the news, and they huddled around it.

Shortly afterwards, the old gong of the East Gate Monastery was struck several times as if for a festival, its deep resonance like a wave of warm air over the town, and people came out of their houses or little businesses asking what it was for and why it was continuing.

Half an hour after the broadcasts were first picked up, citizens were thronging the streets, most shaking their heads and advising caution, smiles of concern on their faces.

Mr Wu, standing in his backyard beside a heavy workbench and with several hens nearby, was one of the many doubters when his pretty daughter ran to tell him. 'They'll not be leaving, Ashenga, the planes will come again, that's a false transmission,' the furniture maker said, thinking of his family's flight into the hills, and the destruction of the Wuyi Court mansion. But his happy-looking daughter kept saying she was sure the war had ended, and he couldn't deny he was now hearing continual shouts and cries of joy coming from the street that led to the Great Gate, the three-tiered bastion that had seen so much history. He went out into the side lane with his daughter - the girl about to become a young woman, who had long ago given up wearing her fragrance pouch - to ascertain the truth for himself.

Huihua was lying in near despair on a sofa; she was in a basement bedroom in the Officers Building, trying to rest in the afternoon, her little girl upstairs with maid Yiying. She hadn't slept a wink the previous night, and her last few days had been nightmarish since the verbal message was received at the repaired main gates, from a man called Chang, that Yuling had been captured and seen taken into the prison camp in south Amoy. The messenger said he was from the Resistance, and he told the civilian guards that on no account should she go there, that the Japanese were sure to take her life. She knew why: she was the daughter of the general who had valiantly resisted them, and she was the wife of the man who had exposed their agent; they had killed her father, and they might already have executed or would very soon execute her husband.

Yet, despite the danger, she had been thinking of taking the risk, going in disguise to find out what she could. Above all she had to think about her daughter, and about ...her hand was on her middle. If she was captured and killed, Jia would have to grow up without either parent, with her grandmother who would then have lost all her family; or she might go to Yuling's mother.

It was old Xuiey, running down the stairs as best she could and calling out 'Mistress Hua, Mistress Hua pet!' that made Huihua sit up and await the strangely animated entry of her dear cook.

Within twenty minutes - after refusing to listen to the concerns of her mother, losing herself and shouting back '...now you'll get your wish to have Yuling out of the way, if he's not been killed yet...' - Huihua was calling out to a civilian guard to open the door in the repaired main gates, and was walking as quickly as she could through the gates, soon passing the empty space where one of the stone lions had stood before the bombing. She was making her way along the road towards the river, towards its landing stages.

Two sampans had already left, but she was in no mood to be turned away from a third that already brimmed with people, people seeking to get to the cities in the east, to be reunited with their loved ones, or to search for them as she had to search for her husband. She invoked her name and used the authority of her voice, and the captain waved her on, hesitatingly she saw but she didn't mind, she could feel the flat-bottomed boat moving under her in the water, and that was all that mattered.

In the early afternoon of the following day, while Huihua was getting close to Amoy, Madame Huang stood just inside the door of the Officers Building, receiving a visit from an excited Elder Han who had tried to run some of the way. She stared at him as he beamed, and she had to look away, feeling the tears coming. She had known that he wanted to proclaim the peace that she already knew about. But his message delivering the words she never expected to hear had brought back her life. 'Master Shanghan's alive and uninjured, my lady, he's survived the camp under another name, he's on his way home.'

Huihua reached the chaos of Amoy in the evening on a warm but cloudy August day. As the bigger boat - her third of the journey - came into the quayside, she caught sight of a body, Japanese she guessed, lying on the ground a few paces from where they were about to disembark; another was floating in the filthy water.

Nearby, a huge Japanese merchant ship had just pulled away; it was surrounded by several Chinese junks in full-rigged brown sails, they were sounding their fog horns, seeing off the ship in hatred and derision. It seemed to be a thousand times more crowded than the little sampan she had started in. She could see Japanese soldiers on board, all looking into the ship, all turned away from the country they had occupied. But most of the passengers were Japanese civilians, and some were looking back at the land they had made their home and many were crying; and even through the horns she could hear some of them in their distress.

People in her boat began waving fists and screaming oaths towards the ship, spitting into the water or in the direction of the body on the ground near the gangplank. The urge in Huihua to follow was great, but desperation and dread were in her heart.

Shots frequently rang out in the city as she made her way to the notorious southern camp. She saw more bodies on the streets and pavements, or lying by shops and tea houses that were closed or boarded up. Some were of Japanese women as well as men. Occasionally a body had been stripped bare, and soon she was trying not to look, walking quickly away or round. She received a further shock when she passed a dead Chinese, a man left sitting upright against a drainage pipe, blood still oozing from a recent bullet to the head - a collaborator or informer she guessed.

There were no policemen about. Hardly a rickshaw was to be seen. Outside a drapery shop with its blinds fully down, two men stood looking alert, clearly intent to protect their property; one held a hand gun, the other a heavy stick.

About an hour after leaving the boat, Huihua walked through the open gates of the prison camp with a stronger sense of foreboding than ever.

The sun was making a brief appearance through clouds; soon it would descend over the horizon. Its rays lit on a wide tarpaulin covering what she thought could be bodies brought in from the streets, and inwardly she shuddered. An unpleasant smell was in the air, making her hold both hands over her nose and mouth.

She thought about going into the nearest of the buildings, to see if anybody could tell her what had happened to the prisoners, give names, whether some might have been rescued or released, still be alive...

But spotting a group of people at a long mound, including workmen with shovels, she walked slowly towards them, well realizing what the workmen were doing, as they had cloths covering their noses.

A number of people mostly women stood not far from the workmen. Others sat on the ground. Some were weeping. No one spoke. Among them stood a thin lad openly crying; a middle-aged man had an arm round him, the father, she guessed, trying to comfort.

She leant down to the nearest woman, excusing herself, and asked if she knew whether any prisoners had survived and where they were. The woman had a black veil over her head, gave no reply, she was staring into the ditch part of the mound.

Then the head starting nodding. 'All dead.'

Huihua went cold. She straightened and looked at the mound, was at a loss to know what to do.

She turned towards some of the other women. 'I'm trying to find my husband Tsai Yuling,' she said a little louder, at once sensing the hopelessness of her utterance. 'Do any of you know...' But she couldn't end her question because nobody was looking her way or taking any notice; everyone was mourning their own.

The workmen on the other side of the group were shovelling earth onto the side of the mound, empty carts nearby. Some of them too must have heard her, but they kept working.

She turned away with a sickening emptiness, and looked down at the patchy grass beneath her feet, again putting her hands to her nose. In the ground, a long wavy run made by field mice led her eyes towards the nearest building. Perhaps she would have to go inside after all, see if there was anyone she could talk with. But there were other buildings in that place of death; she didn't think she had the strength to look into all of them.

Sanchi, the stepsister who helped Yuling recover from his childhood ordeal, came into her mind, and her Communist husband, a decent man Yuling said when asking her to memorize their address. Yes, she'd seek them out after looking into the first building only.

She began walking towards it, seeing again the sinister tarpaulin.

'Who did you say you're looking for?' She turned. The eyes of the thin lad were red-raw. 'My brother's under there,' he said nodding to the mound, 'they pulled us apart, he so nearly survived...'

Huihua wanted to say something to comfort him but she couldn't, she was frozen. His grief-stricken look was the face of all China's suffering.

30

...where's he gone...he was just with us above the escarpment...he's not gone over to the far lands has he, to his father and grandfather...the black kites caught sight of him high high above them, and soared into the vastness of the sky on the warmth of the forest thermals...and when they reached him and found his eyes still shut, they put their great wings under him and began gliding ever downwards in gentle swings and circles...can't you see the Hut yet, it's easy, there, look, on top of the escarpment...but the eyes would not open...we'll place you by the structure your parents built, we like it there, we perch when you're not around, when the bangs are no more and the wind ruffles our feathers...

Eucalyptus ...the smell is strong in his nostrils and in his head ...his head, it feels so heavy, and as if squashed.

His eyes remain closed, but he senses it is not as dark as he first thought when coming out of the unconscious.

He breathes deeper ...yes eucalyptus ...am I really in the land of the living, if so it's a miracle ...what happened to the firing squad...

He can tell he is lying on a bed, and that his head rests on a pillow. And he is hurting, not just the head, but the right arm he remembers was gashed with a bayonet at the train.

He moves his left hand over and feels a bandage ...a bandage ...somebody is taking care of him.

There is stillness all around.

He turns to the light source, and lets his eyelids open. Some old screen obscures a window, but there is sunshine outside, and the very thought warms his heart.

He begins to focus on the screen, late Qing dynasty, seeing apple twigs in blossom, the light affecting the pinks and whites and the dark almost black parts in different ways, in different tones ...the artist was good.

He turns back and closes his eyes; and for a few seconds, as his left hand feels a linen sheet lying over him to his middle, he allows himself a faint smile: he really *has* survived, at least for the time being.

He listens to his own breathing; it is regular and calm, and somehow it comforts him.

He takes a deep breath and holds it. He cannot understand - when he holds his breath he can still hear breathing.

Slowly he turns his head and looks the other way, and comes to another miracle: she is sitting beside him, facing him, asleep, and she is oh so lovely, her presence a hundred times more powerful, more welcoming than the sunshine outside.

He studies her face, what he can see of it; her chin is resting on her chest, the hair he adores partly fallen.

'psst!'

She doesn't react.

He calls louder: 'Chang-o, are you real, are you mine, psst!'

His girl wakes with a jerk, he hears a chair or stool fall away, and she is all over him, gasping and kissing his hand and his face and crying out to someone and telling him how much she loves him and smiling as she kisses him more and is calling out again.

And very soon amongst her cries and touches he can hear a man's exclamations and the loud creaking of a door, and an old gentleman he doesn't know is soon smiling down at him, wearing what he can see is a traditional grey satin gown of old China and a blue skull cap.

'Welcome back to life young man!'

Yuling looks at Huihua; there are tears in her eyes. 'Where am I?'

'We're in Mr Lao's apothecary shop not far from the prison camp. This dear wonderful gentleman has been trying to bring you round for nearly two days, he's been feeding you water and syrup.'

The man is nodding. 'And welcome to freedom!'

Freedom? Yuling doesn't understand, and frowns. The apothecary is bending down and feeling his forehead. 'They've gone, or they're going back to their wretched islands, this time may it be forever.'

He cannot take it in. How can the Japanese be going, they are all-powerful. Yes they are losing the war, being bombed from other Pacific islands; and some of their troops have left to defend their homeland. But they would always be in China, they could never be made to leave his motherland. For a brief and shockingly unpleasant moment, he wonders if he is in the next world and somehow able to imagine life on earth. But he can feel Huihua's soft hands, and his left hand has just touched her amazing face. In disbelief he wants to move his leaden head but dares not, he knows he's been shot.

He recalls the crackling transmission and what he understood in those last terrifying moments in his darkness under the hood.

The apothecary is putting a small bowl to his mouth and telling him to drink, and Huihua is holding his neck and her tears have dried. He begins sipping green tea; it is warm, semi-sweet, delicious.

He lies back on the pillow. 'Aren't I going to die? Don't I have a bullet in my head?'

'No you don't,' the old gentleman says, 'and you're not going to die under my roof!' Yuling thinks he has a kind and wise face. 'A soldier hit you with a rifle at the back of your head, and a hospital doctor has already examined you and is coming back this evening when he can get away. He said you should be alright once you came round. All the medical people and the hospitals have their hands full at the moment, so you must stay with us, and I have told Mrs Tsai that you will remain here for as long as is necessary. At such a momentous time, it will be one of the greatest privileges of my long life to make sure that you do fully recover.'

'But I heard shots.'

'The camp officers killed themselves,' Huihua says.

Killed themselves! *You tricked us, Intelligence say you must pay the price, clever painter!* And now he is being told that the commandant and second officer are dead. He wants to shake his head in further disbelief.

He thinks of Fuguang, feels trembling coming on and quickly gets out '...young lad with me, he died, collapsed, my leg tugged...' He doesn't end his sentence about the connecting rope because Huihua keeps smiling down at him and he can't understand why.

'He brought you here, others helped him, they carried you in a cart, and he brought me here too, his name is Lu Fuguang.'

This is too much, he has to frown again. But Huihua is talking on. 'When he heard the first shot, he let himself fall thinking he was hit somewhere, and when he realized he wasn't, he lay pretending to be dead. He thought the second shot killed you because you fell on top of his legs, you were heavy and he couldn't move. He didn't know what was happening. Someone was suddenly beside him in real anguish, for you he thought, but he was told later that it was a Japanese soldier who was crying because they'd had to surrender. And he heard lots more distress, and thought it must be coming from the mound diggers, except most of the words were in the enemy tongue and he just couldn't understand what was going on.'

Huihua stops. She can see she needs to give Yuling time to take it all in. She places his left hand on his chest and starts caressing his fingers - her hero with a missing finger.

After a short while she continues, smiling gently into his eyes: 'He heard men running away, they were the soldiers and they were shouting in fear, and he realized they had gone somewhere and left him to the Chinese workmen. He lay wondering when to look up and how he was going to get through the barred gates. He said there was an eerie silence, with you dead over him he thought. And then some of the workmen came near, and as soon as they started talking he looked up and got free of you. They were shaking their heads and pointing to the two dead officers, and they said they saw the guards running out of the gates. They told him that a soldier hit you at the very moment when the second officer shot himself, and then the soldier fell to his knees and began beating the ground. They told Lu Fuguang you could still be alive.'

Yuling feels in a complete daze. For a while he says nothing, preferring just to look at Huihua, at every part of her face, at the joy and concern in her eyes. His survival seems extraordinary enough, but so does his love for her.

'A messenger called Chang came to the Court,' she adds, 'he told the guards which prison you were in, he said he was from the Resistance.'

He thinks of the scruffy man who was sick, whose place he took, whose real name he doesn't know. And of the leader running down the other side of the railway embankment; he wonders whether he got away or was caught and killed; he hadn't heard any shot while they were running in their opposite directions.

He comes back to the thin lad. 'Fuguang's brother was killed.'

She nods. 'He's very upset. He goes to the burial mound with his father. But he comes every few hours to check how you are, and he's going to be very pleased when he sees you, he says you saved his life, he hid behind you.'

Saved his life. The horror of the old man in the cemetery comes back to haunt; so does the little girl, and the mother who kept crying out for help.

'They shot a grandfather because of me, in front of his family...' But he cannot go on, cannot make himself describe the scene. And the tragedy of his own grandfather comes to him: the exploding gun on the promontory into the lake; so much has happened to him since then, more than ten years ago.

The old gentleman in gown and scull cap is giving him a rueful look. 'In war terrible things happen, believe me, I know. Are you sure he died?' He cannot answer, tightens his lips. 'I'm going to the temple,' the apothecary continues, 'so if you like, I'll pray for him at the healing Buddha, and for his family.' He is looking at Yuling's right arm. 'We'll need to dress this again, there's some minor seepage, but it will heal. Now you've talked enough, you must rest. We'll prepare some broth, you'll be hungry.' He smiles and turns away.

Yuling hears the door creaking again, and thinks it must have been left half open. Huihua has dried her eyes, and is now leaning close. In her face, in her expression, he reads her feelings for him, and they are balm to his bewildered emotions.

And is there ...is there something else, some playfulness, that glint of hers has come into the eye, she is taking his hand and pressing it to her middle.

Then life and the wonders of life come back to the artist, and he thinks of the little guard Shuzo - his eight children - and prays that the father, the husband, reaches his home and family in Japan safely.

'The birds brought me back to you,' he says, touching a strand of her hair, smiling into her heart. 'Give me your cheek, angel.'

***

In salute to Christopher 'Kit' Whittaker

The author's childhood best friend who died aged twenty. Chris combined joie de vivre with early purposefulness for his love of sea diving, and was inspirational for life to those who knew him well. As a safety diver, he gave his own life off Catalina Island, California, attempting to save two men in a bell during an American/Swiss deep-sea diving expedition (Book: Rosemary Whittaker's moving One Clear Call; Google: The Keller Dive). The men planted flags on the ocean floor at a record 1020 feet, but after two or three minutes one of the divers got into difficulties. They managed to close the hatch, and then were seen on the surface-ship's camera to keel over, as if to go unconscious. The bell was winched up and halted at the necessary decompression level of 200 feet below the surface. Chris and another safety diver were sent down to investigate the bell's exterior for a possible leak. In their first inspection they could not find anything wrong, and Chris surfaced with that news, and with a nosebleed. He was advised not to go down again, but he could not leave the men in the bell without checking once more. This time he and the other diver spotted or felt the edge of a flipper protruding, they cut it, and the hatch slammed shut. The other diver stayed with the bell and sent Chris back up, but tragically he was never seen again. Equally sad, one man in the bell died. The other man survived, without doubt due to the cutting of that flipper and the sealing of the hatch. Chris was a hero.

And with gratitude unlimited

to a wonderful international bunch from Britain, Germany, Canada, South Africa and Taiwan, who showed the way, supported, listened, criticized, and above all kept faith, including particularly (though there were others to whom heartfelt thanks have been given): Julia Adams (London book world, for superb advice throughout), Anton Beaumont, James Beaumont, Cecily Beeton, Isobel Bodie, Peter Ebeling (for Kaffeehaus ticks, crosses, and boundless enthusiasm),

Isobel Fernyhough and Christine Cowie (mother and daughter), David Field, Janice Hambley, Chris Little (London book world, for advice on the first chapter, which became the second!), Robin Porter (who introduced the shop Arthur Probsthain, the Oriental and African Bookseller near the British Museum), Paul Taylor, Sue Waudby-Smith, Wu Su-pin (the author's much respected first Chinese reader), Yen Wen-chian, and last but by no means least Anna, recently deceased, she of lustrous long black hair, beautiful curvy legs, and velvet tender ears, who took her slave on walks through the Bavarian countryside, when ideas flowed and problems miraculously solved, while she chased hare, fox and deer... in vain.

Also admiration for and huge thanks to the brilliant cover designers Annie Hartridge and Charlotte Rutherford of Giant Arc Design, Brighton, UK, and great thanks to AuthorHouse, publishers, Indiana, USA for their excellent help and patience.

Author,
Bad Wörishofen/Mindelheim, Germany,
2011.

ABOUT THE AUTHOR

Nigel Beaumont was born in Yorkshire, England, educated at Oundle, and won a competitive Commonwealth scholarship from the Drapers' Company (an ancient City of London guild) to Canada's prestigious McGill University, Montreal. For many years a London solicitor (lawyer in American parlance), he moved to Bavaria several years ago where he writes, oil paints, und spricht ein bisschen Deutsch. He is a lover of music (classical and the best of old pop), of art in most forms, of history and architecture, and enjoys the richness of the south German landscape and culture. **Crimson in the Water** is his first novel, for which he genuinely felt inspired throughout the composition. He is currently working on his second novel that takes place in the Philippines, and the muse has not yet left his shoulder.

CPSIA information can be obtained at www.ICGtesting.com
Printed in the USA
LVOW042323021111

253298LV00001B/177/P